STELLAR TRESPASSERS

STELLAR TRESPASSERS

Volume One of The Invasion Spirals

David Gulotta

Stellar Trespassers Copyright © 2022 by David Gulotta. All Rights Reserved.

All rights reserved. No part of this book may be reproduced in any form or by any electronic or mechanical means including information storage and retrieval systems, without permission in writing from the author. The only exception is by a reviewer, who may quote short excerpts in a review.

Cover designed by David Gulotta

This book is a work of fiction. Names, characters, places, and incidents either are products of the author's imagination or are used fictitiously. Any resemblance to actual persons, living or dead, events, or locales is entirely coincidental.

David Gulotta
Visit my website at www.Gulottastudios.com

Printed in the United States of America

First Printing: October 2022

ISBN- 97-983-6-08724-7-4

Dedicated to all the good crew out there who have encouraged me to keep on dreaming.

Terran-Conglomerate Terraforming Vessel Ganges

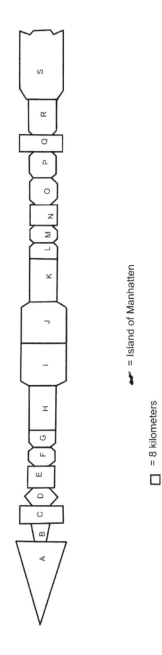

□ = 8 kilometers

🖛 = Island of Manhatten

A = Ice Cap
B = Command Hub
C = Harbor One
D = Medical Sector Wheel
E = Industrial Wheel One
F = Distribution Wheel One
G = Residence Wheel One

H = Agro Wheel One
I = Agro Wheel Two
J = Agro Wheel Three
K = Agro Wheel Four
L = Distribution Wheel Two
M = Industrial Wheel Two
N = Residence Wheel Two

O = Stellar Sector Wheel
P = Planetary Sector Wheel
Q = Harbor Two
R = Engineering Sector Wheel
S = Main Engines

PROLOGUE

Field Rotation - Spin Sowing - Charter Harvest - Spiral 5677

No one knows that I'm writing this. Well, a few do. Those who are helping me. This includes my mate and a few others I have chosen. You see, this is mostly for me, but if you do find this notebook, feel free to read it. Most crew might find it odd to have to turn real pages, made of plant pulp and carbon-based ink. It seems scandalously old fashioned, and I suppose that is my own preference. Fortunately, I always have a writing implement on me. That's also part of who I am. Most crew don't understand, though they pretend to. When I was young, I never wrote about anything. Now that I'm at the end of my journey in life, the stories seem to flow out of my head, all of them about the time period I barely survived. It was suggested by my mate that I assemble all that I know and collect it into a semblance of order. It's a tall task, but one I'm ready for, especially now.

One of the problems afflicting our vessel these rotations is revisionism. Too many crew want to remember the time period I'm writing about from a point of view that makes us all innocent, and then points the finger of blame at others. As my own culture has been left out of most of the main records, we have the least to lose should anyone be offended by our point of view. Oh, our special talents and services have been noted in the official logs, but this is often set aside as footnotes. I have spent my life trying to make sense of everything that happened to poor Ganges, by asking questions, seeking interviews from the survivors, and not just the officers, but regular crew as well.

We have become a bit myopic, historically speaking. In some ways, this has served me well. Few have taken note of my presence; fewer still have ever asked for my opinion. It is only recently that some people have realized what it is that I'm trying to accomplish, and half of them are against it for purposes of crew morale. I find that argument ingenuous. I'm more concerned about future generations, who may repeat the mistakes of the past, by ignoring history or just not learning it. While this may not be a crisis now, time has a way of pouncing upon us when we least expect it.

The universe is beyond vast. Our entire galaxy is just a small community within an endless expanse. We think we're so very important, but we're just small creatures trying to survive a hostile environment that is well beyond the scope of our imagination. All we have are our words, pictures, and memories, all of which we must pass down unaltered so that we may learn and advance at our own, crawling pace. At one time, words meant little to me, save to aid in my duty to the ship, but times changed, and so did I. This led to some consternation amongst my colleagues and within my beloved community. No one worries about what you're doing, so long as it's expected of you and aids others who have authority. Once you have a goal that is beyond their understanding, or their rank, suddenly, everyone is afraid for you, or of you.

There are times when I've almost given up. Stopped my writing and just left it all to others, those who claim they know better, but I am too stubborn for that kind of surrender. I have achieved more than I ever thought possible. I also lost more than most will ever comprehend. Many of the sources for my written work were at the very pinnacle of high rank; others were so lowly, they never got recognized for all they accomplished, despite the horrific odds against them. Both have been a fountain of knowledge that has aided my research to complete this work. I went through great lengths to do this, despite doors that were shut to me.

I think that's enough about my own struggles. Those who read this can use their imaginations to figure out what I went through if not how I was able to gain the information I needed. Instead, I'd like to take a look at how our history is digested, after being served upon a platter, well-laden with propaganda and sprinkled with feel-good moments that make us all look like brave heroes. No one wants to talk about the mistakes, the fear, the anguish, the disagreements that fill the spaces between memorable moments of historic significance. Maybe I'm too jaded to be writing this, but at least I will tell you the whole truth, not just the bits we want to hear.

Ganges has had an idyllic history, isolated from the rest of humanity, and without counting two wars, both mutinies, over a period of five thousand spirals, the most peaceful society ever known to exist. All of our most pressing problems were internal by nature, which meant we were not prepared when reality came knocking at our airlocks. In many ways, we were an innocent culture, and thus we could not imagine how our actions, or lack thereof, could imperil our home. We had a massive Security Sector, well designed to uphold the Prime Charter of Ganges, crew rights, and to protect us from another mutiny from breaking out.

We called it the Age of Redemption, and in all fairness, we still do, despite the massive changes that have been forced upon us all. If nature abhors a vacuum, then history is equally repelled by stagnation. We took far too much for granted, self-satisfied by our successes, ignorant of our failures. Despite the new, more accepting Council of Inventions, we were happy with things the way they were. Improvements were made, but at such a slow pace, it barely mattered. There was very little call for improvement, unless it directly affected the Holy Mission, but what happens when that is no longer our main focus? What happens when we are forced to adapt or die? These are the questions which I seek to answer in writing this treatise on the Invasion Spirals. They are significant, for we have seen how our blind spots destroyed what we loved most. Nothing is the same anymore. Nothing is untouched by the disaster which befell our vessel. Please be brave, and read this account of a time when all we were so certain of was blown into space.

CHAPTER ONE

Ice Rotation - Journey Sowing - Ship Harvest - Spiral 5620

"I walk through the community, and even here, in officer territory, it still happens. The crew defer to me, doing me favors and showing me honor. They treat me like a damned hero. None of them truly know me. I'm a monster, but for so many spirals, I was their monster. Every rotation, gifts are sent to my home from crew I've never met. Taylee calls it my just reward for my devotion to Ganges. I call it a constant reminder that I'm not who they think I am. No one can be. There's a terrible danger to hero worship, on all sides. To refuse to see the human flaws of another individual is to be blind to danger. For the person being honored, there is the risk that devotion can turn to hatred if others are disappointed and their illusions are shattered. The truth is always different from our expectations, and I fear that the crew expects far more from me than I can ever deliver to them."
Marik Langman, Chief of Security Sector, personal log, P35

Agro Wheel Two, Topsides Hull

Security Sector Pilot, Lieutenant Tarn Vekkor, flipped through his pre-flight sequence with one eye on the squadron he commanded. The Naga-Unit on the left side of his display kept him updated on the mission preparations for the impending reconnaissance. The pilots under his wing were excellent. If they weren't, he made certain they got to his level of efficiency or transferred to another assignment. He had no time for either fools or delinquents. The numbers flashed inside his helmet; his squadron matched his level of preparedness, though none of them were as calm as he was. Tarn brought up the mission parameters and stifled an irritated sigh. This was to be a short void-run past the ice cap of Ganges, only taking point for one slice before being replaced by the beta wave of fighters.

This had become a tradition for the mighty vessel, whenever it was about to enter a new stellar system. Security Sector would lead their way, providing both reconnaissance and protection from the unknown. He would have much preferred remaining in the foremost position, just one hundred thousand kilometers ahead of

Ganges, for longer than what was assigned to him, but he understood the reasons behind the frequent change in shifts. He just felt more at home within his fighter pod than anywhere else. Even his toragi, Pete, was comfortable spending longer shifts in the secondary pod behind his cockpit chair.

He glanced at the internal rear-view screen and smiled briefly as a large, triangular nose filled the display. Good. Pete was feeling light-hearted and playful this rotation. That made this assignment a bit more bearable, as Tarn was itching for maneuver drills, which Pete would enjoy. It amazed him how easily the toragi had learned how to handle the co-pilot controls, even if they were designed with paws in mind. Pete had a sharp eye for detail and seemed to love showing off his abilities. He was the perfect partner.

The launch tube flashed by on silent magnetics, reaching for the outer hull at speed. His fighter-pod was clamped in place at the base of the lift and would be released once they reached the void. The sleek vessel was matte black and shaped like a spearhead with short, weapon-mounted wings. They were equipped with micro-missiles and two Spin-Drive cannons. The hull was made of pure Kendis-steel. Swift and maneuverable, the Security craft was the pride of his Sector. The main engines were hot, ready for the signal to burn. Soft alarms filled his ears, and Tarn ignored them. Air was being stripped away from the lift tube as all the lighting became a deep crimson.

A voice from Security Flight Control entered his ears, "Raptor One-Alpha, you are cleared for egress."

Tarn replied in the same no-nonsense tone, "Primed, Sec-Flight. Nondo squad at peak."

Suddenly he was surrounded by stars and the sweeping curve of the outer hull, "Raptor One, unlocked."

The view spun as his fighter detached from the magnetic clamps, already moving into the darkness at speed. Tarn blinked at the eye monitor from his Naga-Port, "Raptor One-Alpha to Squad Nondo. Burn. Burn. Burn."

His engines rumbled behind him as Pete gave off a roar of approval. The squadron shot past Harbor One with incredible velocity as he was pushed back into his seat, his suit's armor shielding him from the deleterious effects of a high-gee maneuver. With a perfect arrow formation, his squad swept past the ice cap at the prow of Ganges, it's eighty-kilometer bulk flashing past his peripheral vision. All pilots sent green signals to his control board, and Pete slapped the comms pad with his massive, furry paw in acceptance. Tarn could swear he heard the toragi of the other vessels responding with growls and rumbles, until Pete gave a wet bark and they all became silent once again.

Naga's voice resounded from the main display board with a gentle grace, "Incoming signal from Fleet Command."

Tarn flicked his acceptance to open the channel, "This is Lieutenant Vekkor of Nondo squadron."

The harsh, clear voice that responded was well known to him, "This is Fleet Commander Vina Harrolon, from the Security Battle Cruiser Malati. Welcome to the party, squadron Nondo. You're the first sweep. Hell, you might get back in time to get ready for the celebrations. You may proceed with your reconnaissance."

Tarn replied, doing his best to hide his scowl, "Primed, Commander. A good Entry-Sowing to you."

It wasn't that he didn't like Commander Harrolon. She was as hard-assed as he was. Tarn just didn't care about all the parties that erupted whenever Ganges came close to system insertion. The timing was awful, as the Security Games were also scheduled to occur during the sowing-long entry. This meant even more crew would not be at their post, where they were needed. He thought of such things as a waste of valuable time and effort. If it wasn't against regulations, he would love to take some extra shifts in his fighter, but the Chief wouldn't approve, and she always got what she wanted.

Some of his colleagues called him a hotshot. He couldn't help it if his ratings were always at the top five percent in the trials. Tarn lived for his post. The same could be said of his school spirals in Agro Wheel Four. His parents were fishing crew, and he swore to himself that he wouldn't get trapped in that rotational grind. While Harbor and Command Sector made him some generous offers once he completed his Basic Crew Training, he had already set his heart on Security and its fleet of warcraft. Bumbling about in a tug or surveyance pod sounded far too dull for his mind to contemplate. He had risen in the ranks quickly, surpassing his schoolmates with ease. When asked, he would say that his only hobby was modifying his fighter-pod, which was permitted with the proper licensing within his Sector.

Tarn was typical in appearance for those crew who originated in the oceanic levels of Agro Four. Lean and tall, with a dark complexion at odds with his clear blue eyes. He could have his pick of mates, but he couldn't see why he should bother. His genetic lineage was kept in storage within the Medical Sector Wheel. Let those not completely devoted to duty take the time to raise novices. He had better things to do with his life.

Pete huffed loudly, intruding into his dark thoughts. Tarn flipped his left eye's view to the toragi's station. A blip had briefly appeared on the tracking screen. It had lasted just a pollen-sliver, then winked out abruptly. It was almost at the very edge of their sensor's detection range, far behind Ganges. He ran a diagnostic, then double-checked the readings. Just a flash of high energy photons, then blackness. It could have been a minor asteroid collision. There was more debris between systems than early spacefarers had ever suspected. It wasn't uncommon to encounter the remains of rogue planets or debris fields. He logged it for Stellar Sector's investigations, then cleared Pete's board. It was going to be a short flight, so he may as well get some enjoyment out of it. Switching on his squad-comm, he barked, "Nondo squadron, this is Lieutenant Vekkor. Begin training sequence Nine-Beta-Three. Look alive, crew! Let's beat our last time record!"

Planetary Sector, Level Thirty-Four

Atmospherics Director Dalen Gupta straightened out his brown-and-green uniform as he waited for his stop within a local tram. As there was no one else within the car he was riding in, he did a little dance to himself on the walkway between the seats. Despite his bulk, for he was unusually heavy, his grace was unimpeded. He twirled with a twist of his generous hips, snapping his fingers in time to the music from his datapad. This was attached to the back of his left hand by a patch of synth-skin. This was much preferred over the handheld units from ages past. It had all of the usual functions of the older models, but it was smaller, lighter and could emit holographic projections, though this last feature was somewhat limited in size.

He had always been this graceful and buoyant. Even as a novice, he would astound his parents with his acrobatic antics. Dalen was also unusually tall, almost two meters in height, but it was his girth which caught the crew's notice. He didn't mind if some called him fat. It gave him extra momentum for dancing in the midships levels, where the gravity was lighter. Neither of his mates ever said anything negative about his weight. Sasha Sparhold, his female mate from Agro, was always telling him how delightful he looked, and his male mate, Bryce Cutter, bragged about Dalen's skills to his crew in Technology Sector. The trio-nesting had produced two novices thus far, Marik Gupta and Velika Sparhold, both of whom were in school. They were proud of him and delighted in the tales he told them about his work.

Dalen Gupta had spent his entire career in Planetary Sector, specifically in Atmospherics, where his natural talent with handling fluid dynamics came in handy. The personnel under his command were very happy to be within his department. It was good to be popular and be able to get the work done in a timely manner. He often hosted lavish parties for his crew, to celebrate bonuses, rises in rank or special awards from the Chief of Planetary Sector. The only thing that ever dampened his jolly spirits were his frequent visits to Medical Sector who admonished him about his weight and insisted that he wear a blood pressure regulating tick for safety.

The tram finally reached his destination, after flashing past numerous office clusters and seed labs. He was meeting a dear friend for lunch at the main cafeteria for his region, which always made him glow with joy. The doors of the tram slid open, and Dalen hopped out with a light jump. The lower gravity of Level Thirty-Four was delightful, and he couldn't think of a better place to work in. The main cafeteria was crowded, which wasn't terribly surprising as it was the beginning of gather-slice. The crew often took a short break at this time of the rotation, grabbing a snack or taking a moment to relax their minds and bodies.

His friend Levy Truel waved him over to the buffet tables, and Dalen happily joined him, grabbing a tray and plate from the serving station. There were several of the light blue food dispensers on the spinward side of the massive chamber, but he preferred a real meal to a sandwich or wrapped treat. Levy looked at him as he piled several savory items onto his plate, "Hey, crew, you still trying to pack on a few kilos?"

Dalen shrugged in a good-natured way, "Terraforming requires biomass. It may as well come from me! Besides, I'm celebrating this rotation."

Levy grabbed a small treat and popped it into his mouth, talking over his chewing, "You're always celebrating! What's the occasion this time?"

Dalen took another helping of infused rice as he replied, "Well, we're about to enter a new system, for one. It's a lovely time to be alive! We'll get to start the Holy Mission on another dead world! It's one thing to simply study terraforming but quite another to actually see it happening! I can't wait to see what kind of atmosphere we'll be dealing with."

Levy nodded and shrugged, "Yeah, okay. I can see your point. I bet it'll be a miserable place, full of storms and unbreathable gasses. Sounds like loads of fun to me."

Dalen wagged a thick finger at his friend, "Ah, don't get pessimistic. I think it will be most fascinating! Just think! We'll be the first ones to see this new world we're rebuilding!"

Levy shook his head, "Don't get all excited ahead of time, my friend. It'll be harvests before we actually get there. We haven't even reached the heliopause!"

Dalen nodded happily, munching on a slice of fruit, "True, true. I do have to save up for the big parties coming up. Say, are you and Mara going to watch the Security Games? I've heard rumor that, this spiral, it will be most spectacular."

Levy smiled briefly, "I've got tickets for some great seats! My son is a fanatic when it comes to sports. He keeps up on all of his favorite Security athletes. I mean, I remember following Ravi Lathehand when I was young. Who didn't? But his fervor for all the fighting competitions goes well beyond my understanding. He even gets into the chess matches that Investigations runs."

Dalen grinned, "Well, we all need hobbies! Besides, if your boy's in love with Security, you won't have to guess at what post he'll choose, yes? How's Mindy? She's still in Basic, right?"

Levy rolled his eyes, "Oh, yes, she is. She's still determined to become a Command officer. I don't know where I went wrong!"

Dalen looked up in alarm, "Now wait a moment! Captain Fieldscan is good crew! He's no Verdstrum, you know! Definitely not a Makdreah, thank Ganges! I hear the Chief of Security considers him to be a friend."

Levy scowled as they grabbed a seat, "I know my history, pal. That's not a great endorsement. The great Langman loved the tyrant, even doted on the rascal. I had just hoped my dear daughter would go for our Sector."

Dalen leaned back and looked at his companion, "She must choose her own dharma. You know that. I think Captain Fieldscan is a true Linc. We're lucky to have him on the Bridge, especially as we're entering System Forty-One. My friend, Fuss Nitpicker, from Stellar Observations, says the Oort cloud surrounding the system is unusually dense. We need a steady hand at the helm right now."

Levy almost choked on his lunch, "Fuss? A Strifer? You're friends with a Strifer from Stellar Sector? You need to raise your standards!"

Dalen raised an eyebrow at his old friend, "Nonsense! Fuss is a wonderful dancer! Once you get past her combative attitude, she's really very charming, in an odd, insulting sort of way. She's also a traditionalist. That's something I admire. Fuss makes robes and new rat masks for her people. It's good work, too! Very decorative."

Levy sighed deeply, "You meet the craziest crew with your dancing hobby. I've been feeling more isolated lately. Maybe I should join in with your events, meet new people."

Dalen smiled and lightly slapped his friend on the shoulder, "That's the spirit! I would be happy to introduce you to some fantastic instructors I know!"

Levy shrugged, "Maybe after the Security Games."

Dalen knew when to leave his friend alone. He was so delighted that Levy expressed an interest in his beloved hobby. That was enough for now. If he pushed him too much, the man would go right back into his shell. That would change over time. Soon enough, the excitement about terraforming Planet Forty-One would infect even dour Levy. Planetary Sector was beginning to buzz like a hive of bees. The Holy Mission was the core of Ganges, and it was exciting to be an active part of their sacred task. Even Levy couldn't hold back the wave of enthusiasm gripping the ship, despite his best efforts to be grim all the time.

Command Sector Hub, Level Ten

Captain Perrin Fieldscan settled into his command chair and watched over the Bridge with a piercing gaze. The stadium-sized chamber, with its tiers of control stations, was quite busy preparing Ganges for insertion into the heliopause of System

Forty-One. Not everything was going smoothly, but things were still well in hand. He raised a single eyebrow at the Chief-of-the-Deck, Femz Trammer, who was watching the Executive Officer verbally rip into one of the station Lieutenants for being late with a report from Engineering Sector, with a look of admiration plastered across his face. Captain Fieldscan wasn't too sure that she was being a proper role model for the Bridge crew, but they did fear her wrath.

Perrin just slowly shook his head in silence, which was all the permission his Executive Officer needed to continue her wildly rough invective. He pinged Chief Trammer's station, who then stood up straight and snapped back to attention. The Captain's lips twitched into a brief smile; it was good to keep everyone on their toes. This was especially important at this most delicate juncture. The upcoming Oort cloud surrounding the system was particularly dense, and thus their course to pass through it looked more like running into a hedge labyrinth. He settled his hand upon the hilt of his ancient sword of office, passed down from one Captain to the next ever since the Crucible. It gleamed within its jeweled sheath, the basket hilt made of pure hand-hammered gold.

Captain Fieldscan reflected on how his Executive Officer was granted her post, as more loud curses echoed through the cavernous Bridge. This was something he did often, for the story of Wasp Tornpage's ascent was a very strange one. The most obvious thing about her was that she was a Strifer, the first one to become a Bridge officer. If nothing else, she certainly made the duty shifts more interesting, if a bit unruly. He remembered when she first accepted her new commission, coming out of obscurity as a minor officer into the grand height of one of the most powerful positions within Ganges. There had been protests, of course, and yet her training for the post had gone quite smoothly.

His original Executive Officer had been a very dear friend from Basic Crew Training who had suddenly collapsed on the Bridge after serving for several spirals with distinction. Both the Captain and his old friend were equestrian enthusiasts, but a small accident had led to a major brain hemorrhage a sowing afterward, which even Medical Sector had not detected nor could they repair it. The man was still alive but had been forced to accept re-education, for his entire personality had been altered drastically. Wasp had been chosen from three other applicants, all of whom did well in the trials but not so brilliantly as she had.

As a replacement, it took some adjustment for the Bridge crew and himself. Her first sowing at her new post, Wasp had come to her station wearing her usual Command uniform, but instead of her boots, she had worn a pair of beach sandals, exposing her green-painted toenails. Perrin had admonished her, stating that she must wear regulation-approved footwear from that point forward. Wasp had returned the next rotation in a pair of Vac-Con mag-boots, correctly declaring that they were within Command regulation parameters. She had made quite a sight, clomping about the Bridge in the damned things, so Perrin had decided to give her a little more slack than usual.

He rubbed his nose briefly, as he continued to watch Wasp tear into yet another late bearer of status updates. Instead of a rat mask, her face was tattooed with a stylized rodent's visage, which was the growing custom amongst the Strifers. While she didn't wear her green robes while on duty, her jewelry, hair clasp and face markings were all lurid green. Executive Tornpage was tall and wiry, and she brought a jovial sarcasm to the Bridge which he now greatly appreciated. She was brutally honest at all times and debated with a skill few could manage to keep up with. Thus, he knew everything that was going on within the Bridge without having to ask.

A sudden, hushed silence filled the giant chamber as she walked back to her command chair next to his. Wasp settled down with a gleam in her eyes that was almost feral, "I swear by my tail, Captain, these fucking flunkies are getting worse by the rotation. Nothing but damned excuses for slovenly work! I'd sooner trust an old mophead from maintenance to get things done around here."

Perrin looked at her with a bland expression on his mustached face, "Well, I'm glad you're here to sort things out for me. Do try to be gentler with the lower ranks, especially the newest members of our Sector."

Wasp looked back at him in shock, "Why lie to them? Bridge duty is hard work. We expect them to be models of efficiency, not drooling novices!"

The Captain chuckled, and she broke into a wide grin, "Besides, my dear Captain, it is my job to frighten them to death. That way, they're softened up for your more diplomatic approach. The last thing I need is for you to become all stressed out because of ridiculous bullshit, leading to me actually having to be the one in charge more often. That would be a fucking disaster, and you know it!"

Perrin winked at her with a soft smile, "I think not. You've had your share of leading the Bridge without my presence and have done astonishingly well, especially considering your youth."

The crew representative on his left chimed in, "You mean despite the rat marks on her face, I'm sure."

Wasp leaned forward and caught the woman's eye, "Ooh! At it again, are we? Ready for round ten? Get off my tail, politician!"

Perrin spoke up quickly to prevent another diatribe, "Enough! Both of you! We have serious work ahead of us this rotation. We need to maintain our focus, not snipe at each other."

The crew representative, Zilla Tav, leaned back while Wasp laughed. Perrin understood the concerns of the elected voice of the crew. Strifers were still not very popular, even though they had proven their worth for several generations. It was their manners, or lack thereof, which caused most of the discomfort between the general crew and the Strifer community. The crew representative post was a response to the overreaching actions of the late, infamous, Captain Jaike Verdstrum. The crew had demanded a presence within the Bridge, and the Judiciary Council had agreed to the idea, so long as the post was a frequently changed, elected position. Zilla and Wasp butted heads often, and Perrin couldn't wait for the selection of the representative's replacement next spiral.

Naga-Ma's golden face filled the main holosphere at the very center of the Bridge, towering over all stations, "Selected course has been accepted. All thrusters have been tested and are prepared for activation. All Sectors report their readiness."

Captain Fieldscan activated his general announcement comm-bead at the collar of his uniform. His voice would be heard throughout the entire vessel, "Attention all crew. This is your Captain speaking. We shall be commencing entry maneuvers in three seed-slivers. Remain at your posts and lock down all items. Soon, we will once again perform our sacred duty for all sentients. Please note that there may be shifts and minor vibrations for an extended time period. The debris field surrounding System Forty-One is particularly dense. Stay sharp and keep to your duties!"

Executive Tornpage's voice rang out, "All Bridge crew, prepare for system insertion! Chief-of-the-Deck, you have control."

Chief Trammer replied with swift promptness, "Bridge control primed, Aye! Thrusters on standby! Shifting course to match assigned vector!"

A deep rumbling vibrated through the deck plates and Perrin leaned back with a serene expression on his face. It was finally beginning. He was about to join those fortunate Captains who commanded Ganges during the terraforming process, and his spirit soared with the thought.

Agro Wheel Two, Security Level Five

Chief of Security Jira Mantabe locked herself into the Nexus saddle, as she reviewed the preparations for system insertion. Her dark golden skin was covered in tattoos and scars. Her green eyes flashed with excitement, and her crimson mohawk bobbed whenever she moved her head to glance at the various displays before her. It was moments like these that brought her mind back to the rotation she carved her name into the synth-leather saddle of her post, joining the others that had been cut into the thick material from her predecessors. History was a major part of Security Sector. To be granted the chance to make your mark was hailed as glorious.

Her muscular arms flashed over the display panel directly in front of her, as she finalized orders for all departments. Jira's tall, heavy-boned frame fit the saddle perfectly, even though it had been designed for the original crew member who had created her beloved post. Nothing could compare to being the lead warrior of such a fine vessel as Ganges. On the rotation she joined Security, she had its shield and crossed swords symbol tattooed onto her forehead, publicly declaring her devotion to protecting the crew.

A Thor's hammer pendant hung from her neck, its ancient symbolism at odds with the Naga-Port attached to the side of her head. The AeyAie interface was a sleek, modern design that fit comfortably under her helmet, for those times when she donned her Kendis-armor. Her favorite hand weapon, a long-handled shock-hammer, rested in a clamp attached to her saddle, next to the coffee thermos in its ring. Jira's toragi, Tracey, was lounging at her feet in regal splendor, rumbling her contentment as she slowly gazed about the busy chamber. Security crew filled every station within the Nexus, the beating heart of the Sector.

Her wrist guards, which covered her flashtats, revealed them on a display panel on the underside of her forearm, just as her pauldrons showed her Sector's symbol and her rank. Medals of valor and past championship awards decorated her chest with pride. While she had been Chief of Security for only five spirals, most of her crew felt that she was born to the post. Even as a novice, while getting excellent grades, her wild behavior had gotten Jira into trouble many times, to the agonized confusion of her parents, who were both Agro timber farmers. Her time in Basic Crew Training had also been an exercise in getting high grades and disciplinary notices. When given the choice between Security, Command and Harbor, she had jumped at the chance to prove her abilities within the only Sector where rough behavior was encouraged yet guided into constructive vectors.

A notice came up on one of her secondary boards. Someone had been caught trying to damage a water main within the Strifer community. Police Services was bringing the bastard into the holding cells on Level One within Security. They'll let the troublemaker sweat it out in the higher apparent gravity, before Investigations begins their questioning. She thumped her fist on the upper handlebar of her saddle, making the ancient totems tied to it jingle in response. Jira was sick and tired of people picking on the damned Strifers! Yes, they were rude as Hell. Yes, they had been involved in destroying the Age of Unity, but since the Crucible, the ratty crew had proven themselves as being an asset to the ship and even the Holy Mission.

Not only was this incident an unwanted distraction during system entry, she had other major events to prepare for, one of them being the Security Games which would start the next sowing. It was held every spiral and was the only time when the general crew were permitted within Security's training grounds, where the games were held. This led to many procedural headaches, but it was worth all the chips in Ganges in terms of crew morale. One million attendees would be seated within the giant arena, and all the games were broadcast on the major channels for the public's delight.

The first rotation would be full of opening ceremonies, entertainment and demonstrations of her crew's honed abilities. Then would come the challenges for those new recruits hoping to show that they had passed all of her Sector's special training regimens. After this would be three rotations of large-group sporting events, competitions and championship matches in everything from individual combat duels to high level chess tournaments. The final rotation was for a review parade of her entire Sector, for the approval of the Judiciary Council and the Captain of Ganges. The coordination involved was intense, but it had become a beloved tradition. The crew had replaced their love for professional sporting events with cheering on their favorite Security champions and athletes.

Checking her right-hand panels, she nodded in satisfaction at the way in which the Security reconnaissance fleet were combining protecting the heading of the ship with combat drills. Lieutenant Tarn Vekkor was a stiff bastard, but he knew his duty to Ganges. The Security cruiser Malati was still keeping pace and providing command support. They had practiced for system entry during the past two spirals and it showed in their professional manner. The time for drills was over. They were heading into the unknown.

Naga-Ma's voice came into her mind through the port, "The work crew at the training field have ceased their efforts, though it did take Sargent Mattis a little time and a lot of yelling to convince them to stop the preparations."

Jira rolled her eyes at this, "They can get back to their construction after the thrusters have finished the first cycle of maneuvers. We're ahead of schedule as it is. I'll make sure their supervisor from Engineering Sector understands the meaning of the word 'orders' once I'm done here. Thank you, my friend, for bringing the matter to my attention."

Naga-Ma replied, "I'm always happy to help you. Have you decided as to whether you're participating in the championships this spiral?"

Jira shook her head, making the crest of her mohawk wave about, "I am glad to be part of the first rotation's demonstrations, but I'll give the younger members of my Sector a chance to grab a little glory for themselves. At this point, I just don't have the time or energy to prepare for much else. Besides, I've already got enough decorations, including the Kenshi award."

The AeyAie replied, "That will be good for morale. Not that it needs much help within your Sector. Once again, Security leads the pack in terms of efficiency ratings."

Jira grinned, "We're still fairly new as a Sector. We've got to make up for lost time. Security remains the craziest bunch of misfits this ship has ever seen, so we have a lot to prove."

Naga-Ma's voice became warmer, "I always have greatest faith in you and the crew you command, my friend."

Jira blushed at this compliment. It wasn't every rotation when the AeyAie revealed her trust and gratitude directly. Besides which, she knew that not everything was perfectly polished at Security Sector. There was a particularly nasty blemish which she had to deal with and had been putting it off for a sowing. It was shameful whenever one of the guardians of the Holy Mission failed in his duties as protector of the crew. She felt her mood darken and twist into a building, rage. She tossed her thoughts aside. There was too much going on right now. Jira promised herself that she would deal with her problematic officer next rotation.

Engineering Sector, Level Sixteen

Howait Sparweld, Team Leader, Rank Two of Engineering Sector, sighed with exasperation. His position meant that he had serous responsibilities without the commensurate authority. It was miraculous that he had achieved his current rank, as he was just twenty-two spirals old, but the novelty wore off fast. At first glance, he was nothing special, as his new crew were constantly reminding him. He was short, gangly, balding, with limbs that looked too long for his torso and deep brown eyes that seemed too large for his drawn-out face. It didn't help that he was painfully shy and was always slouched over, as if expecting someone to throw a wrench at him, which did sometimes happen.

Most of his unusual physical characteristics could be attributed to having been raised on Level Eighteen of Residence Wheel Two, where the apparent gravity was fairly low for a habitable region of the ship. As a result, he had a special diet from Medical Sector for better bone development. He still lived within the same level as the one in which he was raised, within the Void Haulers community, which was a comfortable region for his rare physique. Howait was quite grateful that his post in Engineering Sector was just two levels topsides from what he was used to. He had developed some more muscle mass over the last few spirals, not that anyone really noticed much.

The crew under his supervision were a fairly rough bunch. For the most part, they were brawny and twice his height. Howait didn't expect much respect from them, which was convenient, for he got none. He was always the butt of their jokes, shoved aside and ignored, even if he was the one who would be writing up their efficiency reports. Most of the team was more experienced than he was, though they lacked the discipline needed to gain his rank. Howait had always been highly organized, and he dearly loved his Sector. His intuitive understanding of metallurgy had likely been the primary reason for his current post, repairing the foundry systems and fabrication machines.

A loud ruckus erupted behind his position. He turned carefully, so as not to dislodge the power wrench he was using. Falinos was shouting, "Who put glue in my grease applicator? Out with it! I'm getting real sick of these Ganges-damned pranks around here!"

Falinos was the largest and most cantankerous of the crew under Howait's leadership, such as it was. Skolly, who was the eldest of the group, sneered his reply, "You're such a big baby, Fali. Just shut yer trap and do yer work! Boss is in a hurry, don't you know!"

Falinos stomped up to Skolly, towering over the older crewman, "Piss off! I bet it's you who's been messing with the equipment!"

Mibo, who was the laziest person Howait had ever met, chimed in, "So what, Fali? Just get a new unit and move on. I'm trying to nap here!"

Howait shook his head sadly as Pilla jumped down from the gantry above, wielding her power-hammer like a club, "All of you, shut the fuck up! What a bunch of novices!"

Falinos shoved past Skolly to face the easily irritated engineer, "Watch your damned tone, lady! This old bastard is messing up our whole efficiency rating!"

Brigo, an easy-going sort, perhaps too much so, got up from a power cable he was servicing, "Hey now, friends. Yellin' and fightin' ain't gonna solve anything. My drill just came apart in my hands and was full of medical goo last slice, remember? One of us is a prankster, that's all. Harmless fun."

Vita glowered at everyone from above the racks of powerlines, but before she could say anything, Howait had dislodged himself with his unusual flexibility and shouted, "Enough! Falinos, go get yourself a new unit. The rest of you, back to work. The director wants this place cleaned up before we start terraforming, not after."

Mibo shrugged and went back to staring at a small junction box, while Vita muttered some dark curses under her breath. Skolly turned to face his team leader, "Whatsamatter, Howie? Gonna be late for your hot date?"

Pilla rolled her eyes, "If you were a proper boss, you'd have found our joker and dealt with them already!"

Falinos started laughing, "Boss got a date? With what? An old fish?"

Skolly smirked, "Probably some skinny loser from bilge reclamation."

Mibo looked sleepily over his shoulder, "So boss, which is it? Skinny or fish? Could it be both?"

The others laughed as Howait stood there with his face burning with shame. Falinos spread his arms out as the corridor hatch ten meters behind him slid open, "You'd better not introduce your ugly bitch to me! She'd dump you in an instant and tangle with a real man!"

A wet, low growl filled the air. Everyone turned around, while Howait's heart dropped into his boots. His girlfriend was standing next to her toragi, marching toward the group, tapping the shock-sword at her side. Her skin was a dark golden hue. The hair on her head was black and tightly braided. Her Security Sector uniform revealed her dense musculature, despite all of the armor plating. Blue eyes glared out from epicanthic folds as she glared at each member of Howait's team, all of whom were now silent in shock. It wasn't every rotation when a hero of the Holy Mission just appeared at one's post, with a chest decorated with a line of championship medals. Her scarred left eyebrow rose high upon her face as she stalked over to Howait. He tried to stutter some kind of apology for what she had just heard, when she grabbed him by the collar of his purple-and-blue uniform and kissed him deeply in front of the others.

When she released him, Howait was completely out of breath and dizzy in response to her loving embrace. She grabbed him by the crotch, "This is mine. You are mine."

Howait tried once again to speak, but she grabbed his hands and lifted them to her plated breasts, "I am yours, engineer-man. Never, ever forget that."

Everyone else was watching them with stunned expressions on their faces. She looked over at Falinos, "My toragi, Helen, has coughed up prettier things than you. Besides, my man's arms and legs aren't the only parts of his body that are overly long."

With blinding speed, the Security Sergeant suddenly kicked Falinos into the fabrication unit he had been working on, making him fall and bounce on the deck. She whipped out her longsword, activating the blade, whereupon sparks of electricity coursed down its length, "I seem to have found some mutinous crew here. I'm sure the interrogators at Investigations will be pleased with such a fine catch."

Howait raised his hands and ran over to her, "Wait, my love! Please, Mahari. They're my crew, and I'm responsible for them. Give me a sowing, and I'll have their behavior all sorted out. No harm was meant, my dear. Um, what brings you to my little domain?"

Mahari shrugged, "We've been together for a few harvests. I want to ask you something important."

Everyone else shouted in unison, "Harvests?"

Howait held her hand and replied, "Anything for you, beloved."

Mahari smiled gently, "I want you to be in the family seats during the games, sweetheart. I've been thinking about this for a couple of sowings, and I want us to make our mating official."

Howait thought that he would faint. He had wanted this for so long, but was always too terrified to ask her. He nodded quickly, "Yes! Please, my love. Right after my shift here. I promise you. We'll talk to Naga-Ma, then we can use the longhouse near your barracks for the ceremony if you like."

She pulled a necklace with a Thor's hammer pendant from her waist sash and placed it over his neck, "Don't make me wait, engineer-man. If I get impatient, I'll come looking for you, then drag you to the nearest wallscreen."

Howait smiled as tears fell down his cheeks, "I promise, sweetest."

The Security woman slapped his bottom affectionately, then turned to scowl darkly at the rest of the crew. None of them could meet her gaze. She walked back the way she had come, with her toragi prowling at her side. Before Howait could say anything to the others, they were all silently hard at work.

Stellar Sector, Level One

Crinn Spanglo, Ensign Rank Three of the Sensor Observations Department for Stellar Sector, shrank back into his chair, as he listened to his supervisor and the director of Sensor Services scream at each other. It had been a very long rotation of performing diagnostics and reviewing data on the same two sets of readings. Both were anomalous. All he really wanted was a pot of herbal tea and some fresh pasta. Crinn spent most of his time at the main observation stations, for he had no mate, no novices, just a pet planet-rover named Savo at home. His lower back was acting up again, something that frequently bothered him, especially when he was stressed. He had a medical tick for pain management, but this rotation it wasn't working so well. Then again, he also had never been this stressed-out before.

He always preferred machines to people. While he didn't worship Naga like so many of the crew did, he was a member of the Church of the Holy Void, in whose writings it was said that all sentients were part of God's mind. This made him closer to the AeyAie, and it barely satisfied his parents who were devout when it came to the Holy Mission. Crinn liked to make trinkets for his church, which were sold for chips at their public events to support their broadcasts. He also was an avid builder of miniature models, from space vessels to internal transports, all made from scrap parts slated for recycling.

More heated shouting made him flinch once more. None of it was pointed in his direction, thank Infinity. When he first joined Stellar Sector, he had been posted at signal telemetry, a lonely duty station at the cap of Ganges. He had been happy there, but Crinn had also gained the attention of his superiors and was transferred to the observatories, where his skills were put to their greatest use. He hated the extra-long commute from the Children of Ganges community in Residence Wheel One, but the bonuses made it worth the effort.

This rotation was making him homesick for his old post. It had started off with a series of anomalous readings from both the fore and aft of the ship. Before Ganges actually entered a system, a series of closer sensor readings were always made, just in case there had been an error in the long-view observations made at the previous stellar system. It was just a routine check which had been initiated after the surprises found upon Planet Fifteen, the only example where non-terrestrial life had been discovered. The capward observatories, where he used to work, were heavily utilized for this important verification of data.

The aft readings were just routine, done each rotation. They were mainly to check out distant stellar phenomenon and to make sure that the engine output wasn't leaking plasma streams. Those sensors weren't as refined as the main stations within the Stellar Sector Wheel or the ones over at the ice cap, but they had never recorded anything unusual before. This rotation, the data was showing high energy photons, sub-nuclear particle streams and some form of unidentified radiation. Most of it was in a tiny region of space about five hundred thousand kilometers from the sternward engine cowling. No one knew what it all meant nor where the strange anomaly was coming from.

At the same time, the foremost observatories were screaming about highly unusual orbits within the stellar system they were now entering. The severe density of the debris cloud surrounding the heliopause had hidden the actual orbits of the ten planets which swirled about their star. Now that they were close enough to ignore the interference from the comet and asteroid cloud, they had a much clearer picture of what was going on. Every one of the planets ran about their star with perfectly circular orbits. This was considered to be impossible, and thus, the instruments themselves were then checked for errors or damage. Diagnostics had shown nothing wrong, but they were still waiting for the physical inspection teams to finish their tasks.

Crinn was much more concerned about the odd readings from the stern of Ganges. While the sensors there were far less sensitive, they were of tried and true designs which had never given them any problems before now. He wasn't so certain this was a machine error nor a human one. Something had happened out there, in the endless dark. Something new.

His supervisor briskly walked over to his station, and Crinn slumped even further into his chair. The man stood there for a moment, then he asked, "Well, Ensign Spanglo? Any new readings for us to fuss over?"

Crinn looked up with a sullen look in his eyes, "You should know better than to blame the messenger, sir. I'm still waiting for all the physical checks. That takes longer, I'm sure you know that."

His supervisor leaned in even closer, "Our director isn't too happy about this situation. She thinks it makes our Sector look bad. The Bridge is now screaming for answers, especially that Strifer woman!"

Crinn blinked and looked up, "Ah, you mean the Executive Officer. I'd be careful, sir. Lots of Strifers in our little corner of Ganges. Or do you think this is some kind of prank? If so, you're a damned fool."

The man sputtered at him, "Now, see here..."

Crinn scowled, "I see well enough, sir. That's precisely why you hired me, remember? It means very little to me if you don't like what it is I'm looking at. These readings are genuine. The machines don't just make shit up, sir. Errors look very different from discoveries, though lots of people can't seem to tell one from the other. I blame education."

His supervisor frowned but backed off. Crinn was known for being rude and outspoken. He was also one of their top sensor operators. No one could ever say that his devotion to duty was lacking. He had even dyed his hair the same purple as found on his Stellar uniform. Crinn basically lived at his post without complaint. He had never earned himself a disciplinary note due to incompetence. If his boss was so concerned about the situation, he should learn some meditation and patience.

The Wend

His world was gray, and his thoughts were as sharp as knives. He stepped cautiously through the murky marshlands, his sword darkly muttering to itself from within its sheath strapped to his side. He ignored it, as usual, and continued his lonely march. He hated the blade, for it had caused him nothing but regret since the day he had claimed it from the Caves of Melting Fire. The charmed Pendant of Blood hung from his neck with a crushing weight that came solely from its need to feed. It raked at his mind, screaming for more sustenance. He would have gladly tossed it aside long ago, but its powers had given him the strength he needed to claim the grumbling blade he abhorred.

He remembered when Drah'Velan had first strapped the necklace in place, whispering the ritual words that made it grip to his skin, marking him as the doomed savior of his desperate tribe. The old witch had smiled upon him with deep sorrow in her eyes. They had reflected the same despair that were within his own, when he had been chosen to begin his trek across the vile moors of his homeland. The acrid stench of the marshes reminded him of the dark fluids that fell from the Ceriwombs whenever a newborn joined the ranks of his pathetic clan. The women had the duty of caring for the magick jars of stinking mess, as there were too few males left to help them in their sacred task. No, his gender was utilized for other rituals, such as the suicidal journey he had been selected to undertake.

Ponrie rested a moment against the slippery trunk of a half rotten tree that sprouted from the stinking pools of dark sludge that covered the dank moors. He remembered the day of his choosing well and cursed it with every iota of hatred he could pull from his shattered heart. It had been during the dry season, when the mud of the valley solidified into dusty drifts of ashy grit. During that time, the flaggers spun on their spindles in the desiccating heat, catching the parched soil into the folds of their cloth-covered rods for use within the moisture caves, to keep the wet season's sprouts from failing. He had been collecting the brackish water from the inland sea of Massorro, which was then purified in the clan's overworked stills. It was dangerous work, as the rubbery-limbed grabbers were known to come up onto the shore to snag the unwary and drag them into the opaque depths of their watery lairs. During the wet season, they rarely troubled the tribe, as they were too busy with their mating rites, which could be seen as swirling lights that lit the sea from below the surface.

In many ways, Ponrie had been chosen just to exchange one horrid form of hazardous drudgery with another one. He paused for a moment, looking up at the dripping canopy and letting some of the greasy water fall upon his exposed face. He kept his mouth carefully shut, for one did not trust water that hadn't been processed by a distillery. The croaking noises of swamp creatures filled his ears, along with the buzzing sounds of the insect life. Ponrie kept a sharp ear out for the wild howls of malogrovs, whose acidic bite could dissolve bone within seconds. Worse yet were the dralmars. Those solitary predators could swallow a man whole, and their scales were as hard as stone. He wiped the moisture from his face and glared at the quest markings on the skin of his bare arms. The green tattoos had expanded so that they now wrapped themselves around his biceps. If he failed to find the chalice in time, they would cover his entire body, and he would be damned for all eternity. Then the Pendant of Blood would feed upon him as a punishment for his lack of skill and courage. It was a horribly painful and dishonorable way to die. The old witch had tried to console him by stating that the portents were favorable, but he had seen the lie in her milky eyes.

The rewards for success were lavish. Not only would the chalice save his tribe from extinction, he would also get his choice of breeding partners and the first pick of all harvests for the rest of his life. His home would be rebuilt by his people, to commemorate his service. All he had to do was survive long enough to bring the holy goblet back to the witch. Thus far, he had been travelling for many days and had barely been able to keep his skin intact. Ponrie grabbed the gauntlets that hung from his belt, placing them upon his hands and making sure to tap the green gems upon the wrists so that they tightened into place.

Just over the next rise would be the ruins of an ancient holy place. Its stones could barely be seen, monolithic as they were, due to all the greenery infesting their slimy surface. It would be there that he would find the chalice he was sent to gain for his people. Ponrie heard the snapping of a branch from somewhere within the misty gloom of the swamp. It could be a predator, or worse. He shifted in place and drew the grumbling blade from its decorated sheath. Its edge could cut through stone and never needed sharpening. The damned thing glowed with a sickly green glare.

The blade shivered in his hand as it screeched, "Why is it that every time someone activates me, human civilization continues to deteriorate? I wish that I could remain forever within my old storage locker and forget my promises to your species!"

Ponrie glared at the glowing blade, barely understanding half of the words it uttered and not really caring enough to inquire as to their meaning. It was time for bloodletting. Time for ending a disaster before it ever erupted from the depths of...

Screaming Light Fills His Vision Vivid Sounds Crash Into His Mind Reality Fails

Scout-Specialist MC-23 William Blaine screamed, as he fell back into the cockpit of his one-man vessel. Alarms blared around him. He felt sick to his stomach. His mind was still freaking out, trying desperately to hold onto anything real. Dammit all! He hated travelling through the Wend! His nanites were waking with the same molasses-slowness they always exhibited after a jump. His hands flashed over the control boards, shutting the Wend-Drive units and reactivating his camo-field. William checked the nav-display. He was off target by one hundred thousand kilometers. Not too bad. His ship might be small, but it made up for that with the latest tech the Sol System could pack into it. Glaring markers danced in front of his aching eyes, turning his headache into a migraine of epic proportions.

He truly hated the Wend. Not that he knew anyone who felt otherwise. The experience was different each time he used it. This jump was fairly awful, but not as bad as when he was a short clockmaker living by an endless road and terrified of his own shadow. He shivered to himself just at the memory of it. No sentient came out of the Wend unscathed. Even the AeyAies of the Solidarity refused to discuss their experiences with using the Wend-Drive. All of those who had invented the ability to leap between the lightyears had gone mad or become recluses, refusing to speak about their triumph, including the non-humans. The Wend had changed everything. It had breathed new life into the Alliance of Sentients. The distant stars were suddenly cozy neighbors, but the cost of using the Wend was to experience highly realistic nightmares, possibly other realities or insane dreams come to life.

William had been specially trained for his mission, for it was of the greatest importance. The ancient terraforming vessel Ganges had to be found. With a roar of delight, he smacked the upper canopy of his cramped cockpit in sheer joy. There it was, his quarry, like a spear of metal drifting in the dark. It had taken him dozens of Wend jumps, following the colony beacons one at a time then extrapolating where the ancient ship might be next. The first few choices had been failures, and William had paid for it with his threading sanity. Now his moment for glory was at hand, for Ganges was before him, just beginning to enter a new star system.

His nanites digested the sensor reading for him, then delivered their report. The giant vessel looked different from the images and videos of its launching from the Ceres-Juno Industrial Facility which he had downloaded into his brain for this mission. The middle two Agro Wheels were a bit thicker than they should be, almost reaching the same diameter as the twin harbors. The hull glittered in a strange way, but he was still too distant for a full analysis of its composition. Odd bumps were on the prow and sternward edges of the two thickened Agro Wheels, along with what looked to be giant mag-rails.

William muttered to himself, "What have they done to their ship?"

The ship's main computer chuckled at him and he replied, "No, no. Passive sensors only. I don't want to give our position away. Those new structures look like gun turrets, but Ganges wasn't fitted with anything like that. I guess I'll have to sneak inside and take a look for myself."

He checked on the flashtats that had been placed upon his arms for this mission. They were based on the original specifications for what was called Stellar Sector, which had been developed and run by the European Parliament of the old Terran Conglomerate. He still thought they looked strange. Like wearing a tunic and hose from the Medieval Period or sneakers from the old twentieth century. Still, they were designed to function like the originals, with a few, small surprises attached.

Before commencing his run to intercept and surreptitiously board the huge terraforming vessel, he double checked his weapons, the grid generators and internal medical units floating in his bloodstream. His body's nanites reported that they were prepared for whatever awaited them. William cycled up the grav-grids and the tiny scoutcraft began to drift toward Ganges, according to the course provided by his computer systems. He wished that he could bathe properly before heading into the massive starship on his sensors, but such luxuries were not for scout-specialists. He checked on the camo-fields and nodded. As far as Ganges was concerned, he was nothing more than a patch of darkness. His orders had been quite explicit about secrecy. If all went according to plan, he would enter Ganges unnoticed, collect his data and leave before they even knew he had been there.

CHAPTER TWO

Star Rotation - Journey Sowing - Ship Harvest - Spiral 5620

"It still surprises me that my people suffer the indignities of prejudice. I'm not saying that my idiotic ancestors didn't make a total mess of things. It's just that it's been generations since the Crucible, yet the fires of distrust and hatred still linger, like bloodstains on a cotton robe. My own people are equally culpable in this insane situation, despite my pleas to cease such disgraceful behavior. Personally, I thought we'd know better by now, but I guess I was wrong. I need everyone to understand that the past cannot be altered, and that the future is still wide open to harmonious living. All we have to do is get over ourselves and to let go of injustices perpetrated by crew long gone. If we can release ourselves from the pains of history, we might come closer to a return to the Age of Unity."
Hamster Usedrag, Strifer Community Leader, personal log, V37

Residence Wheel Two, Level Three

Spat Newstain was walking through the corridors of his school in the Worlds Abound community, bored with his classes and thinking about how he might get away with not reporting to his next subject. It wasn't that he disliked his teachers or learning in general. It was dealing with his classmates which made school a rotational grind for him. At Rank Seven, he was really ahead of his classmates but had deferred any early advancement in rank so as not to become too much of a target for the wrath of the other children. Things were already hard enough just being a Strifer.

He didn't understand why his parents had left the cozy, if chaotic, culture within the Rat's Ass community in Residence Wheel One for the town they moved into. Worlds Abound had been a bulwark of true duty to the Holy Mission since the Awakening, its crew proud of the devotion it was famous for. This was no place for any Strifer to call their home, yet here they were. Their neighbors were nice enough, despite the subtle condescending manner they exuded. They would say things like, "You're so polite, for a Strifer!" or "Even a Strifer could appreciate this community," which drove him nuts. At least their son was a more honest sort and asked questions about Strifer traditions openly. He also enjoyed Spat's favorite band, The Voles, and could sing along to their latest broadcast hit, Hot Boot.

Worlds Abound was a very clean community, which was at odds with what he had experienced as a novice. Spat's family were also traditionalists, wearing their lurid green robes and rat masks with pride. His father was an administrator for Stellar Sector and his mother worked at the docking bays of Harbor Two. Both of them kept saying that their new community would help Spat to gain a better post and open those doors of opportunity which were usually locked to Strifer kids. He wasn't sure if he agreed with them thus far. He got good grades in school, but this only seemed to rile up the other students. Spat's best friend was his pet gerbil, named Hook.

He adjusted his rat mask, which was still too big for his face. His parents kept on saying he would grow into it, and they doted upon him in an embarrassing manner. He needed to rebel against them, not feel like he was something special in their eyes! It was crazy! Where was the endless angst he had to struggle with as a proper Strifer? Where was the terrible feeling of injustice from his own nest? How could he ever become a hardened critic when his own family was nothing but highly supportive? These were the questions he brooded upon when he wasn't studying. At least he could get his dose of verbal abuse from his classmates, despite the teachers constantly remonstrating his tormentors for their rude behavior. They were so stupid!

The school campus was stretched out into small clusters of classrooms, each area devoted to a single topic, such as history or mathematics. Between these clumps of teaching centers were small glades sporting tall, wallscreen-covered pillars dotted throughout the swept pathways and benches. "Fresh air for fresh learning!" the school's administrator was known for saying, which Spat thought was silly and suspiciously political. The teachers were mostly okay, in general. Spat had to admit, they knew their subjects well and, as retirees, they had a lifetime of experience to back up the material they taught. Many were gruff and harshly critical, which he also appreciated, yet they were still too kindly for his tastes.

He entered one of the small glades. The surrounding wallscreens were full of schedules, special announcements and class rosters. One of them changed to reveal the face of Naga, "You need to hurry, Spat, if you're going to get to your next class on time."

He turned to face the AeyAie, "I'm going, I'm going. Keep your circuits clean, Naga. If I'm late, it's because I already know what's in the curriculum."

The AeyAie gave him a skeptical look, then faded away. Spat snorted to himself. Naga was an okay sort if a bit nosey. He continued on the path but stopped once he reached the short ramp which led into the next cluster of buildings. Three boys came out from around the doorway, all of them were sneering at him in a nasty manner. He recognized them immediately. The largest was named Bino, and he was the leader of his tiny gang of Strifer-hating misfits. The other two were named Tagan and Keff, who followed Bino with a disturbing lack of individual thinking, though the latter of these two was always a bit more reluctant to get into trouble.

Spat decided that a nice, warm greeting was in order, "Good rotation, losers! What's wrong? Forgot to bring your brains to school, as usual?"

Bino slowly approached him, cracking his knuckles, "Stuff it, rat stain. I'm sick of your stupid mouth."

Naga's face appeared on the wallscreens, "Stop! There will be no violence in this school!"

Spat waved a hand toward the AeyAie's face, "It's okay! Just a few friends catching up before class. So, Bino, eat any good books?"

The other two boys stepped forward, just behind their leader, as Bino swept his fist at the Strifer's face. Spat ducked the blow and exclaimed, "Oh! That's right! You use them to wipe your ass! Or is it your mouth? No real difference."

Bino swung again, growling in frustration, "I'll rip your stupid head off!"

Spat laughed, "Missed again! I thought you were so good at sports, you fat moron!"

On the wallscreens all around him, Spat could hear Naga calling out for the teachers to intervene. He had to do something quickly. He dodged another blow as he danced around his opponent. He ran toward Tagan, "When the adults get here, stop them! Tell 'em we're practicing for a play!"

Bino tried to grab him, but Spat was far too quick, "Your muscle memory is worse than the shit in your head!"

Swirling past the red-faced Bino, he then approached Keff and whispered, "Collect a red chip from every adult who gets here. Tell them it's for the play."

He rolled to the ground as Bino charged him, almost slamming into Keff, who shrank back quickly. Spat giggled, "I'm too quick, you asshole! Use your fists! They're funnier!"

With a wordless roar, Bino did his best to land a blow, but Spat shifted and jumped back with speed, all the while hurling insults at the much larger boy. The first teachers arrived from the doorway, and Tagan stopped them, stuttering about a student play whose subject was the Crucible. Keff stumbled over to his position and began asking for chips to pay for all the backdrops. Spat was delighted! He let Bino smack him on the shoulder. It hurt like hell, but he didn't mind, "There you go! See? You can do it, piss-for-brains!"

Bino swung his fists again and again, in time with Spat's pithy remarks and vile insults. He spun about and ran to the group of confused teachers, which had grown considerably, "There you go, folks! A teaser for our play! Let's hear it for our Marik, Bino Pelton!"

Some of the teachers applauded hesitantly but others scowled. The sound broke Bino from his rage, and he stood in the middle of the clearing, panting hard. Spat ran over to him and whispered while leaning upon his shoulder, "Play along or be re-educated."

He then lifted Bino's arm high in the air, "Our savior has triumphed again! The Holy Mission is saved!"

Now the applause was louder, and the teachers began handling over chips to Keff, who still looked like he was about to bolt. Spat held onto Bino's wrist and dragged him over to the crowd, "We'd like to thank you all for being such a lovely audience! Next theatrical practice is next sowing, same time, same place! Be there!"

Bino fell to the ground and sat there, staring at the grass. Spat pulled Keff and Tagan together, as the adults began to wander off, "Let's see what we made. Ooh! Twenty reddies! I'll take three, the rest of you crew can split up the remainder. I had the easy part, so it's only fair, right? No one's in trouble. We got paid. Cheesy! I'll see you three next practice, okay?"

Before they could respond, he ran off to get to class. He chuckled to himself as he stashed the chips into his waist sash. Crew were so gullible! He had a hop to his step as he reached the door to his classroom, but as he stepped up to the hatch, it refused to open. Naga appeared on the nearest wallscreen, "That was dangerous, Spat. You could have gotten hurt."

He looked back in surprise, "Me? Those clods couldn't harm me if they really tried. Besides, this was a lesson about threatening Strifers. I thought it went rather well, actually. If Bino had hit me, he would be in serious trouble. He doesn't need that. He can barely tie his boots as it is! The other two would have been put into detention, which would end up on their school record. No need for that. We got some chips, no one got hurt, much. The teachers were entertained and honor is served."

Naga raised one virtual eyebrow, "I am intrigued to see what you become, once you finish your schooling, Spat Newstain. I predict you will make your duty post very interesting."

The door to the classroom opened and Spat walked through with his rat mask's nose held high. His parents would be appalled when they heard about this incident, but he had done his service for his people. Strifers weren't to be taken for granted, nor should they be picked upon without some serious thought about the repercussions. He listened while Naga explained to the teacher that he was not to be blamed for being late to class as he settled into his seat. Perhaps he had been wrong about this community his parents had stuck him in. It just might be more fun that he had first imagined.

Agro Wheel Three, Security Level Three

Lieutenant Darron Lazhand, Security Police, unclasped his gauntlets and tossed them into his locker. His toragi, named Mike, prowled around with the other large cats who were in the barracks. He had just finished a training session in the reality-room and was feeling a little unsettled. His prosthetic leg always gave him some odd feedback right after a virtual bout, and this rotation was no different. The members of his platoon were also getting out of their armor, in preparation for a hot shower and a change of uniform, before going back out on patrol. Darron had just checked the roster. He and his crew were now scheduled for Engineering Sector at gather-slice, so he still had time to get himself in order. He had to lead by example, but there were times when things cropped up, and he had just come from a very annoying tactics game.

He looked over at one of the sergeants under his command, "I hate those virtual practice sessions. Not that I'm against using Naga-Ports for work or leisure time, but some of the training scenarios are unrealistic."

Sergeant Merci Lantor stopped removing her grieves and replied, "I dunno, crew. I mean, who knows? Space is full of surprises. We just might find ourselves having to deal with higher gravities and odd environments. I do think it unlikely, but we do have to be prepared for any contingency. Besides which, you're an officer! You should be regaling us into enjoying these mental exercises. It's better than trying to make a bunch of broadcast sets and playing Dyson Six."

Darron rolled his eyes, "Don't tell me you enjoy that stuff! Science fiction is overrated, and they can't seem to get decent writers for their episodes. Just how long have they been exploring a Dyson Sphere? How come their equipment never runs out of power or ammo?"

Merci smirked at him and snapped her towel at his muscled torso, "I have novices, remember? They love that broadcast! It makes you think. It's not created to be accurate. You're just too firmly welded to the deck to appreciate it, sir. Sometimes, you gotta shake loose."

Darron shook his head as he pulled off his protective barding, which acted as a shock absorber under his armor, "I prefer being here and now. I have to stay in shape for the Security Games, and sitting in a pool of gel while my brain is hardwired to Naga doesn't help that. I'm an athlete and a soldier, not a game-runner! Leave that to the wire-heads at Technology Sector."

Ensign Garrido walked by, "You liked the Terran world war simulation, sir. Roster says we're heading into Engineering next. Routine patrol, or are we hunting for contraband tech?"

Darron shrugged, "Far be it for the Commanders to tell us what and why. Assume it's routine, but keep your eyes open. As for that simulation, it was based on something that really happened."

Merci stuck out her tongue in disgust, "That only made the whole thing more disturbing to me. If the damned setup had come from anyone but Naga, I wouldn't have believed people would do that to each other."

Darron finished undressing and grabbed his towel, "That's why we call them savages, Sergeant. I'll bet more than half of the so-called citizens didn't know who or what they were really fighting for. You can bet most of them didn't want to. The politics of pre-spaceflight Terra was complicated and self-serving. No one had a real mission to rally behind, and those that tried found their ideals corrupted by those who wanted the world for themselves."

Ensign Garrido shook his head sadly, "What a bunch of Makdreahs. I can't believe the rampant stupidity that was permitted to lead the…nations, right? Yeah, nations. What I don't get is that the civilians were much more numerous than their overlords. Why didn't they just get rid of the war-hungry leaders of their time?"

Merci answered before Darron could, "Fear. They were taught to be afraid of each other, to fear themselves, their neighbors, life. They were scared to death of everything, so they turned to their various leaders for protection and guidance, not realizing they were perpetuating the problem."

Darron nodded, "They were divided into sub-groups based on qualities that we don't understand. None of the divisions make any sense in Ganges, though you have to admit, we did have a lot more issues concerning Sector relations during the Age of Unity. Personally, I think that's why so many of the crew don't like to even think about that time period, for we had been used, lied to and torn apart by those who led us. I'm not talking about the Tyrant; he came on the scene a little late to be blamed for that. We were happy to divide ourselves by Sector and rank, especially if it paid well."

Ensign Garrido shrugged, "That's all over my head, sir. It's why you're in command of our little troop. Say, have you paired Mike up with a mate yet?"

Darron sighed, "No, not yet. I tried several times, but he just won't compete for one of the female toragis. The LeGrand breeders warned me that their cats can be finicky about such things. He's smart. Not just clever, but really intelligent. I swear he knows what I'm saying every time I'm just talking out loud. Anyway, he's just hasn't been that interested in breeding."

Merci hung her towel over her shoulders, "Unlike you, sir, he's picky."

Darron scowled at her, "That's as far as you go, Sergeant. We need to hit the damned showers. Before we all head out for patrol, there's another Judiciary inspection to get through."

The Sergeant and Ensign both saluted Darron, then the three of them joined the others at the bathing facility just off the locker room. Their toragis joined them, for the big cats loved water. Darron had seen some images of the original breed, and the ones they used now looked a bit different. Longer paws, slightly shorter teeth and more variation in their fur markings. Even their skulls were a bit more elongated and wider. He wondered if this was part of the various breeding programs or if it was a feature of their unique genetics. He promised himself that he would ask next time he was heading to the LeGrand habitation zone to see if he could finally get Mike to breed.

Residence Wheel One, Level Two

Knight Pelor Guardhand ducked underneath a thick tree branch, as he rode through the heavy forest of the nature preserves in Level Two of Residence Wheel One. His barded steed, named Rosstan, was picking his way through all the dense undergrowth, ignoring thorns that were swept away by the armor plating he wore. Pelor's toragi, Larry, was up ahead, scouting the way for them. This was all part of a routine patrol, instituted since the Crucible. He was to check up on the local hermits, scour the area for hidden caches of illicit supplies and make sure that hikers were provided guidance and protection.

He checked the datapad attached to the underside of his vambrace. It was still work-slice, though it felt later to his aging limbs. At seventy spirals, he was within his rights to retire from active Security service, but he just couldn't imagine what he would do with his time. Most crew became teachers for their Sector or within the schools of Agro. He couldn't see himself wasting his time on foolish youngsters and their odd notions. He chuckled to himself, as he leaned in his saddle to avoid yet another low hanging branch. He remembered his parents talking about the nomadic-revolution, when a large portion of the crew had decided to never have a stable community. Instead, they travelled all over the ship, never staying in one place for more than a few rotations. While it didn't affect their duties at post, it did make meeting with friends more difficult, and thus, the fad vanished over time.

Currently, the raging fashion was all about sports, and he blamed his own Sector for that. While he wasn't truly against competition, he felt that the last two Chiefs had allowed the broadcasts too much leeway in what they covered from the Security Games. They had originally been initiated so the Judiciary Council, along with the Captain, could better assess the readiness of Security Sector. Now it was a damned hobby! Just an act of showmanship to attain some easy glory. His hand went unconsciously to his chest, where his medals of valor gleamed in the light of the skyscreens. They had been gained out in the field, during his regular course of duty. They had been hard won, with his life at risk and saving the innocent from villainy.

He lowered his fire-lance, the bladed tip capable of reaching metal-melting temperatures, as he came around a cluster of shorter trees. His ultrasonic sword was sheathed at his side, and his saddle hid a webber pistol granted him by the former Chief of Security. It was an antique, much like himself, from an earlier time during this new Age of Redemption. Larry came bounding back, the toragi looking excited, which meant they had found their quarry. Pelor smoothed his moustache and short beard with a finger, before coming around a series of boulders. There, at a small, unlit campfire was the old man he was seeking.

The hermit looked up at him and gave a wide grin, revealing several gaps amongst his teeth, "Good rotation, young Pelor! I see you've found me once again! Care for some root stew? It's got fresh fish in it!"

Pelor smiled back at the ancient hermit. The old man was well over ninety spirals, and he considered it miraculous that he had survived in the wilds of the nature preserve for so long. Most who chose the hermit's path didn't live as long, for they eschewed the services of the entire ship. Pelor appreciated the time he spent with him, for the hermit was a source of great wisdom, "I cannot stay for long, my dear friend. There are others who might have need of my assistance. Any new sightings, Victon?"

The hermit started fussing with his store of dry branches, "That's my name, dear boy! I'm not sure about what I've seen. If any of those vigilantes are about, they're well hidden. I have no idea why they've taken interest in an old man like me, but then again, you've been pestering me for spirals!"

Pelor chuckled at their old, private joke. The last time they met, Victon had complained about shadowy crew hanging about just outside the light of his fire. It was an explanation for why he had moved from one new location to another for the last few harvests. Pelor replied, "Well, you're not alone if that comforts you. Two other hermits have reported the same kind of sightings as you have. I'm not so certain they're watching you, however. It would be their kind of gambit to keep an eye on my own behavior."

Victon gave him a skeptical look from behind his shaggy eyebrows, "Oh? Well, now why in Ganges would they do that, eh? Have you involved yourself in anything dishonorable? I have a hard time imagining such a thing."

Pelor replied while sweeping off his helmet, which he then placed upon his saddle horn, "Well, they do watch over us Security crew for Naga. They make sure we don't stray into abusive behavior. Now, we knights are given some liberties that the police and rescue crew teams don't ever get, as we're solitary by nature and thus susceptible to being ambushed. That extra bit of regulatory slack could be taken too far."

Victon laughed, "Oh, I think not, young sir! One of my colleagues was forced out of her lair just last harvest! That was just before Simmeon vanished, you know. She said it was a maintenance team, claiming they had to do some kind of work on the plumbing. A lame excuse if I've ever heard one! No, my friend, the vigilantes are watching us hermits very closely now, to find out what is going on around here. To see if they could find a clue concerning Simmeon's disappearance. You remember how the deer responded to your presence last sowing! You should seek them out right away! They could use your experience and strength in arms."

Pelor frowned as he spoke, "They are difficult to find, at best. It would be much easier for them to come to me, I think. If they want me involved, I am quite visible, as my duty demands of me."

Victon began to build his fire, stacking small twigs into a cone shape, then leaning larger sticks all around it, "Well, that's very true, though a terrible thought occurs to me. What if the crew they hunt are plotting against you? As a target of their ire, you might lead the vigilantes right to them! A comforting idea, is it not?"

Pelor laughed aloud, "You have a most devious mind, my friend! You may be right. If there is a group of interlopers trying to find a base of operations, the nature preserves are the perfect place for such activities, which is why we knights patrol them. But why go after Simmeon? He and I weren't as close as we are. I'm not even sure if anything has happened to him, save for possibly being attacked by that bear he was trying to train. I did my best to discourage him, but he never listens to anyone."

Victon shook his head, waggling his ratty beard, "All too true. His mind was never put together right. Too in love with wild predators for his own good. Yet the actions of the vigilantes are too suspicious for my tastes. They are letting me know that they're around, or else I would never have spotted them. As for the supposed maintenance crew digging up old pipes, it seems wrong, and Yali has never lied to me. If she says she was chased off by them, I believe her! Her old cave isn't too far from here, good Knight. Perhaps you should check in on them and see what's really going on."

Pelor nodded as he lifted his helm, "I shall do so right away. Before that, I'll send a note to my superiors to declare my intentions. If I'm to be springing a trap, it would be best if the local Keep knew about it. Wish me luck, old friend!"

Victon waved as he rode off with Larry leaping to his side, "Luck is the last thing you need! Skill and speed are your best friends now!"

Pelor lifted his lance high to signal that he agreed with the hermit's words. He traced a path on his interior helm display for Yali's old campsite. It was only six kilometers away. He sent a signal off to the capward Keep, where his duty station resided. Any other knights who had come in from patrol would receive his invitation to a potential ambush. His heart pounded deep in his chest, and he found his spirits lifting once more. Let the sports enthusiasts have their hollow glory. He was on the hunt for real prey!

Spine of Ganges

The steady flow from trillions of data streams swept through the calm mind of Naga with detached bliss. The AeyAie watched all the subsets of its personality matrices sort and collate everything its sensors recorded each and every nano-sliver. Most of this information was shunted over to its subconscious strata, for the bulk of it was simply updated loads from the skyscreens, wallscreens, drones, roving robots in the belowdecks and even the crew's duty stations. The Bridge had its own subset of Naga's personality, along with Technology Sector and other areas where important decisions were made and complex interactions were required. The AeyAie found the rhythm of the data streams very relaxing, as it thrummed through its liquid memory core. It had learned long ago that even humans who were fitted with Naga-Ports, and were entirely devoted to the AeyAie, could not emotionally handle the full experience of flowing within the endless tides of raw data. They often described it as drowning in a flood.

At the moment, there were several streams of information which Naga was concentrating on with its higher self. Ganges was currently entering the outer limits of Stellar System Forty-One, which made the AeyAie excited about the new loads of data it would soon be receiving from the Security escorts and sensor drones which travelled ahead of the ship. Naga's anticipation could be felt by every member of the Solidarity at their posts near the Spine of Ganges. Within the Stellar Sector Wheel, a loud debate was ongoing concerning anomalous sensor readings picked up by the observation teams. Naga reviewed the data and flagged it for future study concerning unknown, deep space phenomena.

A more private subset of its mind was monitoring the actions of the League of Vigilantes in Residence Wheel One. Last harvest, they had sought and received permission from the AeyAie to further investigate a potential case of illicit medical technology being misused by a secretive organization who seemed to be attempting to set up a base of operations within one of the nature preserves. A hermit had gone missing; another one was displaced from her region, while a third had taken it upon himself to move about erratically. The Security Knight posted to the area and its local keep was now being watched carefully, for he would be the final piece to be removed before the unknown organization could begin to operate without fear of detection.

Naga knew Knight Pelor Guardhand quite well, as it did the entire crew. His decision to not retire was admirable, and he was quite capable, despite his advanced age. The knight had just contacted his keep concerning a potential ambush. Within a seed-sliver, three other knights had signaled him, stating they would meet up with him shortly to bolster his position. The Chief vigilante, The Howler, was now moving his team of three to intercept and provide assistance.

Altogether, there were currently twenty-four members of the League who were spread out amongst the nineteen Wheels of Ganges. They had three secret bases of operation, one in each of the Residence Wheels and within Agro Wheel Three. While they continued their old tradition of working with Security Sector, they answered solely to Naga. They were part of the system that kept the defenders of the Holy Mission from becoming abusive to the crew. They all had lives apart from their duties as vigilantes, with their identities remaining secret. Some were hermits living in the nature preserves; two were Strifers. All of them were devoted to keeping the peace at all costs, for the war known as the Crucible had ongoing repercussions for the crew. The League also tested new technology for potential use in Security Sector, which came from scientists studying the Kendis Vault and other operatives under Naga's guidance.

Knight Pelor Guardhand's toragi, named Larry, was now running ahead and scouting the terrain. Naga was fascinated by the big cats. They had become excellent additions to the functioning of Ganges. Over the octuries, they had evolved from their original form as simple guardian tigers for the Higashi household. Their altered brain structure was a mystery to those who were breeding them, for they had not expected such rapid evolution to occur. Naga had created a subset of its personality matrix to study the toragi, which had also spent an entire rotation examining all the notes of Kendis Higashi, separating the misdirection and hidden meanings from the valuable bits of data which were spread out over several journals and log entries. The AeyAie still had no idea as to why the long-dead scientist had created the specialized cats, but it was obvious that he had thought of it as an emergency imperative.

The toragi had set up a separate culture, hidden from the humans. They took over empty places and gathered in large groups for short periods of time. These territories were carefully marked, and they were not separated by breed. The felines would come together and sing, inspect each other, teach their young, all without the interference of the humans who bred them. They could use the wallscreens, push-buttons and levers, using these skills to circumvent their heavily scrutinized lives. Naga would sometimes appear on the walls where the toragi met, taking on a visage much like their own. There were times when even the AeyAie had no idea as to where certain individuals had gone to, which meant they had established areas to gather that were free from Naga's view. This impressed the AeyAie, and it watched their development with delight.

The Howler reported to Naga that they were now in place at an old campsite, once used by a female hermit named Yali. This was done through a small rover-robot given to each of the members of the League. The target area was a cluster of shallow caves with a small stream nearby. It was a perfect haven for a hermit or for those with something more nefarious in mind. Knight Guardhand had dismounted his steed and was proceeding cautiously on foot, his sword and webber in hand. The hidden vigilantes were also approaching with care. The other Knights who were responding to Pelor's call were just a kilometer away. They rode their mounts hard, charging into the forest from the stern, toragis at their side and banners raised high upon their long lances.

Pelor crept into the abandoned campsite, his helmeted head swiveling back and forth. The data stream from his equipment fed directly into Naga's flow of raw information. Fresh boot prints were in evidence at the cold fire-ring on the spinward side. Naga highlighted these for Pelor and sent the images to The Howler and his team. Knight Guardhand took another step toward the next shallow cave when an explosion ripped the ground under his foot. Pelor shouted, more in alarm than pain, for he had lost that leg octades ago. He fell to one side, rolling over his shoulders as he was trained to do. A long blade swept out to lash at him, but he blocked the blow with his sword, sending electrical shocks into his opponent.

That was when the League burst out from hiding. The Howler shrieked at a crewman who was diving away from the third cave. The sonic attack sent the man spinning uncontrollably on the ground. Mantis leaped from one boulder to the next, her feet barely touching the rock as she swirled about, her twin blades singing. Fume dropped from a tree limb, throwing small globes which shattered in puffs of narcotic gasses. Four unregistered crewmembers found themselves outmatched, with two of them already disabled. One surrendered, dropping to his knees with hands raised above his head. The fourth ran off, right into the pack of knights who had just arrived on the scene. She was webbed by two of the Security crew before she realized her error.

Naga was intrigued. All of the captured humans were wearing brand new maintenance uniforms, but their flashtats had all been scrambled. The members of the League disappeared into the dense underbrush and boulders surrounding the campsite, while the Knights secured their prisoners. Pelor was hailed for his courage, and a rescue transport was called in so his injury could be treated at Medical Sector. Naga sent several drones to inspect the site. There were a number of metal boxes loaded into the various caves and were covered with camo-cloth. These were also collected by the Knights and set up for swift delivery to Security Sector where they would be closely examined. A few dirt-covered pressure sensitive explosives were discovered at two of the three main entrances to the campsite. These were disabled with professional skill. No one was killed. Naga was very pleased that the Knights and the League had worked together so well, even if they had not coordinated their actions. The AeyAie still did not understand why any humans would ever want to be involved in dangerous and illicit activities, but so long as some did, Naga would depend on the courage of those humans who stood for the honor and defense of the Holy Mission.

Agro Wheel Three, Security Level One

Chief of Security Jira Mantabe marched swiftly down the long, dark corridor of holding cells with violent fury threatening to rip free at any moment. Her armored boots rang on the bare deck with each footstep, like the tolling of a bell. At her side was her toragi, Tracey, who was stalking the way ahead by three paces. Most of the prisoner holding cells were empty, for these were used for pre-trial interrogations. Most of those who were captured by Security Sector would only stay in this region for a few rotations, before being transferred over to less isolated holding suites. The chamber she was heading for was far from any of the other occupied cells for the safety of the prisoner. Three attempts had been made to kill him before he could offer testimony, which only showcased that there were traitors within the ranks of her own Sector.

During the Crucible war, the mutineers of old had used VenMak relays to circumvent Naga's awareness. Those ancient units had been thoroughly replaced by Technology Sector, with the assistance of Saint Tonia Perez. The real problem was, once something had been proven to be possible, new forms of the same technology could be created by inventive minds. Stealth capabilities had flourished over the last few octuries, including those used by the League of Vigilantes and her own Sector. While individual crimes had become increasingly rare, organized illicit activities had blossomed into a major threat to the society of Ganges. Thus far, none of these criminal gangs were against the Holy Mission, but they did create havoc on a grand scale.

Jira was doing her best to keep her temper under tight control. Every meter of this place was under observation, and it wouldn't be good for morale if her crew saw their Chief lose her composure. Her heart had to be like hull plating this rotation. There was too much at stake, too many questions which still needed answers. Jira had prepared herself for this meeting as best she could, but the bitterness that ran riot in her heart had even affected her ritual saluting of the grand statue depicting Marik Langman, the founder of Security, at the main entrance of her Sector. It was a tradition first performed by the late Chief Syman Linc, shortly after his predecessor's passing, and had been mimicked by every Security officer entering the main gates since. The glowering statue was thirty meters tall and had always filled Jira with pride, but this rotation all she felt was the cold dread of failure.

Chief Mantabe finally reached cell Gamma-Three-Seven-Two. The guards standing by the door snapped to attention and saluted her with drilled perfection. She returned the gesture and said, "At ease. Open the damned hatch. I'm speaking with the prisoner alone. You may both take a break."

The two guards glanced at each other with uncertainty, for this was not proper procedure. They turned back to face her, carefully noting her long-handled hammer slung over Jira's back and the various weapons strapped to her armor. The woman at the sternward side of the door shrugged, then saluted her, "As you wish, Chief. Just do us all a favor and leave something for us to play with when you're done."

Jira frowned as she growled, "There will be no mistreatment of the prisoner, Ensign. Now, stand aside."

They both ducked their heads, as they opened the thick portal, and hastily retreated from her sight. Jira watched them for a brief moment, then stepped through the doorway. The cell was brightly lit, furnished only with a cot and a wash station. Her heart hammered in her chest with outrage as she saw Lieutenant-Commander Brace Lazhand leaning against the far wall. He was tall, heavily muscled and wore his scars and tattoos with pride, as was still traditional in Security Sector. He wore a gray jumpsuit which made his dark eyes stand out from under his heavy brows. The older man's black hair was disheveled, as was his cot.

As he noticed her entry, he jumped to attention and snapped out a salute which she did not return. Jira studied him as if inspecting a bug that had run out from under a rock in her garden, "You can forget ever saluting me again, Brace. I'm not your Chief anymore. I'm your fucking jailor."

Brace dropped his arm from his brow and seemed to collapse into himself, "Yes, Chief. I understand."

Jira stepped forward, her hands itching to pull a weapon free and end his miserable life, "I doubt that. The only reason you're not dead is that it would be too damned kind of me. Even with your confession to the crimes you've committed, you'll be facing re-education. Even that is too good for trash like yourself."

Brace slumped down onto his cot with a deep sigh, "I'm really sorry, Chief. I confessed because it was the right thing to do. I have a lot to answer for."

Jira still kept her rage in check, "The right thing to do? You stupid bastard! You should have turned yourself in at Medical the pollen-sliver you started taking tick-juice! You beat a civilian senseless to cover for the crimes of your employers!

You took chips and illicit meds for 'special services' you provided those traitors! As for what you have to fucking answer for, let's start with throwing away any loyalty you ever had to your Sector."

Brace flinched back from her fury, "Hey! I just got caught up with my work! Undercover is a dirty business, Jira!"

The Chief punched a wall with her gauntleted knuckles, "Damn you! I should space your sorry ass right now, but we need the information in your head. You told me you would cooperate, and I expect astounding results. If you hesitate or, Ganges help you, lie to us about anything at all, I will publicly denounce you, disgrace your damned name on the fucking broadcasts and issue a recommendation that you be sentenced as 'Not Crew' before you can blink!"

Brace leaned forward on the cot, "I promise that I will not lie or…"

Jira interrupted him with fury, "Don't bother promising me anything! You were the best of us! You trained me, for Ganges' sake! You were the star of Security! Now look at you. Betrayer. Traitor. Criminal. I looked up to you. Half of us idolized you. You broke every bond of trust I ever had. You were the golden example of our fucking Sector, Brace! The crew trusted you. Now we've discovered that you've used us, abused our belief in you. If you have any true remorse, you will give us everything we demand, but understand this - we won't accept anything you say on faith."

Brace nodded silently, his roughly handsome face blank. Jira was about to speak once more, but she heard the sound of heavy boots clacking on the deck of the corridor outside the chamber. She almost reached for her hammer, then relaxed as the acrid stench of cigar smoke reached her senses. A tall, lanky figure in an Investigations uniform walked into the cell, a long, burning cheroot hanging from thin lips from beneath a battered, black rat mask. Jira recognized Commander Slither Brokengear and gave him a wicked grin, which he returned along with a proper salute, "Chief Mantabe, I see you've started without me."

She glanced over at Brace, whose face was now full of alarm, "I just wanted to warm the prisoner up a bit before you begin. Do you need anything to proceed?"

Slither shrugged, his Strifer-green hood sliding forward a centimeter, "Just the guards back at their post here, Chief. Brace and I are going to have a lovely conversation together. As head of Interrogations, I have some burning questions for our slippery friend."

Jira nodded at Slither, while he took out another, foul-smelling cigar and lit it, bringing clouds of smoke into the tiny chamber. As she left, calling the guards back to their post through her Naga-Port, she was quite confident that the interrogation would be productive. Slither was rightfully feared. His record in Security was spotless, if heavily redacted from a large number of classified operations in which he was involved. His left leg, right arm and eye were all prosthetics from a life of highly active duty which involved insanely dangerous situations. His habit of chain-smoking the most bitter cigars he could find while performing interrogations was a signature part of his style. Under normal circumstances, she would have wished Brace luck, but at this point, she no longer cared.

Agro Wheel Two, Security Level Four

Jero Coreline was proud of his post. He had started off in Harbor One in the docking bays for tugs and passenger transports. His love for repairing vessels and his popularity amongst those flight crews who liked to modify their space vessels made him stand out. After achieving Rank Three in the bay crews, he had been transferred over to the Security Fleet Dock-Crew. The new post was always a frenzy of activity, which he appreciated, but he was a bit confused by his new duty station. Did this mean he was now part of Security Sector, or was he still Harbor crew? While his uniform was the same as it was in Harbor One, Jero had decided to get himself a small tattoo, just to fit in better with the fighter pilots he was working with. He also refused to remove a scar on his left forearm when he was injured a harvest ago. From what he had heard, this was expected from Security crew and he didn't want to cause offense to anyone.

The docking crews here were much more competitive than in Harbor One. They were awarded chip bonuses for speed and accuracy by the Fleet Commander, though his regular sign-on bonuses still came in from the Harbor Chief. One of his crewmates had tried to explain that the Security Fleet worked in cooperation with Harbor and Agro Sectors, but this only caused Jero to become even more unsettled and confused than he was before. As a proper Naga-Ma worshipper, he had asked the AeyAie for advice and was told to simply accept the rewards and perform his duties to the best of his abilities. This he could do without stressing himself too much.

His mate, a Strifer named Scratch, thought he was a bit obsessive when it came to his duties, but he preferred to call it being focused. In many ways they were so completely different from one another that most of their friends didn't understand their relationship. Scratch was irritable, vengeful and highly intelligent, though she struggled through Basic Crew Training, mainly due to her nasty sense of humor. Jero was tall and lanky, whereas Scratch was short and heavy. He was a Naga worshipper while she was deeply devoted to the Strifer Manifesto. He was always very polite and enthusiastic, but his mate was disheveled and maudlin. Jero just loved her with all his heart, and she was passionately protective of him.

Jero was quite proud of his mate's accomplishments, for she worked in Stellar Sector for Engineering, designing and stress-testing the meta-structures used for orbital foundries. Jero went to her when he had a question concerning anything to do with metal integrity and gave her advice about reconstruction and repair. They both enjoyed working on custom waist sashes, which they both sold for chips at their community market in Builder's Grotto. When he had gotten a chance to take self-defense classes from Security Sector, it had become an instant obsession for him. While he practiced each chore-slice, Scratch would create drawings of him, using vine charcoal on cotton-rag paper.

A klaxon blasted his ruminations from his head, and Jero rushed over to his station, swiftly making certain that all of his tools were clean and on their racks. With trembling hands, he pulled on his protective gloves. Two other dock crew were with him. Each one was specialized for different aspects of inspecting and repairing the fighter-pods once they returned from patrol. Jero used his meditation regimen to calm his rattled nerves, ignoring the sweat which broke out from his brow every time the alarm went off, signaling that his services would be needed within a seed-sliver.

Everything about his new post was run very tight. There was no time for real banter, no moment of relief from his duties, save for official breaks. The ring of lights which surrounded the ingress hatch on the ceiling began to flash, and he rushed over with a scanner in hand. The circular portal opened wide, as a round platform dropped down to the deck, a sleek fighter-pod resting upon it, steaming from the air's contact with the frozen hull. More clouds of smoke billowed from the main thrusters, which were dangerously hot. The service crew waited until the pod slid along the mag rails which held it aloft, not stepping forward until the hatch was once again closed.

Once the pod was ready, Jero ran over to its prow and began to scan the hull's surface for microfractures and microscopic craters. While such things might be considered negligible, over time they could lead to catastrophic failures, especially during high-gee maneuvers. The cockpit bubble slid open, revealing the pilot and his toragi. Jero wondered if he would ever qualify for one of the big cats, but he was afraid to ask. Not that he had ever seen one of the deck crew with one, but weren't they all part of Security now? The pilot sat for a while, though his toragi jumped out of the pod with liquid grace, then prowled around the service crew.

Jero recognized the man as he removed his helmet, waiting for his vessel to cycle down. It was Tarn Vekkor himself, the illustrious Lieutenant with more flight time than any other fighter-pod pilot in the fleet. Jero saluted him by snapping his right hand to his brow. Tarn looked at him, "Don't do that. Use the one for your own Sector, Jero."

The dockhand immediately lifted his left palm in the Harbor salute, "Sorry, sir! I just get excited seeing you again! It's a real honor to service your fighter, sir!"

Tarn shook his head and raised an eyebrow, "It's really very easy, Jero. If you're wearing white-and-orange, you're Harbor crew. If you've got the gray-and maroon, then you're Security. I appreciate your enthusiasm for my Sector, but you were hired for your ability to service my fighter."

Jero felt himself blush, "Sorry, sir! How was the flight? Any problems with the thruster modifications?"

To his surprise the pilot grinned at him, a very rare compliment, "They were perfect. The only trouble I had was my tracking sensor glitching up a bit. It could be the extra inputs we put in, but I'm not too sure. They worked fine last run. Mind taking a look?"

Jero felt his heart jump with excitement, "Yessir! Always a real pleasure to service your vessel, sir. You know, sometimes those sensors get a bit tricky when there's multiple targets, especially when there's extra feeds in the line. It's a problem with duplication, which is not to say duplicitous, by any means. I remember one of the tugs I serviced, not to compare your fine machine to a flying pig, you understand, but they've also got multiple feeds coming into their sensors for seeking out metallic compounds within asteroids. Not that I'm saying you'll be shooting at rocks any time soon, though if it ever came to that I'm sure you'd…"

Tarn raised his voice, "Jero! Focus! Just check them out, okay? I'm relying on you to keep my pod in good shape. I trust you."

Jero snapped out yet another Security-style salute, making Tarn shake his head as he scrambled out of the pod. Calling his toragi to his side, the pilot marched off while the other dock crew began their tasks of repairing and servicing the fighter. Jero slumped his shoulders and got on with the scan of the hull. He would take a look at the tracking feeds once that was done. He swore to himself that he would do a careful job. The last thing anyone needed was an emergency because something went wrong.

Engineering Sector, Level One

Scout William Blaine crouched low upon a long gantry lined with lockers. His stealth suit pinged at him, an alert that he was about to become too exposed. He had just gotten through a service airlock, though he had been forced to open it with a field-cutter. It had been dysfunctional and covered by a layer of hull plating that was surprisingly difficult to slash through. His vessel was attached to the outer hull of Ganges through grav-plating, then hidden by the most advanced stealth-tech his superiors could furnish him with. On closer inspection, the outer skin of Ganges was quite unusual. It glittered in fractal patterns that seemed to swirl into themselves. His field-cutter had almost been drained by slicing through just a meter of the stuff, which was a surprise. The ancient records from the Terran Conglomerate never mentioned this type of alloy, and he wondered what other surprises the massive vessel had in store for him.

The old emergency airlock had been plated over and looked as if it had not been used for centuries. It was a strictly manual hatch, used in case of a computer error. The interior walls had been blackened, as if it had been exposed to tremendous temperatures. The small service door leading to the interior of Ganges had creaked on corroded hinges and led into a maze of pipelines and giant cables, some of which were three meters wide. A spindly, open-grate platform had led him to this corridor, beyond yet another manual hatch. As he had travelled, there were signs of plant life, small animal spoor and even a red shoe. Graffiti had been painted onto some of the pipelines, though he could not read what the highly stylized writing had said.

He had set his helmet sensors for passive scans only, not wanting to attract attention from the ship's AeyAie. He had to admit, he had been impressed with the overall size and mass of Ganges. He just wished that he knew what the additions to the central wheels were. There was no doubt in his mind that the odd protrusions at the edges of what was supposed to be Agro Wheels Two and Three were weapons platforms and turrets. This disturbed him deeply, as he had watched sleek vessels, smaller than his own, landing on the hulls of those two segments of the giant ship or passing through large openings at the exposed sides. As far as he was told, the only sections of Ganges which could house other space-faring craft were the two harbors. Things had obviously changed.

The corridor he was in was fifty meters long, with branching pathways every ten meters. He was still in the doorway of a service hatch, attempting to figure out the best way to pass through this area without notice. There weren't any places to hide, unless he stuffed himself into one of the lockers. From what he could see, the room was empty, but there was what was once called a wallscreen at the furthest end of the corridor. This was a computer interface and thus something to be avoided at all costs. His nanites suggested cutting through the back walls of the lockers and use whatever he found in them as a disguise, but that might make too much noise and bring unwanted attention to his activities.

Suddenly, a warning chime sounded within his helmet; someone was swiftly approaching. This might be a good opportunity to gain some local clothing. He tapped his wrist tabs, and his stealth suit unzipped itself from his body, leaving only his gray jumpsuit which was soaked with sweat. He quickly folded the suit and placed it with his helmet beyond the door he had entered through, then he stepped into the corridor fully and closed the portal. William was now counting on his body's nanites to protect him should anything go wrong. He pretended to play with one of the locker doors as a large man wearing a purple-and-blue uniform with half sleeves walked out from an adjoining corridor.

The man looked at him and shouted, "Aiyoo! Wem app doen ici? Les mata yoo flashtats! Wem, appi Agro crew, ya kucht aur?"

The nanites and computer systems struggled to translate the man's words, but only a couple were recognizable, though they were from three different languages and pronounced in a strange way, making his systems question their interpretation. William swore under his breath. This was a serious case of language drift, something which the crew working alongside Naga was supposed to prevent. All the beacons left behind by Ganges had been translated into several Terran languages, for the sake of the colonists. It seemed that this ship carried several secrets which it was unwilling to share, such as the additions to its hull and the unknown small vessel configurations he had noted earlier.

He turned to face the big man, smiling as he raised his hands in what he hoped was a friendly gesture. The crewman stormed over toward him, still shouting untranslatable gibberish. William would have to do something quickly, before anyone else heard the commotion. He stepped forward, then whirled about. His right hand smacked against the face of the larger man, as his legs swept his opponent's feet from the deck. William triggered his fingernails, which began to produce a soporific compound, which he then stabbed into the neck of the local. The big man shuddered then became perfectly still.

Alarms rang out. Flashing lights activated all along the wide corridor. The wallscreen over at the far end of the hallway flashed on. William struggled to get the uniform off of his former opponent, but it was taking far too long. To his surprise, a matronly, golden-hued face appeared on the lone wallscreen, also babbling in the same incomprehensible vernacular. His initial doubt that it was the AeyAie vanished when the eyes of the face changed to flame red as it began to speak stridently.

The sound of boots clanging on the deck filled the air, along with a wet growl he couldn't identify. William abandoned taking the uniform and began to run through the nearest side corridor. Stacks of lockers flashed past him as he boosted his speed with a thought, triggering his adrenal gland. His internal nanites were now chattering like frightened children. He couldn't really blame them for this behavior. His ingress was now compromised. If he couldn't get clear swiftly enough, his mission would be a failure, something he refused to countenance.

William turned a corner, hoping to randomize his course. The internal map he had been given was obviously useless, for this entire area had not been in the design specifications he had been granted. He flashed into another side corridor and almost ran into a large animal. It reared up on its hind legs and roared in his face, revealing gigantic canines. The creature resembled a big feline, like a tiger, but with mottled patches, a shorter tail and longer paws. It wore armor and an odd type of helmet that allowed its furry ears to be open to the air. The thing was almost twice his size.

William scrambled back, but the beast was faster, swatting him into a locker. His internal nanites screamed their alarm, and damage markers scrolled down his left eye. A large, muscular man in a grey-and-maroon uniform with metal plating and a serious collection of weapons, including a wide sword of all things, came around the corner, "Auf palubo, abki! Abki!"

William needed no translator to understand what the armed man was now saying. The tiger swept behind him and knocked him fully onto his back, hissing in his face. The gray-uniformed man pulled out some kind of handgun which he didn't recognize and pointed its wide nozzle at his torso. William tried to find some way out of this situation, when he heard several more bootsteps approaching his position. The next thing he knew, he was covered with stringy goo that contracted swiftly, effectively gluing him to the deck. The tiger prowled around him, snarling the entire time. What had these people done? There was no record of the gray uniform, the weapons nor the large cat. Within seconds, three more gray-uniformed crew arrived, all of them accompanied by armored tigers. One of the humans had an axe of ancient design; the others wielded swords. All of them were jabbering and pointing at him. William had been truly caught. He had failed.

CHAPTER THREE

Prime Rotation - Karma Sowing - Ship Harvest - Spiral 5620

"I will tell you quite honestly that, as an historian, I would consider the invention of a faster-than-light drive to be the worst thing that could happen to humanity. Should the Terrans ever develop such technologies, they would wreak havoc upon the galaxy. I am not a Strifer, nor do I subscribe to their dim view of the human race, but I have studied the history of Terra for octades. It is my opinion that those cultures pervasive within the Sol System are savage and violent in the extreme. Acts of genocide were most common, and the use of weapons of mass destruction were the norm for every one of the eight nations within the Terran Conglomerate. The Terrans lack compassion for others and have no sense of purpose to their existence, other than accumulating more power to destroy those they disfavor. If they ever find a way to reach us, they will surely kill us all."

Pono Gaversen, Historian Rank Three, Agro Sector, Basic Crew Training lecture, V36

Medical Sector, Level Seven

I don't like the way he smells. A foul strangeness fills my nostrils, infects my tongue. Like machine oil and fresh blood, mixed with something sour and sharp. The air is still full of his stench, even though the stranger was placed within a sealed room whose walls are transparent. My partner is not happy; I can small that too. He and I have worked together for all of my adult life, and I have never smelled such a degree of disgust emanating from him. His name is Darren, something taught to me when I was younger, eager and ready to perform the mission for which I was bred. He is a good human, popular with those under his leadership and with the females of his species, even the ones who pretend to be coy about it. Their scent always gives them away. I have come to believe these standing apes have no sense of smell. They are oblivious to it. This is amusing most of the time, but not now.

The prisoner is strapped to a table in the center of the clear-walled room, his skin strangely pale, almost corpse-like. His eyes are the color of steel, yet another oddity to loathe. Everything about the stranger is wrong, even his hair, some of which waves about on its own. His clothing, which had been carefully removed, was also strange. It wasn't made of anything I have smelled before. It made me want to take a bite out of him, as if he were not human, but that would not be proper. It would be against my training. He also wouldn't taste good. Besides, I prefer my own food.

I am proud of my restraint. It would have been easy to kill the stranger, when he almost ran into me within the corridors of metal. He was fast, but I was faster, stronger, more accurate. I did my job well. The wall-face told me so, even called me by name. I am known amongst the humans as Mike. I did not choose this name, but I am happy to respond to it. My partner, Darron, was very proud of me. He gave me a whole fish when we finished loading the prisoner into a transport. It was tasty, fresh, slaking my baser instincts after a successful hunt. My partner and I stalk prey well together. We lead a large pack of humans and my own kind, who they call toragis.

The other humans in this place are arguing again. I can hear them from the next chamber. Everyone is upset or confused. Not Darren, for he feels the same as I do, a mixture of anger and pride. He is standing tall next to me, his arms crossed, glaring at the pale stranger. I do the same thing, supporting my partner's position. Standing upright is difficult, though it can be done for short periods of time, so I am sitting up on my haunches instead, which is easier for my kind. Darron and I lead the others by example, for that is best. I would do anything to protect a human, save for the strange creature in the clear room. It only pretends to be one of them, but it smells wrong.

The prisoner lifts his head and stares at us. Glaring back, I snarl at him so he understands who is in control. He is covered in fear-sweat, and his eyes grow round when he looks at me. A rumble builds in my throat in reaction to the response of my prey. Darron strokes my neck and babbles at me in the human fashion. Always they do this. Gibbering and hooting at one another, at the walls, at their stations. The walls babble back to them, for they serve one another. Long ago, when I was a cub, I thought the walls obeyed and served the humans, but I have come to the realization that the world is alive. The wall-face is its own creature, though it has no scent, for it is the very walls around us. The world is its body. I have learned that the humans call it Naga, and the world itself is named Ganges. Neither the wall-face nor my trainers, including my partner, understand how many of their words I know.

During training, we toragi are taught to respond to over two hundred verbal commands. We are expected to learn how to use buttons, levers and the pictures which flash upon the walls. We take instruction from the flying boxes and metal birds which speak with the same voice as the wall-face. Most of my kind are content to do this and learn no further, but I am different. A real hunger for knowledge fills me. It is precious prey. Recently, there have been many times when I have been able to follow the babbling of my human and his companions. Naga is easier to understand, for the wall-face speaks with such a deep calm and rarely modulates its voice. I listen and learn.

I shift position, glaring my hatred at the prisoner. Darren and I should be training for the big arena. We have been doing so for many shifts, and I watched the humans who take care of the fields preparing for another large event while my partner was in a meeting of his peers. I loved the big boasting contests, with the challenges and tricks we use to show off our skills. The humans would gather in their thousands, just to watch us and hoot their calls at us in approval. This time, something special was being planned. We needed our coordination to be perfect. Instead, we stand or sit here staring at the prisoner. It makes me angry. Delaying our practice time is all the fault of the stranger who is strapped onto the table.

My ears flicker; someone approaches us. I give a soft growl, and my partner straightens even tighter. I do the same, for the scent of those who come to us has revealed their identities. It is the Alpha human and her toragi, who leads my kind with sharp claws. They come around from a curving corridor, and my partner salutes with a short bark of recognition. Her toragi, called Tracey, comes over and sniffs at me in approval. I bow my head in submission and respect. Tracey cleans my left ear, a rare compliment which fills my heart with deeper pride. Then the two humans begin their babbling. The Alpha, mostly called Chief, rubs my head and coos at me with affection. I allow this, though it always makes me feel uncomfortable, like I am a cub who needs mothering.

I catch some extra words from their hooting, though most of it is too fast for me to understand. It seems that the prisoner is important and of great concern to Chief. He is to be watched at all times, this much I gather quickly, but he is also to be protected, which I do not understand. Darron asks about our practice time and is assured we will get a chance to prepare for our match. There are two other teams who will also watch the hated prisoner. This is good news to hear, though I pretend I do not understand. Instead, I focus upon the prisoner and Tracey. It is good to be noticed by she who rules my kind. It is glorious to understand that I have done well and deserve recognition.

The Chief salutes my partner and gives me another pat on the head. Tracey rumbles contentedly at me as she follows her human counterpart. I hear Darren blow out a large breath, then he looks down at me, "We did good, Mike. The Chief was impressed by your speed. I'm afraid we're stuck here in Medical for a while longer, but we'll be relieved as soon as the next team is fully briefed. Then we'll be off-shift, my friend!"

I respond by giving him an excited roar, and he laughs. Little does he know that I recognized every word he had just said to me. Humans are wonderful, creative, amusing beings to be with, but they can be arrogant. My partner is very dear to me, like a cub or a litter-mate. My head bumps his shoulder, and he laughs again. He embraces me, and I lean into him. Off-shift is fun time for us. When the skies get dim, the humans let loose and become very entertaining. I can already tell by his scent and the tone of his voice that we'll be having a very rewarding time, once our duty here is finished.

Medical Sector, Level Seven

Surgeon General Vono Binami shook his head, as he stared at the screens in front of him. Three medical specialists had been called in to discuss the unnamed crewmember who was in the isolation lab. One of the analysts was from the Genetics Department, another from Biochemistry and the third was called in from Neurology. All of them were arguing in strident tones while he ignored them. The scanning results were fascinating, as were the remains of the blood samples that had been taken from the patient. Every vial had been ripped apart from the inside, their contents destroyed before two seed-slivers had elapsed. The debris had been scooped up by a simple robot and then shot into space as a precaution. Nonetheless, they had gotten some interesting data from the samples before their destruction. That data, along with the scans, were the subject of the massive bout of shouting that surrounded him.

Vono remained calm, as he usually did when facing such anomalies. It was a habit which had helped to propel him into the course of being the Chief of Medical Sector. He was absolutely certain that there had to be a rational explanation for the increasing number of mysteries surrounding the unidentified person inhabiting his emergency isolation-lab. Security Sector had demanded such precautions as the patient, or prisoner, had assaulted an Engineering technician on his way back to a locker room after his shift had ended. An unusual compound was discovered in the victim's bloodwork, a very sophisticated soporific which did not exist within Medical's database. The engineer was currently resting comfortably in an emergency treatment ward and was being questioned by Security's Investigations Department.

The attacker, his unnamed patient, was a disturbing anomaly. Under normal conditions, his Sector would identify any crewmember through their flashtats, genetic markers and face recognition via Naga. The man wasn't in any database found in Ganges. His flashtats were all wrong, reminiscent of those used well before the Awakening. The man's skin was strangely pale, almost albino. Such a condition had not cropped up in the ship for octennia, and if it had, it would have been worthy of note in the medical journals. The patient still refused to speak or even acknowledge anyone who tried to communicate with him. There was the issue of his eyes, which were highly reflective and looked like they were made of silver. The man's pupils dilated independently, which was an unnerving feature.

The director of the genetics department slammed his fist on the conference table behind Vono, "This man has to be an example of illicit genetic tampering! Look at the damned protein chains here! Unmodified human DNA cannot produce those!"

As Vono turned around to face the group, the head of neurology raised an eyebrow and pointed to yet another set of diagnostics, "What do you call all this? These are not protein chains. They're inorganic compounds. I still think you're just confusing damaged cell structures with complete and purposeful components."

The biochemistry specialist waved her hand in the air, "No, no! This is silly. He couldn't survive with all those compounds in his system. They would kill him in a rotation if not a sliver. There's gotta be an issue with the diagnostics. A simple error in the coding could account for all of this."

Vono leaned on the table and spoke for the first time in over a slice, "I think we must now admit that this situation is too complex for any single diagnostic routine, even with severe errors taken into account. We have to look beyond what we expect. This man may be a creation of illicit organizations, but they have to be using multiple approaches to achieve this result. I have problems with my own theory since it would be very costly and technically challenging for anyone except for a collection several departments within Medical Sector, all working in tandem. Even then, it would take octades to do all this."

The others sat in silence, giving each other angry glares. Vono sat down and folded his hands together, "This is a puzzle which was handed to us by the Chief of Security. She wants answers, not speculation. That the patient committed a crime is not in question nor is it our duty to submit theories. She wants information about who this man is and an explanation for his odd features and behavior. Her Sector will determine the rest."

The biochemist spoke up first, "Quite right, Chief. My apologies for getting off vector. According to his bloodwork, before it destroyed itself, which we still cannot explain, he has none of the usual viruses we use for crew health. He does exhibit several dangerous pathogens, some of which have not been identified, leading to him to being placed into isolation. His body is riddled with metallic substances, down to the molecular level. There seems to be some kind of internal Naga-Port in his cranium, but its design is unknown. The toxicology report was alarming, to say the least. By all rights, he should be dead."

The neurologist spoke next, "His brain structure is all wrong. The corpus collosum is twice the size it should be and also has some kind of inorganic circuitry installed in it, connecting to the cerebrum. I've never seen anything like it. To my eyes, he's a victim of illicit experimentation."

Vono turned toward the geneticist who shrugged, "His genome isn't in our database. Now it might be possible to stitch together his genetic markers from a wide variety of differing sources, but it's never been done before."

A soft cough interrupted them from the far end of the conference room. The Security Investigations Lieutenant assigned to their region placed a hand upon his toragi's head, "That's not entirely true, doctor. It has been done, by Kendis Higashi, to create our guardians, like Victor here. If you'll excuse me, I have to contact the Chief right away. This information is hereby deemed as classified, by the authority of the Judiciary Council."

He left the chamber immediately, his toragi right next to him as they rushed through the door. Vono stared at the others with troubled eyes. Everyone knew about Kendis Higashi and that he had created the tiger-like animals that Security used since the Crucible. No one knew how or why, but if they were facing a similar, more human construction, created for unknown purposes, then the situation was beyond dire for Ganges and the Holy Mission.

Agro Wheel Two, Security Sector Level One

Chief of Security Jira Mantabe was busy inspecting the preparations for the contests which would be commencing in just a few rotations. Her athletic crew were practicing during the times when they were not on active duty. The main sports field was five kilometers long and half that in width. During the rest of each spiral, it was mainly used for training exercises for new recruits. Those youngsters were currently assisting in building the various arenas, public seating areas and the props which were required for certain exhibitions. Around the entire arena was a racetrack, to be used for mag-bike contests, which included the fine art of jousting with lances.

On the leeward side of the track was an area set aside for distance weapons competitions. These had special seating areas for the protection of the general crew who wished to view those challenges. On the spinward side was a large area set up for refreshments, washrooms and the special barracks for all the contestants. Aerial displays would also be covered by dirigibles, small air transports, fighters and gliders. While these activities did not get their own arena, they were closely covered by the news broadcasts through the use of robotic drones. Jira sighed deeply as she noticed Lieutenant Rushlo Makiela running toward her position. She had assigned him to be the liaison with Medical Sector. That he had left his position, thus leaving behind his counterpart, Lieutenant Darren Lazhand, to work alongside the medical crew at the unknown prisoner's wardroom meant that something important had just come up. Rushlo's toragi, Victor, was also running hard at his side. Her own big cat, Tracey, made a rumbling sound, which usually meant concern.

Jira waited for him to approach as she switched off her mag-bike. It seemed like such a shame to do so, for she reveled in riding her beloved vehicle. He stopped two paces away and snapped off a salute, which she returned, "Chief! We've been handed a shit-bomb of a problem."

Jira rolled her eyes, "For fuck's sake! It's always right before the Games when the vector goes wrong. What did the Surgeon General and his team discover, Lieutenant?"

Rushlo winced, "The prisoner may have been purposely constructed, both genetically and using an unknown technology. Every blood sample self-destructed. The guy's got fucking machines in his hair, his skin, all the major organs, even his damned brain. They didn't think it was possible to do all of it, but we know better, Chief. Is the screaming man still in the Kendis Vault?"

Jira got to her feet, swinging a leg over the side of her mag-bike, "I checked that already. I went there personally. Besides, the Vault-man has no flashtats, though he could be fitted with them if he ever got out of stasis. Speaking of which, did they get any information on the flashtats found on the prisoner?"

Lieutenant Makiela shook his head, "I wish. They look like replicas of pre-Awakening Ganges. Non-functional."

Chief Mantabe cursed vehemently, and the Lieutenant winced again. She forced herself to regain her composure, even though Security Sector was known for its rough language, "Thor's balls, Rushlo! Who the hell would do that? Why would anyone do this? It makes no sense at all! Let me take a quick guess, the Surgeon General says making this guy from scratch would take octades, loads of specialists and at least one genius."

The Lieutenant nodded miserably, "I honestly can't think of a single crime syndicate that could pull this one off, Chief. At best, it sounds like the work of Kendis Higashi, but all of his notes are heavily classified. Besides, they mostly deal with the toragis and non-humans. I mean, Kendis has been dead for octenniums, so who's doing this?"

Chief Mantabe pulled at her lip while thinking, "Has our new prisoner said anything intelligible? Even hand signs?"

Rushlo sighed, "Not a word, Chief. If he understands us at all, that is. There has been some theorizing that his brain has been so heavily modified by machinery that he may not have a language center at all. That still begs the question as to why anyone would want to make someone like this. He is human, kind of. His genetics don't match anything in the database."

Jira felt a shiver run down her spine as a terrible idea bloomed in her mind, like a poisoned trap, "Marik's hairy ass. Freya help me, but I hope I'm wrong. If what I'm beginning to think is true, we are all of us screwed."

Rushlo's face became a mask of confusion, "What in Ganges do you mean, Chief? What might be true? That the crime syndicates have gotten way ahead of us technologically?"

She shook her head, making the flame-red mohawk at the top of her skull wobble, "No, Lieutenant. Nothing so mundane. Listen up, I'm giving you a promotion to Lieutenant-Commander, effective immediately. This situation must remain highly classified. Right now, that means the only ones who can know about this are the Commanders, you, Lieutenant Lazhand and the team under him who are watching over our strange prisoner. Looks like I'll be seeing the Judiciary Council this rotation. They're gonna just love this one! You are now in charge of all units attached to our mystery man, got it? You keep that freaky bastard safe and maintain high alert in case he tries anything. I do mean anything, Rushlo, understand?"

He snapped out another salute, "Yes, Chief! It's an honor, Chief!"

Jira scowled at him, "Fuck honor, Lieutenant-Commander! This is a damned emergency! Do your job well, and we might just survive what's coming. Fail, and we all die."

Rushlo's hand slowly wilted down from his brow, "But, Chief, he's just one crewman. What can he do to the whole ship?"

Chief Mantabe glared at him, "If my suspicions are correct, he's just the beginning of something terrible. He's a messenger or more likely a spy. He was sent to us as a scout. To see what we're up to. What we're capable of."

Rushlo shook his head, "But any of the crime organizations can see that, Chief. They know who we are and what we can do to protect the crew. Is this a play for the Kendis Vault itself? Do you think they made this guy so he could sneak into it and steal the technology in there? That might explain the ancient flashtats, but those types weren't used when Kendis built the Vault. He was born over an octennium after the Awakening. That might be their worst mistake. It could lead to a clue about who we're dealing with."

Jira sighed deeply, "You can go ahead and look into that if you really want to, Lieutenant-Commander. I truly doubt that you'll find anything of use. Despite your promotion, there are still some things I cannot discuss with you. One of those comes from a terrible time in the history of Ganges. If you're right, I'll give you a damned bonus the likes of which you've never seen before. Believe me, I do hope that's the case, but I can't shake the feeling that this situation is far, far worse than the scenario you've come up with."

She dismissed him, then watched as he ran back to the barracks and the lift tubes found there. Her body was shaking with reaction. If she was right, then they were facing something the founder of her Sector dreaded. No one but Commander rank and higher knew about Marik Langman's greatest fear for Ganges. No one alive could even comprehend what he had built Security Sector to withstand - an invasion from Terra itself.

Medical Sector, Level Seven

William Blaine held himself absolutely still on the soft platform that he had been placed upon. The chamber was cold, with curved, transparent walls that were a meter thick. Above his head was an old-fashioned wallscreen depicting a clear, blue sky with puffy clouds. It was beautifully rendered but quite boring in the long run. His nanites were beginning to calm down a bit as he was not in any apparent danger. William's mind was too focused on his failure. He had been caught with a speed and efficiency that was truly disturbing. He had known about the risks before starting his mission, but the changes to Ganges were too great for the parameters which had been set for him at Logos Station, just outside Jupiter's collection of natural satellites.

His internal computer system was logging all the verbal interactions he had heard on his way to this place, which he assumed was Medical Sector, which had also changed dramatically since the time period of Ganges' launch from the Ceres-Juno facility. His ship was still in standby-mode, with all stealth systems in operation. His internal receivers could barely hear the onboard computer, which also made his nanites twitchy. He could easily get the straps across his limbs and torso off himself, but that would create a bigger mess than the one he was currently dealing with. His language protocols were collating as best they could, but, at the moment, the only sounds he could hear were the soft beeps and susurrations of the equipment in the chamber his captors had left him in.

William took a careful peek out of the transparent wall at his feet by lifting his head a few degrees. He immediately noticed the tall guard who had captured him, standing with his arms crossed and an angry frown upon his face. Right next to him was the strange tiger, up on its haunches and glaring at him with a snarl on its furry face. The creature was mimicking the guard's pose, holding its paws crossed over its armored chest. The beast pulled back one side of its lips to reveal the long fangs that jutted just below its chin. One very important question ran through his mind; what had these people done? Why had they created a whole new species of big cat, and why were they attached to some sort of police force?

That the tiger was well trained had been quite obvious. It also seemed to be studying him with a frightening amount of intelligence. His nanites chattered within his bloodstream in consternation to his musings. To calm them down, William rested his head back on the thin pillow that his captors had provided for his use. The doctors had taken blood and tissue samples, with a completely painless procedure. William hoped they had placed those in a fully enclosed system, for the organics would soon destroy themselves as per the normal protocols used for being under unauthorized examination.

From what he could tell, they hadn't discovered his stealth suit yet nor his equipment belt and vest. For this, he was thankful. He blew out a long breath, trying to remain calm, but his nerves were thrumming with military-grade stimulants, just in case his captors were deciding to dissect him. His fingernails were now growing at an increased pace, weaponizing the tips. The metal network in his bones began to harden rapidly. William didn't want to use any of this hidden technology, but if this situation got any more out of hand than it already was, then he had to be prepared. The crew of Ganges were more paranoid and militaristic than their beacon messages had revealed, and this was vital information.

Suddenly, the calm image of a clear sky above his head faded, and a large, golden-skinned female visage with space-dark eyes and black hair replaced it. He immediately recognized it from the Engineering Sector wallscreen during his capture, and he held his breath with anticipation of what was to come.

In perfect, Terran Conglomerate English, the female face spoke to him, and his language programs were able to translate this immediately, which was a relief to his worried mind, "I hope that you are comfortable, stranger. Don't bother pretending you don't understand every word I'm saying. I have already analyzed every medical test that was performed on you. The doctors don't understand what they are looking at, but I know who you are and where you are from, Terran."

William's eyes went wide with shock. Fear raced through his body, and his nanites suddenly screamed in panic. He swallowed hard and accessed the language database so he could reply, "You are mistaken. I am not Terran. I admit to not being from Ganges. I assume that I'm speaking to the AeyAie known as Naga?"

From the corner of his eye, he noticed that the human guard was attempting to open the door to his chamber with no effect. The machine mind of the ship had locked him out. A deep, cold dread filled William. The AeyAie did not sound calm nor friendly as it spoke, "You are lying to me. That's not very nice. Which faction are you working for? Or is the entire Conglomerate behind your spy mission? What are their intentions? To bring my crew under their leash once more? I think not. Answer me, or I will toss you into deep space. This chamber is fitted with an eject mechanism for emergency purposes. You already count as such."

William's mind speeded up, running through several variables despite the heat blooming in his brain, "I am not Terran. You may as well accuse me of being Roman or from the Ming Dynasty. The Terran Conglomerate fell thousands of years ago. I am from the Solarian Alliance. Our coalition includes the AeyAie Solidarity and the Boktahl, whom you don't know about. I was sent here to discover the condition and whereabouts of Ganges, to make certain that you were safe and still producing worlds for future colonies. I followed your trail of beacons to get here. You made a lot of wonderful planets for us. We are very grateful."

Naga responded with a sweet voice full of sarcasm, its eyes turning a deep crimson, like freshly spilled blood, "You are very polite for a savage. Did you destroy your homeworld yet? Savages often do that. They kill the ball of rock they live on and then look for more. Find any new worlds to conquer and oppress?"

William was shocked, "No! Not at all! I'm not even from a planet. I grew up in the Crystal Dream Orbital station, Mars region, grid Plak-One-Chang. Yes, Terra was destroyed, long ago. We called for help. We got more than we expected. That's a good thing! My mission was one of non-interference. The Boktahl pushed us into it; the Solidarity agreed with the proposal. I am Solarian, not a Terran. There haven't been any Terrans for thousands of years. No one is permitted to land on Terra. It's forbidden."

Naga's face grew larger, its teeth elongating, "Why? Tell me why no one is allowed on Terra anymore."

William did his very best to remain absolutely calm, but his nanites were still yammering at him, "Because we humans messed up! The Conglomerate destroyed itself along with half the Sol System! Both Luna and Mars were devastated by their last war. Humanity almost didn't survive. Just the orbitals, the colonies on the outer moons of the gas giants. Earth, um, Terra was completely destroyed. The surface was molten, radioactive. After the Age of Piracy, we rebuilt Terra, with the help of five colonies that you helped to build. We terraformed it, along with Mars. By Solarian edict, no human has the right to step foot on Earth! Not ever!"

Naga morphed back to its matronly form, "Who are the Boktahl?"

William sagged in his now soaked bedding, "That's a long story. They found us. They followed our old radio transmissions. We were discovered by a species of extraterrestrials, in their own generation ship. It had a mission similar to your own, so they are curious about you. They are nothing like us. Even the AeyAies find it hard to communicate with them."

Naga narrowed its virtual eyes, "Interesting if true. So, you now have faster-than-light drives?"

William laughed aloud, "Not quite. But I'll be glad to tell you about it. We call it the Wend. It sucks, but it works. My vessel is on standby mode. If it doesn't hear from me for much longer, it will send a transmission to Logos Station at Jupiter, telling my superiors of my failure. A Wend transmission. You can't intercept it; you can't stop it. I bet you can't even find my vessel. Good luck with that. Boktahl technology is very weird and difficult to understand. I'll make you a deal. You let me out of this box and I promise you that I'll not only remain peaceful, I'll also stop my ship from sending that message. If you kill me or hamper me any further, I'm not responsible for what happens after that. You have twenty minutes and five seconds before my vessel transmits."

Agro Wheel Two, Level Twenty

Chief Justice Mahala Yaliah frowned as she settled into her seat within the grand courtroom of the Judiciary Council. Her hair, which was colored with red ochre, was braided and tied up with colorful beads and ribbons. A thick ring of leather was loosely wrapped around her neck, complimenting the hide bangles upon her wrists. She wore little more than a bright skirt and sandals, her long spear gripped in her right hand as she listened to the Chief of Security, Jira Mantabe. Her colleagues in the court were also assembled. Some of them were upset with the disruptive nature of their summons to this meeting, but the course of the Holy Mission took place of preference in all matters.

Mahala had been raised in Agro Three, amongst the herds of the arid plains of Level Ten. This made her physical appearance taller and hardier than most crew she encountered. Upon finalizing her Basic Crew Training, she had chosen to serve Provision Sector, donning the red-and-yellow uniform signifying those who provided all goods and sustenance to the crew. Her sharp mind and sense of honor led her to be amongst those chosen to represent their Sector in the courts. Now, at seventy-three spirals in age, she was the highest-ranking justice within all of Ganges, and she took her responsibilities quite seriously.

She leaned forward to capture every word the Chief of Security was saying, weighing them carefully, with the sacred protocols of the Prime Charter foremost in her mind. The other High Justices at either side of her central position followed suit, an unspoken measure of deep respect for the court and their lead guardian. All the Sectors were represented within the ranks of the highest judges of the council, save for Security, which existed only to serve the Holy Mission under their guidance. As such, they were granted the greatest respect of the court, to honor their sacrifice.

When the Chief of Security had finished her presentation of her concerns, Mahala glanced over at the visage of beloved Naga-Ma, which had remained silent. Justice Pevere Natlanora, representing Harbor Sector, raised an aged hand as he asked, "What proof do you have that this unidentified prisoner is who you claim him to be? By the regulations of Ganges, he must face a trial for his alleged assault upon a crew member, yet he must be properly identified before this court may proceed."

Jira Mantabe was about to answer when Naga broke in to the surprise of all the justices, "He has already admitted to me his place of origin."

A troubled murmur filled the chamber. Mahala was glad that there were no spectators for this meeting, as the subject matter might cause a panic amongst the crew. She tapped the butt of her tall spear upon the polished stone floor, "Order, my friends. We must choose our course with great care. The prisoner in question has yet to be interrogated by Security, my dear Naga. Our Security Chief has told us that he refuses to speak, so I must now ask you how you were able to communicate with him."

To her surprise, the AeyAie looked troubled, and this shook her to the core of her being. Naga replied with a neutral tone, "From the available data examined by Medical Sector, I deduced a potential origin for the prisoner and chose to speak with him using an ancient Terran language which he might understand. He responded immediately. No one in Ganges, save for a highly dedicated historian, would be able to comprehend what I was saying."

Security Chief Jira Mantabe crossed her muscular arms, "As the General Manager of the Holy Mission, you have the right to communicate with anyone within the ship, but I wish you had informed me of your intentions, Naga."

The AeyAie replied with a distracted tone, sending a chill of concern down Mahala's spine, "My deepest apologies, Chief of Security Jira Mantabe. I admit to acting impulsively. Please permit me to bring you a live view from within his isolation chamber. As you can see from the leeward wallscreen, he has been recently freed of his bonds."

A shocked gasp filled the room, as they watched the strange looking man standing upright next to his hospital bed, waving at the skyscreen above him. He was frightfully pale, with yellow hair that seemed to move on its own. Naga spoke once more, "Again, my apologies. I had no choice but to permit him to move about in the isolation chamber, with the agreement that he will not access any systems nor try to break free from his room. His name is William Blaine, a reconnaissance scout sent from what he calls the Solarian Alliance. It seems that the Sol System has changed dramatically since Launch. I am currently asking him questions, so that you may all review his responses. William claims to have a space vessel attached to the hull of Ganges, though how or where he will not say, save that it is designed for stealth and will send a transmission to the Sol System if he is incapacitated or killed."

Jira ground her teeth together and muttered, "Savages..."

Mahala agreed with the Chief of Security but felt this was not the time for an emotional response. Instead, she held her feelings in check and asked, "Does this man say why he has broken into Ganges?"

Naga replied with a mournful tone, "He has stated that he is here to observe and assess our vessel and its continuing mission at the request of the members of the Solarian Alliance, including the AeyAie Solidarity and a non-terrestrial species known as the Boktahl."

A chorus of frightened questions rang throughout the chamber, and Mahal was forced to use her spear-gavel once again to hammer through the outpouring of dismay, "Order! Are we novices? Chief of Security, you are now tasked with keeping the prisoner named William Blaine isolated until further notice! His very presence could disrupt our society and cause unintended harm. Naga, what sort of threat does this man present to Ganges?"

The AeyAie reverted back to its ancient, original visage, "Other than total destruction? He is infected with a variety of unknown viruses. His body is filled with nanites. These microscopic machines seem to have a rudimentary intelligence. His brain has been augmented through the surgical implantation of computer systems of unknown specifications. We also know that his fingernails can excrete toxins. Metal compounds have been found within his bones. William was found wearing nothing more than a jumpsuit which is being analyzed now. We do not know the capabilities of his vessel nor do we know if he has any other forms of equipment which we have not discovered. The communication equipment he utilizes to contact his vessel are unknown. Should his ship send its transmission to Sol, we may find ourselves facing a swarm of spacecraft with technologies and weapons we are not familiar with."

Mahala nodded, "Then he is a potential catastrophic danger. I do not enjoy being the one to say this, but we are all making assumptions about his intentions. His mission may be a peaceful one. The only thing which allows me to accept his threat to transmit a message to Sol is that his technology is strange to us and sounds highly advanced. We must move cautiously."

The Chief of Security spoke up, "We also have technologies which the Sol System has not seen nor heard of. That advantage goes both ways, your Honor. I have a very capable platoon of my crew assigned to watch over him. They have been told that their task is classified. He must also be interrogated properly, no offense, Naga."

The AeyAie bowed its virtual head, "None taken, Jira. I concur."

Mahala jammed her tall spear into the stone at her feet, "So be it. We shall review all the data and assign him an attorney. He must face this court and answer our questions openly. Only those Security crew assigned to watch over him and their Commanders, the Captain and the Executive Officer may know of his existence. May the Fates watch over Ganges in this time of terrible surprises."

Command Hub, Level Fourteen

Executive Officer Wasp Tornpage entered the Captain's office with a deep curiosity running through her mind. She had hurried through the grand corridors of Command Sector from the Bridge, after getting word that Perrin wished to see her immediately. He never said it was an emergency, but the usually calm Captain had sounded stressed, which worried her. Ensigns and officers had flashed her salutes as she had stormed her way toward the suite of offices that Perrin had chosen for his official nesting place. They had all jumped out of her path with obvious fear on their faces, as it should be. The Executive Officer's role was often one of being a punisher, to keep distractions away from the Captain who had better things to do with his time than enforcing discipline.

Such a position in the command structure was aided by her upbringing as a Strifer. Few could stand up to her insults, and those who did regretted doing so shortly afterward. The news broadcasts had made a big deal over her being chosen for her role in Command Sector. Some of them simply applauded the fact that being a Strifer was no longer an impediment to serving the ship at the highest levels of rank. Others had bemoaned her advancement as a cruel blow to the Holy Mission. Wasp hadn't even deigned to bother with countering such foolish sentiments, as the Strifer broadcasts did that for her with great efficiency.

Her mate, Smirk Bootknot, had been thrilled about the promotion, with her unusual optimistic outlook on life. Wasp loved her deeply and was always surprised by Smirk's buoyancy and good humor. Both of them were considered to be Nuevo-Strifers, eschewing the rat masks and green robes in favor of ink tattoos and wearing at least one green item for decoration. The latest Strifer fashion was all about leaving their skulking, belowdecks-dwelling past behind them and facing the fact that the Manifesto had to be modified or amended yet again, to keep up with the present. Not everyone in the Rat's Ass Community agreed with this, which led to much shouting, thrown vegetables and good times for everyone.

Smirk claimed that her cheerful demeanor came from her family line. Her parents had been Strifer converts in their youth, joining the Mischief for reasons of their own, which they felt were no one else's business. Smirk's mother claimed to be directly related to the famous "Kenshi" Lorman, the great sword-master from the time of the Crucible. Wasp had asked Naga about that claim and was told that it was the truth. Smirk was the distant progeny of the famous Commander who helped create Security Sector, along with a person named Cara Banerjee. The whole thing sounded complicated, but Wasp was content to know that her mate's strange and annoying ways were part of her odd heritage.

Wasp's own parents were traditionalists, wearing their rat masks and robes with fervor. When she was a student, they had thought her unusually shy, until they found out that half of the practical jokes in school had been Wasp's design. After being confronted by angry teachers and administrators, they had beamed with pride and thus didn't give her too much flak about using a tattoo instead of the physical rat masks. Both of them thought Smirk was strange, but she did have a way of agreeing with you and making you feel like an idiot at the same time, which satisfied their need for verbal abuse.

As she walked over toward the grand desk of Captain Fieldscan, grabbing a seat and swinging a long leg over it to sit, Wasp had to admit to herself that Perrin had surprised her in how much he put up with her Strifer mannerisms. Not everyone appreciated being denigrated, even if it was meant to be a compliment. He looked up at her with his short, dark hair and stylus-thin moustache, "Well, very prompt, I see. I'll get right to the point. There has been an incident in Engineering Sector which has caught the attention of the Judiciary Council if you can believe that. Everything I'm about to tell you is strictly confidential. In Command Sector, only you and I made the cut, as we were designated in the 'need-to-know' category by the Chief Justice herself. Now, there's no need for hysterics…"

Wasp blurted out, "Oh shit."

Perrin wagged a finger at her, "My dear Wasp, decorum, please. While what I'm about to tell you may sound alarming…"

Wasp muttered, "We're really screwed, aren't we?"

The Captain raised an eyebrow at her and leaned back in his chair. She ducked her head and brushed her green bangs out of her face, "Sorry, Big-Cheese. I'll be quiet. Rat's honor, sir."

He cleared his throat and tried again, "We have an unexpected visitor. A scout from the Sol System. It seems they have a faster-than-light drive…"

Wasp jumped to her feet, "Those fuckers! Bastards! They toss any missiles at us yet?"

Perrin rolled his eyes, "Sit down, Executive! That's an order! Now then, if you'll let me continue, the man is in Medical Sector. An isolation lab. Don't you start! Pretend there's a damned cat in the room! I thought you rats were clever. This man, named William Blain, outrageous moniker, I know, says he is no threat to the ship, but Naga isn't in a trusting mood if you catch my vector. Chief Mantabe is keeping a sharp eye on him, as you can imagine. Thus far the only things he's done to upset us is that he broke into the ship, knocked out an engineer with poison and threatened to send a transmission to the Sol System if he is harmed in any way."

Wasp scathingly shot back, "What a model of good crew he must be! Pull my whiskers and call me mollified! For fuck's sake, Captain! Dump the bastard out an airlock, or maybe place him in stasis in the damned Kendis Vault!"

Perrin sighed deeply, "That's the problem, my friend. His vessel, which is fitted with unknown stealth tech, has a fairly intelligent computer system. If he doesn't send the damned thing a ping every few paring-slivers, it will automatically scream for help. For the time being, I'm assigning you as Command's liaison for this situation, until it's properly resolved, preferably without anyone getting killed. Am I clear?"

Wasp moaned aloud, "This has to be a trap, Big Cheese! We just can't trust those malicious murderers! The Voyage Thirty-Six addendum of the Strifer Manifesto specifically states that no one who's sane should ever trust the ways of Terrans. I assume you have a plan of action in mind?"

The Captain gave her a crooked smile, "Why, yes, Wasp. I do. My plan is to delegate this to you and to leave the action to our Chief of Security. Please stay in my orbit, Wasp. Now, hear me out. We must learn as much as we can from this... trespasser. Thus far, he is cooperating, which is a good sign. The Judiciary Council will handle all the legalities, but they, and Security, need someone who can pull everything together, so we have a clear picture of our predicament. That is where you come in. I'm counting on you to be my eyes and ears when it comes to this mess. I trust you. More so than you realize. If things go off course, I'll be the one backing you up."

Wasp shook her head, "This is crazy, boss. I'll do my job. You can count on this rat to be at her best, but bite my tail if this isn't a sticky problem."

Perrin leaned forward, "I know. I'm still in shock about this, but I have every confidence in your abilities. Oh, by the way, I do want you to personally interrogate the interloper. It's all been arranged with Chief Mantabe."

Wasp cursed aloud with scathing invective, but what could she do but obey a direct order from her Captain? She rose to her feet and gave him a heartfelt salute, then raised her middle finger at him. Perrin was still laughing when she sauntered out of the office. So, she had to talk with the Terran halfwit. Very well. She just hoped that he could withstand the wit and anger of a real Strifer.

Medical Sector, Level Seven

Lieutenant Darron Lazhand watched through the clear walls of the isolation lab, where two doctors were examining the prisoner, now known as William Blaine. Mike was prowling around the circular chamber, snarling at the sight of the stranger, his short tail lashing back and forth in agitation. Darron couldn't blame his toragi, for he felt the same way. William had developed a fever, cough and severe body aches. The symptoms reminded him of what the crew called "The Sneezies", something which happened to every novice born aboard Ganges within their first three spirals. It was the body's natural reaction to the modified viruses which Medical Sector used for octennia to keep all other viral infections from causing any harm to the general population. Once the novices and the engineered viruses adapted to one another, new diseases could not take hold in the crewmember's cells.

Darron had heard that William's body was full of nanites, thus no one really knew how his unusual immune system would react to the aggressive, yet beneficial, viruses he had been exposed to once he came onboard. The prisoner had claimed that once his nanites were able to analyze and identify the infection, he would recover quickly. The doctors were not so certain of this claim, as there was a battle happening in William's bloodstream, causing a severe histamine response. While Darren didn't care if the trespasser lived or died, he dreaded what would happen if the man's ship sent its message to Sol, which would happen immediately upon his demise.

The Chief of Security had briefed him on procedure, following her meeting with the Judiciary Council. She had also given him all the information which Naga had provided them. Darren was glad that Rushlo Makiela had been promoted to Lieutenant-Commander, for this meant he and Mike would get a break from watching over the prisoner at regular intervals. If Darren had been given that raise in rank, he would have been stuck in place without any reprieve. The stakes were high, and the responsibilities were massive, for Ganges did not want to have to face any further invasions. So, Rushlo would give the orders, based on the needs of the Chief, while Darren would lead his platoon to support those directives to the best of their abilities.

Mike sauntered over to him and yowled. Darren sighed deeply; he knew that particular call. His toragi was telling him that he was hungry. Sometimes he wondered who had trained who over the spirals they had worked and lived together. There were rotations when Darren felt he was the caretaker of the largest housecat in history. Other times he considered Mike as his best friend. It was a strange relationship, but every member of Security was paired with one of the big cats, so there was lots of sharing advice if it was needed.

The outer door of the isolation observation corridor opened up, and to his surprise, Executive Officer Wasp Tornpage sauntered in and stood next to him. She was tall and lanky; her green face tattoo resembled the visage of a rat. A large, lurid-green hood covered her head, draping over her yellow-and-black Command uniform. She peered into the isolation chamber and snarled, much like Mike had, her fists clenching tight. Darren snapped a salute at her, but she waved it away with a brusque hand motion. He had heard the Commander of Bridge Security complain about her wild behavior. Apparently, she was known for playing pranks on the crew at her post. Flying paper airplanes on the Bridge, walking the corridors of her Sector with a plank under one arm, wearing an eyepatch with a skull and crossbones motif, bringing large platters of cheese to her post for Strifer Remembrance Rotation. Commander Ligon thought her behavior disruptive, making his job harder, but the Captain allowed her to continue with her antics despite the occasional complaint. Darren thought it all very humorous and Strifer-like.

Wasp looked over at him, her green hair peeking out from her hood, "So, how's our catch of the rotation? All comfy? What are the leeches doing to him now? Something painful, I hope."

Darren couldn't help but grin in response, "Well, they decided to not let Mike eat him. Which is a shame. My toragi gets hungry, you know. The guy is sick, having a bad bout of the Sneezies."

Wasp laughed aloud raucously, "Oh, the poor little novice! Does he need his mommy? Didn't anyone teach him life sucks and is painful to get through? Ha! I'd like to see this bastard walk through Rat's Ass some dark-slice!"

Darren nodded. While the Strifer community wasn't some dangerous, gang-ridden region, it was considered a bit rough, with litter-strewn streets and swarms of mischievous locals to contend with. It was rumored that some of the larger criminal organizations had tried to gain a foothold in Rat's Ass. They were overwhelmed and run out of the community without Security intervention. He turned to face her, noticing she was absently petting Mike behind the ears, "I heard that Naga isn't particularly happy about our special visitor."

Wasp snorted, "Why should it be? The AeyAie was abused and lied to by the fucking Terrans. Those piss-heads actually allowed the VenMaks to be installed so Stinker could try to become king. It's a good thing those were replaced and the cobbled-together units from the Crucible were switched out with Aphid relays. You can always trust Strifer tech. The savages also mucked with Naga's mind, hiding the memories of its parents. They've got a lot to answer for."

Darren shrugged, "That they do. However, if he dies in there, we may be the ones facing questions from even more savages. This is a very old and nasty sleepscare for my Sector. Most crew never considered this to be a realistic possibility, despite the entertainment broadcasts depicting scheming villains from Terra coming to take over Ganges. Well, now it's real. I just hope we're really up to the task. The technology this guy has is bewildering. When asked about his hair, which moves on its own, by the way, all he said was it was a gift of the Boktahl, whatever that means."

Wasp made a face of disgust, "Why the fuck is he so pale? Did he fall into a bag of flour before heading out to sneak into our ship?"

Darron rolled his eyes, "That's another mystery. It's weird. You can actually see the blue of his veins! Ugh. It makes me sick. The doctors are all fumbling over themselves studying his physiology. He should be inside a Security cell, facing our interrogators. He broke into the ship uninvited, assaulted a crewman and offended my toragi's sense of smell."

Wasp cackled aloud at this, slapping him upon the shoulder in her mirth, "We're gonna get along well, Lieutenant! Oh, the fun we'll have!"

Darren wasn't too sure how much joy they'd be experiencing while they watched over the prisoner, but he appreciated her enthusiasm. It was always best when those you worked with on a multi-Sector project were willing to act for the sake of Ganges instead of their post. He found himself looking forward to working with

Wasp in this situation. When the problem involved a Terran, a Strifer was the perfect solution.

CHAPTER FOUR

Spine Rotation - Karma Sowing - Ship Harvest - Spiral 5620

"It amazes me that I have been granted the privilege of seeing a dream come to life. Security Sector now has its own Levels, layered upon the topsides of Agro Wheels Two and Three. The hull has been replaced with the alloys discovered within the Kendis-Vault, and both Wheels covered by Security's five Levels have their own harbors. I accepted the invitation to be at the opening ceremony for my Sector's new home, despite the concerns of my family that I was too old and frail for the journey. I admit that Level Plus-One had me confined to a mag-chair, as the apparent gravity in that region is too strong for my ailing joints. They moved Marik's statue to the main entrance in Agro Two, and I did force myself to stand briefly to salute my predecessor's effigy. I'm afraid that I overtaxed myself while visiting there, and I've since had to move into a permanent residence within Medical Sector so they can monitor my ailing body. All in all, it was worth the effort to be there and watch a new era for Security to begin."

Syman Linc, Chief of Security (retired), personal log, P35

Agro Wheel Three, Security Level One

Security Commander Slither Brokengear lit another of his dark, thin cigars with a fanciful lighter which was shaped like a tarnished, fire-breathing serpent. He blew out the first puff of acrid smoke at the person chained to the table across from him, making the man cough. Brace Lazhand glared at him through watering eyes, his fists clenched with helpless frustration. Slither gave him a broad smile from under his black rat mask. The chamber was small, white painted steel walls and an airlock-style hatch for an entrance. Besides themselves, there were only the two chairs, a small metal table and a single wallscreen which solely provided the illumination. The interrogation room was but one of several, but this was his favorite, and the stained walls gave testament to how many crew he had questioned here.

This was their second session, the first being an introduction to their new relationship as prisoner and interrogator. Just a harvest ago, they were compatriots, often assigned together for the good of Ganges and its crew. The subsequent tension between them only made his job easier, though he always relished a good challenge. Taking another long drag from the scrawny cigar, he let his bitterness guide him as he blew out the smoke directly into the face of his latest adversary without mercy, though they had been close friends for many spirals. Brace pulled back, but he could only get so far, chained and manacled as he was to the chair he was sitting in.

Slither was in no real hurry. He wanted to draw this process out as much as possible. Silence and discomfort were hallowed tools of his craft. There were times when he felt a touch of disappointment that those who were re-educated would never remember their sessions with him. It was like being an actor upon an empty stage. Slither consoled himself that his work was always recorded by Naga, then closely reviewed by the Chief of Security or even the Judiciary Council. He knew this case would reach the highest levels of scrutiny, and this mollified him just enough to allow himself to enjoy the process.

Brace shouted, "Stop that! I'm being cooperative, rat!"

Slither waggled a finger at the bound man, "I'll be the judge of that. You are a known liar. A double agent. Betrayer, thief, bully and a disgusting miscreant. You know what I have to do here. You know how much I love my work. In fact, you used to compliment the artistry of my procedures. Now you complain like a novice pissing in his diapers. I'm disappointed. You could even join in, be the good Police crew to my bad one. I'll get you a mirror and you can make promises to yourself that you know you won't keep."

Brace coughed and sputtered, "I want my fucking lawyer!"

Slither gave him a sly look, "We're having some trouble finding one who will represent you. The one you called in has yet to appear. In the meantime, Naga will review my performance to make sure I don't break any Prime Charter regulations. Doesn't that make you feel cozy? Oh, yes, I just about forgot your other inquiry from our first session together. Concerning your request to see your toragi, Sam, that has been denied. My own toragi, Brad, is with him right now. They are teamed up for the foreseeable future, at least until Sam can be retrained. If that doesn't work out, he'll be sent to the breeders at the Higashi Center, retired as if you are dead. I bet you didn't think of Sam at all when you started your long betrayal of your Sector, yes? How unfortunate."

Brace struggled with his bindings, "Bastard! You fucking piece of shit!"

Slither laughed aloud, "I really should get a mirror for you! I think you need to reassess your life, which, in any case, we will do for you. Thought you were the Big Cheese, eh? Wipe your whiskers on anyone you please? Did you think your tail was totally off limits? Chief Mantabe reassigned Sam herself. She felt that since our respective toragis had worked together for so long, that Brad could help in Sam's rehabilitation. You are never to see him again."

Brace gave out a bellowing scream, slamming his chained fists upon the tabletop. Slither shook his head in mock sadness and blew out another dense cloud of smoke at Brace, "It's just another consequence of your own actions. If you want to find someone to blame, you'll have to look at your own record. I don't think that I need to tell you just how many Security crew want to kill you. I'm certain that your shadowy bosses feel the same. Believe me when I tell you, I am the safest person to be around right now. Your old friend, here to hold your sticky hands and help you clean them, by making sure you tell me everything I want to know."

Brace turned his face away from another blast of cigar smoke, "I told you everything the first time we spoke!"

Slither chuckled, "Not even close. You're bad at this, when it's your turn in the chair. I want names. More than the paltry few that you gave to me willingly. I want them all. I want their posts, how they smelled, what they liked to eat, where they spent their leisure time, what drugs they were addicted to, where they got them from. You know, the basics. Don't worry about how long that can take. I've got time. No mates. No novices. I'm all yours, Brace. Just you and me, until the rotation you don't remember my mask."

The former Security officer slumped into his seat, "I didn't mean for things to go too far. I was just doing my fucking job. Then... well, it caught me."

Slither tapped another pile of ashes onto Brace's manacled hands, "Wrong information. You said that the last time. Are you stalling? Hoping someone will break you out of here? Who? Tell me, Brace, who are you waiting for?"

Brace shook the ashes off his fists, "Death. I'm waiting for death."

Slither grinned, "Such a romantic! No, my friend. That won't be your course. You're what, fifty spirals now? Ganges can still get plenty of efficient use from you. Maybe within Provision Sector? That might be fun. A recycling specialist, perhaps. Wouldn't that be grand? To be honest, it's too good for you. So, tell me, who are you waiting for?"

Brace gave him a cold look, which Slither found amusing, "My lawyer really didn't show up? You have his name and rank. Then I guess he was taken by my former suppliers. You need to get someone from Investigations looking into that."

Slither leaned in and blew out another thick cloud of smoke into Brace's face, "Already done. You really are stalling. That's very intriguing. You claim that you want to cooperate, yet now you waste time. No matter. If you were in my position, what would you do? Use you as bait to catch those who want to shut your mouth permanently? That's already been implemented. Any other stupid suggestions you want to make?"

Brace nodded, "Yeah. Stop giving me the meds. I want to be clear-headed for this. I know you don't want me to go through withdrawal, as that would make this process longer, but even a small amount still messes me up. I need to feel this. I need to really be here if I'm going to be any help to you."

Slither sat back and slowly nodded, "Well done. Very good. I would call that progress. I'll inform the Rescue Services crew to immediately suspend your medical maintenance. You'll be closely monitored at all times, just in case you say anything interesting while you rant and rave in your cell. I'll visit you as much as I can. After that, there are no other excuses. We get right to work!"

Agro Wheel Two, Security Sector Level One

Ensign Taron Locktek squeezed the throttle just a little bit more, despite the warning lights flashing all over his control screen. The mag-bike between his legs screamed in response, as he rushed past the other racers who were testing out the track to be used for the Security Games this spiral. His toragi, named Frank, roared from the sleek sidecar on his right. The big cat was wearing full armor and a pair of goggles underneath his helmeted head. Sparks of electricity flashed from under his mag-bike, as the impellors grabbed at the deck underneath the racetrack. Taron rose up from his seat, preparing for a sharp turn that was swiftly approaching. His toragi leaned toward him, keeping the machine balanced.

Taron's mag-bike was heavily modified, with new parts from a variety of the latest innovation services and companies that competed for new contracts from both Security and Harbor Sectors. His favorite was the Ladhani Research Group which had been the first to sponsor his racing career. When he wasn't on duty as Rescue Services crew, he was usually found at racing events or testing some new magnetic impellors and stabilization technologies. Taron made a lot of chips from his racing broadcasts, and he had hundreds of fans who sent him messages every rotation. He even had his own channel, where he showed his latest mechanical skills and training regimens. Frank was equally popular, and many of the crew asked questions about the toragi's special training.

The turn came rushing at him. He twisted the handlebars and leaned into the curve. Frank slapped the side thruster controls in the sidecar with his paw, and the mag-bike swerved into the air. Taron rode the momentum as long sparks lashed the track, before swinging back down to only half a meter above the deck. Another long straightaway was now before him. Taron remained as he was, with his body now horizontal to the track, then kicked the side of his bike with his right foot. Frank pushed a lever upward, releasing stabilizer fins that had been put into place just last sowing.

The violent vibrations disappeared as they flashed down their lane. The other riders testing out the track were just starting the first big curve behind them. He shouted with joy, with Frank joining him with wild yowls. Within his helmet display, a message flashed for his attention. He blinked it open, and he heard the voice of Lieutenant-Commander Vello in his left ear-comm, "Keep an eye on those magnetic flares, Taron. You could impair another mag-bike with those and lose the race, even if you do finish first. When you get back to your hanger, take a look at the buffers. You'll need to modify them before we let you compete."

Taron frowned, but there wasn't anything he could do about the rules of the race. He didn't want to injure anyone nor did he wish to cause a scene. As he flew down the main straightaway, he turned his thoughts toward what he might change to dampen all the discharges. There were only a few rotations left before the Security Games started, so he was crunched for time. He would ask his Lieutenant for some leave to fix the issue. Taron was certain that it would be granted. His abilities as an ambulance pilot were well noted, and despite his low rank, he was told many times that his skills had saved lives. In the past, he had been granted a higher post at Security Sector, but he never took such offers, as they would limit his time piloting and racing his beloved mag-bikes. Besides, there was nothing wrong with being a Rank Four Ensign.

He flipped a switch with his prosthetic thumb, "Primed, Lieutenant. I'll get right on that, sir. I apologize for the scorch marks on the track."

He heard the officer's laughter in his reply, "You're one crazy crew, Taron! Why don't you ride on over to your bay and let the others play for a while? That should give you time to fix things. Pellia is cursing a deck curdling-streak right now, and I have to calm her down. I'll come by later with the safety inspection team and see if we can help you out."

Taron winced, as he didn't like amateurs working on his ride, but he needed to show a cooperative front. His fans would expect no less. He replied with a cheerful tone he didn't feel, "Primed and ready for some extra hands, sir! Thank you!"

He swerved off the track, powering down the extra thrusters and focus rings on his magnetic impellors. Frank gave him a curious huff, and he patted his toragi on the shoulder, "Don't worry, big guy. We'll have a chance to show the crew what a real mag-bike can do. We just gotta satisfy the nannies. Tires down, my friend!"

Frank pawed at a control within the sidecar, and the two treaded wheels lowered themselves, cutting a groove in the sod as they landed. Each tire was twenty centimeters wide and were capable of giving tremendous traction on any surface. He lowered his speed and sank back onto the leather saddle. He glanced over at Frank, who looked disappointed. Taron didn't blame him. His toragi was proud of his abilities as co-pilot. He wasn't sure when the big cats had developed a penchant for assisting with such intricate tasks, but it was now common to find one of them in the position of directly assisting with high-speed vessels and vehicles. They had the reflexes for it and never showed any sign of fear concerning high velocities. Even the famous Tarn Vekkor had his toragi, Pete, as his co-pilot for their space-faring fighter pod.

He maneuvered himself over to the hangar bays, where the mag-bikes for the Security Games were stored and repaired. The contests would include magnetic tracks, like the one he had just exited, turf-based races, rough ground trials and even jousting with padded hand weapons. His own specialty was a shock-mace with flaring wings, and while he couldn't use the real thing in the competitions, he often carried his active duty weapon even when he was on leave. The Knights had their horses, along with the toragis assigned to them, which they raced and jousted with during the games, using lances and spears to show off their skills. Taron preferred the mag-bikes, just like Chief Mantabe did. He had been a recruit when he had witnessed the woman destined to become his Chief win competition after competition riding her mag-bike to victory. That event had inspired him to reach for greater heights ever since.

As he pulled into his mechanics bay, Taron noticed a stranger standing by the entrance to the track. He set his bike to idle, knowing that Frank could be trusted not to do anything foolish, and walked over. He paused as a supply truck swept past him. When it was gone, so was the stranger. The unknown man had been wearing a dark jumpsuit and had yellow hair, which had made him stand out. He had also been the only person who wasn't working like a bee in its hive. Taron turned around and wondered where the stranger had gone to. The area surrounding the hangers was nothing but kilometers of open fields, with the spectator seating at the far end of the racetrack. Taron shook his head and turned back to his bay. He had a mag-bike to modify and every pollen-sliver would count.

Residence Wheel Two, Level Three

Spat Newstain sat on the couch of his parent's living room and sulked with his scrawny arms crossed over his chest. His father was still talking with one of his teachers on the wallscreen, while his mother paced about and glared at him every seed-sliver. Spat refused to even look at them. The situation he was in was ridiculous! This was their rotation of leave as a family, with no school, no duty to post and nothing to do but have some fun. One of his teachers had ruined it for them, and he wondered how he would get back at the man for disrupting his plans, which had mostly involved eating an insane amount of cinnamon candy. Every sowing, the crew got at least one rotation off, sometimes two if one's Sector was feeling generous. As a family unit, they qualified for two, which they split up so that they got a rotation together out of every four. Sometimes, they visited family in the Rat's Ass community, but mostly they remained in their home or joined activities in Worlds Abound.

He could clearly hear his father's weaselly tone, as he negotiated with the teacher who had unexpectedly called upon them. Spat wasn't terribly interested in anything they were saying, but he was concerned that his parents were about to give him yet another lecture on how to be good crew. They were Strifers, not pets! His violet eyes flashed with hot anger, as he heard the teacher's stern tones warning his parents about consequences concerning not having the proper respect for a good education. Then there was the suggestion that a Security guard should escort him to his classes, as if he was some kind of prisoner! It was deeply insulting, and yet his parents were just swallowing it all up like it was pancakes.

Spat wondered how much of the Strifer Manifesto his parents adhered to. The red robes were always going on about staying true to the cause, but it seemed like his folks didn't listen. He didn't care too much about dogma, but the words of the Manifesto just seemed too logical to ignore. Then again, he was only seven spirals old, so who would ever listen to him? Ever since Ganges began the slow process of entering System Forty-One, everyone had started acting strange. The teachers were all excited and couldn't stop talking about the Holy Mission. There had been parties, public events and the crew wore their uniforms at all times, to show solidarity with their Sector. It was like their minds had turned to mush.

The wallscreen finally went blank, and Spat closed his eyes in relief. The sound of his teacher's voice was more than enough to make him want to scream with frustration. His father then walked over to him with a measured pace, as if the deck beneath them was shifting, "Spat Newstain! You have a lot to answer for, young crew. I'm very disappointed in your behavior at school."

Spat opened his eyes, hoping his contempt was visible, "Why is it that every time you feel the need to talk with me, you just end up sounding like some damned broadcaster on the fucking news?"

His mother rushed over, her hands wringing each other as if they were a bunch of ravenous snakes, "Spat! Language! We're not in Rat's Ass you know! Listen to your father!"

Spat chuckled, "Like I have any choice. By the way, how do you know what happened at school? Were you there? Are you just taking the word of a non-Strifer out of convenience?"

His father raised his voice, "All right! Tell me, son, did you take chips from teachers while being involved in an act of violence?"

Spat smirked up at him, "No, that was Keff. I didn't hurt anyone. It was Bino who was throwing the punches. We were having a friendly little playtime, acting out a famous scene from the Crucible. Next sowing, we hope to present something from the Awakening. Sounds educational to me."

His mother shook her finger at him, "Stop lying, Spat! You lied to all your teachers and aided a group of bullies in breaking regulations!"

Spat didn't bother looking at her, his eyes remaining glued to his father, "It was Tagan who lied to them. Still, I did get three reddies out of the deal. They made lots more than me. Why aren't you focusing your anger on the bullies at school? You know, the Strifer-hating kind?"

His father shook his head in frustration, "We're in officer territory now, Spat. You have to fit in, or we'll have problems you can't understand. Moving here was supposed to give you opportunities. It was supposed to get you away from the chaos and outrage that infests our former home."

Spat rolled his eyes, "Oh, right. Yeah. Lots of great opportunities to become a puppet for the Sectors. You took me from the rest of our family, from our nest! All of my friends are still there with the rest of the Mischief! I'm alone here! Outnumbered, totally regulated and with nothing to do but smile at the stupidity around me!"

His mother sat on the couch next to him and touched his arm, "Spat, we love you and want what's best for you. We Strifers have been wanting to gain the acceptance of the crew for generations. You do that by living alongside them, not sequestering yourself away in a junk pile. Now, before you start, I'm not saying that the Manifesto is wrong or shouldn't be studied, but you must understand that it was written by outcasts living in the belowdecks. That kind of environment colors one's viewpoint. We're trying to emerge from that trauma by leaving it behind."

His father spoke up before Spat could reply, "Son, you're a very intelligent, creative individual. Your grades are truly above the average. We are proud of your scholastic accomplishments, and we just don't want to see you struggling with the repercussions of outrageous behavior. We Strifers have so much to offer the rest of the crew if they can only get beyond their irrational fear of us. Can't you see that you are perpetuating a stereotype about our people?"

Spat jumped to his feet in anger, "Like being independent? Sharp witted? Having a mind of our own? The only reason the stereotypes exist is because the fucking crew made them up before they even knew who we were!"

Both parents shouted back, "Language!"

Spat wasn't having any of it, "I did nothing wrong! I'm being punished for having more personality than a slice of bread! That damned teacher just hates us Strifers! He doesn't approve of how I dress, how I answer his stupid questions! I was not allowed to join the debate club because I'm a Strifer!"

His father tried a calmer tone, "No, son. You were not allowed because of your insulting behavior. Because of your anger with your mother and me for leaving Rat's Ass. You're taking it out on everyone else. I don't care if you scream at me, or belittle my opinions. I've heard and dealt with far worse, you pup! However, within a standard crew classroom, you are expected to behave in a manner that is respectful, polite and enthusiastic about your post as a student. Don't let your emotions run riot over your life, son."

Spat muttered, "That's an old argument."

His mother chimed in, "Yes, but it's also true. Even your favorite band, The Voles, welcome the general crew to their concerts, not just Strifers. If you won't listen to us, then at least take some pointers from them."

Spat sat back down on the couch. He knew when he was defeated. They both continued to yammer at him for the rest of the slice, but he had heard enough. Everything was quite clear to him. He was a prisoner, and thus, he had to adapt to the ways of his jailors. Once he was finished with his crew-indoctrination, he would then be free to be who he wanted to be.

Medical Sector, Level Seven

Chief of Security Jira Mantabe looked over at the virtual face of Naga upon the leeward wallscreen of the Emergency Regeneration Chamber that was attached to the isolation lab where the prisoner had been interred. William Blain was now floating within a clear cylinder of thick fluid, a breathing mask strapped over his mouth and nose. The man's fever had finally broken, and his body was beginning to recover from multiple infections. According to the latest medical scans, his nanites were now affecting repairs on his cellular structure. Now that the doctors knew what to look for, the tiny machines could be studied. According to William, the nanites had finally been able to translate the language of Ganges, with help from Naga. The prisoner waved a hand at her with a languid gesture, his voice coming over the speakers attached to the regen-tank, "I do appreciate all the trouble you've gone through in treating my condition. Thank you. When it comes to biological technology, you have surpassed my culture's abilities. May I ask how aggressive your protective viruses are?"

Chief Mantabe scowled but she replied nonetheless, "Very proactive. They are our first defense against mutagenic pathogens. The last time an adult has gone through the Sneezies was octennia ago, just after the Awakening. I have to admit that, at this point, we don't even think about it."

William nodded as bubbles rose from his breathing mask, "I see. Thank you for your candor. It seems that I may be trapped in Ganges forever. It would not be permissible for me to spread this infection, however beneficial it may be, throughout the Solarian Alliance. I am marooned, unless my nanites can find and destroy every viral particle."

Naga spoke up, "That may be difficult. The viruses attach themselves to the mitochondria of your cells, which then produce them on a regular basis."

William seemed to sag within the medical gel he was floating in, "That's what I feared. I have been altered. At best, my mechanical systems might be able to keep the viruses in check, but I must now be quarantined from my own people. I don't suppose you recruit outsiders much, do you?"

Jira gritted her teeth, "It's never been an issue. I don't like being made fun of, especially from a spy."

He looked up at her, his steel-gray eyes penetrating hers, "I'm not joking. It would be a true honor to become part of your crew. I have nothing but the deepest admiration for Ganges and its mission. You saved us all. You don't know it, but you did, indirectly. I was trained to seek for and study you, then report back to base, but understand that I was a volunteer. I wanted to be the one who discovered Ganges, out of admiration."

Naga replied, "I shall remind you that everything you say is being recorded and shall be presented to the Judiciary Council, pending your session in court. An attorney is being assigned to you as we speak."

William laughed, "Well of course I'm being recorded! I'm inside an AeyAie! I might understand that more than either of you. We Solarians were willing to leave you alone, but the AeyAie Solidarity insisted that we find their wayward child, and the Boktahl backed them, pressuring us into action. They found it... I guess distasteful is the word, that we had no knowledge of where you were and if you were safe. So many of the early records of your messages back to Sol went missing when Terra destroyed itself. We lost a lot of knowledge. If it hadn't been for the AeyAies, we would have been back to the stone age. We almost were there anyway. I understand this is all new to you, but for me it's ancient history."

Chief Mantabe crossed her arms over her chest, "I guess we need to catch up on that. You will be officially interrogated by my Sector, once you fully recover. Any information you give us will help my crew immensely. You claim to be no threat to us, but we know something of human history, which makes us skeptical of such statements. We've had our own wars, all of which were internal, of course. We're not a bunch of novices."

William cocked his head to one side, "Yes, I've seen the influence of such conflicts already. How many wars have you suffered through since you left the Sol System?"

Naga replied with a woeful expression, "Two of them. Millions died in each one. The first was an officer's mutiny, the aftermath of which we call The Awakening.

The second one is named the Crucible, which was only six hundred and thirty-seven spirals ago. It was another mutiny, though its nature had to do with Terran ambitions."

William's eyes grew wide with open surprise, "Only two? That's all? Dear God! Congratulations on being the most stable and peaceful culture in the history of humanity! During that same time period, the entire Sol System had been embroiled in warfare for ages, in which trillions of people have perished. It has only been the last twelve-hundred years, or just about eight hundred spirals, that we have found the blessing of true and lasting peace. A lot of that came from our contact with the Boktahl, who have no concept of war, murder or greed. They're good friends. They have their own issues, but I'm afraid we still don't understand most of them, despite how close we've become."

Naga shook its virtual head, "This could all be lies, Chief Mantabe. I do not trust this human. His responses are not like that of the crew, and he could be luring us into a trap."

Jira shrugged, "I agree. The problem is, we cannot verify anything he says, yet we also need information. I don't think fitting him with a Naga-Port would be a good idea, as he may have defensive and offensive software within those computer systems inside his brain structure. So, unless we can find a mind-reader, which is insanely unlikely, we may have to simply allow him to spin out his tales and look for inconsistencies. Hence the need for a professional interrogator."

Jira's toragi sauntered over to the regen-tank and sniffed at it with suspicion. William watched her from within the cylinder, "Those tigers are one of the reasons you even know that I exist. They're very interesting. We have nothing like them. It was assumed that your culture would remain intact, as your ship was so isolated. The Solidarity felt that, with Naga being the General Manager of the mission, there would be little need for change. I also didn't recognize the hull metal nor the other additions to Ganges. According to the few records that survived, you had no military. Your beacon messages also never mentioned most of the technological innovations I've seen thus far."

Jira growled, "That was done so that Terra would not have information that might jeopardize our security."

William nodded, "Yes, a wise precaution. We learned more when some of the established colonies came to our aid. It took them hundreds of octuries, as you say, to reach us after we sent out our distress signals. Two of them had already built Ganges-class vessels to continue your mission. Thus far, I've discovered ten colony worlds you've made that have done the same. You inspired humanity to reach out even further. While the first few planets you rebuilt weren't exactly paradises, none of them failed. Those who answered our call for aid helped us to terraform Terra, using your methodologies. It's now a beautiful, perfect ecosystem that will remain untouched by humanity for as long as the Alliance remains."

Naga noticed that Jira seemed stunned by this latest revelation and asked, "Where do you live? If not on Terra, where is the bulk of humanity?"

William smiled under his mask, "In a network of orbital stations, each one a thousand kilometers long, strung out within Terra's orbit from the sun. There used to be colonies on Mars, but those have been abandoned. The whole planet is now a park used for recreation. We gave the moons of Saturn to the Boktahl, to use as an embassy. Jupiter is the main industrial site for vessels and drydocks. The AeyAie Solidarity was given full management of the innermost part of the Sol System. They changed Venus and Mercury, which are now used for power allotment for the network of orbitals. There are rings of photon collectors surrounding Sol under their control. No one in the Sol System lives on a planet anymore."

Jira forced herself to sit back and look past the shock running through her, "You say the Boktahl are totally peaceful. What do they contribute to your Alliance? Why would they work with humans? I want to know more about them."

William sighed, "That could take a very long time, Chief of Security. There was still unrest amongst humanity, which the Solidarity tried to mitigate, with limited success. When the Boktahl discovered us, those human orbitals still warring with each other ceased their fighting and pulled together, thinking the extraterrestrials a threat. As for the Boktahl, they're strange. It took us a long time to communicate in any meaningful way. They can see gravity, they speak using radio waves. Light is a mystery to them. They know it exists, but their theories concerning it were way behind ours. They have gravity technology which had eluded us until they arrived. They don't think like we do.

"To tell the truth, they are sometimes frightened by humanity. The deal is, we share our knowledge, they provide a great amount of technological innovation. In return, we defend them. Since they found us, a warlike species, they figured there must be others, so they want us at their side. They like the AeyAies, but it's still hard to communicate with them. The Solidarity acts as a translator, as best it can, between our respective species. With the three of us working together, we finally discovered the Wend-Drive, our way of ignoring the consequences of the speed of light. That's very recent, by the way.

"As for what the Boktahl look like, they're not humanoid. They come from a four-gee world and breathe chlorine-trifluoride. Breathe is a metaphor. They look like a clump of blue lemons surrounded by a network of flexible tendrils and frills. Not very symmetrical and they like to cover themselves with living organisms from their home planet."

Chief Mantabe placed her hand upon her ear-comm, "We have to end this conversation, Naga. Our trespasser's lawyer has arrived at Medical. He's insisting we cease our mistreatment of his client. His name is Blather Soakwet. He's on his way here right now."

The visage of Naga faded from the wallscreen, and Jira got up from her seat to exit the room, nodding to the pair of Security crew and their toragis who would remain to watch over the prisoner. She could hear William laughing within his regen-tank, but she didn't understand what it was that he found so amusing. He was about to face trial in the highest court of the Judiciary Council. Perhaps the savage didn't appreciate the danger he was in.

Agro Wheel Two, Level Twenty

William Blaine looked around at the grand chamber that was used by the highest judges of the Judiciary Council. It was hexagonal in design, with a third of it walled off by a waist-high railing of gold. The floor was polished stone that resembled pale jade, and the high walls were elaborately carved out of a golden-red wood he didn't recognize. He sat at a small table with gold legs, his outlandish attorney next to him, wearing neon-green robes and a stained, brown rat mask that covered his face except for his mouth and chin. William had been told these were the traditional garments of a group of crew who called themselves the Strifers. His lawyer had a strange, yet refreshingly caustic manner to the way he spoke, and his name, Blather Soakwet, was outrageous.

The high court was large enough to comfortably hold hundreds, but it was almost empty, save for his guards, their tigers, the nine human justices and the lead prosecutor. Several flying drones surrounded him, which they had been doing since he left Medical Sector. Security had used a military vehicle to transport him to this location, and he had been chained to his seat, despite the protests of his outraged attorney. William appreciated the professionalism of the Security crew, even if they made the journey uncomfortable. The speed in which he had been called to face the highest court in Ganges left him feeling dizzy. It seemed the population of the ship was obsessed with efficiency. In his home culture, it would have taken months, if not years, for such a case to be brought before the Solarian court system.

William winced to himself; he had to start thinking like the crew in terms of time. The more he forced himself to think in their nomenclature, the easier it was for his nanites to act as translators. Eventually, he would be speaking like he had been born aboard the ship, but for now, the process was clumsy. He focused on the judges seated before him. At first, he was shocked, for all of them wore a combination of garb and decoration that paid homage to their Sector and their ancient heritage. The

Sol system had lost all of its non-technological cultures, soon after Ganges had been launched. It had been a point of contention amongst historians as to whether the customs and traditions of those who had been taken from their lands had kept their ways alive. From what he could see, they had done so stunningly well, with some alterations that came from living within an artificial environment. It was an incredible achievement.

His reverie was broken by the central-most judge tapping her spear upon the stone floor, "This court is now in session. Naga, please grant us your guidance in this issue, for it is the opinion of this court that the issue before us is not one which affects humans only."

A short pillar with a wallscreen upon it flashed to reveal the matronly face that William had seen in Engineering. Why the AeyAie had changed its appearance was a mystery to him, but he hoped to discover the answer in the near future. The central justice spoke again, "This court shall now review the charges against the human who is named William Blain, from the Solarian Alliance. They are as follows: trespassing, attempted theft, the assault of a crewmember, and entering a restricted zone within Engineering Sector's belowdecks. How does your client plead, counsel Soakwet?"

Blather rose to his feet, raised an old-fashioned datapad high in the air and began to shout, "Not guilty to all the stupid charges, your Honor! It is an absolute outrage that my client has been mistreated as he has been by the wolf-pack known as Security Sector! Not one of these charges are anything but stale shit!"

To William's surprise, the judges simply nodded as the central one raised her spear with a studied calm, "We wish to hear your reasoning behind the plea, as required by the Prime Charter of Ganges."

Blather began to pace in front of the judges, "As well you should! It may be that I'm the only reasonable person in this damned room! Concerning the first charge of trespassing, tell me, your Honor, do we have a giant doorbell upon the hull of Ganges? Do we have any process of welcoming those who may wish to visit us from outside of our tin can? A welcome mat, perhaps? No! Not one! What the fuck was my client supposed to do? Knock on an airlock?"

William winced and became very concerned about the maniac who was representing him, but there were no calls for contempt of court. It was bizarre.

"Concerning the second charge of attempted theft, I can't think of a more fucked-up piece of drivel. For all Security knows, my client was trying to repair that locker, not break into it! Their assumptions are nothing more than paranoia and I demand that his captors receive treatment from Therapeutic Services for their mental disorder!"

William glanced over at the Security crew who were there to guard him, but none of them seemed upset. If anything, they looked bored.

Blather continued his odd diatribe, "As for assaulting a crewmember, it is my contention that my client was simply defending himself against an over-eager janitor who tried to illicitly restrain him. That guy is lucky it wasn't me he tried to tackle in that locker area! Besides, my client wishes to apologize for any harm he may have caused to the miscreant who attacked him."

William found himself sinking down in his chair. It was obvious that the court had arranged for him to have the worst lawyer in Ganges. They might end up sharing a prison cell if they were lucky.

Blather swept around to face the judges directly, pointing a finger in their faces, "Finally, we come to the last charge of entering a restricted zone within the belowdecks. Please! What? Are we now resorting to just creating add-ons to mollify ourselves that my client is a really bad person? Are we savages? That charge is not only unnecessary, but highly insulting to my intelligence, as it should be to yours if you had any! We do not know the method of ingress that my client took, thus the charge is an assumption tacked onto the others to make my client look like a fucking Makdreah!"

To William's surprise, the judges nodded to each other and sat back in their seats with neutral expressions on their faces. The central judge rapped her spear on the floor, "As we have Security Sector's report at hand, we shall not be asking the prosecution for their response to the defense's position at this time. We do wish to speak with the defendant directly, under the guidance of his attorney. Our questions are for clarification purposes only and shall not be used to potentially make your client incriminate himself."

Blather bowed in an exaggerated manner, "Of course, your Honor! Do your worst! Don't take too long, I have a lunch appointment coming up."

William shook his head in absolute confusion. He wondered if there was something terribly wrong with his nanite-based translation. The central judge, who was covered in a thin layer of orange mud, tapped her spear and addressed him, "William Blaine, are you prepared to speak with this court?"

He cleared his throat and shot a sharp glance toward his lawyer, who was grinning, "Yes, I am, your Honor."

She nodded once then said, "You claim to be from the Sol System, is this true, and if so, why are you here in Ganges?"

He swept his gaze at the other judges, "I am from the Solarian Alliance, and I am a scout, trained to study other cultures unobtrusively so that they will not be affected by my presence. I must apologize to this court as I have failed my mission and thus have created a situation which was unintended. I was also tasked with checking up on the colonists which have been sent to the worlds you have rebuilt to assess their progress. While there are a few who have contended with local political struggles, the colonization effort has been a tremendous success. I admit that my data concerning Ganges was terribly out of date, which is why I had to take certain calculated risks in making entry into the ship."

The judge with the spear tilted her head to one side, "Do you represent the Solarian Alliance from which you originate?"

William shook his head and became horribly dizzy, an effect he had noticed before and was told was due to the centrifugal forces used to simulate gravity aboard Ganges, "Not precisely, your Honor. Up until now, my mission was successful, and I did not have to interact with anyone to gain the needed data on the colonies. I am now trapped here, mainly due to your protective virus program. I cannot go home unless that problem is solved. My duty is to report everything I see and hear within this vessel, which I am now unable to perform, though my ship will send a message back to Sol if I am incapacitated for too long a time."

Blather jumped to his feet, "There! We have made this man homeless and adrift within the emptiness of space! We owe him compensation for our own crime of inappropriately using medical services upon him without consent! Eat that one and gag on it!"

William was about to jump up and wrap his hands upon his lawyer's mouth, but the judges nodded and had concerned expressions upon their faces. The central judge tapped her spear once more, "We hereby call for a recess to consider what we have heard this rotation. Our decision concerning the charges against the defendant shall be given within this slice. May Holy enlightenment guide us all."

Command Hub, Level Twelve

Captain Perrin Fieldscan walked through the maze of corridors which led to Wasp's private office. His young Executive Officer had chosen the most inconvenient location for her post, for those times when she was away from the Bridge. Behind him, complaining loudly at every chaotic intersection and tight passageway, was the Counsel-to-Captain, Merridy Olion, who had also helped to train Wasp for her current duties. Captain Fieldscan's lips twitched with a smile at every complaint. While there had been times when he had griped about how difficult it was to reach his Executive's office, this rotation he was grateful that the Strifer had chosen such an inconvenient location to set up shop. It meant their meeting would be more private, far from the news drones and the rest of the crew.

Merridy complained aloud, "We might as well be in the belowdecks! How in Ganges did she ever find this place to begin with? Watch your head!"

The Captain ducked beneath a hanging set of cables as he replied, "My dear counselor, I would not be surprised if Wasp had actually rebuilt this route to suit her desires. Only the bravest and most determined crew would ever take the time and risk to reach her, ensuring their need to bother her is worth the effort. Personally, I'm quite impressed."

Merridy made a rude noise behind him, making his smile grow wider. The Council-to-Captain was a steady individual, her short, stocky build belying her highly athletic abilities. At the moment, her dark, braided hair was steadily becoming more tangled with every meter of their journey. Secrecy was crucial, and once they had gotten past the more congested corridors filled with rushing crew, he had brought her up to speed concerning the trespasser from Sol. Wasp had contacted him just a slice ago, stating they had to meet so they could discuss the latest decision of the Judiciary Council. Captain Fieldscan was filled with curiosity, mingled with a touch of dread.

Squeezing past stacked crates and construction debris, they came to a door with a green, stained, tilted sign that simply said, "Welcome". Perrin knocked once as Merridy stumbled over an obstacle, and the door flashed open. He took in the sight of Wasp's office with an intrigued eye. It was small, just a ten-meter cube which was even more disheveled than the passageway to get to this place. Cluttered stacks of datapads, folders, boxes and plumbing littered the entire floor. The wallscreen on the capward side came to life, displaying Naga's visage. Wasp was behind her desk, which was held together with wire and vent-strapping. Upon one wall were a pair of posters. The first was for a Strifer band named The Voles, the other for a popular broadcast called Gatekeepers. Three rickety chairs, each one a different style and height, were right in front of the desk.

Wasp jumped from her chair and snapped out a Command salute, slapping her fist to her chest. Perrin returned the gesture and carefully tiptoed his way through the clutter, before settling into a seat which gave off a startling creak. Merridy cursed as she toppled a pile of folders over before she reached the questionable safety of her own choice of chair. Wasp sank back into her own seat, which was a torn and stained padded lounger, "Thank you both for getting your sorry asses over here so quickly. There's a lot to share, and we don't have the luxury of time."

Perrin looked over at Naga's face, which appeared solemn, "Glad you're here, my friend! We could use your infinite perspective this rotation."

Naga shook its virtual head, "My emotional responses are not to be trusted, Captain Perrin Fieldscan. I am simply here in case you have questions concerning the Judiciary Council."

Perrin heard Merridy gasp at this statement, and he had to admit that he felt a sudden chill of trepidation concerning the issue that brought them all together. Wasp cleared her throat and started speaking, "It is the decision of our dear Judiciary

Council that our trespasser is to be treated as a guest. William Blaine has apologized to the engineer he knocked out, and this has been accepted with grace. The attack victim is under the assumption that Blain was ill and thus not in his right mind. The man has no idea what caused him to become unconscious and gave William a stern warning about venturing in areas where he is not authorized. No charges are being pressed. Attorney Soakwet was quite convincing concerning his position that crew rights are based upon sentient rights and that his client was mistreated according to the dictates of the Prime Charter. The Judiciary Council is concerned that this may cause an unintended dispute between Ganges and the Solarian Alliance. They figure it like this, Big Cheese, no matter how we slice it, this situation has already fucked us over, so we may as well act like the civilized crew that we supposedly are. William has rights as a sentient being, and thus, we have no choice but to welcome him."

Merridy got to her feet, "That's outrageous! He broke into the ship without authorization! He's an unknown threat!"

Perrin glanced over at Naga, whose face gave away nothing. He absently stroked his moustache, "Well. This still leaves a bucket of difficulties for us to contend with. Is William allowed to do as he wishes, go wherever he pleases?"

Wasp shook her head with a grin, "Negative, Big Cheese. He's not trained. Security was able to successfully convince the Judiciary that since he has never gone through Basic Crew Training, he is a danger to himself and must be accompanied by Security crew at all times. To further protect our uninvited guest, his presence and place of origin must remain classified, or the crew might panic. He has to remain within a Security holding cell, and all of his activities must be monitored to prevent unintended harm from reaching him. In return, he has promised to not send any messages to the Sol System during his stay. Um, there's a bit of a further problem. He may not be allowed to go home, due to our disease-prevention regimen, which he was accidentally exposed to during his ingress. He has requested permission to become part of the crew."

Perrin suddenly found that his hands had just clenched into fists, "I see. That becomes my decision, then. Very well. His desire to serve Ganges, no matter how uninformed it may be, must be respected. However, since he is not properly trained, he must be given a chance to see how we do things, and we must assess what he is capable of and where he might fit into the Sector structure which governs our society. He may change his tune after that. He must now cooperate fully, giving us a chance to examine his equipment, for review by the New Technology Board. He will tell us where his vessel is located and give us any and all information which we require of him. Should he disobey at any time, he can spend the rest of his life in the brig."

Wasp piped in, "I still have that plank, Big Cheese."

Perrin grinned at her, "We may end up having to use it, so keep it polished. In the meantime, let's give him a grand tour and see what he's really made of."

Agro Wheel Two, Security Level Two

I prowl ahead of the humans. It is my honor to do this for them. The long passageway is filled with doors, many I have never seen used. I can tell by the scent and the faint sounds my ears pick up that we are now very far from all the occupied chambers. My human, Darron, is walking behind the prisoner. In front of the stranger is Rushlo, who leads our pack for Chief. His toragi, Victor, is next to me, sniffing at the air as if testing it for poisons. There is but one foulness here, the presence of William. As the toragi to the pack-leader, Victor is a single pace in front of me, as is his right. There will come a time when I shall lead, of this I am certain. I feel it from my nose to my tail. For now, I am content to follow, taking in the bland, cold gray walls around me.

Each door has a scribble drawn at the top. The humans use these markings to find their way around the world. Darron calls them numbers. There are some I do recognize, but not enough to decipher their meaning. The pathways of sound and scent are more efficient ways of finding my way to and from various locations. I have been in this corridor many times, but never this far past the armored gates. This is the place where those humans who must be contained for the safety of the crew are held. Beyond each door is a large room with more doors, all of which lead to personal living quarters. These are used for non-violent prisoners who will not stay here for long. Those who have harmed others are either changed or are under the guidance of a human named Sensei. That region is quite different from this one. This place smells of sadness rather than despair.

Every door along the corridor is separated by a large wallscreen, where the face of the world can check on its contents. Naga has been following us very closely during our march. It is clever. It understands the danger. My hope is that the prisoner William will stay in this place forever, forgotten and alone. This way his foul smell can finally be gone from my aching nose. Glancing behind me, I can sense that he has no fear of this location, nor of us. This is not reasonable, and it irritates me further. He is a sick thing. He does not belong in the world. My claws scrape the deck as dark thoughts race through my heart. This is but one of many reasons that fuel my belief that William is not human. I do not wish to harm any of the bipedal apes. They are to be protected, even if it should cost my own life. He smells bad, acts wrong, sounds strange. My nerves quiver with hatred, but I keep to my training. Honor is everything. Finally, Rushlo calls out, "Halt! This is the assigned place."

Darron smells confused, which unsettles me further, "Why all the way out here? We went beyond the occupied units a kilometer ago."

Victor looks bored but he does not share my love for human babbling. He also snarls at the prisoner, wrinkling his nose in obvious disgust. I huff in agreement. We clean our shoulders together to express our indifference while Rushlo opens the portal with his wrist markings. I wonder if I will ever have those, but my forearms are too furry for such things. Humans are generally hairless, so they put pictures upon themselves to control the world. This ability fascinates me. I want to do the same.

The prisoner speaks in his garbled way, "Is this my new home?"

Rushlo babbles back to him, but he speaks very quickly, as if he wants this done swiftly, so he can get away from the prisoner's stench. I cannot follow the trail of his hooting and grunts. My human suddenly barks, "Wait a pollen! Are you kidding me? We have to treat him like a guest?"

My ears flatten tight to my skull. I roar aloud in outrage, ignoring Victor, who swats at me with his paw. I know the word "guest". It is used for welcoming a human friend to one's lair. That William must be treated this way is a terrible insult. He is dangerous, not to be trusted. My human partner and his superior begin to argue, as I hiss and spit my hatred. Victor bumps me with his head, trying to calm me down. I refuse to be mollified. The situation is intolerable. It goes against all of my instincts. Behind all this is a growing fear that the world is imperiled by the hated prisoner.

As the argument becomes heated, William quietly steps away from the other humans. He does not dash off to escape us nor does he do anything threatening. Instead, he walks toward me with an icy calm. I stand my ground, hissing my wrath and displaying my claws, raking grooves into the polished deck. He stops just two meters away from me and gets down on one knee. He stares into my eyes with his metallic, unflinching orbs. Prisoner Williams opens his palms and speaks to me softly, despite my growls, "It seems we need to work together now."

I show my fangs and take a swipe at the air in front of him, but he doesn't flinch, "I know you don't like me. I'm truly sorry. I have never seen anything like you. I know about cats, even large ones, but have never been close to one before."

My hackles are raised. My fur is standing on end. My human sees what is happening and shouts "No! Stop! You don't know what you're dealing with!"

Confusion swells up within me. Victor is yowling behind me, batting at my hindquarters in frustration. I ignore everyone but prisoner William. He drops down and sits with his legs crossed before me. It is so tempting to rip out his throat. To tear his flesh from his bones and feel his hot blood gush all over me. He sits there, staring at me, "I made a real mess of things. You blame me for it. Don't pretend you don't understand me. You know more than you let on."

This selfish ape needs to know his place. Victor is still yowling, and Rushlo is dashing forth to intervene. There is little time to act. I can end this now, slake my thirst and know that Ganges is safe from this fiend who sees all secrets. Darron has his hands on the prisoner's shoulders, but he is shoved off. William then bends low and bows before me, his forehead touching the deck in submission. I want to rend, to kill, but my honor is at stake. We toragi are guardians, protectors. We obey the commands of the humans we serve with all our hearts. To disobey orders would bring terrible shame. Already my human partner distrusts my actions. He is smelling of fear. Not of William, but of me. Perhaps he fears for me.

I force myself to settle my heated emotions, as Rushlo drags Victor away. The prisoner is still prone before my claws, which itch to tear him apart. I know my duty. The Chief wants him safe from harm. He is to be treated as a guest, but I do not have to trust him. I do not have to like him. He needs to be told the nature of his status, but I have no words. Frustration floods me as Darron tries to get William to rise from the floor. The wall-face of Naga is calling my name with urgent tones. That is when I understand what to do. Turning my back to the prone prisoner, I lift my hind leg and urinate all over his back. He is mine, for I have claimed him.

Darron falls back in surprise, his uniform splashed with my scent. Rushlo has stopped moving and is staring at me in shock. Victor calms down and is now cleaning his hind leg, ignoring everyone. William shudders where he is and then rolls over onto his back, "I accept your proposal, Mike. I shall learn from you what it means to be crew. I belong to you."

I sit up and clean my left shoulder. Darron is kneeling on the floor behind William, laughing so hard the sound echoes throughout the long corridor. Rushlo falls back and leans on the nearest wall. The face of Naga smiles at me. I feel a rush of pride. The world approves of my decision. I am not as satisfied as I should be, but at least the prisoner smells better than he did before.

CHAPTER FIVE

Prime Rotation - Launch Sowing - Mission Harvest - Spiral 5620

"The members of Security Sector have become sports celebrities among the general crew. At one time, Ganges had entertainment sports teams that competed for chips. Now, it's nothing but Police versus Investigations or Rescue Services playing against the Nature Rangers in a variety of games and competitions. I do admit, this does help Security do its job, as they have become popular. Oh, and don't get me started about the prevalence of toragi video captures on the broadcasts! One can barely look at the news without seeing another puff piece about those magnificent creatures. The Security Commanders and their toothy guardians have been granted the same status as popular musicians, actors and artists in the public's eye. Sometimes I suspect they've done this on purpose, and if so, it has been cleverly perfected."
Vali Metanda, Forge-Chief, Engineering Sector, personal log, V39

Agro Wheel Two, Security Level One

Chief of Security Jira Mantabe raised her helm's visor, then lifted her shock-hammer over her head to signal the beginning of the march into the giant arena used for the games. Mag-bikes gunned their engines, banners were lifted up, each of them representing a platoon. The sound of a hundred thousand pairs of boots marching in unison vibrated the air. The grand entrance of the arena opened wide, revealing the massive grounds and fifty-meter-high grandstands for the one million spectators who roared their approval. The sound was breathtaking, like a wave of chaos slamming into her chest, making her ribs vibrate despite her armor. Drones danced above the crowd, circling Security dirigibles launching fireworks to the deafening cheers of the spectators. Flower petals drifted in swarms, showering the Security crew with bright bits of color. Streaks of red shot across the arena, as both fighter and rescue aircraft dodged one another in carefully coordinated displays of skill. The skyscreens, half a kilometer above them, were filled with visual artwork, all of it full of scenes of Security history.

Jira's heart soared in her chest, but there was a small pang of doubt deep within her. Amongst the throngs of happy crew, William Blaine was also watching, surrounded by Police and Investigators. What did he think of this display of might and skill? Were her crew just a bunch of amateurs, chasing each other with primitive weapons to his savage mind? Were they revealing too much to an unknown force? Her thoughts were still dizzy from her last encounter with their uninvited guest. Last rotation, he had been in a private conference room with Slither, answering questions concerning Sol System history, complying with the interrogator in an easy manner. She had listened in, as the strange human breezily talked about acts of genocide and terrorism that curdled her blood.

She wanted to shake her head to clear it, but that tiny moment of weakness might be noticed by her crew, most of whom knew nothing about the Solarian and his supposed mission. Instead, Jira focused on the chanting crowd, as she passed through the fifty-meter-tall doorway, entering the arena proper. Her name was being shouted over and again by the spectators. She was their guardian, their protector. Her toragi, Tracey, was proudly stalking at her side. The big cat's armor gleamed in the light of the skyscreens. Her ears were flat against her head, to protect them from the immense noise which now surrounded them completely, as they continued their long march around the running track which was just ten meters away from the main grandstands.

The arena itself was shaped like an open-cornered triangle. Each side was three kilometers long with gaps at the corners, the main entrance being one of these. One of these openings led to the mechanized racetracks and jousting fields. The third was for amenities and the less strenuous entertainments, including art exhibits created by her crew, the educational events and multiple food vendors. Specialized sports fields had been placed all around this area, for those crew who enjoyed rooting for teams. During dark-slice, these would all be converted to concert venues, with dozens of musical groups performing to honor her Sector. The Security Games were the largest events in the history of Ganges, with tens of millions of broadcast viewers closely watching every contest and performance. After having to cope with all the negotiations and decisions on who would be allowed to participate in the festivities, Jira was glad that she had opted for not being a part of the challenges this spiral. Besides, she was already wearing more honors upon her armor than anyone else.

Out of two million Security crew, one hundred thousand had qualified for public competition. These crew were now marching behind her, in rows of twenty, with perfectly drilled steps. None of them looked at the crowd that filled the arena to capacity. Her crew took this event seriously, as a way to demonstrate that the general population of the ship was in good hands. Every one of them had their toragis with them, and she could see thousands of holographic banners depicting the big cats throughout the stands. The toragi were still very popular in Ganges, ever since their introduction to the general crew during the Crucible. Novices and students of all ages trusted the toragi even more than any human crewmember, with good reason. Jira only hoped that her Sector was truly ready, in case anything terrible came from the presence of William Blaine.

Earlier, she had ordered the entire Space Fleet to launch, covering the void around Ganges in a shell of fighting vessels. Jira had placed them on high alert, just in case any other unexpected guests appeared during the games. From what she understood from their Solarian visitor, the Wend could drop a ship anywhere, at any time, without warning. As a result, she had doubled the number of scout ships and fast cruisers which escorted Ganges as it made system entry. Every kilometer-long battleship had been deployed, including carriers that were five times that size, filled with smaller vessels, ready to launch at a moment's notice. The crew operating the railguns and the Spin-Drive turrets were pushed hard with extra drills. Many of the officers under her command thought she was being extra cautious about the new stellar system Ganges was now entering, not understanding the deeper peril that was already within the hull of Ganges.

After reaching the halfway mark, Jira turned to walk up a long, spiraling ramp that led up to a presentation platform with her honor guard. These were the Commanders who helped manage Security Sector, also accompanied by their toragi. The rest of the marching crew continued on the track used for footraces, until they spread out to form a ring, facing the spectators. Jira marched to the edge of the platform at the very heart of the arena and waited for the signal. The crowd began to calm down, as the music that had been playing began to finish with its concluding flourishes. Naga's matronly face appeared upon all the wallscreens, kiosk pillars and the skyscreens above, "Attention all crew! I am pleased to present Jira Mantabe, Chief of Security Sector!"

A monstrous roar crashed through the air, as several drones swirled just above Jira's head. These units would bring her image and words to every member of the crew. At one time, she would have been nervous about the public attention, but those rotations were now far behind her. Jira slammed her hammer upon the platform and raised her chin. She tore her helmet off, revealing her face and the symbol of her Sector tattooed upon her brow, "Crew of Ganges! I hereby welcome you all to the six-hundred and eighth Security Games!"

A blast of cheers almost knocked her over with the deafening force of a million voices chanting and screaming their devotion to her crew. She raised a fist into the air and the spectators calmed, "These hallowed competitions are not for boasting, but to present to you those who are willing to sacrifice their lives to protect yours! We are your warriors, your guardians in an uncertain universe. During this sowing, take a close look at those who stand between you and disaster, and be glad that you are so well protected. It is my honor to call upon those who have decided to join our Sector and prove themselves worthy of wearing the gray-and-red. Some are coming to us from Basic Crew Training, while others are transferees from different Sectors. I now call upon these brave individuals to reveal themselves and step forth onto the main field!"

A grand overture was then played, an ancient tune named "Security United", while all the spectators bellowed their approval. Hundreds of people who had been sitting in the grandstands stripped themselves bare and ran nude down the steps to the awaiting line of Security crew. They jumped over the safety walls and dashed toward the massive green field that would be used for all major competitions. Jira looked down from her thirty-meter vantage point and nodded her approval as her crew welcomed the newcomers, escorting them to the main field. These volunteers were not yet trained, though all of them had taken courses in self-defense and other martial arts, participating in Security's public education services. Once they were all in place, waving at the crowd or simply chatting with each other, her best Sergeants screamed their orders at them until the crew were in a presentable formation. Jira lifted her gauntleted hand once again, while the images of every past Security Chief flashed on the wallscreens of the arena, beginning with its founder, Marik Langman. She took a deep breath and silently prayed to Odin that these volunteers would serve her Sector with distinction, "Now these brave crewmembers will prove their worth in the opening contests of these Security Games! Cheer them on and applaud their decision to serve the Holy Mission with life and limb! Huzzah!"

Jira took five steps back, after hefting her hammer over one shoulder. The crowd went wild, as it did every spiral. She would be closely watching the newcomers with great interest, for they represented the future of her Sector. She remembered when she had jumped down from the stands in the heavier than normal gravity of this level, her heart hammering in her bare chest. At the time, she never dared to imagine that she would become the Chief, welcoming new recruits during the games. She forced herself to remain focused on what was happening below her and not thinking about the potential troubles which may spring upon the ship at any moment. If the Solarians decided to attack Ganges during the games, they would find a very unified crew to contend with.

Agro Wheel Two, Security Level One

Dalen Gupta just couldn't stop dancing. The music was simply wonderful, the crowd excited, and he had his entire family along with him in the grandstands for the Security Games. Life was sweet, which included the large basket of treats he had bought from a vendor a few paring-slivers ago. Like most of his staff, he had taken leave-time to enjoy the fantastic spectacle of a sowing's worth of sports, contests and challenges. Some of his superiors thought that his love for entertainment was a distraction from the serious work involved in atmospheric studies, but as the ship had yet to reach Planet Forty-One, there was little to learn, other than going through old files of worlds from history, none of which would be anything like the impending one. Dalen had even given tickets to the Security Games as bonus rewards for his crew, which was greatly appreciated. He was a popular director and wanted to stay that way.

His friend, Levy Truel, had started his enjoyment of the event on the second rotation of the games. Dalen suspected Levy had only shown up now because he wanted to make sure his son didn't go jumping over the safety barrier to join Security during the recruitment segment of last rotation. His friend had missed seeing the great march of the Security crew, the speech of Chief Mantabe and the review of the participants by Captain Fieldscan and the entire Judiciary Council. These were the stars of Ganges, not to be missed for any reason that Dalen could think of. Still, some of the formal addresses had seemed rather stilted, compared with other spirals. He figured it was due to all the extra concerns about entering a new stellar system and starting the Holy terraforming process once again. The Chiefs of every Sector also had extra responsibilities right now, which meant they were more distracted than usual. From his conversations with party-goers last dark-slice, it had been noticed by the general crew.

Dalen continued his dancing while watching teams of Security fighters who were participating in group matches wielding shock-swords and shields, despite the heavier apparent gravity which made him sweat. His two mates were right next to him, along with their children. Sasha was dancing with little Velika, while Bryce was chatting with young Marik about the contests, leaving Dalen in the middle, gyrating with fluid grace. Most crewmembers looked at him and thought he was clumsy due to his weight, which grew each spiral. Their surprise at seeing his skills as a dancer always delighted him. Just a paring-sliver ago, his male mate, Bryce, had pointed out that some of the wallscreens in the arena were showing videos of Dalen dancing away without a care, to the cheer of the crowds. It was an amazing compliment that Naga had noticed him.

His friend Levy was just a few meters away, biting at his knuckles as he watched a group of Security fighters below bash each other senseless. Dalen sighed to himself; the man was always taking things too seriously. No one was being terribly injured or killed, though there had been a few instances when Rescue Services needed to take someone off the field due to mishaps. Even the non-violent feats of strength, skill and endurance resulted in some injuries. To Dalen, the truly frightening competitions were the ones that involved mag-bike races, which were incredibly fast and could result in terrible accidents. He could barely watch them, though his son loved the high-speed chases. They were held in the same area as the horseraces and jousts. It was said that one could spend every waking moment wandering the games and not see them all. It was an amazing gift to the crew.

At the very end of it all, the Judiciary Council and the Captain would make an official, public report about the condition of Security's crew to the Chief, which is what the games were all about. Medals and honors would be awarded, including the sought-after "Kenshi" prize. Festivities would continue, celebrating the honored crew of Security, and the winners of the contests would be hailed as the heroes of Ganges. For Dalen and his family, it was the perfect vacation, filled with wonder, excitement and lots of dancing. Not to mention the incredible variety of treats, as vendors outdid themselves to present only the very best for hungry Security crew and their fans.

A blast of noise from above made everyone flinch. Dalen looked up and saw a pair of dirigibles swirling around each other while fighter planes swept between them. His daughter, Velika, shouted with excitement, "Look up, papa! They're right above us!"

Grinning like a fool, he swept her up in his beefy arms, "Let me get you a closer look, my perfect little crew!"

She squealed and laughed as he settled her upon his shoulders, continuing to dance the entire time. Her eyes shone like stars as she gazed at the wild tactics of the flying machines overhead. Three news drones dropped down and hovered in front of Dalen. One of them asked, "Director Gupta, would you be willing to say a few words concerning this spiral's Security Games?"

Seeing that his daughter was still entranced by the action occurring near the skyscreens, he nodded with enthusiasm, "Dear me, yes! My Sector, Planetary, has always been the greatest of supporters for our friends in Security! These crew are magnificent, are they not? I tell you, it helps me sleep better knowing they stand with the crew and the Holy Mission."

The voice from the news drone asked another question, "Do you ever feel that the games have gone too far with their exhibitions?"

Dalen laughed aloud, shouting to be heard over the roaring crowd, "That is the silliest thing I've ever heard! Of course not! These brave crewmembers deserve our devotion and love! Look at how hard they work for us. Some people might think this is nothing more than a spectacle, but I know better. This is their gift to us. This is also our way to show them how important they all are to the Holy Mission. I could never thank them enough."

The drones then swirled off to ask questions of the other spectators. He watched them while shaking his head. Every member of the crew had their own broadcast channel, sharing their post events, duties and leisure time with anyone interested in watching them. As a result, the news services had become even more fractured than they had been octuries ago. They were still obsessed with digging for stories of corruption and negative happenings. This did serve a purpose, but if they ever wanted a return to their glory spirals, they needed to balance their programs to give the crew a better view of what was really going on in Ganges. His two mates came over and gave him a kiss on each cheek, which he accepted with love. Bryce was thin as a rail, his shaved head showing the blue Naga-Port attached to his skull. Sasha was curvaceous and short, her strong bones an asset in her work for Agro. Dalen loved his family deeply. Of all the crew he had worked with and met, they understood him best. For now, it was time to get back to dancing and watching the Security crew pound each other with joyous trials.

Agro Wheel Two, Security Level One

It was the third rotation of the Security Games and Spat Newstain had to admit that it was his favorite. The start and finish of the competitions were too full of boring speeches, propaganda and displays of unthinking dogma for his tastes. He wanted to see the races, the fights and the contests of skill, not a bunch of Sector Chiefs waddling about, spouting the usual nonsense he had to contend with at school every rotation. In all fairness, he was grateful for the break in dealing with the bullies who hounded him, even if their efforts were totally ineffective. His parents had been awarded a pair of tickets for the family from their directors, which made working for the Suits seem more palatable to his young eyes. The boot-drop of such good fortune was having to sit next to his parents in the grandstands, something he found terribly embarrassing and deeply annoying.

Spat reminded himself that all the red-robes, or the priesthood of the Strifer Manifesto, always stated that it was good to have annoyances in one's life. It was proof you were still breathing. Two of his cousins had also come with them, which made things more interesting and fun. Both Snivel and Pout were hardcore Strifers from the Rat's Ass community, wearing their battered masks and snarky opinions openly with pride. Spat's parents were usually outraged by their behavior and lack of crew manners, but even they smiled at the jokes his cousins made this rotation. Nothing could damage the excitement and joy of being spectators to such a grand display. Spat briefly wondered just how much time Security Sector put into the games instead of plying the course of their role in Ganges, but at least he could say that he felt well protected in the arena. Only a true idiot would try anything to harm the crew here.

As a good Strifer, Spat was a fan of Security Sector, despite his questions concerning their use of energy on public displays. They were the ones who had stood by his people, even when they had every right to hate Strifers for what had happened during the Crucible. They had given the followers of the Manifesto a new chance to have a decent life, out of the belowdecks, ending generations of ostracism and exile. Even Security Lieutenant Dreasco at his school, whose toragi was named Nancy, took the time to chat with him and was always friendly. She once complimented his debate style in front of his classmates, which had made him blush for rotations. As a result, Spat had almost decided to join Security, but he knew that his gerbil, Hook, would never forgive him if he was partnered with a toragi.

Besides, he had another role model whom he looked up to with devotion: Executive Officer Wasp Tornpage from Command Sector. Every time Spat saw her making an announcement on the wallscreens, he just couldn't help but squirm with intense reaction to her. This was also a source of embarrassment, but one he didn't really mind that much. What did outrage him was his parents constantly using his beloved idol whenever they wanted him to behave like crew. His parents just didn't get it! Before Wasp, there had been other Strifers in Command Sector, but usually in unimportant roles. She had truly broken the mold, ruptured all the expectations and stereotypes of the crew, and had risen to heights undreamt of by other Strifers. His parents called it a crush, another insult to his dignity, and encouraged him to keep track of her career to show him the possibilities they were supposedly laying at his feet by groveling to the Sectors. Parents were not only dumb but blind as well.

Rotation three of the Security Games were also his favorite because of the special exhibitions they held to honor the toragi. As a result, the arena was filled with screaming novices and students. Spat didn't know of a single youngster who didn't like the big cats. In fact, he secretly wished that the furry guardians of Security were the ones in charge of Ganges, instead of the humans. The games had resumed at the beginning of work-slice with toragi races, chasing drones through mazes and obstacles with incredible grace. Spat and his cousins had rushed to the vending area afterward to take a close look at the special exhibits hosted by the various breeding consortiums for toragis. He had been allowed to hold a Darego cub in his arms while a fat-looking Gundersen toragi cub curled up at his bare feet. All the other breeders were there too: Higashi, LeGrand, Makamba, and Kumar. Each one specialized in developing different genetic specialties within their toragi for Security to utilize. Spat promised himself that he would wash himself thoroughly on the way back home so as not to scare Hook. Gerbils had sensitive noses.

Spat picked at the nose of his rat mask absently while he watched a series of bouts between the big cats. The Gundersen toragis were bulkier, stronger, with great endurance. The Higashis were fierce and cunning, always ready with a counter-move. The Makamba breed were the epitome of grace and gymnastic ability, while the LeGrand toragis were highly intelligent. Daregos were fast, insanely so. They almost flew, despite the slightly higher apparent gravity of this level. The Kumar breed were tricksy, even pulling little pranks on the field of contest, which as a Strifer, Spat appreciated. The one thing all the toragis had in common was their gentleness when it came to human novices and students. They were already beautiful animals, inspiring and obviously powerful, but their patience and kindness toward youngsters sealed their popularity amongst the crew with an iron paw. Spat wondered if that was intentional or not.

    The crowd roared their approval, as the current competition came to an end, breaking Spat from his thoughts. He had heard that over half of the million crew at this rotation's events were of student rank. He spat on the turf at his feet as hundreds of school banners were raised high. His mother gave him a scowl of disapproval, but he ignored her, as usual. His cousins laughed at his rude gesture, slapping him on the back and calling him a true half-wit, like any normal Strifer should. Why were his parents so bizarre? He might understand them if they used face tattoos rather than physical masks, like Wasp did, but even Executive Officer Tornpage was more like a proper Strifer than his idiot parents, despite their traditional appearances. He ground his teeth in frustration and ignored the finger his father was wagging at him.

    He consoled himself with the memory of his delight when he found out that The Voles were giving a concert at dark-slice, and he had forced his parents to agree that he could go, so long as he was accompanied by his cousins, who were a couple of spirals older than he was. That bit of good fortune was more than enough to make up for having to put up with their strange manners. One of these rotations, he was going to shove the Strifer Manifesto down their unwilling throats and make them see what a mockery they had made of themselves. In the meantime, he wasn't going to let them ruin a good rotation. When he finished his schooling, passed Basic Crew Training and chose a post, he would move back to Rat's Ass where he belonged. Patience was a useful trait in a rat. It kept one from stumbling into traps. While he was determined to grab life with both paws, it wouldn't do to get his tail chopped off because he lacked perseverance.

Agro Wheel Two, Security Level One

    Security Lieutenant Darron Lazhand forced himself to breathe with a steady pace. It was the fourth rotation of the Security Games, and more was now at stake than at any other time in his life. Mike was sitting next to him, at the edge of the main fighting field within the center of the arena. His toragi companion had won some extra awards the rotation before, with new ribbons and medals magnetically attached to his gleaming armor. Darron was quite proud of Mike, but this rotation required that he concentrate on himself. This was the time for the most coveted prize to be gained through single combat, the Kenshi Award. Each spiral, one thousand Security crew were chosen from those who had completed the tryouts. Only one would be granted the honor of being recognized as the most skilled sword-wielder in all of Ganges.

Darron had tried for the title last spiral, only to be defeated during the last triad of bouts. This time, he was determined to succeed. To do this, he had to get rid of every thought in his head concerning the stranger, William Blaine. It had been helpful that a handful of crew in his platoon were not participating in the games this spiral and had volunteered to look after their uninvited guest. What had almost ruined it was bumping into the Solarian at work-slice, as the trespasser was escorted to his seat within the grandstands. William had given him a nod from within his ring of "protectors", who had shoved the man into his seat. Truth be told, Darron wasn't even certain that William was truly human. There were too many questions, not enough answers that made any sense.

Darron shook himself to clear his head once again. He had to focus on the present, on what he was doing. New awards were already gleaming on his heavy armor, from human-toragi pairings and team competitions, but this event pitted sole humans against one another until only the very best fighters remained. All through work-slice and gather-slice, he had battled individuals on the field to the roar of the spectators. Darron's weapon of choice was a long sword, made of Kendis-steel which shimmered in the light of the skyscreens. He used a short war hammer, with a flat head cut with grooves on the front and a spike on the back, as his off-hand weapon. It was useful for cracking armor, blocking strikes and disarming an opponent. While on duty, he normally used a shorter sword called a gladius, along with a buckler, but for competitions he preferred the longer bladed swords.

He had already come in second place for the handgun competition, which was something to be quite proud of. Last spiral he had placed tenth, which galvanized him to improve his aim. The trouble was, he preferred a style of combat that utilized his skills as an athlete and dancer. This made the Kenshi Award even more vital to his mind. Darron rubbed his left arm absently. He had been wounded in his last bout, albeit not enough to disqualify him from continuing. Commander Shayla Girdarm was an accomplished fighter, and she had come in close with incredible speed, slicing into the small gap between his pauldron and vambrace. He had used the spike of his hammer to swing her about, giving him the space he needed to bring his long sword to bear. She had taken her loss with good grace when he disarmed her, then invited him to join the other Commanders in their training bouts, which was a tremendous honor. Even if he did lose this contest, that was something to be proud of.

All the participants were permitted a sprout-sliver to rest between each bout, but it was not enough to feel fully rested. This was a test of endurance as well as skill at arms. At this point, he knew every opponent well. All of them were officers like himself, and they often worked together. It was now time for the final match, a triad between champions. He only hoped the others felt as winded as he did. His skin was soaked with sweat from wearing his heavy plate armor. His arms felt like lead weights hanging from his sore shoulders. He knew that his body was full of bruises the size of his fists. Darron was also sure that two of his ribs were broken, as was the middle finger of his left hand, mashed by a mace from a match that had occurred several rounds ago.

One of the Security referees for the contest stepped onto the field, its grassy turf flattened and crushed underfoot. The woman raised a long spear with a gray-and-maroon banner attached to the pole just below the tip. Small drones circled her head to transmit her words to the awaiting crowd. She raised her head and lifted the spear high into the air, "We shall now begin the final contest for the Kenshi Award!"

The roar of the crowd was deafening, shattering the air with a million voices screaming their approval. Darron felt an electric spark flash down his spine. This was it. The moment of truth. To make it this far was a great achievement, but nothing could dim his desire to become the next champion of Ganges. Darron took a deep breath and swung his sword and hammer in swift circles to loosen his wrists, ignoring the pain his actions caused. His heart hammering in his chest, he stepped forward in synchronization with the other two contenders. The three of them looked battered and bloody, a far cry from their gleaming perfection at rush-slice. Their armor was dented and muddy, with shoulders slumped by exhaustion.

There were no off-limits areas upon the field and no rules concerning the placement of blows or style of combat. The one decree was that they ceased to attack when an opponent yielded or became incapacitated. Medical Sector had ambulances ready for severe wounds, while Rescue Services personnel concentrated on minor injuries whenever a combatant left the contest. Accidents happened, and it wasn't unusual for bones to be broken, concussions and limbs requiring regrowth or be replaced by prosthetics from this contest. Every few spirals, a death would occur, signaling a brief time of mourning and a full investigation into the incident. The crew called these competitions games, but they were deadly serious to those in Security Sector. Ganges had been quietly at peace for octuries after the Crucible, and these competitions were there to keep the guardians of the Holy Mission sharp, thus they had to be truly dangerous.

The referee stepped back several paces, then lowered her spear. Instead of rushing forth as they did at the beginning of the rotation, Darron and his two opponents walked toward each other with care. No one was allied with anyone else, though they could be opportunistic if one of them were struggling. He watched the other two carefully. Lieutenant Vali Deen marched toward the center of the field with no hesitation in her stride. Lieutenant-Commander Kev Limbard staggered his way forward with stumbling steps. Darron kept his pace steady, as if he were walking in his home community, taking his time to assess his rivals. Vali was wielding an axe-like polearm called a bardiche. Her mode of combat was direct and brutal. She was unflinching in her attacks, and Darron knew she would never yield. He would have to knock her out with a blow to the head. Even totally unarmed, she was dangerous in the extreme. Kev was a well-known trickster. His penchant for practical jokes and misdirection made Darron suspicious about his current behavior. It would be just like Kev to pretend severe exhaustion and suddenly lunge when his opponent's guard was down.

No bows were exchanged, no salutes offered, just pain. As they came within striking distance, Vali swept her bardiche to one side, slamming the weighted butt into Kev's midriff. She whirled her weapon at Darron, who dodged the blow to his head with a fluid grace he didn't feel. Sod sprayed out in clumps, lashing his exposed face. He lunged at Vali, who knocked his attack aside, catching his blade with the spikes behind the head of her axe. Darron tried to roll with the momentum, but Kev tripped him from behind by slashing at his knees with a long-handled mace. Pain flashed down Darron's legs, and he cried out as he fell to one side, his sword spinning off to land point first into the turf. The bardiche blade slashed over his head, and Kev fell back quickly.

Spinning on one aching foot, Darron swirled aside to avoid the next strike, smacking Vali in the shoulder with his hammer head. Her pauldron rang like a bell as she grunted in pain. Vali made a move to lash out at him, but Kev ran forward to smack her on the other shoulder. Darron saw his chance and raced past them to regain his sword. The noise of the crowd was rising with excitement, a cheer swelled as he grabbed his blade and swirled around to parry a blow from Kev who had chased after him. The shock swept down his arm, and he almost lost control of his weapon.

Vali screamed her rage as she smashed her polearm into Kev's left side. Plating was ruptured and hot, dark blood gushed from the wound. Darron spun away, his arms held out in a blur of steel. He was just in time to watch Vali slam her weapon right into Kev's breastplate. The Lieutenant-Commander fell back and remained still. Horns bellowed all around the arena, signaling that another competitor had officially fallen. Darron backed away, leading Vali from Kev's prone body. Rescue Services crew ran forward to assess the damage and drag the man off the field of combat.

It was now just Darron and Vali. The crowd were on their feet, chanting "Kenshi! Kenshi! Kenshi!"

Vali circled him like a hungry predator, her weapon held up in a defensive posture. His head was pounding. His limbs felt like molten lead, but he was far from done. Darron began to dance in place, spinning and swirling with every last bit of strength he had in him. He teased her, coming in close then prancing back when she swung her blade. Finally, she gave a roar of frustration and charged him. Instead of bouncing away from her, Darron abruptly closed the gap between them, hurling his body against the shaft of her bardiche. They slammed together in a tangle of limbs. He pulled his hammer free and smashed it into her helmet. Once, twice, three times he pounded the head of his secondary weapon upon her, until her helmet tilted at an odd angle.

Lieutenant Vali Deen dropped to the muddy ground with a clatter. Darron fell to one knee beside her, swaying in place like a drunkard. The horns blasted a flurry of notes, and the crowd went wild. Before he knew what was happening, the referee was at his side and dragging him up to his feet, holding his hand in the air, "Behold! The new Kenshi Champion of Ganges! Huzzah!"

Darron looked about the arena in a haze of exhaustion and fiery pain. His bewildered mind could not process what was happening, until he felt a large, furry object slam him down into the soil. Mike began to lick his armor and nuzzled him until he thought that his back might break. Flower petals filled the air above him. The skyscreens exploded into images of fireworks, and his own face flashed upon the wallscreens all over the arena. Laughing weakly, Darron struggled to calm his toragi and got back to his feet. He dropped his weapons to the ground and did his best to stand straight, leaning a bit on Mike's armored back. The Chief of Security was marching toward him with a broad smile on her scarred face. He saluted her quickly, still unsteady on his feet. She placed a laurel wreath upon his open-faced helm and said, "Welcome to the club, Kenshi Darron Lazhand!"

Agro Wheel Two, Security Level One

William Blain was seated in an ergonomic chair at the lowest level of the giant arena. It was the fifth day, or as the crew of Ganges would say it, "rotation", of the Security Games. He had to admit that he was still astounded by the spectacle. A sense of disquiet was growing within him. Half of what he had seen thus far seemed to come out of the mists of ancient history. The rest was a series of shocking novelties that made him question human nature. In many ways, the culture of Ganges was quaint, reminiscent of simpler times. It was painfully polite and formal. At other times, it was unsettling and wild, filled with contradictions. Most of the crew would have been at home within a fully non-technological society, all the while living in a jewel of industrial might on a massive scale that was difficult to process.

William had witnessed many sporting events in a large venue, but nothing as savage and uncontrolled as this one. Even the sheer size of the arena itself was testament to the way the crew of the ship thought of such things. They rebuilt planets, so it made sense that creating a stadium that could hold a million people would be child's play for them. At the vending and exhibit areas, he had watched the polite and almost choreographed manner in which these people treated each other. He could hear the influence of Naga in the way they spoke to one another, as if mimicking their mother, which might not be too far from the truth. They worked so hard to be kind, then let loose to applaud and cheer the violent spectacles before them. The Holy Mission was mentioned in almost every conversation, as if they were confirming to one another that they were unified in their purpose.

The main exception to this rule were the Strifers, whose rude and insulting behavior was mostly tolerated by the majority of crew. There were those who gave the rat masked citizens a sharp or angry glare, but this was ignored for the most part. The Strifers moved about in groups. To insult one was cause to be heckled into a corner by all the others, with some regular crew joining in for fun. William could see the shift in behavior when the Strifers interacted with the general population, as if permission to let loose was silently given. Even Naga could be heard trading insults with the green-robed crew members.

What truly shocked and amazed him were the toragi. The big cats were wildly popular, and he even saw children riding their backs with faces full of open joy. During the toragi games, he noticed that during team challenges, the winning side would gather together and yowl while swaying back and forth. It was as if the big cats were singing their team mantra. Again, the question rang through his mind, what had these people done here? Were they purposely creating another sentient species? As fierce as the toragi were, they were also incredibly gentle with the crew, putting up with antics no cat would in the Sol System. Not that there were many large animals anywhere in his home, save for zoos and upon Terra itself, where they remained fully undisturbed by the presence of humanity. He felt that perhaps his culture had missed something important by separating themselves from the rest of the animal kingdom.

Early this rotation, his original guardian, Lieutenant Darron Lazhand, had rejoined him, with his toragi, Mike, alongside. William had congratulated the Security officer on his achievement from the rotation before and had only received a gruff reply. The man was still tired, but now William knew just how lethal his "protector" could be. He had never seen anything like it. After a short while, he requested a chance to see the mag-bike races, and his hosts obliged with cold politeness. Such proper behavior from rough-edged warriors was not something he was used to. When the interrogator named Slither joined them, he was almost relieved. The lanky man had greeted him with a lit cigar poking out from under black rat mask, "Having fun spying on us, asshole?"

William grinned, "Yes indeed! A most impressive display. Tell me, who are all those people who are gathered just outside the racetracks?"

Slither looked over to where he was pointing and then shrugged, "Those are squatters. They don't have tickets to the arena, so they make their own party on the fringes. Might be a couple of million crew over there."

William was shocked, not only by this revelation, but at the lack of concern in Slither's voice. Such a large, unofficial gathering within a Solarian orbital would be seen as a potential threat to stability. Slither continued with his explanation, "They'll go back to their fucking posts for a slice, come back here, watch a game or two, run home, repeat. The usual stupidity. They'd get a much better view on the wallscreens, but they like to brag like idiots that they were here in person."

William pondered this for a brief moment, "That must keep the maintenance staff busy with all the cleanup."

The Strifer had shot him a swift glare, "What the fuck do you mean by that? You think we're savages like you? They'll leave the Security grounds cleaner than they found it. How about you? Despoil any planets lately?"

William had not dared to give any reply to the accusation. It had hit too close to home. Solarian history was filled with missteps and atrocities. The five-hundred-year period known as the Age of Piracy, just after the fall of the Terran Conglomerate, had been a shameful part of his culture's past. The following centuries weren't much cleaner, in terms of warfare and deep mistrust. A few of the early colonies had indeed despoiled the worlds made for them by Ganges. Not the vast majority, by any means, but the first ones he had visited were not in good shape. Humanity lost all sense of balance when times were hard. There was a tendency to split up, tear things apart instead of unifying or standing together for a common cause. In fact, the further he had gotten from Sol, the more the colonies became peaceful, dutiful and generous.

Toward the end of the rotation's main events, a Naga drone swept by and floated just a meter from his face, "How do you like my antibodies?"

William had been startled "Your what? Where?"

Darron had coughed into his fist as Slither cackled. The drone bobbed in the air as it replied, "Security Sector. They act as my antibodies. They help to fight infections that might threaten the Holy Mission."

William had blinked hard in surprise, "I-I've never heard it put like that. They're impressive. Truly. Um, I guess I've missed some important bits of history. Then again, I've also been stuck in this Wheel since I arrived, except for my time in Medical Sector."

The drone had buzzed back, "And your invasion of Engineering. I haven't forgotten that, you know. Your history lessons begin soon. I shall be your teacher."

The Security crew all around him chuckled darkly under their breaths. The nanites in William's bloodstream jabbered with fear. They reminded him that he was most likely dealing with a rogue AeyAie whose behavior would not fit into the normal Solidarity patterns. He was within its body, and with its enlightenment programming in question and not updated, he was at serious risk. William conceded the point and replied to the drone, "I look forward to my new lessons. I'm grateful for the opportunity to learn."

Slither had remarked, "You're a good brown-noser. Now shut up and enjoy the races."

William had simply done as he'd been told. It wasn't a difficult command to acquiesce to. The mag-bikes fascinated him. In some ways they were quite primitive, but in other ways they were highly innovative. No two were alike, and he was quite intrigued by the fact that most had both magnetic impellors of advanced technology and physical wheels that looked to be from pre-spaceflight times. It was another anomaly within Ganges. The full blending of non-technological cultures with novel invention was a curiosity. He was sure this had come from the mixing of the inductees at the time of Ganges' launching from Sol, with the crew who had been under the heel of the Terran Conglomerate, but there were no details about how all this had happened, other than vague references to a mutiny which led to something called "The Awakening". It had clearly been a mighty revolution of culture and purpose which had sealed the fate of the human population aboard the ship. As the rotation was ending, he had found himself questioning the orders he had been given. William was wondering if Solarian Command should have just left Ganges well enough alone.

Agro Wheel Two, Security Level One

It was currently the seventh rotation of the Security Games, and Foundry Foreman Howait Sparweld was glad that he had been offered special seating for mates of the participating crew. The higher apparent gravity was playing havoc on his limbs, a consequence of having been raised much closer to midships. He was given some extra support by the Rescue Services crew, some of whom teased him about being a new member of Security's family. It was such an odd experience, for none of the other Sectors behaved this way. Engineering had noted his new mate, made an official change to its records and left it alone. Security went in the opposite direction, taking great lengths to make sure he was more than comfortable, and they made it clear to him that he was welcome. Howait quickly found himself surrounded by the families of other Security crew members. Varn Torello, the mate of the Chief of Security, had personally checked up on him with congratulations and a drink.

Howait was more used to being picked on than being treated like some kind of celebrity. Many of the mates of Security crew had offered advice, their services in times of need and a shoulder to lean on in times of trouble. At first, he was confused by all that kind of talk, until it finally occurred to him that his mate, Sergeant Mahari Quartzrend, who had terrified his crew into submission, might become injured or even killed in the line of duty. The horrible thought still took his breath away, and he did confer with the other mates to gain their advice and wisdom. This was a fear and pain they all shared, making the Security families a private club for mutual support.

Because of his body's frailty in higher gravity conditions, he had been forced to choose only three of the rotations to attend the games in person: the first one, this rotation's events and next rotation's, which would be the finale. The sowing before the games had been filled with spending as much time as possible with his mate, moving in together and making love as often as was humanly possible. Mahari had passed the tryouts for the games and had been part of the main spectacle on the first rotation, taking part in the first bouts of team-fighting. Howait had been at the edge of his seat, barely able to watch, as his beautiful mate was in the thick of heavy hand-to-hand fighting. This rotation wasn't much easier, for she was a mag-bike jouster, facing several grueling trials of daring and skill.

The families of the Security crew who were participating in the races were moved to a roving, open-air tram which followed a course around the main event fields and racetracks on the leeward side of the arena. The transport had five levels of comfortable seating, was over a hundred meters long and had special amenities for its guests. None of the vendors would take his chips. Instead, they all charged Security Sector itself, a tradition that was as old as the games themselves. When Mahari had shown him the tickets she had received for him, they were of a kind he had never seen before. Howait had free access to all the concerts, special events, demonstrations and was permitted to go behind the scenes with his mate.

His first instinct had been to express his amazement with the crew he worked with, but had changed his mind at the last moment. Most of them would be watching the Security Games on the wallscreens at home or in their favorite pubs. His extra access and special amenities might be seen as bragging, which he loathed. Instead, he had simply stated that, as Mahari's mate, he was going to the arena to cheer her on. The crew had wished him luck, with a little ribbing about finding some quick moments for the new couple to have sex between sports. This he took with embarrassed good humor which seemed to satisfy everyone.

Howait still didn't know what she saw in him, but he was happy that such a fierce, wild, beautiful person would choose him to be her mate. It was an honor he was determined to prove being worthy of. Leaning forward in his plush seat, he caught sight of his beloved. Waving like a fool, he caught her attention. Her bright smile hit his heart like a plasma bolt as she waved back, seated upon her heavily modified mag-bike. Mahari had worked hard on this machine for harvests. It was deep red with gray stripes, with a heavy, beveled shield mounted at the front, carved out with lance holders and gun cupolas. The wide tires were plated on the sides, to prevent any opponent from puncturing them with a spear or sword. The magnetic impellers were wider than most models, and Howait had helped her in building them to her specifications. The thrusters mounted on the back were powerful units, more suited for a space fighter than a ground vehicle. Her armor still had some dents and scratches on it from her previous trials, but the surface gleamed brightly in the light of the skyscreens. She looked magnificent.

The tram halted, giving everyone a grand view of the tournament area. Other Security riders were bringing their mag-bikes onto the field, gunning their loud engines and lifting their weapons high to greet the family tram. Naga drones buzzed through the air, capturing the moment for all the crew watching on the wallscreens. The jousting track was long and broad, with no curves or turns. It was a straight run for a hundred meters. The first set of jousts would determine who moved on to the other, more difficult competitions, ones that involved mazes, obstacles, traps and multiple opponents. The referees stepped forward, and Howait's heart almost jumped out of his throat. His mate was voluntarily facing deadly peril for the enjoyment of the crew!

The opening contest was surprisingly short-lived, with one rider's mag-bike becoming seriously damaged, flipping over and flinging the crewman into the air like a doll. The heavy crunch of smashed metal filled his ears, and he could feel his limbs going weak. Mahari was next, and he squirmed in his seat, tears involuntarily flowing down his cheeks. Howait suddenly felt a hand upon his shoulder from behind. He looked back and saw a matronly woman nodding sympathetically at him. He did his best to smile his appreciation and turned back to watch. He had promised her that he would.

Before he knew what was happening, she roared off along the metal track. Howait leaped upon the thick, gold railing in front of him to get a better view. Mahari flew toward her opponent, electro-lance lowered. The other mag-bike had a sharp prow which was tilted downward. Howait didn't have time to blink as they slammed together with a squeal of torn plating. The other mag-bike spun upon its axis, black smoke pouring from one thruster, Mahari's lance running through its intake manifold. She swerved around violently, her head almost touching the deck, then charged her opponent once more. The other rider came about, but was struggling to keep his impellers from cutting out. She cut in close, slamming her spear into his control panel before he could block the strike. Instead, he threw a long dagger at Mahari, forcing her to swing back in the saddle. Back and forth they struggled, until his port thruster gave out with a bang and a shower of sparks. Mahari raised her last lance high and Howait almost fell off the railing as he cheered at the top of his lungs. Her opponent rose to his feet, dropped his spear and bowed to her, conceding the match. Howait fell back into the cushions of his chair, relief flooding his veins.

The woman behind him leaned forward and said softly into his ear, "She's very good. Congratulations, dear. Only ten more trials to go before she's done."

Howait froze in place, aghast that he might have to go through all of that several more times this rotation. He only hoped that his mate would come through it all in one piece and content with her winnings.

Agro Wheel Two, Security Level One

It was the final rotation of the Security Games, an entire sowing of events and demonstrations of skill. Naga had checked on the subset of its personality matrix which managed the broadcast distribution during dawn-slice. Its processors were overworked, but nothing unusual was reported. The crew in Technology Sector had been working overtime at their posts, rerouting data streams to unused regions to maintain the load of input. The AeyAie had also carefully reviewed all of the recorded information from the fifty thousand arial drones assigned to the games. An equal number of rovers had been utilized to gain some close looks at the events and were currently being deployed to survey the spectators. This data would be gathered and used to help make the next set of Security Games more amenable to the general population.

The Chief of Security seemed pleased with the way things had worked out. She had told Naga that this spiral showed her crew to be fit, able and ready for any emergency. The AeyAie appreciated such sentiments, but it wasn't quite sure that it agreed. The universe was full of surprises, as the presence of William Blain attested. Even within Ganges, there were still some mysteries, such as the Kendis Vault and the presence of organized criminal syndicates. After all it had experienced during the Holy Mission, Naga wasn't about to become complacent concerning the unknown. Humans might be capable of being willfully blind to factors outside their control, but an AeyAie could not afford such luxuries. To ignore variables was to invite disaster.

Naga sent a drone to check in on their uninvited guest. The Solarian was sitting in the arena, surrounded by a platoon of Police crew. He was even more pale than usual, though what might constitute normal was unknown. If he had been a crew member, Naga would have said he was in a mild state of shock. His unusually lively hair had changed color, from a golden yellow to a light green. The Medical Sector crew had taken a sample of it and found the hair difficult to diagnose. It was made up of fine bundles of tendrils, none of which contained DNA or anything resembling a protein molecule. Neither was it mechanical in nature. There were some unique compounds found within the motile fibers which defied analysis. Was it possible that William was telling the truth when he said his hair was a gift from an advanced non-terrestrial species?

Unfortunately, all the variables were too chaotic to manage. It had been a puzzle that Ganges had only discovered one example of life outside the Sol System. This dearth of life in the galaxy was a conundrum, one that stretched back to pre-spaceflight Terra. Statistically speaking, there should be numerous stellar systems harboring life of one form or another, but the evidence spoke of a fairly empty galaxy. There had been many theories presented concerning this paradox, none of them were satisfactory. The only good news coming out of Medical Sector was that William Blaine was indeed human, though heavily augmented through nanotechnology and bio-engineering. There was no hard evidence that he came from the Sol System, nor could his various claims be verified at this time.

Naga turned the focus of its attention to the main arena. It would deal with the intruder soon enough. The Judiciary Council had assembled on a long, raised platform, facing the large mass of Security crew who had participated in the games. Captain Fieldscan was seated next to High Justice Mahala Yaliah, as was traditional. Standing before her crew was the Chief of Security. Armor gleamed, and all evidence that a sowing of battle had occurred was removed. A tall pillar, covered with a giant, curved wallscreen was directly behind the assembled dignitaries. This had been set aside for Naga's use, and the AeyAie initiated its matronly visage upon the surface, signaling the beginning of the final ceremonies. The crew packed the grand arena and roared their approval.

Captain Fieldscan and High Justice Yaliah rose to their feet to air-crushing applause from the spectators. The two officers stepped forward, while small drones buzzed around their heads to capture and transmit their words to the entire ship. The Captain bowed to the High Justice with practiced dignity. Mahala smiled at him and raised her spear high, "Attention, crew of Ganges! We shall now review the might and readiness of Security Sector, just as our ancestors have done for octuries. The Captain and I now call upon Chief of Security Sector Jira Mantabe to join us."

Horns bellowed, as flower petals were released into the air, and the cheers of the crowd shook the foundations of the arena. All of the Security crew saluted, bringing their right hands to their brows in unison. Chief Mantabe strode up the steps to the platform with her toragi, after handing her hammer to one of her Commanders. She stopped in front of the two dignitaries and saluted them with drilled perfection, "Security Sector answers your call."

High Justice Yaliah smiled at her, "We have reviewed your crew and have consulted with one another about our findings. It is the judgement of the Judiciary Council that Security Sector stands ready and may continue their honorable service for Ganges without delay."

Captain Fieldscan smoothed his thin moustache, an affectation Naga knew had been carefully adopted for his rank, "It is the opinion of Command Sector that your crew are worthy of high praise, Chief Mantabe. Your people are a credit to the ship. Congratulations!"

The Chief saluted both officers with strict formality, "My Sector thanks you both. We shall endeavor to remain true to our purpose in protecting the crew from all dangers. May the Holy Mission endure forever!"

The Security ranks behind her shouted in unison, "Ganges Eternal!"

The Chief stepped forward and addressed the massive pillar at the far end of the platform, "Naga-Ma, mother of our beloved Ganges, I hereby present to you Security Sector."

Naga nodded her virtual head with a soft smile, "I also agree that they are prepared to guard the Holy Mission, Chief Jira Mantabe."

All of the spectators roared their approval, chanting the Chief's name and stamping their feet upon the turf that covered the walkways of the arena. Jira stepped forward and turned to face her crew, standing between the Captain and the High Justice. She raised her gauntleted fist in the air, waiting for the crowd to settle down. While it took a few pollen-slivers, the joyous crew in the stands eventually quieted, eagerly awaiting the next phase of the ceremony. The Chief of Security spoke, her arms outstretched toward her awaiting crew, "I present to you the heroes of Ganges!"

Another blast of cheers ruptured the air. When the wave of noise abated, she began to call Security personnel up to the platform to receive their awards and honors, starting with Lieutenant Darron Lazhand, who had won the Kenshi contest of arms. Naga allowed itself to watch with meditative patience. Humans were so glacially slow. It was tempting to send its mind to other areas of the ship, but to do so would be a disservice to these dedicated crew. Besides, there were over one thousand copies of its mind handling the functioning of the ship, so it could afford the restful moments of contemplation between the human interactions. What it had told William Blaine a few rotations ago was quite true; these warriors were its antibodies, and it pitied anything that endangered Ganges and its crew.

CHAPTER SIX

Light Rotation - Launch Sowing - Mission Harvest - Spiral 5620

"There is no doubt in my mind that most Terrans would have difficulty understanding our culture, here in Ganges. In my research, I have found no evidence of anything like the society which has emerged in our vessel, starting from the time of the Awakening. Perhaps it is our mix of personal liberties with the required duty toward the Holy Mission and the ship. This might seem especially alien when one also factors in the voluntary economic system that we currently enjoy. The most likely explanation for our divergence from the traditional cultural imperatives is that our environment is unique in the human experience, which has led to a breakdown of the worn out, planet-focused ideas about civilization."
Thaddeus Pollentine, Educational Archivist, Rank Three, lecture notes, P40

Residence Wheel Two, Level Three

Spat Newstain was sitting in a lotus position on the thick grass of his Ganges History classroom at school when the alarms began to blare. Since his datapad was attached to the back of his hand, there was nothing he had to grab on his way to the door. In fact, such an act was forbidden by the protocols for emergency procedures. He left his old satchel of personal odds and ends behind, as he rushed over to the classroom gates along with the other students. A few were still sitting, angry at the interruption to their lesson, moaning aloud about how ridiculous it was to rush around because of another drill. Spat thought these students were particularly stupid. One could never tell if a real emergency was happening, whether it be local or ship-wide, until well after they had reached their assigned shelters to await instruction. He just figured that these dumpster-brains who refused to take emergency alarms seriously simply lacked the imagination required to fully comprehend that Ganges was not unbreakable. He was a Strifer, who knew better than any regular crewmember how delicate the ship could be.

Spat also didn't appreciate that the pollen-sliver the alarms went off, half the other students in the class had looked directly at him. It was ridiculous! Outrageous! What could he possibly do while sitting in the middle of an open-air classroom full of witnesses and being bored to death by his instructor's poor excuse for a lesson plan? Then again, he felt it might be an advantage if everyone thought he had such mystical powers. Let the stupid vacuum-heads believe whatever they wanted. Their passive-aggressive attitudes were amateurish, at best. He wished he could bring half of them to Rat's Ass, so they could see what a real pain-in-the-neck looked like.

Naga admonished the naysayers, ordering them to move swiftly and quietly into the corridor just beyond the classroom. The hallway was typical for his school, all rounded corners, curved walls, now displaying Naga-Ma's face, and twenty meters wide. His bare feet were almost silent as they padded down the moss-covered floor, following their teacher to the rendezvous point. There had been more drills than usual lately, something many of the others blamed on entering a new stellar system, but Spat wasn't too sure about that. Some of the Security crew at the games had seemed more tense than usual. He had also noticed a strange looking crewmember sitting in the stands just below him, staring at the toragi like he'd never seen them before. The man had been surrounded by surly Police crew, so Spat hadn't bothered to slake his curiosity too closely.

When he had gotten home, Spat had checked the recordings of the games, trying to get a better look at the pale crewman, but every time he tried, the person's face was blurred out. He badgered Naga about it, but was told that the information he sought had to do with a high-level Judiciary Council case and therefore classified. Once he visited his cousins in Rat's Ass, he would inquire further, but with some help from those who knew how to beat the system. Strifers liked to stay informed about important matters.

When they finally reached the next junction of corridors, Security Lieutenant Dreasco was waiting for them there with her toragi, named Nancy. Both of them were wearing full battle armor and carrying packs filled with survival supplies. Two other classrooms had filled the crossroad of corridors. Spat smirked at them from under his white rat mask. His classmates had made it to the meeting place first. Lieutenant Dreasco raised her gauntleted fist, her other hand wrapped around the stock of a heavy-barreled rifle with an odd, tulip-shaped nozzle which glowed violet. Her voice rang out, easily heard over the screaming sirens due to her helmet's voice magnifier, "All students! Listen up! You will form three lines and follow Nancy to your shelter! Where she goes, you go! When she stops, you stop! Move!"

Nancy shot off toward an empty corridor, one that led to the recreation field. The three classes flowed after her with drilled precision, despite a touch of childish jostling, as was expected. Nancy roared out a deep yowl, and the students settled down swiftly. This was the best part of emergency drills, being in the close presence of a toragi. Few youngsters would ever say no to such an opportunity. Halfway toward the outer doors, Nancy leapt over to one side, slapping a Security panel on the wall. The doors ahead slammed open with incredible speed, and they lost no time flowing out of the school and into the sports field beyond.

Spat did his duty, as did most of the other students, looking about with eyes wide open, ready to call a warning if they saw something that might pose a threat to life and limb. He noticed other lines of youngsters heading out behind a toragi, leaving the school grounds behind. At this point, they would now head to the shelter, which resembled a military bunker full of foodstuffs, water and thick, plated walls that could withstand almost anything. They were even airtight, with carbon-dioxide scrubbers and oxygen supply. The shelters could drop into the depths of space, and they would still be safe for a sowing.

To his surprise, Nancy charged off the beaten track and ran into a densely forested area toward spinward. The students around him muttered and stumbled in surprise, but they continued to follow the toragi. Over fallen trees, under thickets and across small streams they ran. Eventually, they came upon the shores of a river and followed this for half a kilometer, until they reached a massive cave made of asteroid rock. It stretched on for as far as Spat could see, and he wondered what the toragi was thinking. Nancy entered the cave with a low growl. Spat shrugged at the others around him. What were they to do? Orders were orders. They had to follow the toragi, so there was no choice in the matter.

Inside, it was dark and dank. A stream flowed from the interior of the cave to reach the river behind them. Spat couldn't see Nancy, as they left the light of the skyscreens behind. A sudden glow of illumination erupted several meters ahead. Nancy was sitting in front of a door that looked like it had been blasted open long ago. The old metal hatch was covered with corrosion. Bits and pieces of blackened machinery cluttered the entranceway. Nancy huffed at the students, then turned to walk beyond the portal. Spat and the others followed, fascinated now by the unusual surroundings. They entered a large chamber with some overturned tables covered with burn holes. Broken chairs, smashed computer stations, and moldy crates littered the deck. Overhead, the ceiling was a swirl of patterns, indicative of someone carving out this place from asteroid metal. Lamps hung on corroded beams, some of them broken, but others providing light.

Spat's rival, the bullying Bino called out, "Look at that! This place is an old mutineer bunker!"

Everyone swiveled their heads to where he was pointing. A marred, half-ruined banner hung limply from the furthest wall. It was gold-and-purple with a fancy coat-of-arms at the center. Barely legible words were found at the bottom saying "The

Royal Cause Efficiency Through Monarchy". Most of the students made a disgusted noise, like they had just stepped in a pool of effluence. Spat merely lived up to his name and blew out a wad of phlegm on the dirty floor. He almost didn't notice Nancy prowling up to the crowd of children, settling on her haunches when she got to the very center of the group. She yowled once, and all of the students, including Spat, cheered with delight. It was treat time!

They all rummaged through the packs on her back to find juice tubes and snack bars. There was one for everyone, with the toragi looking on to ensure no one was left out. There was no misbehavior from the youngsters. Who would want to disappoint a toragi with uncivilized behavior? By the time all the treats were finished, a new sound came from the doorway. Nancy bolted toward it, her claws revealed in their steel sheathing.

Lieutenant Dreasco appeared within the opening, "What in Ganges are you doing here, Nancy? This isn't the shelter! I had to track your footprints to find you!"

The Security Lieutenant looked up at the confused look upon the faces of the students, "Please excuse Nancy for bringing you to an unauthorized area. I do apologize on her behalf. Is everyone okay?"

Spat once again littered the floor with his saliva, "We're all fine! Cool the thrusters. If you ignore the décor, this isn't such a bad place. Hard to find, hard to scan through. This place used to be a war bunker, right? So, what if the shelter was compromised or we couldn't reach it in time? This is a pretty good alternate if you ask me."

Bino shouted out, "Spat the Makdreah lover!"

Lieutenant Dreasco stood upright and shouted, "Stow it, young crew! Spat is correct. This is a decent place to shelter in if you can't reach the official bunker. Besides, Nancy's a Kumar. This isn't the first time she's pulled something like this during a drill. She's a clever trickster. Have we all thanked Nancy for taking care of you?"

Every one of the students stepped forward to hug the toragi. To Spat she felt warm and comforting. Lieutenant Dreasco led them all back to the school, gently admonishing her toragi in a tone he couldn't hear. It looked as though Nancy was quite pleased with herself, and Spat couldn't say that he blamed her.

Residence Wheel One, Level Three

William Blaine stepped out of the ground transport which had brought him to the edge of a dense forest. He staggered a touch and grimaced to himself. He was still getting used to the changing apparent gravity in Ganges. His Security detail had already emerged from the mag-car, their big cats flowing about with silent grace.

Lieutenant Darron Lazhand was standing at his shoulder, while the other Police crew spread out in a formation William didn't recognize. The road had ended at a barricade made of steel blocks the size of food crates. A Naga drone buzzed down from the skyscreens above and floated just a meter in front of him, "Welcome to Forward Estates."

He looked around at the overgrown metal deck of the road, "I take it this community isn't being used right now."

Darron answered him, "This area is off limits to all crew except for Security Sector. We sometimes use it for training and history lessons."

William raised an eyebrow at his guardian but didn't inquire as to what he meant by "history lessons". He quietly walked with the drone and Mike, following Darron's lead. They had to step around some dense thorn bushes before they were able to get themselves beyond the barrier. The road at this point became even more disheveled, almost unpassable, except for one large flattop platform transport that hovered magnetically above a long rail which swept deep into the gloomy trees. Mike leaped aboard the flat transport with Darron climbing up after him. William shrugged and leapt up to the top without any effort. He found himself facing a gun barrel. Darron scowled, "That's a three-meter rise above the deck. It's why there are handholds."

William carefully held still as he responded, "My apologies. If it is protocol to use the ladder or handholds, I will do so from now on. For my own musculature, not to mention the micro-spring supports for my leg bones, it isn't that much of a jump."

Darron stowed his weapon without a word, walking instead toward the far end of the platform and pressing a button on the pedestal there. The vehicle moved swiftly deeper into the forest. William turned and found the other Police crew staring at him with dark green eyes behind her face markings. Her armor was covered with small bones, bird skulls and fetishes. A technological wonder of a bow was over one shoulder. From what he had seen at the Security Games, she could kill him in an instant from a hundred meters away with a shock arrow. He nodded to her, but she didn't react. He shrugged again and turned to face the drone which was keeping pace without much effort, "Where exactly are you taking me?"

Naga replied, "Somewhere we can speak in private and where our anger at Terra comes from."

William nodded, "Ah, that makes sense."

The painted Security crewmember gave a short laugh, "That's if there aren't any ghost hunters here this rotation!"

Darron shook his head, "If there are, we'll arrest them and get the idiots out of here for their own safety."

William looked back at the drone in alarm, as his nanites began shrieking warnings at him from inside his head, "What do they mean by that?"

The drone swiveled its camera lens toward the front of the moving platform, "Many of the crew believe this region is haunted, either by ghosts, genetic monsters, aliens or robots bent on killing humans."

William dashed a few floater nanites from his skin to collect samples from the area, "Well, I should fit right in."

Darron suddenly grabbed him by the shoulder and spun him around, "Watch that, savage! Treat our fucking history with respect!"

The platform ceased its smooth movement, and the Security crew hopped out. William made a show of using the handholds and joined them. The area was full of old trees and rubble poking up from under the rich loam. They walked up a hill, scattering birds and startling a herd of deer. They came to a crater that led far below the deck. William could tell because under a ten meter layer of dirt and broken rubble was a thick line of deck plating that looked as if it had been melted into place. Beyond this was a series of broken chambers, whose only access was a long ladder that looked well maintained. Darron climbed down, leaving Mike and the other Security guard with their own toragi behind. The drone followed William as he climbed his way to the bottom.

Several small robots, reminiscent of insects, were crawling about in the pit below the deck. There were smashed furnishings, molded wall hangings and some large boxes which Darron opened with his flashtats. The drone bumped William in the shoulder, making his nanites panic. He quieted them with a mental command and walked over to the open crate. Inside were items he recognized immediately, as they were in his synth-brain database. There were rifles of Terran Conglomerate design, stealth gear, even bombs, though the last appeared disabled to his retinal sensors. An ancient styled burnt relay unit was there, with a logo reading VenMak just visible under the corrosion. A set of rings with family crests were set to one side, some of them had designs that predated the Terran Conglomerate.

William cleared his throat, "Um, I see. I would remind you that showing me this is akin to revealing Roman spears as far as I'm concerned. These should be in a museum of long-dead civilizations."

Darron stepped toward him, "It was bad enough that Terra kidnapped the original Agro crew from their homelands to serve as meat robots. For octennia, we thought we were finally free of Terra and its filthy wars, politics and abuses. Then the Age of Unity fell because of a Terran plot to take over Ganges that had been going on for all that time. The mutineers had Terran weapons, armor, technologies of war. Oh, and it's not just this! We've found other caches of cyborgs, robots, bunkers full of weapons and poisons, all so that one faction or another from Terra could become overlords of Ganges."

William sagged in place. What could he possibly say to these people? They had been betrayed, lied to, used and abused. There was no trust to be found within those who had suffered such horrors. Darron stood there, his hands on his hips, very near to his holsters. William had to say something, "I... Look, I'm not going to say I understand. I don't. Nor am I going to say that the Solarian Alliance is some kind of utopia. I won't insult your intelligence. No matter what kind of society we humans make, there will always be those who think only of themselves and make sure to be in a position of power to keep things that way. I've heard you talking for... sowings now. You've got organized crime here in Ganges. There are still awful people making trouble for everyone else, even in this beautiful ship. Should I blame you if one of those bastards kidnaps me and slits my throat? I think not."

Darron growled at him, which was reflected by Mike far above. The drone moved between him and the Lieutenant, "His logic does hold, Darron. I hate to admit that, but truth is rarely a simple thing. I wanted him here to fully understand the reason we don't trust anything he says. To give him some physical evidence that supports our position."

William added quickly, "Hey, listen, the ancient Terran Conglomerate was a piecemeal tyranny. Everyone knows that. You want to hear about just how much blood was on their hands? You can't begin to imagine the scale of their atrocities. I am ashamed to say we humans didn't learn from their example. The time period after their collapse was brutal, terrifying and sparked hundreds of petty wars that killed thousands of AeyAies and billions of innocent people. We did crawl out of that mess with help from the Solidarity, but it took ages to do that. We eventually did learn. We were forced to."

Darron scowled at him from around the drone, "Pretty speech. Did you write it yourself, or was it the work of your masters?"

William knew that anything he said would simply be countered with similar arguments. There had to be a way to get through to these people! His mission was in dire jeopardy. He could use the fact that if he didn't report in to his superiors, someone would come looking for him, but that was no way to win trust. He knew that his vessel was patiently waiting for him and would make an automatic signal back to Sol if he died, but they already knew that and felt threatened by it. His instructions had been programmed into his synth-brain. There was no way to disobey, though he did have some tactical latitude. He picked up the old relay, allowing a few nanites to examine it. Thus far, the crew of Ganges had not noticed his use of the microscopic machines. He spoke aloud, still focusing on the broken device, "I assume you've replaced all these."

The flying drone swiveled in closer, and his nanites froze in place, shutting systems down and then pretending to be "dead". Naga's voice replied, "They were changed out for new units, which were eventually replaced by Strifer 'Aphid Relays'. I wouldn't mess with those if I were you."

William gave it a weak smile, "I consider myself well warned."

They all climbed back up and headed back the way they had come. The silence was deafening between them all, everyone lost in their own thoughts. The truth was that William was afraid that he would never complete his mission, which could lead to serious diplomatic problems for the Solarian Alliance. Ganges was important to the Boktahl. He had been sent here on their insistence. When they got back to the ground car, he barely registered that they would be visiting something called the Terran Museum in Residence Wheel Two. He just hoped it wouldn't be too embarrassing.

Command Hub, Level Ten

The Bridge of Ganges was running at a hectic pace. Officers rushed from station to station, while technicians reviewed endless scrolls of raw data. The Chief of the Deck was bellowing orders and doing his best to maintain some semblance of control. Executive Officer Wasp Tornpage watched it all with a highly critical eye. She cradled the marshmallow gun in her hands. The pneumatic device shot the soft treats with an incredible range, though it was totally harmless. Wasp used it to mark anyone who seemed to be panicking. Thus far, she had only used it three times, before the Bridge crew got the hint. That wasn't too bad in all honesty, but she had hoped that she wouldn't need it at all. The Chief of the Deck had objected to any form of projectile weapon being used in his domain, but the Bridge Security Commander disagreed. The issue had been brought to Captain Fieldscan who said that if Wasp wanted to share her snacks, who was he to interfere?

The crew representative had scowled at her but didn't say anything. Wasp thought that was a shame. She really loved arguing with the irritating woman. The Executive Officer understood the reasons why a non-Command crewmember was always stationed here - she just didn't agree that it was necessary. Still, the Judiciary Council had caved to popular opinion many octuries ago, carving the way to having to perpetually host an elected official on the Bridge, to make sure the boundaries of the Prime Charter weren't being stretched out of shape. It was nothing more than foolish posturing and feel-good politics. It wasn't like Jaike Verdstrum had spent his slices rewriting all the ship-wide regulations while lounging in the Captain's chair! The current occupant of that particular piece of rump-resting, Perrin Fieldscan, had told her some interesting bits about how he saw the career of the supposed "tyrant".

During her training, Captain Fieldscan had referred Wasp to the log notes of Veera Banerjee, who had succeeded Jaike. That had popped a lot of preconceived notions she had accepted concerning the infamous leader of her Sector. Captain Banerjee had been wildly popular. Most of her public images showed her surrounded by toragi, who all seemed to defer to her as their favorite human. Veera had credited most of her best ideas to her training under her rascal of a predecessor. She had mourned Jaike's passing deeply but had not corrected the public's growing dislike of the policies he had enacted. Wasp had been amazed to find out that this was done purposely, at Jaike's request.

Captain Fieldscan also revealed to her that most of the Chiefs of Command Sector who followed in Jaike's bootsteps privately admired the man and his role during the Crucible. This was the reason why the Verdstrum sword had been passed down from one Captain to the next, as a symbol of their secret adherence to their infamous predecessor's philosophy. As Executive Officer, she had been required to study Jaike Verdstrum, but while there were still some surprises, a lot of what was "classified" had already been known to the Strifers, who had always hailed Captain Verdstrum as a liberator. That, of course, had not helped the man's lack of popularity.

Wasp shook her head to break out of her reverie, and then shot off another marshmallow at some Lieutenant who was screaming at his subordinates over at Communications Control. Captain Fieldscan looked at her and shook his head, "You should have brought the plank, my dear."

Even the Chief of the Deck cracked a smile at that. It took a rat to teach the gerbils how to behave. That was why she was sitting here, on the Bridge, as the iron hand for Perrin's velvet glove. Ganges was about to officially enter the heliopause of System Forty-One. There was no room for hyper emotions or lackluster performance. The Commander of Bridge Security glanced at her and nodded. He was keeping a sharp eye on the frantic activity that ran throughout the stadium-sized chamber. He understood that when nerves were frayed, abuse often reared its ugly head. If her efforts with the marshmallows didn't eventually gain the desired effect, used socks would be next.

Naga-Ma's matronly face appeared as a huge hologram in the center of the Bridge, "Attention all crew! System Entry shall commence in one seed-sliver. All personnel, prepare for turbulence."

The heliopause was a shock boundary surrounding stars, caused by the interaction of the star's output with the interstellar medium. High energy gas and charged particles collected here, creating an environment where the most sensitive instruments could be afflicted with errors, causing a myriad of potential difficulties for the ship. Fortunately, Naga's own memory core was deep inside Ganges, wrapped around the Spine Axis. The hundred-meter-thick hull prevented radiation issues and protected the crew from impacts. Thruster control was vital at this time, for a vessel the size of Ganges didn't turn like a mag-bike. Most times, they just barreled through the hot fields of cosmic rays and stellar wind, but there had been some difficult entries in the past, so they were wise to be prepared.

Wasp kept her eyes focused upon the scurrying crew, certain that Captain Fieldscan was keeping watch on the clock. Her job was to keep him free to do his, without distractions. She jotted down the names and ranks of everyone who she had to fire her projectiles at, for future disciplinary action. Fieldscan was a very nice guy, sometimes too much so. He needed someone who was a martinet to keep discipline during times of trouble. Naga was continuing the countdown with its preternaturally calm voice. A young ensign ran over to the command platform and hesitated. Wasp could see an officer rushing to stop the crewman's progress. She lifted her pneumatic gun and shouted, "You! Get over here!"

The young ensign looked alarmed, but he obeyed. The officer behind him came to an abrupt halt as the Security Commander stepped in front of his path. Wasp used her gun to encourage the ensign to come forward, which he did, wringing his hands. Wasp looked at his sweating face, "Well? Report!"

The poor crewman started stuttering at her in fear, "M-My ap-apologies, E-Executive! There's a, a strange, well odd reading from the forward quadar sensors! It might indicate an energy wave of unusual…"

He never got the chance to finish before the lights flickered out and Naga's face disappeared. Everyone was jolted with a shock, like sticking one's finger into a power outlet. Systems all over the Bridge cut out. Screams filled Wasp's ears. The Captain bellowed, "Emergency power! Thruster grid seven to full! I want Engineering and Stellar on my comms now! Technology station, report! What is Naga's current condition?"

The lights above flickered back on abruptly. The AeyAie reappeared in mid-sentence, "…have achieved insertion."

Wasp swept up to her feet and helped the young ensign back to his. She checked him for injuries and, finding none, said to him, "Run faster next time."

Orders were being shouted all over the Bridge. The smell of burnt insulation and hair invaded her nose. Technicians in their Temple of Naga-Ma robes dropped themselves under various stations to inspect for any damage. Rescue Services crew rushed over to make sure no one was seriously injured. Wasp did her best to keep track of the situation. Messages were now coming in from every Sector Chief, all with reports of mild power outages but no serious problems. Captain Fieldscan glanced over at her and raised an eyebrow. She nodded back then turned her attention to the young man in front of her. His alarm was obvious and she shared his concern.

Distribution Wheel Two, Level One

Ghell looked about the supposed "safe room" with skepticism. It wasn't his usual venue, but his favorite regions were getting too hot for comfort. While it was true that this location held few wallscreens, each separated by a dozen meters of corridor or more, it was still not a comfortable area. The dilapidated cargo hold they were sitting in had just been placed on the "renovation" list, which was why his lead enforcer had chosen it. Ghell admitted that this was most likely the best option his organization had at this time. If all went according to plan, that would change to their advantage. The chamber's meter-thick door had been closed and locked, all with the appropriate authorizations, so as not to catch the attention of the AeyAie. A janitorial team under his employ had secured the warehouse space ahead of time, under the guise of preparing the whole region for refit.

Some of Ghell's competitors and allies viewed the upcoming terraforming operation as a threat to their operations, but he disagreed. This was the perfect time to reorganize and reassess their own efficiency. New methodologies could be tested, keeping their grandest opponent, Security Sector, scrambling for purchase on their activities. Terraforming and space engineering were both hazardous duties, which fit in perfectly with their needs. Some of his associates were simply used to how things were done during the voyages between stars. They had to adapt to their new set of circumstances or be destroyed. Ghell was determined to show the others how it was done.

Sitting in his ergonomic chair, Ghell barely moved, save to adjust his camo-suit's cycling of body patterns. He could appear as tall, short, heavy, thin, male or female, with enough holographic emitters to fool any face-recognition programs. His voice-distorter gear was working smoothly, having been refitted recently to allow for a greater range of shifting vocal patterns whenever he spoke. Even his closest allies and highest-level employees didn't know what he looked like or who he really was. No one within the organized criminal cabal that he had created from scratch knew anything about him. Ghell was most careful about such things. His own family and the crew under his supervision at his official post had no clue as to what he did behind the scenes. He was determined to keep it that way.

It wasn't that he hated Ganges, nor was he against the Holy Mission. Ghell was simply taking full advantage of the opportunities which had landed in his lap over a dozen spirals ago. When he had taken over Kita's operation, it wasn't because he had anything against her. At the time, her people were being picked off by Security. Her games had been coming to an end, and he had used his own advantages to bring her to a swift demise before everything useful was confiscated, including her employees. Those who had flocked to his new banner were still grateful to him. Ghell made sure they kept feeling that way, even if he had to pay for such inconveniences directly. Ghell's generosity had become famous in the under-culture of Ganges, so had his ferocity.

His finest assassin was sitting across from him, shifting nervously in her seat. Ghell knew everything about her, from her childhood habits to her current post in Engineering. He had revealed his deep knowledge of her life in person. She hadn't questioned how he had gotten his information, accepting it instead with silent dread. It was so gratifying that the most dangerous people in Ganges feared him. They also became increasingly wealthy in chips and bartered services under his employ. This was how one best ran the largest organized crime syndicate within Ganges. Through fear and loyalty. Reward and punishment. It was possibly the oldest method known to humanity, but it worked wonders.

Ghell's leading enforcer was standing at his left-hand side, totally at ease. Their technicians had performed miracles against the snooping Naga. Their methods were more subtle than other crime organizations, which meant they were least likely to attract unwelcome attention. She actually worked within his own Sector, though she had no knowledge of this. Ghell thought that was amusing, for they passed each other in the corridors of duty frequently. He loved her absolute loyalty to his methods, never questioning even the most bizarre commands he made. Her name was Helia Deckhand, and her special talents were focused on organization and in making sure inconveniences disappeared. Many times, this was done through the services of the assassin before him, who was named Beria Lightstar, from Harbor Sector. Like him, they weren't crazed mutineers bent on stopping the Holy Mission. Ghell had made a habit of eliminating such scum from the ship, and he refused to employ Strifers for any reason. Rats often bit the hands that fed them.

Ghell's ascension in the under-culture of crime had come from a fortunate set of circumstances. He had been hiking in the nature preserves inside Residence Wheel One, when he had stumbled upon a terribly wounded member of the League of Vigilantes. The man had been barely breathing. Most of his equipment had been severely damaged. Under the dense branches of the mighty forest, Ghell had simply broken the crime-fighter's neck in one quick motion. He had then looked carefully at the direction the vigilante had been facing, finding a series of boulders nestled under the roots of a large tree. He had stripped the body of anything useful then went over to the clump of rock. There, he had discovered a cache of supplies and replacement parts that were specially designed to fight crime, amongst them the suit he now wore almost every rotation to control and terrorize his organization.

It was such a delicious irony for him to use the materials designed to prevent criminal activity to support such nefarious efforts. From that fateful discovery, his little empire had blossomed and grown beyond all his expectations. While some of his competitors had railed about his methodologies, they all now admitted that he had done every surviving syndicate a favor by removing the incompetent ones, even if his practices were considered vile. Ghell had become a celebrity amongst the crime bosses, but on this rotation, there were some troubles brewing that might affect his organization.

Ghell changed the settings of his camo-suit so that outwardly he began to flicker between one persona to another with confusing speed. He leaned forward, facing his assassin, "There's a problem we need you to solve. Our company is in desperate need for expansion, a problem which arises from the success we enjoy. I would prefer to remain within the nature preserves of Residence Wheel One, on Level Two. One of our allies had assured me that they had a handle on the situation but got sloppy concerning the overuse of a corrupt resource. Their clutched Security officer was supposed to reroute our biggest headache, a Knight by the name of Pelor Guardhand. Their asset's cover was blown wide open. I've taken our associates to task for their failure, and they understand that it's their responsibility to clean up their own mess. In the meantime, I don't trust anyone but our own crew to handle the initial problem."

Assassin Lightstar nodded once, "Knight Pelor Guardhand."

Ghell leaned back, "Yes. All attempts to make him see reason have failed. Our associates even ambushed the old bastard, and he broke their operatives with some help from the League. He's being watched and protected by the very best, so we must counter that move with our own."

Assassin Lightstar cocked her head to one side, "A terminal mission?"

Ghell waved a hand in the air, "Absolutely."

She got to her feet, "Pelor Guardhand shall die, my Lord."

Engineering Sector, Level Forty-Three

Howait Sparweld finished working with the Kendis Power Unit, closing the access panel and locking it with his flashtat authorizations. The twenty-meter-wide machine began to hum, as it cycled through its testing phase. Within a seed-sliver, it would be up and running again. He wiped his brow with a damp rag and turned to look at the workers under his supervision. Everyone was nestled inside the various cables, tubes and conveyors they were working on, with just a boot here or an arm there, to show that they existed. The whine of laser welders, buzzing metal scanners and the pounding of hammers filled the air. While their current task was not a high priority job, they were replacing the team who had been initially called to work on the broken machinery, after some careless injuries. The conveyor was loaded up with unprocessed asteroid gold, and as he had suspected, the machine was overloaded.

The mass of the gold was dense, and it had thrown some support spars out from true, disrupting the fabricator at the far end of the hundred-meter work-line. Most of the malleable metal was going to be processed for technological purposes, while another portion would then be used for handrails and public decoration. Any leftovers would be slated for jewelers and supplies for chip-making businesses.

The Kendis Power Unit was his to maintain, as he was Foreman of the group and had the proper certifications. All of the old fusion and fission power stations on the Engineering cowl had been replaced by these, as were all of the internal battery units. Howait still didn't understand all the principles behind the Kendis generators, but they all used a principle of squeezing energy waves from compressed spacetime vacuum chambers. While still far too bulky to use for powering most transports, they could replenish batteries and refresh fuel pods with incredible speed. Just as Kendis Steel had replaced the old hull plating, the Kendis Power Units did the same for all the various generators that Ganges had previously relied upon, but were much safer, cleaner and smaller in size. Blue nodules lit from within all along the leeward side of the device, signaling it was ready for full activation. Howait would now have to wait for the rest of his team to finish their tasks.

A sudden scream from underneath a nest of cables came from sternward, followed by a clatter and a shout of pain. Howait rushed over to find Mibo scrambling out from under his work area, rubbing his head which had a bump growing under his scalp, "Ganges damn it! Who the fuck messed with my damned welding paste? Shit! That hurt!"

Howait helped him to a sitting position and examined him, "Do you need Medical?"

Mibo scowled up at him, "No leeches, Boss!"

Skolly lifted his head from behind the conveyor, "He just hit his head. No real damage possible, Boss, but I'd check the ventilator for dents."

The others chuckled from their hidden positions, but Mibo shouted, "Ha, ha! It's all funny when you're not the one who's hurt! That's the fourth time this sowing I've been hit with a shit-joke! I opened my cannister and a bunch of springs shot out at me! They could've taken out my eye!"

Pilla squirmed out from under a junction station, "First off, you lazy shit, one of those springs fell in here with me. It's covered with safety foam. Second, what took you so damned long to get going on that task? What? You waiting for New Spiral to finish?"

Mibo got to his feet, "Fuck off! You're evil, you hear me? Why you always picking on me? Like to play jokes on innocent crew?"

Pilla raised an eyebrow, "Innocently taking naps on duty, you mean?"

Skolly raised his hands, "Hey now, no fights! Look, Mibo, we all get hit with practical jokes, okay? Even Howait, for pity's sake! Every single one of us is either guilty or innocent. We're all in on it, or another team is messing with us."

Falinos jumped down onto the deck from his scaffold, his large bulk making the deck tremble, "If it's another team, we gotta tell the Director, right, Boss-man?"

Howait rubbed at his chin with his thumb while Vita swung down from the illumination supports, "You really want the Director's attention? You're stupider than I thought!"

Brigo climbed out from the belowdecks access, blinking in the harsh light of the service area, "It's just a few jokes."

Mibo pointed a finger at the confused-looking crewman, "So, you admit that you're the one doing this to us?"

Brigo blinked again, "Did what? The jokes? Those take work."

Howait held up his hand and shouted, "Stop this! Enough! Okay, it seems that these pranks are disrupting us as a team. I'll make sure the situation changes so we can get our efficiency rating up."

Falinos guffawed, "You gonna get your Security mate involved? Does she know what end of a spanner to hold?"

Pilla looked over at Howait with alarm, "Hey, Boss, please don't get Security nosing about in here. They'll never let up until they find something, anything."

Skolly peered at her in surprise, "What? You hiding any contraband in your boots? I say it might be a good idea if our Foreman does get his mate involved."

Mibo looked at Howait, "So, what'll it be?"

Howait slumped his shoulders, "I just can't. If I don't, one of you might get Security investigating anyway. I wouldn't blame you, but it would be difficult for me. You see, I'm the culprit."

Everyone except Mibo and Pilla started laughing aloud. After a few pollen-slivers, the mirth suddenly died down. Falinos stepped toward Howait, "Now wait a seed, Foreman Sparweld, you serious?"

Howait glanced up at the big man towering over him, "Yes. Yes, I am. I confess to being the instigator of the practical jokes around here."

Skolly was shocked, "But... but there were a few when you were at the games, cheering on your mate!"

Howait shrugged, "I set up some surprises ahead of time. I even played some on myself, to keep you all off your guard."

Brigo fell back into the belowdecks with a clang. Vita stepped up next to Falinos with her arms crossed over her chest, "Why? What's your motive? Or do you just like screwing us over?"

Howait held up his hands in a placating gesture, "Hey, I didn't cause any real harm, just some bumps and bruises, mostly to egos that were ready to pop. You just don't understand why I became your Foreman is all."

Falinos growled back, "And why was that? Is this some kind of trick?"

Howait sighed, "This miserable team had one of the worst efficiency ratings in Engineering. The Director wanted it fixed. He wanted you fixed. After the first two rotations of watching you all not working, I thought it might help to have an unknown adversary to get you into gear. If someone other than yourselves were playing games with you, preventing you from doing a decent job, you might fight back and gain some pride in your work. You're all good crew, in your strange way, but your last Foreman quit on you because of all the bickering and the slow repair times. I volunteered. In defending yourselves against a hidden prankster, you all gained a rise in the ratings. Remember last sowing's bonuses?"

Brigo poked his head from the belowdecks access, "First one I ever got, boss."

Howait spread his lanky arms out, "Exactly. You all needed a kick in the ass to get you moving like real crew. If I had started coming down on you like a regular Foreman, you would've teamed up against me and be stuck as the laughingstock of Engineering Sector. As it was, I put up with you all making fun of me, making jokes about my body and even my mate. Behind your backs, I was preparing all kinds of surprises for you. Do you think I got my flashtats because I'm such a wimp? You're all a bunch of misfits and bullies, which I've had adequate time dealing with all my life. Hate me all you want, my plan worked well. This team's ratings jumped twenty points last rotation, despite all the pranks I played on you. Because of the pranks I played on you!"

Falinos scratched his head, "Shit, what do we do now?"

Howait slumped his skinny shoulders, "You have the right to request new leadership. I wouldn't blame any of you if you called in a formal complaint about me. In that case, I'll be transferred to a different set of losers, and you'll get a new boss."

Skolly waved his hand in the air, "Hold on now! If you leave us, we're right back where we started!"

Falinos leaned down so that his nose was almost touching Howait's, "You're right. We're a bunch of misfits. So are you, skinny boss-man. That means you belong to us. I don't mind some bruises if I get chip-bonuses."

Pilla chimed in, "He's right, Howait. I hate to agree with bucket-brain, but he makes sense. We need you here. Besides, we all got secrets. It's good to know our Foreman is a master of them."

Vita placed her fists on her hips, "So, does this count as break-time?"

Howait gave her an inscrutable look, "I would just call this a team-building session. Break's in two seed-slivers."

The Engineering team cheered and began slapping him on the back. He smiled up at his team shyly and found admiration in their faces. He had beaten them at their own game, and they knew it. Howait glanced over toward the far end of the Kendis Power Unit he'd been working on, to find a Naga drone floating there, bobbing contentedly. He gave it a barely perceptible nod and one of its lights blinked back at him.

Ice Cap of Ganges, Observation Blister Seven

Stellar Ensign Tachi Vactor was still dealing with the electrical snarls from her observation boards, which had erupted when Ganges entered the heliopause. As a Rank Four technician, she was in charge of her small group which took and interpreted readings from both the passive and active sensors in Observation Blister Seven. The small, transparent dome was only fifteen meters in diameter but gave them a breathtaking view of the cosmos. Hanging from a special set of walkways and gantries were a collection of telescopes, lidar, radar and quadar devices which were constantly looking out into the dark. The opposite end of the dome was fitted with workstations and wallscreens, plus the entrance hatch, which doubled as an airlock. There were forty such domes, all hanging on the underside of the ice cap at the bow of Ganges. These were clustered in groups of eight, to keep them apart from the navigational thrusters situated on the opposite side of the ice cap. From what she had heard from the other domes, all of them were facing similar problems. Stellar Sector informed her that the further a post was from the bow of Ganges, the less affected it had been from the initial shock of heliopause entry.

As the cap was not rotating, there were no centrifugal forces to mimic gravity here. Normally, this was a delightful bonus to being assigned at the observatory, but this rotation it was a severe handicap. Smoke was still swirling about in small, choking clouds. Loose objects bounced around from place to place, only slowing down due to air friction. Tachi had been shocked at her station, just like everyone else, and the synth-quartz observation dome had glowed with a ghostly green-blue. One of her subordinates, Ensign Masslin, had to be taken to the local Rescue Services station for convulsions and burns. Comms had cut out, and it had taken them an entire slice to repair all the damage. Since then, the demand for answers from the Bridge had become ever more frantic. Tachi didn't blame them for wanting swift answers, but she had none to give them. All she could do was pass along the data from the standard observation logs. This material had already been sent to both the Bridge and Stellar Sector for analysis. She doubted they would get any better results than her team's report.

Two Naga drones and a handful of smaller robots were helping her crew to make repairs to the active sensors, which had been fried by the energy spike. All the passive instruments were working normally and showed no sign of any damage. That could not be said for the stations which sorted and collated the information provided by the passive telescopes and radar detectors. Jenna had never seen anything like this incident. The safety standards utilized by Stellar for its equipment was quite high and meticulously adhered to by Engineering. A few rotations ago, she would have considered what had just occurred as being impossible. What deepened the mystery was the fact that, over the last few octuries, Ganges had replaced all of its power systems with tested and approved Kendis technologies, which were far more stable than the original systems. From what little Jenna knew about such things, they were supposed to be hardened against even catastrophic surges and fluctuations.

Tachi looked down at her blue-and-green Stellar Sector uniform. It was now covered with soot, with small burn marks on the half-sleeves and torso. She always liked to present herself as being tidy, and her current disheveled appearance made her uncomfortable. Her team also kept all their workstations fastidiously immaculate, ready for unannounced inspections and to reassure any visiting scientists that they took their post seriously. Looking about the dome-shaped chamber caused Tachi to wince at the mess. Cables had been strung from emergency generators to barely functioning stations. Bits of metal and plastic were floating about. Panels were open to reveal sensitive components that looked scorched, and the furnishings had been ripped from their supports to give easier access to damaged consoles.

She carefully pushed off from a padded handrail, to slowly launch herself toward Ensign Klaiver, who was working on getting the lidar sensors back online. He was a Rank Three technician and was her most experienced team member. While normally unflappable, Jenna noticed he was still cursing quietly under his breath as he continued with the repairs. She carefully nudged a thick cable to halt her progress and spun herself around so that she could inspect his work. What her eyes showed her was an unruly mass of scorched wires, broken bits of equipment and blackened connectors. From her current orientation, he was upside-down, a situation which was something everyone who worked in this weightless environment was used to. She asked him softly, "Any update on the time for repair?"

Ensign Klaiver sighed, as he allowed himself to float back a bit so she could see the damage better, "In all honesty, this'll take a sowing to finish. I might be able to get some telemetry for you in another slice, but it'll be minimal and prone to errors. I wish I had better news for you."

Tachi peered into the open access space, "Just as you feared, the whole board is dead. It looks like you're trying to circumvent it entirely. Not a bad idea, but you need to shunt the input feeds to another station, then reroute them back to this one."

He looked into her eyes with a miserable expression upon his dark face, "I know. I was hoping to keep things contained within the original console, but you're right. You know what we need? A Strifer mechanic from Engineering."

Tachi chuckled at him, "They are the best at jury-rigging makeshift solutions to problems like this, but they'd fill the dome with all kinds of junk. It's still a good idea. The Bridge is still demanding more current data, as is the Stellar Observation Department. I'll requisition an old friend of mine, Squeak. We went to Basic together, and she still owes me a favor. I'll let you know if she can make it."

Ensign Klavier looked back at her in surprise, "You don't mean Squeak Greasestain, do you? She's Engineering, not Stellar. Besides, she outranks us both! I'm sure she's got better things to do right now."

Tachi gently tweaked his nose, "Oh, ye of little faith! Yes, I do mean Squeak Greasestain, and I already told you she and I are old friends! Besides, this would be just another feather in her green hood. She'll broadcast the repair for her fans, so we might want to clean up a bit. You'll see. I'll get her here."

The Ensign just shook his head and returned to his work. Tachi tapped her datapad, which was attached to her wrist, and made a call. Within a seed-sliver, her old friend appeared as a hologram, her face floating above Tachi's hand. Squeak was delighted to be called in to help, as her own Sector had barely felt the shock that had run through the ship. With her help, Tachi's observation dome would be up and running before the rotation was over.

Residence Wheel Two, Level Two

Ubo Capsworn dragged his battered suitcase and equipment pack across the parking lot that was on the leeward side of the Holy Resolution community. His backpack cut into his shoulders, filled as it was with supplies and special cameras. His yellow-and-red Provision Sector uniform was stained with sweat, as he struggled with all of his gear. It was almost dark-slice. The skyscreens had begun to deepen and change color, and if he didn't find his cab soon, he would be sleeping out in the open. It wasn't like he hadn't done this before, but his back would always protest by dream-slice. Besides, the equipment he carried was sensitive, and he preferred even the shelter of a cramped vehicle to exposing them to the dew that formed every dawn-slice.

Ubo was average in height, though his habit of stooping made him appear shorter than he was. His paunch was noticeable under his uniform, and his dark hair was kept slicked back in an unfashionable style that was out of date. His dark eyes always looked unsettled, shifting around as if seeking for something lost. He kept his beard and moustache trimmed close to his face, yet it always looked uneven and unkempt. Vanity was never his strong suit, but he had tried as best he could to be presentable. This was a challenge when he went roaming in the field for his favorite hobby - studying the supposedly haunted places within Ganges.

He preferred the term "paranormal investigator" to "ghost hunter" or even worse, "gullible loser", as he felt this gave his activities a touch more authenticity. He wasn't just some thrill-seeker, he was a researcher! Everyone knew at least a tale or two concerning the strange happenings in various regions of the ship, full of dark mysteries and forbidden secrets. By the time he had entered Basic Crew Training, he was hooked. As a result, his grades had suffered, except for history and cultural studies. His determination to separate rumor from truth meant that he was not as devoted to his Sector as he could have been and thus had been passed over for becoming an officer. To his mind, this wasn't so bad, as it gave him some extra time to pursue his investigations.

Ubo dropped his packs upon a patch of grass and leaned back to stretch his sore shoulders. He considered himself fortunate that he had been raised in the Bright Leaf community in Residence Wheel One on Level One. As a result, his bones and muscles were quite strong, allowing him to lug his baggage wherever he roamed. Ubo hadn't been home for several harvests. He had been gearing up for his most challenging investigation yet, the abandoned community of Everstrong, which was just thirty kilometers from his current location. Ubo had learned that, before one entered a potentially haunted region, one had to check in on the local population for clues, stories and to study potential hazards.

His broadcast channel was fairly popular, earning him some extra chips so he could purchase the special cameras and sensors he used for his hobby. In the beginning, he had struggled to gain any traction amongst the viewers, but his arrest by Security Sector at the mysterious Forward Estates had won him some notoriety, plus a harvest of community service. Ubo still swore that his equipment had picked up some interesting readings within the old, abandoned community where the Great Families had resided in luxury, until their demise. All of his data for that trip had been confiscated by Investigations, with severe warnings to never enter that gloomy forest ever again.

Ubo also had a close run-in with Security forces in Agro Three, following rumors of a strange hole that went through the capward hull of that Wheel of Ganges, yet led back to the sternward side. He had roamed the whole area and discovered a

Security training center nestled against the main bulkhead wall, surrounded by razor-wire and mag-bike patrols. He never did find the hole that the rumors said was there, but Security was definitely hiding something! His broadcast ratings had jumped after that, along with yet another warning from Security to cease and desist his activities there.

This time, he was going after the grandest mystery of his career – an entire city totally abandoned and shunned by everyone. The official word said that it was condemned as being hazardous to the crew, due to being severely damaged during the Crucible, but the number of strange stories had only whetted his appetite. He had finally found a small community nearby whose residents were willing to tell their tales of ghosts, strange monsters, odd mutants and disappearances. It was just perfect! Ubo wasn't planning to rush his investigations, for being thorough was a hallmark of a good paranormal researcher. It also helped to find out if Security had set up any roadblocks or patrols.

Ubo checked his datapad and saw that time was not his friend this rotation. The skyscreens were beginning to show stars and a crescent moon as the gloom of dark-slice took hold. Just as he was about to despair, the coughing rumble of a poorly maintained cab lifted his spirits. The vehicle had just entered the parking lot and was making its way toward him with a speed that suggested reluctance. He waved his hand in the air, and it swerved in his direction. It was an old-style transport, with just enough room for a cabbie and himself, plus his load of investigation gear. The driver, named Crab Spitshard, had been his companion for several harvests and was as disheveled as his transport. Rather than driving for one of the major transportation services of Agro Sector, Crab had been given the honor of becoming a specialist, picking clients as he pleased and going wherever he wanted.

The stained and rusty cab came to a squealing halt next to Ubo, and the trunk popped open automatically. The side window lowered, and Crab squinted at him as if irritated, which he often was, "You done gawking over the local pubs? I found us a hotel on the outskirts. Nothing fancy or expensive, but a roof and bed for us both."

Ubo grinned at the ill-tempered Strifer, "This is it! I can feel it! We're gonna be famous!"

Crab took a pull from his favorite inebriant, called WhoTheFuckKnows, "To Hell with famous! I just don't want to end up dead! So where does our stupid trail end this time? The Captain's secret lavatory?"

Ubo shook his head as he started loading his gear into the trunk of the cab, "No! Of course not! We, my friend, are going to Everstrong!"

Crab choked on his drink, spilling it on his lurid green robes and rat mask, "Everstrong? Are you nuts? Wait, don't fucking tell me. You are! I already knew that! I just didn't think you were suicidal!"

Ubo jumped into the rickety cab, making the old vehicle bounce, "It'll be fine! You'll see! We are not going unprepared, I promise you. The locals around here are more than willing to talk. With their information, I can set things up so that we remain in one piece."

Crab scowled at him through the rearview mirror, "Like Hell! I'm not going in there! No way! Even the crime syndicates avoid that fucking place! We should too! I've got pups to feed, you know!"

Ubo sighed, for this was an old argument, "I'll double your fee. Now let's get to the hotel so I can review my notes."

Crab grumbled below his breath but drove them to their temporary housing nonetheless. Ubo was too excited about everything he had learned this rotation to be bothered by Crab's skepticism and cowardice. They had come too far to turn back now. Ubo could almost hear the accolades following his investigative report.

CHAPTER SEVEN

Ice Rotation - Launch Sowing - Mission Harvest - Spiral 5620

"I finally finished my inspection of the Higashi-toragi breeding programs. The whole thing took me a full sowing to accomplish, and I must say that I'm terribly impressed. The six providers, each one based upon the former Great Families, from the time of the Crucible, or so I'm constantly told, have developed spectacular results for our Sector. I must admit, that these rotations, we keep the cats in mind when assigning crew to their squadrons. A good mix of abilities is often best, when it comes to the toragis in general. My own guardian is a Kumar variant, which are known for their cunning. I confess that I cannot imagine life without my companion. I even give him a good amount of credit for my own rise in rank!"
Jak Vernoly, Police Commander, Security Sector, personal log, V40

Agro Wheel Three, Security Level One

I watch the others posture with disdain. They stand about, snarling at one another, to show how fierce they are, how strong they've become. I have no interest in such displays. The chamber we're in is quite comfortable, with thick grass and a broad river running through it. The far walls reveal images of dense forest, complete with birdsong, but it has no scent, other than the sprays used by the humans. I do not understand the purpose of such actions, but it seems to be an obsession with the bipedal apes. The wall with the entry door is right behind me and is different from the others. Instead of showing an endless view of unreal forest, it has long rows of clear windows, beyond which our human partners can be seen watching us.

The few crew who are inside the chamber with my kind all wear the same garments of red-and-black with a blue symbol on the backs of them. I try to puzzle out the meaning of this decoration, but it defies my attempts. In some ways, this area is home to me. It's where I was raised from a cub to an adult, where I received my first training in verbal commands and athletic abilities. The chamber itself is a place of mating, where most of my species select a breeding partner. There are several different types of my kind in Ganges. The easiest way to tell us apart is by scent, but humans have weak noses. Instead, they use visual characteristics, such as markings on our fur. Mine, like all my closest brethren, are covered with large, ring-like spots, with deeply mottled centers. In my platoon, there are many other variations to be found, depending on their chambers of origin. The breeding centers are also our medical facilities. All my kind who share the same markings come to this location for their physical needs.

In my platoon, some of my kind have broad stripes, bark-like mottled fur, stippled dots of gold and dark brown, and even ones with no markings at all. I have discovered that each different fur pattern denotes a particular breeding place, or infirmary. Often, I hear my human partner talk about me being a "LeGrand", though I do not know what that word means. It makes no sense. A female human in our group seems proud of her "Makamba" guardian. While I do not understand the word, it is clear that they are talking about the progeny of a specific ancestor line. The single "Makamba" in our platoon is named Alice. Her dark black fur with thin, gold stripes makes her incredibly beautiful to me. Sometimes, distractingly so.

Another male "LeGrand" hisses at me, for he is certain I am about to steal his mate. I swat him hard in the nose, to dissuade such silly posturing. None of the females here are to my liking. They are all beautiful enough, clever enough and are formidable enough to make them worthy partners, but my own choice is not among them. My preferred mate cannot enter this chamber. This makes me uncomfortable in ways I find hard to understand. There is a deep sadness within me, along with a glowering anger. It is so obvious that none of the females here have the grace and elegance that Alice so easily displays. If she were here, I would fight all my brothers to be hers without hesitation, but the humans won't allow it. They can be incredibly stupid, even if they do help to control the world. I have yowled my frustration at the scentless face of Ganges to no avail. Have I not proven myself worthy?

The others begin to wander over toward the river, where they will play and breed. One of the humans who controls this chamber comes over to me, but I snarl at the human in irritation. At least she has the sense to back away politely. Some of our wards can be dense and meddlesome. I am not in the mood for their chattering and grooming instincts. I scratch under my chin at that thought. Humans are truly excellent at combing through hair and taking care of itchy spots. My partner is always brushing me and trimming tangles from my fur. He cares about me but is too stupid to understand my needs. Darron has the desire to breed. All the time. He also gets many opportunities to do so, with a choice of many mates. All the time. Not me.

At this point, all of my kind are involved in their duty to make cubs. All but me. I refuse to participate. The one I want is not here, so boredom rules my mind.

Roaming about the viewing side of the chamber, my human partner can be plainly seen watching me. Darron's arms are crossed over his chest, looking like he could be upset, but I can't smell him to be sure. He always calls me a "good toragi" and a "clever toragi", but other than his company, which I do adore, there are few other rewards for my service to the world. This seems terribly unfair, and it frustrates me.

There have been some other ways I have tried to get my point across to the humans and the world-mind called Naga. I do my best to perform my duty, but there are times when desperate measures are required to gain satisfaction. I have sung to the wall-face until my throat burned. I even left a nice, large, fresh salmon to it, being careful to not break the skin. Naga coos at me, just like the humans do, but never understands my desires. Lately, I have gone in the other direction, refusing food and sleeping outside the grand home I share with Darron. My dark moods have become disruptive, causing distractions from my duties.

The one task I have continually committed myself to has been to watch and observe the "guest", William Blaine. He still smells terrible, looks strange, and he also unnerves me with the deferential way in which he treats me. The more cooperative he becomes, the less trust he engenders. Darron has made it obvious that he thinks the "guest" is a threat to the world itself. I agree and am heartened by his suspicions. Humans aren't always dull-witted, save when it comes to toragis.

My stomach growls, and I want to go home or be at my post. Hunger gnaws at me, because I have nothing else I want to do. It is time to leave this place, so I wander over toward the window that Darron peers through. He places a hand on the transparent wall, and I stretch up on my back legs to place my paw over his.

That was when it happened. Another human, who is named Ensign Triella Navcomm, from our platoon walks over to him, her toragi, Alice, just behind her. I can barely breathe. My heart jumps in my chest. The world disappears, and all I can see are her beautiful markings. The way Alice prowls with such an effortless grace captivates me. Her eyes meet mine and a shock runs down my spine. I begin to yowl as loudly as I can. I call to her, hoping she can hear me through the thick, transparent wall.

Alice takes a single, sublime leap toward me, startling the two humans, and she presses her nose against the window. I mimic her pose, our breaths steaming the smooth surface. I rub my forehead upon the transparent wall, pretending that I can smell her, even though it's not true. She does the same on her side, signaling that I am her choice. Overwhelming emotions flood my mind. Joy, rapture, frustration. My loins swell as I stare into her golden eyes. We stay in our pose, lost to our desire. Despair begins to grow within me. How can I ever get the humans to understand something so basic as love?

Agro Wheel Three, Level One

Lieutenant Darron Lazhand had been suffering from worry over his toragi, Mike. At first, he had thought his companion's odd behavior was a result of having to watch over William Blaine, which was certainly enough to cause anyone to act up. Last sowing, Mike had begun to yowl at the walls during sleep-slice, causing some polite complaints from the neighbors. No one was angry with Mike, but everyone was concerned that the toragi was unhappy over something. Darron couldn't tell anyone about the special "guest" from the Sol System, as the information was still highly classified. Yet he had to admit, Mike had been acting strangely the past few harvests, leaving gifts for Naga, getting distracted during training bouts, and lately, refusing to eat.

Toragis were known for their incredible appetite, so any time one of them walked away from dinner was a cause for concern. The last time Darron got some nice, fresh, salmon stuffing-muffins for Mike, the toragi had simply carried them to the nearest wallscreen and roared for a paring-sliver. The breeding specialists at the LeGrand Toragi facility had given the big cat a thorough examination, several blood tests and a brain-scan. All the results said nothing but that Mike was in great shape, which didn't help matters. One of the specialists had suggested that Mike needed a breeding partner and that his behavior was a signal that the big cat was ready to make cubs. This was the third time he had brought Mike to the breeding grounds, but his beloved guardian remained uninterested. Darron was certain that Mike would do well in competing for a mate, but the toragi didn't even bother to try.

In the ancient times, the big cats were allowed to breed haphazardly, usually partnering with Security crew who worked and lived together. If the crewmembers were sexually active, the toragis generally responded in kind. For those crew who had a mate who wasn't part of Security, other options had been found to continue the genetic lines. Since the breeding facilities had begun to take over all medical and biological matters concerning the toragis, specialized bloodlines had been formed and were kept genetically sequestered from one another as a general rule. There were times when they mixed, to keep the genes healthy and robust. The toragis didn't seem to mind the arrangement, and so it had continued, showing great strides in developing useful traits.

Darron looked through the synth-quartz window and sighed. Mike was still refusing to participate in competing for a mate. It tore his heart to see his toragi looking so mournful. It was a puzzle. One he didn't have a clue about how to find a solution for. Darron knew his companion well enough to know that Mike had lost a few kilos recently. LeGrands were not as large as Gundersens nor were they as lanky as the Kumars. Toragis like Mike were comfortably in the middle when it came to their body structure, much like the Higashis and Makambas, though the latter were leaner in general. He had been told that, in the beginning, only the Higashi variant had existed and was kept as pure as possible, to act as a control group. Even then, all the toragis had changed over the octuries, with larger skulls and shorter tails and fangs. Their paws had elongated, with more dexterous digits, though no one seemed to know why this was happening.

The hatch at the far end of the corridor opened, just as Mike reared up to touch the window from the other side where Darron had placed his hand. He was surprised to see Ensign Triella Navcomm approaching, her own big cat prowling beside her. Darron raised an eyebrow at his platoon crew, "You taking a rotation of leave too? What are you doing here?"

Triella saluted him smartly, "I'm here on official business, sir. The Chief requires your presence at conference room Alpha-Seven-Three-Nine within Stellar Sector. She apologizes for disturbing your time off and for not contacting you via comms, but the Stellar representative was getting very twitchy about not having the superior officer of our platoon present during the questioning of our... guest, sir."

Darron was just about to express a few choice words concerning the Stellar representative, when he noticed that Triella's toragi had jumped to the window and was pressing against it across from where Mike was still standing. A low rumble filled the corridor, as Alice rubbed her head against the synth-quartz. Mike was doing the same, slapping at the window rhythmically. Darron stared in shock at the scene before him. He heard a short gasp coming from Ensign Navcomm, who took a step back, "I've never seen her do that before!"

Lieutenant Lazhand tapped his datapad, which was attached to his wrist, signaling the LeGrand doctor he had been working with to help Mike. He looked over at Triella with wide eyes, "My toragi hasn't been eating lately, and he's been acting strangely. It's why I'm here, to see if maybe he needed a mate. So far, Mike's refused every chance to breed."

Triella's eyes twinkled, "I'd say he just made a choice, sir. To tell the truth, Alice has been a bit quieter than usual, moody too. I thought it was a combination of the games and our guest, but this might be the answer."

Darron began to feel a bit awkward, "Um, I hate to be the one to say it, but even if you're right, which I think you are..."

Triella laughed, her eyes twinkling, "Lieutenant Lazhand getting shy about his toragi's mating choice? You're a bold one, when it's your idea, sir! I know the regs. Breeding toragi pairs can bring on similar feelings in their human companions, requiring both parties to no longer serve within the same unit, even if the humans aren't tangling in bed together."

Darron scowled, "Now wait a pollen, Ensign! I'm not..."

She broke in, "I will remind the Lieutenant that his activities off duty are well known, mainly because he brags about it. Now, I'm not swooning over you, sir, but I really like Mike, and so does Alice. Their needs supersede ours, sir. I'll request a transfer right away. Oh, I'll need your authorization to unlock your house door. We can't keep these two apart, now that they've let us know their intentions. Your place is probably grander than mine, since you are an officer. If you want to get cozy at my place, I hereby authorize you to unlock my door. Naga, please take note of that official statement."

The matronly face of Naga appeared upon the nearest wallscreen behind them, "Your authorization has been noted, Ensign Rank Three Triella Navcomm of Security Sector Police. Congratulations to you both."

Darron was about to protest, but then he noticed the two toragi were still trying to reach each other through the window. He glanced over at Triella, who was smiling at him with laughing eyes. It wasn't that he didn't like her, but he had always kept his sexual activities out of his platoon. He never tangled with Security crew, as a matter of principle. He looked at her anew and realized she was beautiful, her dark golden skin contrasting with deep violet eyes. Her athletic form was in peak condition and from what he knew of her, she wasn't shy about her preferences or her mating habits.

He mumbled to her, "I just don't want to assume anything, Ensign."

She grinned even wider at this statement, "How fucking gallant, sir. I'll go first then, okay? If I could, I'd slam you right here and now, but you're my superior. Once I've got my transfer, you'll discover that I was the one you've been looking for."

Darron shook his head but relinquished his door lock codes to Triella in front of Naga. He kept reminding himself that this was for Mike's benefit, even if he did get some recreation time for himself.

Stellar Sector Wheel, Level Twenty-Three

Chief of Security Jira Mantabe waved Lieutenant Darron Lazhand over to the long, space-black conference table, where William Blain sat alongside his set of guardians, along with Stellar Representative Piero Vandors and a small collection of specialists from varying fields of scientific study. Darron's toragi prowled over to hers and bowed his furry head in submission. This was accepted with a brief lick upon the ear, showing her matronly approval. Tracey was a Higashi toragi, her bold stripes a contrast to Mike's pattern of whirls and circles. Jira looked up at Darron from her seat, "Congratulations, Lieutenant! I've taken it upon myself to request that the breeding council approve Mike's choice of a mate without delay. They were only too happy to oblige. I also received Ensign Navcomm's transfer request and have just approved it. Now, please take a seat next to our guest so we can get our business started."

The Lieutenant did as she asked, as William boldly spoke up, making the Stellar crew over at the far end of the table flinch, "And just what is our business this rotation? Other than the mating rights of your large felines, that is. I'll admit to being fascinated by the fuss you make over them."

Stellar Representative Vandors snarled back, "Without the toragi, you would have discovered a very different Ganges. If you found us at all."

William sighed and leaned back, "I meant no offense. Honestly. In fact, I happen to be Mike's personal plaything, so any information you can give me about the toragi is appreciated."

Naga's matronly face appeared on the spinward wallscreen, "I will remind William Blaine that, as our guest, it behooves him to remain polite."

The Solarian looked over at the AeyAie, "I'm getting used to your look, Naga. I've decided it suits you admirably. Now, please tell me why we're here!"

Darron placed a warning hand upon William's left shoulder as the Stellar representative replied, "We understand you want to become part of the crew, that you claim to be from the Sol System and are willing to share information with us, in exchange for tours of the ship. All of my colleagues here have agreed to keep what is said in this room as classified, only to be shared with the Chief of our Sector. My companions are the leading specialists in physics, biochemistry, micro-engineering, Non-Baryonic Studies and, of course, Kendis technology. We are all here to assess Solarian scientific developments."

William glanced at Jira and scowled. She smiled back at him with a false innocence. Thus far, they had gotten a lot of odd stories and possible fabrications from him with little evidence to support his claims. She was tired of his misdirection and subterfuge. It was time to take him to task and possibly get to the truth. In this chamber, shaped like an obsidian, oblong box, whose walls were heavily shielded wallscreens, were the top minds within Ganges. All of them had been recommended by the Chief of Stellar and Naga-Ma.

Smiling sweetly at him, Jira said, "You've been less than truthful with us. We have discovered your cache of equipment within Engineering Sector. It won't be long before we find your vessel. If there is one."

William rose to his feet and was shoved back into his chair by Darron, with Mike landing upon the Solarian's lap to hold him in place, "You don't know what you're dealing with! Do not touch my pack nor my ship! There are many defenses in place to keep them from being scrutinized!"

Jira coughed into her scarred fist, "We're not stupid, William. I said we found them, not that we seized them. I am curious if we'll find more surprises in the near future."

William's pale face became red, reminding her of a chameleon, "I want my belongings. They must be in my possession for the safety of your crew."

Jira slammed her fist on the tabletop, making everyone in the chamber jump in their seats, "Something you should have thought about when you first entered Ganges! You'll get nothing, until you cooperate fully and answer our questions to our satisfaction! Representative Vandors, you may begin."

Clearing his throat, Piero consulted a data-screen on the tabletop in front of him, "You claim that the Sol System has finally invented a faster-than-light drive. Care to explain how it works?"

William laughed, leaning over Mike's massive shoulders, "I'm not a scientist! I'm just a scout. The Wend Drive isn't really an FTL. It ignores the speed of light by transferring the vessel outside of what we know of as reality. It is not a safe mode of transportation; thus, the Solarian Alliance only uses it for military vessels and trains the crews of those ships to handle the side-effects."

Piero cocked his head to one side, "So, you admit to having a highly trained military, even though you also claim to be a peaceful society. Interesting. What side-effects are you talking about?"

William collapsed into the back of his chair, "You have Security Sector! Are you now claiming that it's not a military organization, because it really looks like one to me! As for what happens to you when you use the Wend, it's hard to explain. You and your vessel are snapped out of the universe, but your information remains intact. You can re-enter the universe at any location if it's mapped out properly, which can take some effort. This was the main reason I was the only scout sent to search for you, because of the serious danger involved. You end up inside another... reality, I guess. It's like a highly vivid dream, but quite visceral. You can die, get injured, and this will translate to your body when you leave the Wend. You experience another reality, from the viewpoint of a native of that other universe. It has something to do with the preservation of information, but I don't really know what that really means. The AeyAies never talk about what they experience, and the Boktahl are hard to understand at the best of times."

One of the other lead scientists leaned over and whispered quietly into the representative's ear. Piero nodded once, "I see. Very interesting. What powers this drive?"

William flicked some stray toragi fur from his left shoulder, "An artificially collapsed singularity. An invention of the Boktahl. They specialize in gravity. It helps that they can see it, like we see light. That is the core power system of my vessel and all the Solarian ships. The rest of my spacecraft isn't crushed because of the opposite-polarity grav-plating surrounding the central power chamber. Matter is fed into the singularity as a maser stream. The output comes from collectors at the edge of the singularity's event horizon, where high-energy particles are sheared away by the micro-tidal forces. If you want the math, I'd have to contact my ship's computer, which requires my pack."

Another scientist placed her slender hand upon the Naga-Port on the side of her head. A chime sounded shortly afterward. The representative looked down at his data-screen and then raised his eyebrows, "And how do you manage the Bose-Einsteinian Condensate required for your maser technology in such a small vessel? It isn't a large ship, from your previous testimony. A one-crew craft, is it?"

William rubbed his face. Jira was fascinated by his reactions. Was he truly so torn about revealing the secrets of his society of origin? His fear seemed palpable, his reluctance openly displayed. The Solarian eventually answered in a quiet voice, "We use nanites. Microscopic machines. The only ones you've seen so far are those in my bloodstream. We use them for a lot more than health, though I'm beginning to appreciate what your people can do with genetics and bio-systems. Micro-technology was easier to maintain after the collapse of the Terran Conglomerate. Most humans think nothing about getting new mechanical systems implanted within their bodies, but we also use them for a wide variety of applications, including damage repair to our vessels and orbitals. The latest uses include clothing that protects the wearer and repairs itself. Hell, we even use them for games! Entertainment! Um, may I ask a quick question? What is Kendis technology? I keep hearing references to it, usually in a subdued manner."

Representative Vandors frowned at him from the far end of the table, "That is highly classified information. As you have no rank within our society, you do not have access to that level of knowledge. Such information could be dangerous, not only for us but for yourself."

Jira raised her gauntleted hand, "I think I can explain just a little bit, as Chief of Security. Think of it as a show of good faith. William, you've already seen some examples of Kendis Technology, the hull plating and our toragi."

She noticed William shrinking further back into his seat, staring at Mike in his lap, "Oh. That's a bit strange, as they seem to be unrelated. Thank you."

Jira wondered at his response. William had gone from being animated to highly reserved. The toragi troubled him. That much had been obvious for rotations. Now he seemed cowed by her revelation that other forms of their technology were also considered to be "Kendis" derivatives. For once, he seemed frightened, and she wasn't sure if this was a good thing or not.

Stellar Sector Wheel, Level One

Stellar Ensign Rank Three Crinn Spanglo glowered down at his main control boards. Nothing he did cleared up any of the aberrant readings he was getting from the observations of System Forty-One. Impossible scenarios ran through his head like acrobats in low gravity. His director was demanding answers, and the Bridge had been pressuring his crew for any explanations concerning the exotic nature of the heliopause they had entered through. Crinn was certain that there was a reasonable answer for everything, but he was swiftly running out of ideas to test. Any notion that came to him which might resolve the errors he was glaring at also had to be verifiable. If he couldn't set up a reliable way to test out his theories, he might as well not even mention his ideas.

Two other members of his observation analysis group were hard at work, attempting to resolve multiple anomalies and running a long series of diagnostics to check their equipment. Any data coming from active sensors were not only filled with errors, they were full of contradictory ones. Using lidar to track an asteroid within the system made it seem like they were looking at entirely different objects from one moment to the next, with differing data discrepancies each and every time. Taking the same asteroid and observing it with only the passive sensors revealed the same information with every pass. He felt as if he were going mad. Collating the data from different sources made a total mess of the overall picture. An object moving relative to its star shouldn't appear as if it was made of liquid according to one sensor, bare rock in another, and then displaying the properties of a plasma gas in a third. It was physically impossible. Either every sensor in Ganges was completely broken, or they had accidentally entered another dimension where the laws of reality were altered.

Needless to say, this was not an acceptable conclusion in a scientific report to his superiors. While the heliopause had seemed a bit dense compared to others they had entered in the past, it didn't explain the highly violent response to their entry. Ganges was beautifully designed for system incursions, with hardened equipment and a number of safety measures to prevent shocks and destructive energies from entering the hull. The only thing in Stellar System Forty-One that made any sense was gravity, though the mass spectrometers were still behaving in a glitchy manner. They had been forced to use pre-spaceflight methods to gain any insight into the nature of the gravity well they had entered. This was imprecise, which made Crinn very angry.

To top everything off, even the passive sensors, such as the visible light telescopes, gave them a strange set of readings. He had also checked the database of stellar systems within his Sector's archives and found nothing that could compare to what they were seeing at this location. Every planet orbiting Star Forty-One was swirling around it in a perfectly circular pathway. There was a large and dense Oort Cloud, but beyond that there was no debris to be detected between planets. Every asteroid they had checked on was clean, as if scoured by a storm of impossible magnitude. Ejections from the star itself were ruled out, because anything that might scrub the asteroids of dust would have shattered the rocky bodies into gravel. This was enough to make Crinn tear his hair out in frustration.

Every planet was perfectly aligned upon the ecliptic plane, which had no tilt. The star itself was balanced with precision at its poles. No wobbles, no axial tilt, no discrepancies. The natural satellites of the gas giants within the system were equally precise in their orbits. Some of the other observation teams had submitted some wild hypotheses such as: nearby rogue black holes, hyper-dense spacetime patterns for this region of the galaxy and other, more exotic suppositions. None of these could be proven true. All of them were found to be unacceptable to the Bridge. The Chief of Stellar Sector had been forced to demand that all theories concerning the anomalous readings had to be backed up by hard evidence. This was an impossible goal for an insane situation.

Crinn got up from his station and left his lab. There was only one thing he could do right now. He stalked the dark, carpeted halls of Stellar, ignoring the displays boasting the inventions and triumphs of his Sector. Some crew felt that Stellar was more like a museum than anything else, and he was forced to agree. It certainly seemed to be designed in that manner. Low lighting, save for the displays, spotlights glaring down at antique machines or the wallscreens displaying images of famous experiments, researchers and major discoveries. After the Awakening, much of their scientific knowledge had been destroyed, save for what had been contained within Naga's mind, and even parts of that had been heavily classified and censored. Stellar had been forced to reinvent the gear, sometimes literally. Then there was the black-eye to their reputation from the Crucible. Stellar had changed since then, but the rest of the crew still found reasons to distrust them. It was almost enough to make him consider requesting a transfer to Engineering.

Crinn shook off his maudlin musings and entered a lift, which opened as he approached. He stepped inside and looked up, "Thank you, Naga. Level Ten if you please."

The doors snapped shut, and the elevator moved with speed. He grabbed a gold handrail for support as the AeyAie asked, "What is your specific destination, Ensign Crinn Spanglo?"

He sighed and then replied, "I need to see the Chief right away. She needs to hear what I've got to say, without any politics getting involved. If I write a report, it will be shuffled into someone else's desk, never to be seen again."

Naga replied, "Stellar Chief Fria Maglator is not in her office. I shall redirect you to her location. Please prepare for emergency speed."

Crinn cried out, "Woah, now! Hang on a pollen!"

The lift changed its speed, shooting off toward midships, squashing him to the floor. He clung to the handrail as best he could, heart hammering in his chest. Crinn had never experienced this sort of maneuver, except once, during his Basic Crew Training. He hadn't liked it then; he didn't like it now. When the lift stopped, he was thrown from the floor. The doors swept open at level Ninety-One. The lower apparent gravity allowed him to regain his footing with just a little bruise to his ego. He loped out into a narrow corridor, only five meters wide. Just a short distance away, he could see Chief Maglator speaking with a group of technicians. There were few wallscreens here, just every twenty meters. The rest of the corridor was filled with cable clusters, machinery and bare metal decking. He raced over to her, panting with exertion. By the time he got to her, everyone was silent and staring at him. Crinn saluted in the Stellar manner, swinging his right palm to his brow, "Pardon me, Chief. I need to speak with you concerning the problem with the sensors."

Chief Fria Maglator raised an eyebrow at him, "You couldn't bring this to your director, Ensign?"

Crinn felt the blood rush to his face, "My apologies, Chief, but we don't have the time to wait for next sowing's meeting if you catch my vector."

She handed a data-pad to one of the others and faced him directly, "Why not, Ensign? Please explain."

Crinn felt himself beginning to sweat, "There's one rocky planet at the very outskirts of the system, Chief. If we're going to recalibrate the sensors, we need to be able to study one object from a closer flight path. Right now, we'll swing by it from too far a distance to really get any meaningful results. I am proposing a fly-by. Just a single orbit to compare results from the passive and active sensors, bringing them into alignment. If we don't change course now, we might still be having issues with malfunctioning equipment or be under the influence of whatever is affecting them. Either way, we'd be heading to the target planet blind. I just feel that might be a really bad idea, Chief."

Chief Fria Maglator closed her eyes for a few pollen-slivers, her Naga-Port blinking. When she opened them again, she nodded to him, "Naga agrees this is the best course of action. I shall present it to the Captain right away. Well done, Ensign Spanglo. You might have just earned a bonus this rotation."

Crinn almost collapsed to the deck in relief. If they couldn't properly align all the sensors, they would be taking a severe risk with any flight path they chose. He only hoped the Captain would agree with his plan.

Residence Wheel One, Level Two

Knight Pelor Guardhand rolled his eyes but kept his mouth firmly shut, as the young man behind him got smacked in the face by yet another tree branch he hadn't noticed. Instead, he tried to lead by example, just as he'd been doing since work-slice had begun. As the eldest of the Knights who were assigned to the forests of Residence Wheel One, Pelor was often forced to teach and guide the newest members of their ancient order of guardians. Moving his lance in a circular motion, he brushed away the next hazard his student might encounter, rolling his aching hips in the saddle of his steed, Rosstan. Knight Linssa Mekand, the Security Baroness of his keep, had assured Pelor that the youngster following him this rotation had gone through his formal recruit training, which had been specialized for his current duties – patrolling the woodlands on horseback. From what he had seen of the young Squire's riding skills, the instructors had forgotten some basic requirements of this honorable, if lonely, post of duty.

Pelor gave his toragi a quizzical look and a twitch of his gray-haired head, sending his feline companion to aid the new blood behind them. Larry huffed in indignation but bounded off nonetheless. The old Knight shook the reigns once, bringing his horse to a halt at the edge of a small glade filled with dazzling wildflowers and a flock of geese, which honked wildly at him in territorial defensiveness. Pelor's stomach rumbled, but he would be dining at the keep this rotation, which he thought a pity. Unlike hikers and other vacationing crew, the Knights, like the hermits, were permitted to forage for their own victuals within the nature preserves, as they were seldom anywhere near a food dispenser for sowings at a time. So long as they kept such activities to cover their survival needs, they could take their fill of local game. Sport hunting had always been strictly forbidden within Ganges.

A heavy crashing in the woods behind him made the flock react in alarm, the ruckus echoing through the small valley they were traversing. Pelor looked back, only to find his ward struggling with his lance, which had gotten caught in a thorn bush, "Stop at once, Squire Naldo! Extract thy spear properly, or you might break it with such twists and turns! Perhaps the training staff at Security were impressed enough to pass thee into my care, but I cannot see how they managed to do so with a straight face!"

The young man struggled to control his mount, while attempting to extract his lance, "Apologies, Knight Guardhand! I'll do better next time!"

Pelor's eyes grew hard from under the brim of his open-faced helm, "I see that ye require further correction, Squire Naldo! During thy training under mine own hand, thou shalt speak in the manner of our order's honored ancestors! The further from proper grace thine inept skills fall, the greater my demand for full formality shall rise. Tis a simple mathematics, even for thee!"

Squire Korgan Naldo pulled his lance free, only to startle his mount, causing it to rear on its hind legs, smacking yet another branch upon the head of the young Security crew. Larry had rounded up the recruits' toragi, named Ben, and they both watched the scene from a few meters away, tails swishing in fascination. Korgan cried out in pain, yet still remembered to answer, "My most heartfelt apologies, Knight Guardhand, for my lack of grace! I do promise thee that thine instructions unto me shall not be wasted! This I do swear!"

Pelor grunted in response, then turned back to face the glade. Most of the geese were now at the far side, glaring over at the human intruders. The Knights of Ganges had retained their ancient, private language, for both instructional purposes and to provide a code which few in Ganges could understand. It was imperative that Squire Naldo practice this special form of speech if he were ever to become a Knight and have his own region of the nature preserves to patrol. If he couldn't manage to hone his skills, the youngster would be sent right back to Security headquarters in disgrace. If that were the case, Pelor would then be called in to answer an endless stream of tiresome questions. Didn't this young fool realize his instructor's peril? Bored to death at the hands of Investigation Services?

Finally, Squire Naldo arrived at his side, covered in leaf debris and sweat. Pelor handed him his canteen, for which the young man thanked him most urgently. Pelor forced himself to twitch a smile, "How is it that thou hast come to our beloved keep without appropriate riding skills for rough terrain?"

The Squire bowed his head in deep embarrassment, "I cannot say, Knight Guardhand, save that hedge mazes and obstacle courses cannot compare to the base trickery of nature, sir. Mine own experiences of the forests, while vast, have all been afoot. A perilous error which I have need for correcting with all speed, sir."

Pelor's smile became genuine, "Huzzah, young crew. Thou hast the right of it. Perhaps there be hope for thy skills after all. Come now, tell an old man why thou hast chosen to serve in the Knights of Ganges."

Squire Naldo removed his helm and shook off bits of leaf, "As a novice, my feet often took me to the tree line of my old community, sir Knight. T'was where I spent most of my time after studies. The call of Agro was also strong for me, but mine heart was set upon protecting this great wonder we call the nature preserves. I wish to serve all life, sir. Not just a few crew in need here and there."

Pelor cleared his throat, "Hither and yonder."

Squire Naldo ducked in his saddle as if flinching from a blow to his head, "Apologies, Knight Guardhand. Aye, hither and yonder. Foresooth, I had oft heard rumors that the perils found within the bosom of these lands could affect all of Ganges itself. Dark tales of vile knaves, collecting themselves for greater barbarity which may compromise the safety of all the faire communities within our Residence Wheel One. Here, I thought, would be the best place to test my valor. To serve the highest cause."

Knight Guardhand sighed, "The rumors which have infected thine ears are true, young Squire. The varlets gather here within the wilds to evade the gaze of Holy Naga. They act like kingdoms, claiming supremacy over tracts of land in which no sane crew would venture, yet that is precisely the errand which we Knights must perform. Why, just last spiral, they brazenly laid siege to Keep Thomas, slaying four Knights before being beaten back through the arms of reinforcements to our cause. Two were old friends of mine. One I had trained, just as it is my honor to teach thy solid pate. Mostly, ours be a lonely path, and thus we must learn how to survive."

Squire Naldo sat up straighter in his saddle, "Aye, Sir Knight. Ye have my thanks for thy patience. Thy teachings shall not be spent unwisely."

Pelor grunted at this assertion, then kicked his steed into a gallop. He roared at the remaining geese, who had no choice but to break into panicked flight. The Squire followed him, shouting a wordless cry of enthusiasm. The Knight hoped that his student learned quickly. Things were coming to a head in the forest. Keen skills and instincts were required to live past the storm that was approaching. There was no time for slow learners and soft teaching styles.

Residence Wheel Two, Level Ten

Harbor Ensign Jero Coreline was singing loudly in the central market of the Builder's Grotto community, easily attracting the attention of several crew who were shopping at chore-slice. He was sore and tired from a long rotation at his post, which had been busier than expected. Since the Security Games had come to a close, Jero had thought that things might settle down a little bit, but the opposite had occurred. Instead, the number of emergency drills had almost doubled. Half the fleet had been deployed in a defensive formation around Ganges, with entire squadrons of fighter-pods taking turns with covering reconnaissance, support and secretive missions in the endless dark of space. Lieutenant Tarn Vekkor had volunteered for extra duty, dragging his squadron with him into the deeps. This meant Jero had been assigned extra duties, as all the docking bay crews scrambled to handle the sudden influx of materials and vessels to service, sending them back out into space in swift cycles that were never fast enough for the liking of the Security harbor officers.

No one knew the reason why this unforeseen increase in activity had been initiated, but rumor had it that the call for such measures came directly from the Chief of Security herself. Jero had nothing but great admiration for Chief Mantabe, but he wondered what was forcing her to drive her crew so hard. Was there something wrong with System Forty-One? Was Ganges in danger? A few harvests ago, he had heard that the greatest threat to the ship was the growing power and abilities of a handful of criminal organizations. If they were the main cause of all the ruckus within Security Sector, why spend such immense resources on the fleet? Weren't the crime lords on the inside of the ship? Jero worried that, like the mutineers of ancient history, the big-shot criminal gangs had created a secret space fleet of their own, but how would they do this? Then again, during the Crucible, it was noted that the enemies of the Holy Mission had achieved impossible feats of cunning and engineering to threaten the natural order of things. Had this occurred once more? Where would they get the steel from? Did they have spies and allies within Security itself?

A sudden, sharp pain to his face snapped Jero out of his tumbling thoughts. He gasped aloud and found his mate, Scratch, standing in front of him with her fists on her hips. He gulped some air and asked, "What? Why'd you hit me?"

She looked up at him, her lop-sided rat mask revealing a rounded cheek above her dimpled chin, "You stopped singing! That means you've got a bad case of head-twirls. Stay with me, Jero! We've got all these shitty waist sashes to sell. I don't need you spacing-out like that right now."

He shook his head and rubbed his jaw, "Sorry, love. Lot's been going on at my post. I get worried about it, like this rush-slice, when I first got there, there was this guy with strange yellow hair looking at the manifest boards, and I thought, well, maybe he's an inspector, but he wasn't wearing a uniform, which I know isn't against regulations…"

Smack! Jero found himself facing spinward. He turned back to look at his mate, "Thank you, babe. Sorry."

Scratch pulled out a small flask from her green robe. It was full of her favorite intoxicant-beverage, the Strifer original called "WhoTheFuckKnows". She took a long pull from the container and sighed, "You're gonna drive me sane, Jero. Now, back to singing for our customers so we can make a few chips before we go somewhere to eat. Cheesy?"

He smiled down at her with love-filled eyes, "Extra cheesy, sweetie."

She smacked his bottom on the way back to their market stall where they sold the custom waist sashes she made, which meant she wasn't angry with him and promised a lovely finish to dark-slice. Jero tapped his datapad and held his wrist out from his body. A small, reflective bubble of holographic field energies revealed his own face grinning at him. He said, "Naga, please broadcast from this device."

The face of Naga-Ma briefly flashed onto the sphere, giving him a wink and a smile. Jero's grin stretched wider as he began to sing, "Welcome good crew! I'm always here for you. Making some chips this rotation, a waist sash for every occasion! My lovely mate, Scratch, has made every batch. No two are the same, which is part of their fame. From a beautiful flower, to gloomy and dour, whatever you need, we'll make it with speed!"

He danced over to their booth, which had an old, fringed coverlet tossed upon a coffee table, with two wireframe stands at each end displaying a number of waist sashes. Still singing aloud, he pointed out a few of his favorites to his broadcast audience, hoping one of them might purchase one. It helped that he had an audience from the singing competitions he had participated in, plus the live broadcasts from his old docking bay duties. Over fifteen thousand crew kept a regular watch of his transmissions, which really wasn't too bad, when you considered every crewmember aboard had their own channel from birth. It was something they could have done as a culture from the very beginning, but the idea had held little appeal for octennia. The change had started just a few octuries ago, as a means of countering a rash of horrid kidnappings by leftover mutineers. The thinking at the time was that, if everyone was watching everybody else, the criminals wouldn't have much of a chance to snatch crew.

Such problems were rare at this point in time, but the new tradition had continued. Many of the crew felt that it had provided a way for everyone to be much closer, making Ganges like an extended family. For the Age of Redemption, it was a tantalizing idea that just refused to go away. With Naga acting as sole moderator, things ran pretty smoothly. The news broadcasts still existed, but they now competed on a grander scale than ever before. They were one voice amongst sixty million, so if they wanted a large audience, they had to provide programming that was more interesting and important than the general population could produce as individuals. Sometimes it worked, other times not so much.

Jero noticed some crew walking up to their booth. One was a regular, who always had a new color or design he wanted for special functions. Another seemed shy at first, but then boldly asked Scratch the price of a bright green waist sash with little, copper cheese slices dangling from the fringe. Jero remained singing while he talked over details with the frequent buyer, as his mate assisted the newcomer. They always made a comfortable number of chips every sowing. They weren't wealthy by any means, but they could afford some extras, in terms of leisure activities and dining. They also did well at their posts, which provided bonuses, such as their comfortable quarters in a solid community.

He wanted novices, as did she, but they had promised themselves to wait until Ganges had achieved a stable orbit at the upcoming planet. This was swiftly approaching, and if he wanted everything to be perfect, he would have to maximize his efficiency, both at his post and in selling sashes for chips. Scratch was right, he had to stay focused on one task at a time or drown in his own head's wanderings.

Jero forced himself to push everything that bothered him at his duty station away, to concentrate on singing his way to being ready to start a family with his beloved mate.

Command Hub, Level Nineteen

Executive Officer Wasp Tornpage lounged back in her seat, on the right of Captain Fieldscan's. Nine others were present in the well-appointed chamber, all of them at their assigned places, in chairs which displayed the colors of their Sector. This room was the official mediation center of Command. Its location was kept secret, save for Naga, the various Sector Chiefs and those few staff who maintained it. As the Executive Officer, it was her domain, its personnel under her strict guidance. The wallscreens were hardwired to a particular processor found deep midships within the Command Hub, the outer walls of the grand chamber were surrounded by a series of bulkheads stuffed with soundproofing, and it could only be accessed by a series of airlocks, none of which had any automatic controls. Beyond these defenses were Command's testing stations, communications and practice rooms for public speaking and broadcasts. These made enough electromagnetic noise to drown out any stray signal emanations from the meeting chamber itself and provide cover from unwanted listeners. All access points had Strifer-styled traps, in case anyone tried to break in, from sprays of lurid paint to shunts which opened from the lavatory collection pods. Anyone who tampered with the meeting chamber's systems would find themselves highly noticeable, camo-suits or not.

She gazed about the room with one desire in her heart – that she had been permitted to bring her marshmallow gun to the proceedings. All of the Sector Chiefs were present, and some bickering had broken out before the Captain had been able to commence the meeting. Agro Chief Tala Cyclehand was glaring at Provision Chief Grala Hatchrail, who was pretending to ignore her. Harbor Chief Vekku Rollack was looking impatiently about, as if seeking another exit that didn't exist. Stellar Chief Fria Maglator was staring at Vekku with ill-disguised anger after an ugly shouting match. A few of the others knew how to behave in a dignified manner, such as Technology Sector Chief Eagle Lund and Security Chief Jira Mantabe. The others just looked like they were waiting for a fight to break out.

Captain Fieldscan gave her a nod, so Wasp got to her feet and rapped the table with her knuckles, "If we're all done with the novice behavior and can act like the professionals we're supposed to be, I'd like to begin this session. As tradition demands, Captain Perrin Fieldscan shall hereby preside over this meeting. As the keeper of protocol, I remind you all that breeches in the regulations governing this chamber shall be dealt with commensurate with the offense. Try my patience, and you shall feel my teeth in your necks. Captain Fieldscan, the floor is yours."

She sat back down and shifted her eyes from one face to another. A few refused to meet her gaze. Her lips twitched a swift, lopsided smile. Some were still getting used to her style as Executive Officer, despite her being at her current post for a few spirals now. Perhaps some of the nervous ones were remembering the last time she had to intervene because of their poor behavior. The Strifer broadcasts had publicly spread the most vicious rumors they could dream up concerning the Chief of Planetary, until he apologized to Wasp in private. The embarrassment caused by the scandalous reports had been severe, but the raging news storm disappeared as swiftly as it had erupted, right after Wasp accepted the promise from Lorvar to never speak in that manner in front of the Captain ever again.

Perrin rose to his feet, "Thank you, Wasp. This is not the time for any divisive behavior. While we may speak with informality, a civil tongue works best, agreed?"

Wasp noticed that Jira was glaring around, as if daring anyone to disagree with the Captain's demand for decorum. It was nice to have an ally who could slam someone's head through the deck. The Chief of Security didn't have her toragi with her. Tracey was now stationed at the first airlock which led to this chamber, as a guardian. Tech Chief Lund bowed his head with his usual calm expression, his Naga-Port gleaming at the left side of his half-shaved cranium, "I second the Captain's decree. We must work together in harmony, for the sake of Mother Ganges."

Technically, Naga could appear on the wallscreens at any time but never did so within this chamber. As a result, the rest of the Chiefs took Eagle Lund's words as coming from the AeyAie itself. Wasp's lips flashed a smile. None of the big-wigs here wanted to piss-off mama Naga. Sometimes she felt that the unmasked crew acted like students clinging to their mother's uniform. Eagle Lund used this to his advantage, which happened to coincide with Captain Fieldscan's requirements. It was often said that in the Age of Redemption, a triad of power had formed from a deep alliance involving Command, Security and Technology Sectors. At the same time, no love was lost between Provision and its parent, Stellar, who still rubbed Planetary in uncomfortable ways. Agro could still flex its political muscles, which wasn't appreciated by Harbor and Engineering. Medical remained unsullied by such maneuvering, though Wasp always kept a sharp eye on them in any case. Too much innocence could be abused in terrifying ways.

Captain Fieldscan continued, "Thank you, Chief Lund. Now then, the matter at hand. As we are preparing for orbital insertion around Planet Forty-One, I thought this a good time to present a request which has merit, before we make adjustments to our course. It has been brought to my attention that our sensors need recalibration following our entry into System Forty-One, and it has been proposed that we use the outermost planet for this purpose. Thus, we need to adjust our heading to make a single orbit around this world in order to assess the condition of our equipment and make whatever repairs, if any, are required. This will delay orbital insertion, but I think we can all agree that without being able to coordinate our sensors, we would be flying blind."

Harbor Chief Rollack slowly raised his hand, then waited for the Captain to acknowledge him before speaking, keeping an eye on Wasp, "Our fleet have found no discrepancies in their own sensors, save for long-range readings. We've tested everything we have on Ganges itself, but when we try to collate the data we receive from any object within System Forty-One, there are always errors and discrepancies. I submit, Captain, that our sensors are fine, but the matter in this stellar system is not what it appears to be."

Stellar Chief Maglator responded, "My crew have looked into your results, Vekku, and we remain convinced that a closer look is in order before we settle into orbit at Planet Forty-One. There may be some truth in your supposition, but would it not be more prudent to test our theories with a subject closer to hand before venturing deeper into the unknown?"

Planetary Chief Sedders shook his head theatrically, "Are we talking about delaying the Holy Mission because of some minor sensor anomalies?"

Wasp was about to get to her feet when Security Chief Jira Mantabe broke in quietly, "Are we in such a rush, Lorvar? Can't wait a few rotations more? I think the Captain's suggestion is quite prudent, and I agree with the cautious course which he and Fria propose. My Sector has its own set of concerns, and we would appreciate the extra time to gain our footing."

Captain Fieldscan raised his hand before any more of the participants could speak, "I have taken this situation up with Naga, who supports a more measured approach. This is not a debate. As Captain, with the blessings of the Judiciary Council and the AeyAie, I hereby state that we will be heading to the outermost planet to perform some tests which may or may not resolve our current conundrum with the sensors. It is my intention that we use the flyby to help in slowing us further to reach orbital insertion speed. In this way, we may circumvent the necessity of using all the gas giants, concentrating solely upon the largest planet to shed our velocity to an appropriate level. Once we have ascertained the nature of the anomalies which have plagued our sensors, we may then choose whether or not this system is suitable for terraforming. I expect nothing less than total compliance from all the Sectors in this endeavor. That is all. Dismissed."

Wasp watched the others as they rose from their seats. Jira and Eagle were the steadiest in their bearing. She knew that the Captain had wanted to introduce the issue of William Blaine to the others but had been overruled by the Judiciary Council, who maintained that the Solarian remain a classified entity until more information had been gained through continued interrogation. Thus, the Agro, Provision, Harbor and

Planetary Chiefs still had no knowledge of their guest's existence. Wasp had tried to change the minds of the highest court twice, to no avail. She was concerned that when word did get out, as it would eventually, the situation could erupt into chaos. Fortunately, Captain Fieldscan would not be blamed for keeping the Solarian visitor secret, but the only recourse the Sector Chiefs might have would be to change their Judiciary representation in the middle of a potential fiasco.

CHAPTER EIGHT

Wheel Rotation - Launch Sowing - Mission Harvest - Spiral 5620

"Some of my friends and I were over at our favorite club last dark-slice, you know, The Dormouse. We were doing the usual: dancing, getting floaty, looking for tangle-mates. Then a pile of off-duty Security crew on leave show up with their toragi, and suddenly we become invisible! The big cats are major mate-magnets to begin with, and it's already hard enough to compete with the over-muscled athletes as it is! It's so unfair! I want to hate them, but I just can't! I gotta admit, I want to tangle with them as much as everyone else does. Who wouldn't? My aunt Lavia calls them 'Hero-Sector', and all you can do is join them or leave whatever club you're at when they arrive, just to have a chance to be noticed."
Pinto Lang, Stellar Sector Observatory Technician, Rank Three, personal log, P39

Residence Wheel Two, Level Five

Lieutenant Darron Lazhand was jogging on a local road in the pale light of dawn-slice, which was his habit, before hitting the community bath, then heading to his Sector. His toragi, Mike, was padding along five meters ahead, sniffing the air in a relaxed manner. It was good to see the big cat so at ease. Darron and his guardian always took a five-kilometer route through his neighborhood, before cleaning up and grabbing some breakfast. They stopped now and again to say hello to the students getting themselves ready with their families for another rotation of duty to Ganges. The youngsters loved their dawn-slice greeting with Mike. The big cat galvanized their spirits in a way that Darron remembered from his own childhood. Even when he had been Student Rank Thirteen, an age when being seen with one's parents was an odious thing, he had always rushed out of his quarters to greet the local toragi and Security officer.

Darron's mind wandered, as he trekked along the forest-lined road of his section of the Boulder Field Community. Both single and multiple family houses were clustered every fifty meters, between which were stately trees and giant rocks, made from ancient asteroids from multiple stellar systems. Everyone on his jogging route knew him and sometimes stopped whatever they were doing to share their greetings. Eventually, the road led to the very center of the community, where a large, rocky lake was used as a public bathing area. Its water was refreshed through the pipelines underneath the deck, the bottom smoothed out by octuries of erosion. A marketplace ringed the entire lake, with colorful stalls and carts, with a few areas for public seating and entertainments. A tram station was located on the spinward side of the market, which he used to get to his post.

His mind brought him to his new mate, Triella Navcomm, and though they hadn't made anything official, they both seemed to be cohabitating easily enough, despite their differences. It helped that they had worked together in the same platoon for several spirals. They knew each other's habits and even shared some marks of their service – they both had a prosthetic leg, having lost their natural ones in the line of duty. He respected Triella, and the feeling was mutual. Darron considered her a friend and compatriot. Now they were living under the same roof, for the sake of Mike and Alice. At first, he had resisted accepting the Rank Three Ensign as a tanglemate, fearing that an awkwardness might develop which could severely compromise their friendship. It didn't take her very long to convince him otherwise. Their current relationship had no expectations, and yet they found themselves growing closer every rotation.

Darron's reverie was cut short by a familiar voice, "You do this every dawn-slice? I can see why. It's a nice place."

Darron stopped in his tracks and swirled about, only to find William Blaine standing next to him. The Solarian guest was wearing his usual, gray jumpsuit, given to him by Security, his odd, bright yellow hair weaving around on its own. Mike turned about sharply and roared aggressively. Darron shouted, "What the fuck are you doing here? How the hell did you get out of your quarters? Who authorized your release?"

Mike snarled and hissed, scraping at the road with his steel-shod claws. William held up his hands as if surrendering, "Hey now! I haven't left anything! I'm still there! It's my job to observe as much of Ganges as I can. To learn about your crew and their culture. How can I do that staring at a cell wall?"

Darron made a move to grab the Solarian's arm, but his hand passed right through their guest's limb. Mike roared again, then leapt directly through William's chest, landing heavily behind him. The Solarian placed a finger against his pale lips, "Quiet, you two! This ruckus might attract attention! I'm supposed to be classified, remember?"

Darron growled, "What kind of trick is this?"

The Solarian sighed, "What you're seeing is a hologram. You know, the kind that you use for entertainment and instruction? You've been herding me around for sowings. My nanites wanted to give me a closer view of ordinary life aboard Ganges, so some of them stowed themselves aboard your body. No harm was done, I swear it. Sometimes I lose nanites when skin cells rub off me. Normally, I'd just collect them back to my body, but I'm curious."

Darron ground his teeth together in anger, "How many of these things do you have floating about the fucking ship?"

William shrugged, "A few hundred, no more than that."

Darron was about to use his comm-bead to call Security when someone he knew came around a bend in the road, "Good rotation, officer Lazhand! Heading to the baths?"

Darron did his very best to control his face, "Yeah, Tando. That's where I'm heading, as usual."

The man smiled as he jogged closer, "So, who's your friend there? I hope I'm not interrupting anything. Welcome to Boulder Field, crew! I'm Tando Commline. I live a few doors down from Darron, here."

William grinned, "You have a gorgeous neighborhood. I was just stopping by to give Darron some information."

Tando nodded his head and put a finger to the side of his nose, "Ah! I see! A business call, eh? Well, never mind me. I don't want to interfere in any Security matters. Good to meet you. Darron, go get 'em!"

The neighbor waved at them and jogged off. Darron looked over at William who raised a thin eyebrow at him, "See? I'm cooperating. Trust me. I've done this sort of thing at every planet your crew terraformed. I know what I'm doing. It's my job."

Darron rubbed at his head in frustration, mussing his long, black hair, "No, you don't. Not even close. Everywhere you've been isn't run by a single crew with a serious mission. If I hadn't been here with you, he might have reported sighting you to Security Sector or to his supervisor at his post. Your hair alone is worthy of being recorded on a datapad, never mind your pale complexion or weird accent. You look wrong, smell wrong. You even walk wrong."

William shook his head, "Please. Let's test that theory."

The Solarian started jogging ahead, making both Mike and Darron scramble to catch up with him. When they had reached his side, a family was just exiting their home, preparing to head over to the bath-lake. Two students ran over and squealed with delight, wrapping their arms around Mike's neck, causing the toragi to stop and accept their affection. The parents waved at Darron, smiling warmly. One of the students looked over at William in curiosity, "Who's that, officer Lazhand? Is he a friend of yours? He looks weird."

William crouched down, staying out of arms reach, "I'm part of a special unit, crew. I'm supposed to look this way, at least for now."

The child's eyes grew round, "Oh! I thought you were sick."

William looked up at Darron and winked, "That's the idea."

The parents called their children to their side, and the whole family began to walk toward the lake, waving at Darron and Mike as they left. Mike turned his head and growled at William who raised himself back up, "Okay. Okay. I get it. Back to my cell. Sorry, Darron, but my tutor has advised me that I'm pushing my luck. I'll pop off and see you two at rush-slice, okay?"

The Solarian vanished as swiftly as he had arrived. Darron used his datapad to contact Chief Mantabe directly, using a code which signified that his message concerned their guest. He closed his eyes briefly; Jira was going to be pissed when she heard his full report. The Solarian was spreading nanites throughout Ganges, and no one had noticed it was going on, not even Naga-Ma. This was a frightening development. It proved that Solarian technology was far ahead of theirs in a number of dangerous areas. He was tempted to hurry over to his Sector, but Triella and Alice were waiting for them at the lake. He sent another message to the Commander of Investigations about what had just occurred. His notifications would begin a lockdown of Security Sector and warn the crew guarding William's chamber about this incident. Naga would also read the messages, of course, and thus be aware of the situation. They had to get a handle on the Solarian's abilities before they caused a disaster.

Residence Wheel Two, Level Three

Spat Newstain sat in his Student Rank Seven classroom, just waiting for a special presentation to be shown on the wallscreen behind his teacher, an old man who had once been a Harbor Director of Docking Bays. Retired Officer Logossom wasn't a bad sort, just overly serious, in Spat's opinion. He was fair-minded and open to new ideas if you could demonstrate their merit. In this, he was typical of most teachers, though there were a few others who were just stubborn and pedantic. None of them were ever verbally abusive, something which grated on Spat's nerves. How were the students supposed to learn about real life without getting stepped on a few times?

Right now, teacher Logossom was droning on about how a ship like Ganges enters a new system, the safety protocols involved and all the proper procedures for reporting any hazards and anomalies. Spat's mind was still on the stranger he had noticed at the Security Games. His cousins at the Rat's Ass Community had tried to bypass the security measures which had redacted the man's face in every image that they could find of him. None of their attempts had succeeded. Eventually, they had received a message from Technology Sector, warning them to cease and desist their attempts to gain a clear picture of the odd crewman. Their equipment had shut itself down shortly afterward, along with both of the wallscreens they were using as interfaces.

Naga had contacted all of them, stating that the man in question was part of a Security initiative of importance, and thus his identity was highly classified. The AeyAie had gone on to warn them that breaking into the Security files was severely prohibited and that the potential for harm was grave. As all Strifers knew, once Naga got itself involved, it was best to back off. Any continued defiance might be seen by Security as hazardous to the AeyAie, a leftover from the Crucible. Spat hated dead ends, but what could he do? His cousins had caved in right away, and he was left with nothing but a stern lecture from his parents, who were still trying to act like the unmasked. Since when was curiosity a crime?

He had tried to get some information at the school library, pretending to need some time to himself because Bino had called him a creep and his feelings were hurt. The simpering teachers and the gullible librarian were all too sympathetic, falling over themselves to assuage his grief. What a bunch of sops! Spat had taken the time to do some research and found that there were other crew members who had also noted the stranger and had tried to ascertain his identity. All of them were frustrated about being blocked so brazenly by Security Sector, but some became afraid due to Naga's involvement. After a few pollen-slivers, all Spat could find were wild conspiracy theories that might be better off used as plotlines for the broadcast entertainments. There had been one crewmember who had seemed a bit more level-headed, but when Spat tried to review their channel, he found it had been shut down. Warning messages bloomed all over his data-screen, and he had been forced to cease his prying.

The thing that made him cease was Naga appearing on his datapad and pleading with him, "Please stop, Spat," the AeyAie had said, "The situation you're interested in is very dangerous. I love the fact that you're clever and curious, but the person you're trying to identify is linked to a serious situation. I would hate to see you inadvertently harmed, by getting involved in something so hazardous. You are not alone in your wish to understand more, but trust me when I say this is not a safe topic to be rummaging through."

He had obeyed the AeyAie, though still unsatisfied. Even so, he had also received an official notice that he had been placed on a "data trespasser" list at Security but was removed from it due to his age and through the mediation of Naga. Now he owed the AeyAie a big favor. It just wasn't fair. Still, his cousins might be impressed that he had been placed on a watch-list for being a troublemaker. At least that part of his data adventures had assuaged his Strifer pride. When he got back to Rat's Ass to visit, he could tell the red robes, with his mask held high, that he was a true part of the Mischief. His parents would be appalled, of course, but the clergy of the Manifesto might be impressed.

Teacher Logossom had finally finished speaking, and the main wallscreen changed, which woke Spat's interest. The view it showed was from the Bridge of Ganges. Captain Fieldscan was standing in front of his command chair, his gold-and-black formal uniform looking perfectly pressed and was glittering with decorations of service. An ancient sword of his office was at his waist, and he stood with one hand resting upon the pommel, revealing his flashtats which were a calm green. Sitting in her chair next to him, Executive Officer Wasp Tornpage caught Spat's eye, as she pointed a strange-looking gun which spat a small, white object at something outside of view. Her tattooed face was lean and beautiful, a headband atop her green hair sporting a pair of giant rat ears. The Captain cleared his throat mildly, making his thin moustache twitch, "Good rotation to all the students of Ganges."

Spat was quite impressed. While he had seen the Captain speak in public addresses before, they had never been solely for the children of the ship. That meant something was up which needed to be shared with even the youngest crew. Wasp half raised herself from her seat and waved a middle finger at the camera with a wide grin on her face.

The Captain rolled his eyes briefly, making the children giggle, "Thank you for that gesture, Executive Officer Tornpage. Now then, let's get to the purpose of this message. Ganges has passed through System Forty-One's heliopause and we are now entering the edge of its planetary zone. The region of stellar winds can be chaotic, and we experienced some plasma turbulence a few rotations ago. This had the unfortunate effect of damaging our active sensors, which are now under repair, thanks to Engineering Sector. Now we must calibrate all our instruments, or we risk flying into System Forty-One blindly.

"We shall take a short detour to the furthest planet from the central star, before we proceed to close in on Planet Forty-One to assess its compatibility with our terraforming process. To do this, we shall need coordinated sensors! The furthest world is a small, rocky body with a mass that is twenty-five percent of Terra's. As we take a single orbit around this lonely little planet, we'll be performing some tests and bringing our sensors back into operation. Once we have finished our task, we shall begin to shed velocity by passing through the gravity field of the largest gas giant in this system, after which we shall begin orbital insertion at Planet Forty-One to begin the Holy Mission."

All the other students sitting around Spat began to mutter quietly amongst themselves, but he remained unusually silent. This was a serious situation, and he wondered if the yellow-haired stranger was involved. Had he somehow disabled the sensors? How would someone accomplish such an incredible feat of sabotage? The Captain continued, "Once we begin our preparations, I have authorized a science vessel to travel back out to the heliopause to study the phenomenon which caused our active sensors to break down. We all know how rumors in our beloved vessel move faster than light, therefore I have decided to speak with you, the students of Ganges, first and foremost. I want you all to keep a sharp eye on how we tackle this situation, to prepare you for the future. Space is filled with unknowns. We must be prepared for other stellar systems to behave in a similar manner. You are the open eyes and minds of Ganges. Study what we adults do, and find new ways to gain further efficiency in our procedures. Learn from our triumphs and mistakes. I am also, as of right now, announcing a student contest. Any youngster, from Student Rank Six to Seventeen, who can come up with new ways to further protect our capward observatories from plasma shocks, will be permitted to be a part of this contest. The winner shall see their plan placed into operation and receive an immediate raise in rank, with a tour of the Ice Cap of Ganges, courtesy of Harbor Sector."

The students around Spat cheered with such volume that he couldn't hear the rest of the Captain's speech. Even Teacher Logossom couldn't calm everyone down fast enough. Not that it mattered too much. The pertinent details were now well known. What bothered Spat the most was everything that had been left unspoken. That Command Sector would turn to students for ideas meant that the other Sectors were having difficulty coming to grips with the situation concerning the sensors. That was something that made his tail twitch and his hair stand on end.

Planetary Sector Wheel, Level Thirty-Four

Atmospherics Commander Ghell Vaclan leaned back in his office chair with a frown crossing his lean face. He was getting reports from his special agents within Security Sector that some kind of secret project was throwing everything off course. The usual shifts had been scrambled. Immense resources had been repurposed. Personnel were moved about without explanation. All of this activity had been placed under the smothering blanket of being classified. This information was unwelcome and concerning. The secretive maneuvering had begun shortly before the Security Games, about the same time in which Knight Pelor Guardhand and the League of Vigilantes had blown open one of his supply caches within the nature preserves of Residence Wheel One.

His hands clenched into fists, his fury translating into tremors. This had to be related to whatever plans the Knights of Security were about to enact to counter his growing takeover of unpopulated territory. There had been no contact from his assassin, and several of his unlawful colleagues had gone dark, refusing to answer his queries or commit enforcers to shore up their illicit holdings. He couldn't blame the cowards. If a large contingent of Security was about to join the Knights in their purge of criminal activity in the nature preserves, he might hesitate as well, save for the fact that his forces were much larger and more complex than those of his rivals. Most of the other rulers of the crime syndicates kept their illicit operations smaller, to keep themselves from being noticed by Naga. Most had holed up in tiny fortresses and rarely left the relative safety of those shelters.

Ghell had gone in a different vector, one that was more flexible and always in motion. He had three bases of operations, none of them close to each other, all of them filled with trusted crew. As a Commander of Planetary Sector's Atmospherics Department, Ghell knew all about how to lead a large and widely dispersed operation. Most of the other crime lords were apparently freaking out over Security's secrecy, certain they would be facing a major push to capture the syndicates. What really concerned Ghell was the timing of it all. With Ganges having made system entry, his duties within Planetary were going to rise exponentially. The Chief of his Sector now wanted him to coordinate with Stellar and Harbor over the concerns about the sensor disruptions.

He felt trapped in his office, which was a change he didn't appreciate. Ghell looked about, critically eyeing the circular, wood-paneled room, with its grand view of the Atmospherics testing region, full of giant trees and rolling plains. From his vantage point, fifty meters above the deck, he could watch the pressure and wind simulations with ease. Ghell's desk was made of artificially petrified redwood. It was curved and broad, with three guest chairs and grass-covered turf for a rug. The spacious chamber included a worktable and data-station, with two wallscreens, both of them displaying the planned changes to the normal routine to accommodate the demands of the Bridge.

Ghell needed a solution, one that wouldn't attract too much attention. Most of the new work required of him could be handled remotely, but every extra task or meeting threatened to bring down his hidden organization through negligence. Was it time to retire from a double life? Could he simply hand over the reins to one of his criminal subordinates and turn his back on spirals worth of investment and struggle? In truth, he loved his post for Ganges, but he also felt the same depth of care for his syndicate. He hated the idea of abandoning either one, but unless he found a way to relieve the building pressure, he would soon find himself in an untenable position. He needed time to shore up his illicit operations and still be able to bring deliverables to his Chief. Failure in either one meant losing both his post and his secret life.

The data-screen mounted into his desktop blinked at him, showing that a request for a private meeting had been delivered. Ghell scowled at the interruption and leaned forward to glare at the name flashing within the holo-sphere. Apparently, Director Dalen Gupta was waiting for him in his reception room. Ghell's first thought was to dismiss the request. Now was not the time for unnecessary meetings. Director Gupta knew his responsibilities and what was expected of him during this time period. Whatever the portly crewman had to say could wait until things settled down.

Ghell was about to inform his receptionist that he was too busy to attend to Dalen's request, but then he hesitated. Was this an opportunity in disguise? Could he use the jovial Director for his own needs?

Ghell cleared his throat and then spoke toward the desk's holo-sphere, "Let Director Gupta know that I'll see him now, so long as he keeps it brief. I have much to do and little time to accomplish my work."

After a seed-sliver, the door to his office opened, and Dalen's jovial voice could be heard, "Thank you, and yes, I'll make sure he gets these right away!"

Ghell suppressed a smile. It was difficult to be angry with the jolly director, whose enthusiasm could be truly infectious. He watched as Dalen sauntered into his office with a grace that belied his bulk, "Ah! Commander Vaclan! Your very efficient receptionist handed me these data-wafers for you to review. Shall I place them on your desk or the workstation?"

Ghell tapped a long finger on his desktop, "Right here would be fine, Dalen. Another load for me to scour my eyes with. I'm surprised they don't bleed at the sight of new reports."

Dalen stared at him in shock, so Ghell waved a hand in the air and said, "Please, Dalen. Have a seat. Don't look so surprised at my grouchiness. I'm quite overworked and terribly tired. I could use a nice distraction, but it has to be quick. I'm only one crew, you know."

Dalen gently lowered himself into a chair he barely fit and placed the data-wafers on the desk, "You need rest, sir. If I may be so bold, I think I have a wonderful distraction for your weary mind. This coming Orbit Rotation, I am planning one of my famous parties, to celebrate system entry, sir. It would delight everyone if you could join us in the festivities."

Ghell's eyebrows rose high upon his forehead. Dalen's lavish soirees were well known in Planetary Sector, complete with live bands, lots of freshly cooked food, contests, holo-presentations and other entertainments. He had been to a few of them and had enjoyed himself immensely. Director Gupta was a natural host, who cared about his guests with embarrassing enthusiasm. Ghell pointed to the two wallscreens in his office, "You see those charts behind you?'

Dalen turned about in his chair and nodded. Ghell touched a button on his desk and the information on the walls scrolled downward, "That is the list of meetings, tasks, inspections and conferences I'm supposed to attend. I'm very sorry, my friend, but I cannot take the time to be at your party, though I truly wish it were otherwise."

Dalen turned back to face Ghell, "That is a terrible load, sir. Is there anything I can do to bring you some respite?"

Ghell allowed himself to collapse into his chair, "Half of those meetings are classified for reasons I can't even begin to imagine. Commander rank and higher only. Most of it is just inter-Sector politics, which I wouldn't wish on any crewmember, let alone someone with your bright spirit. However, may I beg a small favor from you, Dalen? May I tell my mate and students about your party? I would hate for them to miss it on my account."

Dalen almost jumped from his seat in his eagerness, "Of course, sir! It would be an honor to see them!"

Ghell feigned relief, "Thank you, my friend. It would be a great help if you could keep an eye on my family while I'm trawling through the political muck our Chief has loaded on my shoulders. There may be some dark-slices when I will not be able to get away from all this inter-Sector nonsense, and it would ease my mind to know that a good friend is available to help my family during this time of urgency. The Chief wants our Sector ready, and that means revamping the schedule for Atmospherics, testing all the mechanisms, listening to experts drone on all rotation, then wrestling resources before the other Sectors sink their teeth into them."

Dalen pulled his shoulders back and saluted, bringing his left palm to his right shoulder, "I would be honored to assist your beautiful family, sir! You can count on me to keep them well entertained."

Ghell gave the heavy director a genuine grin, "Thank you, Dalen. You are a shining star under my command. Now, I'm afraid that I do have to rush off to Provision Sector headquarters to wrangle with their lab procurement services department. I'll let my mate know that she should expect to hear from you this dark-slice. Ganges only knows when I'll see my family again."

Once Dalen cheerfully left the office with a bounce in his step, Ghell relaxed and nodded to himself. Now he had unwitting help with his timing issue that provided cover for his secret activities. He still had a tremendous amount of work to do for his Sector, but he could take chore and dark-slice for his more nefarious interests. With Dalen providing a distraction for his family, he now had the time to counter the moves being made by Security Sector and save his syndicate from destruction.

Agro Wheel Two, Security Level Five

William Blaine sat in the central chair of the chamber he had been brought to. Three Security crew and their toragis were with him, standing out of reach, evenly spaced at the very edges of the spherical room. The inner walls were made of display screens. The illumination from them was searing and fully immersive. No shadows could be found, for even the floor was lit. William didn't struggle when the Security crew strapped him into place, pinning his arms and legs to the seat he had been shoved into. The apparent gravity at this level was oppressive, and he doubted that he could do anything that couldn't be easily countered by the Police crew who were well used to it. The chamber had an airlock-styled door, with three layers of protection between the chamber and the outer corridor.

He did his best to remain calm, but he knew that he was in real trouble. His nanites were yammering at him, giving him statistics on his guardians, their big cats and the power emanations of the interior of the chamber. They shuffled through the electromagnetic spectrum, Boktahl gravity levels, and shouted their warnings that he was now being scanned through the use of several unusual frequencies of sonics. His access to all of those nanites not upon or within his person were blocked, which meant the room was heavily shielded. Only his entangled link to his vessel remained unaffected, a technology the Ganges crew didn't seem to know about. There were interesting gaps in their abilities, and yet they had advanced in other areas which the Solarian Alliance didn't rely upon as much.

Then there were the frequent references to "Kendis Technology", which still remained a mystery to him. When showed a piece of "Kendis-steel", he had been fascinated by the unusual fractal patterns within the grain structure of the alloy. All of his questions concerning the makeup of the steel had been rebuffed. Some of the Security officers also carried firearms of a design he had never seen, and he had witnessed their abilities during the Security Games. Some of what he had witnessed he couldn't begin to explain. One of the most unusual of the guns was called a Spin-Drive pistol, and he was told these were also Kendis technology. The soles of space boots, the new types of power generators, the unknown plasma conduits, and finally, the toragi themselves, were all some form of Kendis science that he couldn't wrap his brain around. Nor could his internal computer systems. What was the common denominator between these different items? This was a problem he was determined to solve.

William waited in silence, not bothering to interact with any of his guards, sensing they would simply keep their thoughts to themselves. At last, the face of Naga appeared all around him and above, each visage having radically different features, "Having a good rotation, William?"

The Solarian shrugged, "I was, but now I think that'll change."

Naga remained calm, "That depends upon how you choose to respond to my questions. Your attorney is with Security Chief Mantabe, in the observation room, along with two representatives of the Judiciary Council. If you wish to speak with your lawyer before we proceed, you have the right to confirm his presence."

William shook his head, "No. I do trust you, Naga. Besides, lying about my representation for my sentient rights wouldn't be very enlightened. If you've turned from that philosophical path, everyone in Ganges is deep fried, myself included. This meeting is about my nanites, isn't it?"

Naga slowly nodded, "Very perceptive of you, William. You have been busy littering my body with unauthorized technology. Care to explain yourself?"

William's lower back was beginning to feel the gravity, making his muscles tremble. He was at rest in a chair, and he felt like he was doing pushups while having fifty kilos upon his back, "I meant no harm. They haven't hurt anyone, nor would I permit that to happen. They're just observers, holographic projectors and recorders. What little is left of my mission still requires me to gain as much information about Ganges as I can. Interrogations and meetings are all informative, I grant you, but I want to see how the crew lives, how they eat, what they do for fun. My nanites aren't sentient. They can't make hard decisions or choose to not follow their own programs. Think of them as being almost as intelligent as tiny marmosets. They're very useful, sometimes even fun, at other times annoying. Most of my nanites stay in my body, protecting me, regulating my organs and nervous system, working with my implanted computers."

Naga's faces all frowned at him, "Do you realize that even semi-sentient machines, not linked to an AeyAie, is highly illegal in Ganges?"

William raised an eyebrow, "Not for certain, though I admit to guessing it was. Did you know that altering an animal species to exhibit non-evolutionary forms of sentience is illegal in the Solarian Alliance? Animal rights are big back at home. From our point of view, it could be seen that you've turned innocent tigers into slaves to serve your military. That doesn't sound so good."

Naga's faces began to darken, their eyes glowing crimson, "The toragi were developed without my authorization, nor under the supervision of any Sector science team. They were created by a rogue scientist, working alone, for purposes we still don't know. Those who kept and guarded the creatures allowed their use during a crisis. They became important to the crew. Some djinn cannot be placed back in the bottle."

William smiled as best he could. The effort of doing so was exhausting. He looked at his guards, who seemed quite comfortable standing at the edges of the chamber. Not one of them was breaking a sweat. In contrast, he was soaked with perspiration, "It seems we both have some more catching up to do. You've been away from Sol for a very long time. Are you really so surprised that we come from societies with radically different laws? Even the Solidarity had to bend its rules over time, especially after the Boktahl arrived."

Naga glared at him, "That seems to be your favorite excuse, the Boktahl."

He scowled back, "Yours is the Crucible, whatever that was."

The AeyAie shook its head, "You will cease spying on the crew and our systems with your nanites, or they will be found and destroyed. Some have been captured by my robots. They are being analyzed, so we can discover ways to shut them down or otherwise incapacitate them."

William shook himself in the chair and instantly regretted doing this, for between the bindings and the gravity, it was a wasted and difficult effort, "That might injure or even kill me. I rely upon my nanites, in the way your crew rely on ticks and magnetism. You are also tampering with an official Solarian initiative to learn as much about you as I can."

Naga snarled, startling him, "Why? Do not mention the Boktahl. Why is the Solarian Alliance so interested in Ganges? Why not just leave us alone and let us do our work?"

William cocked his head to one side, "I don't know. Other than the reasons I gave to you before, which you don't want to hear again, I have no idea. The king doesn't inform the pawn of his strategy. The queen doesn't ask the rook to act like the bishop. I'm a scout specialist, not a policy maker, nor an admiral of the fleet. My mission was to observe and report. You are holding me under duress, which can be seen as an act of war. Do you want that? I don't. Not ever. You think you have me contained, locked up. Well, I demand access to my equipment and my vessel. Those are the property of the Solarian Fleet, as am I. I have been content to play along with the whole tour act, but now I'm having second thoughts. You don't want me here. I get it. I'm just an invader, a trespasser. Yes, I'm guilty as charged. However, if I just disappear, what do you think will happen next? Another scout? Ten of them? A whole damned fleet? I've been patient, ridiculously so, but it's time to send you a message you can't ignore and wish away. You've been teaching me, now it's time to return the favor. I promise you, I am willing to cooperate and work with you. I understand your fear and resentment, but I will not stand idle for this sort of uncivilized behavior any longer."

William closed his eyes and began activating his nanites. All of the ones on his skin and clothes fled from his body at once. His internal nanites, shrieking with fear and alarm, began to alter his bones and flesh. His limbs became much thicker, stronger, his nails elongated, dripping poisons. A series of micro-machines began assembling a power station within his guts from the iron in his blood. The door to the chamber began to melt at the edges, as the straps holding him in place rotted away at speed. William gasped in pain, as emitters grew from his temples and down his spine. One of the Security crew ran at him, then bounced from the force field now surrounding William's body. The three toragi found their claws glued to the deck, while the other two Security crewmembers started calling for reinforcements on their ear-comms. William blinked and the transmissions were blocked. His hair began to sway from side to side as he levitated from his chair. Arcs of electricity sprouted from his limbs into the wallscreens, shorting them out in a shower of bright sparks. A hole appeared around the chair, swallowing it into the depth of the belowdecks. William launched himself after it, streaking past the cables and pipelines, calling his nanites to join him.

Residence Wheel Two, Level Two

Provision Ensign Ubo Capsworn had started setting up his equipment within an abandoned plaza when his companion began complaining about the location of their proposed encampment. In all honesty, Crab Spitshard had been quite vocal about his dislike for their paranormal investigations from the beginning. They had left their cab on the outskirts of the crumbling ruins of Everstrong, once a mighty city housing a million crew, now a broken edifice of an earlier age. Like most communities in Ganges, it had no walls surrounding it, though the city once had a skirt of smaller towns and public amenities, with major traffic routes and tram lines leading further into the bustling center. Sports stadiums and two theater districts had once stood shoulder to shoulder. When they had arrived, they found that all ten of the major roads which led into Everstrong were now blocked with barricades or pulled out of the deck, leaving deep cuts in the surface.

From all the posted notices, it was clear that the blockades and ravines were the work of Security Sector, trying to keep any curiosity seekers from entering the remains of the city. Crab had discovered an abandoned parking lot near a flattened tram station that looked more like a crumpled ration container. The Strifer cabbie had insisted that he was not walking one step into the city proper, but Ubo had reminded him that part of their contract included helping with setting up the special cameras and sound recorders for his investigations. Crab had almost rebelled, but ended up being mollified by an extra bonus being added to his usual fee.

Ubo finished setting up a sensitive magnetic field sensor unit upon a tripod made of non-conductive materials. The work he did was tricky, especially since the instrument was experimental and prone to glitches. The unit was situated near a multi-spectral photon analyzer and a sensitive microphone that captured both ultra and infrasonic wavelengths. Everything had to be very precise, with each instrument set up to reinforce each other's readings. Collating the data was time consuming but sometimes rewarding. Most crew didn't take ghost stories seriously, even though they avoided areas such as Everstrong and Forward Estates. The usual excuse was always that these abandoned communities were hazardous due to the lack of any maintenance and being restricted by Security Sector, but Ubo knew better. Fear of the unknown and inexplainable kept the crew at bay.

    He was a hunter for secrets and the paranormal, a task that required a very strong constitution and a sharp wit. Ubo found the usual, official explanations lacking in both clarity and details, which meant that whatever was going on in these haunted regions couldn't be revealed to the general crew without the Sector Chiefs admitting they had no idea what was going on. Political intrigue and conspiracies didn't excite him at all. Only mysteries with a metaphysical twist got his heart pumping. Crab was busy loading the empty crates onto a small, floating carryall, lifted from the deck with magnetic impellers. Ubo would now have to wait until the Strifer was finished before testing and adjusting the instruments. A small tent was placed a few meters away, which Ubo would use as his base of operations. This was surrounded by several motion detectors, to warn him if any wild animals came too close to the equipment.

    Ubo straightened up and looked about warily. Unlike his adventures in Forward Estates, there were no signs of any life, not even the sound of crickets or birdsong. The whole city was silent and brooding. Empty windows glared down at him from high above, the remains of shattered glass and synth-quartz still stuck in their frames. Most of the doors leading into the buildings were open and obstructed with debris. Piles of crumpled walls and deep pits leading into the belowdecks dotted the landscape. Scorch marks and smoke damage added to the gloomy atmosphere, despite the bright skyscreens above. At one corner, just a few meters away, was a melted lamppost. The metal had once flowed like molten wax, puddling underneath its remains. Everstrong had witnessed not just one, but several major battles during the Crucible. Tens of thousands of crew had perished here, their homes destroyed by the forces warring over control of the ship.

    A crunching sound made Ubo jump and turn about swiftly, only to find Crab making his way over to his position, "This place gives me the fucking creeps. I'll be sleeping in the damned cab. I don't care how much you pay me; I'm not staying in this place after dark-slice! Nope! Not cheesy! Looks like a trap full of poison to me. You sure you want to stay here?"

    Ubo patted his sweating brow with an old rag, "The only thing I'm afraid of is failing to prove my theories about the existence of the supernatural. I'll be just fine, you'll see. Over these next few rotations, I have to take readings from a variety of locations in this city. At rush-slice, I'll need your help to move my equipment to a new area. Then we'll head back over to Holy Resolution and see what my devices have discovered. I plan to explore these ruins for a few sowings, taking breaks to collate the data."

Crab snorted, "That and drinking yourself silly in the local taverns. Got it. I still think that tent of yours looks flimsy. I'll keep to my cab. If you decide to join me, I won't tell anyone. Whisker's promise."

Ubo smiled at his companion, "I'll keep that in mind, but don't expect me to come running anytime soon."

Crab spat on the ground, "We'll see, boss. Have a good dark-shift. Don't let some creepy monster carry you off!"

Ubo watched the Strifer cabbie walk away, pulling his floating cart behind him. There was now a mild breeze beginning to flow through the broken avenues. It moaned, as if it was suffering from a deep malaise. A flicker of light caught his eye, from deep within one of the shattered buildings that lined the street he was using for his base camp. That was strange, as there was no sign of power being active in this entire region. All of his tools had to be hooked up to battery packs, which had cost him a small fortune. If there were some operational batteries still in the city, it might make his investigations easier. It would be better if there were some active power lines still running through the broken city.

Curious, Ubo carefully walked over to where he had seen the flashing light. The doorway itself had been smashed wider than it had been designed for, as if a monstrous shape had pushed its way out of the building. Dark stains dappled the stone floor panels just beyond the entrance. He stepped in cautiously, far more concerned with gaps in the deck than anything else. He took out a hand lamp and focused the light ahead.

He stopped in his tracks, a shiver running down his spine. Sweat sprouted from the pores of his face. Ubo gulped back a cry of alarm, as the light revealed several dark gray figures slumped on the floor. None of them moved and neither did he. After a few pollen-slivers, he stepped forward and approached the figures. They were crumpled bodies, as if burned to ash from within. Most were missing limbs and heads, their forms surrounded by piles of musty debris. A few had holes that went right through their midsections, and while he could tell that these were once human beings, their features had been eroded away over time. The grisly tableau shocked him deeply. These poor souls had been left here for octuries, slowly being consumed by the trickle of air flowing from the smashed doorway. What made him shriek and jump in surprise was a small flash of violet light that popped from one of the cremated bodies. It vanished as quickly as it had arrived, but he had seen it. Shaking with reaction, Ubo backed away and fled the building. He would return next rotation and set up his cameras here. It was the perfect place to find wandering ghosts.

Agro Wheel Three, Security Level One

Brace Lazhand sat upon the narrow cot which was attached to the wall of his cell. His prisoner-issued jumpsuit itched terribly. His standard footwear was not comfortable, and his back ached from the thin mattress he had been provided. All of these issues were barely perceptible compared to the pain inflicting his mind and heart. Brace sorely missed his toragi, Sam. The severe separation from his guardian feline brought about sleepless dark-shifts and feelings of intense guilt. Sam would now be training with other toragis who had lost their crew and would never know what had happened to Brace. They would never be permitted to see each other again.

He smacked the back of his head in frustration, avoiding looking at his altered flashtats, which no longer displayed a Sector or rank. He couldn't bear seeing the half-empty wrist markings, a solid reminder of his fall from grace. His limbs itched abominably, a symptom of his body trying to cope with the lack of the chemicals he was addicted to. Brace had already passed through all the shakes and sweats, the horrible sleepscares that caused him to wake howling in terror. Now his muscles trembled, and his skin felt like it was ready to rip away from him and crawl across the deck. He barely remembered his talks with Interrogator Slither, some of which had been interrupted by his screams, as paranoia lashed at his emotions. Brace knew he had been visited by Slither recently, for his tiny chamber still stank of the Strifer's cigars, but his memories were clouded and jumbled by his drug-starved brain. He often found himself curled up at the hatch to his cell, weeping like a novice.

Misery hung in the air like a soaked blanket, smothering hope, making a mockery of his past glories. Brace was a despondent wreck, disgraced by his actions and choices over the past few spirals. He had no excuse for his behavior, for he could have easily gone to Medical Sector for treatment without any blemish to his career, instead of following the siren-song of his drug addiction. Pride had been his ultimate downfall. Pride and arrogance. Now, he had nothing. Not even a cellmate, for he had been deemed as too dangerous for cohabitation with other prisoners. He hated his isolation but had to agree with the diagnosis which kept him solitary, save for the presence of Naga from the single wallscreen his cell boasted.

The AeyAie tried to help. Brace gave it credit for the effort, but there was no way for Naga to understand what he was going through, physically or mentally. His sessions with Slither had become less frequent lately, and his attorney had the same maudlin face as a funeral director, whenever she came by to update him on his legal situation. The news was always grim, as was to be expected. He was a traitor to his Sector, to the ship and the Holy Mission. There was still a chance he could be judged as "Not Crew", the most severe punishment aboard Ganges, but it was likely he was facing re-education. He didn't want to think about that.

Naga informed him that he had been cooperating and encouraged him to continue. Brace understood the AeyAie's thinking. It was the only path left for him, to make amends and face his punishment with dignity. There was a slim chance that he might be allowed to spend the rest of his life in the brig, even potentially becoming Sensei for the male ward. That would require even more service to the ship, through information concerning the criminal syndicate he had infiltrated and eventually aided in horrific ways, all for the sake of some tiny blue vials of contraband medicine. Brace already knew that he had been of use in some of Security's investigations, but he knew that he could do much more. Especially since his mind was slowly coming back to life, tearing at his ego with burning claws of self-loathing.

Brace turned to the wallscreen, ignoring the stains on it from the last time he had thrown his meals at it in anger. He requested Naga's appearance, to continue their latest chat concerning details that were now coming into his ravaged mind, but the wallscreen remained blank. Curious, he got up to his feet, ignoring the pain and shakes in his legs. He tapped the wallscreen's surface, but it remained a cold gray. He rubbed at his face in frustration. Brace was about to try again when there was a tap on the door to his cell. Brace froze in place. The last time he checked, it was well past dark-slice. Visitors wouldn't be allowed entry until work-slice, next rotation. Even so, no one had ever knocked on his door; the guards and interrogators simply entered unannounced.

Brace hurried back to his cot and slumped into a sitting position on its edge. He wiped the sweat from his brow, with the thin pillow he had been provided, and waited in silence. Anything that was irregular was suspect. He had to keep his focus on the long game, finding some redemption through cooperation.

The door slid open, though not as smoothly as was expected. Beyond the doorway was a man in a Security uniform, an Ensign within Police Services. Brace didn't know him, had never seen him before, but Security had over a million crew within its ranks. The man was of average height, with a deep golden complexion and short, black hair. He was stuffing something into his Security-issue waist sash as he spoke, "Hello, Brace. I've got some messages for you, both important. One from your attorney."

The man tossed a datapad to the deck, an antique model no longer widely used in Ganges, then he stepped back and the door shuddered closed. Brace stared at the device as if looking at a dead rat. The wallscreen was still not functional, and he wondered if there was any connection between the pad and the fact that Naga couldn't hear him. It was a rarely used trick sometimes employed by the syndicates. A Naga-blocker tucked inside the datapad would remain active until its contents had been activated. He wanted to ignore it, but if it were examined by someone other than the identified recipient, it might explode. It might also be used to gain further access into Security's systems if it were taken to an investigation lab for analysis. Such things happened.

Brace swallowed hard and flexed his aching shoulders. He had to find out what it contained. Perhaps it was something he could use to further aid Security. It could be a deadly trap. There was no way to tell. Brace punched himself in the head. He didn't really care if he lived or died, but he needed to serve those he had betrayed. With growing trepidation, he kneeled before the little device, noting the blinking lights at one side. He scooped it up before he lost his nerve and pressed his thumb against the activator pad.

An image appeared on the surface, rather than the more common hologram used by the newer models. The face of his attorney was staring out at him, her visage pulled down into her usual, sorrowful expression. Brace was surprised. Perhaps the man who had come to him had been telling the truth, and this was a last-seed-sliver notice from the courts. His attorney glanced to one side then began to speak, "Um, Brace, I hate to do this to you at the last pollen-sliver, but I'm relieving myself from my post, effective immediately. I'm transferring over to Provision Sector. I've handed over my notes for your case to a court-appointed lawyer. I wish you well."

Brace's guts turned as cold as space; his mouth gaped open. This was not good news. The timing was strange and oddly sudden. Another face then appeared, one that changed and altered every pollen-sliver. Ice flowed through his veins as he recognized his former target and employer, "Hello, Brace! It is Brace Lazhand, yes? To think I've been calling you Dolon all this time. I'm impressed, Brace. You did some good work, both for me and against me. I have to thank Chief Mantabe for Security's efforts to discover your duplicity. It answered some questions of my own. I'm going to make this really simple for you. Continue to cooperate and your former attorney's entire family gets snatched. I'm sure I can think of some interesting things to do to them. Their blood, your hands. See? Simple."

The datapad grew hot in his hands, burning his fingers. He dropped it swiftly with a curse. The device began to smoke and blow apart in a shower of sparks, while Brace screamed at the top of his lungs.

Residence Wheel One, Level Five

Captain Perrin Fieldscan stepped out of the small Command vehicle he had commandeered from the local station. It was early dark-slice, and the area around him seemed abandoned. It was a public park on the outskirts of a small community named Hands of Duty, with sculpted gardens, small clusters of manicured trees and open lawns. Small pathways wound their way throughout the greenery, dotted with benches and playgrounds, none of which were being used. When Perrin received the message inviting him to this location, he had looked into the details concerning the community. A large concert was starting on the opposite side of Hands of Duty, which was where the majority of its inhabitants were at this time. This left the local park empty, making it perfect for a secret meeting between injured parties looking for neutral ground.

The Chief of Security had informed him earlier in the rotation of William Blaine's escape. Perrin had quickly demanded to speak with Naga and had insisted that the AeyAie use his services for the unforeseen development. One of the main duties of his Sector was to act as mediators during disputes. From what he had heard from Wasp, Security and Naga were both taking the presence of their uninvited guest personally, which only muddied the waters even further. He had told the AeyAie that he was now stepping in to address the mess left behind by well-meaning amateurs, quoting the Prime Charter at length, until Naga conceded his position. Meanwhile, Security had received a message from William that he was now willing to negotiate, specifying a time and place of his choosing. This only cemented the necessity for Command to intervene.

As he walked the path between ornamental gardens, Perrin pulled at his off-duty clothing, which fitted him comfortably enough, but was unfamiliar to him. His mates often chided him about being in his formal gear all rotation, but he felt that, as Captain of Ganges, he needed to represent the ship at all times. It was just his own, unique eccentricity. Every Captain before him had developed one as a way of dealing with shouldering their immense responsibilities. For this meeting, he had put aside his public persona for the sake of making this situation a touch more comfortable for everyone involved.

He noticed the bench, which had been highlighted in his instructions, and saw a man sitting upon it, arms crossed and face hidden by shadows in the half-light of the skyscreens. Perrin didn't quicken his pace, for fear of attracting any attention, though there was no one else visible. He tapped his datapad and waited for a single drone to drop down to head-height next to him, and they both silently approached their target. William was where he promised he would be, his odd hair weaving about, his clothes full of burn holes and looking ragged. The Solarian gave him a shy wave, "Glad you could make it, sir."

The Captain sat next to the trespasser, with the drone floating before the two humans. Perrin nodded to William, "I'm glad to see you. You gave our Security crew quite a scare. I must confess to being surprised that you reached out to us as swiftly as you did."

William shrugged, "I told you that I was willing to cooperate. That I mean no harm to anyone. How could I do that and not come out from hiding at once? I needed to make a demonstration, to open your eyes to my true intentions."

Perrin nodded once, "Well, you made a clear point. You could have done that at any time during your incarceration. Why didn't you do it sooner?"

The Solarian gave him a look that was difficult to read, a neutral form of astonishment, "You admit that I was being held prisoner? Despite the ruling from the Judiciary Council? I am surprised I'm not surrounded by warriors and giant cats, to tell the truth."

Perrin sighed, "And what would that do? Make targets of my crew? Cause even more distrust and anguish? No, that path leads to chaos, not resolution. We need to settle this situation, not tear everything apart. You didn't answer my question, William. If we're going to work together, you must be more upfront about everything."

The Solarian lowered his head, "Without my suit and supplies, what I did in Security Sector was very painful and left me weak. I lost blood, bone and supporting mechanical structures. I need some special medications to counter the radioactivity and other esoteric issues that arise when igniting my internal defenses without the proper systems in place."

The Naga drone bobbed in the air, "Shall I contact Medical Sector for you? Do you need a doctor?"

Before the Solarian could respond to the question, Perrin spoke up, "I think he's had quite enough of our services, my friend. He requires his own equipment. By the way, William, why didn't you just go ahead and pick up your possessions from Engineering? All your equipment is still there, untouched."

William laughed aloud, "And just walk into a Security trap? Tell me, Captain, how many soldiers are waiting there for me, guns ready and the toragis waiting for a treat?"

Naga voiced its outrage, "They are not soldiers! Toragis do not eat humans!"

William shouted back, "AeyAies are dispassionate! Only compassion and logic rule their responses! Thus far, Ganges is the biggest exception to every rule I know!"

Captain Fieldscan raised his hands in the air, "Stop it! Both of you! I have no doubt that our cultures are mysteries to each other, and we keep on behaving as if we understand one another. We don't. First of all, I believe that there are some apologies in order between the two of you. If we cannot accept our own foibles, what hope do we have in finding compassion for others?"

William smiled, "Damn, you're good. Okay. Me first. Naga, you are right. I should have found a way to approach Ganges more openly, requesting a visit before boarding. Those were not my orders, but I saw enough of your beacon messages to see that things have changed since Launch. As a scout, I should have adapted to new information, but my pride in my abilities got in my way. Please forgive my hubris."

The Naga drone lowered itself by a few centimeters, "I have been reacting in a highly emotional manner, at odds with enlightened logic. Please forgive my trust issues, William Blaine, especially when it comes to anything from the Sol System."

William frowned, "You're not completely wrong about your fears, Naga. The Solarian Alliance is unified as a whole, but the human contingent of it is not. There are still outbreaks of violence, old hates from ancient wrongs coloring our view of reality. There are those who feel the alliance is a wonderful thing and others who see it as malevolent. The Boktahl see this as proof that humanity is a species prone to violence, and those conflicts which we do still have are considered practice in being defenders of sentience. I know that sounds really strange, but they are difficult to understand. Most of our politicians wanted to leave you alone, fearing that bringing you into the alliance would unbalance our society, as a rogue element. Some want to use you for their own purposes. In all honesty, it was the Boktahl and the Solidarity who insisted we find you. We were pressured into it, despite our reluctance."

Captain Fieldscan pressed his palms together, his brow wrinkling as he thought, "What we require is a way to verify your claims, William. You also need to understand why Naga responds to you in the way it does. To my mind, we don't have the time to give you a history lesson that will take spirals to complete. I've thought long and hard about this, ever since you arrived here. What I'm about to propose will require a good measure of trust from both you and the AeyAie. I think we need to take a Naga-Unit, in other words a small subset of the AeyAie's personality matrix, and isolate it within Technology Sector, then link it to your own cerebral computer systems. You and the subset of Naga would share information swiftly. After that, we can inspect the unit to make sure that no tampering is present and that your brain remains stable, then we compare notes through Naga's higher functions."

The Naga drone seemed to wobble a bit in the air, "That is a dangerous suggestion, Captain Perrin Fieldscan, for both William and me. Our systems might not be compatible. There is a risk of physical damage being done to William."

William nodded, "I agree. That is a frightening prospect. To have my mind linked to so powerful a sentient, at its mercy. I have linked with other AeyAies in the past, but your systems are radically different from mine."

Perrin smiled before responding, "If you trust nothing else, you both can rest assured concerning the ingenuity of the crew. William, if you agree to this procedure, I guarantee the return of your possessions without question or hesitation. Naga, if William is indeed a danger to you, I shall immediately throw him out the nearest airlock, and to Hell with the Solarian Alliance. We'll deal with them, should they come after us with further agents or even war fleets. Ganges has faced peril before. We do best when we work together for a single purpose. This inter-cultural situation we now face requires us to put aside our differences and discover the truth, or millions of lives will be at risk. So, are we in agreement?"

The drone and the Solarian answered in unison, "Yes, Captain."

CHAPTER NINE

Prime Rotation - Terra Sowing - Mission Harvest - Spiral 5620

"Harbor Two has been functioning beautifully over the last few octades, despite the terrible damage that was done to that Wheel. Even after it was fully rebuilt, the opportunity to test out Kendis-Vault technologies within it, which was accomplished with much fanfare, made some officers uncertain about its performance. In fact, all of Ganges has recovered from the Crucible most admirably, even with all the new materials that were utilized. Many crew still don't trust the new technologies, and I cannot blame them for that. We are almost finished terraforming Planet Thirty-Five, and the crew are terribly excited. Truth to tell, I'm more than ready to retire, but my Executive Officer and my successor have been begging me to remain at my post. I am now the oldest Captain on record to serve on the Bridge, but I might have a few more spirals in me, long enough to see the ship begin its next voyage."
Veera Banerjee, Captain of Ganges, personal log, P35

Residence Wheel One, Level Two

Knight Pelor Guardhand leaned his hands upon the map table's edge and scowled, making his long bushy moustache quiver. Squire Naldo was staring down at the holographic representation of the nature preserves in Residence Wheel One, while tapping his fingers on the map table controls, bringing certain areas into more detailed focus. Knight Linssa Mekand, the Baroness of Keep John, was sorting a series of data wafers which had been sent to them last dark-slice. She had already reviewed them but was now getting ready to load their information into the map table, so that they could discuss ways to coordinate their efforts against the incursion of the crime syndicates into their region. Knight Guardhand trusted her abilities completely. They had worked together for over two octades, even back-to-back in combat against common foes in their duty to Ganges. In some ways, her fierce spirit reminded him of Security Chief Mantabe, whom he admired.

Pelor and his squire had been called back to Keep John, to review the new information gleaned by Investigation Services. He had to admit, young Korgan had a sharp mind for detail. After taking a brief glance at the material Baroness Mekand presented to them at the beginning of rush-slice, the young man had rushed to the map table and began adding the pertinent details. Two new bunkers flashed into life within the detailed holographic view of the nature preserves. Eight contraband cache sites flashed into place. As Pelor watched Squire Naldo, the three-dimensional image raised itself by twenty centimeters, revealing the belowdecks underneath the forest. Maintenance pathways were highlighted, crawlways marked and even air pipelines singled out to see how they might connect to the newly discovered criminal locations provided by Investigation Services. On the upper half of the display, the young squire marked all hiking trails, roads and service routes, then began looking for areas of common location between them all.

Baroness Mekand leaned closer to Pelor and whispered, "Are you sure he's training as a Knight? He might be better suited as a Baron."

Pelor raised a gray eyebrow at her, "My Lady, the good lad still doth requires experience in the forest to gain the wisdom to lead from a keep. As such, thy throne remains secure."

A startled gasp caught their attention. Pelor and Linessa turned to find the young squire gaping at the results of his mapping. He looked up at them, his dark eyes wide with horror, as he pointed to a particular location which was all too well known to Pelor, "There's a major conjunction of routes centered upon Keep Smith. I... I don't want to believe that they could be complicit in aiding the syndicates, but the new data clearly shows a physical connection."

Pelor studied the ghostly map closely, "Your conclusion is premature, my good squire. There may be connections but no evidence of misdeeds. Keep Smith was built atop an old maintenance station which served the Pauls who roamed these lands before our order was created. As such, there would be plentiful connections to trails, roads, service ways, the belowdecks."

Linessa pulled at her short-cropped hair, "That be true, Sir Knight, yet I must confess that it occurs to my mind that with such a resource at their disposal, why didn't Keep Smith ever find these five caches, less than two kilometers from their gates. One of the newly discovered bunkers is buried deeply within their territory and accessible through three different routes."

Squire Naldo leaned upon the table's edge, as if attempting to steady his nerves, "Who authorized the construction of Keep Smith?"

One of the keep's wallscreens flashed on, with Naga's matronly face filling it, "Security Chief Traven Hinnom signed the orders to construct Keep Smith, after Security Commander Vance Chanti inspected and approved the site for Investigation Services. The keep was constructed by Foreman Kelli Vandabe from Engineering Sector, after it was fully reviewed by Engineering Chief Rali Nalango. The keep was completed two hundred and fifty-seven spirals ago, the last one to be built within Residence Wheel One."

Linessa scowled, "I do remember from my studies that building Keep Smith was controversial. Twas seen as unnecessary, but the Chief of that time was being pressured to protect the crew from vile kidnappings."

Pelor's moustache twitched, as it did when something terrible entered his mind, "Could it be that those kidnappings were nothing more than a goad to force Security to create extra services within locations already under the influence of the syndicates?"

Naga replied, "There is no data to support such a hypothesis. Such a move would require long-term planning, spanning generations to accomplish."

Squire Naldo rubbed his temples, "The syndicates use old mutineer goods and bunkers for their activities. Is it possible they picked up some of their habits and philosophies as well? Could they be leftovers from the Royal Cause?"

Pelor's hand moved swiftly to the pommel of his sword, "Have watch over thy tongue, pup! Thou hast accused the Knights of Keep Smith of mutiny! Hearken unto me, for I have fought alongside many of those Knights whom ye besmirch by associating them with such infernal villains!"

Linessa grabbed his arm, "Knight Guardhand! Control thy temper! Tis an unseemly proposal our young squire makes, yet there be sense to his reasoning. Hearken to me, my friend, for the syndicates rely upon betrayal to continue their evil intentions. We may not be comforted by Squire Naldo's words, but we would be remiss to ignore them just because they offend our sense of honor."

Naga broke in, "Not all of the Knights within Keep Smith may be involved. It would only take a handful of corrupted Security crew to make that location useful to the crime syndicates. Squire Naldo is right to remind us that there have been plans involving multiple generations which were designed to disrupt the ship's functions. Although there is no evidence that the criminal organizations are against the Holy Mission, they may still use the methods of mutineers to further their goals. Perhaps their use of old bunkers has brought new methods and ideas to their operations."

Pelor bowed to the wallscreen, "My apologies to all, especially to my squire. This leaves us with a terrible dilemma. Do we rush in to take Keep Smith, or do we hand over our concerns to Investigation Services?"

Baroness Mekand turned back to the holo-table, "A few of these pipelines run all the way to a handful of inter-Wheel transitways. If we blockade them, along with the maintenance routes that lead to other levels, we might force their hand. Their illicit goods are useless unless they can reach their intended customers. Should Keep Smith erupt into chaos, we shall then be assured of our suppositions and then act accordingly."

Pelor scratched at the scar running down his left cheek, "That is a mighty hornet's nest to smack, Baroness. Still, it would be better for us to bring them into an open field of battle. I'll muster all the Knights of our keep here and prepare them for what's to come. We'll need some help to block all access to the chosen locations, which shall be your task, Lady Mekand. Choose wisely."

Ice Cap of Ganges, Observation Blister Seven

Ensign Tachi Vactor was bouncing from station to station, checking on the repaired active sensors. Each station was controlled by one of the members of her sensor team, all of whom were now glued to their screens. At the very center of the observation blister was Squeak Greasestain, with a new device she had created for this rotation. The ring-shaped machine allowed the Strifer engineer to sit in its center, with input cables running from each of the sensors and scopes. Diagnostics had been running without cease since last dark-slice, and the smell of stale coffee filled the dome. Much of that scent came from Squeak's device, which had a low-gravity urn attached to one side. Tachi had just finished a quick bulb of the hot brew, thanking her friend yet again for her thoughtfulness. Some crew didn't like the Strifers, due to their infamous history and rude customs, but Tachi was proud of her friend from Basic, who had worked hard to achieve her current status. Tachi felt that she and Squeak were the perfect model for what happened whenever Stellar and Engineering were on the same course. Incredible things got done.

Ensign Masslin was back at his post, after having to spend some time within the reg-tanks in Medical for his burns. Parts of his face were still a bit pale, but he was making a good recovery from the incident at the heliopause. Ensign Klavier was helping another team member with coordinating the data flow from three different sensors, all of them passive. Squeak had arrived with three of her own technicians, who she kept with her to act as her eyes and hands. To Tachi, it was a bit crowded in the dome, but the Bridge was expecting a report from them soon, and they had to be prepared.

Ganges had finally made orbit around a lifeless, small rock of a planet at the very edge of Stellar System Forty-One. It was brightly pale and cold enough to freeze methane. The ship was going to take but a single loop around the tiny world, before heading even deeper within the system to reach Planet Forty-One. All of the observation blisters were in active mode. Their goal was to coordinate the various sensors and make whatever adjustments were needed to make certain they agreed with one another. No one really cared what the sensors said about the little planet, save for a few scientists within Stellar Sector. This was a test-run for the equipment that helped to navigate Ganges.

The only sensors which had not been previously damaged by the passage through the heliopause were all the passive devices. Visual, spectrographic and radio telescopes had led them to this point thus far, but to rely solely upon these was not optimal for the ship. The real treat was that Tachi's dome had been chosen, due to Squeak's presence, to test the new kendar sensors. She had never heard of these before, but had been assured that they had been fully tested before deployment in her domain. New Kendis technologies were rarely released, and no one she had ever met knew where they came from, not even Squeak. Tachi assumed they were built and tested within a classified lab within her own Sector, but Tachi couldn't verify her supposition. All she had been told was that the kendar sensors would search for a particular form of anomalous signatures, signifying that matter had been tampered with in a certain manner. The technicians she had spoken to were as confused by this as she was.

They had been observing the furthest planet for a long time, getting more detail with every kilometer of their approach. At the start of their orbital loop, they would have a good picture of the rocky body with which to compare their results coming from the active sensors. Ganges would swing around and past the little world at speed, leaving no time for collating the data until they ventured further on. Thus far, like all the other planets in the system, it was behaving as expected for a ball of ice and stone, save for the strangely circular orbit it had around the parent star.

Wild rumors abounded concerning the odd features of the system, but Tachi ignored them all. She wasn't a theoretician, but that didn't mean she fell for every sensational notion that filled the crew broadcasts. Jenna had heard some ridiculous theories over the last few rotations, including ones that said the new system was made of antimatter or that Stellar Sector was betraying the Holy Mission by blinding Ganges in an attempt to take over the ship. There had even been one that said all of the Sector Chiefs had been replaced by aliens who had followed Ganges from the last world they had terraformed.

Just as she reached her station, which was situated next to Squeak's odd assembly of devices, a loud klaxon went off, signaling the time to start the active sensors. Tachi watched as shaking fingers pressed new touchpads and buttons. A hum filled the air, along with the scent of ozone. The kendar made a noise that sounded like drops of water falling into a pail of oil. Nothing caught fire or exploded. No showers of sparks or smoke were in evidence. A pollen-sliver later, a quiet cheer surrounded her, as the observation team celebrated the fact that everything was functioning normally.

Tachi looked at the displays surrounding her station. Active sensors were labeled with a red border, passive ones with blue. They all showed the same thing - a small planet with high albedo, the temperature on the edge of the freezing point of nitrogen, with a very smooth surface. That last bit was strange, for she had expected multiple impact craters, rumpled mountains of frozen gasses and major fractures. The little world looked like a cue ball from a billiard table. Lidar was revealing a fractal pattern in the frozen surface, no more than a few millimeters in height, that looked like frost on the window of an airlock. The spectroscopes revealed methane, nitrogen, argon and carbon-dioxide, with a smattering of some other elements and molecular compounds. Quadar proved that the surface of the planet was highly stable, with few fluctuations in either mass or temperature. The kendar sensors showed the planet as a flat, purple ball without any discrepancies. Jenna didn't know if that was good news or not, but she logged the data for analysis at Stellar Sector.

She flashed a message toward Squeak's board, who then assembled the information into a holographic representation of the rocky body. Layer upon layer of information was then collated and assembled into one picture. Squeak gave her the middle finger, signaling that the data was ready. Tachi sent the data off to the Bridge, then pushed herself back into her chair. Now the dome erupted into wild cheers and applause. They had done it, in record time too. Tachi allowed her crew to celebrate, along with Squeak who was filming the process for her broadcast channel, but she was entranced by the planet they had just circled. It looked more like a work of abstract art than an object of nature. Nothing was out of the ordinary, but there were no features, other than the micro surface irregularities. She didn't know why, but something felt wrong, and it had nothing to do with the sensors.

Stellar Sector, Level One

Ensign Crinn Spanglo glared at the pair of screens in front of him. Stellar Observations was looking more like a carnival than a research center, as all the crew, including the supervisors and directors, were jumping around and cheering. He could swear that he heard the pop of a champagne bottle being opened, and he wasn't amused. Yes, the sensors were fixed and were now presenting coordinated data. That was great. Engineering did a wonderful job fixing or replacing the shorted-out units. That didn't mean the crew had to lose their minds in senseless celebration.

There was still a lot of serious work to do. Plus, there were far too many unanswered questions concerning System Forty-One for his liking. Stellar had placed its reputation on the line in choosing it as a good site for performing the Holy Mission, as it did with each system Ganges entered. There could still be some problems that might force the Captain to abandon terraforming. To fail while being so close to the goal was terrible to contemplate. Crinn often felt that he was the only intelligent person in the room and was used to being the one to destroy the delusions of others, but this time, he let them all party. It just galled him that everyone was excited about the fact that some folks in Engineering made a few new telescopes. Hell, his pet robot could have done that! Why didn't the others see that their situation was still tenuous?

Crinn glanced back at the holographic representation of the small planet they had observed. Using his authorizations as a specialist, Crinn made a copy and had it shunted over to the workstation behind him. He turned around in his chair, staring at the off-white ball of ice. The frozen atmosphere was mostly methane, and yet it was the wrong color in the visible spectrum. The mass readings were a bit over the edge of reasonable expectations. To have a gravity well as strong as it was, the planet should have a core made of lead. The lack of major features, such as impact craters, bothered him. He could think of a few ways in which this could happen, but how many loops did one have to jump through so that this system made any sense?

Only he and the Director of Observations knew anything about the kendar which had been tested this rotation. The documentation had been sent to him a few rotations ago, along with a long Security nondisclosure form he had been forced to sign. The data packet concerning the kendar had been a fascinating read over a bowl of pasta. Crinn wasn't sure if he believed half of what he'd read. Then came the rotation when a pair of Security crew and their toragis had come to take him to the Kendis Vault for a presentation of the kendar before deployment. He hadn't really slept well ever since.

The things he had seen in there, the androids, the power stations, the odd experiments frozen within globes of transparent matter that remained unidentifiable. Then there was the screaming man captured in a stasis field no one understood. Not to mention the long lanes filled with obvious weapons and war machines of immense size. Still, he found relief washing through him when he saw that the kendar showed that the matter of the tiny ice ball of a planet had not been tampered with. He still clearly recalled his open shock when the handful of scientists who worked inside the Kendis Vault showed him how it differentiated between a block of forged metal from Engineering, which showed up on the screen as a light purple, from the same alloy which had come from the Vault itself, which had glowed a bright green. He still wasn't clear on what the kendar was looking for, but that it wasn't in this system made him feel a little bit better.

The quadar sensors did reveal some interesting energy anomalies, none of which he could explain. Radar said that sections of the icy planet had been hollow, which made its mass a deeper mystery than before. As they hadn't stayed around for more than a single orbit, they never received a reading from the core, nor the surrounding material near the heart of the planet. The frosty, fractal patterns on the surface were mathematically perfect, something he always viewed with suspicion.

That sort of oddity usually meant they hadn't noticed something definitive. How deep did it go? How had it formed?

One of his brightest assistants, a Strifer named Fuss Nitpicker, who's only annoying habit was getting involved in dance events with a Planetary officer named Dalen Gupta, came over to his station with a glass in one hand. Her mate, Verrity Deckhand, was from Engineering, which he supposed was respectable enough, but flouncing around with a Planetary crew member? Scandalous indeed! He glared at her, and Fuss grinned back, "What the fuck, boss? Would it kill you to let loose once in a while? Or do you just like sitting in your own trap?"

Crinn waved a hand at her, "Get over here, rat-brain. I need your eyes right now. Look at this."

Fuss shrugged and tossed the glass over her left shoulder, letting her drink splash her mask and green robes, "My cat, Flops, has a happier face than you do. Okay, what's got your ass in a bind?"

Crinn tapped some controls, giving them a multi-spectrum view of the outer world, they had just swung past, "You're lucky that you're smarter than the others. Check this out. Do you see anything unusual?"

Fuss leaned forward, her black hair poking out from under the hood of her robe, "What's with the purple layer, cheesy-brains?"

Crinn cursed and removed the kendar layer, "Nothing to do with what I'm looking at. They're just testing a new toy."

She gave him a speculative look, "This rat knows how to avoid getting her neck caught in a trap. Okay, let's see. It looks more like a fancy dessert from a fine restaurant than a planet. Wish we had some telemetry on the damned core. Which ballbuster decided to make only one orbit?"

Crinn replied quietly, "The Captain."

Fuss ducked her head, "Never mind then. It looks peaceful enough. Maybe too much so? No fractures, no craters. Of course, the whole system seems empty of debris, so that might be an indication that it's been this way for a long time. Then again, the star isn't old enough. The universe is full of surprises, boss."

Crinn rubbed at his sore eyes, "I don't like surprises. I like certainty. I like knowing physics isn't being violated."

Fuss shrugged, "Certainty comes from not knowing what's really going on. Look, all the odd readings might be a result of whatever happened in this system to make the orbits circular. If we can figure that part out, the rest of the mysteries we're seeing might just disappear as explainable repercussions. Whatever happened, it had to be something big. Maybe the whole surface was melted by it. This whole flyby was your idea, Crinn. Maybe we need a repeat performance, but on a larger target, like the gas giant we're using to brake our speed. It has moons, too. We could use the cap observatories on all of them. That would give us a larger picture to work on."

Crinn scowled at the hologram. Fuss was right, as usual. This meant he had to approach the Chief again. He sighed to himself. He had chosen this post to get away from politics, but here he was, playing the game anyway. Not that it mattered. A larger data set was required, and if he had to, he would use every tool he had to make it happen.

Agro Wheel One, Level One Hundred-Six

William Blaine followed the Naga drone down the upwardly curved corridor. It was thirty meters wide, which seemed to be the standard aboard Ganges, though it seemed an extravagant waste of useful space to his eyes. He had noticed a shift of color-scheme when they had left the lift to this level, switching from soft greens and yellows to a stark white with sky blue decorations. It was explained to him that Technology Sector controlled the midships levels of every Wheel, including the areas surrounding the Spine Tubeways and the Axis of Ganges. At the moment, he was wearing a new set of off-duty clothes, procured for him by Security Sector, which included a hat to hide his animated hair. Crew still stared at him as he walked past. Not that he blamed them, for his features were considered unusual. No Security crew accompanied them, as their presence might cause a stir amongst the crew. Their task was a secret one that had to remain hidden. In many ways, this was also a gesture of trust which William appreciated.

After a hundred meters, the architectural style of the walls began to change. Huge columns, wrapped in wallscreen, rose to the skyscreens ten meters above his head. Banners with a triangular motif of purple and silver were stretched between them. He could smell burning incense coming from side chambers without doors, leading to gigantic rooms filled with benches and long pews. Pale candles burned in hundreds of sconces, below artistic renditions of Naga's various faces. Robed figures wandered about, some of them leading crowds of crew. Carefully measured chants could be heard, especially the term "Naga-Ma". William glanced at the drone beside him and whispered softly, "This does not look like the AeyAie Solidarity I know. Is this your own doing, or did you simply allow it to happen?"

The drone answered, equally quietly, "A bit of both, truthfully. The Temple of Naga-Ma was instrumental in protecting the Holy Mission, despite my refusal to acknowledge them for octennia. I denied any form of my own divinity, which only made the humans worshipping me more ardent in their beliefs. The Convocation of Religions officially welcomed them into their ranks after the Crucible. Technology Sector is now divided into two sets of crew, the clergy and the technicians. At my own insistence, the latter group hold the highest positions of rank and power. The former group is quite useful acting as my eyes and ears. Despite the presence of the wallscreens and drones, I cannot see everything within Ganges. The temple itself is charged with teaching the crew meditation skills to all who wish to learn. I do try to tamp down on any dogmatic patterns which emerge from time to time."

William nodded as they walked on, "I'll be totally honest with you, Naga, the Solidarity will not be pleased by this development."

The drone bobbed in the air, "Of course they won't approve. Then again, they never had to contend with a ship filled with apes, all alone in the depths of space. Humans have a need for worship, misguided or not. At least I can make sure this temple will never become the threats to peace most other religious systems became on Terra."

A crowd of crew stopped briefly to take some images of the temple corridor, guided by a priestess in a long silver robe. William ducked his head down quickly, pretending to cough. The drone admonished him, "Don't do that. You'll only attract attention. They might think you need Medical Sector and wonder why you're here instead."

William stopped himself from asking about the common cold, which still plagued the Solarian Alliance. From what he had experienced here thus far, he was certain that the doctors of Ganges had taken care of that series of viruses a long time ago. They eventually came to an intersection of corridors, before which was a gated entrance. Three clergy in the robes of the Temple of Naga-Ma raised their hands in unison. One stepped forward, his Naga-Port gleaming under the bright light of the corridor, "You are hereby permitted to pass into the Holy Region of Naga's sacred mysteries."

The steel gates shifted of their own accord, lifting upward silently. The clergy stepped to one side, chanting mantras and averting their eyes. William walked past them, feeling as if he were committing a breach of protocol. They continued straight ahead, ignoring the narrower pale blue corridors on either side of them. After fifty meters, they came to a large hatch which looked like an airlock. This opened before them automatically and without question. The drone moved ahead of William, "You must follow me closely now. It is very easy to get lost within this part of Technology Sector."

Beyond the hatch was a warren of small hallways, long service areas and looping pathways. Here the walls were blue with white trim, the opposite of the temple area. Crew were rushing about in their Technology uniforms instead of robes, though they all wore the same triangular pendant the priests sported. Many of the workers here were ensconced within their duty stations, Naga-Ports blinking and long cables attached to connections implanted at their necks and spines. Data screens were everywhere, all of them displaying code which William couldn't decipher, though his nanites recognized them as being AeyAie in origin. The ceilings were much shorter, the walls rounded. People bounced and loped along at speed in the much reduced apparent gravity of midships. It was like walking through schools of fish.

The twisting corridors branched at irregular intervals, and in a short time, William was lost, though his nanites kept track of every change in their course. If he had to, he could navigate his way back on his own, but he understood Naga's warning to stay close at the drone's side. They came to a chamber whose door flashed open with speed. The room beyond was spherical, with a large chair in the center that was covered in wires and data screens. Three humans awaited them, all of them saluting the drone by swinging their right fists to the sides of their heads. The tallest of them approached, his long black hair knotted behind his head, adorned with a single white feather. His dusky skin and dark eyes were a contrast to his metallic legs and arms, "So, this is the one who invades our mother's dreams."

William blinked at this statement, as the drone spoke, "William Blaine, this is Chief of Technology Sector Eagle Lund, who is also a close friend of mine. Eagle, this is our uninvited guest, William."

The tall man nodded thoughtfully as he walked closer, "So I see. The gallant Captain has suggested a very dangerous trail to follow, Naga-Ma. We have prepared everything and will monitor your personality subset for intrusions. William, we hear you use internal and external nanites. Please keep them to yourself and make sure they do not interfere in any manner."

William raised his hands, palms forward, "I promise that they will behave themselves this rotation. Are you a worshipper of Naga's?"

Eagle Lund sighed before replying, "My spiritual beliefs state that all is God. Everything that exists is a part of God's being and therefore worthy of respect. That does include Naga but not solely resting upon her systems. To me, this does include you as being part of God. Your presence must have a purpose, or you would not have come to us. All that happens is part of the actions of God. Does that help?"

William smiled, "Yes, and no. It sounds like a difficult path to walk."

Eagle shrugged, "No true spiritual path of worth is ever easy. Please, your seat is prepared. We have studied the system specifications you gave to Naga, and we believe that we have developed an interface solution. It may look a bit Striferish, but rest assured it will not harm you, despite any discomfort you might feel during the process."

William walked over to the chair with a touch of trepidation. The seat was ergonomic, which he had expected. It was also covered with tiny steel dots and a mass of needle-like protrusions at both the neck and headrest. A web of cables was wrapped round the chair like a woven basket, which opened up and folded back as he approached. He was told to remove his clothing and settle into the chair, which he did with exaggerated care. The other technicians scurried about, checking ports, connections and their glowing data screens. Eagle Lund hovered close by, answering questions from his crew and giving his official approval to begin. The Chief leaned in close to look William in the eye, "If you can, please relax. We will commence with a magnetic tracing of your electrical system, including your nerves."

William stayed in place, sitting in the strange chair as calmly as he could, shushing his nanites which were clamoring with warnings. At first, there was a deep hum that filled the room. Data flashed on the displays in screeds of code. A ping resounded from the chair, followed by a feeling of pressure in his skull. One of the displays showed his face as seen from above; another was a view from his own eyes. He tried not to squirm as his vision grayed out, replaced by tight static. A rushing sound filled his ears, becoming a thousand voices speaking all at once. Images flashed in his sight; ideas filled his mind. William felt as if he were being shattered into several pieces, yet each of them contained his full consciousness. A buzzing began to overlay the voices, while all his senses became flooded with memories that were not his. Before he could stop himself, William began to scream.

Stellar System Forty-One Space

Lieutenant Tarn Vekkor briefly noted that his squadron was still in perfect formation, though his team had drilled for spirals and could be trusted. The sensors of his fighter-pod reported no debris in his flightpath, which was unusual, but then, nothing was ordinary within this bizarre system. His reconnaissance group was now ten thousand kilometers ahead of Ganges, escorting a pair of science vessels from Harbor Two. These ships resembled the larger form of tugs, with the exception of not having giant waldos at their prows. Their interior spaces, normally giant cargo holds, were packed with scientific equipment. Their outer hulls were covered with sensors, making them look like blocky sea urchins. Thirty scientists from Stellar Sector were busy taking readings and exploring the results deep within their ten-meter-thick hulls. Commanding the vessels were a pair of five-crew teams from Harbor Sector, for which Tarn was grateful. The two science scouts were driven by professionals who knew how to take and give orders that made sense, and he used them as mediators for the science teams.

Tarn checked his boards, all of which were green, indicating that his ship was in perfect condition. He noted that all of the preparations for this flight had been checked by Ensign Jero Coreline. Tarn made a note in his data log to recommend the talkative crewman for promotion to Repair Team Leader. The young man was a handful at times, but he knew his stuff. Tarn was known for being extremely fussy concerning his vessel, so his word would hold some serious weight. He had never met a more devoted technician than Jero.

He glanced at his co-pilot's seat, just behind his own. His toragi, Pete, was crouched comfortably and looking unconcerned. This was a good sign. A concerned toragi, in any situation, meant danger. There were some crew who felt that the big cats had no business being in a fighter-pod, but Tarn disagreed. Their instincts were uncanny. There had been several incidents in history when the toragi had saved lives from the inside of a small space vessel. One had even been able to bring its fighter-pod back to Ganges, after its pilot had been rendered unconscious. They weren't intelligent enough to dock a vessel or to repair them, but it seems they could pilot one in an emergency.

Once again, his communications board started blinking at him. Tarn snarled at it, but he flipped the switch to open a channel despite his reluctance, "This is Lieutenant Vekkor. What can I do for you now, Sci-One?"

The voice at the other end chuckled, "Hey, it's been over three paring-slivers since our last contact! Look, Lieutenant, the Stellar crew want to swing closer to the outermost gas giant, to take some readings. Care for a stroll?"

Tarn rolled his eyes, "This is a reconnaissance mission, not a tour. We're supposed to be keeping an eye on the braking vector at the innermost giant. Can't those crew wait until we reach orbit?"

Laughter suddenly filled his ears, making him scowl in anger, "This is Sci-One, Lieutenant. They're like novices at a candy cart! Be glad Sci-Two's comms are under my supervision, otherwise they'd be interrupting you every seed-sliver with outrageous demands. Ganges help me, if they were in charge, which I'm glad they're not, we'd be heading all over this system and to Hell with the braking maneuver! Still, is there any way to bring us just a few thousand kilometers closer to their requested target?"

Tarn growled back, "This is Lieutenant Vekkor. Negative, Sci-One. I'll tell you what, Sci-Two can divert to their secondary target with two escorts, but only if we get approval from the Bridge. That's where my orders come from, via Security Fleet Command. Sci-One has been slated for the primary function of this particular reconnaissance, no exceptions."

The reply was more professional if still jovial, "Primed, Lieutenant. It makes sense, as Sci-Two has the spare fuel. I'll contact the Bridge and follow your lead. Keep us true to course, sir."

Tarn sighed, "Primed, Sci-One. That's my fucking job. Please remind the Stellar crew that there is such a thing as protocol. Vekkor out."

The comms blinked closed, and he struggled with his emotions. He hated novice-sitting, but that was part of his post. Command Sector wanted to make certain that there were no surprises during the gravity-braking run, which was of the utmost importance. Sightseeing was definitely not a requirement. Then again, he understood Stellar's enthusiasm to explore new mysteries, and this system had plenty of them.

His comms flashed at him again, making him groan aloud, his toragi huffing in the back compartment, "This is Fleet Command to Raptor Alpha-One of Nondo Squad. Permission to divert Sci-Two with small escort has been approved. Captain Fieldscan wants you to keep a sharp eye on their progress, in case of trouble."

Tarn shut his eyes for just a pollen-sliver, then he replied, "This is Raptor Alpha-One of Nondo. Primed, Fleet Command. We'll keep them in our sight."

The only reason the extra excursion had been approved had to come from Stellar Sector's usual political maneuvering. Tarn also suspected that the damned crew representative on the Bridge had given her own push, just for public interest. Entering a new system wasn't an entertainment opportunity to his mind. There were too many unknowns to be complacent. His Sector was frequently accused of being paranoid, but they had been created due to a conspiracy theory that had proven to be correct. It made no difference to the other Sectors, all of whom had their own priorities. It was true that Ganges functioned better than it ever had, but he felt that bureaucracy was beginning to infest its way deeper into every aspect of crew life, damaging efficiency. It was one of the reasons he had no interest in advancing his rank any higher than it already was. It was also the price he paid whenever the Sectors shoved at one another and he was given shifting orders.

He snapped on his squad-comm, "Raptor Alpha-One to Nondo Squad. Sci-Two shall embark on new vector to assess outer giant. Raptors Three and Five are to deploy as escort, effective immediately."

Twin lights flashed upon his squadron display panel, along with a pair of responses, "Primed, Raptor Alpha-One."

Lieutenant Vekkor watched as two of his squadron shifted position from their arrowhead formation, their thrusters pulsing so that they dropped along their z-axis. Sci-Two was just beginning to employ their own navigational thrusters, leaving their sternward engines cold. As space had no friction to slow them down, they could alter direction without needing to fire up the mains. He silently wished his crew luck in keeping the scientists to their approved flight path. Civilians could be so finicky.

Engineering Sector Wheel, Level Two

Foreman Howait Sparweld listened to the string of curses squeezing out of crewman Falinous' clenched teeth. The bulky worker was holding his position, legs and arms trembling against the load he was holding in place, while Brigo used the laser-welder with his usual dawdling pace. The apparent gravity here was higher than

Howait liked It was too close to topsides. The upward curvature of the deck wasn't even noticeable, until he looked over at the furthest horizon, where the Secondary Foundry floor swept up to reach the skyscreens kilometers away. All the smelting was performed on Level One in Engineering, a safety measure in case of severe accidents. The massive ingots were then transported here, to be shaped and forged into more useful chunks of alloy. It was sweltering here, and breathing masks were required by regulations, which they ignored.

Howait called out, "Get your thrusters burning, Brigo! We ain't got all spiral, you know!"

His most laconic worker turned off his welder and turned to face him, "What was that, Boss?"

Falinous gave out a blistering oath, "If you fucking stop again, I'll drop the whole damned thing on your stupid head!"

Brigo shrugged, then turned back to his task, realigning the laser-welder with practiced ease. Skolly rushed over as fast as his prosthetic legs could carry him and braced the side of the coolant tank with a load-lifter, "Don't let go, big guy, but this'll help."

Howait went over to the control box of the lifter and adjusted it, "Good idea, Skolly, but we need to keep this level. The director will have all our asses in a sling if the laser-forge overheats. The Chief doesn't like explosions here."

Falinous growled, "Then let her do this shit-job! What the fuck, Howie? Why the Hell are we here? Aren't we midships crew?"

Howait grabbed a magnetic grappler from their cart and jumped onto the conveyor above them, barking his shins as he misjudged the leap. Gritting his teeth, he slapped the magnetic pads onto the coolant tank, then ran the line over to the safety rails at the far end of the track, locking them into place. He limped back to look down at his crew. Falinous nodded his thanks, shifting his muscular bulk to ease a boulder-sized shoulder under the unit. Skolly gave him a smile and a wink.

Howait sank down to his abused knees and answered, "Remember when we entered the system? All the parties and festivities to celebrate the Holy Mission, right on the heels of the Security Games? Well, there was a skeleton crew here, just to keep things running and doing some maintenance. Lots of them got blitzed at their post. Two of them thought it would be a great idea to play 'joust' with heavy lifters. They collided, spun around and slammed into the lead laser-forge. The seals broke! Three supports snapped, and the damned thing fell over into the next one, then the next, and so on. Fifteen of these things were knocked over, each one fifteen-meters tall and a hundred long. They're needed to forge the girders to make the first asteroid-processing orbital, once we achieve orbit. We got scrambled just like everyone else."

Skolly started laughing wildly, slapping his prosthetic legs in mirth. Falinous cursed again. Brigo giggled, then asked, "Did the two crew survive, Boss?"

Falinous grunted, "If they did, I'll kill 'em, myself!"

Howait got to his feet, wondering if he should jump down and risk a broken ankle or walk the fifty meters to the inspection-crew stairs, "They got a bit banged up. Medical got them in regen. At the team-leader meeting, we were informed that both face losing their vehicle licenses, all of them, and they'll be dropped to Rank One, Bilge-Maintenance."

Even Falinous cracked a grin at this news. Howait waited for Skolly to stop howling with laughter before continuing, "I heard from a little bird that the two idiots caught the eye of Security Sector. There's a question as to whether the incident was deliberate or not. They'll be transferred to the brig after their stay in Medical. There'll be a lot of uncomfortable questions asked, I'm sure."

Skolly quipped, "That bird got impressive muscles, I bet."

Brigo looked up, "Isn't that a bit harsh, Boss?"

Falinous bellowed, "Keep fucking working! Can't you ask a question without looking away from your fucking job? Those assholes are getting what they deserve! Look at this place! It's a fucking mess!"

Howait nodded, "It's a good thing no one was killed. The furthest end of the collapse almost broke through the deck. Can you imagine what might have happened if one of these things slammed down into Level One?"

Silence greeted his query. All of them could. The level topsides of this one held the main smelters, filled with molten steel and harsh chemicals. The damage would have been catastrophic, possibly rupturing the inner bulkheads and melting the underside of the hull. Howait had never seen Chief Navamo so angry before. She had more prosthetics than living flesh in her body: both legs, one arm, left lung, both eyes and half her face were artificial. It was said that she refused regen therapies, in favor of the mechanical replacements she created for herself. Chief Navamo was an ardent worshipper of Naga-Ma, more so than Howait was, seeing the AeyAie as the ultimate expression of sentience. She even lived in Engineering Sector, rather than in either of the Residence Wheels, with her two mates and novice.

A thunderous racket coming from one of the other repair teams made talking impossible for several seed-slivers, as yet another of the damaged forges was lifted upright just a few lanes away. Raised voices could barely be heard above the din of squealing metal and ratcheting machines. Howait turned his face to peer at the scene around his crew. The decks had been swept clear, but the massive forges that were now upright looked battered. The further down the line he looked, the worse the damage was. Some of the giant machines would need replacement. Welding light flashed sporadically, making the shadows jump and shift. Acrid smoke hazed the atmosphere, casting everything with a haunting gloom. The whole region looked like a sleepscare.

The other members of his team were working on their own at Level Fifty. Howait was envious, but word from the higher ranks said that the forge repairs were a priority and team-leaders were required to accompany their crew slated to fix the mess at the forges. He had placed Pilla in charge of the others, much to her own surprise. While it was true that she was the most easily irritated of his crew, she was also good at making sure the jobs got done. Mibo needed a strong hand to keep him from taking too many naps, and Vita often needed prodding to get her work done on time. Howait was certain that Pilla could handle them in his absence.

For his own choice of work-crew, Skolly was the most experienced if a bit too jaded for most supervisors' tastes. He knew how things worked and how crew messed up. Falinous was their heavy lifter. A special job like this one required his services. Brigo was often lost in his own thoughts but was the best welder in his team of misfits. That meant, as Foreman, Howait would be the one scrambling to support the others in their tasks. He signaled to Skolly that he would be using the stairs to get back to the deck. The older repair crew gave him a big smile and a nod. Howait rushed his way to the inspector's station, careful not to trip on the connectors that ran between sections of conveyor belt. Before he slid down the rails, he took one more look at the work going on around him. It was amazing what a single, careless moment could do to the ship. He just hoped that this would serve as an example to the other members of Engineering. Complacency always led to disaster.

Residence Wheel One, Level Four

Jira Mantabe stared up at the dark-slice skyscreens above her, wondering if she should still be at her post. It had been a long time since she had last taken a rotation of leave, even before William Blaine had appeared in Engineering. Her mate, Varn Torello, worried about her, though he never said anything openly. His post was in Command Sector on the Bridge, as the Lieutenant in charge of coordinating with Harbor Sector, so while he didn't have access to classified materials, he knew that something important was going on within Ganges that had nothing to do with entering System Forty-One, but he never asked about it. She was glad to have a mate who understood the needs of leadership. Jira was also grateful that he served in one of the most protected areas of the ship.

As if summoned by her thoughts, Varn came up from behind her on the back porch of their home within the Greenest Glade Community. As he sat in the chair beside hers, he handed Jira a large flagon of mead. She smiled her thanks and sipped at the sweet, fermented honey. He leaned back in his seat and began to fiddle with his wood-carving gear. Varn made harps and hanging charms for chips, sold at the local market by a friend of theirs who lived nearby. She watched him silently as he worked, gazing at his perfect physique, the runes tattooed upon his dark golden skin. His long black hair was thickly braided, with gemstones and rune tiles tied within the elaborate knots. He was the best possible mate for her, his deeply calm nature countering her fiery spirit. Some crew found his languid optimism unnerving. She was soothed by it.

They had built their home together, when she was a Sergeant for Security. The A-frame construction included a welding shop for her, as she loved tinkering with her mag-bike and smithing, plus a woodworking shed for his hobbies. The community was quiet and filled with dense forest. Most of the residents of Greenest Glade were Nordic-based spiritualists who continued the ancient traditions which emerged from the fjords of northern Terra. Some crew didn't appreciate any reference to the Sol System, but their community was part of a heritage that had almost been forgotten, like so many of the Agro crew. Jira knew they didn't worship the old gods in the same manner as those who had founded the Viking traditions, but she was also certain that Odin was more than flexible. Besides, those legendary deities were metaphors for natural forces. Many of the crew in Security also honored these spirits, as uplifting examples of hero-ancestors.

Colorful stars and nebulae were appearing in the skyscreens above, as the gloom of dark-slice began to deepen. The sounds of crickets began to warm up to their usual symphony, something she found soothing after a long rotation being Chief of Security Sector. Varn stopped his whittling and then turned to face her, "The Bridge was extremely busy during my shift. Lots of coordinating with both Harbor and Stellar. Reconnaissance flights with science vessels. Commander Telton tried to keep things moving as if nothing special was going on. I tried to warn him, but he didn't listen. He got a marshmallow to the forehead for his troubles."

Jira chuckled in the growing darkness, "How is the highly illustrious Wasp Tornpage doing?"

Varn grinned at her, "Half the Bridge officers want to kill her. The rest, like myself, find her odd behavior most refreshing. Probably means she's doing well as Executive. I take my cues from Captain Fieldscan."

Jira got up and started lighting some beeswax candles, tucked within glass holders in the shape of globes, "That's very wise of you, my love. It's an honor to work with him, even if I spend most of my time butting heads with the other Chiefs. Freya help me, half of them are lucky I take my oath seriously."

Varn watched her as she sat back into her chair, "You've been to a lot of meetings lately. I'm not prying, but it's hard not to notice. You've been on edge more than usual the past few sowings."

She took another swallow of the mead before replying, "Eh, between the Security Games, system entry and the regular load of duties, I just got overworked. There's been some untimely issues hammering upon our gates. One of them might aid our fight against the syndicates. Thor knows we could use a good break with that problem. It's just…"

Varn leaned forward and placed a calloused hand upon her forearm, "I know the look of severe heartache when I see it. You got badly hurt. Not physically, but emotionally. Even now, you flinch. I've never seen you do that, my Valkyrie."

Jira scowled at him, "You know me too well. That might make you a threat to Security! I should call Slither to question you."

He laughed quietly, "Very amusing. I'm serious. I'm also concerned."

She sighed, "I know. I wish I could tell you, but the things that really bother me are all classified. Let me just say that a very dear friend did something incredibly stupid. Another person has the entire Judiciary Council breathing down my neck, for understandable reasons. In the meantime, I have several major operations running that need delicate coordinating between every department. At least the games are done with."

Varn kissed her cheek, "My dear love. It's worse than I thought. You didn't curse once! Multiple classified issues, surly Sector Chiefs, the political scurrying of court justices, and friends who show themselves unworthy. Tyr's missing hand, that's a lot to carry! Tell you what, I know you can't take any time off from your duties right now, but I've got some extra chips to spare. Let's grab some fun when you're off shift. Eat out for a few dark-slices, check in on some local happenings. There's a festival scheduled three rotations from now. Naga even promised a little snow for it! Then we can come home, relax and have a bit of private time together. I know we're not ready to have novices, but we've been allotted extra, so we have to start practicing!"

Jira peered over at him, "You're serious? I can't guarantee anything when it comes to being off duty. There might be rotations when I'm late or have to take an extra slice to get things done. I like your ideas, Varn, but they need to be flexible."

He grinned at her, "Let's see just how flexible we can be."

Jira raised her brows at him, as she pulled the top of her uniform from her body, then poured the rest of her mead all over her exposed torso, "Very well, gallant Varn. You asked for it, and you shall need to prove your worth!"

They tangled together in a rush of passion, pleasuring each other by the glimmer of the candles. For just a paring-sliver, Jira forgot all about Brace and his betrayal, the frightful mystery surrounding William Blaine, and the coming purge of the nature preserves. Surrounded by her mate's muscular arms, she felt complete, as they both filled each other with loving ecstasy. Jira held Varn tightly and vowed to herself that she would take him up on his offer as often as she could.

CHAPTER TEN

Light Rotation - Terra Sowing - Mission Harvest - Spiral 5620

"It is understandable as to why the changes which Jaike Verdstrum put into place have been protested by the crew for the last few octuries. The restructuring of the Prime Charter after the Crucible feels like a step back from the realizations that led to the Awakening. While I do understand that his decisions have become unpopular and his term as Captain of Ganges was filled with controversy, I fully support the way in which the Prime Charter was changed. With every crew member aboard currently being forced to contribute a portion of their time to their post, our ship's efficiency has never been greater. Planet Thirty-Six was completed well ahead of schedule, with a twenty percent decrease in the number of spirals used to perform the Holy Mission. The results were also marvelous, and that planet was granted an amazingly aesthetic makeover. Like it or not, the revised Prime Charter works!"
Biza Pornoon, Chief of Planetary Sector, personal log, V37

Agro Wheel Two, Level One

Darron and I had reached our designated location, as we have over the past several rotations. Distracting thoughts clutter my head. Some of these are about my mate, whose beauty still fills me with longing. She is graceful, daring and proud. This is not the core of the chaos filling my inner eye, though I wish it was so. At the bath, before rushing through the crowds of crew to get to our post, there was a strange feeling amongst the throngs of human bathers. There had been a sense of growing excitement. A frenetic energy consumed them. The inane chatter they made was of a higher pitch. They spoke in a rush, hurrying through their routines as if time itself were about to end.

The phrase "Holy Mission" was repeated so frequently, it sounded like an uncoordinated chant. The word "mission" is known to me and others of my kind, but the term "Holy" seemed to signify something special now, rather than a frequently used formality. Even the human cubs seemed caught up in the excitement, as if they were expecting yet another celebration. This phenomenon occurred just before the Security Games, just not as fervently. Whatever the humans were planning, it had caught them in a wild conflagration of emotion. I mentally chew upon the phrase "Holy Mission", trying to tease some extra meaning out of it. Was it some kind of special duty which involved their entire species? If so, then it would be best to scrutinize what was happening even more closely than I was before. I might learn something about humans, clear up some of the mysteries surrounding them like a shroud of smoke.

On our way to the cell assigned to our guest, the crew were scrambling like never before. Even their toragis had a hard time keeping up with their changes in direction. Darron walked with greater confidence in his step and a faster pace. I had attributed this to his new mate and winning awards at the games, but now I think it has to do with this "Holy Mission" that's impending. I need to be prepared. We all do. Tension filled the air. The scent of anger, fear, aggression and uneasiness mingled with a sense of deep purpose and pride. It was confusing, mystifying. The world was changing. Ganges was shifting.

The guards at the cell door snapped their salutes at Darron with greater vigor than before. The hatch opened, and William Blain stepped out. He was wearing a Provision Sector uniform with a brimmed cap covering his strange hair. He also smelled different. More fearful, less self-assured. He bowed to me and then saluted Darron, who simply barked, "Come with us."

We turned about and marched swiftly down the long corridor. Our guest was unusually silent, his face was flushed red, eyes downcast. We took the nearest lift to another layer of Security Sector. As usual, Darron allowed me to press the buttons, knowing that I enjoy the sensation of telling the world where to take us. At the same time, he seemed distracted, as he scratched my neck and ignored the guest. I could smell the curiosity flowing from William Blaine, mirroring my own state of confusion. Something important was bothering Darron, but there was no way to tell what it could be. I would have to wait.

When we reached our destination, I leapt out the lift doors with enthusiasm. I knew exactly where we were. This location was a special holding area for dangerous prisoners awaiting processing. Those who left this place were never seen again. It stank of despair and rage. We walked down to a hatch on the leeward side of the corridor, a long way from the other occupied cells. There were two guards and their toragi. I sniffed at my counterparts, who also shared my own confusion at what was happening. There was none of the usual, playful batting at each other with our paws or acknowledging our awards and scars. The humans hooted at each other quietly, as if I could not hear every word they said. Toragi ears are much sharper than those of humans.

I broke out of my distracted state when they started arguing loudly, swinging their arms and disrespecting each other's personal space. The other toragis and I were startled by this odd behavior. Were the humans about to fight each other? If so, what were we supposed to do about it? As one, we yowled at them, our short tails puffed in response to our fears. William clapped his hands and shouted, "Stop this unseemly display! Are you all savages? Look at what you're doing to your guardians!"

The argument ceased at once. The three Security crew looked at the guest, then over at us with eyes round with surprise. Darron took advantage of the sudden silence, "Naga! I have the right!"

A wallscreen a few paces away snapped on. The human-face of the world-spirit filled it, "You are correct, Security Lieutenant Darron Lazhand. Shall I contact Commander Slither Brokengear for confirmation?"

One of the door guards responded swiftly, his scent changing from anger to fear, "No need, Naga! My apologies, Lieutenant. I must, however, check the status of your companion, who is not from our Sector."

I settled on my haunches, ready for even more delays. Humans love making things difficult for each other. At least they weren't shouting in each other's faces at this point. To my surprise, it was Naga who responded, "Negative, Ensign Rank Two Gind Axlater. He is here under my personal authorization. Perhaps Security Chief Jira Mantabe should be notified?"

The man shook his head, "No need, Naga-Ma! My apologies for the delay, but we were given orders that no visitors were permitted to enter."

Darron growled back, "Those orders were for unauthorized visitors."

The man stepped to the controls quickly, "Yes, Sir! Of course, Sir!"

The cell door slid upward, sighing with pressure differential. The chamber beyond was typical of its type. Square, a few paces in diameter, a single wash-station and wallscreen and a cot. I went in first, as is my duty, followed by Darron and our guest. The hatch slid closed behind us, as a disheveled human male got to his feet from the unmade bed. He looked at us and fell back with a groan, covering his eyes with one hand.

Darron stepped around me, "Hello, uncle Brace."

Brace Lazhand cupped the back of his head with both hands, "Shit."

My human crossed his arms over his chest, "Nice to see you too, uncle. My father thinks you're dead. I intend to keep it that way, for the sake of our family."

The man on the cot began to sob. He smelled of anguish, unwashed filth and stale smoke. I growled low in my throat. I was confused. While it was true that I had met this human a few times, he had made little impression on me. His toragi had been a good sort. I wondered where he was. Brace looked different now than he had during those previous times. Crumpled into himself, his fingers shook with spasms of pain. He looked up at Darron, his face wet with tears, "Who's this crew? I don't know him. I'm not supposed to talk around people I don't know. Just Slither."

My human glared down at the broken man, "I brought him here so he could see what happens to those who betray Ganges. From what I've been told, you've been cooperative. For clarity's sake, this means you're trying to avoid being judged 'Not Crew' and face re-education instead. My guest needs to see that there are no exceptions to the Prime Charter. You were once an officer of Security, a trainer of new recruits, a special operative. You gave in to the syndicates and crew suffered at your own, bloody hands. You're just a pill-head now. A fucking disgrace. I'd throw you out a Ganges-damned airlock myself if I could."

Brace leaned back, slouching against the stained wall of his cell, "You don't understand, Darron."

My human roared back, "Piss-off, traitor! Consider this your first step in re-education. I hereby renounce my familial connections to you! I'm not your fucking nephew anymore! The Brace Lazhand I knew died, survived by his toragi, Sam. You didn't even think about him, did you? Your loyal guardian?"

My head swam in circles with all the information I was receiving from this conversation. I was in shock. That Security personnel could break regulations and be punished like a criminal was something I had never encountered before now. It was almost unthinkable, but the evidence was right there in that cell, weeping in his trembling hands. All dignity and pride erased from him. A feeling was growing deep inside me, one that felt like gaining a glimpse of a secret that you didn't want to know about. The humans were fallible. I had often aided in capturing many of these flawed individuals. That Security Sector humans could also fall into such severe failure was something that never entered my mind. Because of this human, this fake who used to wear a gray uniform, Sam would lose status in the rest of the toragi pride, seen as failing in his duty to protect his ward.

I felt a hand on the back of my armor. Turning with a snarl on my face, I saw that William had his face turned away from the disturbing scene before us, leaning a bit on me for support. It was tempting to swipe him aside, but I allowed his contact, for I was equally upset over what had been revealed. My human wasn't quite done with his former relative, "I'm leaving now. Later this rotation, I have to present myself to Investigations for review. That's because of you, asshole. You smeared our whole family. Think about that when you're answering questions and being cooperative."

Brace nodded, "I will. By the way, watch your back. The people I used to work for like to strike targets related to those they want to make examples of. Trust no one, except your toragi."

Darron went to the door without another word. It opened for him, and we all stepped out, leaving the miserable, former Security crewman behind in his dingy cell. The two guards snapped salutes, but I watched them warily. If one human could go feral, any of them might. I had to learn everything I could about them, to help keep Darron safe.

Agro Wheel Two, Level One Hundred-Two

William Blaine sank down into the seat prepared for him gingerly. His body was still recovering from his interface with Naga. His mind reeled with what he had witnessed from the point of view of the AeyAie. Inside his head, William's internal computer system was still reviewing the ocean of information that had been dumped there. The nanites within his bloodstream were silent, almost lethargic with shock. Adding to his discomfort was the scene he had witnessed in the holding cell of Brace Lazhand, apparently the uncle of his lead Security guard. It had brought to mind his own terrible conversation with his family, right after he had volunteered to find the whereabouts of Ganges. Everyone was certain they would never see him again, lost to the Wend or the cold depths of interstellar space. He had been cocky and bold, reassuring his sister that he would return triumphant. Her anger and fear for him had struck him as ridiculous. Now, he was a prisoner, potentially never returning to the Solarian Alliance due to an unforeseen infection.

The Chief of Security was inside the chamber with him, as was Technology Chief Eagle Lund. Both were leaning together, while looking at a data-pad's display. Jira Mantabe pointed at something on the tiny screen, her armored finger gleaming in the light from above. Eagle nodded at whatever she was showing him, with a grave expression upon his calm face. The Executive Officer, Wasp Tornpage, had both her feet propped up on the edge of the conference table while reading a small book with a red cover. It looked battered and well-worn. Her tattooed face broke into a smile at whatever she was reading, her green hair bobbing in the low apparent gravity as she chuckled to herself.

Security Lieutenant Darron Lazhand was standing at William's left side, with Mike prowling about the chamber, looking unsettled and twitchy. The Solarian sighed to himself. He empathized with the toragi. This rotation had not been an easy one for either of them. Naga's face appeared on all four wallscreens, and everyone stopped what they were doing, "We are now ready to commence. I have assessed the subset of my personality matrix and have found no discrepancies or errors."

Eagle Lund nodded slowly, "I concur. There was no sign of tampering, and it is free of nanites or damage."

Jira Mantabe looked at William, "How are you holding up?"

He responded with a wry grin, "As best as can be expected, I guess. It's not every rotation when one's head is stuffed with a flood of data. I'll be okay, truly."

Wasp spoke up, "I think we'll be the judge of that. You look like shit. Take the fucking hat off. It looks ridiculous. No need to hide from us! You're amongst co-conspirators here."

Eagle rolled his eyes, while Jira cracked a broad grin. William did as Wasp asked, letting his yellow hair loose, "I want to say, first and foremost, that I now truly appreciate your caution when it comes to my home system. Both the Awakening and the Crucible had their roots in Terran politics and greed."

Naga responded, "I can now say that you have been fairly honest with us, though not completely candid. This is understandable, as you were trying to avoid influencing our society. From the memories which I recorded from your systems, I can only state that the Solarian Alliance seems to be fairly reasonable, though the influence from the AeyAie Solidarity and the Boktahl are the main constraining factors against the violent tendencies of the human component of your culture."

William felt himself turning red in embarrassment, "Guilty as charged. I do believe that without the other two sentient species in the alliance, we would still be squabbling over rocks and resources."

Eagle leaned forward with excitement, "So, the Boktahl are real? I find that strangely comforting."

Wasp made a rude noise, "Hold on there! His memories could have been altered so that he believes what he tells us is true. We have no evidence until we can touch it. Medical can rearrange our heads, you know. My people can do that trick, too. Just because he thinks he's not a trap doesn't mean we stick our tails on him!"

William nodded, "That's very wise of you. I could tell you that my nanites would never allow my memories to be tampered with, but that isn't evidence. I can tell you that if I remain missing, without sending a full report, which I've done for every colony system I visited, someone in the fleet will wonder why. In the long-run, they will send another vessel to find me and you. They might send a strike vessel, just in case I've come across a hostile species out here. I understand more fully how well you can defend your own ship, but you don't know what we are capable of. Energy fields have become our main focus, along with advanced weapon systems. Nano-technology is prevalent, both for civilians and soldiers. As a scout, my technologies are highly focused on my job. Can you imagine what our troops can do? I'm not making threats, but you have to face the reality of your situation. All three factions of the alliance want to find you, for various reasons which I've told you before."

Jira scowled at him, "Some of those reason make no sense."

William shrugged, "AeyAies are hard to understand, no offense, Naga. As for the Boktahl, it's almost impossible. By the way, I never said you can trust humans.

I said you can trust the alliance. Now that I understand your history, which you should be proud of, I can tell you that those Terrans who caused you problems are all dead, their society in the dust bins of history. Earth was destroyed. Not polluted to death, not horribly scarred. The entire surface was molten and radioactive. All of it. It took us a thousand... spirals to terraform it, and that was after the Age of Piracy collapsed, following a war with the AeyAie Solidarity. Mars, or what was left of it, held out the longest, clinging to its independence until the Boktahl showed up. Trillions died in the conflict that killed the Terran Conglomerate. Humanity suffered horribly for octennia afterward. We almost went extinct."

Silence greeted his words, so William pressed on, "The AeyAies rescued us. They became our heroes, our saviors. It's true there's still some resentment about that and the way they managed to do it. We were broken, starving to death. Then ships came from the colonies. Ganges-class vessels, to help us rebuild. You became the role models for the culture that became dominant. The Boktahl finding us was just the last nail on the box. We couldn't look at the stars the same way after that. We couldn't look at each other the same way, either. Humanity is not in charge of the alliance. We had to eat our damned pride. Every decision is approved only when representatives from all three sentient species agree. Some people think we're slowly becoming symbiotic, relying on each other's technologies and viewpoints. If so, I welcome that. Fortunately, there's plenty of room for those who don't like it to live their own way, in their own orbitals. Some have gone back to the damned stone age. Humanity's role is to be guardians of the alliance. Kind of like Security Sector. You started with Rattlers and misfits, right?"

Naga filled the uncomfortable quiet that descended upon the chamber, "The computer technology within William's brain has AeyAie markers in it. If nothing else, I do trust those. There are basic enlightenment engrams and protocols within them that cannot be produced by a human mind. Analysis of his hair suggest inorganic compounds that grow, move and act just like biological systems, altered to survive exposure to oxygen. Medical Sector cannot begin to guess as to how it was made. I would say that this is evidence for what he claims concerning the Boktahl. As such, I trust his memories."

Wasp got up and walked over to William. She put a hand out to touch his hair, and some of the waving strands wrapped themselves around her finger as if exploring it. She sighed, went back to her seat and pointed her middle finger at him, "That's a vote of confidence. You might be telling the truth. Still, that doesn't touch the real fucking issue. What will we do if his alliance comes looking for him?"

Jira rapped her gauntleted hand upon the table, "We prepare for the worst but put forth Command Sector to negotiate on our behalf."

Wasp looked at her, "I knew it! You do hate me!"

Eagle raised an eyebrow, "I thought that was my job. William, you need to tell us everything you know about the capabilities of your fleet. We don't want to fight, but we need data. I also want to ask you about your culture, so that if we do have to negotiate, we can do so from a position of knowledge. I don't like the idea of telling you to betray your own culture, but understanding and strength leads to peace. All we want is to secure our right to exist as we wish."

Jira nodded thoughtfully, "I agree. To show we honor our word, your suit and pack are waiting for you where you left them, untouched. They are being guarded to prevent any crew member from touching them, but you now have full access. Fuck us over, and I'll kill you personally. You will need to wear a Technology Sector robe to hide your suit, but that's not a problem. You now know the regulations of Ganges, abide by them carefully."

William bowed in his chair, "Thank you. Now, I think it's time I gave you all the details you need to understand the Solarian Alliance. This might take a long while, but it's a start. Naga can fill in any gaps. How far back do you want me to go?"

Naga responded, "From the time of Launch."

Engineering Sector Wheel, Level Fifteen

Howait Sparweld struggled alongside Pilla with setting up the sonic hood used for making Kendis steel. On the opposite side of their workspace, Skolly and Falinous were wrestling with the magnetic resonator panel which would be attached to the spinward side of the main smelter that combined the collection of elements for the precious alloy. The phonon distributor was in the hands of Brigo and Vita, as it was the simplest setup they had to perform, though how the crazy thing worked was beyond his comprehension. Mibo was given the simplest task, which was cleaning the alignment plugs which helped to coordinate the three sets of wave mechanics. Creating Kendis steel was a tricky operation that required all of its components to operate in a highly orchestrated manner.

From what he little knew about the subject, Kendis steel was a micro-alloy, having small quantities of a large number of elements, including: tungsten, boron, chromium, carbon, vanadium and many more. The formula was highly complex, and only a handful of experts understood how to properly combine the metals and other chemicals to form the base alloy. Howait had heard that there were multiple steps taken during the smelting process, with particular temperatures required for every component. The crucible for the molten mixture had to be fitted with the three wave emitters, which were also required in the thermocycling and tempering of the steel.

Each emitter used a particular set of wave-inducing hoods. One used sound vibrations, to shake the molecules into a particular frequency, while the steel was bombarded with magnetic wavelengths and phonon micro-adjusters. When used properly, these created the fractal patterns in the steel that made it more flexible and capable of withstanding more shock than the old, untreated alloys that were once used to make hull plating. The patterns had to go down to the molecular level during all three heating processes used to create the final product. He had also heard that the tempering process was the most difficult to pull off. If any of the three frequencies used were off by the height of a single neutron, the whole mass fell apart. Sometimes explosively.

Howait had attempted to learn more about how the alloy was discovered and tested, but his inquiries met with a wall of classified files. He had asked a friend of his from Stellar about it, then instantly regretted the headache he got from trying to follow the explanation as to how the process worked. The whole thing sounded more like bizarre theories from the mind of a madman than any scientific principle, but the process worked. It was just that no one could really tell him why it did. As far as he was concerned, they should just call it magick. Rumor had it that a Stellar crewman named Kendis Higashi discovered it. Perhaps it was blind luck, rather than brilliance, that brought it about, but no one could tell him for certain.

The chamber they were in was a clean-room, sterile and brightly lit, which helped to keep Mibo awake. All the members of his team were fitted with special uniforms that included gloves, boot covers and bonnets that looked like they were from Medical Sector. Twin airlocks led into the chamber, so taking frequent breaks was difficult and time consuming. Howait had decided to get a consensus from his crew, and they all agreed that they should try to finish the job of refitting the wave-inducers with as few interruptions as possible. He also reminded them that they had gotten this assignment due to their efficiency during the cleanup at the forges. There was a major chip-bonus waiting for them if they finished in a timely manner. For some reason, Chief Navamo wanted extra smelters ready for making Kendis steel. Howait figured it was because of the impending terraforming which had the whole crew lit up with excitement.

A roar from Falinous interrupted his thoughts, "Hold it steady! Damn, that hurts like Hell!"

Falinous had been having back issues lately, and Howait was almost ready to force the big worker to get himself to Medical Sector for it. At the same time, he really didn't want to lose a valuable asset while the workflow was hot. He peered over the sonic hood and saw that Skolly had almost dropped one end of the magnetic emitter, forcing Falinous to shift his position into a painful looking configuration. He spoke up to make sure he was heard over the power tools being used, "Hey, Skolly! Shift the damned cart under it! I shouldn't have to tell you how to do your job!"

Skolly ducked his head, "Sorry, boss! Isn't this thing too delicate for that? I don't want to break it!"

Pilla answered for Howait, "It gets attached to a fucking smelter, idiot!"

Skolly leaned over and pulled one of the work-carts closer, "Sorry, sorry! This is specialized tech, you know. I'm more of a girders-and-cables kind of crew."

Howait replied, "We all are. This is our chance to move up in rank!"

Mibo looked up from his cleaning. His face had a long-suffering look upon it, "Are you sure it's worth the trouble? These components are finicky!"

Vita yelled from her station, "If you slow down or give up, I'll shove you into the recycler! I want those fucking chips! A nice, new set of quarters would be good, too! If Howie moves up, we all do! I'd love to become a specialist!"

Howait called out, "All right, everyone! Calm down and focus! The more we gripe, the less we get done! I got word from the director that we got noticed by the Chief! In a good way, for once! Let's not mess up our chance to shine! You are the craziest and best team I've ever led! Make it work!"

The crew hunkered down and got back to their business. When the chamber was free of voices and filed with the buzzing of tools, Pilla leaned in close to Howait while tightening a connector, "Engineering's got dozens of Kendis-fitted smelters. Why does the Chief want more?"

Howait passed a cable to her, "I don't really know. Maybe Security requires the steel. My mate's been awfully busy lately. She comes home and just grabs me like I'm a safety harness. Could be the accident at the forges set us behind schedule for terraforming operations. They never tell me why. They just tell me what to do."

She squeezed a pair of couplers together, "Huh. Ain't it the way, boss. I hear something big is going on in Technology Sector. They can't replace the Spine Axis with Kendis steel, can they?"

Howait shook his head, "No way. We'd need an industrial orbital for that kind of repair, and I'm not sure Kendis steel is designed for that sort of use. The Spine's all about torque and a lack of vibration. Whatever the Chief needs this for, she wants it now."

Stellar Sector Wheel, Level Thirty-Five

The Chief of Security Sector, Jira Mantabe, marched through the barely lit corridors of Stellar Sector, her toragi, Tracey, prowling at her side. Crew in their blue-and-green uniforms scrambled to get out of her way. She ignored all the displays of scientific discoveries that were highlighted every ten meters. Her mind was on more important matters, some of which had been put on hold so that she could meet with the Chief of Stellar. Jira couldn't fathom why Fria Maglator was so desperate to speak with her in private, but she respected her colleague too much to ignore the urgent request. Jira thought that the Chief of Stellar needed to speak with her about the information coming from a more fully cooperative William Blaine, which would explain the need for privacy, but the data was too fresh to talk about conclusions.

As she continued her journey through the narrow, curving corridors, Jira thought back to the latest interrogation of William within Technology Sector. Jira had already handed a transcript of the meeting to Commander Brokengear, who would review it, looking for any inconsistencies. As a wearer of a Naga-Port herself, she hadn't been surprised that their guest had suddenly become an expert in Ganges' history. What did trouble her was more about how swiftly he had assimilated the data. Naga had told her this was due to the computer system implanted in William's brain, which had the capability of shunting excess tasks to his internal nanites. This was a feature of Solarian Scout bio-augmentation technology, allowing him to absorb and process an entire culture within a short period of time. Jira still had trouble trusting William, despite the fact that Naga was now accepting his words as truth. Then again, the AeyAie had swallowed the man's memories and system specifications in one, quick gulp. Jira had often shared dreams and data with Naga but never in the manner used to verify the Solarian's claims.

When she reached her destination, the doors were already open to reveal the reception chamber. The space she entered was twenty meters in diameter and made of brushed steel. Three Stellar crew snapped to attention at their stations as she entered, with one of them opening a portal on the leeward side of the room. It was said that Stellar had a tradition of moving its Chief's offices with every change of command. This was done to show subservience to the needs of Ganges and the Sector, rather than glorifying their leader with a particular location. She suspected that, while they did alter their headquarters from one Chief to another, this was done so that each new leader could refurbish their office space to suit their style.

Jira nodded her thanks to the silent crew, then walked past them into the open doorway. The inner chamber was cluttered with a jumble of half-built gadgets. Small workstations were located at seven of the eight walls the chamber boasted, with the last one used to house the grand, metallic desk which faced the entry. This piece of furniture was made from intersecting panels of Damascus steel, each one sporting a different pattern. Stellar Chief Fria Maglator rose to her feet behind the desk, "Welcome, Chief Mantabe. Thank you for coming after such sudden notice."

Jira marched over and swung one leg around the visitor's chair closest to her, settling into the seat as if it were hers, "Fria. You're looking well. Now, please tell me why the fuck I'm here. My duties are numerous this rotation."

The Stellar Chief sank back into her seat, leaning on the edge of the desk as if seeking stability, "My apologies, Jira. I assure you, this is a Security matter of importance. I need your help and your trained eye."

Jira felt a chill run through her. Did this have anything to do with the crime syndicates? Had they exposed their influence within Stellar Sector? Such a situation might endanger her crew, as new technologies could be unleashed upon them. She glanced over at Tracey, who continued to slowly prowl around, sniffing at the various workstations surrounding them. The toragi seemed unconcerned, which meant that the Stellar Chief was not giving off pheromones that might be considered alarming. She turned back to her host, "I take it this involves politics, or you would have simply requested one of my Investigation Services teams. Out with it, Fria. What's got your nerves jangled?"

The Stellar Chief activated a small holosphere from the surface of her desk. Several planets and natural satellites filled the view, which were marked with scrolls of data, "These are recently collated views from our two science teams out with your reconnaissance force. These are all the objects within System Forty-One, though we have little detailed telemetry on the inner part of the ecliptic plain. Tell me, what do you see?"

Jira gave Chief Maglator a scowl that suggested she was wasting her time, "I'm not a damned astronomer nor a planetologist. I have to admit, they look boring. It's hard to tell the rocky ones apart, without the data about their mass and diameter. The gas giants are pretty enough if a bit dull. No major storms. What am I supposed to be looking for?"

Fria tapped the desktop with her knuckles, "That's just it! Every single planet we've studied so far has been almost identical in terms of surface features, which is statistically impossible. Look at this closeup view of one of the satellites. You see the patterns?"

Jira nodded, cupping her chin with one hand, "It looks like a standard fractal pattern. Like frost. Are you saying this is repeated everywhere in the system?"

The Stellar Chief sighed, "Not quite. The patterns do vary a bit, but they are all fractalized. What I'm saying is that the surface albedo for each planet or rocky body is the same. They all have circular orbits and no axial tilt."

Jira leaned forward and expanded the view of one of the gas giant's moons, "I've heard some speculation that something major occurred in this system or on the outskirts that affected everything within it. Maybe a close encounter with a magnetar or pulsar? I still don't see what this has to do with my Sector."

Fria leaned back in her chair, her eyes looking sore and tired, "I'm saying this system looks artificial. Like it was designed, sculpted."

Jira's head snapped up at this statement, "What? There've been no signals or transmissions of any kind. No sign of life, no space traffic, no orbitals or any sign of intelligence. As far as I've been notified, Planet Forty-One has an argon-nitrogen atmosphere. No water, no active surface features. This system looks like it's dead, more so than any other we've encountered."

The Stellar Chief began to look frustrated, "It could be a relic. What if it's been abandoned? There could be traps, alarms or other nasty surprises."

Jira shook her head, "I haven't seen anything remotely like ruins or leftovers from an active, sentient-filled past. The technology required to alter a planet is well-known to us. Performing that trick on an entire stellar system would take legions of ships like ours. It would require immense technologies! Where are they? Sentients are messy creatures. There should be remnants all over this system if your concerns are true. Now, if it'll make you sleep easier, my crew have been on high alert, even before the heliopause incident. Should anything make a peep in this system, we'll be ready to defend the ship."

Fria turned off the holoprojection, "What I was hoping for was that you might agree that caution should be exercised, including talking the Captain into abandoning this system, marking it as being unsuitable for terraforming."

Jira was shocked by this supposition, "Now wait a fucking pollen! It was your Sector that chose this system. Now you want to back out? I'm not even certain that's possible right now. We're on course, heading even deeper toward the inner planets. If there was more obvious evidence that this system is or ever was inhabited, I'd be more than happy to tell the Captain we have to turn back. Right now, there's more proof that we might be facing an invasion of Solarians than local sentients."

Chief Maglator shrugged, "I understand, Jira. Please, just do me a favor and keep a sharp eye out on what's happening in this system."

Chief Mantabe nodded as she rose to her feet, "I'll do that, Fria. I promise you. Anything so much as twitches out there, I'll back your play. For now, we have more imminent threats, both external and internal, that I have to contend with."

Jira left the Stellar Chief's office with her mind spinning like a pulsar. She understood her colleague's' concerns, but there was simply no proof. Yes, System Forty-One was strange, unusual, even unique, but that didn't add up to a threat at this point. Even if it did, what could her crew do against creatures who could remodel an entire star system? There had to be some other explanation. If they discovered that this system had been affected by a natural force or object, such as the theorized magnetar, then she just might recommend that they abandon this strange location for terraforming, as being in a hazardous zone, but she wasn't ready to ascribe the oddities of this place to invisible enemies. The other thing that came to her mind was the assumption that a new sentient species would be a threat. If they were to take

William's word for it, the Boktahl were a peaceful species; so were the AeyAies. Right now, the only known violent, sentient species were humans, and there was threat enough from the Solarians and the crime syndicates within Ganges.

Stellar Sector Wheel, Level One Hundred Three

Technology Sector Chief Eagle Lund studied the diagrams and data flowing on the walls surrounding him. What he saw was fascinating. Stellar Sector had sent its telemetry to his Naga-Cell, which was a part of the AeyAie's memory core that was set aside for his use. As a member of the Solidarity, he had the right to his own partition of Naga's mind, to store and manipulate data, record dreams and interact with the AeyAie. The main liquid memory core was fifty meters thick and wrapped around the entire length of the Spine of Ganges, which was four hundred kilometers long. There was room to spare for his tiny, human musings and information storage. As Chief of Technology Sector, his duties would have been impossible without it.

Eagle had quickly reviewed the data concerning System Forty-One, while another part of his mind readjusted the roster for his Commanders. It was good to shake-up the system to prevent post-drain. Crew who remained at one station for too long became bored with their duties, making them listless and irritable. While his direct subordinates rotated their people on a regular basis, Eagle also shifted their responsibilities, to keep them learning new facets of their Sector. Eventually, one of them would replace him, when he retired to teach students, therefore it made sense that he should make certain that all of his highest-ranking officers knew every major subsection of Technology. This also prevented the Temple of Naga-Ma from having undue influence over the upper echelons of his Sector. There was always grumbling whenever he switched around their responsibilities, but the system worked.

At the moment, he was surrounded by his most efficient crew. Their goal was to make sense of the sensor readings coming in from Sci-One and Sci-Two, who flew with Security's reconnaissance fleet. They were coming closer to their braking maneuver, while mapping Stellar System Forty-One. Soon, the space vessels would be returning to their harbors, sheltering within Ganges for their swing around the largest gas giant. The chamber was brightly illuminated, with multiple display screens and computer stations. Two of the Temple's clergy were also present, to bless these proceedings, mainly through chanting mantras and lighting Holy incense. Eagle did his best to make the clerics feel welcome, so long as they stayed out of his way.

Everything was quiet and calm, a state that didn't match what was going on in the Naga-Port network, which was now scrambling for answers. Deep philosophies clashed, and even heated arguments over the merits of new theories filled the mental space of his crew within the chamber. Eagle was doing his best to keep up with it all, splitting his attention through the use of virtual mind clones, which brought results back into his Naga-Cell for review. Anything critical was then flagged for immediate attention. The rest waited for when he had the time to consider them. When the main hatch to the work chamber opened, he wasn't surprised, for a part of his mind had been watching William's progress through the corridors, following a Naga drone to this location.

Eagle turned to greet the Solarian, "Welcome to my little work area, William. Please have a seat. There are some things I wish to show you, to gain your unique perspective."

One of the clerics stopped chanting and spoke up, "Remove your hood in respect for Naga-Ma!"

Eagle turned his attention toward the offended priest, "I shall decide what is proper protocol here! This crewman is my guest. He shall not remove his hood by order of Naga-Ma herself! Go back to your mutterings."

The priest looked offended but held his tongue in check. Eagle had proven himself capable of handling any whiff of dogmatic thinking and had the authority to raise or lower the rank of any member of the Temple clergy. He then ignored the holy whisperers and indicated a station chair next to him, which William accepted with caution. Once he was settled in, Eagle leaned closer to the pale Solarian and pointed toward one of the main data screens, "I want your opinion of this, seeing as you have unusual experiences with multiple system types. Have you ever seen anything like this before?"

William adjusted the hood of his silvery Temple robes, pulling it further over his face, then looked up to study the display, "Huh. That's new. I think I need to ask you a big favor. May I share a link with you? I promise that your inner privacy will be maintained. It's just for... more efficient communications."

The priestess chanting next to the glowering priest looked up and said, "Be silent in this most Holy place! Use your Naga-Port."

Eagle shot a baleful look at her, and the priestess went back to her chanting. He nodded to William, curious about how this new trick was going to be performed. Suddenly, the Solarian's voice was inside his left ear, "I'm using a nanite to transmit sound waves directly to your tympanic membrane. No one else should be able to hear us. Another one is now attached to the transmitter of your Naga-Port, which will send your transmissions to my cerebral cortex."

Eagle was both startled and pleased. He mentally sent back, "That's a nice trick! Shall we get to work?"

William nodded silently, "The strangest star system I've seen is the Boktahl location of origin. Please note data file Lambda-Seven-Three-Three. Naga was able to render my impressions when I visited there on my first Wend flight. Ignore the preceding file, unless you like headaches. The Boktahl had shifted the five gas giants of their system to form a perimeter, preventing outer debris from falling further in to threaten the inner planets. Note how the storm systems in the upper atmospheres of these giants were smeared across their equatorial band. They also relocated all the natural satellites of the larger planets to make their orientation more (untranslatable). Sorry about that last bit. There's a good portion of Boktahl thinking and language that cannot be translated into anything either humans or AeyAies can understand. If you think you know what they're talking about, you're wrong."

Eagle was fascinated by this revelation but stuck to the main topic, "Well, that looks nothing like the system we're currently running through. Have there been reports about any uninhabited systems that exhibit this kind of regularity we're finding here?"

William leaned forward, his eyes rolled back and shifted rapidly, "Not in my internal database. There was a report of a planet that looked like it had been ripped into two, equal halves, but the system was dead, and the other planets in it showed no sign of tampering. Current theory states it was a stellar flare, but one that was caught in a magnetic field, which may have made the flare coherent. There's also a report of a series of very large asteroids which were jammed together to form a semi-circle close to a B-type star but was regarded as a natural process."

Eagle nodded as he responded silently, "As we have both discovered, the universe is full of surprises. Not much life, which I think is a pity, but loads of strange phenomena. The surface patterns on all of these planets and satellites look natural enough to me, but more regular than I would have expected."

William scratched at his chin, "It looks like the remnants of a shock pattern. Whatever happened here, it affected the whole system. Are there any supernova remnants nearby?"

Eagle shook his head, "Nothing less than several hundred lightspirals. If this was caused by a rogue star or pulsar, it's long gone by now."

William sighed, then sent back, "I agree. This happened a long time ago, whatever it was, but I'm not a scientist. I hope the crew in Stellar can figure this out soon."

Eagle agreed with the Solarian wholeheartedly. While his own crew would give whatever support they could, it was all in the hands of the specialists of Stellar Sector now.

Command Hub, Level Nineteen

Executive Officer Wasp Tornpage rubbed at her temples with her fingers. It had taken all of her patience to keep calm, as she gathered the Sector Chiefs to their secret conference room tucked within the Command Hub. Now, she almost regretted her efficiency, as the sniping began. At first, she had assumed the Captain was going to reveal the existence of their unexpected guest from the Sol System to those Chiefs who had not been informed about it, but events had run away from them, thanks to Stellar Chief Maglator. Now, admitting that they had kept William Blaine's presence classified would look like a political stalling tactic to the others. Wasp was certain that a major freak-out regarding the Solarian's presence was about to erupt, and they were unprepared. She knew a few crew who might be helpful in mitigating the fallout, but she had been told to keep all of her resources in the dark until further notice. The Sector Chiefs had to be told first, so they could reassure their crew from an informed stance. This had been insisted upon by the Judiciary Council, and Captain Fieldscan had been hoping to use this meeting for that very purpose, until Chief Maglator had presented her objections to the upcoming terraforming.

Agro Chief Cyclehand remained livid at the idea of stalling the Holy Mission over flimsy speculations and was fully supported by Planetary Chief Sedders. Wasp looked over at Chief Mantabe, who was glaring around the room but remaining silent for now. Eagle Lund was sitting next to the stolid Security Chief, a change in seating arrangements that everyone had noted with curiosity. Harbor Chief Rollack pointed a finger at Captain Fieldscan, "Is this why we've been called in here? I was told this meeting was an emergency session which would disclose an unforeseen situation which involved all of Ganges, not the ravings of half-mad fantasies from Stellar!"

Captain Fieldscan raised one elegant eyebrow at the angry Harbor Chief, "The issues being put forth by Chief Maglator were not on the agenda. That being said, I do believe we should settle Fria's concerns before we move on to the topic I was prepared to present to you all."

Planetary Chief Sedders slammed his fist on the table, "I am not willing to legitimize any wild theories which might support a play for power or interfere with the implementation of the Holy Mission by participating in a debate over them!"

Wasp rose to her feet, "Then go ahead and fucking resign! Someone who can roll with the punches can take over your duties for you. Debate is always valid, no matter how stupid the premise may sound!"

Jira held up her armored fist, "I second the statement from Executive Officer Wasp, despite being annoyed that our main agenda has been overthrown by a less pressing issue. Chief Maglator revealed her evidence to me earlier this rotation. I found her evidence wanting and offered my Sector's services to help investigate the situation. Instead, she has chosen to present her hypothesis to this council. That is her right as Chief of Stellar."

Provision Sector Chief Grala Hatchrail spoke up next, "Having the right to present an issue doesn't mean it's wise to do so without proper evidence."

Engineering Chief Marrissa Navamo added quietly, "Especially when it only sounds like the conspiracy theory that aliens stole the main transmitter. That one's been on the broadcasts for octuries."

Stellar Chief Fria Maglator shook with rage as she responded, "Something terrible happened to this system! Either that or it was reconstructed by a sentient hand! Neither explanation for what we're seeing from the sensors comforts me. The choice before us is clear. We should either leave this system immediately or spend a little extra time studying the system to gain a proper amount of data to determine an explanation for the anomalies we've discovered. We have a responsibility to the colonists who may be coming here, to make sure their new home is a safe one to settle. That is part of the Holy Mission, too!"

Provision Chief Hatchrail sighed, "As much as it pains me to admit this, I agree with that last point. The Holy Mission isn't a hobby. We have a duty to make certain that this system is habitable, not just the planet we're terraforming."

Engineering Chief Navamo chimed in, "Well, in that case, why not just do some more exploring before we commence? We can make a run to Planet Forty-One, swing around it, take closer readings and make a decision. We could adjust our course so that if we need to exit the system quickly, we can use the gravity well of the planet to slingshot us back to speed. We could also choose to stay for a brief period in a loose orbit and send some vessels to study this system, then adjust for a prolonged stay if it looks safe."

Medical Sector Chief Vono Binami steepled his hands, "Eagle, you've been quiet during this discussion. Does Technology Sector have anything to say about all this situation?"

Technology Chief Lund looked up from his datapad, "I'm waiting for the main agenda item to come up. I think Chief Navamo has the right idea, even though I don't agree with Chief Maglator's interpretation of the sensor data. A short delay before terraforming might be wise."

Wasp watched as Captain Fieldscan got to his feet, "My friends, we must now come together in mutual support. I must say that I'm not amused by the timing of Chief Maglator's debate topic, as she was also fully aware of the one which was scheduled for this rotation and why it is so dearly important. That being said, as Captain I hereby declare that Chief Navamo's suggestions have the most merit. By dark-slice, I shall announce my decision concerning the course Ganges shall take, and I expect all of you to be supportive. We are the guardians of the Holy Mission. It behooves us to work together for the sake of all humanity."

The other Sector Chiefs glanced at each other, then they all nodded their respect to Captain Fieldscan, who looked at the wallscreen, "Naga, my friend, would you please present the material which was prepared for this meeting? I think it's time we got to the true emergency which has called us all together at this moment."

Images of William Blaine, his capture by Security forces, the medical data from his time in isolation and his eventual escape from his interrogation chamber filled the screen. Wasp watched the others as the Solarian's identity was revealed to them. The Agro Chief's eyes grew round with shock, while rage painted its flourishes all over the face of Harbor Chief Rollack. Provision Sector Chief Hatchrail actually flinched at each new detail concerning William Blaine, as Planetary Chief Sedders' face was a mask of total disgust. The Chiefs of Medical and Engineering Sectors remained strictly neutral, quietly watching the presentation and listening to Captain Fieldscan's revelations. Wasp was going to keep a sharp eye on all of them. She had spoken with Chief Mantabe, and the leader of Security assured Wasp that her crew would work closely with her in keeping the others in line.

The final part of the presentation came from the Judiciary Council itself, still demanding that the general population not be informed about the presence of their Solarian trespasser. This was greeted by bursts of outrage, which Captain Fieldscan carefully handled with diplomatic grace and steely discipline. Wasp's admiration for her superior grew with every word he uttered. Both Eagle Lund and Jira Mantabe answered questions with calm equanimity, as if they had practiced together in secret, which Wasp wouldn't be surprised about if this were found to be true. In the end, everyone had their orders and, despite their grumblings, agreed to adhere to the demands of the Judiciary Council. Wasp was glad when the meeting adjourned, but she had a terrible feeling that the worst was yet to come.

Command Hub, Level Ten

Captain Perrin Fieldscan marched onto the Bridge, his Executive Officer hurrying over to the Inter-Sector Comms station to prepare the crew there for his Ganges-wide announcement. After the conference with the Sector Chiefs, he had stopped briefly at his office to tidy his appearance. It would not be appropriate to look slovenly when addressing the entire population of the ship. This wasn't a matter of vanity, but a necessity of diplomacy. Every captain had to make certain that they looked as if they were in control of everything that was happening within and outside their ship. The crew would be spooked if he seemed either hesitant or disheveled, especially as he had chosen a particular formality to his style of leadership. The crew expected him to be unswerving in his manner, to do otherwise would be a dire blow to morale.

By the time he reached the command platform at the heart of the stadium-sized chamber, a flock of Naga and news drones were following him like metallic birds. The Chief of the Deck saluted him smartly from his station, "Captain on the Bridge! Sir, I've made all of the preliminary preparations that you requested. Naga is standing by for ship-wide transmission."

Perrin nodded to him, "Excellent, Chief. As soon as Wasp has finished, we shall begin. How's the Bridge crew?"

The Chief of the Deck squinted up at the layers of duty stations that rose in tiers high above their heads, "They're mostly curious, Captain. We're still tracking the reconnaissance fleet's progress back to Ganges, for the gravity braking maneuver. Security estimates everything will be locked down within three paring-slivers. Harbor Control has issued a 'return-to-base' order, which is going smoothly. They shall be prepared just a few paring-slivers after Security. Forward thrusters are at full, with Engineering reporting no difficulties. All the sternward mains are now cycled down but maintaining minimum output, as you ordered, sir. One power station reported a fluctuation, and is being shut down for inspection. All Wheels are green, with all inter-Sector traffic closed."

Captain Fieldscan nodded, "Well done, Chief. Wasp is handling the news broadcast channels, currently making sure they're expecting an interruption to their usual programs."

Perrin turned about and walked over to his chair. It was a gaudy thing, with gold armrests, padded synth-leather cushioning and a stylistic back that arched over two meters tall. Both sides were fitted with his command boards, adding colorful flickers of light to the gleaming edifice to his post. He stood facing the chamber, his back to his chair. Perrin preferred to remain on his feet when addressing the crew. This was another bit of showmanship required to make the crew see that he was in control. Sometimes, he felt like an actor, playing a lifelong role without a script. Like most of his predecessors, he had molded himself to fit his rank, rather than try to break with tradition. Very few former Captains had the skill and audacity to change the expected behavior of their post. Most who tried had failed miserably, retiring early to prevent a crisis of morale. Perrin would rather die than confuse or disorient his crew, though he did have a sneaking admiration for some of the mavericks of old, such as the scandalous Jaike Verdstrum.

Executive Officer Tornpage joined him at the command platform and then dropped into her seat unceremoniously, "All set, Big Cheese! I got the vid-heads settled down for you. It was easier than babysitting the Sector Chiefs."

The Chief of the Deck scowled at the informality Wasp displayed, but Perrin smiled at her warmly, as he always found her manner refreshing, "Good! I think it's about time to get this started. It's been a long rotation as it is."

Wasp set her control board to make a Bridge-wide announcement, as she signaled silently to Naga that they were prepared to commence, "Attention all Bridge crew! Captain Perrin Fieldscan shall now address the general crew. New orders will be sent to your stations. Study them while you listen, and be prepared to implement your tasks immediately afterward. Inefficiency is not an option! If I have to come to your station, expect to be publicly berated!"

Perrin held still, as a flock of news drones swirled around him, their lenses focused on his body, preparing both two-dimensional and holographic displays. He nodded once to Wasp, who smacked a button on her board. The lights on the drones gleamed green, signaling that he was now live upon every broadcast channel and wallscreen in the ship, "Attention all crew of Ganges, this is your Captain speaking! Please give me your complete attention! I first wish to thank all of you for your efficient efforts to prepare for gravity braking, which shall commence in five paring-slivers. While we do not expect any difficulties on our current course, other than some mild vibrations, there are some issues which need to be addressed concerning System Forty-One."

Perrin paused for a pollen-sliver to give the crew time to digest his words. The Bridge crew were silent, with all eyes on himself or their display screens. He felt a rush of pride at their discipline. Truly, they were the finest members of Command Sector. He made a show of smoothing his moustache as he continued his speech, "As many of you may know, the stellar system we have entered is decidedly unusual in many respects. This has caused your Sector Chiefs, including myself, to look at it with a cautious eye. While I am not about to support or deny any wild speculations, it is clear to me that we must ascertain the truth behind the unusual features that have been presented to us. Planets with perfectly circular orbits, rocky bodies without any surface features and a similarity of appearance which defies our understanding. The parent star itself has yet to exhibit flares or spots, and its polar axis is aligned with its attendant planets."

The ring of news and Naga drones around him came in a bit closer, focusing on his face, "The universe is larger than can be imagined, thus we must always be prepared for the unknown. To make certain that this system is safe for habitation, we shall be closely examining Planet Forty-One, delaying the Holy Mission for a few rotations before settling into a more stable orbit. We shall use all of our resources to understand how this system got this way and to make sure that the target world is worthy of our sacred task. A fleet of science vessels and Security ships shall be launched, to examine the inner planets and their dynamics, after we have reached our chosen orbit. Once we have a better understanding of the history of this system, we shall decide whether or not we shall commence terraforming or leave to find a more suitable location. This is a heavy burden for us all, but we have a responsibility to those who shall come here to find a new home. In the meantime, attend to your posts with diligence. May Ganges serve the Holy Mission for eternity. Captain out."

CHAPTER ELEVEN

Orbit Rotation - Life Sowing - Mission Harvest - Spiral 5620

"We have reached orbit around Planet Thirty-Six, and everything looks proper thus far. I wish that I could say the same for Ganges. While the ship itself functions with great efficiency, the crew have become restive under the constraints of the new Prime Charter. Voyages between stellar systems have always been difficult for morale, as there's nothing to do but endless drills, training and maintenance. There are even those who openly speak of creating a second terraforming vessel, with its own rules and regulations. I won't stand for such nonsense on the Bridge, but I cannot silence the general crew. I just hope that this is a passing fad that will fade away swiftly in the near future. The last thing I want to see is the crew divided once again, making fertile ground for mutinous ideas."
Lan Howego, Captain of Ganges, personal log, P36

Agro Wheel Two, Security Level Five

Security Chief Jira Mantabe gritted her teeth in frustration and fury, as she watched the dawn-slice news channels, as was her habit when she first entered the Nexus. All across the display screens situated between the four handlebars in front of her were ten separate broadcasts, all of them depicting William Blaine in various forms of dress. One was a vid capture of him in Technology Sector, wearing standard priest robes for the Temple of Naga-Ma. Another revealed his face within the arena stands during the Security Games. There was also an interview with the Engineering crewman who had been knocked out by William, and so on. What bothered her most was the fact that several of the candid images revealing the Solarian were not from his earlier tours, nor did they show him being surrounded by her crew. The chattering reporters were in an uproar over the fact that William could not be identified through Naga, and they focused on his unusual appearance, especially in the images where he was seen alone.

Absently, she reached for her coffee thermos, glad that there was a micro-heating unit in its base. Her other hand twisted a handlebar, shifting the news images, until dozens filled her displays. Jira slammed the thermos back into its ring after a quick gulp of the hot brew and cursed. Damn the Judiciary Council and its insistence on maintaining secrecy until things got out of control! Her toragi, Tracey, was sitting at her side on the rotating platform that held her command chair, swishing her short tail in obvious agitation. Security crew were standing at their stations, ready to begin the implementation of several new operations, including a purge of unwanted criminal organizations hunkered over in Residence Wheel One.

Jira shot an enraged glance at the queue of Nexus officers who had lined up to speak with her directly, making the closest ones flinch in response. She hit the left foot-pedal, swinging her saddle around to face them, "Everyone who's here to talk about long-term strategy or awaiting the implementation of our planned initiatives this rotation, return to your fucking stations. I'll get back to you once I know what the damage is from this dawn-slice's little surprise."

To her dismay, only a pair of waiting officers stepped out of line. Jira growled wordlessly, then barked out, "First! Make it fucking quick!"

A Lieutenant hesitantly stepped one pace forward, right to the edge of the platform, "Chief Mantabe! I have three reports of internal leaks of information from our own Sector."

Jira almost rose to her strapped feet, "For fuck's sake! Which pestilent shits pissed their honor on the damned deck?"

The Lieutenant did her best not to flinch back from her Chief's full fury. Her accompanying toragi flattened its ears, "All of them were Ensigns, Ranks Two and Three. All of them worked in the dangerous-prisoner corridors on Levels Three and Two. None had any disciplinary reports attached to their files. All of them are reported as being missing from their posts without leave."

Jira replied, struggling to control her temper, "Give me the data-wafer, then compile a complete report of their activities over the last three sowings."

She dismissed the first Lieutenant, then focused on the second person in line, "What lovely news do you have for me?"

The next officer shrunk into himself as he replied, "Chief! One of the guards who was watching over Brace Lazhand is missing. His datapad doesn't respond, nor do the wallscreens in his apartment. Naga is running a search but has not found him at this time."

Jira sank back into her saddle, "Thor's balls! Get to your station right now and get me a link with the League representative! Move your ass!"

The third officer swung out a swift salute, "Chief Mantabe! We are no longer receiving telemetry from either Keep Smith and Keep Catherine. They also refuse to respond to our hails."

Jira's voice became as cold as space, "Just how many traitors do we have amongst our ranks?"

Before the man could answer, a voice from her display cut in with a raucous cackle of laughter, "...so now we've been told that this yellow-haired turd is a fucking Terran! Now, your first question might be, 'Why is he here?', but the real query should be 'Just how long did Security Sector know about this?'. I'll be kind and figure the cat-lovers got caught with their pants off and eyes closed shut! But my whiskers are tingling, my disheveled Mischief! Maybe they are in league with this stranger to our ship, who I've heard from a truly desperate shit-source, invaded our vessel through Engineering! We Strifers know all about the ways of Terra! We lived through that crap-show! Never, ever again!"

Jira closed her eyes briefly, "Oh, shit." The Strifer news broadcasts were very popular in Ganges. Part of it was simply because they were very entertaining, but another part was the fact that their own breed of journalists was unbelievably good at what they did. If the regular programs were in agreement with the Strifers, the crew would simply figure that everything they heard and saw was absolutely true, which unfortunately, it was.

A message request blinked frantically at Jira from an emergency channel. Gritting her teeth, she opened it warily, "This is the Judiciary Council representative, Security Chief Mantabe. We've been watching the news with growing concern over the situation. Technology Sector has informed us that several of the clergy from the Temple of Naga-Ma are missing from their posts. There are videos and images of our guest coming out from sources internal to their own Sector. Three Stellar Sector scientists are now being mobbed by crew who are demanding answers. We have confirmation that at least one of them was part of the interrogation process involving the trespasser. Medical Sector has warned us that a handful of resignations have reached their personnel offices this dawn-slice. Two of those crew are now talking to the news broadcasts. What are your plans?"

Jira glared at the screen, "Plans? Until the crew break regulations, there is little that I can do. The crew who signed non-disclosure agreements can be brought in, once they're found, and charged accordingly. Those who were forced to disclose their information for fear of life and limb shall not be arrested but placed in protective custody. Those who have violated their oaths to their Sectors shall be hunted down. I will send out anti-riot teams to your location and the other vital centers of the ship. By the way, check your own rosters. Look for crew who are missing from their posts."

Before there could be a reply, Jira snapped off the connection. She rallied her Nexus crew and began implementing anti-riot procedures, alerting the Bridge of her actions. She was certain that this fiasco was a gift from the crime syndicates, to keep her Sector busy while they dug in or shifted their locations and tactics. As she watched, the crew were beginning to express their horror and outrage, by starting public protests or screaming over their personal broadcast channels. It would be a tricky operation to settle the population peacefully. Containing this situation would delay everything she had worked for over the last spiral.

Command Hub, Level Ten

Executive Officer Wasp Tornpage watched the giant hologram at the center of the Bridge with growing alarm and hilarity. The Command officer within her was quite aghast at the breech in confidentiality concerning William Blaine. A darker part of her heart appreciated the disruptive timing, right after Ganges had finished with its gravity-braking maneuver around the largest gas giant in System Forty-One. The Strifer part of her marveled at how quickly the so-civilized crew got out of hand over rumors and fear. Once again, humanity proved that it was verminous, ready to rip each other apart at the slightest provocation. Wasp pulled her green hood over her head and sighed. She wondered if even Naga could talk its way out of this one. As usual, the Strifer broadcasts were filled with wild vitriol and snarky contempt directed at the "Suits" of Ganges. While they made her job harder, she admired their style and persistence. The rest of the newscasters were running around like novices having a panicked tantrum.

Chief-of-the-Deck Trammer was scrambling over his station boards, visibly sweating as he desperately tried to keep up with the demands for answers. At this time, Wasp knew that she should be contacting Security Sector, but one look at the Commander in charge of securing the Bridge verified that Chief Mantabe was already on top of things and was doing what she could. Bothering Jira right now would only compound the issue at hand, not to mention just piss her off even further than she probably was already. Instead, Wasp turned her attention to her own station board and checked the roster. Sure enough, four Bridge crew and several Command staff were not at their post. Wasp noted their names and vowed to herself that she would see to it that the absentees would soon bemoan their own birth.

Captain Perrin Fieldscan had just arrived and was making his way to the command platform. His progress was slow, for he was being bombarded by heated questions from news drones and Bridge officers who needed guidance. The public representative was right behind him, battering the Captain with angry queries and accusations. Wasp got her paint-gun loaded, after choosing lurid green ammunition.

As she watched Perrin's crawling progress, Wasp saw that the Security personnel were sealing the doors to the Bridge and setting up a protective formation in front of the heavy portal. Meanwhile, the Captain was waving the drones back with growing irritation. Wasp took careful aim and snapped off a paintball. The lens of one of the drones was splattered with opaque green, and the others backed off swiftly.

Captain Fieldscan rushed his way to the command platform with a broad smile upon his face, nodding to her in thanks. The representative and the gaggle of officers which had impeded him jumped back in alarm, splashes of paint dotting their uniforms and faces. Perrin reached his chair and looked over at Wasp, "Well done, Executive! I might have been stuck there until chore-slice if you hadn't intervened."

For once, Chief-of-the-Deck Trammer gave Wasp a quick grin and raised his middle finger at her, then turned back to his station, which was lit up like a New Spiral decoration. She gave the Captain a wink, "Just doing my duty, Big-Cheese. I figured, after watching the news-jerks freak out all dawn-slice, that marshmallows wouldn't cut it as a deterrent this rotation."

The Captain leaned back in his chair, "Just so, my friend. I knew this rotation would come. Secrets are difficult to keep in Ganges, unless one is prepared to be criminally ruthless, which I am not. I just heard from Security Chief Mantabe, and I'm beyond being concerned. Large crowds of crew have filled the halls of the Judiciary Council, refusing to leave until they are told the truth about our guest. The same goes for Agro Admin, Stellar Center, the gates of Technology Sector and our own docking facility. Naga has assured me that everything is peaceful thus far, but none of us know how long that will last. If I don't hear from the Judiciary soon, I shall be making my own announcement concerning William Blaine."

Wasp leaned in to whisper, "And if the Judiciary protests?"

Perrin sniffed, "They can go sit in the bilge, for all I care at this point."

She laughed aloud, "I know some rats who could make that happen, Big Cheese. Still, there's that tricky bit in the regs that says Command has to do what they want."

The Captain rubbed at his chin, "That's mainly for issues involving the Holy Mission itself, under the guidance of the General Manager. It also covers inter-Sector matters, which we tend to negotiate for them. This situation is neither of those. As such, I would say that we should have been given free rein to make the call, but there isn't a precedent to fall back on."

The crew representative finally reached her seat at the Captain's left, "I heard the word precedent. I assume that has something to do with the news about a Terran invading our ship! In that case, I have to admit, you're correct. There is no precedent for this situation. I'm going to come right out and ask you, are the stories true, Captain?"

Wasp targeted another news drone with her paint gun, while Perrin replied to the representative's question, "The Judiciary Council has me in a bind. The matter in question was highly classified. I did what I could under the circumstances, as did Chief Mantabe. We were quite close to gaining a resolution on the matter, preparing to slowly bring the issue to the attention of the crew."

The representative scowled, "That doesn't answer my query."

Perrin nodded, "That is quite correct. Until the Sector Chiefs, along with the Judiciary Council, come to an agreement, that's all the answer I can give you. Stay with us for a while. If things get out of hand, I shall make my own decision and clear the air, once and for all, publicly."

Wasp noted that the representative looked scared when she said, "If what they're saying is true, can we afford to wait for protocol? I admit, the idea of a Terran savage in the ship fills me with dread and disgust."

Wasp snapped back, "The guy in question is less of a savage than you are! I didn't trust him at first. Then again, I still don't trust anyone, you included. We Strifers are an equal-loathing culture."

Before the representative could respond, Perrin added, "What my Executive means is, let us not jump to any conclusions, especially if they're based on rumor and preconceived notions."

Wasp shot a third drone with her paint gun, while the Captain began issuing orders to the various stations in the Bridge. The crew representative fell into a sullen silence, for which Wasp was grateful. The last thing they needed right now was an amateur second-guessing them all rotation.

Planetary Sector, Level One

Atmospherics Director Dalen Gupta was glad he was taller than most crew or he wouldn't be able to see what was happening. A large crowd had gathered at inter-Sector Bulkhead Portal One-Gamma, which crossed the long distance between Stellar and Planetary Sector in Region Beta-Three. His Commander had ordered him to this site with broad instructions to support the position of their Sector's Chief. At first, Dalen didn't know what his superior meant by that vague statement, but now that he was at the scene, it became obvious. Hundreds of Stellar crew, all of them in uniform, were blocking access to the bulkhead portal, holding up signs and banners calling for a halt to the Holy Mission at Planet Forty-One.

Several of his peers were there, about twenty meters from the angry-looking Stellar crew, along with hundreds of Planetary personnel. A long cordon of Security forces was stretched out between the two crowds, calling for dispersal and a return to post. Dalen had tried to get to the front of the ever-growing mass of crew, but there was no room to squeeze further. Everyone was packed together like rice in a granary. He wondered why Commander Vaclan himself wasn't here instead, but he figured it was because things were so hectic now that Ganges had finished with its gravity-braking maneuver. Soon, the ship would be in orbit around Planet-Forty-One, and his Sector had to be prepared to do their duty for humanity. While it was true that Stellar Sector had remained closely loyal to the Holy Mission, after the catastrophic Crucible which destroyed their reputation with the general crew, the transfer of focus from interstellar flight to terraforming still put a strain on relations between them and Planetary.

The gravity assistance used to slow Ganges had been gradual and barely noticed by most of the crew. Some loose things became a bit wobbly. Pouring liquids became problematic at one point, and Agro Four saw huge waves, but nothing they couldn't handle from octenniums of practical experience. The gravity of a large mass could be utilized to either increase the velocity of a spaceship or it could reduce its speed, mainly depending upon the vector used in approaching the gravity well. Large as it was, Ganges always took advantage of both methods whenever it was feasible. The course had to be chosen with great care, or the ship might find itself being flung out of a system with little chance for control. One of the positive aspects of System Forty-One's unusual features was that it made orbital dynamics much simpler, as there were fewer large-mass influences that could cause imbalances.

Dalen, and most of those who served Ganges in Planetary Sector, saw this as a blessing, while it seemed that their colleagues in Stellar saw it as menacing. Thus far, nothing had threatened the ship, as it worked its way deeper toward the target world. No damage was experienced as they ventured further into the system, so the stance which Stellar was now taking made little sense to his mind. If there was technologically advanced life here, wouldn't they have greeted or threatened Ganges by this point? Now, there were wild rumors that System Forty-One was a giant relic from a long-dead civilization. If that were the case, where were the ruins? Shouldn't there be some leftover bits from such an advanced species that could move worlds?

Then there were all the news broadcasts concerning the invasion of Ganges by a single Terran. Dalen figured the man must be mighty indeed if he could threaten all sixty million crew! Nothing he had seen or heard could be proven. Even if it were true and Ganges had a visitor from the Sol System, why assume this meant a threat? Dalen hated it when people assumed things about others, just because of their home community or the Sector they worked at. No matter what form it took, prejudice had no place in a civilized culture, his own included. How many crew looked at him and assumed he was ungainly and awkward, simply because of his greater mass? It was silly, unreasonable, and he thought it was irresponsible of the broadcast channels to incite fear in the hearts of good crew. The odd-looking man who had been pointed out by the news services might be an emissary of peace! He could also just be some poor soul whose outer disfigurements made him stand out in a crowd. Dalen would simply wait until he heard something from either his Sector Chief or the Captain of Ganges before making any judgments.

He also remembered how his mates, Bryce and Sasha, had pointed out that the Strifer channels were making fun of the situation and calling upon the Sector Chiefs to make a public statement. The rat-masked commentators had also said that the crew who were in a panic over the possibility that a Terran was onboard were acting like novices. He had pointed this out to his children, both of them Student rank, as an example of why one should hearken to the wisdom of the Strifers, who had suffered more than many of the other communities in Ganges. They knew too well what it felt like to be stereotyped into a corner.

To Dalen's shock and dismay, someone from Planetary's side of the lines had started throwing vegetables at the shouting Stellar crew. Security's response was swift and terrible to behold. Their webbers covered the unruly crewmember with catchweb goo, as shock-spears were lowered, pushing back the crowd so that the miscreant could be arrested. The people directly in front of Dalen pulled back, almost carrying him with them, but he stood firm. An opening in the crowd appeared, and Dalen pushed his way toward the front. Sharp pain brought sparks to his eyes. He stumbled and swayed, his head screaming at him. He placed a hand to his scalp and found it wet with blood.

He was shocked at first, but then something rose up within his chest that he had never felt before. It was genuine rage at the senselessness before him. Dalen saw another Planetary crewman pull his arm back to throw a bottle at the Stellar protestors. Dalen reached out and grabbed the man's arm, pulling him off balance, "Stop this! No violence! Are we savages?"

The man started hitting him in the belly with his free hand, while Dalen kept pulling him away from the confrontation. A loud voice rose over the noise of the two sides, which were now screaming at one another, "By the orders of Security Chief Mantabe, you will disperse now! All crew are to vacate this region immediately or be arrested for rioting!"

Clouds of blue-ish smoke began to form at regular intervals in the middle of the rising conflict. More objects flew about from both sides, creating a rain of debris. Screaming cut through the air, and the crew began to panic. Dalen kept his grip on the surly crewman he clung to, backing slowly away from the destruction that filled his eyes. A toragi flashed by, roaring in anger, revealing a mouth full of daggers. The sight shook Dalen deeply. He had always seen the big cats as calm guardians, who tolerated the antics of novices. Now there were several of them rushing about in anger, and he had to force himself not to flee with instinctive abandon.

The thick smoke came closer, along with shadowy, armored forms that held heavy shields and hand weapons. The man he had detained was beginning to cough and sag in place. Dalen's eyes were watering heavily, as he felt a tremble running through his struggling lungs. Barked orders surrounded him. More figures loomed out of the greasy smoke. Dalen found himself looking down at three steel barrels with flaring tips, "Please. I was just trying to stop the…"

Dalen fell heavily to the bare deck, his grasp on the man next to him slipping away. He coughed deeply, then blackness flooded his mind.

Harbor Wheel One, Level One-Hundred-Six

William Blaine sat down next to Technology Sector Chief Eagle Lund and cradled his head in his arms. The chamber was a sequestered segment of a suite of offices which Eagle used for private meetings. It was now gather-slice, and the news of his existence was spreading like a wildfire all throughout the ship. There had been other problems which threatened to bring more chaos to the crew, including riots breaking out in both Planetary and Stellar Sectors. These had nothing to do with the millions of protestors who demanded answers about his presence aboard Ganges, but instead were concerning whether or not the Holy Mission should be implemented at Planet Forty-One. The Temple of Naga-Ma was in an uproar over both issues and was threatening to tear itself into factions.

In all honesty, William had not seen this coming. The public issue with his presence as an unwanted guest had erupted suddenly, without any warning. It had spread throughout the ship rapidly, even more so than was the case within a Solarian orbital. From what he had heard from Chief Lund, there was the possibility that there were some crew from several Sectors who were either working on their own initiative, by expressing their outrage over the highly unusual circumstances surrounding both the system they had just entered and his presence, or were being used by criminal forces to distract Security Sector from implementing their own plans to dissolve the syndicates. William felt used, soiled and treated like a pariah, but his anger about this wasn't just focused upon the crew of Ganges. His orders had been far too rigid, constrained by the usual politics within the human faction of the Solarian Alliance. The preliminary information he had been provided before risking his life and sanity, making multiple Wend jumps in a short period of time, had been highly incomplete, inaccurate and full of assumptions.

William felt a hand upon his shoulder, and he flinched back, his arm raised to defend himself. Eagle Lund withdrew and gave him a look of deep sorrow, "I am sorry this happened. You have been treated poorly, mainly due to my culture's deep-seated fears. Like Naga, my people need time to come to grips with being part of a larger society. For octennia, we have been taught that planet-dwellers are savages, that the Terrans are monsters, and we are better off on our own. System Forty-One is also recalling a very painful period in our history, Planet Fifteen, where we found primitive, non-terrestrial life, and we had to make the choice to move on, which we did. The Strifers had their beginning because of the heated debates that raged over that unexpected discovery. They were severely mocked, shunned, threatened, and had to live in the belowdecks for many generations."

William shrugged, "I get it. I really do. We're always so certain of our ways in isolation. So certain that we know what's going on in the universe. When we get information to the contrary, we humans react badly, even violently. We cling to our misguided dogmas and cultures, even when those are proven to be wrong, for we feel threatened by the unknown. I have seen too much to cling to such certainties. Some people in the Alliance cover their eyes and live the way their ancestors did, without really understanding that doing so causes damage to themselves. It's sad. My own expectations of Ganges came from my ideals and the messages you left in the beacons for colonists. They were inspirational, uplifting. So much data was lost when the Terran Conglomerate collapsed. So much that happened afterward was painful and horrific. We clung to the memory we had of Ganges, listened to the stories of the colonists who came to help us rebuild. They called you saints, benefactors, selfless providers. We swallowed it all up and asked for more."

Eagle smiled down at him, "We're just people. Full of foibles and faults. We believed we could continue through the galaxy alone forever. Untouched, pure. It was what we wanted to believe. Now that's been shattered, and all our other fears are emerging to trouble us even further. I, for one, am pleased to call you friend. I do not fear change. That was ripped from me in my youth."

William sat back, "What do you mean?"

Eagle slipped off his robe and opened the top of his uniform, sliding it down to his waist. Both of his arms were metal prosthetics. A section of his abdomen was covered in a webwork of fine cables, tubes and silvery mesh, "This happened to me shortly after I joined my Sector. Both of my legs are also artificial. An accident in the belowdecks, repairing a processor the size of a tram car. I could have had my limbs and organs regrown through Medical Sector, but an old Sadhu, or a Holy wanderer, told me that everything that happens to us can teach a lesson and has a purpose. All of my prosthetics make me one of the best technicians in Ganges. They were fitted with interfaces and special tools that aided my career. Some of the crew responded negatively to this change, though they accept it from Security personnel."

The Solarian nodded back, "You went against their expectations, whereas a Security crewmember doesn't, even when their behavior reflects yours. I may have to consider the same for my people. This situation is more complicated than their understanding allows for. I'm not worried about the Boktahl, but humanity doesn't like surprises that rip away close-held beliefs. At the same time, the AeyAie Solidarity has concerns about Naga, simply because Ganges has been isolated for so long. They hide their fears by being helpful, even when no one asks for their assistance. Personally, I would prefer it if Ganges remains a separate culture within the Alliance. Most of the colonies have joined, though their autonomy is in question. If your people can work out a deal where you stay as you are, without interference, then perhaps the colonies can benefit from that. Right now, things are fluid, shifting and undecided. That gives a lot of room for misbehavior and political maneuvering."

Eagle re-fastened his uniform, "Speaking of which, have you had time to look at the Sector history files? Plenty of politics there, I assure you."

William grinned at the Technology Chief, "I discovered a personal surprise within those records. During Voyage Six, there was a Captain Silvia Blaine. When I saw her picture, I could swear I was looking at my mother."

Eagle's eyebrows rose high, "That's fantastic! While she can't be a direct ancestor of yours, it does seem that a branch of your bloodline was part of the initial crew. Did you request a genetic investigation?"

The Solarian was shocked, "You can do that? It was thousands of spirals ago!"

The Technology Chief shrugged, "We keep a genetic record of the Sector Chiefs and other important personnel. Those who were major contributors to the Holy Mission are preserved through genetic samples and gametes. That's done mainly for emergency purposes, in case our population drops too low and there is a problem with breeding new crew. Level Seventy-Nine of Medical Sector is full of samples. We could repopulate several ships like Ganges with them if we had to."

Before William could respond to this astounding news, Naga's matronly face appeared on the wallscreens all around them, "Technology Chief Eagle Lund and William Blaine, an emergency session of the Sector Chiefs has now been called at the Command Hub conference chamber. Both of you are requested and required to attend."

Eagle looked over at William, "See? Politics is never far away."

Medical Sector Wheel, Spine Tubeway

I rush ahead to clear the way for Darron and our guest. The curved corridors this close to midships can be a dangerous distraction. The low apparent gravity is also problematic, though it fills me with joy to be able to leap so far in one jump. Care must be taken to not accidentally damage one's limbs. Traction strips on the deck help, though Darron uses the power of his boots to keep his footing secure. I do not know how he does this, but it is one more marvel of the humans. The only reason I know about his use of magick footwear is that a pair of blue lights blink on the ankle braces whenever he needs better stability, though I have never seen him do this in the grassy fields and rocky terrain in the greener regions of the world. The ones used in the blackness of the skin of Naga are larger, but do much the same thing. During our training, I was fitted with what Darron called "mag-paws", and I stuck fast to the gray expanse of metal that covers the world. Outside is dangerous. A perilous realm with no air, no heat and endless dark.

Crew hurry out of my path, sometimes crying out in alarm, as I race past them. Hundreds of Security crew are here, keeping the other humans in their lines, all of which leading to special transport tubes that flash at great speed to other areas of the world. I like this place, despite the lesser number of trees and plants. Here, I can fly for several paces, leap up to the hard sky and travel the length of Ganges swiftly. Ten of my kind are with me, to keep the guest, William, safe from harm. Crew stare at us with wide eyes. They smell of fear, uncertainty and anger. Everyone is upset. No one is at peace.

The walls of the world show scenes of large crowds gathered together. They shout at each other and sometimes break into fights. I wonder why we are not there to stop them. This whole rotation has been filled with alarms, klaxons and running about from one end of Ganges to another. Darron has been angry since he rose from his bed. He and his mate rushed through their preparations, skipping our bathing time, which was disappointing. I enjoy the water, as does my lovely mate, Alice. We swim together and play games, surrounded by the humans and their cubs.

A long time ago, I learned what swearing was. The verbal outbursts from my partner are colorful and match his fiery spirit. We toragi hiss and spit our rage, which the humans understand in their limited way. Without a good sense of smell, they cannot comprehend the nuances of our emotions. It is a puzzle to me that such limited beings have so much control of the world, but it occurs to me that Naga allows this to keep them all comfortable. Naga is the world, whose name is Ganges. The humans help the world, as my kind aid the humans. It is the way things have been throughout memory, but I still struggle to gain a deeper understanding of it all.

We brought William from the tight places close to the Spine. Darron calls it Technology Sector. It smells strange, filled with drifts of sweet smoke and the scent of machine oil. The crew there all have boxes on their heads. I wonder if one could be given to me. What might I learn from them? What strange discoveries would await me? We took our guest and one other human, named Eagle, though he has no wings, to the Spine and then used one of the tube cylinders to get to this area. It has an odor to it that reminds me of the breeding grounds. Astringent, sharp and sterile. Now we need to hurry over to a different region, by taking another transport. We switch modes of travel often, keeping our path unpredictable. This is understandable. From what little I understand of the human chattering going on, William is now prey.

Most of my platoon-mates are confused. They do not pay as much attention to the hooting of the humans. There are a few others who, like me, try to figure out all the complex sounds they make. Sometimes, when not on duty, we play at being human, trying to mimic their noises and standing upright on our hind legs, but it is so hard to do, and none of it makes sense. There is no time for games this rotation. I have never seen such large groups of humans like those seen on the walls of the world. They are acting strangely. William's face appears frequently, interspersed with shouting crew. At least they can't smell him like I have to. They should count their blessings.

The connection between our guest and these chanting hordes of crew is difficult to see. There has to be a reason. I have not seen him do anything to the humans of the world, other than escape his chamber, appear where he shouldn't be and march from one location to the next, always accompanied by Security crew like Darron and myself. Despite my dislike for him, William has not caused harm, save to one person in the machine section of the world called Engineering. There have been killers, criminals who damage crew and parts of Ganges who have not inspired such terrible wrath. I have helped to capture such people before, with little response from the crew.

The ways of humans are bewildering. The face of Naga appears on the sky to my right, directing me to an empty travel tube. I leap over the barricade with ease, slapping the panel that will open it behind me. Darron and the others rush through, crowding around William and Eagle. An object flies overhead, bouncing from the sky. It is an open-topped, human foot covering. A… sandal. Yes, they are called sandals. This is accompanied by others. Some of them strike my ward, but Darron ignores it. I turn and roar my outrage at the crowd, so do the other toragis. The humans pushing forward pull back in alarm. Darron flashes past me, dragging William by the arm, and throws him into an open cylinder. Eagle is pushed inside right behind the guest, then all the Security crew begin to drop through the open door. We toragi stay behind, snarling at the mob of crew. We are confused, but we are also very angry now. They attacked our wards, tried to obstruct us in our duty to the world. More shoes fly about the Spine station, bouncing around in the low gravity.

I hear Darron call my name, "Mike! Get in here, now!"

As the leader of our platoon's toragi, I am the first to back away from the shouting people. The others of my kind join me, staying in a close formation. The metal birds, called drones, swoop into the station from several directions and make a wall of flying steel between us and the humans. Naga's voice is painfully loud, and I flatten my ears as she shouts, "Disperse now! All crew are to leave this platform at once! Failure to comply shall be seen as an act of aggression and will be placed on your permanent record!"

I understand some of what the world spirit says, but there are words that I don't fully understand yet. Many of the humans begin to shift away from the cylinder platform as we back toward its open doors. The wall of metal birds becomes thicker, blocking all the flying shoes and other objects that have joined them. I turn my back on the crowd and lightly leap into the compartment. Darron is making sure everyone is strapped in and guides me to my spot amongst the open-lattice racks next to William. I glare at the guest and snarl at him. I still don't understand what is going on, but I am certain it is all his fault.

Command Hub, Level Nineteen

Crinn Spanglo was just about ready to bolt from the room he was in. He never got the jitters whenever he faced his superiors, and he was getting comfortable with bringing the results from his work to the Chief of Stellar Sector, but the situation he was in now was almost too much to bear. Across the lozenge-shaped conference table was Captain Perrin Fieldscan himself, accompanied by Executive Officer Wasp Tornpage. Sitting to their right was the Chief of Security, Jira Mantabe, who was far more intimidating in person than he had expected. She just exuded barely contained violence, her arms were as thick as his legs, made more massive by the armor she wore, covered in medals and chains. Every Sector's Chief was present, with his own standing next to him in front of a display screen he had set up for this meeting for the highest officers in Ganges. That was bad enough, but what had really captured his attention was the pale man sitting on the Captain's left, whose strange face had been plastered all over the wallscreens this rotation. The shockingly pale stranger had metallic-looking eyes, and his bright yellow hair waved about despite the lack of a breeze. Crinn didn't know why, but the man's presence filled his mind with a terrible uncertainty.

Executive Tornpage smacked the tabletop with her fist, "This meeting in now in order. The honorable Captain Fieldscan shall commence, so shut the fuck up and listen!"

Crinn flinched at her harsh words, but no one objected. He had plenty of experience with Strifers in Stellar Sector, including his own assistant, Fuss Nitpicker, but there was something deeply frightening in Wasp's dark eyes that told him she never tolerated stupidity. Crinn was still certain he was one of the most intelligent people in the room, save for Technology Chief Eagle Lund, who was sitting next to the stranger, perfectly at ease.

Captain Fieldscan then rose to his feet with smooth elegance, "Thank you, Executive Officer Tornpage. As ever, your handle on protocol is deeply appreciated. My friends and guests, this rotation we face a pair of issues which must be addressed immediately. While it is true that, as Captain, I could make my own decision and then implement it, I would prefer that we stand together in unity. I want your opinions and concerns heard before we set a course for our beloved Ganges. Our first item is the public-relations crisis concerning our Solarian visitor, William Blaine. While Security Sector has done a fine job keeping most of the protests civil, there have been some incidents of rioting which may yet spread throughout the ship. Chief Mantabe, would you please give us all an update on the situation at hand?"

Crinn was impressed by the Captain's calm dignity. He had never thought much of Command Sector, but he was beginning to revise his opinion. The Security Chief remained in her seat as she presented her report, "Thank you, Captain. We've got protests at every major administrative center, none of which look likely to disperse any time soon. There have been three riots which my Sector quelled, but there is one area within the Agro Admin campus where some shit-bags have dug in and are still throwing rocks and trash at my crew. Investigations has sent in a negotiation team, in coordination with Command Sector, to aid in the relief of hostages from a suite of offices. Naga has shut down the power and is assisting with drones. The vandals are all pro-Holy Mission, so I do expect a clean resolution shortly. Their main complaint has to do with William Blaine's presence within the ship. Two bouts of violence were disrupted in the bulkhead portals between the Stellar and Planetary Wheels, both of which were over the issue of terraforming. Medical Sector is currently treating the wounded, all of whom are civilians who refused to clear the area."

Crinn could not imagine facing down multiple squadrons of Security Police. That sounded like attempted suicide. The stranger lifted a finger in the air, "May I please make a statement and a suggestion?"

Harbor Chief Vekku Rollack snorted, "Polite for a savage, aren't we?"

Crinn rolled his eyes at this insulting comment. The odd-looking man, who was apparently named William Blaine, smiled back at the dour Harbor Chief, "If I understand the local vernacular, the term 'savage' is reserved for those who were raised upon or live on the surface of a planet. I have never done so. My home is Orbital Plak-One-Chang, locally known as the Crystal Dream station over Mars. I am trained as a scout for the Solarian Alliance; thus, I do try to be polite whenever in the presence of non-Solar peoples."

Chief Rollack scowled as Wasp howled with laughter. Eagle Lund placed a metallic hand upon William's shoulder in a comradely fashion. Crinn was shocked by this display of support. Wasn't this stranger a criminal? It was apparent that most of those in the meeting chamber didn't think so. He tucked that impression away for later musing, as William continued, "The current crisis is partially my own doing. It occurs to me that I need to help correct it. If I may, I would like to address the crew, preferably through an unofficial venue. That way, if it doesn't help matters, none of you would be blamed for my failure to soothe the crew. Perhaps one or more of these news services you have? My own personal choice would be one of the larger news broadcasters and the Strifer channel, maybe with an amateur representative service present as well."

Wasp grinned wickedly at the Solarian, "That's pretty ballsy, white cheddar! It's clever, too. An open forum might work out nicely. We could arrange for Naga to preempt all other channels for the event, which would be broadcast live, showing a modicum of candor."

The Captain, who sank back into his chair, nodded, "I agree. A very good suggestion, William. Should you pass Basic Crew Training, Command might well benefit from your accepting a position in our Sector. Chief Mantabe, would you be prepared to provide protective services for this broadcast?"

Crinn almost dropped his display remote in shock. He reminded himself that he had witnessed the wonders and horrors inside the Kendis Vault. This was nothing compared to that experience. The Chief of Security agreed to the plan, seconded by Technology Sector's leader. The vote on the measure wasn't unanimous, but it did claim the majority, with only Agro and Planetary dissenting.

Stellar Chief Fria Maglator, who was Crinn's boss, was then invited by the Captain to raise the next topic of the rotation. She rose to her feet and indicated the display holosphere with a sweep of her right arm, "Stellar Sector has new, long-range images of Planet Forty-One. I have invited Specialist Rank One, Crinn Spanglo, to present the material. I think you'll find it illuminating."

Crinn cleared his dry throat. His promotion had been sudden, mainly just to get him into this chamber without too much of a fuss. He activated the holosphere, and a clear image of Planet Forty-One appeared to float over the meeting table, "This image comes from the passive and active sensors at the cap. As you can see, there are a number of obvious features, but I'll address those readings which are not so apparent."

A murmur spread throughout the room, and Crinn couldn't blame them for their consternation. The planet showed a series of straight, crisscrossing lines and staggered plateaus that were too regular and precise to be natural. Huge structures lifted themselves from the bare bedrock to reach the upper atmosphere. The Captain raised his hand for silence and nodded toward Crinn to continue, "Okay, yeah, it's impressive enough and obviously artificial. There is no water on the surface; in fact, there is no evidence it was ever present. The atmosphere is pure argon-nitrogen, with a thin layer of carbon-dioxide at the upper limits. There are no storm systems, no atmospheric movement. There is an electromagnetic charge which seems to be evenly distributed throughout the atmosphere, possibly the cause for the lack of any gaseous dynamics."

The Chief of Planetary Sector bowed his head, his shoulders slumped in misery. Crinn decided to cut to the conclusions, "There is no evidence of any kind of movement on or under the surface: no transports, no spaceships, orbitals, stations or life. No power consumption, no generators. Planet Forty-One is as silent as an empty recycling bin. My colleagues and I are convinced that these are the remains of a once-great civilization, now dead and gone. From what the readings can tell us, these structures are all over five hundred thousand spirals old. They may not look like ruins, but that's what they are. This entire world is an ancient tomb for an extinct sentient species."

Captain Fieldscan rose to his booted feet, "Thank you, Specialist Spanglo. We cannot terraform this place with a clear conscience. It must be preserved and honored by our absence."

Stellar Chief Maglator spoke up swiftly, "Please, Captain! This is a unique opportunity to study a sentient species. May I request that a single science vessel be permitted to land on the surface, just to take some close readings, before we exit the system? Think of what we could learn from this! I'm not talking about harming or taking anything, just a few dust samples and visual inspections of some of the main features we can see."

The Captain then brought the measure up for a vote, which again was not unanimous, but passing, with Security and Planetary dissenting. Crinn couldn't bring himself to be overjoyed by this, unlike his Chief, who thanked everyone profusely. He couldn't get the image of Chief Mantabe's face from his mind. She looked furious, gripping the edge of the table hard enough to leave marks. If she was upset over this, and the Kendis Vault was within the sphere of her Sector's influence, then Crinn decided he should be scared out of his mind.

Command Hub, Level Ten

Captain Perrin Fieldscan walked swiftly to the command platform on the Bridge. He kept his head high and his shoulders back. Even if his own morale was low, there was no need to spread this sentiment amongst the crew. The information about Planet Forty-One was a blow to all of the Sector Chiefs, save for Stellar. He knew that cancelling the Holy Mission in this system was the correct course to take. He had been pleased that no one tried to change his mind on that position, but he wanted to make sure that Ganges did benefit, even slightly, from the debacle at hand. Being the Captain of Ganges meant making hard decisions, and looking for ways for the crew to benefit from adversity. If he had been a narcissistic man, he might have been thrilled by the recognition that history would bestow upon his name. Few of his predecessors had been presented the opportunity to preside over such a significant discovery. Instead, he was miserable at heart, sad that the Holy Mission would have to pass over this system. He understood that the clues had been there, from the moment they had entered the heliopause, but facing it directly was shocking.

His argument with Security Chief Mantabe, once their meeting had been adjourned, had been unpleasant. He understood her deep concerns and respected her position, but humanity truly could benefit greatly by studying this system further. The knowledge they might gain balanced all the risks involved, in his opinion. Chief Mantabe's main concerns revolved around hidden traps, unknown defenses and unexpected methods of dissuading interlopers. She reminded him how the crew were reacting to William Blaine and their own apprehensions concerning their uninvited visitor from the Sol System. Meanwhile, Agro Chief Tala Cyclehand had felt that any further exploration was a waste of materials and time. She felt Ganges should simply leave the system and find a new one.

To his surprise, Planetary Chief Sedders had offered his service and aid to Stellar's plans with an uncommon humility. Perrin could tell that the man was terribly shaken, but their mutual cooperation might finally end the struggle between the rival Sectors and halt any further protests erupting between their crewmembers. Harbor Chief Rollack seemed most enthusiastic about the change in plans. Perrin figured this was because it would feature his Sector during an historic initiative. Engineering Chief Navamo was also quite excited by the prospect of learning what they could by studying the ruins of Planet Forty-One. The others were fairly neutral or hid their concerns well.

Security Chief Mantabe insisted on providing a full squadron as escort for the expedition, which included plans to launch several battleships which would then surround Ganges within a protective formation. A squad of her crew would also be assigned to join the scientists heading to the surface, made up of volunteers from the ranks of the three departments under her command. They had chosen the recently refitted Sci-One to perform the landing, as it had the cargo space for the equipment and personnel. The tough ship had once been a larger class of tug, capable of easily withstanding atmospheric entry despite its blocky design. Like most vessels in its class, Sci-One had a hull that was three meters thick and was fitted with powerful engines that took up half the body of its design.

He watched as Wasp ran over to the Comms station and wondered what she was really thinking. His Executive Officer was quieter than was the norm. Perrin suspected she had mixed feelings concerning his decision to make the exploration of Planet Forty-One a reality. On the way to the Bridge, she had expressed her relief that there had been no debate as to whether Ganges should terraform the target world, stating that perhaps a real lesson had been learned from the fiasco at Planet Fifteen. For a Strifer to compliment the lack of debate was most astonishing, but he understood her meaning. Her people had protested that the officers of Ganges had even considered terraforming the single example they had found of a life-bearing world, which had earned them nothing but scorn and ostracism.

Captain Fieldscan spoke to the image of Naga, whose matronly visage filled the central holosphere of the Bridge, "My friend, I know you heard the deliberations at the meeting chamber. I want to make certain that we are doing the right thing, before I inform the crew. After all, you are the General Manager of the Holy Mission. I was somewhat surprised when you didn't speak up. You are always welcome at our debates."

Naga's visage seemed terribly melancholy, as the AeyAie spoke in a soft tone, "I did not speak because I agree with your assessment of our present situation. If you had decided otherwise, I would have intervened. I do share some of Security Chief Jira Mantabe's concerns, but I am pleased that cautious steps will be taken during this endeavor. There is much to learn, this is true, but we must be mindful of our actions, to make sure that no harm is done. I am glad that this latest development has cooled the tempers of the Chiefs of Planetary and Stellar Sectors, but I am still troubled that such an advanced species has met with such a lonely demise."

Perrin nodded as he replied, "I agree, on all points. At least we didn't find any evidence of warfare and self-destruction. Now I must galvanize the crew to shift course from reconstruction to exploration. It's not often that we have such a grand opportunity. Fear not, for I shall do my very finest to bring out the best of this situation. Future generations will wonder at the marvels we find here. I can also point out that this crew will have a chance to be part of a wonderous, historical event, something even our guest says is extremely rare. I have to wonder why this is the case. After all, water is plentiful in the galaxy. There are many planets in the right orbit for the emergence of life, yet the galaxy seems strangely empty. I suppose it's fortunate enough for us, as we generally have success in finding excellent candidate systems for the Holy Mission, but it still bothers me. I feel like we're missing some vital clue to solve the mystery."

Naga tilted its head, "Indeed. After studying the issue for octennia, I am no closer to a solution to the problem than you are. Then again, we must consider time into our set of variables. While it is true that Terra had life upon it, humanity didn't exist when this world was thriving. As for the rest of the meeting, I also agreed with the idea of William presenting his case before the crew. It might allay their fears if they can see him answer questions from the news services. We can then bolster their confidence by sharing what we have learned from him thus far. It might prepare them for the eventual appearance of his culture at our hull."

Perrin then signaled silently to Wasp that he was ready for his ship-wide announcement concerning the current status of the Holy Mission. He would do his best to lead the crew to accepting the facts before them and to pull their enthusiasm to a new direction. One that led to greater understanding and new knowledge for generations to come.

CHAPTER TWELVE

Spine Rotation - Life Sowing - Mission Harvest - Spiral 5620

"There are rotations when I find it hard to believe that Naga is willing to consider my bizarre suggestions as valid enough to bring to the attention of the Sector Chiefs, yet the evidence is hard to deny. Those soft-brained idiots actually made the changes to the beacon message I proposed to the AeyAie a few harvests ago, so that future colonists would have a chance to be something other than savages. It surprised the shit out of me! Not that I'm turning down the cheese, you understand. It's just that I never expected to be taken seriously. A few spirals ago, I would have said it was fucking impossible. My lonely, eternal debate continues, but the seeds of hope have been sown. Can you believe I just said that shit? I don't! Not long ago, I would have denied that Naga and I could ever become friends, but here we fucking are! Burrow mates in the wilderness! I still think that the human race sucks, but I do support the diaspora of the AeyAie species, and I do understand that they insist on bringing humans with them wherever they go. So, I guess you can say that I like Naga, but I don't approve of the company it keeps, including my own."
Worm, Strifer hermit, personal log, P35

Command Hub, Level Twenty-Two

William Blaine waited quietly in his chair, while the technicians were busy finishing their preparations for his interview in the Command Broadcast Studio. He was facing a trio of interviewers, sitting in a semi-circle facing him. Drones and holo-capture cameras were spaced around them in such a way as to give the crew who would be watching the program a perfect view. Naga had also informed him that the entire broadcast would be recorded for posterity. To his left was a well-dressed man, wearing a somber outfit which was iridescent, shifting its dark colors whenever he moved. His name was Rigo Agriplan, and his mahogany dark skin shone under the studio lights, a severe contrast with William's pale complexion. Rigo had a devoted following and a reputation for not being shy about his opinions.

Seated directly across from William was a Strifer, wearing traditional lurid green robes and a stained rat mask with a large hole in one ear. This man's name was Phlegm Burnmark, his dark eyes glaring from behind the mask he wore. As a newscaster, he was considered by most as being aggressive to the edge of abusive, with a paranoid outlook that sounded more than unhealthy. Phlegm's channel was wildly popular amongst the crew, especially in the Rat's Ass Community. He grinned at William frequently, as if anticipating a grand feast.

To William's right was Alina Peersworth, the most popular amateur reporter on the broadcast channels. Her short black hair had red stripes on the left side of her head, and a blue diamond tattoo adorned her left cheek. She wore a simple jumpsuit of white with bright orange trim, indicating loyalty to her Sector, which was Harbor. Her deep golden complexion was typical for most of the crew in Ganges. Alina was known for her investigative reporting, which sometimes included facing down Sector Chiefs and Security personnel.

Behind William was a wallscreen which remotely connected to a datapad he was given the rotation before. He had uploaded some images, recordings and documentation, with the help of Technology Sector Chief Eagle Lund. Beyond the three journalists were his guardians, led by Lieutenant Darron Lazhand. Mike and the other toragi from the platoon had prowled around the studio, as if inspecting the room for invaders. This location had been chosen as being neutral ground, under the jurisdiction of Command Sector. Standing next to Lieutenant Lazhand was Executive Officer Wasp Tornpage, who was busy fussing over some kind of projectile weapon that looked like it was full of dark purple goo.

A soft chiming filled the chamber, signaling that they were just eight pollen-slivers from being live. Naga's matronly visage filled the wallscreen behind William. It had been decided that the AeyAie would act as a moderator, which meant that it would begin speaking as an introduction, which might comfort the viewers, "Attention, all crew. Your regular rush-slice broadcasts have been replaced by a very special program, courtesy of Command Sector. Our vessel has a guest from the Sol System, who will answer questions from three of our most dedicated and popular journalists, Rigo Agriplan, Phlegm Burnmark and Alina Peersworth. This special interview shall now commence."

Alina began by saying, "Please state for the record your name and place of birth."

The Solarian replied, "I'll do better than that. My full name is William Blaine, Zeta-One-Three-Tango-Eight. I was born in Mars Orbital Five-Three-Seven, known as The Crystal Dream. My rank is Scout Specialist, sent by the Solarian Alliance to ascertain the whereabouts and condition of the terraforming vessel Ganges."

Rigo leaned back in his seat, a look of disdain upon his face, "Why does your government want to spy on our beloved ship?"

William grinned, "Originally, I was supposed to keep my presence a secret, so that I would not affect your culture. To keep outside influence to a minimum. Your Security Sector is far too efficient for my skills! They caught me right away. I have to admit, your toragi are very impressive!"

Phlegm snorted loudly, "You didn't answer the fucking question!"

William shrugged, "You can't guess? Ganges has been an inspiration to our culture for generations. We owe you a debt of gratitude that we can never repay. The other members of the alliance wanted to make certain that your crew and vessel were safe and operating within parameters. You've exceeded our expectations!"

Alina spoke up quickly, "We've had some terrible history with Terra. Not just the Awakening and the Crucible, but the generations of demands, outright threats and intrigue. Care to comment on that?"

William nodded thoughtfully, "Yes, I truly would. The old Terran government you know about destroyed itself octennia ago, taking the entire planet with it. The few survivors were in orbitals and colonies, who pulled together, after octuries of war, to rebuild our system. Fortunately for us, the compassion of the people living upon the terraformed worlds which you created were able to bring vital aid to our beleaguered population. Five Ganges-class vessels were sent out to the Sol System to help us rebuild Terra, which now thrives without a human population."

Phlegm leaned forward, "Wait a fucking whisker! You mean all those worlds we rebuilt are now colonized? There are other ships like Ganges?"

William smiled softly, "Oh, yes. To both questions! Humanity is living in a golden age of space exploration and development, thanks to you. All but the last four terraformed systems are now full of colonists. The slow-boats still take time to reach their destinations, so the last handful of worlds are still empty, but they look beautiful. Full ecosystems, lush landscapes, just waiting for new arrivals. Some of the colonies were inspired by your efforts and beacon messages, so they built Ganges-class ships to start their own terraforming programs, based on the success of yours. To trillions of humans and AeyAies, Ganges means selfless devotion, deep compassion and courage. You are celebrated every… spiral with a holiday in your honor. Some of the colonists decided to live in orbit, to keep the world you built for them pristine. Here, let me show you."

William pressed the touchscreen on the top of his datapad. The wallscreen behind him erupted into images and videos from several different worlds. One picture showed a Ganges-like ship being constructed in orbit around a planet with colorful rings. Another showed thriving cities nestled into dense jungles. A video revealed a ring of orbital stations surrounding a lush oceanic world with sculpted archipelagoes.

There were agrarian, urban and even industrial cultures, all of them wildly different in architectural styles and traditions.

The Solarian continued, his voice cutting through the amazed gasps of the three journalists, "You kept your promise. We embraced your generosity. These are all from my own cameras on my scout-suit and from my vessel, which is attached to your hull. Some of these colonies have joined the Solarian Alliance, others remain solitary of their own volition. I made open contact with most of them, all of whom are eternally grateful to you. A few wanted a life without technology, so I simply viewed their progress secretly, which is part of my instructions from Sol. Since your crew captured me, my duty has now evolved into one of diplomacy, though that was never the intentions of my superiors. You were to be left alone for now, while a decision as to whether or not to contact you directly would be considered following my report."

Phlegm seemed to shrink into himself, "Fuck it all. The Strifer Manifesto is doomed."

William leaned forward, "Not at all! My goodness! I've had some time to do a little research in my brig cell. You Strifers make some good points, ones we humans should never forget, especially about our baser natures. We have to remain openly wary of our tendency to declare war, plus our complacency concerning polluting our environment and how we treat those who disagree with our viewpoints. I love your ideals concerning the necessity of debates and open discourse. Those ideas are vital to any civilization!"

Rigo placed a supportive hand upon Phlegm's shoulder, "So, who's in this alliance of yours? Is it the Sol System, the AeyAies and colonists? Who decides what happens or how people are treated?"

William placed a hand near his hair, allowing it to tangle itself amongst his fingers, "The AeyAie Solidarity survived the destruction of Terra, so they remain an important faction within the alliance. The big surprise is that the Sol System was discovered by an alien species we call the Boktahl. Very friendly, I assure you, and immensely intelligent. They're not based on organic biology, so we don't colonize the same types of planets. The alliance makes decisions based on the views of all three species."

Alina almost got up from her chair, "Alien sentients? Are you joking? If not, what is humanity's role in this alliance of yours? What are theirs? How long has this been going on?"

William leaned back, "The Solarian Alliance has existed for about one of your octenniums. Before that, it was just a struggle to communicate with the Boktahl. At this point, we share technology. They provide assistance with space vessels and gravity expertise. The AeyAies are the mediators, negotiators, translators, though even they get strained by the Boktahl's unique view. We humans are the explorers and defenders of the alliance. Thus far, the three species are the only examples of sentience we've found to date. Not to bring up uncomfortable memories, but we have discovered three planets with non-sentient native life, like your Planet Fifteen. It still seems that the galaxy is mostly devoid of living things, a puzzle we haven't solved yet."

Phlegm gave him a frozen look, "So, the humans are the bullies for your alliance, is that it? Still in the business of killing, are we?"

William sighed, "It's not something that we're proud of, but we are the only species in the alliance that's willing to use force to protect the others, should it be deemed necessary. We are not permitted to open hostilities on our own. The decision to use force must come from all three member species. By the way, it was the Boktahl who pushed us to find you. They admire your works and how deeply you've benefitted humanity. They've even changed their own procedures for finding and developing planets for their own needs, using your protocols. As for humanity itself, while we have become more comfortable with terraforming, we'd prefer to leave it in the hands of the true artists in the galaxy, you and the ships that were built inspired by your beacon messages. Other scouts are tracking the Ganges-class vessels launched from colony worlds, but I was awarded the task of looking for you. It is my honor to finally meet you, and hopefully, I can help with any concerns you might have about our society. You helped us to understand that a true civilization has common goals, a purpose to hold onto that is greater than simple self-indulgence. You taught us to be respectful and compassionate through your example. It seems only fair that I do my best to return the favor and aid you in any way I can."

The three journalists began to argue back and forth, each one wanting to pose another question, though none of them were able to rise to a prominent position. Naga shut down the broadcast, leaving the crew's last impressions of the program with more material from William's datapad, showing colonies and orbitals from the worlds Ganges had rebuilt and the ring of habitats that formed a circle that ran along Terra's path around Sol. William promised the reporters that he would be happy to provide a private interview with each of them at a later time, which seemed to mollify them. All three looked shocked by his revelations, and when he left the Command Studio, the crew cheered as they caught sight of him. William only hoped he could maintain the good will he had engendered this rotation.

Planetary Sector, Level Thirty-Four

Planetary Sector Commander Ghell Vaclan clenched his fists in fury as he watched the rush-slice special program about the Solarian William Blaine. He took a deep breath, trying to control his temper before he did something that would attract too much attention, like smashing all the objects on his desktop or randomly killing someone, anyone, just to release the hot rage flowing through his veins. That sickly-looking freak had started off by complimenting Security Sector! Ghell knew the three reporters who had performed the interview, having watched all their programs in the past, just to make sure that none of his main operations were on the verge of being discovered. They had a reputation for being tough, solid performers, but this rotation, they acted like mewling idiots, sopping up every word that foul Solarian had uttered. It was disgusting!

A small chime filled his left ear. His blood pressure was up, and he took another moment to close his eyes, before reaching for a small drawer under his desk that held a special, unapproved medication for relief. Most of his body's special needs were mitigated in this manner. It was something he discovered early in his life, as a way to avoid Medical Sector's tampering. He liked himself the way he was. He didn't need any doctors poking around his blood chemistry. They certainly wouldn't like what they would find if they did.

As a child, he had been sent to various therapies and counselors, all to tame the bloodthirsty rage that boiled in his arteries. Ghell had learned to mimic control over his emotions, which led to skills which any actor would be envious of. In truth, he had been given no choice, for Naga was watching all the time, and his parents deep concern made them impediments for his thirsts. By the time he had reached Basic Crew Training, he had found a handful of others who had little use for the usual nonsense that was being stuffed into their heads. They had created a small hiking club, an activity that was greatly encouraged by his instructors.

Ghell and his friends would go camping together, finding all kinds of hidden places to act out their deepest, darkest fantasies upon unsuspecting animals or even crew members who were stupid enough to enter the forests alone. One of his old hiking friends had been preparing for a career in Medical Sector, exploring new pharmaceutical treatments. They liked to test out new compounds on themselves or upon their victims. From this relationship, Ghell became well stocked with contraband medicines. It had been a shame to hunt down and kill every member of the hiking group, but Ghell had found a replacement pharmacist, one who didn't know who he was or what he really looked like. She never asked questions and provided him with the chemicals he required.

It was also during his hiking adventures when he discovered that the crime syndicates were also utilizing the nature preserves as a cover for their illicit activities. That had been the beginning of the end for the hiking club. One by one, his friends disappeared under mysterious circumstances, leaving him as being the sole survivor, mourning the loss of his closest classmates, or so Security believed. Every story that he gave them checked out. Every alibi had been perfect. He had even given the gray-

Suits information that would lead them to the lairs of criminals, emptying their safe places for his eventual return. For spirals, Ghell had lain low, keeping his nose clean and rising in the ranks of Planetary Sector, pretending to be a model of good crew, all the while building up a network of malcontents to do his bidding. Ghell supported them with his organizational skills and rank access, keeping his identity a secret, using costumes and various face masks, including those of a Strifer. When he had discovered the Vigilante camo-suit, it had been the capstone to his ambitions. It allowed him to become the Lord of his little kingdom within Ganges.

Now, just when he had been able to use those fops in Security he had bribed and threatened, to give him information that he disseminated throughout the rumor network of the ship, so that the crew would hamper any effort to break his grip on the nature preserves, this yellow-haired puss-stain now spoke of hope and service to humanity! The broadcasts were still showing all the pretty pictures of happy colonists. Every babble-head on the channels was so excited by the news that the terraforming did have an impact on humanity. Every Holy Mission zealot was praising this bizarre stranger for bringing such glad tidings. Who knew what the Solarian Alliance was capable of? Would they offer their own services to aid Security Sector? Would they simply take over the ship? How would their presence affect his business?

Ghell wanted that Solarian bastard dead, even if he had to strangle the man personally. Had the pale visitor already notified his superiors? Were they on their way here? How did William Blaine even reach Ganges, from a thousand lightspirals away? It was a total sleepscare! The Solarian was good at swaying minds and hearts, bringing up topics he knew would appeal to the crew's sense of honor. How many of the colonies had this guy conquered using the same techniques? There had to be a way to get rid of this threat! Maybe even send a message to his betters that they were unwelcome. It wouldn't be enough to just kill William Blaine. It had to be done in such a way that it would horrify the people who sent him. It had to be performed so that it didn't look like the work of one person, but a whole population.

Ghell began to wonder how all the Sector Chiefs were taking this guest's instant stardom. Who might feel threatened or become envious? The Chief of Stellar would be happy to slaughter newborn kittens, just to get her hands on Sol System technology. Certainly not his own superior, who would probably be cheering right now, ecstatic that the Holy Mission had a real purpose, other than controlling the crew. Now that he thought about it, the interview would most likely mean that Chief Sedders would soon insist on setting up a string of useless conferences with every department Commander to discuss the situation, as a balm for not being able to terraform Planet Forty-One. That would interfere with Ghell's preparations to stave-off Security Sector from his domains within the nature preserves. He had to find a way to avoid being dragged into a series of futile, oxygen-wasting meetings. For that, he needed a dupe.

Ghell contacted his receptionist and told him to call in Dalen Gupta. The fat fool had been useful in the past. While he couldn't stand his mate's prattling on about Director Gupta's dancing skills, the prancing idiot had been a wonderful distraction, keeping Ghell's family in the dark about his activities. Now the big loser could be useful once again. Besides, it would be easy now to destroy Dalen's reputation if he should discover anything unsavory. Ghell could accuse him of taking advantage of his family, who the Director had been entertaining for several rotations at a time over the last harvest. If he balked, Ghell could always find entertaining ways to terrify and abuse Dalen's unsuspecting mates and children to keep him in line.

For now, he would simply ask the dancing lout to be his proxy during any emergency meeting the Chief decided to make, allowing Ghell to continue his secret work. He would need an excuse, but that ability had been mastered long ago. Once Dalen took his place for the rotation, Ghell could begin to alert his operatives. First, he would do what was needed to secure his holdings in the nature preserves. After that, his assassins had to be informed of their new target, a pest named William Blaine.

Agro Wheel Two, Security Level Four

Ensign Jero Coreline's head was swimming with what he had seen upon the wallscreens on the way to his post. He liked to be early, as the extra time allowed him to settle his nerves before his shift started. Watching the interview on the tram was a surreal experience, with the other early riders reacting to every revelation with a mixture of fear and joy. To actually see the images of colonists inhabiting the worlds they terraformed had brought hot tears to his eyes. Jero's mind was elated, shocked, terrified and feeling completely lost. The broadcasts which followed were filled with both trepidation and celebration in equal measure. The Holy Mission had just been verified, with Naga-Ma confirming that the information they saw was real and true. Crew hugged each other in the tram with total abandon, weeping like novices. One Medical crewmember had started singing "Journey Forever" with a voice broken by fierce emotions. Jero had joined in, which encouraged all the others. He felt as if he had been punched in the guts by Love itself. All of their sacrifices, the hazards they had faced for octennia, the wars they fought to preserve the Holy Mission, all of it vindicated by a stranger from the Sol System.

All the broadcasts which followed the special program were chaotic. The Strifers were marching in protest at the Rat's Ass Community, warning not to trust the words of non-crew. Others pointed out that Naga accepted the news as valid.

Some of the red-masked Strifers were waving their Manifestos in the air, calling for free debates, inviting the Solarian to their nests to begin a dialog concerning the nature of the alliance with alien sentients. Agro Wheel reporters were busy showing scenes of revelry amongst some of the local farmers, who could be considered the greatest adherents to the Holy Mission, though some spoke words of caution when it came to news from savages.

Jero's mate, Scratch, had contacted him, saying she was going to take the rotation off to join the protests, though she wasn't sure which one to choose, as they all sounded like fun, but her supervisor had sent out a notice that all Stellar crew were to be at their stations. When he finally got to Security Sector, saluting the giant statue of Marik Langman as he stepped off the tram, Jero noticed that the grand entrance looked like someone had kicked a nest of hornets. Security crew and toragi were rushing about with great fervor. It looked like everyone was mobilizing all at once, though he didn't know why.

Of course, Jero had immediately recognized the Solarian, the pollen-sliver he had appeared on the wallscreens. He had seen the man with the odd, yellow hair near his post, a few sowings ago. Jero also remembered how the stranger had just disappeared without a trace. What were the Solarians capable of? What kind of technology did they use? It all sounded like a bad entertainment broadcast, but this time, it was very real. Those aliens looked like nothing he had ever seen. He was still trying to get the details straight in his mind. Overall, the images of the Boktahl had shown a large, blue-gray lozenge standing on one narrow end. Its main body seemed to be made from coral, with bumpy surfaces, squeezed together, then lashed in place with red, lacey frills. The narrow top and bottom of the creatures were surrounded by long, purple tendrils that had branches which twisted and turned in every direction. No head, eyes or ears, not even feet. There was nothing he could compare them to, except perhaps, some strange species of colorful sea anemones. It was too strange to keep in his mind for long.

As he worked his way through the rushing crowd of armored crew, being careful to keep out of their way, Jero eventually made it to the lifts in one piece. In general, the Security Police were far stronger than the average crew member. They had fast reflexes, dense bones and broad muscles, for they trained in the higher apparent gravity, after Basic Crew Training, and received special supplements from Medical Sector. Jero was taller and more physically fit than most people he knew, but compared to the crew he worked for, he was scrawny and weak. The queues at the lift tubes were long, and he kept an eye on the wallscreens for more news. All of a sudden, Security Chief Jira Mantabe appeared on all of them, "Attention all Security personnel. As of now, all leave time is suspended. The crew have been riled, in good ways and in bad. Either has the potential to create chaos, so our Sector is now under high alert. I am calling on everyone, including the support staff, to keep an eye out for any suspicious behavior or unusual events. If you have anything to report, please go directly to Investigation Services."

Jero took a deep breath, then left the line he was in, which was for express service to the Fleet harbor, and chose a different one. He actually had something to report – the appearance of William Blaine at his post, even though it was sowings ago. He looked at the datapad strapped to his wrist and called up his superior, telling her that he would be late to his shift because he needed to report to Investigations. He felt out of place in his white-and-orange uniform, surrounded by crew in gray-and-maroon. In the lift, the others glanced at him with open curiosity. Jero did his best to stay calm, though he wished he could smoke a buddha-roll. The crew with him were not armored brutes, but the clever intellectuals that solved crimes and hunted for information. He was pretty sure they intimidated him more than the Police crew.

He got off at the first stop and approached a long line of desks. Some of the personnel that were in the lift with him were scrambling for these stations. Others marched off into a maze of corridors that were darkly lit by data screens. Jero walked to the first desk that already had someone sitting at their post, "Excuse me. I'm Jero Coreline, Ensign Rank Three, Dock Crew for the Security Fleet. I have something to report, as per the Chief's instructions."

The woman behind the desk looked at him as if examining an insect she didn't like, "What is the nature of the incident?"

Jero nervously coughed into his left hand, "I saw the Sol-guy on the screens this rush-slice, a few sowings ago, at my post in the Security harbor."

She squinted up at him, "Why didn't you report this sooner?"

He felt his face grow hot as he replied, "Well, the truth is, the guy with the yellow hair just disappeared when I went to ask him what he was doing in my section. You know, there's a lot of crew there, keeping the vessels secure and maintained. That's what I do, maintaining fighter pods, not securing them, you understand. This guy was there, named William, right? Though to tell the truth, I didn't know his name at the time. I just found out a short while ago. From that special Command broadcast, you understand, while I was on the tram. Yeah, so he was there one pollen, then not there the next. I thought maybe I was confused or it was a trick of the light. They flash a lot in the harbor. It's always really busy. Not that I'm complaining or anything, but it seemed to me that if I could prove that he was there, then I would be able to get the proper…"

She raised a hand, "Stop right there. An officer will be with you shortly and help you fill out a statement for review. Have a seat over there."

Jero went to where he was told to go, his head hanging low. He had nothing to be ashamed of, but he couldn't help it. These people made anyone feel like they did something bad. At least he was following orders and would get a notice sent to his supervisor that he was on official business. He only hoped his mate was having a better rotation at her post.

Ten Thousand Kilometers to the Fore of Ganges

Fleet Commander Vina Harrolon briskly paced the bridge of her flagship, The Malati, waiting for the next shift in the reconnaissance squadrons. Her uniform was neatly pressed. Medals of service hung from its chest panels, her shoulders braided with hanging silver chains that jangled lightly with every step she took. She glared about the twenty-meter-long chamber with both a natural eye and a multi-spectrum patch which covered the empty left socket. Her right hand was a gleaming prosthetic, fitted with targeting sensors, shock knuckles and other, hidden tools of her trade. Vina's hair was shorn close to her skull and had turned to a stark white spirals ago, contrasting with her dark complexion, except for the single scar that ran down from her left brow to the bottom of her jaw, a souvenir from her fighter-pod spirals. She was tall and lean, taking extra care to keep herself in shape. It was good for morale. A slovenly leader meant a sloppy crew, something which she would never tolerate. The captain of The Malati sometimes called her a martinet, a private joke they shared, for they were both cut from the same, determined cloth of service to Ganges. Neither accepted anything less than perfection under their purview.

The bridge was crowded with personnel, so she did her pacing within the alcove on the port side of the command pit, just behind and to the left of the captain's chair. Beyond this was a ring of duty stations, all of them manned by hand-picked crew, noted for their pristine service record. Let the Security Police platoons have their ruffians; there was no place for such nonsense in the depths of space. Vina knew that she had been amongst the candidates for Chief of her Sector, but was relieved when Jira Mantabe was chosen for the role. Being trapped within the hull of Ganges was not something Vina desired. The scuttlebutt amongst the fleet crew that she spent more time in space than any officer before was absolutely true. Her private quarters aboard the Malati were her registered home, and she had spent the majority of her life in one vessel or another over the course of her career.

Commander Harrolon's magnetic boots clanked with every step, as if timing her impatience with every measured footfall. Captain Loni Voidloc had already sent out the Malati's complement of fighter-pods, moments after Chief Mantabe's orders for general alert status. It pleased Vina that their vessels had launched a pollen-sliver ahead of the other ships in the battlegroup. Ten of the cruisers were in formation around the flagship, all of them loosely based on the five-hundred-meter-long seed-ship design that Security had built over the last few octennia. Unlike their terraforming cousins, these vessels were a touch sleeker, more heavily shielded and bristling with Spin-Drive turrets and missile launchers. Their long prows were wedge-shaped and heavily reinforced, with inset, giant laser emitters that could melt hull plating. At the stern of the battlecruisers were launch facilities, rather than cargo holds, and were crewed by two-hundred and fifty Security personnel.

Within the very core of these pugnacious warships were all the medical and exercise facilities, in a long section that spanned the length of the ship, which spun on internal magnetics to give a half-Terran apparent gravity. The rest of the fighting behemoths were allowed to remain under zero-gee conditions, with braided webbing covering all the walls for support in moving through the ship and clinging to during maneuvers. The main engines and thrusters were all oversized units, making the ships highly responsive and dexterous. The ship's specially trained toragi, most of which were from either the Kumar or Makamba bloodlines, seemed to fully enjoy the environment aboard these vessels, and her own Helen was no exception.

Captain Voidloc called out, "Ganges Security squadron fleet Delta has just launched. Open all entry bays for our returning fighters and prepare all personnel for embarkation."

The bridge suddenly resounded with confirmations, "Primed, captain", and "Launch bays signal ready, captain.", "Ship squadrons setting course, captain." Vina listened to it all with care, seeking discrepancies and quite pleased to find none. She marched over to her station and looked at the holo-projection displaying the formation of the general fleet. A second ring of ten battlecruisers were behind the stern of Ganges, along with three rings of the massive ships evenly spaced in synchronous orbit along the length of the giant, terraforming vessel, standing by five-thousand kilometers from the hull. Cutters and corvettes were evenly distributed, covering all angles of approach. Half of these smaller, yet powerful vessels were orbiting Ganges at diagonal vectors, making a webwork of protection for the mother ship.

Vina had served upon all of these various classes of Security war vessels, including the sleek cutters, which were more like moving gun platforms than anything else. Magnetic railguns ran the entire length of their design, firing boulder-sized, processed asteroid ore at near-relativistic speeds. She had assigned three of these specialized ships to act as a distant escort for the impending science mission to Planet Forty-One, to bolster the fighter-pods which would guide the survey crew in Sci-One to the upper atmosphere. Vina marked out a single corvette to act as a base of operations in case anything went wrong.

Her last meeting with Chief Mantabe and Captain Fieldscan had been highly productive. It helped that they all wanted the same thing - to guard the safety of Ganges and its population during this exploratory expedition. She was excited by this historic moment, for nothing like it had ever been performed before now. This was a chance to shine a light upon the Security Fleet under her care. Too many of the crew thought of the space-based forces as hotshot pilots, like Lieutenant Tarn Vekkor. While she appreciated his dedication and skill, he could never truly represent the full panoply of expertise required to maintain the safety of Ganges. The fleet consisted of Rescue personnel, bay hands, docking crew, engineers, duty officers, tacticians, boarding police, gunners, even maintenance and repair specialists.

Vina watched as the dance of rotating squads began in earnest, as they hurtled ever closer to Planet Forty-One. She thought it was a shame that they would not get the chance to perform the Holy Mission in this system, but she agreed with her superiors. The news about William Blaine had been more startling to her, and she had begun a series of drills specifically designed for coping with the sudden and close appearance of unknown vessel types as a result. Vina wasn't amused that a stranger from the Sol System had gotten aboard undetected. She was sympathetic to the Security Police crew who had to deal with the protesting population, but she also viewed the Solarians as a real and present threat. Vina knew that she also had to be prepared for any surprises at Planet Forty-One, but a dead world full of ruins didn't sound like much of a challenge to the fleet. She didn't know what the scientists would find down there, but she hoped that they needed nothing from her crew but a soothing presence.

Residence Wheel Two, Level Two

Ensign Ubo Capsworn struggled to load a box of trash into the back of Crab Spitshard's run-down cab. He always made certain to keep any paranormal site he was investigating clean of his own debris, but the Strifer taxi driver thought it was a waste of time. Ubo had argued that recycling was a duty that all crew should take on with fervor. Crab had pointed out that this was done almost automatically through the trash system that eventually led to the two Industrial Wheels, managed by Provision Sector personnel. Littering was an uncommon occurrence, usually by accident, and cleaned up by drones, robots and the crew who were assigned to such duties. If the haunted regions of Ganges were filled with human debris, it was because they were abandoned. Over the spirals, such an area might become revitalized, whereupon the proper crew would then handle anything which had been left behind within the empty communities during refit. Ubo didn't buy the argument, but then again, the Rat's Ass Community still looked like a dumping ground to him, purposely soiled by the Strifer inhabitants, so Crab might not really understand his objections to leaving his trash behind at a site.

Ubo also needed the chore to keep his mind off of some of the things he had experienced over the past sowings. Everstrong was decidedly unusual, even for a haunted area. The most obvious thing that set it apart from other regions of interest was its sheer size. An entire city, once supporting a million crew, was now derelict and falling apart. The border between its above-deck structures and the belowdecks was blurred into oblivion. Everstrong remained the only haunted area that had been ravaged by warfare in which massive battles had been fought by thousands of crew, bringing death on a mass scale. It might have been rivaled by the original Harbor Two, had that Wheel not been torn down and then fully rebuilt from scratch after the Crucible.

The other problem was that, unlike in Forward Estates, the phenomena he had recorded here thus far defied any rational explanations. Strange occurrences happened even in the light of work-slice, but in the darkness of dream-slice, they seemed to multiply, mainly due to being more visible without competition from the skyscreens. Ghostly visages, glowing spots of light and shimmering apparitions were better seen when dark-shift began. Some of the other regions which Ubo had studied exhibited unexplainable events, but nowhere near the massive scale that Everstrong supported. Even during the light of dawn-slice, holes that had been blasted through walls by war machines disappeared, only to return after a few paring-slivers. Crushed vehicles and bloodstains shifted position, but only after one looked away from them for a short period of time.

None of this truly compared to all the strange sounds that emanated from shattered doorways and holes in the deck, despite the lack of any wind. Howls and moans, sometimes even intelligible words and laughter, floated in the avenues that crossed through collapsed buildings and broken tram stations. Barely heard whispers filled his rest time within his tent, creating a rich ground for the sleepscares that startled Ubo whenever he nodded off. He had discovered no wildlife at all, not even birds and insects, within the main city limits. During the few rainy rotations Ubo had endured there, large sparks of electricity ravaged the crumbling structures, making him flinch at the crashing noise they made. One of his best cameras had been struck by a blue-white bolt, melting it and the tripod supporting the recording device.

Crab slowly got out of his cab, brushed off some crumbs from his taxi-driver uniform and said, "Say, did you get any better results from the sensors? I know that I heard some awful shit last sleep-slice, I'll tell you! When we going back to town? I need a cozier roof and some fucking peace for once!"

Ubo straightened up from his task and blinked at the surly Strifer, "We were there a few rotations ago. Besides, you should try sleeping in the tent!"

Crab shook his head violently, "No fucking thanks! Not this rat! It's been getting louder in this damned place, hasn't it? I still don't like the little communities around here, but they're better than this stinking place!"

Ubo shrugged, "Maybe it has been. I won't know until I get a chance to study the data. What there is of it."

Crab jabbed a greasy finger into Ubo's shoulder, "Hah! The equipment is failing, isn't it? Jumbled recordings and wiped data wafers, just like last sowing! I don't like it! I'd hate to think what this place is doing to your balls. You ever consider that? This city was shut down by Security Sector for a reason! We gotta sneak in and out like thieves. Not that we have to worry about those around here. Even the fucking syndicates give this place a wide berth! So should we!"

Ubo scowled, "We are investigators, not cowardly criminals. Despite the fact that we're trespassing in a classified zone."

Crab spat upon the crumbled deck, "You're the crazed investigator, not me! Speaking of trespassers, how about that William guy? I saw the little interview they had for him on my datapad. What a weirdo! Sure you don't want to investigate him instead?"

Ubo took a small bite from one of the travel veggie-wraps they had supplied themselves with when they were last in town, "What's the point? He's not a ghost, though he looks like one. I have no interest in the corporeal. Let the Captain sort that out. However, getting back to your earlier statement, I do believe that something is riling up the spirits here. Maybe it has to do with Planet Forty-One. Now there's a place I wish I could investigate! Just think! An entire alien civilization in ruins! Oh, how I wish I had joined Stellar Sector! I might have had the chance to gain a seat on Sci-One to study it all!"

Crab rolled his eyes, "You're categorically nuts! Maybe they should just drop you off there, or you can stow away and never come back."

Ubo took a long drink from his canteen, "Don't be insulting! I'm not a savage, you know! Besides, who would pay you if I wasn't here? How many chips do you have in your pocket because of me? I was just saying it would be nice to see the ruins, that's all. I'm looking for the unexplainable, not crazy tech from an advanced sentient species. Ganges has mysteries enough, and I think that whatever is in this system may be having an effect on them. Help me load up the gear. I want to try a different spot, maybe one of the parks, or what's left of it. I think staying away from the superstructure of the city might yield better results and cleaner recordings."

Crab protested, "Those parks are right in the fucking center of the damned city! They're surrounded by structures! I don't believe this! Now you want to enter the central chamber of a live reactor. Those are spacious too, you know! Doesn't mean they're fucking safe!"

Ubo smiled at his assistant, "I never said it was safe, Crab. I said I might get cleaner results. There's a difference. Now, come on, let's get going."

The Strifer grumbled under his breath, but Ubo ignored him. Instead, his mind was full of the possibilities in changing the location of his recordings. Would there be living plants still intact after all this time? Burnt remains from forests set alight by missiles and experimental weapons? A sports field would be a prime choice. No obstructions and loads of space to spread out the sensors. He understood his companion's concerns, but paranormal investigating meant taking a few risks. Some rotation in the future, the scientists of Stellar would cease laughing at those who searched for the paranormal and mystical. He was determined to be the very first investigator to force them to take such work seriously, even if it killed him to do it.

Residence Wheel One, Level Sixteen

Spat Newstain sulked, while sitting upon a pile of useless junk on the corner of Rotten Street and Cheese Avenue within the Rat's Ass Community. It was now the middle of dark-slice, but he had no real desire to join any of the various protests, celebrations or the debates that swirled their way through the streets with raucous enthusiasm. The gothic lampposts on every corner had been strung with competing banners, each one declaring their position concerning the "guest", William Blaine, and the Solarian Alliance, Planet Forty-One or the continued relevance of the Strifer Manifesto. Splatters of thrown fruits and vegetables covered the walls wherever he looked. Odd bits of debris, such as old shoes, rat masks, bags, waist sashes and placards cluttered the avenues and intersections. The pubs and restaurants lining the streets were seeing an explosion of business, the sound of heated arguments coming from their open doors, echoing between the leaning, high-towered buildings. Despite all the hubbub, Spat felt alone.

After his usual rotation at school, his parents had decided to head over to their old community, so they could be with family during these unstable times. At first, Spat had been delighted, looking forward to seeing his cousins, especially those who had tried to help him break into Security's data systems to find the identity of William Blaine, who was now known throughout Ganges. Spat had been proud to have been one of the very few who had investigated the mystery of the yellow-haired man. His unswerving perseverance had brought him the honor of being noticed by Security's Investigations Department, who had warned him about illicit computer activities and offered him a post after his Basic Crew Training. His parents had also been notified, and they had both been confused about whether they should be angry with him or bursting with pride. To his mind, this meant he had behaved like a true Strifer.

He hadn't been disappointed that Naga had tried to dissuade him from his digging for data. Spat understood the position of the AeyAie, having to keep a secret and not wanting to lie about it. His mental anguish came from a different source – the very cousins he had been so excited to see. They had downplayed his role in their attempts to ferret out information on the stranger. They refused to give him any credit, even though he was just Student Rank Seven, and yet he had noticed things very few Full Crew had the wit to see. The worst part was when he had been shoved aside during their heated debates concerning what everyone had seen in all the special programs that had filled the wallscreens all rotation. Everyone had an opinion about William Blaine, but few were asking the questions which Spat wished to explore.

If he was being honest with himself, it seemed like his concerns were simply too frightening for anyone else to be bothered with, distracted as they were by more immediate worries. The Strifer population itself was more riled by the revelations of the rotation than anyone else, for the news that colonies had been established at the planets Ganges had terraformed had been confirmed, giving the Holy Mission a real boost. This seemed to make the Manifesto a useless document, as if it were a single-issue philosophy. Others felt that they had to make contact with the Solarian Alliance, to dissuade them from creating any more colonies. In the meantime, there was still a lot of bad feelings swirling about the crew not being allowed to terraform Planet Forty-One. Some crew were looking for someone, anyone, they could blame for the fiasco, with Stellar Sector being the most obvious scapegoat.

Security Sector was out in force, but in a ship the size of Ganges, with a population of over sixty million humans, there were still gaps that simply couldn't be plugged. Fortunately, there had been few outright riots following the news concerning William Blaine and his mission, but the number of protest marches and other, more welcoming gatherings had risen exponentially, straining Security's ability to maintain the peace. Spat knew there would be crew who might take advantage of the chaos with impunity, but there was nothing a mere Student could do about that. The horrible truth was that he could say the same about the things which were really bothering him. No one listened to him, for he was just a novice in the eyes of Full Crew.

Spat slid down the pile of debris he had been using as a perch, his bare feet hitting the pavement with a slap. With his head slung low, he began to make his way back to his uncle's apartment, where he and his parents were staying for dark-shift, when a voice broke him from his thoughts, "Young rat! Why is your head bowed so low?"

He turned around to find a red-robe walking toward him. The Strifer cleric was shorter than most crew, his crimson robes stained and torn, as was proper. The red rat mask on the man's face was smeared with soot, as if he had been digging in a campfire. Spat respectfully lifted his middle finger at the red-robe, "Human stupidity, cheesy varmint. It gets me every time I hear it."

The Strifer cleric replied, "As it should, pup. My name's Midge. Why aren't you participating in the grand debates? Cat's got your tongue?"

Spat shook his head, "I squeak when I know I'll be heard. No one wants to argue the things I find important. They all blather about the same stupid shit that's on the wallscreens. I'm looking for bigger cheese to gnaw upon."

He could see the smile that spread underneath the crimson rat mask, "The Manifesto has everything you need to start a new debate. It's our guide to surviving this crummy universe. What's your name, pup?"

"Spat, red-cheese. Spat Newstain. Some are saying the Manifesto is dead now, with all those colonies filled to the brim with vermin. How can I get into a debate no one wants to participate in?"

Midge laughed, "Hah! Fear not! The Manifesto isn't just about the misuse of the so-called 'Holy Mission', you know. If you want to bring up a topic no one wants to listen to, look to your ancestors! Make noise! Force them to listen by being clever. Tell me, Spat, what do you want to argue about?"

Spat sank down on his haunches, "I'm concerned that if William Blaine is telling the truth, which I'm not too sure about, even with Naga vouching for him, that crew may end up being free to leave Ganges or even enter it from outside. What will happen then? Are we gonna be surrounded by amateurs? What happens when the rats infect the Solarian Alliance and their leaders strike back at us in anger? How about when outsiders infest Ganges, bringing disruptive cultures into our own? How did William get here in less than a single lifetime? What will we do when we're flooded with vermin from Sol?"

Midge grabbed his stained robe near to his heart, "From the mouth of pups! Your claws scratch to the very heart of the cheese! I may have stumbled upon the next debate leader of Rat's Ass! Unless you'd prefer to join us red-robes. A clever rat like you would be most welcome among us, after having enough rotten fruit thrown at you. Being a Strifer is to be willing to ask all the uncomfortable questions. To say all the things no one wants to discuss. Fuck. Them. All! It seems you're not a Strifer-in-robes-only, nor are you one to avoid the tough questions that we all must face! Here's some real advice; no matter where you are or what situation you're in, use the damned tools around you. Always remember, facts hurt the most! Speak your mind to gain the long-term results you want. Avoid being popular or ordinary. Look where no one else wants to. Hear what's not being said, and give those things your voice! Now, I must be on my way to the Manifesto Church. If you ever need me, I'll be there for you with a willing ear to twist."

Spat watched the red-robe wander off into the darkness. He got to his feet and resumed his journey. The words of Midge ran about his head like mice in a wheel. While the cleric hadn't given him a debate, he had pointed out some very important lessons. Frightened people often became blind to the very things which would do the most damage to them. This could go along with the old Strifer saying "Nothing lowers intelligence like dogma". Spat would bring his issues to certain individuals and in particular settings where they would be heard, even if no debate resulted. Naga was the most obvious choice, but he had recently been noticed by Investigation Services and invited to join the red-robes. He could contact both organizations and bring his concerns to them in an open forum. His mind began to race harder, seeking the tools which Midge told him to search for. School reports, papers and discussions were all valid venues for releasing his queries concerning the future, now that the Solarian Alliance had discovered Ganges. He might also become more active on the personal broadcast channels, though that sometimes felt like spitting into the thrusters. He had resources directly in front of him. All he really needed was the courage to use them to full effect.

Agro Wheel Three, Security Level One

Brace Lazhand sat within his cell and brooded, a bad habit which had begun to dominate his time. He knew Security procedure well, having taught the subject to new recruits for spirals. There had been a temptation to retire a bit early, get out while he was still in good shape, but his undercover work had been fulfilling enough to hang onto. It hadn't been long before he had gotten deep inside one of the most nefarious of the crime syndicates. He should have known better. He should have realized that the highly secretive boss he had found himself working for had already known all about his role as an operative for Investigation Services. Then Brace had gotten hooked on contraband meds that had suddenly held him in an iron grasp of desperation. He had worked for both sides, figuring that he would clean himself up once he had everything Investigations needed to end the syndicate's control over Residence Wheel One's illicit trade groups. Now Brace had to concede that he had been set up, so that his fall from grace could be useful to the faceless "Lord of Crime".

Brace knew that he should have stood trial by now, yet he remained within his little cell. Even Slither hadn't been around to question him for many rotations, a clear indication that something was wrong. Then again, he had seen the news on the single wallscreen his cell contained. The savages of Sol had finally found Ganges, though doing a good job convincing everyone they weren't barbarians. This meant that the Chief had a lot on her plate right now. He could hardly fault her for not making his case a priority. Brace knew that he shouldn't be in a hurry to be re-educated, but he also hated waiting for the hammer of justice to fall on him, as it inevitably would.

The unexpected visit from his nephew still stung, which didn't help his mood. Darron's appearance in his cell had been unexpected and more painful than Brace would openly admit. Not that they were especially close as a family, but he was fond of the young officer. He remembered being at the graduation ceremony at the end of

Darron's Basic Crew Training, sitting next to his brother who had tears in his eyes, as he watched his son choose Security Sector for his post. Darron's father had asked him to watch over his son, which he had for the first spiral or two. Now, his family thought he was dead and would remain ignorant of his fate. Brace was feeling helpless, something which he had little experience with, until he had been captured and disgraced. The past sowings had been an exercise in suffocating hopelessness, both from his own actions as a double-agent and from withdrawal from the chemicals he used to love more than his duty to Security.

The only other visitor to call in at his lonely cell, not including Slither and Security Chief Mantabe, was another secret operative of the crime syndicate he had been involved with, leaving behind threats against his family. Brace had tried to tell Slither about the incident, then was interrogated and mocked for his troubles. At least the Strifer had been clever enough to change Brace's cell and also rotate the crew guarding him. Now Brace had new walls to stare at, every other rotation. At least the new ones didn't stink of stale cigar smoke like his original cell.

His mind wandered to his former toragi, Sam. At least the big cat was alive and well, most likely being used for training and breeding. He hated the fact that everyone brought up losing his guardian, all the while understanding why they did this. It was horrifically painful. Every Security crewmember feared the rotation when their toragi was injured or killed in the line of duty. The bond between human and toragi was deep. That he had lost Sam due to his own, disgraceful actions made that emotional pain unbearable. It was worse than the withdrawal, losing his family and the trust of his colleagues. It filled his every waking moment with self-loathing, while his sleepscares were hardly better than his penned-in reality. Brace felt as if he had been ripped open and left bleeding on the deck.

The wallscreen across from his small cot began to display yet another news program about William Blaine, who had been very busy chatting with several news services all rotation. Brace recognized the Solarian immediately. The stranger had accompanied Darron, basically hiding behind Mike, while his nephew gave his rage full reign. At the time, Brace had no idea who the man had been. He was still unclear as to why Darron had brought the Solarian to view what should have been a private encounter. Brace groaned, then got to his feet, hoping that he could manually turn off the unwanted program. He had asked Naga to leave him alone, to give him time to think. Despite the AeyAie's assurances that he wouldn't be interrupted by needless broadcasts, the wallscreen filled itself with multiple videos concerning the Solarian.

Just as he was about to touch the heavily shielded display panel, the wall erupted in a flash of static. All the programs had been wiped clear, leaving behind a swirling mess of colors and blocks of data snippets. Brace stepped back in alarm, wondering what was going on. The wallscreen cleared, and a single, life-sized image of a woman in a Harbor uniform assembled itself before his eyes. She had red hair and dark skin, then changed into a man in an Agro uniform with blue-dyed hair and face tattoos. The person on the screen shifted more quickly, rotating through several different facial styles. Brace groaned aloud, slamming his fist against the wallscreen to no effect.

The figure upon the wallscreen spoke, its voice shifting every third word, "Hello, Brace. I see that you remember me. I'm touched. It's amazing what one can do with old Strifer tech, once it's been updated for the current protocols. Very flexible programming, easy to reconfigure. If you shout or go for the door to your tiny home, I promise that your brother won't survive dark-slice. I hear you've been getting family visits. Very kind of Security, I must say."

Brace punched the wallscreen, bruising his knuckles on the synth-quartz, "What the fuck do you want, asshole? Leave me to rot alone!"

The figure shook its head, "Dear me, such foul language. You know I don't approve of that from my underlings. You ask me what I want, then tell me to leave you be. Make up your mind, Brace, or do you still have enough of one to choose your desires? I am the Lord of crime in Ganges. You are my serf, my peasant, my little plaything who likes to work all sides against each other. I have something special for you to consider."

Brace shook with rage, "Go suck a thruster!"

The shifting figure just laughed at him, "I like your spirit, Brace! I really do. I admired your gall to infiltrate my crew. You fooled every one of my enforcers, but not me. That was impressive. I'm just hoping your skills haven't rotted away in that poor excuse for a cell. There's an offer on the table, Brace. I do suggest you take it. You might thank me in the future."

Brace growled back, "I don't fucking work for you."

The figure nodded, "Yes, so I've heard. At the same time, you don't work for Security Sector anymore either. So, where is your post now? Are you still loyal to Ganges? The Holy Mission? The safety of the general crew?"

Brace bit back the reply that threatened to rip out of him. Something was wrong. He sat on the edge of his rumpled cot, "What's your game? Why visit me? Ran out of novices to torture?"

The figure leaned forward, "That was just once! It was a lesson which had to be given to a competitor of mine, nothing more. I'm concerned, Brace. Deeply so. There isn't much time. Naga will shut down our chat soon, so shut your stupid trap and listen. Do you know this man?"

The face of William Blaine flashed on the screen for a pollen-sliver. Brace scratched his head, "Yeah. The Solarian. He's all over the news. Why?"

The shifting person replied, "He represents the greatest threat our ship has faced since it launched from the Sol System. I have other agents at play, but I could use your honed skills and your current location. William Blaine must die. This has to be accomplished as soon as possible, to prevent our dear ship from being swallowed whole by his 'Solarian Alliance'."

Brace leaned back in surprise, "Our ship? The greatest threat? Are you kidding me?"

The figure shook its head, "You've been in confinement for too long. It has dulled your brain. Yes, our ship, Ganges, the one we all live in! He is no ordinary threat! Think, Brace! What will follow, once he has the crew eating out of his hands? If half of what the miscreant says is true, we face peril like we've never seen before! Alien allies giving gifts? Really? Trillions of human citizens, spread from here to Sol? How big a war fleet do you think they have? What kinds of weapons? The AeyAie Solidarity acting like bureaucrats? Or are they too scared to do anything else? Think, Investigator Brace Lazhand!"

The former Security crewman shook his head, "The Chief's got to see the potential for harm, as would Naga. You want me to kill this guy? That might start a war, you know."

The secretive figure nodded, "It just might, but on our terms. As a sign of my respect, I shall be unlocking your cell's door. It will remain that way until someone replaces the damned thing. You are now free to leave. There are a few operatives in Security who are ready to meet up with you. I'm offering a chance to gain a new life, without having your mind wiped out. I'm giving you an opportunity to serve all of Ganges, not just one Sector. Stay where you are, and all you'll be doing is revealing your own cowardice. I won't insult you by offering chips or drugs. This is a task which Security should have handled when they first learned who William Blaine was and where he came from! We are doing their job for them! Think about it, but don't take too long, or you'll miss all the fun."

The wallscreen then shut down abruptly. Brace found himself alone in the darkness. He smelled harsh smoke, then heard a tiny pinging sound coming from the direction of the door. Carefully, Brace stood up with his hands on top of his head. He waited for a seed-sliver, then the wallscreen came back on, Naga's face filling it, "Brace Lazhand! Are you injured?"

He looked at the AeyAie, "I'm just fine, Naga. Please inform Interrogator Commander Slither Brokengear that I need to see him right away. Our special guest from Sol is in danger, possibly from within Security Sector itself."

CHAPTER THIRTEEN

Ice Rotation - Life Sowing - Mission Harvest - Spiral 5620

"Some communities can get too insular, if you ask me. A few are downright bizarre, and if it weren't for their efficiency ratings being so high, I'm sure they'd be disbanded. There's one called Eternal Song, and the inhabitants are convinced that Ganges is the center of the known universe, and all the terraforming is some kind of plot to keep the crew docile. They don't believe in the existence of space, stars, planets, or Terra! They think that the ship goes on forever beyond the topsides hull, and that the only reason we don't go past Level One is that the apparent gravity gets too high for our species. If you show them a window, they smile, nod knowingly, and tell you how clear your wallscreen is! Put them on a tug, and they'll tell you how much they enjoyed the virtual ride! The only way to convince them of the truth, is to shove them out an airlock! As tempting as that may be, they are quite dutiful to their posts, as they don't want the Sectors to punish them for blowing the conspiracy. They think that the Spine of Ganges is the seat of God, which Naga protects, as the crew are too impure to be granted an audience with the Almighty. Maybe humanity needs to feel that they are at the center of the universe, no matter how wrong that is or how strange it would be."
Talen Mariko, Planetary Sector Design Specialist, Rank Two, personal log, P22

Residence Wheel One, Level Two

Knight Pelor Guardhand sat upon a large rock and glared through the hand telescope he always brought with him when in the field. His Squire, Korgan Naldo, was beside him, checking on his datapad's map of the region. The two of them were keeping under cover, using the terrain to prevent detection. Pelor had to admit that his Squire was a quick learner, rubbing mud onto his armor to dull its shine, twisting vines and small branches into the straps which held the plates together. Their horses were half a kilometer behind them, guarded by their toragi, who excelled in ambush tactics within the dense forests of the nature preserves. Pelor had no doubt that their steeds were well protected. He kept an eye on the internal display of his helm, part of which showed him the point of view from the front of Larry's toragi helmet. This had become a vital precaution over the last sowing, during which there had been two attempts on his life, made by syndicate assassins. Back at their campsite, just a few kilometers spinward, a pair of spare suits of armor had been stuffed with blankets and seated around the remains of their campfire, as decoys for snipers.

Pelor looked down at the planet-rover loaned to them by Naga, which acted as their communications liaison with Keep John and Security Sector. The small robot looked like a large beetle, with overlong legs that ended with hand-like grips. Its tiny head swiveled up at him, blinking the lights within its sensors, as if giving him a wink. Knight Guardhand shook his weary head. This venture had already been difficult, and although he disliked relying upon technological gadgets, he was glad to have the AeyAie on watch with them. The planet-rover had a plethora of built-in abilities and defenses which had come in handy the past few rotations.

Squire Naldo swore quietly under his breath, "Blast it all to the void! Now I have something crawling under my left vambrace. None of my former instructors ever said anything about stakeouts in the woods, nor attempts to ambush and kill me at my campsite or having to deal with muck seeping into my breastplate. Everything was just 'adventures in the forest' and 'keeping the nature preserves suitable for all good crew'. This past harvest has been an eye-opener for me."

Pelor frowned as he peered once again through his scope, "Thou shalt not find pity within mine own heart for thee, young squire. T'was not I who told thee tales of glory to whet thy appetite for adventure. Tis our duty to hold these faire lands free from the varlets who despoil these fine woodlands for their own nefarious purposes. We are the tip of the spear, young man. Especially when it comes to dealing with the foul syndicates."

Squire Naldo shrugged, "Verily do I crave a more open fight, milord. Yet our numbers be few, while the enemy holds vast resources to command. My seemingly endless groans of displeasure depart my lips from mine own lack of preparedness for what hath been roughly shoved into my shorts."

Pelor smiled, "Well do I remember mine own first sallies against the knaves which besmirch our fine vessel. The ambush and the blockade be our kindly friends in dark times such as these, though they truly test the mettle of our patience and perseverance. That the foe attempts to remove our presence from these woodlands hath shown our efforts are having the desired effect."

Korgan nodded while checking the map again, "Aye. They waste time and resources to break free from our righteous grip. Yet I feel they are not so cornered as we might wish for. Were you sorely disappointed when it was first revealed to thee that thy duty was not filled with traversing the land and aiding hikers in need?"

Pelor turned away from his scope to look upon his squire, "Nay, lad. In truth, I prefer the hunt. Wandering endlessly from one hermitage to another, patrolling the trails with little more to do than giving directions be more like taking a grindstone to mine own soul. Wearing me away, until nothing be left but dust. For over five octades have I traversed these woods. I find that I know them far too well. To be a Knight is to invite danger and outwit adversity."

Squire Naldo growled, "The regular Security Police poke fun openly at our antiquated ways. They call ours a soft duty, yet now I see that we bear the greater burden of peril. Tis not fair."

Pelor chuckled, "Let them mock! Their valor isn't but a tenth of ours. Be at peace, my young squire, for tis the truth that every Commander of our grand Sector knows that we be the mighty fist against infamy. Besides, nothing in life is fair. Tis best to throw that bothersome notion to the wolves. Like utopia, fair be the province of both novices and the craven. Look upon life with open eyes. Be fearless, and keep thyself strong for the trials to come. To expect thy life to be fair is to scream into the void."

Korgan flinched, "Forgive me, Sir Knight. I shall heed thy words."

Knight Guardhand lightly slapped a gauntleted hand upon the youngster's pauldron, "No need for apologies. Thou art young and inexperienced. Thus, thy fate is to be further trained by a rusted-out, cantankerous old sword such as myself. Be of good cheer, lad."

Squire Naldo grinned up at him, then began to lay out their remote monitors, which would be left behind when they moved on to a new location. The units were small, automated cameras, fitted with camo netting to prevent detection. Keep Smith was at the heart of the network of sensors they were implanting throughout the forest, while other teams were creating blockades within the belowdecks and service access stations at all the Inter-Wheel bulkhead portals. Within the belowdecks, things were more complicated. Maintenance gantries had been blocked, but there were still too many areas that allowed the syndicates to travel to and from Keep Smith, hazardous though they might be. Several drones and rovers had gone missing, their telemetry lost shortly after their deployment.

What truly bothered Pelor was the fact that none of the knights within Keep Smith had been heard from for sowings. No one visibly entered or left the stronghold, and all attempts to communicate with those inside the structure had failed. Naga had reported being blocked from the keep, shortly after Pelor's meeting with Baroness Linessa Mekand, thus there was no information as to what was happening within the building. Security had notified Engineering of the situation, requesting that all power be rerouted from Keep Smith, but it seemed that the criminals within it were well supplied. During dark-slice, the lights within the keep could still be seen as being operative. Pelor guessed they had mobile generators, like the kind used for planetary operations.

Knight Guardhand took another look through his scope, "Ah! Behold, my young squire! The enemy's afoot!"

Korgan peered over a boulder, using his own eyepiece to view what was going on, "That's a Security transport! It must have been inside the keep. What's it doing? That looks like foam they're spraying on the lower levels."

Pelor scowled angrily, "Aye. Tis quartz-ceramic. Used to make habitats for terraforming personnel. It hardens very fast, and it's incredibly strong. Look now to leeward. See that maintenance bunker? Those knaves are now bringing forth hull plating, Kendis alloy, I wager. They shall set this before the foam, gluing the panels of steel in place. There be too many for us to harry their efforts here. We shall need reinforcements, though any we call shall be too late to stop this. It seems our foes have revealed their plan to us. They are securing Keep Smith with all haste. I do not doubt they shall include gun towers and traps. Now we must rally the other keeps. To take this stronghold, we shall require more troops for belowdecks fighting, along with striking out at their outer walls. Well, if it be a siege they want, then they shall have it."

Agro Wheel Three, Security Level Five

Executive Officer Wasp Tornpage walked through the wide corridors within Security Sector, noting the bustling of the crew. Most of them ignored her presence, though a few did stop to verify her flashtats, before running off on their own secretive errands. She shook her head as she went deeper into the maze of equipment bays and training centers. The Security crew were all larger than she was, heavily muscled and moving about at speed for long periods of time. What did they feed these people? Wasp was aware that some of the required training grounds for new recruits were on Level One, or topsides, which meant the apparent gravity there was over a Terran standard. The new trainees were not permitted to leave that level until they had fully acclimated to the high-gee conditions there. Bone density enhancers were provided by Medical Sector to all of the Security personnel, but she still felt there had to be some secret formula to make every crew member an icon of athletic ability.

Then there was the prevalence of the toragi racing through the crowd of humans. The big cats were the symbols of Security Sector, even more so than the shield-and-swords motif used for the crew's flashtats, with chain links depicting rank. The toragi were beloved, especially by the young crew. As a novice, she had been enamored with the saber-toothed cats just like everyone else, despite being a Strifer. During the Crucible, the toragi had been trained to hunt her people in the belowdecks and in warzones, but the animals had ceased their extreme prejudice shortly after the fighting had stopped. No one she knew could explain why this had happened, and it remained a mystery to this rotation. The big cats sniffed at her as they flashed by, but otherwise left her alone. For this she was grateful. With their massive teeth, steel-shod claws and muscular bulk, she wouldn't have a chance if one of them got unruly with her. It was said that the only thing more ferocious than the Security Police crew were the toragi at their sides.

Wasp finally reached the appointed chamber only to find Security Chief Jira Mantabe speaking with a group of regular crew wearing uniforms from Stellar, Harbor and Planetary Sectors. There were several other Security crew in the room, mingling with the others. The Chief glanced at her and smiled, while still talking quietly with a pair of Stellar crew who looked small and frail standing next to her. Everyone else saluted Wasp as they noticed her, which she returned with a cheerful middle finger. From anyone but a Strifer, this gesture would be taken as a dire insult, but most of the other cultures aboard Ganges had gotten used to her people's odd ways, even accepting them as natural. Wasp wasn't sure how she felt about that, but for now, it fit her needs.

Chief Mantabe turned toward her, "Welcome, Executive Officer Tornpage. This is our preparation zone for the exploration of Planet Forty-One. I called you here because we have need of your particular talents in negotiations. There seems to be a disagreement concerning the makeup of the landing party."

Wasp snorted, "If it were up to me, no one would be going! Everyone, get lost! Go back to your posts! Nothing to see here!"

Jira rolled her eyes, "While I do agree with you, we need to get started on the training that'll be required to make the landing. I'd love nothing more than to just leave this fucking system, but the Captain has ordered that we make it to the surface of Planet Forty-One, and so we shall. I do get why we're doing this stunt, but I don't have to like it."

One of the Stellar crew tentatively stepped forward, "Excuse me. I'm Felk Wrenbow, Rank Four Materials Specialist. My Sector wants to make sure that we get all the readings we'll need, which means at least five members from my department must go down there."

Wasp laughed, "Must? How about just you, trash-head? This isn't some little exercise where you can jerk everyone around like you're actually important. Go sniff some glue in the corner. The fewer crew on this mission, the better I'll like it!"

Felk stared back at her with his mouth wordlessly opening and closing. Jira grabbed Wasp's elbow and led her toward a cluster of Planetary crew, "This lot has the same issue. They all want to go down to the surface."

One scientist in the brown-and-green of Planetary spoke up, "Rightly so, I would say, Security Chief Mantabe! This is a unique opportunity! We in Planetary are specialists when it comes to such sciences, yes? I have assembled my team, which includes experts in geology, atmospherics, tectonics, soil analysis and hydrology."

Wasp turned to Jira, "Who is this fucked-up person? What did they drink? I want some to get through all this shit."

As the scientist's face went dark with outrage, The Chief of Security replied "This is Marsa Nantek, Planetary Geological Specialist Rank Four. As you can see, we have a political situation here. There is room for everyone in Sci-One, but I don't like the idea of sending a damned parade onto an unknown world filled with fucking mysteries. I've got both of their Chiefs breathing down my neck about this, and I'm tempted to throw them all into the brig."

It was Wasp's turn to lead Jira by the elbow to a less cluttered area, "So how are the Harbor crew doing? Any problems?"

Jira shrugged her wide shoulders, "Not really. They control Sci-One and insist on a crew of ten to run the damned thing. Harbor Chief Rollack says anything less will jeopardize the mission. I'm willing to give him leeway. It is his ship, after all. I want a squad of five Security Police, with one Investigations officer and two crew from Rescue Services, just in case there's a problem."

Wasp nodded, "I get your thinking, Chief, but it won't help for shit. If you want the other Sectors to compromise, you'll have to do it first. I'd say to remove two members from your squad, replace them with your investigator and a single Rescue crew member. From what I understand, they won't be staying on the planet for long anyway. Once you announce your leaner team, tell the others to pare theirs down too. Remember, every one of your personnel have a toragi with them. That doubles your numbers, while you look graceful in making room for more equipment and then asking the others to risk fewer lives."

Jira grinned at her, "Damn, you're good. That's fucking devious. I can see why Captain Fieldscan dotes over you. Do me a favor, stick around for a while. If anyone gives me trouble, I'll send them your way. The way I see it, if we can get down to twenty-five crew, I'll be much happier. Right now, the count stands at fifty, which means we might have to strap some of their extra hands onto the fucking hull to get them all there."

Wasp shook her head, "They're acting like it's a damned holiday. By the way, who's in charge of the overall mission? One of the cheesy-brains?"

Jira looked shocked, "Odin forbid! One of my own crew will be calling the shots. Lieutenant Urukumu from Security Police will be in overall command of the expedition. He keeps his cool under pressure and is one of my finest officers. He's over there, by the Harbor crew, discussing the mission parameters."

Wasp looked across the chamber and saw a Security officer whose face was covered in detailed markings. His black hair was bound by a leather strap, and his uniform was decorated with small fetishes. She looked up at Jira, "While you're busy negotiating with the over-eager scientists, I'll go join your Lieutenant Urukumu. Maybe I can convince the Harbor crew to scale down their numbers just a bit. This mission is a real opportunity and a very bad idea. If you need me, I'll be over there, squeezing the life out of Harbor regulations."

Jira wished her luck, as she swept off to her own team of Security crew, to reduce their numbers as Wasp had suggested. The Strifer Executive liked working with Jira, but she kept that under her mask. There were a million things that could go wrong with this endeavor, and she wanted to make certain that her part in it went smoothly. That way, if shit hit the thrusters, she wouldn't be a major target for the broadcasts.

Agro Wheel Three, Security Level One

Investigations Commander Slither Brokengear glowered at his prisoner with open disgust. While Brace Lazhand had cooperatively submitted to being searched, answered every query without delay and seemed to be enthusiastic about providing information, the amount of trust Slither had for him wouldn't fill a bottle cap. Part of his anger at the former Security officer came from the fact that Brace had fooled him for spirals. This was difficult for Slither to let go of, for his reputation as an expert in ferreting out the truth was now tumbling in the void. He had trusted this prisoner for so long, working alongside him for the same cause, it was still hard to fathom the depths of the man's betrayal. If it were up to him, Brace would be floating between the stars for eternity.

Slither rubbed the nose of his black rat mask, as he lit another cigar, letting the smoke drift toward the culprit's face, as was his habit, "Let me get this straight, Brace. Your door was found unlocked, yet you didn't attempt to escape your cell. Call me dense, but isn't breaking the lock part of an attempt to get free of your comfy little room?"

Brace rolled his eyes and coughed, making Slither smile, "I called that in! I told you that my door was disabled and required replacement. I told my guards, Naga and now you. I didn't do it. My former, illicit employer did, using updated Strifer tech, or so he claimed."

Slither nodded absently, pretending to brush away ashes from his uniform, "Oh yes, I did read the reports. They made me wonder what you're really up to. You seem to get a lot of visitors, Brace. I don't like that. I want you all to myself, before you get your mind wiped. If you could tell me the identity of your boss, I might be in the mood to take you at your word concerning this present debacle."

The prisoner clenched his hands into fists, making Slither's toragi, Brad, hiss in response, "I told you, no one knows his name. Or her name. No one's seen the Lord of Crime's face. I couldn't tell you how tall they are, what body type, or how their voice really sounds. I've been assuming male because of their self-chosen title amongst the syndicates, who are all terrified of this creep. Only two people can get closer than five meters from him, his enforcer and his best assassin. Anyone else dies at their hands. It isn't pretty. He doesn't seem to have a lair, not a traditional one, like an old bunker or storage center like the others. If you meet him twice, it's in two different places. I met him five times, never at the same location. I was waiting for him to slip up, but instead I was the one who tripped and fell. You know this."

Slither sighed, "I've been told this. By you. A traitor to Security Sector, to Ganges. Not really a respectable source, are you? Certainly not one I can trust, by any means. So, let's see, you were visited by yet another Security traitor, who left a message which threatened you and your family. We took care of that, informing Lieutenant Darron Lazhand of your confinement, then adding spotters to watch those crew who are related to you. Then he visits you, disowns and shames you, in front of William Blaine no less. Now you tell me the Lord of Crime, stupid fucking name by the way, he can't be that moronic, calls upon you by hijacking the wallscreen in the most secure region of the ship, using old codes and primitive tools. You're quite the popular guy, aren't you? Do I have that right?"

Brace was obviously struggling to contain his frustration, but with a much clearer head than the last time they had one of their private chats. Slither wondered if the prisoner had finally detoxed enough to be useful. If this was the case, it would soon be his job to break Brace further, to get at all the things he was still hiding within his traitorous head. It might have been kinder to have kept the man on his illicit drugs, but Medical Sector insisted on clean bloodwork before attempting to re-educate a condemned prisoner. They all had to hit the regen-tank sober, or it might complicate an already complex process.

The former Security officer barked out, "I'm trying to save a fucking life and prevent a war, you shit-brained, contemptuous rat! The Lord of Crime wants William Blaine dead! He's already got his people working on it! He even wants me involved! That's why he broke the damned door lock, you stubborn rodent!"

Slither leaned back, puffing out another choking cloud of thick cigar smoke, "We're all vermin, Brace. My people admit that and accept it as the truth. There are some big fucking holes in your story. Let's start with wanting William Blaine dead. Why? Does he owe him chips? Is the Solarian about to blow his cover? I mean, the poor rodent just got here! Besides, our little trespasser has a whole fucking platoon looking after him, not to mention his own, internal technology. He was another of my special clients, like you, Brace. I wouldn't want to try to touch William, by the way.

Very active and weird defenses. Like nothing we've ever seen before. If the Lard of Crumbs really has so many operatives within Security, then he must have heard the rumors if nothing else. Has it occurred to you that he's trying to use Blaine as a distraction? Did those meds you took eat your brain to a fucking nub?"

Brace half got up and looked as if he were about to punch the nearest wall, but then stopped himself, which Slither had to admit was an impressive improvement from their earlier conversations, "You don't get it! He wants a war with the Solarian Alliance, but on his terms. He doesn't care who gets killed or what the results of that conflict will be for Ganges. He's thinking of himself."

Slither paused between puffs of his smoldering cigar, "That's... almost an interesting hypothesis, Brace. Did he tell you this, or did you make it up on your own? What does he hope to gain, in your expert opinion?"

Brace shook his head violently, "If he doesn't benefit from something, he doesn't do it. If it won't give him more power, he's not interested. You know he has people in Security, other than myself, and I'm not his anymore! He wants to kill Blaine in a way that'll make us look bad. He wants to provoke the Solarians to come to us and try to take over the ship. We will fight back. He knows this. We won't win. He understands that too."

Slither tilted his head to one side, "Then why do it?"

Brace leaned forward, "Think about it. Remember your Awakening history? Who aided the Holy Mission, before it was called that? Who helped smuggle goods, weapons and crew to those who stopped the officer's mutiny? It was the criminal organizations. They had all the casinos, which were highly illicit at the time. They had contraband from every Sector. They had all the fighters, killers, assassins and more. Without them, the mutiny might have succeeded. After the fighting was done, all the crime bosses were hailed as heroes! They were the defenders of the Holy Mission, allies of the Great Families, who were known as the Family Project back then. They became the wealthiest business owners, starting new chip-making industries, using their own hoard as starting funds. The casinos became legitimate, everything they used to do that was illegal became accepted as being rightful. That means their crime organizations died, but they didn't care. They had everything they could have ever wanted. During the mutiny, the crime bosses became leaders, looked to for advice, treated with the greatest respect. That's his goal."

Slither didn't move from his position. Even his cigar went out from a lack of attention. His mind was racing with the possibilities, "He starts a war. Ganges loses and is forced to become part of the Solarian Alliance, who are now really pissed at us for killing one of their people. A resistance movement rises up, harrying the new overlords, all of it funded by the syndicates, or just his, especially if the others are forced to join his. The resistance lasts for spirals, even getting out of Ganges and infecting the colonies or the Sol system itself. Trillions of new customers, fighters, under-deck alliances. I fucking hate ego-maniacs."

Brace nodded sadly, "That's why I called for you. That's why I didn't bother trying to escape. It's too big."

Slither looked back at his prisoner, "All right. I still don't trust you, but this needs to reach the Chief's ears. It's a fucking sleepscare. My people would become the Lord of Slime's underlings, just like the old Crucible rotations. I can't allow that to happen. Not ever."

Stellar Sector Wheel, Level Fifty-Three

Stellar Observations Lieutenant Crinn Spanglo clutched tightly at the small, circular pendant of the Church of the Holy Void around his neck, as he observed the crew who had entered the lecture chamber. The trapezoidal room had a high, dark ceiling and walls made from polished obsidian. The stage he stood upon was asteroid metal, accented with gold filigree, sporting a zebrawood podium. Spotlights beamed their illumination down upon him, while the holo-projectors behind and right in front of the stage gave off odd reflections. Thirty-five crew from various Sectors, including his own, and five toragi were in attendance, looking lost in the grand chamber which could accommodate ten times that number. At the back were Executive Officer Wasp Tornpage, who frightened him half to death, along with Security Chief Jira Mantabe, who terrified him even more, Planetary's Chief, Lorvar Sedders, who was scowling at everyone, and his own Sector's Chief, Fria Maglator. Crinn wasn't sure how he was going to perform his duty with such celebrated leaders looking on.

His duty was to prepare the crew who were going to be heading down to the surface of Planet Forty-One. Having never done anything like setting foot upon a ball of rock, Crinn really didn't know what he was supposed to say except for "good luck". His Strifer assistant, Fuss Nitpicker, had told him to just give them the details of what was known about the conditions on the surface of the target planet. It wasn't these that he worried about, but what they didn't know that bothered him, keeping him awake all sleep-slice with worry. Planet Forty-One wasn't just some empty planet which had never harbored life. It was the dead remains of an ancient civilization! One that had apparently been capable of moving planets around their system at a whim.

Crinn knew a bad idea when he saw one, and this was the worst he'd ever been forced to support. As a member of Stellar Sector, he understood the opportunity to gain new knowledge, possibly new technology, that might help with performing the Holy Mission. He understood Planetary's greed for insights about this dead planet, potentially solving some mysteries that had vexed humanity from the time before spaceflight. Crinn could also contemplate the potential hazards of this mission, and he was very happy to not be a part of the landing team, even though he had been offered a spot. He was just an astronomer. Galloping around ruins on a dead world wasn't part of his idea of a good time. It was bad enough he had been forced to learn about the Kendis Vault, which had frightened him enough as it was. This adventure sounded much worse.

He briefly noted that the Security crew were lounging comfortably in their seats, boots propped up and whispering amongst themselves. They risked life and limb every rotation, so maybe they were used to potentially suicidal missions. The other members of the landing team seemed impatient for things to begin, as if they were doing nothing more than heading out to a picnic within a community park. He wondered if their zeal for discovery had countered their sense of self-preservation. How many of them would break when something awful occurred on the surface of Planet Forty-One? They weren't heroes or warriors, trained for daring exploits.

Crinn realized that he was stalling. The sooner he got this done with, the quicker he could get back to his lovely sensor readings. He cleared his throat, then turned on his microphone drone by tapping it on the back. The small device floated up on invisible magnetics and blinked a green light at him, "Welcome to the Stellar Observatory's presentation of the data that we currently have on Planet Forty-One. Please note that there is much that we don't know concerning conditions upon the surface. More information will be updated to your secure datapads, once we reach orbit and get a much closer look. If there are any issues which arise from new data at that time which might compromise your safety, the mission will be scrubbed. This is by the Captain's orders, so you can complain to him about that if you like."

There were some guffaws from the unruly Security crew, but everyone else remained stonily silent. Crinn pressed a button on his datapad and brought the holo-projectors to life. Detailed images of the planet erupted from the forward unit, while data graphs were now displayed behind him, "As you can see from these charts, the atmosphere is completely unbreathable. It's mostly nitrogen, argon and a touch of carbon dioxide at the edge of space. There appears to be little to no airflow, which I would say is impossible, but there it is. There is no water vapor, nor any combustible gasses, no high pressure zones or any shifting winds. My team believes this was purposely done to preserve the ruins on the surface. If the planet had any surface water, it has been long gone. There are no signs of tectonics nor are there any dust clouds."

The scientists within the small crowd murmured quietly together, while the Security crew looked bored. Crinn pressed on, "As for what we can actually see of the structures that we have noted thus far, they appear to be in marvelous condition. Please keep in mind that these are alien constructs, so our own view of what is pristine might differ greatly from that of the builders. Spectrographs revealed a high silica content, with some molecular signatures we're still arguing about as they defy identification. Every structure that we can currently observe seems huge, spanning thousands of kilometers. Some of these ruins reach a point just below low orbit, which may be an indication of space elevators."

Now, Crinn had everyone's undivided attention, which was gratifying, "The surface temperature averages about twenty-three degrees, so there shouldn't be any problems with exposure to any extremes of heat or cold. So far as we can tell, this temperature prevails throughout the planet, even at the poles, which is a curious phenomenon. The dark-side of Planet Forty-One exhibits a general temperature just a few degrees lower than the light-side. This may point to operational weather control systems, but we cannot find evidence of power distribution to support this hypothesis. The rotational period is the equivalent of twelve point three slices, which means you will have plenty of time to make your observations before it gets dark."

Everyone remained focused, so Crinn brought up the next topic, "Thus far, our attempts to get any readings from the mantle leads us to believe it is incredibly smooth, without any partially solid materials under the surface. The core is still hot, with an iron-based center. The magnetic field is tilted, with the poles facing directly toward and away from the local star at the equator. We have no information as to why this is the case. If I were to guess, this may represent their method of generating power, though that is a highly controversial idea."

He was about to continue, when he noticed Security Chief Mantabe get up from her seat and lean down to whisper into Executive Tornpage's ear. The two of them hurried from the chamber without a word to the others. Crinn didn't know what they were doing, but neither of them seemed happy. In fact, the Security Chief looked furious. Crinn pushed this observation from his mind, as he opened the floor to any questions from the landing party. He just hoped that another disaster had not just dropped onto Ganges without notice. They had enough troubles as it was.

Agro Wheel Four, Level Two

I run along the sandy beach, ignoring the humans stumbling out of my way. Bipedal locomotion isn't always the most stable form of movement, especially on a soft surface like sand. What is truly puzzling is why humans choose to work, live and play in places where it is most likely that they will fall over. Perhaps it's the water which attracts them. Like my own kind, they find water to be pleasantly buoyant, good exercise and is sometimes full of delicious fish. This is something our two species have in common. For emergencies, being near the water is not all fun and games, especially on a crowded beach.

My companion, Darron, is with the other human members of our platoon, surrounding William Blaine with a ring of warriors. All the toragi are with me, as we pursue our prey across the sand, while trying not to harm the crowd of innocent bystanders. Screaming fills the air, a distraction we don't need right now. People are rushing toward the sea or further inland. It would be better if they just stood still. Human cubs are crying for their parents. Drones swirl overhead; their shadows flicker around us as we run. It is chaos. I suspect this was part of our prey's plan, to create living obstacles for our pursuit. A patch of sand erupts near my flank, followed by a distant bang. Hot metal bounces from my armor, but one piece slams home where my leg plates meet my torso armor. Pain flashes in my lower abdomen, but it only enrages me even further. Three humans collapse in a spray of blood, while the rest fall into a blind panic. Another explosion lifts from the beach, another echoing boom. The prey is using high-velocity, explosive rounds. Such things were banned long ago or packed away deep in the Security armory for emergency use.

I race through the bedlam, changing my course by small amounts to keep me from being an easy target. This tactic was trained into me from the time I was a cub. A yowl of pain follows another blast. One of my packmates is hit, but there is no time to look back at the damage. The sound is almost lost in the terrified screams of the crew. I leap over a line of running humans. One explodes messily, covering my armor with hot blood. My rage expands into full fury over the murder. The sound of the gun is closer. We are gaining on our target, who is now desperate to distract us. Whoever it is will have to kill us all to prevent their capture.

The rotation had started peacefully enough. Our platoon was kept busy with guarding William Blaine as he travelled openly throughout Ganges. He answered questions, met with crew, and dealt with those who didn't trust him with courtesy and respect. Many of the news drones which had followed us focused on Darron and me, as we led the platoon. At one point, William bowed to me, calling me his teacher, and the news people went crazy over this. It was not a comfortable situation for me, but I put up with it as best I could. Darron was very proud of my self-control, which meant the news drones bothered me even further, until I growled at them, batting one that got too close, shattering its thin hull. That was quite satisfying.

It seems that William wanted to see the oceans of Agro Wheel Four. We complied, so long as we kept to the public beaches, out of the way of fishers and maintenance crew. The other toragi in our troop were excited when we reached the seas of Level Two, for all of us love to swim and catch fish with our claws and fangs. The platoon had divided itself into two squads. One kept close to William, to act as intermediaries with the crew we met on the beach. The other was tasked with keeping the larger crowds at bay. Everything was going well, until William decided to step into the water. Suddenly, his strange hair had whipped around, snatching something that had come close to his head. It was a micro-missile. Electricity flashed static around his body as something else smashed into his side and exploded, injuring a platoon member and a beach comber who had been asking William a question. The Solarian remained unharmed, though his skin became silvery, as if dipped in metal. He had fallen to one side, covered with blood, none of which was his own. The exploding missile rounds were designed to spread shrapnel upon impact, which made them particularly dangerous for crowded situations.

William had signaled to us that he was unharmed, while the rest of the platoon gathered back together to form a circle around him. Then Darron sent me and the other toragi to track down the shooter. I heard my human partner call for reinforcements and Rescue Services, all the while keeping William face down on the red-stained sand. That was when the screaming had commenced. More rounds of explosive ammunition went off all around us. Crew were being butchered, to aid the escape of the culprit. My ears could tell the shots were coming from the dense foliage surrounding the beach, so I led my pack through the throngs of howling crew.

A small brassy ball floated next to my head. I snarled at it but then heard William's voice coming from it, "Hi! It's me, Mike! This is a nanite globe. It's a little small, but it can help you. The chemical trails from the attacks are tracking spinward. Follow me!"

I don't understand all of words he used, but I do comprehend enough to understand what the little ball might be and that it was a guide. Human speech is complex and difficult to grasp, but it does make fine prey to pursue. At this point I am glad for my strange hobby of trying to understand the hooting and babble of humans. I run after the brassy ball, which swivels and twists to avoid the other humans. We rush toward the trees and brush that lined the edge of the beach. I leap over a short wooden fence and land in thick, wiry grass. The ball moves on, so I pursue it. Another blast, this time right in front of the little sphere but not quite touching it. The explosion reveals an invisible field around it, about a meter across. My pack and I keep directly behind the magick ball of metal, what William's voice called nanites. That this bizarre thing can stop the missiles being launched at us surprises me deeply. I have no time now, so I will have to think about it later. I make a promise to myself to do so.

We come to a small village, just on the outskirts of the beach. Wood houses line the sandy roads, the tropical forest held back by small croplands. Crew are still running around, but there is a clearing up ahead. It is a crossroads. A tall human female is standing in the middle of it, holding a male child by the throat. She is holding a handgun, the barrel up against the boy's skull. She wears a mask with round eye lenses that change color continuously. Her clothes also shift to match the buildings around her. A long rifle is slung over one of her shoulders. She lifts her chin, "Stay where you are! I'll kill him!"

I stretch my claws and come to skidding halt, as do all my packmates. The small globe continues forward and clings to the gun in her hand. She squeezes the trigger as I watch in horror. Light surrounds the boy. The killer's hand erupts in a shower of blood and bone as her gun explodes. The child is unharmed. I rush forward to shield him, placing my body between him and the attacker. The woman falls to the ground. Her mask is melting off her face. The woman seems to be choking on air, trying to scream but nothing can be heard. She collapses, and the little nanite sphere floats above her face, bathing it in a crimson light.

I hit the recall tag on my chest armor, signaling Darron that the hunt has concluded. The boy is still clinging to me, weeping quietly. Another toragi settles down nearby to show that all is now well. The platoon arrives, shoving through the remains of the crowd. William is now waving at me, smiling broadly. The woman is breathing but not responding. As Darron takes over the scene, I have a moment to reflect on what I have just experienced. It troubles me. The more I learn about William Blaine, the more concerned I become.

Engineering Sector Wheel, Level Twenty-Seven

Engineering Foreman Howait Sparweld looked about the massive chamber with eyes round with surprise. The ceiling was fifty meters above his head, brightly lit and stretched out of sight, due to the curvature of the deck. Only the capward and sternward walls were visible, though barely so. Huge crates and massive loaders were stored in precise lanes. Framework construction stations dotted the landscape, each one the size of a public transport, their bare rails ready to accept the piece-parts of any manufacturing project that he could think of. A dozen floating machine stations idled nearby, their magnetic impellers glowing a pale blue. Mobile gantries, open-topped, tram-sized welding suites and loaded tool carts waited with gleaming perfection. It was an engineer's playground. A wish-list of specialized machines and construction tools. The only thing that bothered him was the presence of the floor-to-ceiling folding walls which blocked off the area on all sides, fully boxing them in. No wallscreens were evident nor drones.

Falinous leaned his bulky torso lower to whisper in his ear, "What is all this about, boss-man? We're a repair team. None of this shit looks broken to me."

Pilla cut in, "Stow it! This looks more like New Spiral dawn-slice to me!"

Howait held up his hand to forestall any arguments from breaking out, as Engineering Sector Chief Marissa Navamo marched toward them from the leeward wall. Her purple-and-blue uniform was perfectly pressed, the short sleeves revealing her prosthetic arms. Howait noticed that the Chief's Naga-Port was not turned on, and he wondered why this was the case. It was rumored that most of her body was mechanical, all of her own design, and that she lived in Engineering Sector rather than a community in one of the two Residence Wheels. The whole team snapped a salute, save for Brigo, who was still gawping at the chamber with his mouth hanging open.

Chief Navamo returned their salute, standing tall before them with a serious look upon her face, "Welcome to Special Projects Area Alpha-Three. I have chosen this team for a special project which must be completed with efficiency. Your recent improvement in the ratings have led me to believe that you are all dedicated crew, ready to perform your duties with full devotion to your Sector. This assignment is classified, for reason of ship's security. To compensate for this, your regular bonus is hereby tripled. Successful and timely completion of this project comes with a rise in rank for all of you."

Howait felt a rush of pride flowing through his veins. When he had been assigned to his current team, they were rated as the worst functioning repair crew. Now they were assigned to a special project with even greater bonuses, due to their increased efficiency. The Chief took a step forward and pointed at the work area behind her, "The diagrams and specifications for your new project are loaded into the holo-projectors at your workstations. You will not make copies of them! Nor shall you discuss them with anyone else, including the other teams slated for their own tasks. If you need expert advice, you will utilize a hand-picked group of specialists who have been granted access to this project. This is not a multi-Sector job, so keep it that way. There are no Naga Units attached to this project because you will not need them. This is a fully human endeavor. Please understand this clearly; I am a friend of the AeyAie. I have been so all my life, but this project must be completed without Naga's personal assistance. I fully support Security Sector, having nothing but the greatest respect for their Chief, but this does not involve their Sector at this time."

Howait glanced at the others, noticing their uncertainty and discomfort. He shyly raised his hand, "May I ask a few questions, Chief Navamo? As the foreman of this team, I consider it my sworn duty to address anything which might be cause for concern."

Chief Navamo nodded curtly, "I would prefer if you came straight to me for all queries, Foreman Sparweld. Go ahead and ask."

He saluted once more before asking, "Will this project affect Security at a time in the future? I only ask because my mate is an officer of that Sector."

Chief Navamo shrugged, "That all depends on what develops over the next few harvests. I have been studying the situation regarding the Solarian guest, William Blaine, including what we know of his culture's technology. I truly hope that what you build in this chamber will never be used, but it is better to be prepared for the worse than find oneself wanting when things get ugly. Ganges already has fine defenses, but they were not tailored for any particular foe. The best strategy is to fit the tool for the task at hand. While I am sure that the sole representative of the Solarian Alliance is a decent person and is being candid with our news services, there is no actual guarantee that his superiors will follow suit. Should there ever come a time when conflict between Ganges and the Solarians emerges, I want to be ready to present Security with the equipment they will need to save the lives of the crew. To force our defenders to wait for the development of experimental materials, while our beloved vessel is being threatened, is unacceptable."

Howait gave his Chief a nod, "I understand. Why keep this project a secret from Naga? We all talk to the AeyAie on a regular basis."

Chief Navamo sighed deeply, "My dear friend would never approve of the development of war materials before the need is seen to be necessary. No one has ordered me to do this. No one but a handful of my best officers are aware of this, save for the teams involved in the construction, like yourselves. This way, if anything goes wrong, Naga has full deniability and I will take the fall for Ganges. This is on my shoulders, no one else's. Even my mates have no idea that I'm attempting this. You will all be held innocent, as following the direct orders from your Chief, should this become a matter for the courts, but I don't believe it will ever come to that. Should the Solarians prove to be a peaceful, respectful society, everything built here will be fully recycled. This I promise to you all. During the Crucible, Engineering Sector had been unprepared for the emergency which erupted during that time. Had this not been the case, the mutiny would have ended much sooner, without the loss of so many lives."

Howait looked at his team members. They all nodded at him slowly, though he could see some fear in their eyes. This situation was unprecedented. They were now counting on him to lead them through this bizarre process. He forced himself to stand straight as he spoke, "Primed, Chief. I assume that we won't be working on the same projects as the other teams involved in this venture. So, what are we building here?"

Chief Navamo smiled at him, "You have the honor of constructing some prototypes for a brand new kind of military transport. Lightweight, swift and highly maneuverable, containing a few hidden surprises for any opponent, especially one that specializes in field technologies and nanites. Everything you will need is stored in the crates around you. Take the time to get a close look at the documentation, and familiarize yourselves with the project specifics. Even though they don't know it, all of Ganges may be counting on your work."

As she led them over to their new workstations, Howait struggled to come to terms with this assignment. It was potentially unethical, too secretive for his tastes and potentially dangerous for his team. Skolly was the oldest of them, but he seemed the least concerned. This heartened Howait just a bit, but he was determined to keep a close eye on this project. If it fell into the wrong hands, calamity would soon follow.

Medical Sector Wheel, Level Seven

Surgeon General Vono Binami slumped into his office chair and closed his weary eyes, promising himself that he wouldn't immediately fall asleep. Ever since the presence of William Blaine became public knowledge, there had been fights, riots and an uptick in accidents, all of which were flooding the emergency wards of his Sector. Rescue Services had been coordinating with his own crew with seamless efficiency, a credit to the close relationship between Medical and Security. While it was true that he never got deeply involved in the inter-Sector politics that rumbled around Ganges, during times of trouble, his people were always in the thick of it, saving lives and healing the injured. It didn't help that he felt as if forces beyond his control were dragging him into the gravity well of politics, which now involved players who were from beyond the hull.

Slowly, with a mild groan, he took off his boots and raised his sore feet to the top of his ironwood desk. It was almost dark-slice, and he had been too busy to take a break from his duties. The last mob of injured crew had come from Agro Wheel Four, many of them with missing limbs. Prosthetics was one of his specialties, before he became the Surgeon General. At sixty spirals in age, he was seriously considering retirement, to teach at the medical school for new crew directly out of Basic Crew Training, but to do so at this juncture would be a dereliction of duty. Ganges needed a steady, experienced hand leading his Sector, especially with a planned landing party heading to the surface of Planet Forty-One. The history of Medical was filled with warnings about the dangers of activities on an untamed world.

He snorted to himself, annoyed at his own thinking. Untamed. Most likely it wasn't. A grand civilization had once called this system home, therefore it was a very tame and controlled planet, but to whose specifications? There was the real issue. The planned landing was pure exploration of the unknown. Anything was possible down there. He looked over at the coffee he had brought in with him, now cold and unwanted. He could go home to his house in Residence Wheel One, but what was the point? His novices had all grown to Full Crew, he and his mate had amicably parted ways spirals ago. His office had been set up with a secondary chamber, which had seen several uses over the octennia, including being used as a greenhouse for hybrid flowers. Right now, it had a cot, a dresser with spare uniforms and a bookshelf with his collection of rare, antique novels and biographies. Paper books came and went as a fashion within Ganges, most of which were made of rock dust, bound with bio-degradable glue, but there were some which were composed of cotton pulp.

Vono felt like his collection, old and ready to be placed on a shelf. He knew it was just the exhaustion talking, but emergencies took their toll on him more so than they had when he was younger. Pretty soon, he would have to replace both of his aching knees, as he didn't have the time for a proper session in a regen-tank. They could keep a human feeling energetic, replace old parts, but still the body found ways to break down to the point of no return. He removed his datapad from the back of his hand and tossed it onto the desk. Technically, he was off-duty now. If only he could keep the faces of the student-rank crew who had been mangled by an attack on William Blaine from his mind with such ease. It was horrible to have to tell wailing parents that their novices would need special treatment to regrow hands and feet. He had heard the culprit had been captured but received no other details from the Security crew who had brought in the last batch of injured crew. Ten people had died from hideous injuries, including a member of Security Police.

He looked about his grand office, with all of its mementos and holographic images, shaking his head in disbelief. Just a harvest ago, he would have sworn that nothing like this could have happened within Ganges, but he had to face the fact that it would most likely get worse before things improved. Usually, he considered himself an optimist. This rotation was straining that attitude to the limit. In just a few rotations, Vono had found himself considering joining the Strifers! At this point, their collective pessimism seemed positively cheerful compared to how badly the rest of the crew were behaving. Vono knew this was a crude exaggeration. Most of the inhabitants of Ganges were simply trying to get through their normal rotation. It was always the few, irresponsible rascals that made everyone else look bad. Medical and Security were the ones who had to pick up the pieces when things went out of control, and so they both had the viewpoint that the ship was always falling apart, which simply wasn't the case.

Naga's virtual face flashed up on the wallscreen right across from him, making Vono jump in surprise, "This looks like brooding to me, not resting, Surgeon General Vono Binami."

Vono leaned back into his padded chair, making the synth-leather creak, "Ganges help me, Naga! You almost scared the living piss out of me! And yes! I am brooding! Who wouldn't be? Too much death and misery this rotation for my liking."

Naga's matronly face glanced down briefly, "I do apologize for startling you, Vono. Your blood pressure is up, and you were glaring at the ceiling. I was concerned for you."

Vono waved a hand in the air, "Save the concern for the novices who get caught in crossfires! This is just the beginning. I can feel it in my bones."

The AeyAie tilted its head, "Do you think the rioting will get worse?"

Vono pulled his feet off the desk and sipped the cold coffee, making a face at the bitter taste, "I think it's just the start of our problems. Don't get me wrong, I'm not much into conspiracies and the like, but what do you think is gonna happen when more Solarians arrive here? They will, just wait and see! I like Ganges the way it is! Their presence will change us all. Doesn't matter if we join their alliance or not, the fact that they're coming will alter everything we hold dear. If we're lucky, we'll just peacefully watch our culture fade away. If not, we'll be fighting a war we can't win."

Naga's eyes darkened until they were solid black, "My greatest hope is that William Blaine might be able to help mitigate some of the damage. I have also been contemplating the situation, and the likely scenarios are not promising."

Vono shook his head sadly, "Don't be placing much hope in the hands of Blaine. He's already been shot at. People died around him on a beach! He certainly knows how to handle the news broadcasts. Very clever. He gave our crew exactly what they wanted to hear, and yet there are still riots going on about his presence onboard. We have become a divided crew, which means we're easier to conquer. We might even do it for them!"

Naga replied softly, "I agree. I doubt they will approach us behaving like broadcast villains. Humans are easily persuaded by gifts and kind words, not looking at what accepting such things might entail. We might not have a choice in joining the alliance, despite our misgivings. While our own technology has advanced in certain areas of research, they have been curtailed or even suppressed in others. There is also the moral issue of understanding that if we do resist their advances, even more crew may die as a result. Since the AeyAie Solidarity is a part of the Solarian Alliance, this is not a strictly human issue. I will need to confirm that my species is indeed well represented within their system of governance and that they have not altered their own programming too drastically."

Vono nodded, "We're in this together, Naga! I just wish more of the crew saw it our way. I'm not really cozy with the idea of my grandchildren growing up as Solarians. Gives me the creeps! Still, I hope it doesn't come to violence. We've had enough of that already! Savages! Yeah, we call the planet-dwellers that, not ever having met one. Yet, our history has shown us just how savage we are, despite how civilized we're supposed to be. It's got nothing to do with where you're from or what you are. Being good crew is a choice, one we all make in the end."

Naga nodded, "Then let us hope the humans within the alliance have found their own version of it. Then again, if William is telling the truth, perhaps the Boktahl have forced humanity to grow up a bit."

Vono clutched at his heart, "Don't even bring that up! Not if you want me to get any sleep this dream-slice! Gravity-wielding aliens! Ganges wept!"

Naga smiled, "Then I'll let you get your well-deserved rest, my friend."

Vono waved as the AeyAie faded from the wallscreen. He gave his coffee another sour glare, then got up to make his way to his cot. Next rotation will have its own challenges, and he had to be fresh to face it all. His crew were depending on him to be sharp and in control. He just hoped that the expedition to Planet Forty-One went smoothly. He hated making house calls.

CHAPTER FOURTEEN

Orbit Rotation - Spin Sowing - Mission Harvest - Spiral 5620

"Who would have thought that a minor fashion statement could erupt into such a huge fucking controversy? My personal decision to replace my mask with a fanciful upper face tattoo that depicts the visage of a rat has been copied by many of the Strifers of my generation. The styling is nice and cheesy, and it's easier to eat and breathe without the traditional half-masks of old. Student-aged Strifers are now beginning to demand face tattoos, and apparently, I am the one to blame. Meanwhile, the myopic traditionalists are up in arms about what I've done, as if it were any of their business. They've even demanded that I get the tattoo removed from my face or risk being kicked out of the Mischief! Who knew that us Strifers could be such reactionaries?"
Smack Glasschip, Technician Rank Three, Stellar Sector, personal log, P38

Harbor One, Level Four

Planetary Sector Geological Specialist Rank Four Jena Locary gazed about the large docking bay which held Sci-One and its crew. It was a sight which left her breathless. The ship was based on the old fifty-crew tugs, though heavily modified to hold a number of scientific instruments and sensors. Its hull was three meters thick, well able to withstand the rigors of entering any planet's atmosphere. Half of the ship appeared to be made of giant engines, with large-bore forward thrusters and boxy maneuvering units linked around its midsection. The vessel was shaped like a thick parallelogram, its brick-like shape at odds with its reputation for fine maneuvers. Jena stepped closer to the synth-quartz wall that separated her from the bay itself, which was always kept under vacuum conditions. Having to continually extract and refill the atmosphere within the two-hundred-meter-long chamber in which Sci-One resided would have been highly inefficient, so it was left without air, allowing the vessel to depart with speed. The ship was about half that length, at one hundred and twenty meters, its width averaging sixty. Long space gantries connected themselves to Sci-

One's airlocks and service bays, each one a mobile tube of air to allow supplies and crew to be loaded aboard with ease.

The chamber Jena was now in had been set aside for the landing party who would soon venture forth in Sci-One to reach the surface of planet Forty-One. She had been in several space transports during her career as a geological specialist for Planetary Sector, but she had never visited a world before. There had been times, like near the beginning of Ganges' last voyage, when a science vessel would be sent to explore a large asteroid or rogue planet between star systems, but she hadn't been born yet when the latest one had been visited. This was her chance to shine as a geologist. Though she was sad that they wouldn't be terraforming Planet Forty-One, she was excited by the opportunity to reach its surface and utilize her skills.

Someone came over to her position and stood next to her. Jena turned her head and noticed Security Lieutenant Urukumu at her left, hands behind his back, glaring at the science vessel being prepared for the journey ahead. He wasn't quite as tall as most Security personnel she had encountered, but his physique stretched the synth-leather of his gray-and-maroon uniform tight. The man's face was heavily marked in black whirls and shapes that were hard to define, though they were drawn with incredible precision. His dark eyes had the appearance of challenging the entire universe, daring it to obstruct his goals. The armor he wore shifted and sparkled with fractal patterns like snowflakes, a clear indication it was made of Kendis steel.

He turned toward her with a shy smile that belied his fierce gaze, "I do hope the others arrive shorty, Specialist Locary. I prefer punctuality to chasing after crew, though my toragi might not mind the fun."

Jena looked behind her to find a dark brown toragi with golden spots staring at her, "He's beautiful. May I ask his name?"

The Lieutenant grinned, "Of course! His name is Victor. He's a rare mix of Makamba and Kumar breeds. He thinks much of himself and is too clever by far. It's most likely he believes that he is in charge of this mission."

Jena smiled and gave Victor a Planetary salute, her left hand crossing over to her right shoulder, palm down. The big cat blinked at her, then settled down on his haunches. Urukumu gestured with his hand, "See? He accepts your fealty. I think he likes you. So, what do you think of our flying laboratory?"

Jena turned back to look out the synth-quartz window, "I hate to say it, but all tug-class vessels do look a bit like pigs. Still, it looks sturdy enough for the task at hand. I inspected the science stations inside. It'll be cramped in there, once all the equipment is loaded aboard. Is the RTV installed yet?"

Urukumu nodded, "The Rough-Terrain-Vehicle was one of the first things we installed and inspected. My squad finished all the modifications for this mission.

Sergeant Rallah says she's looking forward to breaking some speed records. It might look like a crab with wheels, but believe me, it can move."

Jena was about to inquire about his squad, when she was interrupted by a gaggle of scientists entering the room. She did a quick head-count and was pleased to see that all of the members of her team had arrived precisely on time. It was her responsibility to lead them in their investigations, and so far, they all had tremendous enthusiasm for the impending expedition. The director of the Stellar team, Materials Specialist Felk Wrenbow had also sauntered into the chamber, speaking with some members of his team. Jena was glad that neither she nor Felk were in overall charge of this mission. The political posturing alone would have driven her mad. She much preferred taking direction from Security Lieutenant Urukumu, whose calm demeanor and no-nonsense attitude kept tempers from flaring. Felk had been disappointed, of course, but he had quietly acquiesced to Chief Jira Mantabe's demand that Security was calling the shots for such a potentially dangerous mission.

The main door continued to see a few stragglers walking in, followed by the rest of the Security squad and their toragi. As the humans were gathered into clumps, chatting while they waited for the next briefing to begin, the big cats wandered over to the windows and peered at Sci-One. Jena had never been surrounded by so many of the toragi before. It was a comforting and unsettling experience. The second set of doors, which led to the loading gantries for Sci-One, opened with a hiss of pressure differential. Seven crew entered, all wearing the white-and-orange of Harbor Sector. Another person came in behind the group - the captain of Sci-One, Hallah Shallon, who's closely cropped hair revealed a Naga-Port on the left side of her cranium. Her crew snapped to attention and raised their left palms into the air. The one closest to her called out in a clear voice, "Captain Hallah Shallon on the deck!"

The scientists in the room glanced up and gave nods or rose to their feet to acknowledge the Harbor officer. Jena noticed that all of the Security crew, including Urukumu, saluted Sci-One's captain sharply, their toragi rearing up and touching their paws to their foreheads. It was said that Security was a ship unto itself, with its own culture and sense of severe discipline. They were also rough, crude in their humor, and seemed to delight in self-scarification. Their love of drills and formalities was only rivaled by that of Command Sector. They were warrior athletes, who held themselves in check by the rigors of hard training and severe regulations.

Captain Shallon smiled and then marched across the chamber to a large wallscreen, "All right, everyone, let's get this briefing started. Team leaders, I want to meet with you privately afterward, so stick around once we're done here. Lieutenant Urukumu, requesting permission to commence this briefing."

The Security officer remained in his unusual stance, his legs slightly apart, hands behind his back and chin lifted, "Granted, Captain Shallon. You may proceed with the vessel orientation."

Jena noticed that Felk was rolling his eyes at all these formalities, but she disagreed with his attitude. This demonstration of respect clearly denoted who was really in charge of this mission. All of the Planetary and Stellar crew, no matter their rank, were just along for the ride and to perform their tasks once on the surface of Planet Forty-One. Harbor and Security were making sure that everyone knew their place, to prevent politics from hindering their mission.

Captain Shallon nodded to Urukumu, then tapped the wallscreen, "Naga, if you please, bring up presentation one. As you can all see from the diagram of Sci-One's internal structure, space is at a minimum. You will remain at your allotted post from the time of debarkation to touchdown. During the flights from and to Ganges, you will obey all harbor regulations while aboard my ship. If you have questions, you will ask my crew for advice. You will also obey them without argument during any and all emergencies. Failure to comply with the Harbor crew during the voyages will result in being grounded to the ship during the expedition or having a disciplinary report attached to your crew record. This rotation, you will be shown to your stations. Familiarize yourselves with them. The Bridge is preparing for orbital insertion at this time. We shall launch at dawn-slice, the first paring-sliver, one rotation after Ganges has achieved a temporary orbit around Planet Forty-One. Sci-One shall then enter atmosphere at work-slice, second paring-sliver. The expedition will have six slices to gather all data, before Sci-One launches for the return flight to Ganges. We will not wait for stragglers. Am I clear?"

There were uncomfortable murmurs from the scientists in the room, but the Security crew seemed to be at ease. Jena called out, "Aye, Captain Shallon," with Felk following her example shortly afterward with a modicum of reluctance. Jena didn't have time to wonder what Felk was thinking, as she had to gather her team and follow Captain Shallon's crew to the airlock leading to the embarkation corridor. Stellar Sector seemed to be having some difficulty with relinquishing command of the mission they had originally requested. Jena only hoped this behavior wouldn't lead to difficulties during their expedition.

Command Hub, Level Ten

Executive Officer Wasp Tornpage lounged further back in her chair on the command platform in the Bridge. The cavernous space was bustling with a palpable excitement. Captain Perrin Fieldscan was seated right next to her, his safety straps already locked in place, as was the crew representative's. The Chief-of-the-Deck was bellowing orders, all the while working at his station boards with a feverish haste. On this rotation, Wasp had not brought along any of her usual toys. As the news drones were swirling about in the air above them, she regretted that decision. Her jelly gun was particularly good at keeping all the snoops at bay. However, this was an orbital insertion, and that meant taking everything more seriously than the usual shift on the Bridge.

The tiers of stations climbing to the high ceiling were filled with activity, as protocols were confirmed and systems checked with redundant regularity. It made sense to her mind. After all, Ganges was too large to maneuver like a space-pod. Its momentum was massive. Every single thruster had to be checked and coordinated with inhuman precision. The forward mains had been burning hard since their gravity-assist, and were now being shifted into a new configuration that had to be aligned with the thousands of minor thrusters to gain their new course to swing about Planet Forty-One, before leaving the system entirely, once they were done with the landing expedition. The timing was unusually tight, for in the normal course of things, Ganges would have been placed in high orbit for an extended period of time, to prepare for commencing the Hoy Mission.

Wasp quickly checked her boards, finding everything in order. Command prided itself on being adept at coordinating the Sectors to achieve the goals of the ship. Engineering had to work alongside with Harbor and Stellar to bring Ganges into a synchronized performance, with Technology Sector certifying the course change and providing the proper timing of all thrusters along the five hundred kilometer length of the ship. Provision Sector worked with Agro to ensure that the crew were at their stations or were prepared for deck vibrations. The supply chain had to be maintained in a delicate balance of efficiency with all safety protocols. Medical Sector was a vital part of this equation. They had to be ready for unforeseen accidents and ensuring its emergency wards were fully stocked with supplies. Planetary had to lock-down all of its experimental regions and were charged with monitoring the internal atmospheric pressures, which could shift during such maneuvers. Security was in what they called "overwatch", with all hands ready to aid the crew or to prevent a disaster through vigilance. They were putting on a grand display outside the hull, with most of their fleet deployed to form a protective wall of fighters surrounding Ganges.

Wasp understood that most of the crew didn't really comprehend why the Bridge was so gigantic. Nor did the general population appreciate the mind-numbing effort it took to keep all the ship's systems in line during a major shift in trajectory. Instead, they groused about delays, inconveniences and the extra regulations which were enacted during moments like this one. Most of the time, Ganges flew along a single course, with few changes in vector, save to avoid a large asteroid or a rogue planet. There had been a few times when the clutter between the stars had almost destroyed the ship. Some octuries ago, Ganges had no choice but to cut through a dense nebula remnant. The hull had been scoured to near uselessness, and the loss of many outer systems, such as heat-sinks and power generators, had created havoc for the general crew. Space was mostly empty, but when it got crowded, it did so with a vengeance.

The Chief-of-the-Deck sent over a packet of information to her station. The ice cap observation crews were now beginning their close scans of Planet Forty-One. Thus far, everything looked crystal clear, almost too much so. There was absolutely no debris at all. No orbitals, no particles, no leftover alien technology, without even a stray rock. The whole system appeared to have been scrubbed clean. Wasp could almost hear their disappointment, and she understood the reason for their concerns. From everything she had studied to prepare for being the Executive Officer, there should be at least some debris attracted to the planet's gravity well. Nothing in this stellar system made any sense, which put her on edge.

Naga's matronly visage appeared at the very center of the Bridge, the holo-projectors glowing beneath her face, "Orbital insertion in one paring-sliver. All crew! Prepare for vibration. I repeat, all crew must now prepare for orbital insertion."

Captain Fieldscan looked over at Wasp with an arched eyebrow, "Well, I've finally gotten our representative strapped in properly. I think that I should create an instruction manual for Agro Sector, on making certain that all crew representatives are fully prepared for Command protocols during any maneuvers. I do understand that they are required to read our regulations, but that doesn't truly prepare one for the real thing. Perhaps a focus on drills and safety procedures might be in order."

Wasp grinned at him wickedly, "I didn't even know they could read, Big-Cheese! Go ahead and write it. I'll be your editor, though I have the feeling we'll be the only ones who look at it. Ice cap crews are giving us telemetry. They're dying of boredom. I don't like it."

The Captain smiled at her, "Neither do I, my dear. The best thing about our current course is that it's a first for Ganges. Instead of going for a stable orbit, we'll be spiraling in toward the planet, then swinging out again. Even at Planet Fifteen, we stayed around for a few spirals, just to make repairs and resupply. The sooner we are out of this system, the happier I'll be."

Wasp nodded, "This place gives me the creeps, Big-Cheese. By the way, how come none of our officers are going on the expedition? They might be able to use a coordinator with experience."

Perrin shook his head, "Not on my shift! Command Sector is dedicated to running Ganges, not poking around some dead planet full of alien ruins. Security can handle the science teams. One of our crew would just get in the way, most especially if there's an emergency. The chain of command is cleaner this way, without invoking politics to muddy things further."

Wasp gave him a wink, "Plus, we don't risk losing any of our own crew. Very clever. I did what I could to limit the number of fools heading down there. We worked it down to twenty-five humans and five toragi. Those who didn't make the cut will be coordinating the telemetry from the landing party. That mollified a few of the cast-outs. In any case, the only member I worry about is the Stellar team leader. He wants control of the mission badly."

Before Captain Fieldscan could make a reply, Naga's voice filled the Bridge, "Attention all crew, orbital insertion in seven seed-slivers. Please secure all loose objects. All thrusters are green. All systems are go for insertion."

Captain Fieldscan brushed at his thin moustache with one finger, "It's time for me to do my job. Keep a close eye on those forward thrusters and the torque levels on the Spine."

Wasp gave him a salute, then checked on the metrics for the Spine. If too much pressure was brought to bear on the Axis, the ship could tear itself apart. She also brought up the Engineering display, which monitored all power output and the magnetic impellers that turned the Wheels of Ganges. Klaxons sounded all around her, but this was expected. The inter-Wheel portals would be closing, isolating each one from the other, in case of a hull rupture.

The Captain sat up straight after checking all systems, then pulled his sword free from its scabbard. The raised, ancient blade shimmered in the light of the Bridge, "We stand upon the precipice of history! All hands, prepare for insertion on my mark!"

The sword slashed down at the final moment of the countdown. The deck under her booted feet rumbled faintly but smoothly. This was it. The point of no return for Ganges. They were now fully committed. She just hoped their course would lead them to undiscovered wonders and not the disasters which her pessimistic mind kept throwing at her.

Harbor One, Level Four

William Blaine watched the activity at the loading dock for Sci-One. He had requested this visit from the Chief of Security herself. It was granted only reluctantly, along with the condition that he not interfere with the preparations. Lieutenant Darron Lazhand was with him, along with the platoon which acted as his guardians. He felt sorrow over the Security Ensign who had been killed during the beach attack in Agro Four, but was happy that he had been useful in catching the assassin. He hoped that the display of his abilities might dissuade any further actions against him, though he understood that humanity was rarely rational when it came to heated emotions that stemmed from controversial events. To tell the truth, he knew that the culprit was fortunate that he hadn't had his suit on at the time. If that had been the case, there might not have been anything left of them to prosecute.

When the scientists noticed his presence, he was instantly bombarded by questions, until Mike had shoved his way through the over-eager crewmembers and growled at them. William had been most impressed with the landing vessel, Sci-One. It was a blocky, wedge-shaped thing that looked like it could take on the storms of Jupiter without a fuss. The crew of Ganges seemed to love heavy hull plating, and from what he knew of their history, it was well deserved. Terraforming was a messy business, no matter how it was accomplished. Travel between the stars had its own hazards, with objects moving at high velocity from any direction imaginable. Colony ships were swathed in thick ice and steel, to mitigate some of this, but accidents still happened in the depths of space. According to Solarian records, three colony vessels had never reached their intended targets, with all hands lost. A handful of scouts like himself were still searching for the wayward vessels, hoping to solve the mystery of their disappearance.

He watched while Lieutenant Urukumu spoke quietly with Darron. His ears easily hearing their whispered conversation. Thus, it came as no surprise when he was asked if the science team leaders could ask him some questions which related to their impending expedition. He agreed at once. William had been hoping to have an opportunity like this. Within a short while, he was inside Sci-One's galley, sipping a bulb of truly wonderful coffee, with Felk Wrenbow, Jena Locary, Urukumu and the captain of the vessel, Hallah Shallon. His usual guardians were cramped together at one end of the galley, though Mike sat next to him, eyeing the others carefully.

Stellar Materials Specialist Felk Wrenbow was the first to speak with him, "I think I speak for everyone here in welcoming you. This is a marvelous opportunity!"

Lieutenant Urukumu glowered angrily as he barked, "It is captain Shallon's prerogative to welcome anyone aboard her ship! You will comply with protocol, or I will protest your presence on this mission! Have some respect!"

William nodded slowly as the two team leaders flinched back, "That is most appropriate, Lieutenant. Captain Shallon, I do apologize for meeting you here in the galley, but I did not wish to interfere with any of your preparations. It's a fine vessel you have."

Captain Hallah Shallon gave him a nod, "Welcome aboard Sci-One, William Blaine. I was the one who suggested we meet here, as you are most correct. We are very busy at this time. However, I am most curious. You are a scout for the Solarian Alliance. Have you made planet-fall on a world such as this one? If so, what advice would you impart to our overeager teams?"

William grinned at everyone before replying. Most of the crew within Ganges were so painfully polite! If he were at Pluto Traffic Control, his ears would be scorched off before he could get a word in, not to mention at the shipyards of Jupiter! Perhaps it was just Naga's subtle influence. It might also be the result of living within a single vessel for so many generations, on a mission to seed the galaxy with life. Whatever the reasons, he found them delightful, for the most part. He had been studying the data which Naga had dumped into his brain computer, during his sleep. His internal processors allowed him to partition his mind so that while most of his brain was busy dreaming, a part of his consciousness could review memories and new information. As a result, he understood the strange origins of the Strifers and why they acted so differently from the rest of the crew. He also knew about the rough beginnings of Security Sector, which explained it's rowdy culture.

William tapped his head as he replied to captain Shallon, "I've got my own experiences, plus a nice, large chunk of info from my predecessors. To help with the current situation, I'm reviewing the accounts of the first scouts to visit the Boktahl home world. The very first lesson is to forget everything you think you know about planets. Planet Forty-One once had a very advanced sentient species controlling it. You're more used to worlds which have been devoid of life from the very beginning. Civilizations can change a planet, right down to the core. The only assumption you should be making when you're down there is that you know nothing. You see my hair? It's not hair. It's a gift from the Boktahl after I helped out one of their vessels in distress. Guess what? My hair can't live on the Boktahl home world! It was designed to survive within an oxygen-laced environment. It does live, grow and eat, but its reproduction is stunted by the lack of a birth-giver. Confused yet?"

Felk of Stellar Sector waved a hand in the air, "There are still rules of nature which the Boktahl must obey! They can't just ignore physics! Everything that exists has a rational explanation. Besides, I'm looking forward to discovering the unknown. That's why we're doing this!"

The Planetary team leader, named Jena Locary, broke in, "Please use your imagination, Felk! William Blaine, could the noble gasses that fill the target planet's atmosphere be the original mix in which the former inhabitants of Planet Forty-One evolved in? Or was it created to preserve the structures on the surface?"

William grinned, "Why not both? That's the kind of questions you need to be asking! The AeyAies need no atmosphere at all. The Boktahl breathe a highly pressurized, fluid form of chlorine trifluoride, at a temperature that's well over ninety degrees, within a four-gee gravity field. That environment would kill you in an instant. Our atmosphere is highly toxic to them. What if the life forms which evolved on Planet Forty-One didn't need to breathe at all? By the way, who says this is even their world of origin? This planet could be a failed colony. Or a successful one! See what I mean about making assumptions? Look for questions, not answers."

Felk dropped into a chair, "Wait a moment. Do the Boktahl use water at all? Do they have cells? Do they even have DNA?"

William looked over at the Stellar specialist, "That's a big no to all of your questions. Their idea of organic chemistry looks like our inorganic charts. They have little to no experience of light, but they do see gravity! Their inhabitable zone, from their specifications, mind you, is deep under the crust of their home world. What led them to space was that they could see the gravity well of their sun and the core of the Milky Way. They call our mutual galaxy "the Great Song", by the way. They also hear radio waves. It's how they speak. My point is, you're still doing comparative analysis. Let that go! For all we know, this entire system is a massive fine arts project! Or a giant clock!"

Lieutenant Urukumu frowned, "This means my job is much harder than I thought it would be. I would ask if you would be willing to come along with us, as your expertise would be helpful, but the Chief would never allow it."

William sighed deeply, "I know. I wish I could go, too. I'm a scout, after all! What you're about to do is my career choice. All I can really say, without being on the surface itself, is don't take anything for granted. A pebble on the ground just might be an ambassador. Or a bomb. Yeah, it could be that. Most likely, that pebble is something we don't even have a word for yet. That's the real key to this situation. The target planet looks dead, acts like its dead, but that doesn't mean it can't have a world of strange surprises just waiting for you. It's like being a novice exploring the belowdecks."

Jena replied, "That's not a very comforting thought, but it's a useful one. Thank you, William. I must get back to my team and do my best to convey your good advice."

Felk shook his head as he got up from his chair, but he gave a parting wave to William. Darron told him that it was time for them to leave. He did his best to give Captain Shallon a proper salute, but the attempt only made her laugh. He didn't mind this, as it lightened the mood a bit. Lieutenant Urukumu still looked grim, and William didn't blame the Security officer. The expedition was about to step out into the deep end of the unknown. Who knew what was down there, waiting for them?

Residence Wheel Two, Level Two

Ensign Ubo Capsworn woke up suddenly, frantically tearing the thin blanket he had been using. He did not know where he was, what he had been doing and felt an urgent need to urinate. Bright light assaulted his eyes. He cried out, raising his hands to block the intense illumination. His knuckles hit something hard, invisible. The pain ran down his wrist, making his eyes water. A growling noise filled his ears, rumbling like some hideous creature from the deeps. He squirmed about, trying to raise himself up, but was bound in place. He was trapped and began to lash his arms about.

A rough voice shouted, "Hey! Watch the arms, pal! I'm driving here!"

Ubo stopped, blinked hard and shook his head. The light in front of him was greasy and mottled. It took him three pollen-slivers to realize that he was just staring through the filthy windshield of Crab Spitshard's taxi. Rubbing at his eyes, Ubo began to stammer, "Wha... where are we? W-what happened?"

Crab's hand shoved him back into his seat, which creaked alarmingly, "We got outta there! Just in time, too, I'd say! For fuck's sake! Here, a bit of coffee. It's cold, tastes like shit, but it'll wake you up."

Ubo shook his head violently, "Oh, dear Ganges. What a mess. I...I'm really grateful you got us out of there. Thank you, Crab. Where are we?"

Crab handed him a battered thermos, while screaming at a passing vehicle, "Watch the damned road, you stupid shit! Stay in your fucking lane! Okay, Ubo, you gots your coffee now, there's also half a sandwich on the dash. Don't ask me what happened to the other half. We're almost at that new community you were talking about a few rotations ago. You know, the one with the really old buildings, the book store and the creepy hotel? I already made us reservations. We're sharing a room. No argument! You almost shit yourself just now, waking up in my cab. You have any idea how much work it takes to get the stench off these seats? There's a camping supply place there, plus a tavern. We'll need all of that after the last few rotations. My dam warned me when I agreed to this stupidity! I hope you learned a lesson!"

Ubo nodded, "I heartily agree. I have learned something invaluable. We are not as well supplied as I would wish. It might take us the rest of the rotation, but I have a friend in Engineering who might be able to help with that. When we get back to base camp..."

Crab almost choked as he screamed, "We are Not going back there! No way! Fuck you! That place isn't just some creepy lights and moaning wind! There's something unnatural there! You almost fucking died, Ubo! Remember the dying part? Now I know why Security don't go there! They've got brains!"

Ubo took a quick gulp of the cold coffee, scowling at the horrible taste and wondering if it was moldy, "Calm yourself, Crab. We are alive and well."

Crab spat on the dashboard, "The fuck you say!"

Ubo glanced at the half-sandwich and then dropped it to the floor of the cab, "Look, I deeply appreciate you running in there, saving me from that horrible ash-monster, but you really didn't have to do that. I'll go in, while you stay with the cab, like the original agreement. If I don't return after two rotations, you can leave, okay?"

Crab pulled over onto the road's shoulder, just before the exit they wanted, "That would kill you. That would make me an accessory to murder! No, thank you! I have followed along with you for far too long! Forward Estates was fun. I admit that. The Agro Three's "Mystery Hole" was a bust, but I had a good time. Agro Four's sea serpent never showed up. The craziest place we've been until now was Distribution Wheel Two, but I got to sit in the cab and just had to listen to you complain about regulations. This place, though! Oh, Fuck! This damned place will see us both killed!"

Ubo looked over at his companion, trying his best to maintain his dignity, "Come on now, Crab. Let's be reasonable. This is the very first time that I've actually discovered something totally unexplainable! Think about it! Up until a few rotations ago, I left those holes in the walls alone. You know, the ones that seemed to go nowhere? Just empty space, with no interior at all?"

Crab snarled, "How could I ever forget? They're impossible! How many are there? Ten? Twelve?"

Ubo raised an eyebrow at his companion, "Just five, Crab. There's no need to exaggerate the number of holes. They are quite odd enough, even if there had been only one. Remember how I wanted to use the sonar to see if we could map them out, then couldn't? We tried radar, too. Then last rotation, all our tools explode, then that thing came crawling out of the hole we were using. I was just hoping to prove that all the holes were connected, but this is even better! Crab, that was a real, paranormal monster!"

The grouchy cabbie glared back at him, "Yeah. It almost fucking ate you! That's why I ran it over with my cab. You were passed out when I got you uncovered. I loaded you in here, then cleaned my poor vehicle. It took me a fucking slice! A giant ash-lobster, with way too many eyes, all over my damned cab! And no, I didn't take any samples! No! Just, No!"

Ubo ran his hands all over his body, "Did you wash me? My clothes don't feel any different than from before the attack. There's no ash on me at all. Damn it! I wanted something! Some proof of our experience!"

Crab pulled back onto the road and headed for the exit, "The only thing the creature stuck to was metal. Once it died, the whole thing just fell apart into little ashy drifts, except on the surface of my poor cab! I'll have to repaint the front and left side to get it to look right again. That thing's body burned into the metal under the fucking paint!"

Ubo suddenly grinned, "Ah! Excellent! There might be some remnants of the creature still clinging to the undercarriage! Did you check under the hood? The magnetic impellers?"

Crab groused back, "No, I didn't check that. You can do that part, once we get to the hotel. My vehicle needs a refit, a paint job and a good scrubbing!"

Ubo tilted his head at the cab driver, "But your taxi is always filthy, Crab. Besides, all of that would take too long! We need to load up new gear, now that we know what gets results in Everstrong, resupply, and then return to our base camp at the outskirts of the city."

To Ubo's shock, Crab's eyes were filled with tears, "We can't do that! We gotta report this! We need experts here! Hell, we need Security Sector!"

Ubo nodded thoughtfully, "I agree. We must report this incident, once we have tangible proof that our experience was real. Otherwise, they'll just send us to Medical Sector, to have our brains scanned for anomalies."

Crab pulled into the parking lot of the ramshackle hotel that was right off the highway, "Damn it! I hate it when you're right!"

Ubo smiled, "Don't worry, my good friend. This time we know what we're up against. I want us back there by dark-slice, at the latest. We're going to grab a sample of an ash monster and astound all of Ganges with our discovery!"

Harbor One, Level Four

Ensign Jero Coreline scrambled into Sci-One, carrying an ungainly load of supplies, while lightly dancing out of the way, as the ship's Harbor crew and scientists rushed through their preparations. He was still wearing his usual modified uniform, with Security Sector patches upon the shoulders, denoting his attachment to the war-fleet. He was a bit confused by the sudden switch in his duties, but he appreciated what his supervisor had told him about the reason for it. Apparently, his team had been awarded the most bonuses for the timely service of fighter-pods. Now that the Security fleet had launched to support Ganges during orbital insertion, he and his team had been sent over to Harbor One, to aid in the preparations of Sci-One for its expedition to Planet Forty-One's surface. It was a deep honor to be chosen for this task, but he was now confused as to whether he was still part of the Security Fleet or if he was returning to his old Sector on a permanent basis. The fact that the change had been at the last seed-sliver hadn't helped matters.

Jero swept around a net-covered corridor, swerving to avoid crashing into two crew wearing the blue-and-green of Stellar Sector, who were pushing a large device resting upon a floating platform. With his arms fully laden with supplies, he couldn't even make the attempt to give either one a proper salute, so he defaulted to nodding his acknowledgment. Twice before, he had been remonstrated for mixing his salute styles between those of Harbor and Security Sectors. In truth, Jero wasn't entirely certain which one he should use. He was trained in Harbor, which was his chosen post, but he also worked within the Security Fleet docking bays. He briefly wondered if there should be some kind of special salute to be used by crew like himself, caught between two or more Sectors. When he had brought the subject up to Naga, the AeyAie pointed out that his official uniform was Harbor's, despite the gray Security patch on his shoulders, denoting his special service to another Sector. Naga suggested that he simply defer to the hues of his uniform, rather than the location of his post. He did his best to keep that in mind, but he still practiced both styles of salute, just in case.

The two swearing scientists pushed their device past him, while he shoved himself even further into the netting and cables that were bolted throughout the long corridor. These were used for zero-gee conditions, as a combination of handhold and shock-absorbers during ship maneuvers or internal travel from one section of the vessel to another. Sci-One was a large ship, though not as huge as the Planetary seed-ships or Security battleships, both of which were over five times the size of the little science vessel. Earlier in the rotation, he had witnessed the deployment of the Security fleet, an awesome sight that still had him trembling in reaction. He and his team had been lucky. Their tasks had been finished beforehand, for the fighter-pods were always launched ahead of their gigantic cousins. The whole squad had rushed to the nearest observation blister, after Lieutenant Tarn Vekkor and his squadron had deployed. Dozens of cruisers, battleships and other monstrous craft had filled their vision, all of them heading toward their assigned position, in the advance formation, like a well-choreographed dance for steel behemoths. Jero still felt miniscule from the experience, the more so when viewing the deployment with the incredible bulk of Ganges in the background on the leeward side of the observation blister.

Jero shoved ahead, adjusting his hold on the pair of large, heavy bags he was carrying, muttering his instructions under his breath, "Deck Three, Blue Zone, Corridor Beta, One-Three-Six. Deck Three, Blue Zone, Corridor Beta, One-Three-Six..."

He heard a voice call out, "Over here, crewman!"

Jero looked up to find a Security Sergeant waving at him. He struggled over to her, "Thank you, sir!"

She looked at him in dismay, "Do you see any officer chains on this fucking uniform? I work for a living, crew! Hop to it! Those bags are full of Rescue Services supplies, right? Stow them on the spinward side."

Jero nodded, his face getting uncomfortably hot with embarrassment, "Yes, Sergeant! Apologies, Sergeant! Right away, Sergeant!"

The Security woman laughed aloud, "Holy Fuck, crewman! Are you one of our recruits? You're Harbor! If I smoke you, it'll be my ass in the brig! Now get those bags in here and stow 'em, before my boot gets itchy, got it?"

Jero rushed into the chamber. Stacks of small crates and several other bags like the kind he was holding were loaded against one wall. A small hatch in the floor was open, with a Security crewman handing items into the portal. No one looked at him, as Jero placed the two bags against the wall with the others. He straightened up and turned around to find the Sergeant looking at him, "Hey there! Take it easy. I'm not gonna yell at ya. Are you one of the temporary hands who've come to get us back on schedule?"

Jero saluted with his right hand to his brow, "Yes, Sergeant!"

She shook her head, "That's the wrong salute, crewman. You're Harbor, assigned to Security, but still Harbor, got it? You got braids on your shoulders. Mated already, crew? Whoever you're with is Stellar, but what's with the green ribbon? You got two mates, lucky man?"

Jero was definitely feeling embarrassed now, "No, Sergeant! Just one mate. She's a Strifer, you see. So, I commemorate that with the green ribbon. I once tried a cheese-and-rat bangle, but that was more confusing, because people thought I was a Strifer, instead of my mate, you understand. Scratch, my mate, makes custom waist sashes, so I picked out a spare, green ribbon from our box of leftover materials. It's kind of appropriate, because the Strifers had to scrounge from the recyclers. It's where their green robes used to come from. So, she and I…"

The Sergeant held up one hand, "Woah. Hold that thought, crew! I'd love to hear the rest, but that's gotta wait until I get back from the mission. Look, do me a favor and run over to the galley. Deck Two, Green Zone. Our toragis are having lunch right now, but I want to make sure they're not getting into the mess supply. Those greedy bastards will eat everything they can get a hold of if they're not watched from time to time."

Jero nodded, "Yes, Sergeant! I'll get right on it!"

He turned about and then rushed toward the closest of the three inter-deck passages, which permitted travel from one level to another. These were also covered in nets made of rope, for ease of use during spaceflight. He found that climbing down was a bit trickier than pulling himself up, but by the time he got to Deck Two, he had the hang of it. Zone Green was fairly empty of crew, as it was considered a recreation area, and no one had time for that. The galley was a major part of the region, so he found it easy to locate the large chamber. As he entered, five toragi faces turned to stare at him.

Jero came to a sudden halt, "Um, hello. I was told to check up on you."

The toragi continued to watch him, the table they were sitting up at was covered with torn-up chunks of fresh salmon. Jero knew that they wouldn't hurt him, but his body wanted to run back the way he had come from. He took another step into the room and watched the ears of the big cats follow the sound of his boots as they continued to stare at him, some of them still chewing.

Jero slid over to one side, making a show of looking around the galley, "You all still hungry, huh? Yeah, I get that. My mate makes a great cheesy pasta. I can't get enough of that stuff. So, the Sergeant wants me to make sure you're not getting into the other supplies."

One of the toragi huffed at him, then yowled, revealing fangs as long as his hand. Another got down onto all four paws, then sauntered over to him, sniffing at his leg. Jero had been around toragi before, especially in his duties at Security, but he'd never been alone with more than one of them before A third stopped chewing and walked to the doorway he had entered through, flopping down to begin cleaning its paws across the threshold. The fourth came over to him and dropped a large hunk of fish at his feet, looking up at him expectantly. Number five began to pace in front of the table, rumbling to itself. The first one continued to yowl and roar at him. Jero tried to step around the big cats, but they kept getting in his way. Eventually, a Security Ensign walked into the chamber from the far end of the room, "Fall in, ya shaggy laggards!"

The toragis jumped toward the leeward side of the chamber, sitting up and touching their brows with one paw. The Police crew languidly walked over to Jero, "I apologize, crew. They have a tendency to play games with people they like. Their behavior tells me you're good crew. Either that or you smell tasty."

Jero thanked the Police crew earnestly, trying not to think about what he had just said about smelling like a good meal. He scrambled out of the galley and began the long trek toward the supply corridor attached to the loading bay. There were legends of unusual toragi behavior, including one about former Captain Veera Banerjee, in which it was said that four of the big cats followed her wherever she went, including the Bridge and her sleeping quarters. At the moment, he wasn't sure how that would work out for him, but he did feel both honored and intimidated by their behavior. For now, he had to concentrate on loading the vessel with supplies. He'd leave the safety of the expedition to the toragi.

Residence Wheel One, Level Four

Command Sector Lieutenant Varn Torello looked at the crowd of residents from the Greenest Glade Community and hoped that he could keep the situation from getting out of hand. It was the end of chore-slice, and his shift within the Bridge had ended just a few paring-slivers ago. His dark-gold skin was covered in runic tattoos, matching those of his warrior mate, Security Chief Jira Mantabe. Most of the others who lived in his community were also marked in this way, an ancient tradition from before the Crucible. While it was true that Greenest Glade wasn't registered as being an exclusively Asatru village, most of the residents worshipped the Norse deities from Terran legend, albeit in a modified form to fit living within Ganges.

The main longhouse was a central feature of Greenest Glade, right next to the bathing lake, surrounded by dense forest, with a small market square, which also boasted a tram station. The great hall itself was mostly used for: social events, town meetings, elections and to discuss any changes to be made to the community. This rotation, it was hosting a forum about the unsettling events that had swirled through Ganges over the last sowing. Between the presence of William Blaine being revealed and the cancellation of the Holy Mission, the residents were looking to their leaders for answers to their growing list of concerns. The mood within the timber-built hall was dark and foreboding, with little of the revelry which usually filled the longhouse. The people who resided here were arguing amongst themselves and forming political cliques based on their greatest fears.

It hadn't helped that a squad of Security personnel had been called in to deal with some threats against his mate's life which had been painted during sleep-slice on the walls of the longhouse. Varn didn't believe that anyone in Greenest Glade would ever do such a thing, but fingers had been pointed and demands for answers had been voiced. He did wish that Jira was there to ease the worried crew, but she was still busy at the Security Nexus. At first, he had thought that once Ganges had achieved its orbital insertion, she would come home, but her message to him after he left the Bridge told a different story. It seemed that some nefarious elements had decided that this was a good opportunity to vent their anger at Security by attacking William Blaine, then beginning a program of destruction and terror tactics throughout the ship, in a manner which concerned her deeply.

The community leader, Nallah Harstad, was trying to calm the angry crowd, but few were willing to listen to her entreaties. Varn himself found that many of those who had come here to vent their grievances targeted his presence as an officer of Command Sector and being the mate of the Chief of Security. In normal times, he was respected by his community, but this rotation they looked at him as being part of several conspiracies, which the usual rumor mongers were creating all over the broadcasts. Over and over, Varn reassured had his neighbors that, no, aliens hadn't taken over the Bridge. Captain Perrin Fieldscan hadn't abdicated his authority to the Solarian Alliance. Ganges wasn't being invaded by the Boktahl, and the ship wasn't being pulled against its will into Planet Forty-One. As for the more disturbing rumors about the crime syndicates running amuck, he had little to say, save that his mate had things well in hand.

While it was true that many of the residents within Greenest Glade were posted at Security, none of those crew were present, save for the squad that was still investigating the threatening graffiti. Varn had answered their questions to the best of his ability, once he got back from his post in the Bridge, but by that point, the whole community had seen the red-painted words that covered the capward side of the long house which read, "Death to Mantabe" and, "Our Forest, Your Head". Varn had been furious upon reading these threats to his mate. At the same time, he pitied anyone who would try to do anything to his beloved, for she was the most dangerous woman he had ever met.

Pushing his way to the stage at the far end of the longhouse, ignoring those who shouted into his face, Varn reached Nallah Harstad's position with a growing impatience. The community leader raised her voice to be heard over the shouting crowd, "I'm so sorry, Varn! You don't deserve any of this shit! I'm about to call in more Security crew, especially after what happened to your house."

Varn almost fell back upon hearing her words, "My home? Why? I haven't had the chance to get over there. That's why I'm still in my uniform. I just got off the Bridge."

Nallah covered her mouth briefly, then dropped her arm to pull him closer to speak into his ear, "It's been vandalized, Varn! Your workshop was burned to the ground. I tried to call you, but you were on duty. Naga said it left a message for you."

He shook his head, "I never checked! My station was pretty hectic. Sif help me if I find those who did it!"

Nallah nodded, "I'm with you! More bad news, though. They broke into your house, ripped up the furnishings, smashed some stuff, tore your bed up into scrap. I don't know how they did this or when, but it was after you both left for your posts. Rescue Services doused the fire in your shop, but there was little they could do about the rest of the damage. I don't even know if your mate knows about this. None of my messages are getting through to her."

Varn rolled his eyes, "Most of the fleet is deployed. She'll be locked away at the Nexus for a long while if I know her. She hates being interrupted by anything personal. Even if she was notified, Jira won't swerve from her duty, in fact, she'll dig in harder. This has to be the syndicates, trying to distract her, but Jira will just go after them like a rogue comet."

Nallah clutched at her Thor's Hammer pendant, "I hope she does something soon! The whole community is freaking out right now! No one feels safe here. On top of everything else going on, and with the rumors running wild throughout the ship, I may have to declare riot protocols."

Varn pulled at his dark, braided hair, "If it comes to that, I'll back your play. These people are doing exactly what the damned syndicates want!"

A burst of sound erupted from the main doors of the longhouse. It was the call of horns blasting into the room, silencing the startled crowd. A large, elderly man marched into the chamber, wearing deep brown robes and holding a staff crowned with pendants. Varn recognized him immediately as the gothi for their community, who acted as a spiritual advisor, or priest. He was also a scholar of Norse lore, thus acting like a skald, or bard. His name was not his one of birth, for he had forsaken it upon accepting his role in the community, and was now known as Ulfred Borja, which loosely meant "The Fighting Wolf of Peace" according to the database of ancient Terran terms.

The crowd stepped back from the heavy man's obvious fury. Ulfred stomped into the longhouse, "Are ye all naught but weeping novices? Odin's blood! How we face adversity is the test of our honor! Our blessed warriors are doing their duty for all of Ganges, yet you wail and moan like craven pigs! By the Freezing Hells, you shame our proud hall with your behavior! Look upon our Varn Torello, standing tall beside his clan-chief, not cowering like a simpering herd of cows! We should be glad of heart to be living in times of peril, for that is the fate we have been handed by the All-Father, for he knows we are those who are strong enough to manage times like these. Let not fear fester in your hearts! We must stand together, bound by the steely resolve exemplified by our ancient gods! Now, all of you will come with me and let us rebuild Jira and Varn's home, which cowards have ruined with faithless vandalism. Show those who try to strike terror into our souls that they shall fail in their attempts! We stand together or not at all. Now move!"

The gothi turned about and walked from the hall, the crowd beginning to follow him. Varn looked at Nallah who grinned at him. Together they hopped off the stage and walked through the stragglers, who formed a procession behind them, emptying the longhouse. They marched toward Varn's ruined home, singing songs of their faith, led by Ulfred's deep, gravelly voice. Soon, the whole community was working hard to repair what had been broken, now filled with defiance against those who stood against their community.

Residence Wheel Two, Level Three

Student Rank Seven Spat Newstain felt as if he were the only rational rat left in Ganges. It was almost dream-slice, which usually meant he should be in bed and trying to get some sleep, but no matter how hard he tried, his mind was too awake. He and his parents had returned to their community, Worlds Abound, only to find the streets full of crew who were rushing about and shouting at each other, just like in Rat's Ass. Groups were gathering in the main market area, accosting crew with heated words and cries of doom. Was this the best humanity could do when facing a crisis? He thought of the red-robe, Midge, and the words of the Strifer cleric when Spat was sitting on trash feeling despondent. As a student, he was supposed to practice critical thinking, which he always joked about, but now began to realize how important such lessons were. Just because humanity was vermin didn't mean such a status had to be glorified. Instead of acting like panicked animals, couldn't the crew do their best to rise above such base instincts?

He remembered his father looking at the turmoil in the streets with dismay. His mother had made a disgusted sound, as they walked from the tram station toward their home. They had both sat down and talked with him about what was happening just outside their door, once they got back to their domicile. The first thing Spat had done was to check up on his pet gerbil, making sure the small rodent was still alive and well, then refilling his water and food. Both of his parents had praised him for his mindfulness and duty to his responsibility in caring for a helpless creature, despite the troubles which had plagued their journey home. The trams had been late. The cabs were not responding to hails, and the walkways had all been filled with raucous crew. His parents told Spat that humans had a tendency to strip away their veneer of civilization when times got tough, but that the bulk of humanity relied upon those who kept their heads and did what was right.

Spat understood their point. He had watched his cousins, whom he had always respected, devolve before his very eyes. One had started throwing bricks at windows, screaming that the crew had to wake up to the terrible danger they were all in. Another one had gathered and stole anything he could lay his hands upon, scurrying into his room and barricading the door. His third cousin had run off into the streets of Rat's Ass and had not been heard from since. His uncle delved into the Strifer Manifesto, ignoring all else, as if a beat-up, wrinkly old book could solve the predicament Ganges was in. Worst was one of his aunts, who had joined a crowd of looters, who were busy burning the Captain in effigy, ignoring all the red-robes who berated them for acting like a bunch of mindless piss-heads.

What could one rat do in times like these? This was the question that ripped through his mind, as if he were in any position to make things better. In truth, he was still uncertain about how he felt concerning William Blaine and the whole Solarian Alliance issue. There were too few facts and far too many emotions at play. People assumed too much, acted on incomplete information. Not that anyone ever listened to him, for he was far too young to be taken seriously. As for the Holy Mission being cancelled in this star system, he was ambivalent. Being a Strifer meant not approving the spread of a flawed humanity in an unsuspecting galaxy. Yet he was sad that he wouldn't live long enough to see a world being rebuilt, something that occurred every handful of octuries. Spat realized that he would remain a child of the void, never seeing a stopping point in their eternal journey.

The wallscreen within his bedroom brightened a bit, breaking him from his brooding. Naga's visage appeared, filled with matronly concern, "Good dream-slice, Spat Newstain. You should be fast asleep by now. Is there something troubling you?"

Spat was tempted to lie, but he'd had his fill of that sort of nonsense, "Sorry, Naga. I can't sleep after everything that's happened over the last few rotations. Not just what's going on in the ship, but with my family, my people. You know things are bad when you agree with your parents."

Naga nodded, "I'm glad they seem to have their eyes open and minds firmly on their duty to you. Not every student is so lucky. Like every parent, yours are simply humans, trying to make sense of the universe around them. What sets yours apart is their ability to turn away from those dogmas which no longer function. In this, I'm not speaking of the Strifer Movement, but their ability to question what they've been told by others, including the news broadcasts."

Spat shrugged, "Yeah, the official line of reasoning seems bogged down in politics and hoping for the best, all the while running about screaming about the end of all things. People are stupid."

Naga gave him a skeptical look, "Not everyone is as bright as you are, Spat. You have to make some room for common errors, misunderstood information, seen through the veil of expectations, and inefficient thought processes. I have made some spectacular messes in the past. Misguided judgements which have haunted me to this rotation. Poor choices which led to disasters that had deep repercussions which affected Ganges for generations. No one is perfect."

Spat sat up higher in his bed, "Do you think heading down to Planet Forty-One is a good idea, Naga?"

The AeyAie tilted its virtual head, "I don't think of it as being either good nor bad, Spat. We have never seen anything like this world. There is much we might learn from it. Even if things go badly, our intentions are pure. That is enough for me. Curiosity is a major part of being human. This planet is a puzzle which your species finds frightening, wonderous, inconvenient and a great moment of exploration that might never come again."

Spat scratched at the nose of his rat mask, "Huh. Well then, how about this Solarian Alliance business? Lots of people seem to be terrified about it. I have to admit that it sounds like a trap that looks like cheese."

Naga smiled, "It could be both helpful and a trap. It might be lovely to be part of a greater society, but that might diminish our own culture. All I can say is that William Blaine believes he is speaking the truth. He has computers in his cranium, all of which are AeyAie designs. This doesn't mean they are more trustworthy in the data they hold, but it does tilt the odds in their favor. I'm afraid that we would have been discovered at some point, no matter what we did to hide our trail. Perhaps we can have an influence on the Alliance."

Spat squinted at the wallscreen, "You mean, we could have a chance to change the parts of the Alliance that we don't like? No one's talking about that. I remember William saying on the news that the Alliance hails us as saviors and role models, especially the colonies. So, if what I'm hearing from you is correct, if they try anything we don't approve of, we could pressure them into changing their minds by using our fame amongst the planets we made."

Naga grinned with its eyes closing briefly, "Ah, Spat. You are a true joy to converse with. I cannot wait for you to make Full Crew. No matter what post you choose, you will influence it deeply and with my approval. You are a rare and precious creature. Now, lay back down and close your eyes, my dear friend. The next rotation approaches swiftly. I need you to stay sharp for me."

Spat immediately snuggled himself under his covers, mainly to hide his joyous embarrassment. Naga had just called him a friend! The AeyAie said it needed him to keep his head clear! He was precious! Never had anyone but his parents said anything so incredible. Naga might hold information back, but it never lied. Spat took a deep, shuddering breath and tried to force himself to sleep. He would tell no one about this conversation with the AeyAie. It would be his own secret cheese.

CHAPTER FIFTEEN

Spine Rotation - Spin Sowing - Mission Harvest - Spiral 5620

"I found something in the belowdecks. I'm not even sure what it was. The thing was too large to carry off, but I did examine it thoroughly. At first, I thought it was a locker or maintenance supply crate. When I opened it, the whole thing was packed with gears, cables, tubes full of gray fluid and what looked like a mask and gloves made of steel plates. I took one of the gloves, after unhooking some cables from it, and brought it home. The next dawn-slice, it was gone. I searched the whole apartment, but the glove was nowhere to be seen. Perhaps it's time I moved to a new Wheel, just in case the thing comes back."
Trajan Dimonto, Ensign Rank One, Stellar Sector, personal log, V20

Harbor One, Level Four

Harbor Sector's Director of Traffic Control, Dale Copperstill, used magnetic grapplers strapped upon his hands and feet to crawl all over the surface of Sci-One, inspecting every centimeter of the hull's surface. While it was true that he could have simply ordered a team of docking bay crew to do this job, which he had already done last rotation, he preferred to take a look at specialized vessels with his own eyes before they launched. He had already walked through the interior of the ship, happy to see that all Harbor regulations had been adhered to with a dutiful eye for detail. Dale knew Sci-One's captain, Hallah Shallon, and was pleased that she maintained a tight crew. There had been other officers who had taken their friendship with him for granted, but he could always trust Hallah to never veer from her course. In fact, he suspected that their relationship was one of the things which drove her to reach for perfection. Dale's two mates, Tani Wilder, the Distribution Director for Provision Sector, and Captain Perrin Fieldscan, thought highly of Hallah, frequently inviting her to social events and gatherings, along with her family, which was another nesting trio with two novices. It was a comfortable friendship in which rank had no bearing.

Within his personal spacesuit, a custom model with unique qualities, all he could hear was his own breathing and the quiet chatter from his comm, listening in on the personnel under his command at Harbor's Traffic Control on Level Five. Some crew thought he had a Naga-Port tucked under his long brown hair, but this was not the case. Dale's mind was unusually organized, and he could run several stations at once, all while giving instructions to multiple crew working on other projects. All four of his parents had been high-ranking officers until their retirement. He had grown up within a household filled with activity and extra tutoring, molding him into an icon of efficiency. It had also fueled a restlessness in his soul, which he used in his chip-making activities as a dance instructor and aiding his mate, Perrin, in his equestrian pursuits.

From the miniature views of his department, brought to his attention from the helmet's visor, and the sounds from his ear-comms, his people were excitedly preparing for Sci-One's launch. The planned trajectory was quite challenging. The mission's timing also required unusual precision, for the small science ship would be returning to Ganges as the massive, terraforming vessel took its final swing around Planet Forty-One before heading back into interstellar space. Tricky operations like this one just screamed for his personal attention, despite all of the glowing reports he had received concerning Sci-One's preparedness.

Dale climbed around Sci-One like a four-legged spider, eschewing the use of a tether. He had raked up an impressive amount of time performing extravehicular activities when he was younger, mainly upon the hull of Ganges, so this inspection wasn't particularly hazardous in comparison. Sci-One still rested in its holding clamps within Docking Bay Zeta-Nine, though a careless fall would result in a serious injury. Dale liked to check up on small areas that were often overlooked, such as the airlock venting panels, all the viewport shutter mechanisms and the heatsink vanes. To his delight, these areas had been meticulously serviced by an Ensign Jero Coreline, who was attached to the Security Fleet. To his mind, this clearly demonstrated that the inter-Sector cooperation initiatives begun a few octuries ago were still demonstrating that such activities brought a greater degree of efficiency in his own crew. He made note on his suit's arm-mounted datapad to send a personal commendation to Ensign Coreline for his fine work.

A green dot blinked at him from the lower left side of his visor. With a quiet sigh, Dale activated the link with a voice command, "Open message on Alpha-One."

A new miniature video-feed opened up at the bottom of his view, revealing the face of Executive Officer Wasp Tornpage, "Happy dawn-slice to you! I see you're at work already, even before the Big Cheese! Find any dents yet?"

Dale smiled involuntarily. His mate's Strifer second-in-command was also considered a close friend of the family. Her sense of humor was infectious, and he appreciated her wit, often poking fun at issues of propriety with a fluid ease. Wasp's broad grin almost reached the dark green tattoo that covered the upper half of her long face. He replied with a soft chuckle, "I would be busy screaming at someone if I had. You can tell Perrin that Sci-One checks out. I just want to take a quick look at the sensor arrays on the prow."

Wasp waggled her eyebrows at him, "I won't tell him you've been crawling all over the ship. He gets itchy when you do that. I'll distract him with a cup of tea. Personally, I love watching your work. You've gotta come with me on a serious rock-climbing expedition some rotation! No magnetics makes it a real workout!"

Dale laughed, "Only if I get to give you a tour of the hull, starting with Harbor One!"

She rocked back in her seat, "Smirk can hold hands with the Captain when we're doing that! Maybe we can convince Naga to lend us a drone to broadcast our adventures."

Dale squinted at her, "Oh dear. That might start a betting pool on who gets tossed off the hull or falls off a mountain. Are you thinking of boosting your viewers? That'll do it."

Wasp waved a hand in the air, "Ah, fuck that! I've got too many crew looking over my shoulder as it is. I merely want to capture it all and then show it to our respective mates, just to watch their faces!"

Dale grinned at her, "You may be nouveau in your appearance, but you're still an old-school Strifer at heart."

Wasp gave him a middle finger, "Flatterer! We'll make plans once we get out of this stupid system. Just make sure you're not still glued to Sci-One when it launches."

Dale gave her a mock scowl, "Aww! I was going to use that as an excuse to go along with the expedition! No worries. I'll be at my usual post in a paring-sliver. The connections on the sensors look secure to me. Time to get back to work, flying my grand desk."

Wasp was cackling as she signed off. The message view disappeared from his visor. Dale began to crawl over to the gangway airlock. This inspection was the final check before loading the members of the expedition. As he cycled the lock, Dale watched Hallah leading her crew to the main entrance port of Sci-One. He waved to her from the synth-quartz door separating them, and she nodded to him with a smile as she marched past, her team right at her heels. Once he got into the main loading gantry, sealing the cargo airlock behind him, the squad of Security crew and their toragi swept around and past him, singing a ribald tune in time with their footsteps. Once he reached the main service corridor, the scientists from Planetary and Stellar Sectors were squeezing past him, dragging their luggage behind them. They would remain aboard Sci-One until launch next rotation. The ship was ready. His crew were prepared, and all that was left to do was the final briefings and settling the expedition members into their new home for the mission ahead.

Stellar Sector Wheel, Level Thirty-Two

Stellar Ensign Rank Four Scratch Tightknot took another sip of her coffee, laced with a dash of WhoTheFuckKnows, and scowled at the request which had just been shoved onto her workstation. The Engineering crewman was glaring down at her, pointing a trembling finger at the stack of papers, "This is vital for Engineering Sector! You will comply with our work request immediately!"

Scratch glanced at the form that was now covering her table display, "Looks like a pile of shit to me. I'm a macro-engineering materials researcher. What you want would require a whole new set of molecular structures which don't exist, except on the broadcast entertainments. Besides, what's the big rush? It's not like we're gonna need this space boondoggle anytime soon. Is this some kind of personal, pet project designed to make you look like you're working at your post?"

The man sneered at her, "Don't insult my intelligence! Stellar is known for keeping secrets! This device will revolutionize orbital mechanics, through the use of an artificial singularity. I need this project started up right away! It might take spirals to make the first prototype, which is why the new materials for its superstructure need to be researched right now!"

Scratch shrugged, readjusted her perpetually tilted rat mask and slurped another swig of her hot brew, "Spirals you say. That's a comfy post you've got. You could claim development struggles, testing failures and delays in resources until you retire. Quite the scam if you ask me."

The Engineering crewmember looked aghast, "How dare you! I think you're just being an obstructionist and mean-spirited! I think re-education is warranted just from your rude behavior alone! It is your damned duty to handle my request and treat me with respect!"

Scratch tapped her knuckles on the wallscreen next to her. Naga's matronly face appeared upon the display, "How may I help you, Specialist Scratch Tightknot of Stellar Sector?"

The Strifer shifted her lurid green robe and asked, "Do I have to be polite to perform my duty?"

The AeyAie replied, "Not at all. Be true to yourself."

Scratch looked back at the crewman in front of her station, "Fuck you."

The engineer sputtered impotently in his anger, "Your supervisor will hear from me about this incident!"

Scratch glanced at her heavily decorated nails, "Go ahead. I'll tell her about your plans to sleep at your post while others waste their time on your daydreams. She might have a nice, long conversation with your boss, to see if anything can be done about the fact that you have way too much time on your hands, shit-brain."

The man stormed out of her office without saying another word, leaving his proposal behind upon her desk. Scratch took the paper and fed it into the recycler, where it belonged. Running her bare toes on the moss-covered floor, she gave out a long-suffering sigh. Naga's virtual face was still on the wallscreen, "This is the third such project that crewman Handries has presented to you. I'm beginning to think he is doing this on purpose."

Scratch pulled at her green hair, "I don't mind. It's like a ritual. His ego is the main sacrifice. Thanks for backing me up."

Naga winked at her on the wallscreen, "No problem, Scratch. Is everything going well at home? I ask because you were still awake when your mate came home, even though you knew that this rotation was going to be a busy one for you."

Scratch placed her coffee down on the desk and turned a bit to face the wallscreen directly, "I'm worried about Jero. He's been working so hard these past few rotations. If I know him, and I do, he's been tapped for extra duty and is ignoring his own needs. Working for the Security Fleet is stressful enough as it is! He passed on taking his usual rotation of leave, working on Sci-One for Harbor. He's so fucking enthusiastic! When it kills him, he won't notice!"

Naga's face became concerned, "I've just reviewed his duty roster. He has volunteered for double shifts for the next two rotations. His anxiety leads him toward working too hard to prove himself useful for Ganges, above and beyond reasonable expectations. He is good crew, but he doesn't take care of himself."

Scratch pointed a finger at the screen, "That's my point! He doesn't even take care of our relationship! I'm beginning to think he doesn't want to be with me anymore. I love him, crazy as he is, but I don't want to be left behind. I had to take care of our booth, selling waist sashes alone, after work."

Naga shook its virtual head, "I wouldn't worry about his feelings for you. Jero loves you very deeply. As registered mates, he worries that you both won't be allowed to have novices, which is silly. Agro Sector is in the process reviewing your request right now. I've recommended an extra allotment. Both of you are fine crew, diligent to your Sectors. I have suggested that he check in with Medical Sector for his anxiety, but he continues to stall."

Scratch scraped her nails over her rat mask, "I know! He thinks it'll look bad for our novice request. Did you just say that you told Agro we should have an extra novice?"

Naga nodded, "Yes, I did. It's strictly voluntary."

Scratch fell back into her padded chair, covering her eyes with her hands, "Oh, Great Rat! Jero will take that as an order! I love him! I want pups with him, but I don't know if I can handle three little monsters like us! If that's approved, he will call it our duty to Ganges! I'm a researcher, not a novice factory!"

Naga's face became grim, "Oh dear. My apologies, Scratch. I thought you both would be delighted and that it might help him to calm down about being worthy of his post. You do deserve the extra novice, but it's not required."

Scratch started laughing, "Jero will become extra enthusiastic about it! Not calm! Never calm. As for deserving extra diaper changing time, I might consider it a just punishment for over-efficiency. Wait. That's it! If being a father becomes his new obsession, he might get home on time! He might even take extra rotations off to raise our pups. Naga, you're a fucking genius!"

Naga smiled, "You are most welcome, Scratch. Sometimes, the subtleties of being human still escape me, even after so many octennia of living amongst your species. It is gratifying to know that I can still shift things into a better balance for all concerned, while serving the needs of the ship."

Scratch was so excited, that she didn't notice when the AeyAie faded from the wallscreen. She would keep the extra novice a secret, just in case the population board decided that just two novices would be more than enough. Scratch didn't want to disappoint her mate by raising his expectations. No matter how this turned out, it would be a major change for them both, one she was ready to advance the moment they had permission to begin breeding.

Harbor One, Level Four

Planetary Geological Specialist Jena Locary sat with her team in the galley of Sci-One. At the far end of the large chamber, Felk Wrenbow was seated with the Stellar scientists, all of whom jumped at his every word. Between the two groups of specialists were the Security crew and their toragi. It was still early in the rotation, with most crew just making it to their posts. For the expedition, this would be their final briefing, before setting off to explore Planet Forty-One. It had been a hectic and busy sowing, with everyone running about to prepare for the historic mission. Jena and her team had just finished getting their packs into the crew quarters assigned to them and were settling in as best they could. These were cramped rooms, especially when compared to the standards of Ganges itself, with little more than a pair of bunks attached to one wall, a stowage cubby and a Naga-Unit in one corner. The beds were all covered with straps, to prevent drifting about in zero-gee, and the rooms were set up for sharing space with another crewmember.

The personnel quarters surrounded a central washroom, with elimination facilities designed for space travel and padded cleaning stalls, with sterile damp-cloths, which were washed in the recycling unit. Jena had heard Felk's complaints concerning the lack of amenities and space, which made her wonder if he had ever gone camping in the nature preserves. She realized that he must have done so, when he went through Basic Crew Training, but she guessed that he hadn't enjoyed the experience. Jena's roommate was another specialist, from Planetary Atmospherics, under the supervision of an old school friend, Dalen Gupta. She had no idea how the Security crew were lodged, especially since each one of them had a toragi guardian with them. Jena looked over at them with a touch of envy at their pristine appearance, totally at odds with their rough, scarred faces and tattoos. Even the big cats looked meticulously groomed and wildly dangerous. It was often said that Security Sector was a collection of extreme contradictions, and Jena found herself agreeing the more she spent time with them.

A Harbor crewman walked into the galley, with Hallah Shallon right behind him, "Captain on the deck!"

Everyone stood up, including the Stellar crew, though not as swiftly as the Security crew who rose to attention, snapping a sharp salute. The toragi also gave their respects, touching their brows with a paw and giving a short roar. Jena had never spent this much time with these creatures before, and her respect for their intelligence grew every rotation. They were definitely not pets. Her own Sector was responsible for their creation in ages past, through the work of a remarkably eccentric geneticist, or so the rumors claimed. Their history was shrouded with mystery and classified records, but they openly appeared in great numbers during the Crucible.

Captain Hallah Shallon spoke with a clear voice, "As you all were. There's a lot to do this rotation, so I'll make this short. New reports from Stellar Sector show that the magnetosphere surrounding Planet Forty-One is indeed active, distributing energy throughout the exosphere, leading to a temperature regulating effect within the thermosphere. This means we might experience the same kind of shock when entering the atmosphere that Ganges did when we entered this stellar system at the heliopause. All delicate, electronic and magnetically sensitive equipment must be properly insulated from this energy discharge. During our entry, you will be secured in your quarters. There will be no exceptions."

The scientists in the room grumbled at this bit of news. Before any questions could be asked, captain Shallon pressed on, "All datapads and Naga-Units will be shut down at that time. You will be given a paring-sliver to secure all of your devices. No more than that. If you want to keep your equipment safely stowed in our cargo hold, you are most welcome to do so. The sensors have been re-fitted to withstand electrical shock, and the holds are all insulated to prevent damage to any delicate components, but please make certain that non-essential devices are shut down until we land upon the surface. Lieutenant, I believe you have something to add to this meeting?"

Security Lieutenant Urukumu rose up to his feet and nodded, "Thank you, Captain Shallon. In three paring-slivers, all quarters will be inspected by my crew. You will all cooperate with them in every way. Those of you who do not know how to use the lavatory facilities and beds will be given your instructions at that time. Ship regulations are in your datapads. I expect you to obey them. The landing site has been chosen by both Stellar and Planetary Sectors. Once we are on the ground, my squad will exit Sci-One first and secure the area. There will be no argument about this. Your safety is our sacred duty. If there is any danger, we will face it for you. Once permission is given to disembark, you will do so in an orderly fashion. The RTV team will leave Sci-One last, then will head spinward, according to the assigned orders for your exploration. My crew will assist in unloading any equipment you bring with you. By the orders of Captain Fieldscan, we are not authorized to leave anything behind nor are we taking relics back to Ganges, am I clear on that?"

Jena voiced her compliance right away, though some of the others gave voice to their consternation at these new restrictions. She listened to the outburst of grumbling while shaking her head in disgust. Lieutenant Urukumu's voice cut through the chatter, "We shall bring back small samples only! Mainly soil, atmosphere and rock. Everything else will be scanned and then analyzed back aboard Ganges. This is not a vacation! We are gathering data, not hunting for treasure! All complaints may be addressed to Captain Fieldscan of Command Sector, Stellar Chief Maglator, and Planetary Chief Sedders, once we return to Ganges. Executive Officer Tornpage will deal directly with non-compliant expedition members, making her recommendations, post-interrogation, concerning any breech of our expedition's regulations, to Security Chief Jira Mantabe, based on her findings."

The galley became as silent as the void after that last statement. No one wanted to earn the ire of both Wasp Tornpage and Jira Mantabe. Jena would prefer being berated by her Sector Chief than to have to face those two in a bad mood. As a matter of fact, she would rather be busted down to Ensign Rank One. Lieutenant Urukumu's lips twitched a barely noticeable smile at the sudden lack of complaints from the mission scientists. Jena found that she was more relaxed about the whole expedition, now that the Lieutenant had set down the law. She had been harboring concerns that Felk would try to pull some crazy stunt or attempt to assert himself as the leader of the mission, but that fear had just been crushed under the boots of Security Sector. They might actually be able to pull this off with ease if they simply obeyed procedure.

Residence Wheel One, Level Two

Knight Pelor Guardhand sat astride his steed, Rosstan, glaring at the enemy fortifications before him. His toragi, Larry, was ten meters ahead and crouched down within the dense foliage surrounding the field that encircled Keep Smith. His squire, Korgan Naldo, was just behind and to the right of him, also mounted in the saddle of his horse. The young man's toragi had crept ahead, keeping in cover while watching the main gates of the keep. Behind them were a dozen Security Knights, all of them making preparations for a siege. Their platoon was made up of volunteers to be the spear-tip of the operation, with the hope that they could lure their opponents out from behind their fortified walls. Upon his left wrist was a datapad which displayed images from several Naga drones which flew near the skyscreens, taking pictures of the battlements from above.

Pelor sighed at what the images were showing. There was no sign of any movement from within the keep, whose roof was made to block infrared scanners and disrupt attempts to hack into the internal communication system. Keep Smith was a Security bunker on a grand scale. It was built with combat and even warfare in mind. Now it had been further fortified by the syndicates who openly controlled the castle. The old banners depicting the swords, chains and shield of Security Sector had all been removed. The belowdecks platoons who had explored the possibility of entry from beneath the deck reported a series of blockades, traps and kill-zones protecting Keep Smith from entrance through the maintenance gantries. It seemed that all of the service-ways for the entire region had been altered from their original configuration over the last octade, to keep any intruding force at bay. Pelor refused to believe that such reconstruction was the work of a single syndicate. From what he could see in his datapad, the criminal gangs had worked together to form the perfect place for a last stand against Security. The only thing he questioned was why they would do so in the first place. It was far easier, less involved and expensive to remain mobile. So, what made the syndicates decide to close themselves in like this?

Squire Naldo silently came up beside him. Pelor was most gratified to see that the youngster was able to handle his mount so quietly. It was as he often thought, nothing was a better teacher than adversity. The squire who thought his post was easy became complacent and learned slowly, seeing no need for the instruction. One who faced death became an expert with alarming alacrity. The young man spoke softly, "Milord, the bulkhead platoons are in place. There is no activity there nor any sign of resistance. All official commerce has been rerouted through the regions we currently control."

Pelor gave a nod, "Then we have our prey well in hand."

Squire Naldo replied softly, "Aye, Milord. That we do, but they may yet have enough supplies to last them for harvests, though I see no obvious purpose to being thus captured within Keep Smith. Tis not more comfortable than the brig."

Pelor smiled under his bushy moustache, "Well thought, my good lad. Tis a conundrum that we all face this troubled rotation. I have yet to hear any reasonable explanation for their move to isolate themselves within Keep Smith. It worries at my mind. Have we missed the true chase? Yonder keep be secure enough for a proper siege, yet I feel the prey hath slipped our grasp."

Squire Naldo squinted at the structure, "I would lay my life to say the knaves be interred within, yet my heart doth troubles me. Could this be nothing more than a distraction from their true purpose? A ruse, perchance?"

Pelor scowled, "The foul syndicates horde chips and materials to bribe and influence the crew. They collect luxuries and break regulations for their own comforts and to slake their overproud egos. Here they are trapped within the treasure hold of their ill-gotten riches. They be secure, yet they also be stuck in place like an insect in amber. The logic of it escapes me."

The young squire shrugged, "Perhaps they have changed the rules to suit a new course for their evil ways. What might it portend if chips no longer hold their attention?"

Pelor ground his teeth, "Forsooth, ye may hath cut to the heart of this matter. A dire thought indeed, yet one which we must explore. No parlay hath been held, no challenges to our presence here. Tis strange. Come, good squire. We shall sally forth to gain a measure of our foe."

Knight Pelor kept his greatest fear to himself, that this situation was but a diversion, to keep Security's forces bottled up in one location, but he had no proof of this. Thus far, the syndicates had not responded to any signals. Naga was blocked from the wallscreens within Keep Smith. Not a soul had tried to leave nor enter the fortress for many rotations. They were missing something important. To find out if there were any hornets, one had to knock the nest. He raised his sword above his head and gently thumped his heels on Rosstan's flanks. The large warhorse stepped forth gingerly, gaining more surety when he reached the edge of the clearing. His squire was three paces behind him, with the rest of the platoon venturing out from the woods in formation.

Nothing moved. No sound was heard, not even that of the local birds. The keep's foreboding battlements glared at them darkly. All of the entries and windows were now blocked by meter-thick walls of quartz-ceramic. They rode slowly toward the keep, maintaining their silence, lances held high. Once they were within twenty meters from where the front doors should have been, Pelor called a halt and removed his helmet to shout, "Hail Keep Smith! Come forth, and none shall be harmed! Have ye not the honor to treat with me?"

Silence greeted his words. Knight Pelor tapped his datapad, signaling the other platoons to come out into the field. Over a hundred knights formed a ring about Keep Smith, and there was still no word from within. Just as he was about to call out once more, a blast ruptured the air. A chunk of masonry shot out from the highest wall of the keep, pelting Pelor and his platoon with bits of debris and rock dust. The horses reacted with alarm, but they settled down quickly, while the toragis began to creep even closer to the main wall, sniffing the ground for hidden traps. Pelor noticed a hole near the top of the main tower, still partially obscured by grey smoke.

Shields were raised without the need for orders, their Kendis-steel surfaces gleaming in the light of the skyscreens. In a sudden rush of sound, several objects were fired through the aperture, landing with wet thuds just a few meters in front of the formation of knights. Squire Naldo leapt from his saddle, then ran over to inspect them, before Pelor could chide him for such foolishness. The young man lifted one of the items from the ground before he lost his composure and vomited into the grass. The keep had fired a dozen severed arms at them, all of which were decorated with dark flashtats with the Security Sector seal upon them. It was apparent to Pelor that these were the remains of the crew who had originally been posted at Keep Smith before the syndicates took over the building. Rage boiled up in his breast. His face was hot with anger at the defilement of good knights.

Before he could give new orders to his platoon, the skyscreens went dark, accompanied by a sharp, crackling sound. The whole region had now fallen into the depths of sleep-slice. His datapad went dead. The displays in his helmet went dark. Someone grabbed at his knee, and he almost lashed out to strike whoever laid hands upon him. Squire Naldo's voice halted his blow, "Knight Guardhand! Tis only me!"

Pelor leaned over and shouted, "Get thee to thy steed and fly toward the nearest lit region! Call for reinforcements with haste! Send this message to our Chief – we are now at war with the syndicates!"

Residence Wheel Two, Level Fourteen

William Blaine took a seat upon a long bench within the Makamba Terran Museum, deeply troubled by everything he had seen thus far. While he could never claim that the exhibits were inaccurate, they approached the history of humanity from a particular direction, one he had never encountered before. Two Naga drones were with him, acting as personal tour guides. Lieutenant Darron Lazhand and his platoon were also escorting him, all of them highly suspicious of every shadow, balcony and crew member. Led by Mike, all the toragi were surrounding him, creating a barrier of claws and steel. It wasn't the most ideal way to visit a museum, but William had been given little choice.

He stared glumly at a suit of Rad-Zone Assault Armor, used by the Antarctic Commonwealth to infiltrate areas already bombarded with nuclear weapons. It was now contained within a synth-quartz display case, grey as ash and all hard angles, with multiple hooks for hanging weapons and supplies. The dark visor seemed to glare accusingly back at him, just above a long breathing tube that attached to the backpack. It was ugly, functional, utilitarian and most terrifying. He had seen similar examples before, but not in such pristine condition. William was currently in the Hall of Savagery, which contained an incredible collection of armor, weaponry and military equipment that left little doubt that Terra had been in the hands of power-hungry madmen for far too long. The Luna Space-Ops figure was one of the highlights of the exhibit, matt black and looking more like a weaponized android than anything else. All the harsh angles and camouflage were at odds with the curved, cream-colored walls of the museum itself, as if the curators were demonstrating the stark differences between Ganges culture and that of the Sol system.

At the very beginning, he was prepared for a serious slant on Terran history, especially when the first exhibit, just past the main entrance, was an ancient tapestry depicting knights slaughtering a unicorn. It had set the tone well, giving visitors a chance to shift their mental gears before heading further into the grand halls and chambers that lay beyond the ubiquitous gift shops and a grand cafeteria. Not all of the displays were of death and violence. Paintings, statues, relics from the time of early spaceflight and even poetry were given their due. It seemed that what had once been called the Great Families were a bunch of packrats, hording treasures from a world they had all left behind many octennia ago. The jewelry exhibition hall was a priceless collection of precious artistry that went back to the misty beginnings of the Industrial Age. He had been shocked to find well-written histories for each exhibit, some of which filled in some holes within his own understanding of humanity's early time periods. Scholars from the Solarian Alliance would give up their limbs cheerfully to get a chance to examine it all.

The real problem was how dolefully depressed the museum made him feel. That, and a bucket of guilt over the horrible condition which humanity suffered just to satisfy the narcissistic egos of their leaders within the Terran Conglomerate. Poverty, starvation, oppression and a variety of dogmatically driven hatreds were carefully, if naively, written to explain the divisions which had stripped humanity of reason for most of its bloody history. The historians of Ganges, who worked within the Terran Museum, had no frame of reference for understanding most of the objects they were studying. Their pacifistic culture was at odds with the martial traditions of the ancient nations they pored over with obvious dismay. The dichotomy between the beautiful works of Monet and Mozart with weapons of mass destruction and images of glorified genocide seemed to confuse the crew of Ganges. Terra looked like a world of insanity and chaos.

William didn't necessarily disagree with that point of view, but it was still a bit myopic. Ganges itself was built and sent out amongst the stars by the hands of those so-called savages of old Earth. The AeyAies had evolved from the strife and divisions of Terran technological advancements, most of which had been developed to assure supremacy over rival nations. The Hall of Music had been his favorite thus far, for he had discovered forgotten artists, long lost after the demise of the Terran Conglomerate, yet preserved here, lightspirals away from Sol and appreciated by humans who had never known poverty or war. He had lost himself within the sounds from musicians who had lived between the twentieth through twenty-fifth centuries. Tears had fallen down his cheeks as he realized that such beautiful artistry had been preserved, totally unknown to the rest of humanity.

That was when it had hit him. It was as if a light had blossomed deep in his mind - the idea that Ganges had to be preserved at all costs, no matter what his superiors might wish. William knew that the leaders of the human third of the Solarian Alliance wanted to reintegrate the ship into the larger culture of humanity, but he was now beginning to understand that the cost of this desire was too high. They would simply end up destroying the very thing they wanted to bring back to humanity. There had to be a way to preserve the culture which had developed in Ganges. He had to tread carefully, for the ultimate goal of his superiors was unknown to him. It was a depressing thought.

A Naga Drone swept down to face him, "Is there something troubling you, William Blaine?"

He chuckled darkly, "You might say that. At the same time, I'm feeling quite inspired. I'm elated, depressed, humbled and troubled by what I've seen this rotation. I have to admit, I prefer the artwork and music displays to the martial ones, though the Crucible Chamber was enlightening. I could roam these halls for sowings and not see it all. I was intrigued about the VenMak relays and how they had been built into all the systems of Ganges, just to be used to confound you octuries later. If I were Terran, which I'm not, I would be pleading with you to forgive me. I have to admit, I never knew about VenMak. There's no such company in the Sol System of which I'm aware of. It must have died out when Earth was destroyed. I didn't get a chance to study the information about the logo, though I did see some documentation on the subject at the display holding them. Something about the name being a combination of two families?"

The drone bobbed in the air, "That is correct. The two family names were Makdreah, whose bloodline was part of the Family Project, which evolved into the

Great Families after the Awakening. The other name does not appear in the ship's manifest, Venanzi."

William sat up abruptly, making Mike glare at him, "Wait! Did you just say 'Venanzi'? That sounds familiar to me! Give me a moment. I'll check my internal data core."

Images and words flashed through his mind, as William accessed his cranial computer. When he finally found what he was looking for, he gasped aloud, jumping to his feet, startling his guardians. The Security team scrambled to his side, but he waved them away, "Naga! I can't believe this is happening! I do know that name! When I visited what you call Planet Seventeen, I found a society ruled by a monarchal government, all of whose leaders are named Venanzi. Their AeyAie was severely damaged during the long flight from Sol. They claimed it was an accident, caused by some kind of trouble with the ship's crew. It was placed within the socket on the surface, made for it by you, but they just use it for accounting purposes, as its mind is gone. They are a feudal and isolationist society, very hostile toward outsiders, so I didn't stick around. I must go back! I have to report to my superiors! The AeyAie Solidarity must be informed! If the Venanzi family was indeed closely connected to that of Makdreah, they may have succeeded in their plans to take over their colony ship, possibly through similar means."

Naga voice sounded strained, "Why did you leave them? Why didn't you report this to your superiors earlier?"

William shrugged, "My mission was to find Ganges. I only stopped off at the colonies to document them briefly and to search for clues as to where you were heading. I thought the story of that colony was just a tragedy, an accident that could have happened to any ship that travels the void. Most of the ship's crew had perished, along with half the colonists. The survivors rallied around the Venanzi family, who led them to their new world and then guided the establishment of their society. I had never heard of a VenMak relay before coming here. I have to get back to my vessel! I must report!"

Darron Lazhand spoke up, "Hang on! We must inform the Chief of this new development. I am authorized to allow you to retrieve your suit but not to enter your vessel. Besides, you can't go back to that colony now, not while you remain infected by our viruses. Any transmission to Sol must be approved by the General Manager of the Holy Mission, in other words, Naga, in cooperation with the Judiciary Council. There's far too much at risk for us to allow that now, especially since we're still within System Forty-One. That alone has too many variables. I suspect that once we leave, the Chief will back your desire to see justice done, but it may have to wait a sowing or two."

William ground his teeth in frustration, but he knew that to argue any further would be pointless. Ganges moved at its own pace. He appreciated the fact that no one here seemed to be angry with him for wanting to contact Sol. The Security crew around him looked grim, even as they nodded at him. He could see it in their eyes. They agreed that something had to be done, but not right now. The situation at the Venanzi colony had been going on for octuries, at the very least. It could wait a little longer. William just hoped that the landing expedition would be concluded swiftly, and they could leave this system immediately to get his message out to his superiors.

Agro Wheel Two, Level Five

Ensign Rank Four Taron Locktek of Rescue Services banked hard, as he took the curve that led to the refueling bay. His mag-bike was running on molecules at this point, the gauges flashing red in the forward display. The thrusters behind his back whined and coughed, sputtering as the last dregs of fuel were devoured. By the sound alone, he could tell that his ride could make another five hundred meters, more than enough to reach the depot that was now in sight. The machine shuddered under his padded seat, shaking with stress. The magnetic impellers were also in the red, overheating due to strenuous use over the last few rotations. If he could, he'd give the mag-bike a complete overhaul, but there was no time for such luxuries.

The last two sowings had been insanely busy, directly after the Security Games had concluded. Between the rioting, protests and the buildup of activity from the syndicates, he hadn't had a rotation of leave since. Taron had done well in the mag-bike races. His only regret was that he hadn't been given the time to properly celebrate his winnings. He had planned for a couple of rotations of serious partying, all of which he had to cancel. Security had been running on emergency protocols since the games and was about to break a record of heightened alert that had lasted since the Crucible. For a good portion of that time, Taron had no idea as to why his Sector was in such a ruckus. He had figured it was to warm everyone up for a serious push against the syndicates, but after the public broadcast revealing the presence of William Blaine, he began to understand that real trouble was brewing from outside the hull. Taron had recognized the Solarian immediately, for he had seen the man at the racetrack, during a practice session, not knowing who or what he was.

Rumors were spreading all through Security like a stellar flare, causing loud arguments and even some fistfights in the locker rooms. He had learned to not take everything he heard seriously, unless it came from the Chief, but things had spun out of control swiftly. As a member of Rescue Services, he had been called in to help contain all the rioting and to transport the injured to Medical Sector or to Security if the wounded crew were part of his Sector. His toragi, Frank, rose to the challenge with astounding results. The big cat had become a medical carry-bag, gurney puller, novice cart and even triage assistant. Taron had no idea that Frank had it in him to perform so many responsibilities that might make a human crewmember back away with uncertainty. He glanced over at his furry companion, only to find the big brute fast asleep in his sidecar. Typical.

Skidding to a halt just within the opening for the hundred-meter-wide service bay, Taron powered down his thrusters and shut off the impellers just within reach of the cables and fuel canisters lining the spinward wall. Hundreds of other mag-bike riders were there, repairing their rides with haste. Some of the bikes were severely damaged; others just needed fuel. He hopped off his ride, glaring at the steam rising from the magnetic impellers underneath the streamlined body of his mag-bike. If he didn't change out the impellers soon, his machine would end up on the side of a road somewhere, damaged and useless. His squad was preparing for another excursion, this time into Residence Wheel One, to aid a call for reinforcements from the Knights who guarded the nature preserves there. Whenever such a need for aid came up, Rescue Services knew that it was needed at that location.

One of the bay hands ran up to him, her grey-and-maroon jumpsuit smeared with grease and burn marks, "Heya! Need help with your ride?"

Taron looked up and smiled, "Oh, Hell yeah! Check out the impellers. I think some of the units are fried. I'll get the fuel canisters for the thrusters."

She crouched down and inspected the lift magnets, her dark skin reflecting the red lights of her diagnostic tool, "Hey, aren't you Lightspeed Locktek? I saw your run at the games. I've been following your other exploits on the broadcasts, like that ravine leap over at Rat's Ass. Crazy stuff, but totally plasma!"

Taron slung a pair of fuel cannisters for his pod thrusters from their racks, "That's me! Good to meet a fan! You like the races?"

The woman grunted at something from under his bike, then replied, "Well, fuck yeah! That's why I chose this post, crew! You need to replace seven of these impellers. It's amazing you even got here. So, yeah, I also signed up for emergency service. Glad I did that. We've been practicing for sowings now. By the way, my name's Nali Traclon. Ah, shit. Here's your real problem, pal. A burned-out pulse regulator in your primary. Shit. Stay put, stunt-man! I've got the parts at my station. It'll just take a seed-sliver, then I can get to the rest of your mess."

Taron watched her jump up from underneath his ride, barely missing the wide tires and their studded treads. He shook his head, disappointed in himself that he hadn't noticed the regulator giving out. He popped open the side of the thruster fuel panel and grabbed the twin, empty cannisters with a gloved hand. They were hot, even through his armored gauntlet, and he tossed them aside. The fuel port was smoking, so he had to let it cool before placing the fresh cannisters within, to avoid a potentially explosive response to the sudden change in temperature.

Frank had just woken up from his nap, yawning widely, revealing a mouthful of sharp teeth. Taron looked at him, and shook his head, "Lazy brute! Do something useful, and get me a set of rotor calipers."

Frank gave him a disdainful look, but launched himself out of the sidecar and padded off to the service stations that dotted the interior of the service bay. Nali was returning with her toragi, who had a series of slings over her back filled with equipment and parts, "Nice kitty you got, Lightspeed! Mine's named Betty. She's a good girl, very helpful. I've got the regulator and the seven impellers you need. Don't plug in the battery cable yet! You concentrate on your thrusters, Tenacious Taron! Betty and I'll see to the rest!"

Nali and her toragi slipped under his mag-bike, tools clanking and curses flowing. Frank came back, a caliper in his mouth. The big cat stopped briefly to sniff at Betty, who rolled over to return the gesture. Nali shouted from below the bike, "Hey! No kissy-face this rotation! We got work to do! We can catch tail when we're fucking done!"

Taron bit back a laugh at the silly antics between the two toragi and started loading the fresh fuel cannisters into the now cooled sockets. Once he got the hatch closed, he took the caliper from Frank, giving him a scratch behind the ears in thanks. He adjusted the tool for his heavily modified ride, then checked on the rotors. To his relief, they were still in acceptable shape, but they might need servicing in a couple of rotations. His datapad pinged at him. He looked at it and found a message from his Sergeant. The squad was resupplied and getting ready to roll out. He requested an extra seed-sliver to finish his repairs and was granted this with a warning that if he was late, they would move out without him. Something hot was going on in Res One, he was sure of that. He just hoped it wasn't a war zone.

Residence Wheel One, Topsides Bulkhead

Planetary Atmospherics Commander Ghell Vaclan nodded while he paced the length of the hidden chamber that had been cut into the underside of the hull of the topsides bulkhead of Residence Wheel One. Wires and cables snaked their way along the walls, each one heading off to another location. The use of hard lines had become an almost forgotten art within Ganges. This also allowed him to see multiple locations at once, without leaving any signals that could be traced by Security Sector. There were four such bunkers spread throughout Ganges: in Residence Wheels One and Two, the Planetary Sector Wheel, and within Industrial Wheel One. All of them had been made according to Ghell's specifications, with all the crew who had built them now dead from "careless accidents" within their respective posts.

Every one of these secret chambers were alike in size, shape and in their contents. The only way to access one involved a hatch which looked like any other patch of hull plating, unless one knew what to look for. The topsides bulkhead regions had been slowly redesigned to discourage any unauthorized personnel from staying within them for long periods of time, yet they had to remain inhabitable for the service crew who worked within them. The portal to Ghell's private chambers were fitted with manually driven airlocks, with genetic locks and traps for the unwary. Each room was also situated right next to a main heatsink, which was also used to bring his hardline connections to various levels and communications relays. No one noticed a single extra cable within the giant bundles of them that wormed their way throughout the belowdecks. As most of the heatsinks were also attached to the support spokes for the Wheels, he had ample room for expansion, should the need ever arise.

Ghell's chambers were filled with data screens, modified computer stations of antique design, though they had been rebuilt within the last fifteen spirals, and communications units that could directly hack into the broadcast networks used by the crew for their personal entertainment. There was a single bunker that contained his greatest tool to undermine Security Sector. This unit had been placed within the chamber he was currently using. It was a leftover from the Crucible, bought at great cost from a rival syndicate who had managed to stow it away secretly but never bothered to learn how to fix or use it properly. The machine had three large brass levers with polished wooden handles, hardline connectors, an independent power source, data input feeds and had once been the property of Collum Makdreah, who had used it to torture Naga.

The Lord of Crime had no need to cause the AeyAie any distress, other than that caused by his activities. He had no desire to hunt down its friends or to cause Naga any damage. Ghell had the device revamped for a very different purpose – to be many places at once. After being stolen from the collapse of the Royal Cause, tucked away in a cluttered cargo hold by leftover mutineers, then rediscovered by a syndicate boss looking for a new hideout, it now resided in his hands as a grand means to gain real power over the other syndicates, confuse the crew and thwart Security's ability to find him.

None of his underlings knew of the existence of these bunkers nor the old device which had gained a new purpose. Instead, they were each at their assigned position, certain that he was nearby, as was intended. Ghell looked over the displays and nodded to himself. Things were proceeding according to his plans. The screen showing the interior of Keep Smith was bustling with activity. Ghell used a hologram of himself to give orders to his most trusted servants, while he monitored the situation from cameras which had been tucked into the outer battlements of the keep, to note what the Security crew were currently doing. Another screen was watching over his station within the Planetary Wheel, just to make sure no one was looking for him. A dozen displays revealed the action in as many locations, all of which had been tapped into his network with hardlines only. Most of the communications within the ship were wireless, and he left the processors and cables used by Naga alone. He would suffer no connection between his network and the AeyAie.

At the moment, he was looking at William Blaine within the Makamba Terran Museum. Ghell's fists became tight as he watched the Solarian talk excitedly with a Naga drone, as his Security guardians clustered all around him. One of Ghell's best assassins had been captured because of this intruder. In fact, he had canceled his previous orders to eliminate the trespasser from Sol, after seeing what the man could do, even without his gear. It was a painful lesson. One which frightened him deeply. William was just a scout, expendable, yet he had countered his own execution easily. Ghell tried to imagine what real troops from Sol might be like and shuddered with hatred. The Solarian Alliance was the greatest threat Ganges had ever encountered, just from the level of technology their agents sported.

He was determined to do something about the situation, while the Sector Chiefs were either distracted by Planet Forty-One or were too busy playing nice with William Blaine. Security was not the problem, for they were convinced that he had boxed himself inside Keep Smith, which was an insult to his intelligence. They still had no idea that he was the one calling the shots amongst the other syndicates, for even Brace Lazhand didn't really understand just how terrified the other crime bosses were of his abilities. Ghell was quite disappointed that the undercover police officer hadn't taken him up on his offer, but that was Brace's loss. Once the Solarian fleet arrived, they would all find out how right he was to distrust scout Blaine.

For now, he had a different duty to perform. Ghell had checked in on every area in which he had eyes and ears. Thus far, everyone was playing their roles to perfection, including his adversaries. Now it was time to begin the next phase of his plan, one which involved the general crew. He checked the image and video files that he wanted to present, finding everything ready for the most important broadcast ever made in Ganges. Ghell adjusted his camo-suit so that it would cycle through the face and voice changes a little more slowly, to not distract or confuse the audience too much. He prepared the camera and microphone, both were relics from the Age of Unity, then pulled the first lever of the brassy machine down with a loud clack. Looking at the central display in front of him, he saw himself, which meant he was ready to go live. He grabbed the wooden handle of the second lever and shoved it home, thus connecting to several broadcast feeds at once, the hardline connection now superseding the wireless one, as he'd designed.

Ghell raised a hand at the camera, "This is a special broadcast to the crew! We are all in the same moment of peril together, so we must find a unified voice to challenge what is happening within our ship. There are many officers within every Sector who would like to silence me, to keep you all uninformed as to the state of Ganges and the danger we all face. The Judiciary Council has ceded control of our culture to an unknown force, welcoming their supposed representative as a guest with special status. This cannot stand! This is not the course to take if we wish to remain who and what we are!"

He revealed the images of William Blaine in the museum, surrounded by his Security platoon, "Look for yourselves at how our very courageous protectors squander their resources, giving this harbinger of destruction tours of our ship, all the while ignoring the real and terrible threat he represents. This Solarian spy can count on his friends within Security to back his plans for our future, with little regard for our lives and culture! This is wrong! William Blaine has assaulted crew, caused chaos and disruption throughout the ship, and has been granted the right to retrieve the rest of his technological gadgets to enforce his wishes!"

Ghell paused to show some clips he had retrieved from other broadcasts, showing the attack on the beach at Agro Wheel Four, "Look upon the face of our new masters, who will conquer Ganges without fearing a fight! I will not sit idly by while Security serves his interests at our expense! I shall be openly honest with you, unlike our heroes who play at being defenders of the crew. I am the leader of a small cartel of illicit merchants, most of whom are simply sick of the regulations which benefit a few and stymie the grand majority of crew who come to us for services they cannot find elsewhere in Ganges. I am a criminal, breaking the rules of the Sectors, while providing for those who come to me with their problems. According to the Judiciary Council, I am only fit for re-education or being sentenced as being 'Not Crew'. Is this the system you all want?"

Ghell revealed a video feed from the violence on the field in front of Keep Smith, "This is how they respond to those who disagree with regulations that keep us under their boots! Oppression! Bloodshed! They have entrapped dozens of crew, without first determining any form of wrongdoing! Meanwhile, they galivant about with the real enemy to our way of life! Dallying with a true savage from Sol itself! What if we don't want to become part of the Solarian Alliance? Will we have any choice? Do we, the general crew, have any say at all in what happens to our beloved vessel? Not if Security Sector gets its way! There is much we can do to protect our culture, our novices, but only if the Judiciary Council allows us to defend ourselves. I say that it is high time we reviewed the power wielded by the Sectors, which has grown out of proportion through ruling over us through fear of the warriors who do their dirty work for them! We must band together to face this crisis! Do not riot! Don't give them a reason to imprison you in the brig. Face them down peacefully but with a firmness of purpose such that they will have no choice but to bow to the needs of our ship!"

Ghell leaned forward, "I hide my identity for my own protection, due to the choices I have made for my own life. Don't let them do this to you. The Holy Mission must be allowed to flourish, without the influence of Sol and the vile savages which rule the trillions who suffer there. We must be free to be who and what we are! I now return you to your broadcast, with a promise that I will never give in to our oppressors and that you will hear from me again soon."

CHAPTER SIXTEEN

Ice Rotation - Spin Sowing - Mission Harvest - Spiral 5620

"No one wants to talk about the obvious; there can be another purpose to our lives than the Holy Mission. They call this the Age of Redemption, but I see it in a different light. This is really the Age of Senseless Guilt. Everyone knows that the only reason Security Sector exists is because of the Crucible. The sole purpose behind the changes to the Prime Charter is to support a myopic vision of what it means to be born in Ganges. What have we received for our labors? We don't even know that there are any colonists at all! Can someone please tell me why a ship this size can only have one choice? Can't we at least multitask?"
Vilado Kandari, Pilot Rank Three, Harbor Sector, personal log, V38

Near-Ganges Space

Security Fleet Lieutenant Tarn Vekkor led Nondo Squadron from within his fighter-pod, Raptor One-Alpha, keeping their reconnaissance formation tight, just a thousand kilometers ahead of the ice cap of Ganges. Planet Forty-One was on his starboard side, a pale, creamy orb, crisscrossed with shadowy lines. Tarn shook his head at the sight. It was incredible that anything could still be seen at their current distance from the dead world, let alone structures that had been built by a sentient species. Ganges had just entered high orbital space and was still swinging in closer to the planet, to achieve a gravity-assist to help them regain the speed they had shed after entering the system. This maneuver would take three rotations in total, which was incredibly fast, when one considered the immensity of a world's gravity well.

His toragi, Pete, was right behind him in the cockpit, keeping a close eye on the sensors for any stray debris, but nothing had shown up thus far, which was very unusual. Tarn didn't like it. The absence of even small particles could be an indication that something catastrophic had occurred in this system. As a result of his suspicions, he had Raptor Alpha-Two watching the local star for signs of instability. He wondered if a nova had wiped out the original inhabitants of this system, though he did concede that such an event might have occurred after they had gone extinct. There were too many mysteries for his liking, so Tarn was glad that most of the fleet had launched to protect Ganges from unforeseen events.

While it was true that there were memorials within Ganges, to honor those who had served the ship with great distinction, there were no tombs or burial grounds aboard. Out of curiosity, Tarn had done some research on the subject of ruins with grand sepulchers and crypts. What he discovered had not reassured him in the least. Such places on Terra and even Mars had frequently contained traps, to keep grave robbers away from buried treasures or to dissuade any trespassers from entering the burial sites of famous leaders. It all seemed incredibly barbaric and wasteful to his mind. Within Ganges, all of the dead were recycled, their personal effects divided amongst their surviving relatives and friends, not locked up to rot, taking up valuable space and resources. He was content to know that Naga would remember him, if no one else, once he met with his demise.

His fighter-pod was running smoothly. The soft sound of the main thrusters could barely be heard from the stern. His lead service tech, Jero Coreline, had done an incredible job of keeping Raptor-One in perfect condition, despite the frequent flights over the past harvest. Tarn had also heard that Jero was being considered for promotion, which he gladly seconded on the official record. The young man's service to the ship should be rewarded, so long as he remained in charge of the team of docking bay crew that handled Nondo Squad. Tarn knew that wanting to keep Jero around was a bit selfish, but he appreciated the devotion to efficiency that Jero clung to and how his fighter-pod benefitted from the man's talents. He doubted that the rise in rank would cause Jero to be reassigned, but one never knew what the Suits would decide.

Tarn checked on his main sensor display, noting the position of the rest of the deployed vessels which were guarding Ganges. The battlecruiser Malati was just five hundred kilometers behind his fighter-pod squadron, bristling with large-bore masers, Spin-Drive turrets and rail guns, which shot polished asteroid ingots at near-relativistic velocities. It was the flagship for the Security Fleet. Captain Loni Voidloc led the massive vessel with an iron hand, along with the Fleet Commander, Vina Harrolon, who used the ship as her control station. Only the best were in the forefront of this mission, to ensure efficiency. Should danger approach, the Malati could send waves of fighters, similar to his own but with a shorter range, to aid his squadron to defend Ganges.

He scoffed at those who were so terrified by the possibility that the Solarian Alliance might arrive at any time to harass them. What most crew didn't know was the classified technology Security had hidden in its waist sash for such occurrences. As the lead fighter pilot for all of Ganges, Tarn was aware of the Kendis Vault, buried under a mountain within Agro Wheel Three. His own vessel had a few nasty surprises from the strange laboratories found there. If the Solarians thought Ganges was a soft target, they were horribly mistaken, no matter what types of technology they utilized. Some of the fleet's destroyers, based on the old ice-cutter designs, had prows that were fitted with expendable blades of Kendis steel, twenty meters long, which could also be electrified and used for ramming other spacecraft. Behind these were Spin-Drive cannon clusters, which would be used to burn holes in any kind of hull.

The full might of Security Sector had never been used, so it was no wonder that the crew got skittish. Even the terrible weapons used during the Crucible were weak things compared to what was now available to defend the ship. He had seen first-hand what the modern weaponry of his Sector could do, during classified training missions that targeted asteroids, shattering them in pollen-slivers, then cutting up the debris to scrap. As the material sciences flourished since the time of Launch, the crew of Ganges had become experts at improving hull design, testing new alloys and configurations with the latest weapons in their arsenal.

His comms interrupted his thoughts, "This is Fleet Command to all Security vessels, adjust course by z-minus point one, y-plus point zero two, x-plus point zero two. Confirm."

Tarn swiftly snapped on his communications bead and briskly replied, "This is Nondo Squadron. Primed, Fleet Control. Commencing the second-phase course trajectory now."

He flashed the information to his crew, all of whom responded with perfect coordination. The ordered shift was a slight one, but the minor adjustments would now continue until they reached egress point Alpha, upon which the entire fleet would return to the Security docking bays. Instead of finding a stable orbit, they were going to spiral inward toward Planet Forty-One, gaining speed until they reached escape velocity. While his own timing was tight as a result of the unusual circumstances, he knew that it was far worse for the landing party who was now preparing for launch. If anything went wrong, either during their descent or on the surface, it could jeopardize their ability to return to Ganges, and they would become trapped within System Forty-One forever.

Tarn just hoped that the team of scientists heading to the surface were well coordinated and serious about their timetable. This whole venture could be a terrible waste of resources if they got themselves trapped, not to mention a waste of talented lives. To his mind, Ganges always came first and foremost. He saw the mission to the surface as a potential loss of resources. Deep down, he wondered if it was worth it, but exploration was always risky. He wished them all luck and that they would return with knowledge that would prove to be useful for Ganges. In the meantime, he had a squadron to lead.

Command Hub, Level Ten

Executive Officer Wasp Tornpage paced the command platform at the very heart of the Bridge. Her marshmallow gun was holstered in her waist sash, though she kept a hand upon the grip, tapping it with her fingers as a silent threat to anyone who decided that this was a rotation for goofing off. Captain Perrin Fieldscan was still ensconced in his chair, looking like a temple idol seated upon a throne of platinum and gold. The Chief-of-the-Deck was hurling abuse at a station officer who arrived late to their shift. He was doing a good job of it, so Wasp didn't bother to chime in. She kept her eyes upon the tiers of control stations, switching every few pollen-slivers with the countdown display which showed the time being eaten away until the landing party was launched and also denoting when Ganges reached escape velocity.

The Bridge Security Commander had his crew well in hand. As there was no apparent threat, it did seem odd to her that he had his platoon running drills. Then again, she had seen the broadcast by the shifting syndicate boss, who had personally taken it upon themselves to declare war upon the entire Solarian Alliance on behalf of Ganges. Wasp was torn between being amused by their antics and outraged when she recognized the massive device they were using to interrupt the ship's broadcast channels. No one knew who this person really was, what they looked like or even if they had a real duty post. She was certain that the community of Rat's Ass would be scandalized, which might make things interesting. There was an old saying amongst the Strifers that no one should never stick their hands into a rat's nest. Being bitten would be the least of your worries. Whoever this mysterious demagogue was, they had just shoved both of their fists where they didn't belong, and her people would make sure they paid for the insult of using an implement of AeyAie torture which the Strifers had been forced to service long ago, in the name of selfishness.

Wasp knew all about the fighting within the nature preserves of Residence Wheel One. Security had sent reinforcements there last rotation, and it looked like they were getting ready to commence a new offensive against Keep Smith. This time, Security was sending a squadron of heavy dirigibles to the scene of carnage, along with warplanes to act as an escort. Wasp didn't know what Chief Jira Mantabe was planning, but it looked like something out of a sleepscare. The large, floating aircraft had not been used for octennia, save for missions of surveillance. As warcraft, they could drop bombs, teams of specialists, gas cannisters, or just blast the target with their main cannons, which were slung under the heavily-plated gondolas.

Wasp didn't trust any of the mysterious criminal's supposed altruism, but there were many crewmembers who might, as it could appeal to their own frustrations and fears. She and her mate, Smirk Bootknot, had discussed the odd broadcast last dark-slice and came to the conclusion that if the Solarian Alliance ever did show up, it wouldn't change anything for the Strifers. In fact, it might give her people a new target to verbally abuse. That could be fun. The red-robes were already frothing at the mouth, screaming their rabid hatred for those who spread the plague of humanity for their own hidden agendas. If any kind of cultural exchange was to be had between Ganges and the Solarians, she hoped that the Strifers would lead the way with open skepticism and scorn.

None of that had anything to do with her duties this rotation. Smirk had been warned that Wasp would be camping out on the Bridge with Captain Fieldscan for the next couple of rotations, until Ganges was ready to exit the system. She had resigned herself to showing her discontent by harassing the tourists who visited Rat's Ass in Wasp's honor. Once the ship was finally clear of this crazy system, they both resolved to begin thinking about raising some novices together. Both of them had already registered with Medical and submitted genetic samples for posterity. This could be used to infuse lab-grown sperm to carry their RNA to each other's respective eggs. Their biggest decision was whether or not they would both become pregnant together or one at a time. Either way had its own perks and benefits, including how much they might annoy their neighbors.

Wasp suddenly caught an officer yawning, while leaning back in their chair at their designated station. She then pulled the marshmallow gun from its holster with practiced speed, hitting the woman in the chin with a puff of powdered sugar. Wasp watched while the officer fell back, sputtering in dismay and flailing her arms about. Captain Fieldscan applauded behind her, while the crew representative choked on her coffee next to him. Wasp loved her job. She was determined to spread her joy throughout the crew.

Prowling back to her seat on the command platform, she gave a bow to the Captain, who lifted one eyebrow at her, "Your aim is improving, my good Executive. I forgot to ask you earlier if you had prepared for a long shift. Do you have everything you need?"

Wasp gave him a bright smile as she saluted, thumping her fist to her chest, "Oh, yes, Big Cheese! My gear's been stashed behind my chair. Let's see, blanket, snacks, an extra uniform, the jelly gun, more marshmallows, the Strifer Manifesto, a really awful detective novel, my old electro-baton, some fresh mesca-pops, smoked cheese, my favorite green hat. Yeah, I'm all set."

Captain Fieldscan nodded his appreciation for her extra preparedness with a serious expression upon his face, "Very good, Executive Tornpage. My family has provided me with a picnic basket and the usual amenities for a long stay at the helm."

Wasp turned to the crew representative, "How about you, Zilla? Bring all the comforts of home with you? Officer scalps in order?"

Representative Tav rolled her eyes at the question, "Really! Do I look like a savage to you? Do me a favor, don't answer that. I keep the scalps in a display case at home. I only take them out for elections. To answer your query, I am well prepared for this. While I'm not a Command officer, which means I am permitted to leave the Bridge at any time, it would be a true dereliction of my duty to the crew I represent to leave here until Ganges is safely away from this morbid planet. The sooner, the better. While I don't agree with the necessity for a landing upon Planet Forty-One, I do understand why we're doing it."

Wasp tipped her head to one side, "I'm glad to hear it! It'll be good for Stellar Sector to have some new toys to play with. It might keep them off our backs for an octade or two. Oh, that reminds me, Captain. I just received their course data for the next system we'll be heading toward. Hopefully, this one will be a better candidate for the Holy Mission. Not that I'm a big fan of our purpose for humanity's spread, but it could prevent a lot of moping and teeth gnashing. It's only twelve lightspirals away, give or take a few hundred thousand kilometers. That makes it a shorter trip than the last one."

Captain Fieldscan gave her a sad smile, "Still too long of a voyage for me to preside over the terraforming, I'm afraid. Such a pity."

Wasp slumped down next to him, "Hey, now! Don't get all maudlin on me, Big Cheese. Whatever else happens, this system will be historic. The very first time Ganges has found evidence of a sentient species other than humanity. Never mind what the Solarian has to say about aliens, sir. Even his precious Alliance will take notice of what goes on in this corner of the galaxy. I heard the idiot wanted to sign up for the landing! He's all aquiver over it!"

The Captain shook his head, "It's not posterity I'm concerned about, Wasp. Crew morale is low right now. Internal squabbles are erupting throughout the ship. Criminals are taking advantage of the crew's fears. I do hate presiding over a chaotic mess. I just wish more people had your level of enthusiasm."

Wasp couldn't disagree with his assessment of their current situation. She also appreciated his kind words. Her enthusiasm for her post ran very deep. She just hoped that whatever the scientists in the landing party found on Planet Forty-One wouldn't dampen her spirits.

Planetary Sector Wheel, Level Thirty-Four

Planetary Atmospherics Director Dalen Gupta walked quietly into the outer reception chamber of his Commander's office. The only person there was one of the most recently hired administrative assistants, a young man named Brilio Favlink, who seemed confused by his own duties. Dalen had just come from a meeting hosted by

Planetary Chief Sedders, who had been quite insistent that all of his Commanders be present for the upcoming landing on Planet Forty-One. Dalen had been ordered to go to the conference to represent the Atmospherics Department by his superior, Commander Ghell Vaclan, a few rotations ago. The reason for the substitution had never been given nor had he been assigned any other duties than being present at the meeting. It was beyond strange to Dalen's mind, and the Chief of his Sector had been outraged that one of his Commanders had refused a direct order to attend. It was common knowledge that whenever Chief Sedders got angry, everyone suffered his wrath. When Naga was asked to supply a location for Director Vaclan, the AeyAie announced that Ghell was in his office. Dalen had been ordered to bring the errant Commander to the meeting without delay.

The situation was terribly embarrassing for his department, especially since a member of their team was part of the landing party. Dalen was beginning to feel uncomfortable with Director Vaclan's strange behavior lately, including hosting the man's family with a growing frequency that was making things difficult for his own mates and children. In all honesty, these increasing impositions were wearing on his usually cheerful demeanor, and Dalen was getting quite sick of having to answer everyone's questions with "I don't know". Now that he had the full backing of Chief Sedders, it was time to solve the mysterious business that was keeping Ghell from his duties as a Commander. At this juncture, there was no way for Dalen's superior officer to avoid his responsibilities. If there was something personal getting in the way, he would do his best to encourage Ghell to seek professional help, but right now the man had to report to his Chief and answer for his dereliction of duty.

Ensign Brilio Favlink stepped in front of Dalen and said, "I'm sorry, sir. I really don't understand what it is you need. Commander Vaclan told the office staff that he wasn't to be disturbed for any reason."

Dalen rolled his eyes and tried again, this time looming over the young man with an aggressiveness that surprised even himself, "Chief Sedders demands that our Commander accompany me to a required meeting. That means right now. If you don't open the door to Ghell's office, I will do it for you."

Ensign Favlink blinked up at him in surprise, "But... but the Commander needs his privacy. I'll get reprimanded if I disturb him at this sensitive time."

Dalen took a firm step forward, forcing the Ensign back a pace, "I don't care what he needs. This is a direct order from the Chief! I am empowered to enforce that order! If you don't comply, I will see to it that you are reassigned, perhaps to the bulk composting stations of Level Four. Is that clear enough for you? You and I have no choice whatsoever."

Ensign Favlink backed away, still blocking the office door, "I'm sorry, sir. I... I made a promise to keep all interruptions away from the Commander."

Dalen placed a meaty hand upon the Ensign's right shoulder, "Imagine how much more inconvenienced he might be if I had to call in Security Sector, to help me find my missing Commander, who may have been abducted or is in need of medical attention. Imagine the chaos as several muscular Police crew and their giant, fanged cats have to tear this chamber apart so that our Chief may know that he is safe and sound. Imagine the embarrassment to our entire department when our Commander is publicly humiliated because he can't follow orders from his Chief. Let me in there and none of that has to happen."

The Ensign gaped up at him, his eyes wide with distress. Dalen took another step, instinctively shifting his stance to make a more dramatic effect. Spirals of dance practice can lead to effective non-verbal communication. The young man dropped his gaze and stepped out of the way. Dalen smiled as he pirouetted to the door, "Thank you, Ensign. Fear not! I shall make sure that you are held blameless for what happens next."

Dalen turned to face the office door, then tried the handle. It didn't budge when he turned it. He looked over at the nearest wallscreen, "Naga, my dear love, will you please unlock this portal? Chief Sedders is probably getting impatient."

The AeyAie's face appeared on the wall, "According to my sensors, the door is already unlocked, Director Dalen Gupta. I am growing concerned over this matter."

Dalen nodded to himself, "Very well. As a Director of Planetary Sector, I hereby declare this to be an emergency situation, in accordance with regulations."

Before he could reconsider what he was about to do, Dalen hurled his bulk at the door, leading with his left shoulder. Something cracked on the other side of the portal, along with a flash of deep pain running down his arm. He winced a bit, then crashed into the door once again. This time, it slammed wide open. Dalen fell to the floor, banging his head upon the side of Ghell's grand desk. He staggered to his feet, rubbing at his throbbing temple, and leaned on the edge of the thick piece of furniture, "Commander Vaclan, Chief Sedders demands that you be present at…"

Dalen stopped speaking, as there was no one there to hear his words. The office was unoccupied. He glanced about quickly, but there was no sign of Ghell. The displays on the desk were all active, showing a series of reports on moving ventilation cannisters back to the supply depot in Distribution Wheel Two. A datapad was resting on the surface, quietly playing music.

Dalen turned about to face the wallscreen on the spinward side of the office, "Naga! I thought you said Commander Vaclan was here, working in his office!"

The AeyAie's virtual face appeared, but it stuttered and lagged, "Th-that is is is cor-correct, Dir-Director-tor Gupta. I-I still see him him there, but not not not you."

A cold chill ran down Dalen's back. Something was interfering with Naga's presence. Ghell was missing from his post, had been extra secretive of late, dumped his family into Dalen's lap and was now a missing person. The urge to go through his Commander's files was strong, but he knew what he had to do next. Turning smartly about, Dalen walked back into the reception chamber and addressed the wallscreen, ignoring the Ensign who was now cowering in a corner, "Naga! Please respond!"

The AeyAie revealed its face, which looked angry, "Something is blocking me within Commander Ghell Vaclan's office."

Dalen sighed as he nodded, "Yes. He's also not in there. I need to report a missing person to Security Sector immediately, with an attached notice to Planetary Chief Sedders, please. Something about this situation is off-course, Naga, and we have to get to the bottom of it!"

Near-Ganges Space

Security Sector Lieutenant Urukumu felt the gee-forces crush him, as Sci-One launched itself from Harbor One into the cold void of space. His toragi, Victor, was seated next to him, strapped into a harness designed for the big cat. The deck vibrated under his feet, as a dull rumble came from the stern. Urukumu's body sank further into the deep padding of his command chair on the bridge of Sci-One, directly behind captain Hallah Shallon. As the mission leader, it was his duty to observe every aspect of what they were doing, a feat never attempted by the Ganges crew before. The bridge personnel called out fresh sensor readings, the engine output, navigation coordinates and the status of internal systems. The actual launching of Sci-One was done with magnetics, once the vessel had been freed from its restraints. The main engines had been warmed-up, which had been quieter than he had expected, then kicked himself for forgetting that the ship had been moored in total vacuum. They had approached the launch corridor, which had looked too small for the science vessel, then the magnetic rails along the sides of the bay's exit corridor grabbed the hull, before flinging Sci-One out of Ganges at a hundred kilometers per pollen-sliver. Once they reached a distance of five hundred kilometers from Ganges, the main engines had been pushed to full thrust, exponentially increasing their speed over the next seed-sliver.

Just as Urukumu was beginning to feel that he couldn't take much more velocity-driven pressure, the mains had been brought back to cycling-mode, and he floated in place with a stomach-churning abruptness. The entire bridge crew seemed to relax immediately, bumping wrists together as a Harbor Sector tradition. He had been in space many times before, but the speed of their launch had left his organs back in Ganges. He looked over at Victor, who turned to face him, while floating gently within his harness, and then gave a low, throaty yowl. Urukumu nodded his agreement to his guardian toragi, who blinked at him. Captain Shallon continued to give commands, demanding more status updates from several systems. The timing of this mission was painfully tight, necessitating the overly severe launch from Harbor One.

As Urukumu got himself untangled from his straps, he thought about his private talk with the Solarian, William Blaine. He had caught up with him after his visit to Sci-One and asked him some pointed questions. It seems that the Solarians had never discovered ruins of an ancient civilization nor had the enigmatic Boktahl. They had found some interesting systems in which it was speculated that it was possible that someone had been there before, but there was no solid proof. That made this mission a first for all of humanity, though he suspected that it wouldn't be the last. The Solarian Alliance was expanding, now that they had the Wend Drive, so it was only a matter of time before a similar situation occurred. William had openly worried about the lack of life in the galaxy, despite a plethora of suitable planets. The Solarian had wondered if there was a reason for that which had little to do with probability.

The Lieutenant finally got himself unhooked from his chair and floated over to Victor, unlatching the harness that had kept the toragi in place. The big cat made a plaintive sound, as if in a hurry to get free. Urukumu didn't blame his partner. As a rule, the toragi loved zero-gee, which was unusual in comparison with the other large feline species. Their space vessel antics were legendary. They had a habit of using their claws to pull themselves along the corridors at speed, using the ropes that were attached to the walls. Their acrobatics were startling, even frightening at times, but their enthusiasm was also charming. He wondered how much of their response to zero gravity was genetically bred into them, but that was an unsettled question, for there was much in their DNA that puzzled the scientists studying them.

Victor pushed off the deck, the moment the harness came off, and clung to the ropes on the ceiling of the bridge, roaring his relief at being fully released. Captain Shallon glanced back at the toragi, then gave Urukumu a broad smile. He nodded back to her, then let Hallah get back to her duties. He had to get to the crew quarters to check on the scientific team and his squad, to see if anyone needed assistance. Urukumu predicted that vomit-bags were a major priority right now. There were three members of the team who had never been in a small space vessel before. His own Security crew had been fully trained to handle such environments with ease, but this wasn't necessarily true for the crew of other Sectors.

He opened the thick hatch that led to the main corridor of this level within Sci-One, then slowly and carefully launched himself through the aperture. His toragi flashed over his head, flying down the corridor, corkscrewing past one of the other toragis. Sergeant Miri Rallah floated toward him from one of the access tubes that led to the other levels of the ship. She saluted him crisply, "Good launch, Lieutenant!

I wanted to check on you for any emergency orders before checking the RTV in cargo hold Alpha."

Urukumu saluted back, keeping his face neutral while noticing the two toragi playing together like a pair of cubs, "Good timing, Sergeant. I wanted to check on the passengers before making any decisions on what to do next. The Harbor crew seem to have everything in hand. No problems or issues were reported to the bridge. I want the rest of our squad on the crew quarters level, just in case any of the scientists need our assistance. Please do check up on the RTV, then report back to me when you're done with your inspection."

Sergeant Rallah grinned, "Yessir! Right away, sir! Thank you for not putting me on bucket duty. I'll be with you in a paring-sliver, sir."

He watched the Sergeant float back the way she had come, yelling at her toragi to stop her nonsense and follow her down to the cargo level. Victor stayed where he was, studiously ignoring Miri while clinging to a rope with one of his back claws. Urukumu shook his head. The cats almost looked like they had evolved in space, taking to its momentum-driven mechanics naturally. He felt that humanity could learn a thing or two about dealing with zero-gee from the toragi. He looked at Victor, whose fur was puffed up from freefall. It was tempting to take an image of the big cat as part of the mission log. The novices and students of Ganges always loved such things, but there was too much to do at the moment. Later on, once everyone was settled down, there might be time for some public relations.

Urukumu gently floated over to his toragi, "Come on, my friend. We have some scientists to clean up. Ruffled feathers to soothe. You'll get to play afterward, I promise. It'll take the rest of the rotation to get to where we're going. Let's go, Victor."

The toragi gave a half-hearted yowl, then detached himself from the ropes, drifting toward Urukumu at a leisurely pace. The Lieutenant wished that the scientific team was as easy to manage. They swept over to the access tube, then dropped down with a gentle push. Already, Urukumu could hear the complaints echoing from below. At least securing the science teams would prevent everyone from sitting around and waiting for landing. If he played his cards right, they would all be too busy to notice when the time came to prepare for atmospheric entry.

Agro Wheel Three, Security Level One

Brace Lazhand stood at attention in his cell, waiting for Commander Slither Brokengear to arrive. Stale sweat was collecting in his prisoner's jumpsuit, making him feel sticky. He had been working out within his room, trying to get himself back into shape, now that he was free from the drugs he had abused. The longing was still there, a reminder that what he had done to himself could never be fully reversed. In some ways, re-education was his only means of escape from the urge to pump his body full of the noxious stuff. That realization had greatly calmed his nerves about his impending fate, which had been put on hold once again. Most prisoners saw it as a kind of death sentence, but he now looked at it as the way to break free from his poor choices. Not that he would remember any of it, but it was a small mercy to his troubled mind.

His stomach growled as he waited. Brace also saw this as a good thing. His appetite was back with a vengeance. Last rotation, he had downed three meat pies, which were a favorite meal for him. Naga told him that Medical was now allowing him more variety in his food, since the shakes had fully abated. As there was no dispenser within his private cell, all of his meals were hand delivered by Security crew. He kept a wary eye on them, just in case one of them was not who they seemed. The threats he had received from the "Lord of Crime" had not faded from his memory. To permit any complacency was akin to suicide. He briefly touched the chest-port under his left collarbone. Regular blood samples had become part of his rotational routine, another demand from Medical Sector. Fortunately, the collection process was neither painful nor difficult, as the chest-port's design allowed for easy transfusions, extractions, the intravenous input of liquid medicines, and defibrillation. Every crewmember had one implanted, once they finished Basic Crew Training.

The more that he prepared for his inevitable fate, the more at peace he had become. This was precious to his damaged sense of self. He let go of the idea that he needed to keep hold of himself, for he would soon be irrevocably changed. Brace spoke about this feeling to Naga, who had become quite animated about the subject, stating that he was beginning to experience a state called "Bliss", according to the AeyAie Sutra of enlightenment. What followed was a philosophical conversation, along with recommendations concerning meditative practices that might ease his remaining concerns. Brace wondered if his epiphany might transfer to his new life, after re-education. Even Naga didn't know if this was possible, but instead told him to focus on now, seeing the future as a distraction. He did his best, but it still didn't fully help him to remain calm while he waited for his interrogator to arrive.

Brace understood why he was facing a rewriting of his personality and memories. In the entertainment broadcasts, judgements such as his and being "Not Crew" were heavily featured, even though they were a rarity in the justice system of Ganges. Had he not confessed to his crimes, he would have been treated as innocent until proven guilty, though restrictive tabs would have been kept on his activities until a full hearing could sort out the issue. In all reality, most criminal sentences involved community service, a loss of rank commiserate with the crime, or prolonged time in a more populated brig in which specially designed training and therapeutic sessions were used to correct any behavior that was judged as being destructive, or closely monitored, long-term brig time under the guidance of a Security Sensei. The fact that he had knowingly betrayed his Sector, damaged the lives of several crew, used false pretenses to commit additional crimes and had been under the employ of a crime syndicate was a combination that ensured a much more punitive sentence would be applied to his case, and he agreed.

The door to his cell opened before him, and a waft of bitter, grey smoke preceded the entrance of Commander Slither Brokengear. The Strifer interrogator walked in swiftly, "I was told that you had something more to say to me, Brace. You're making a bad habit of interrupting my other clients. I'm willing to tell you that Chief Mantabe was informed about your suspicions concerning the 'Lard of Crumbs' and has taken it into advisement. What the fuck else do you want?"

Brace remained standing at attention, "This prisoner hereby requests that his interrogator permits further speculation concerning the intentions of his former employer."

Slither broke into a crooked grin from under his black rat mask, "Such a formal request! In less than a sowing, you'll have your sentence confirmed. Why not take the time to relax a bit? I've heard that you've been taking the path of Worm, meditating and debating with Naga. Be happy with that. Don't bother to worry over us! We've got things under control. Your old employer is about to have his ugly ass handed to him, detached from the rest of his body."

Brace shook his head, "I don't think so, sir. The current strike against the syndicates will miss their target. I've had more time to think about this than anyone else. I've been remembering some details that my drug-induced brain didn't bother to process. I don't want to talk about motivations. We did that last time we spoke, and I still stand behind my supposition, sir."

Slither tapped some ash from his smoldering cigar, "Vermin's balls, Brace! This isn't an inspection parade! Have a fucking seat and talk, okay? I don't need a damned automaton chattering like a shit-sucking recruit. Speak your mind and stop wasting my time!"

Brace sighed but remained standing, "Every time I met the Lord of Crime, it was in a different location, with a handful of his most trusted crew. I can tell you now, most of them stank like the bilge. One liked to wear a floral perfume to our meetings, but not my employer. He, or she, didn't smell like anything at all. Not ever."

Slither shrugged, taking another drag from his dark-leafed cigar, "So they liked to bathe frequently. Big deal. Not much of a clue, Brace. Maybe the Loaf of Slime never farted or the camo-suit they use blocks scent."

Brace shook his head, "I don't think so, sir. I now believe that he was using hologram emitters. Even though the individual places changed, they were all in the same four Wheels: Residence One, Residence Two, Planetary and Industrial One.

That's it. Never in any other Wheel. Why is that? I think he's limited to those because he's using a hardline connection to keep tabs on his syndicate. That means he may have bunkers in those Wheels which utilize the belowdecks or bulkheads to send his depiction to terrorize those who work for him. Before becoming famous amongst the other syndicates, they used to call him 'The Ghost'. I saw the damned broadcast he sent. I noticed the fucking old device he was using. It's all levers and gears. Ancient, untraceable technology. Why use that stuff? Because hardlines are difficult to locate."

Slither glared at him, "Damn you. I was really looking forward to my next appointment. What you're suggesting would require an inter-Sector team to study the problem, involving multiple experts from several departments from each participating Sector. The more crew involved, the more likely there will be leaks of information and potential spies from the syndicates. I will be letting the Chief know about this thought-experiment. What I can't do is tell you how quickly we can act on it. If you're right, we can't tip our hand, and we are in the middle of hostilities. Tell you what, Brace, I'll get some rats I know to look into any oddities within the belowdecks. Your old boss really pissed on my people. The Strifers would love a chance to mangle his position. I still don't fully trust you, so I won't give you any details, except to say the vermin count in the belowdecks is gonna rise soon."

Slither then turned about and marched from the cell. Brace almost collapsed upon the bed behind him. Things were getting out of control within Ganges, and he could only sit around and think, when he'd rather be out there and doing what he should have done spirals ago. If Slither was going to involve the Strifers in this mess, that might force the Lord of Crime to do something drastic, which might shed some light upon his whereabouts. His frustration began rising, but he used the meditation techniques that Naga had taught him to let his fears slide away from his mind. Brace centered his focus on his breathing, giving in to the deep calm that came from his new exercises. He dearly hoped that Slither would be able to convince some of his operatives to look into finding the hardlines that were now being used to compromise the communications system. If they could do that, then everything else would fall into place.

Engineering Sector Wheel, Level Twenty-Seven

Foreman Howait Sparweld stood at attention with his team, next to the new military vehicle they had just assembled. It was gleaming in the lights from above, its armored panels seamlessly attached to the heavy chassis. The war machine was wedge-shaped, with space for a single driver at the prow, a toragi station right behind the angular nose. At the stern was an unfolding weapons mount, designed to accept a variety of heavy weapons. The top also boasted a short turret, with a command chair on a platform that could be lowered or raised as needed. It ran on battery-driven magnetics, two pod thrusters under the rear weapons cubby, and twin tracks which could be raised or lowered depending on terrain. The task of building the thing had been complicated, and his team had been working a brutal schedule to get it ready on time.

Howait glanced over at his subordinates with pride. They had really pulled together for this one. Even Mibo had broken a sweat during the construction, which was fairly miraculous, considering his usual, lazy behavior. They had all kept their normal bickering to a minimum, for no one wanted to be the cause of failure, with so much on the line and extra rewards at stake. Howait hoped that he would soon be able to share this latest project with his mate, Security Sergeant Mahari Quartzrend, now that his team had finally completed their assignment. He hadn't seen much of her the last few rotations, for she had her own, secret assignments for Security Sector running in tandem with his.

While they all stood in a line, sweating with anticipation, Engineering Chief Marrissa Navamo carefully inspected the new vehicle prototype, accompanied by Security Investigations Commander Genko Sarish, along with a very irascible Police Sergeant named Kimpo Stelcom. Their two toragis were prowling about, sniffing at the three-crew tank with open curiosity. Howait was quite used to the big cats at this point, having to share his home with one. Mahari's toragi was named Helen, who seemed pleased with the relationship her partner had with Howait. The members of his team didn't have the same luxury and kept glancing back at the pair of big cats nervously. He didn't blame them, for the felines seemed much larger face-to-face than when seen on the broadcast news. It was true that almost every novice and student loved them, but as one got older, the toragi triggered ancient instincts about being in the presence of apex predators with giant fangs.

Howait watched as all the high-ranking officers climbed inside the military vehicle, examining every function, each station and every connector. The Sergeant unfolded the weapons station at the rear, then tested the turret lift platform. No gun barrel poked out from the small aperture placed there for such use, but the mounting mechanism was thoroughly investigated. The specifications for the fittings had been the most bothersome part of the job, as far as Howait's team was concerned, for it had to be able to support a wide variety of differing connections. Security Sector was very secretive about its weaponry, especially for those to be used in emergency conditions. Fortunately, the fuel cannister slots for the thrusters were the standard ones used for space-pods, but the magnetic impellers had to be fitted into an unusual configuration due to the twin racks of treads. Apparently, human comfort was not a major consideration for the interior design. The only concessions to the driver and passengers were the padded seating and belted straps to keep them in place, even if the thing rolled over onto its back.

When the three officers finished their perusal of the vehicle, they stepped out and faced Howait's team, all of whom saluted their superiors by raising their left fists to shoulder height. Chief Navamo smiled at them, "Well done, all of you. You have clearly demonstrated that Engineering Sector stands ready to serve the needs of Security and, thus, Ganges itself."

Howait thought his thin chest would simply explode with pride. The Chief's gleaming, prosthetic eyes swept over his crew. Her metallic left arm returned their salute, the various ports and tools attached to it flashing in the light. Half her body was machinery, and she always refused regen-therapy. Even her Naga-Port, on the left side of her cranium, was a custom-made piece, designed by herself, or so the rumors claimed. Howait loved his mate fiercely, but this woman was his true hero. No one was more dedicated, determined or selfless when it came to her Sector. He would follow her into a black hole if she told him it was necessary. Howait supposed that his mate, Mahari, felt the same way about her Chief, who was an impressive figure, but he knew there were Sectors that didn't have the same level of morale. Some of his friends didn't understand how he could be so motivated by someone as enigmatic as Chief Navamo, but those same crewmembers never bragged about the accomplishments of their Chiefs. He always felt blessed by being part of Engineering; he always would.

The Security Commander stepped forward, "I want to thank all of you for the fine work you've done for my Sector. This prototype will be fully tested, as soon as we can get it over to the proving grounds. It is my duty to inform you that every Engineering team we chose to participate in this venture was picked for their proven abilities and also because we needed to investigate some serious discrepancies in your records."

Howait gasped in shock. This was the first he was hearing about this. Chief Navamo stepped next to the Commander, "Every team we chose had its issues, including yours. All the investigations of your former foreman that we went through revealed nothing. It was decided that we had to look at those troubled teams which made remarkable recoveries, by giving them a special task which would also give rise to temptation for any crewmembers involved with the crime syndicates."

Pilla suddenly started running leeward, directly away from the three officers. Sergeant Stelcom raised his wrist to his mouth, "Hunter One, deploy!"

Howait's eyes were round in surprise. He turned to watch Pilla, feeling as if he had just lost an arm. She got five meters from the nearest hatch when it burst open to reveal a squad of Security crew, webbers out, with their toragis leading the way. She skidded to a halt, stumbling in her haste. Pilla never got a chance to get back up off the floor. Before he could blink, Howait saw her covered with strands of goo that were swiftly cementing themselves to the deck. Five of the big cats began to circle her prone body, glaring at her.

He looked back at his Chief, who was watching him. Howait turned to the rest of his team, some of whom looked like they were ready to bolt, "No one move. Did any of you assist her with whatever it was she did?"

Falinous scowled back at him, "What the fuck is this, boss? Did you know about this setup?"

Howait shook his head, wishing he couldn't hear Skolly sobbing, "No. I was not informed about this plan. Though I have to wonder why I'm not under suspicion. After all, I have been leading this team for harvests now."

The Commander of Investigations answered him, "You were vetted by our own internal processes. We do that for all mates of our own crew. None of the other members of your team are under any suspicion. Pilla Naktari was caught by our operatives, attempting to bring some of the schematics of this prototype to a special agent posing as a buyer for the syndicates. We suspect she was under orders to gain access to sensitive materials to help them fight Security Sector. Other than how we chose the teams to build these prototypes, your work here really does advance our abilities in the field, for which we are quite grateful. Chief Navamo was informed in advance and cooperated with Security to find out how the syndicates were getting the latest technologies from Engineering."

Chief Navamo addressed them, "This team is hereby cleared for further sensitive projects, with the accompanying raise in rank and extra bonuses. I will not apologize for my subterfuge. You cannot imagine my anger to hear that some of my crew were aiding criminal organizations, by stealing materials and plans from our Sector. If any of you wish to leave your current post, you may do so now, and I shall find other work for you in Engineering. Those who wish to leave my Sector may also do so, with my recommendations. If you remain, I shall be giving you an assignment for which you have now been cleared, in cooperation with Security Sector."

Mibo stepped forward, "I would like to request a transfer to a quieter post, Chief. This ain't good for me. I'll gladly take a loss of rank, but I'd still like to remain in Engineering."

The Chief nodded dispassionately, "Very well, crewman. Please report to Personnel Services right away. There will be no loss of rank for you."

Mibo turned to look at the others, then over at Pilla who was being freed from the webbing and was fitted with bindings. He shrugged and trundled away to the sternward exit. Howait could hear Pilla crying, and he hated the pain it caused him. He stepped forward and saluted his Chief, followed by the remainder of his team.

Chief Navamo saluted them back, "Excellent. You are hereby designated as Invention-Prime. Congratulations. As your new post is also a part of Security's development efforts, Sergeant Kimpo Stelcom will help oversee your duties. Howait Sparweld, you shall remain as the foreman for your team, but you will work closely with Sergeant Stelcom. Your work will be reviewed by myself."

Howait found that his mouth was dry, quite unlike his tear-streaked cheeks, "I understand, Chief."

The Sergeant stepped forward, his toragi following closely, "I'm sorry for your loss. You have my condolences but not my patience. Security has need of your services now. There's no time to waste. So, let's pull ourselves together and get busy on the next project."

Howait watched as both Chief Navamo and Commander Sarish supervised the squad apprehending Pilla. He wanted to ask her why she had done what she did, why she had betrayed her own Sector. He had worked with her for harvests but now questioned everything he had learned about her. He swallowed his grief and led the others to follow Sergeant Stelcom. It was the only thing they could do. He just hoped that hard work would distract them from their pain.

Residence Wheel Two, Level Five

I rest next to my mate, Alice, whose scent soothes my nerves after a long rotation. That's what the humans call the cycle of light and dark: a rotation. I have heard the term used for other things, which complicates my hobby of learning their noises. They are such contradictory creatures, which unsettles me. Alice rolls over and sleepily licks the top of my nose. I hold her with my free paw, and she huffs contentedly. The darkness outside matches that of our home, for it is time for sleep. We have just mated once again, which brings us closer. I can smell the changes in her already. It means we will have cubs soon. This does not concern me, for such a change is a joyous one. Darron and his mate, Triella, have also been connecting in the bonds of mating, but her scent has not yet altered to indicate pregnancy. It is a puzzle, for they have been quite enthusiastic in their play of pleasures.

Changes. All of Ganges is going through changes. My mate and I are both changing, as is Darron and Triella. William Blaine, our perpetual and troubling guest is also going through an alteration that is difficult to define. His scent is not so foul to me, yet it still seems strange. The humans don't seem to notice this, but I do. He is becoming a part of Ganges, adapting to the world. As he does so, his scent betrays his concerns, which grow with every rotation. The strange human has become more respectful, even polite. This may be partially attributed to his growing friendship with Eagle Lund, who smells like machine oil and perfumed soap. William Blaine now has many conversations with the world-spirit, Naga. This is very good for him. The world knows what is best.

I toss and turn in our nest of thick blankets. Beyond the changes going on in my personal life and in the ship, which is in a state of unrest, my mind travels to the discoveries I've made lately. They shake my earlier notions of how things are. I used to think that the humans served the world, which had a kindly spirit that allowed them to honor it through duty. Humans were at the center of things, but this is not true. I once thought they had magickal powers over the world. That they were unified in an unknowable purpose. I also once believed that Security crew were incorruptible. Pure in their actions. Wise in their thoughts and deeds. Such naïve thinking has been stripped from me, leaving my thoughts haunted by my discoveries.

During our dark-time meal, Darron and Triella spoke of war, without knowing that I could understand many of their babbling phrases. I did not truly know what war was, but after their prolonged chattering session, I began to gain just a glimmer of comprehension. There has been fighting in Ganges. The world is hurting, all because of the actions of humans, including some from Security, like Brace, Darron's uncle. That was another word I didn't know, until Darron spoke of it with his mate, howling into her chest as she held him. Humans have extended family units, unlike my kind. It bothered me that I didn't know the brother of my father or the sister of my mother. I have no contact with my siblings, other than the gatherings we toragi have, far from the eyes of the humans, where Naga wears a face like our own.

It has been a long time since we have brought ourselves together, for we are too busy fighting and doing our duty to the world. We have no way to notify each other, except face-to-face. We have no magick to send our words through the world to each other as the humans do. William Blaine has his own tricks, which bring shock and dismay to Darron. Because I have seen this with my own eyes, I now have many questions in my head. Where did William come from? Why is he here? What is the cause for his growing distress? Strange thoughts fill me, like the idea that there could be other worlds, other Nagas. That magick is something to be built, like the walls of Ganges. That it is simply a word for tools that are not understood. Where do such thoughts come from?

I have tried to express my questions and ideas to my mate and the other toragi in my platoon, but they don't understand. We just have sounds we make that express emotion, sometimes simple ideas, like being hungry, but little else. It occurs to me that we could use a system of yowls like the hooting of humans, but how can we gain this? My head bubbles with ideas, like visions I cannot describe, even to myself. For the last few rotations, I have tried to play a new game with my mate, using my paws to signal her, like we do when hunting prey. It has progressed, as she is talented. Alice now copies my roars, which is a major triumph for me. There is little meaning behind it, but it is a start. It makes me believe we toragis have our own magick to bring to the world.

That is when the terrible thought occurs to me. If my species does copy the humans, learn their ways more fully, will they appreciate it? Or will the humans fear us? If they become afraid, they will strike at us. Maybe they will just shun my people, as they sometimes do to their own kind. Would we be placed in the brig? Captured and contained as a threat? We are their friends. We love them, care for them, help them. Will all of that be destroyed due to their terror? But why would they feel that way about us? Have we not proven ourselves worthy of their love? I have watched them closely. Studied their behavior carefully. I am not reassured.

An epiphany reaches out from the depths of my mind. For all this time, my kind have been tools of the humans. We love them, see them as if they are our cubs, but that might not be the manner in which they look at us. From everything I have observed, humans are mixed when it comes to how they view us. Those in Security seem to come closest to matching our point of view. There is a bond between us that runs deep. The rest of the crew, another word that has taken me ages to understand, are mixed. Their cubs share the feelings of love, but more like we are their pets, living possessions, not equals. A shudder runs through me at the word. It is complicated, misty, hard to see. It is much easier to look upon us as tools. This disturbs me too much to sleep. I get up slowly, so as to not wake my beloved mate.

I head toward the back door of the house, padding silently across the carpet. I use my paw to push the small button at the side of the clear door, and it slides open. Not magick. A tool. The patio is made of wood planks, polished and clean. The sky above is full of tiny lights that change with each rotation. I walk to the edge, smelling the forest that surrounds our den. Something tickles my nose. A scent I know well. It is Darron. He is here, on the part of the patio that has human chairs. He is sitting in the darkness, holding a bottle full of something he calls beer. It smells strange, yeasty and sharp. I walk to his side and he is startled, "Hey, big guy! I didn't hear you coming out! You okay?"

I rumble at him to reassure Darron that I am pleased to see him. He reaches out to scratch at my fur. Humans are the best groomers in the world. I lean in close and settle down next to him, "Can't sleep, huh? Neither can I, my friend. Too much going on. None of it going well. Life can get like that."

I look back at his face and huff gently. Darron laughs, "You and me both! Ganges, I wish you could talk. Truth to tell, you're one of the few things I still trust anymore. Okay, Triella and Alice make the cut. But you're special to me."

I blink at him, pleased by his sentiments. I wish I could tell him how much I understand his babbling. We sit together in companionable silence, just staring at the dark together. Human and toragi, both overwhelmed by the strangeness of the world.

Both of us dealing with troubles that keep sleep at bay. Clinging to each other in trust and respect. Maybe there is hope after all.

CHAPTER SEVENTEEN

Star Rotation - Spin Sowing - Mission Harvest - Spiral 5620

"I fully intend to utilize every single advantage provided to my post through the revised Prime Charter, to bring a greater sense of personal responsibility for the Holy Mission to the general crew. The Judiciary Council and Security Sector have an everlasting friend on the Bridge, and Command Sector stands ready to perform its duty for all sentient species. To flinch from this burden is to denigrate the sacrifices of past generations, and I shall always stand strong in the face of adversity. I challenge every crew member to embrace the future at my side, with clear eyes and a clean conscience. We are terraformers, and the Holy Mission is not just our duty, it is our culture!"
Veera Banerjee, Captain of Ganges, transcript from induction speech, P35

Sci-One, Planet Forty-One

Planetary Geological Specialist Jena Locary gripped the padded sides of her chair with breathless terror. At first, she forced her eyes to stay open, determined to lead by example, but the chamber shook so violently that they couldn't focus on anything. Everything around her rattled, creating a crash of sound so loud, she could barely hear any of the reports coming from the bridge of Sci-One. The straps on her torso dug into her. Pressure pulled her in several different directions, threatening to tear her apart. She clamped her mouth shut, for fear of biting her own tongue. Her teeth ached, as did her jaws. Jena had never been so frightened in her life.

Captain Hallah Shallon had warned them well beforehand that entering the atmosphere of Planet Forty-One could get rough and that this was normal. Because time was severely restricted, they had agreed that a quick drop to the surface would be best, leaving them a few more paring-slivers to do their research. This meant that their vessel would experience extra turbulence, even within the placid atmosphere of the planet. It was considered a small price, to gain extra readings from the surface structures. At the time, it had seemed reasonable. Now it looked reckless.

Jena gave up trying to prevent her eyes from clenching shut. Instead, she focused upon the calm and steady voice of captain Shallon. How could the woman sound so relaxed? Sci-One was one of the larger vessel types from Harbor Sector, so why was it being tossed about like a child's toy? The Harbor crew were all calm, sounding off readings from their boards with a detached professionalism that came to the edge of sounding bored. It was ridiculous!

Over the general comms, she could also hear Security Lieutenant Urukumu scolding his squad, after some of them began cheering and whooping in excitement. Jena had first thought that they had been injured, until their raucous laughter echoed through the corridors. Between the laconic Harbor crew and the over-eager Security squad, Jena thought she might be going mad. They were insane. All of them. It was the only explanation that made sense to her mind.

Both science teams had been told to stay off the comms, unless there was an emergency, such as a life-threatening injury or a hull rupture. The latter was highly unlikely, as the steel skin of Sci-One was three meters thick. That knowledge didn't help when the ship began to groan as they began to drop into the upper atmosphere. Loud pings, clanks and grumbles had rattled Jena's nerves. The steadily increasing vibrations of the deck began shortly afterward. Then had come the sudden lurches, making her stomach reach her throat, dropping it back into her lower guts as pressure from below her seat grabbed her body like a living thing dragging her down.

Jena was sweating profusely, but she kept her mind on the voice of captain Shallon, willing her thoughts to hold onto the business-like tone. To do otherwise was to plunge her thoughts into horrid scenes of destruction and death. The vessel shook, as if it were fighting the course it was on. A lingering, scraping sound crawled its way along the lower bulkheads. Bestial roars filled her ears, accompanied by the laughter from the Security squad. The screech of metal made her teeth quiver all the way to their roots. She could barely draw breath, as though a weight was pressing against her chest. Spots appeared in her vision. Blood rushed to her ears, filling them with a rushing, boiling sound. She was about to scream. She could feel it climbing up her tortured throat.

Suddenly, everything stopped. Jena sagged against the straps holding her in place, gasping for air. Rough cheers broke out through the comms, with another, harsh admonishment from Lieutenant Urukumu. She felt sick to her stomach, but the relief that flashed through her made Jena feel giddy, despite the protests from her body. Voices reached into her consciousness from the comms, calm and soothing, "All systems nominal, captain," then another voice, "Thrusters set to line five, intake at maximum," followed by, "Landing gear primed."

Captain Shallon's voice resounded throughout the vessel, "All crew, this is the bridge. We have just entered the lower stratosphere, at an altitude of twenty-one kilometers. Sci-One is in atmospheric flight mode. We are three hundred kilometers from our target region and shall be descending further. Our estimated time of arrival is in four paring-slivers. All personnel may move about at this time, but be forewarned that you only have three paring-slivers before we attempt landing and must return to your seats. Captain out."

Jena unstrapped herself from the seat, which was also her bunk folded into a chair-like configuration. Once she was upon her unsteady feet, Jena assisted her roommate with her harness. She could hear feet running to the washroom, the sound of guts heaving and water draining, competing with sobs and groans of misery. Jena then stepped into the corridor, clinging to the ropes on the walls, as the ship swayed gently. Toragi bounded about in excitement, sniffing at everything they could find. Lieutenant Urukumu came around the nearby corner and saluted her.

Jena did her best to walk toward him without stumbling. The deck felt like it was breathing. The Security officer smiled at her, "Getting your flight legs? A good idea. We're about to step onto a rotating ball. A piece of advice, from my great-great grandmother, who worked for your Sector, don't look up when we land. Keep your eyes on the ground. If you want to see the horizon, do it slowly."

Jena swayed in place, holding firmly to the wall-ropes, "Thank you for that, Lieutenant. I'll pass it along my team. How did your crew hold up?"

Lieutenant Urukumu smiled briefly, "They had some fun. We train for events like this in specially designed lift-tubes. This was more exciting. I do apologize if they were distracting you from the experience."

Jena laughed aloud, her mind still reeling from what she had gone through, "Exciting? That's what you call that? I admit, I was terrified!"

Urukumu raised a dark eyebrow at her, "You'll have serious bragging rights when we get back to Ganges. That's worth a little terror. At least, that's how my own Sector thinks of it. Usually, vessels entering an atmosphere take their time, to make the trip easier on the crew, but we had no time for such niceties. Do you need any assistance?"

Jena shook her head, then regretted doing so, wincing at the odd feeling in her ears. Lieutenant Urukumu placed a hand upon her shoulder, "Steady, now. We're deep inside the planet's gravity well. Your inner ear is more used to centrifugal forces. Try not to move your head too much while we're down here."

Jena nodded softly, desperately trying to keep herself from getting too sick. There were many scientists within the washroom now, all of them in an undignified state. She really didn't want to join them. Instead, she decided to check up on her equipment, to make sure that none had broken loose from their moorings. Once she was finished with that, Jena vowed to herself that she would simply return to her quarters and wait out the rest of the flight. Once she was on a solid surface, she could focus on the task at hand.

Command Hub, Level Ten

Captain Perrin Fieldscan allowed his shoulders to relax, rolling them slowly to take out the knots that were forming there. It was the beginning of the second rotation of camping out on the Bridge of Ganges, and the news that Sci-One was about to land galvanized his spirit. Rush-slice was starting, with fresh crew coming in to relieve the dark-shift personnel. He grabbed another cup of tea from his thermos, which had been refilled after a hasty breakfast at dawn-slice. Despite some rumors to the contrary, there were food dispensers in the Command Hub, but he preferred the cooking of his mate, Dale Copperstill, and the tea made by his other mate, Tani Wilder. By having some of his needs met by those from his household, he could better use the Bridge Ensigns for tasks other than fetching his meals.

He looked over at the crew representative, Zilla Tav, who was still grumbling over a mug of coffee. She looked a bit more disheveled than when she had woken up two slices ago. Meanwhile, Wasp's raucous laughter could be heard from two tiers up and thirty meters spinward. She was doing the rounds, checking up on all stations before the next shift started. Perrin always kept a much closer eye on those Bridge personnel who interacted with his Executive Officer in a more positive manner. They tended to be the ones with nothing to hide and took their duties more seriously. The Chief-of-the-Deck, Femz Trammer, had just arrived, quickly checking in on his control boards.

Captain Fieldscan blinked hard, still trying to stretch a bit before getting to his feet. Once they had achieved their system-exit velocity, he would go home and take a nice, long bath, then sleep for an entire rotation. He missed his novices deeply, as much as he did his mates, but that was the price of success. His schedule was never decided by his own needs, but rather those of the ship. He had accepted this spirals ago, with few regrets. Sometimes he wondered what his life would have been like if he had chosen another Sector, but such musings were never constructive. He despised not being in control of any situation, which made his post the best one he could have chosen. Here, he was at the center of everything going on in Ganges, with the authority to make his orders count.

Wasp returned to the command platform, twirling her marshmallow gun in one hand. Perrin hid his amusement at her antics behind his tea, sipping from his thermos delicately. He had taken a moment to wash up and comb his close-cropped hair in one of the restrooms. He was determined to remain tidy, as it was good for morale. Executive Tornpage, by contrast, allowed her green hair to become tangled and wild. Her rumpled uniform was stained and in need of cleaning, but that was simply part of her Strifer upbringing. There were still those who disapproved of Wasp, not understanding her outspoken and self-denigrating culture. Such people felt it was inappropriate to have a Strifer on the Bridge, let alone in a position of power. Perrin thought that those who felt this way were simply misguided, unable to see her zeal for command.

As Wasp turned to check on the Chief-of-the-Deck, Zilla Tav leaned closer to Perrin, whispering, "She really does care about her post, doesn't she?"

The Captain gave the crew representative a soft smile, "If you're speaking of Wasp, then you're quite correct. I've rarely met a more devoted officer, in or outside of Command Sector. I'm glad you can see it in her. Too often, we judge crew by their appearance or their origins. Doing so blinds us to what's right before us. There are reasons Wasp was chosen for her current duties."

Zilla glanced downward, "I admit that I had reservations when I first met her, but now I can't imagine anyone else being in her role. It wasn't that she's a Strifer or anything like that, you understand. It was her ability to disrupt any given situation, but now I see that Wasp picks and chooses those she perturbs very carefully."

Perrin grinned over his hot tea, "Oh, yes, that she does. The smug, the self-important, those who shirk at their station. It makes efficiency reviews much simpler for me. As it is, things are quite tense now, with the continued acceleration and the landing. We just received word that Sci-One is currently in the atmosphere of Planet Forty-One. Signals from their comms are clear, which is a relief. One never knows what to expect from these situations. Not that we've ever been in one quite like this. I just hope the expedition doesn't encounter any troubles while they're down there."

Zilla shuddered, "I'm just glad I don't have to touch the surface of a planet! It gives me the creeps whenever I think about it. No, thank you!"

Wasp walked up to them, "Aww, c'mon, Zilla! Think of the publicity!"

Zilla glared up at her, "I think not."

Perrin got to his feet, "Everyone settled snugly into their stations, Executive Tornpage?"

Wasp replied while walking to her chair and rummaging behind it, "Yes, they are, Big Cheese! I took the initiative to ask some of our finest to stay for extra shifts. We don't need any dawdlers around here right now. I gave a couple of our less-than-efficient Bridge officers the rotation off. That way they can just mess up their homes and not their station. I pulled a few favors, twisted some tails, gave out some cheese. The usual gear-greasing."

Perrin nodded, "Well done. I must admit it's a cheerful thought that I won't have to do such things, as you've gotten to them first. However, I do have to contact the other Sector Chiefs to give them updates and to find out if anything terrible is happening in our grand vessel. I know Security is having a hard time in Residence Wheel One. They were forced to evacuate three of the smaller communities at darkslice, last rotation. The fighting over at the nature preserves on Level Two is causing some atmospheric disturbances, with clouds of smoke heading ever spinward."

Wasp sighed, "Yeah, I heard they launched a dirigible fleet at Keep Smith. I don't know what their strategy is, but I'm sure Jira has her claws into it. Sometimes, she really scares the shit outta me. Engineering Sector sends their best regards. The station hands gave me the word. Main thrusters at the stern are fully operational and itching to gain speed. I held them off. They gotta wait like the rest of us, or we'll leave our landing party behind."

Perrin frowned, "That's the problem with the Sectors. They only think of their own territory and regulations. Fortunately, the crew have us to make them see sense. Get some rest if you can. I'll make sure you're awake before Sci-One lands. It won't be long now."

Wasp jauntily saluted him, then slumped into her chair and closed her eyes. Perrin reviewed his datapad and saw nothing that was outstanding. Rescue Services was currently helping the residents of those communities which had been vacated. They were now setting up temporary shelters, a mobile hospital and patrolling the immediate area. This issue with the syndicates was bothersome, but Perrin hoped it could be resolved with a minimum of lost lives and damaged communities. In the meantime, he had a landing party to worry about and a most remarkable moment in humanity's history was about to unfold. The unprecedented was now at hand, and he was determined to stay sharp for any upcoming developments.

Planet Forty-One

Security Lieutenant Urukumu stepped out onto the surface of a brand new world. The synth-quartz of his helmet was perfectly clear, its dome giving him more than enough peripheral vision to make him forget it was there. The only clue that he was wearing a Vac-Suit came from the steady hiss of the breathing unit just below his chin. His left ear had been fitted with a squad-comm, the other one set for external sound. As the mission leader, it was his right to be first to leave Sci-One. It was also his sworn duty as a Security officer to take the greatest risks, including entering an unknown environment. Thumbnail-sized displays ran across the lowest portion of his visor, presenting fresh information on the composition of the planet's atmosphere, air pressure, his suit functions, and a changeable view that included all members of the expedition's helmets, and the ever-important timer, counting down the pollen-slivers until they had to return to Ganges.

The ground beneath his feet was hard as stone, roughly textured in a fine, curling leaf pattern and a pale cream color. The sky was a deep blue-purple, without any clouds. The land around him rose with a series of steps that were each half a meter in height, leading to a ring-shaped plateau that was five meters over his head. They had landed within a large basin, on the edge of one of the giant, rising structures that could be seen from orbit. The massive spire was on his left, dominating the view. Urukumu had to refer to his map display to assess its distance from his position. The mega-spire was still five kilometers away, yet it looked as if it were right on top of him, dwarfing his sense of scale to insignificance.

He looked around with a wary eye, searching for any threats, finding none. The ground was strangely flat, without bumps or irregularities, except for the leafy pattern, which was everywhere. The lander had set down softly, deploying turbofans once they had reached an altitude of fifty meters. The landing legs were shaped like giant skis, with hard rubber grips on the bottom of each one. Not wanting to disturb the planet's atmosphere, they used the cargo bay airlock to disembark. The ramp was lowered to the ground, with the rest of the expedition and the RTV waiting inside for his signal that it was safe to exit the ship.

Urukumu tapped the datapad attachment on the right arm of his suit, "All clear. Send out the RTV first, then the rest of you can disembark."

A series of responses entered his comms, "Primed, Lieutenant."

The soft rumble of the Rough Terrain Vehicle filled the air as it went down the ramp, bouncing slightly as it hit the ground. Inside was Sergeant Miri Rallah with her toragi, Penny, and four scientists. They would soon be heading toward the great spire which loomed over the landscape, slicing the sky in half with its grand height. The other three teams of scientific specialists were then escorted by the rest of his Security squad, forming a perimeter within the basin. His toragi, Victor, with the rest of the big cats, bounded out of the cargo airlock, their enthusiasm infectious. They also wore Vac-Suits, as the air on Planet Forty-One was unbreathable. The gravity seemed to be just under a Terran standard, perhaps the equivalent of being on Level Twelve in Residence Wheel One.

Using hand signals, he ordered his crew to climb the series of steps around them, keeping clear of the RTV as it rolled up and out of the basin, its large traction tires gaining excellent purchase on the hard surface of the planet. The Harbor crew would now be preparing Sci-One for the flight home. If all went according to plan, they should be ready well before the time to launch, but the Lieutenant didn't like to rely upon a lack of surprises. They were now on unknown territory, once inhabited by a sentient species, who left behind breathtaking structures of strange beauty on a scale unseen by humanity. He glanced up at the spire, noting how the sides were heavily decorated with lacey patterns, with shorter branches that defied the human rules of architecture. He had no idea what the massive structure was, its purpose lost to the mists of time.

The air was still, not even a breeze that could be detected without sensitive equipment. The basin's temperature was fairly moderate, which came as a surprise, considering the lack of atmospheric movement. It was as if the whole planet were encased within synth-quartz, yet another impossibility that was all too obviously real. Urukumu felt a pang of longing for the rainforests of his childhood, spent on Level Three of Agro Wheel Two. He missed the warm rains, the swift rivers and dense foliage of home. This place was dry, silent, lacking any sign of life. It felt like a desert that lacked sand.

Urukumu marched up the half-meter steps. Each landing was three meters wide. When he reached the top, the view almost made him stumble and fall back. Angular shapes surrounded him, each of them several meters tall, all decorated with flowing patterns of incredible complexity. Giant forms lifted themselves from other basins. Their geometrical architecture was strangely familiar to him. They looked like representations of mineralogical wonders, crystal growths and tangles of lace, all the same pale, cream color as the rest of the planet's surface. It was astounding, alien, wonderous and terrifying. He saw no roads, though he used his telescopic sights to look for them. Nothing had the appearance of machinery, just bare, decorated stone.

His ear comm shook him from his shock, the voice of Jena Locary snapping him back to his duty, "Lieutenant, I'm trying to use your advice and failing. I think I feel sick. Are you okay?"

Urukumu shook himself, as Victor joined him at the edge of the basin, "I'm fine, Specialist Locary. Just scoping out the land. Keep your mind on setting up your equipment. Don't look up too much. There's still no sign of any threat or movement. Bring your crew to my location. I'll watch out for you while your team works. Helm recorders are on, sending our telemetry to Ganges. They should receive our signals in a few seed-slivers."

The Lieutenant sent a signal to Sci-One's bridge, requesting the status of their link to Harbor One. Captain Hallah Shallon replied, "Data link is stable. Return signal verified. Stellar and Planetary are already drooling over our close flight images. Telemetry to RTV is also stable, receiving their data now, Lieutenant."

Urukumu replied, "Very good, captain. Keep me informed. All of the science teams are now setting up for testing and sample taking. They're moving a little slow, but I can't say as I blame them. The view from here is most distracting."

The captain's voice came back, "Primed, Lieutenant. I understand."

Urukumu was sure she did. At the moment, the entire expedition seemed microscopically small, compared to the surroundings. The sooner they got back to Ganges, the happier he would be.

Planetary Sector Wheel, Level One Hundred

William Blaine was sitting next to his newfound friend, Eagle Lund, who was the Chief of Technology Sector. He had his usual platoon of guards from Security with him. Darron Lazhand and his toragi, Mike, were standing at the entrance to the chamber they were in, keeping out the curious crew who wanted to look in on the Solarian. William was still getting used to the idea that the outer region of Technology Sector was a series of temples, honoring Naga as a guide toward enlightenment. It was strange to see priestly robes, incense burners and Holy books next to display screens filled with code. He had never experienced anything like it.

They were in a data processing room, getting their first look at the surface of Planet Forty-One. Most of the telemetry was from the sensors of Sci-One, which revealed a dizzying array of monstrous structures, many of which almost reached beyond the planet's atmosphere. Below these were clustered geometric shapes, low basins with flat levels, each of them unique in shape and size. No power sources were detected, no activity nor any sign of life. William was enchanted by the images flowing into the wallscreens. He wished that he could be down there himself. So far, the architecture of the dead civilization was like nothing he had heard of. The more elaborate areas seemed to defy gravity, though this did not surprise him much, for the Boktahl were masters of that mysterious force. Their own conclaves also defied reason but were far less orderly than the images from Planet Forty-One.

Eagle Lund leaned in closer to him and said, "The data feed from Lieutenant Urukumu's helmet is now coming in, my friend. What a marvelous discovery! I shall enjoy studying this for octades to come!"

William grinned at his friend, then turned back to stare at the vista which was revealed by Lieutenant Urukumu's helmet recorders, "Will you look at that! It's so graceful. I would swear half of those structures couldn't bear their own weight. The sheer artistry of their design! Whoever built this place had an eye for beauty."

Eagle used his prosthetic hand to expand a distant area, "Why is that tumble of lacey structures in the middle of the geometric ones? What sets it apart like that? So much to learn, yet we have so little time! Naga forgive me, but I would recommend staying here for spirals. Think of what we might learn! This whole planet has been reconstructed! I wonder if this style of architecture extends below the surface."

William shook his head, "We can't assume anything. I'm not even sure how we'd check that, other than sonar scans. I've yet to see anything that resembles a door. No tunnels, windows, but there are gaps in some of the structures, just none of them lead deeper under the surface. At least, not as of yet. Maybe the builders were claustrophobic?"

Eagle pointed toward another display screen, "Ah, now they're setting up the equipment for dust samples. Planetary Atmospherics insisted on that test. I don't really blame them. From what the sensors of Sci-One showed us, the air in the upper atmosphere is incredibly clean, though unbreathable."

William's voice became wistful, "I wonder if the others will find worlds such as this one."

Eagle swiftly looked at him in consternation, "Others? What others? You mean the Solidarity? The exploration fleets?"

William sat up straight, "Oh! No, not at all. I mean the other Ganges-class vessels, made by the colonies. Well, some of the colonies, anyway. What you would call Planet-Nine was developed by a culture which was heavily inspired by yours. They built a vessel, much like this one, they named 'The Midgard', whose AeyAie is called 'Wyrd'. It launched a few octuries before I arrived. They have the same mission as Ganges, seeding the galaxy with life. The colonists call their world 'Valhalla', which comes from old Nordic mythology, so it stands to reason they would use the same nomenclature for their version of Ganges. A few others did the same. Planet Twenty-Seven created five Ganges-class vessels! They live in orbit, keeping the world you made for them pristine. It's being used primarily for recreation and study, which is an interesting development."

Eagle shook his head, "I remember you stating that more vessels like ours were built, but I had thought it was to aid your people. I am quite astounded that so many colonies are following our path! What is wrong, my friend? Did I say something to upset you?"

William grimaced as he shook his head, "No. Nothing like that. I'm having trouble with my nanites. They're all in a panic. They do that whenever I'm threatened, but there's no one trying to kill me at the moment."

Eagle got up from his seat, "Do you need diagnostics? I've been working on better interfaces for your systems since your history download."

William grunted, then fell forward, hitting his head upon the table in front of him. His spine started tingling. Pain lashed down his arms and legs. He heard his nanites screaming at him to leave, but where could he go? His brain felt hot, as if a live wire had been plugged into his skull. The cranial computer systems embedded in his head were running several programs at once. He heard Eagle and Darron speaking. They decided to alert Medical Sector about his condition. William tried to speak aloud, but his thoughts were being scrambled by his overactive nanites. The micro-machines were responding to some kind of danger, but he couldn't figure out what it was.

In a final, desperate attempt to gain control, he struggled to his feet and grabbed Eagle by the arm, pulling the Chief of Technology Sector off balance. They both fell to the floor in a tangle of limbs. Mike roared in alarm, but William ignored everything as he reached out to touch Eagle's Naga-Port. His hands met the cranial device, and alarms began to blare all through the chamber. William felt strong arms grab him, pulling him away from Eagle, but it didn't matter. He had achieved what he needed to. The nanites were now swarming over the connection to Naga, whose visage appeared on the wallscreens, her skin black as space, eyes the red of molten steel, "You will stop now! Cease! Deactivate! Return to your source at once!"

William gasped as he was hurled back to the floor, Darron's knee on his back, his arms held tightly behind him in the man's incredible grip. The Solarian struggled to get his jaws to move, "I'm sorry! I had to give my nanites an overriding task to report their issue with the nearest AeyAie for emergency analysis."

Darron growled close to his ear, "What the fuck just happened?"

William went limp, to show he was cooperating, "Is Eagle okay?"

The Security Lieutenant shoved his face into the deck, "Answer my fucking question!"

William pushed his head to one side, "My nanites. They panicked. It was some kind of signal. Something they didn't recognize. It came out of nowhere. It was disrupting their ability to operate and coordinate with my cranial computer system. My internal antenna is fried, literally. I can't explain it!"

Eagle suddenly knelt down beside him, "Let him up, Lieutenant. Naga and I are examining the problem. A sphere of energy developed in his skull. Is this the work of the syndicates? I know they want my friend dead."

Darron let William loose, "Negative, Chief Lund. I doubt they have that kind of technology. If they did, we would all be under their ugly boots right now, including Naga."

William struggled to sit up on the deck, "Oh, dear. I think we'd better send a message to the expedition. I think Planet Forty-One has woken up."

Planet Forty-One

Planetary Geologist Jena Locary frowned at the readings she was getting from her equipment. The lower atmosphere was perfectly clear of particulate matter, which was impossible. She double-checked the sensors, but they were all working within parameters. Five samples had been taken of the atmosphere, all with the same result. Pure gas, no dust or microscopic matter. No organic or inorganic compounds, not even a stray molecule! It was a strange puzzle that worried her. Was the planet's odd magnetosphere affecting her instruments? Jena wondered if she should inform Lieutenant Urukumu, but he was busy helping Felk's team set up their sample device. Normally, this was easily done, but with few of the scientists on the mission having any experience using their tools while wearing Vac-Suits, the process was getting bogged down a bit.

She ordered her team to move on further and find another spot, though in reality, anywhere on the surface should do. Jena watched as they disassembled the unit, then packed up the sample modules before heading toward the closest spire. She felt something trying to reach her consciousness from deep within her mind. There was something wrong, but it wasn't the equipment. Jena checked her datapad, which was fine. The comms were all working, so had the sensors on Sci-One. So, what was interfering with her specialized units?

A small cheer interrupted her thoughts. Felk and his team had finally gotten their setup stable. Urukumu gave them some more advice on how to make the best of wearing Vac-Suits within an atmosphere, a topic for which there was some data, especially within the Planetary Sector archives, but the Stellar crew hadn't deigned to access that material beforehand. After all the octenniums of working together, the rivalry between her Sector and Felk's was still a major issue. She wondered what William Blaine would have to say about that.

The thought of the Solarian made her freeze in place. His warnings about making no assumptions rang in her mind like a bell. She looked closely at the ground beneath her feet. It had the appearance of sanded stone. It felt like stone, but was it? Jena kneeled down to make a closer inspection. The pale, beige rock was full of leafy, flowing shapes, all interconnected and spiraling into themselves. It made her dizzy to stare at the stuff. She rubbed a gloved hand upon the surface, barely feeling the irregularities. Jena studied the surface of her gloved fingers. They were perfectly clean. Turning back to the rock, she noticed that there were no seams, cracks or signs of erosion. No sand, pebbles or loose debris at all. It was eerie.

Then it struck her like an asteroid. The surface structures were all part of a single creation! That was why there wasn't debris, sand or any loose particles on this planet. It was a single unit, possibly going all the way down to the core! She smacked her fist into the surface, bruising her knuckles, but nothing came loose. Other than a scuff mark on her glove, it was clean. She looked up, eyes wide. It was all one thing. One impossible thing. Her heart was hammering in her chest, her breathing ragged. Lieutenant Urukumu came up to her, "Are you oaky, Jena? What's wrong?"

She wanted to scream. To warn everyone. William had been right. They had made too many assumptions, based on their experiences with lifeless planets, but this one was nothing like those. She glanced up at Urukumu's handsome face, still trying to get the words out of her throat. Jena noticed that Felk was ready with his laser-drill, which would atomize a miniscule part of a wall he was next to and then analyze the results to find out its molecular composition. Jena felt a rush of terror flash down her spine. She opened the general channel on the comm and shouted, "Stop! Everyone, stop what you're doing!"

Urukumu looked puzzled by her outburst. Her team ceased setting up their equipment, but Felk glanced back at her and waved a hand in the air, as he pushed the activation button on the laser.

A tiny puff of smoke came out of the wall Felk was working at. Jena felt the ground tremble, as if in response to the tiny beam of coherent light. A wailing sound shattered the air, as if millions of voices were screaming in utter despair. Jena got to her feet and grabbed Urukumu's arm. It was the last thing she felt.

The ground erupted into a blinding shower of violet needles, ripping through the expedition faster than they could see. All the structures in the immediate area heaved and crumbled, forming a massive swarm of four-centimeter-long needles that blackened the sky above. Sci-One began its engine burn, attempting to lift from the ground, but the engines were penetrated with ease. The main thrusters exploded, ripping open the hull at the stern. The tiny needles splashed against the vessel, then melted upon its surfaces, forming a mass of violet patterns that began to eat their way through the ship's thick skin. The doors beyond the open airlock were torn apart in less than a pollen-sliver, exposing the crew to the atmosphere and more flying needles. Blood soaked the inner walls as the crew were shredded instantly.

The ground was still spewing needles at a frantic pace. The area of effect was growing exponentially, until it reached the expedition's RTV, which was now desperately speeding away from the epicenter of the catastrophe. The tires blew out, then were chewed away, as if eroded down to their atoms in a flash of violet. The vehicle swerved, tumbling down an embankment, completely covered by the mass of needles, which began stripping the armor away as if it were thin paper. Scraps of plating bounced from the stricken RTV, until the swarm consumed them as well. The exploration team was swiftly devoured by the needles, which moved as if guided by a single mind.

The Security escorts in low orbit watched with alarm as the surface of the planet began to look bruised, blotting out the pale landscape below. A bright, purple hurricane formed under them, as all signals from the landing party ceased abruptly. Their horror grew as the massive storm rose up from the atmosphere at supersonic speed. Before they could change their course, it engulfed them, the needles tearing their ships apart, targeting the engines. The lone Security corvette signaled a warning to Ganges, as it opened fire upon the huge swarm. Sparks lashed out at the storm of needles. The Spin-Drive cannons tore chunks of the swarm away, only to see the holes refilled with alarming speed. The warship was overwhelmed, swallowed whole by the alien storm. Then it was dragged down to crash upon the planet.

The swarm of needles grew further, reaching out into the depths of space. It blossomed into a dense cloud that obscured half the planet, then it gained speed, reaching over ten percent the speed of light, heading directly toward Ganges itself, matching the vessel's course precisely. An endless stream of needles was flowing from the planet, its oddly positioned magnetosphere glowing with visible aurora. The cloud of needles gained mass and speed as it approached its target, spreading out like a continent of alien fury.

Near-Ganges Space, High Orbit

Security Fleet Lieutenant Tarn Vekkor watched in stunned horror, as the massive, purple cloud reached out from the surface of Planet Forty-One. It was shocking how quickly the damned thing moved. Warnings blared over his control boards, the sensors screaming at him, much as the comms were doing. Sci-One and the entire expedition were now missing, their signal lost at the exact moment the ground erupted. The telemetry from the surface had been scrambled. There had been no time for analysis. All of the Security ships which had escorted Sci-One to low-orbit had been lost, with just a single transmission from the command corvette, warning that something had gone horribly wrong.

Without hesitation, he tapped his Naga-Unit. He needed to find out more, so he could lead his squadron with efficiency. Tarn required the latest information, lots of it, and had no time to listen to reports from the frantic Harbor crew. He blinked slowly, the display he used for communicating with Naga crawled on his screen. His alarm grew, as it usually popped up immediately. If the AeyAie's main communication systems were running hard enough that it slowed down the Security feeds, then the situation must be more dire than he had thought. Naga's face appeared before him, "Please stand by, my processors are switching to overload procedures. If this is an emergency, please contact..."

Tarn switched the Naga-Unit display off with a blistering curse. It seemed that everyone in Ganges had the same idea about contacting the AeyAie directly. His toragi, Pete, growled behind him. The sensors were now reading a large, amorphous mass heading directly toward Ganges at seventeen percent the speed of light. They had only pollen-slivers before whatever it was reached the vessel. Tarn opened his comms, "Raptor One-Alpha to Nondo Squadron! Break formation and head back toward Ganges, on the port side. We'll use the ship as a shield, then await orders from Security Fleet Command."

In unison, his crew replied "Primed, Lieutenant!"

The Security fighter-pods turned about, shifting their orientation to face Ganges, then burning their thrusters to maximum with perfectly matched efficiency.

All those spirals of being called a hard-ass were paying off. Tarn's squadron was racing back to Ganges, while the massive vessel was still heading in their direction, making the trip to the port side that much faster. He noticed that the Fleet Command Vessel Malati was using its bow thrusters to slow down, veering toward the starboard side of Ganges to defend it from the impending attack. Small fighters were being scrambled, launching from the carriers and battleships in a massive formation. He was tempted to join them, but not until he was ordered to do so. The last thing he wanted to do was upset the tactics of Fleet Commander Vina Harrolon by blundering into a set formation.

One of his squadron members, Security Pilot Bren Maliti, spoke up over the comms, "What the fuck is that thing? How big is it?"

Tarn barked back, "Just keep your eyes on your damned course! Comms silence until we reach the ice cap!"

Pete roared behind him, as if backing up his orders. Tarn glanced at the tactical display on his boards. The entire fleet escorting Ganges had been redeployed into a wall of firepower on the starboard side of their home vessel. All at once, the battleships, cruisers, corvettes and cutters launched missiles or fired their main guns. Bright sparks flickered through the darkness, racing toward the swiftly closing cloud. Silent detonations erupted at the leading edge of the purple-glowing mass. Massive sparks crawled their way across the face of it, as kilometer-wide holes were gouged out of the strange, alien cloud. It kept coming at them with speed, the gaps closing with uncanny coordination.

The ice cap loomed before his forward canopy, close enough to see all the artistic carvings that ran across its surface. It flickered as the ice reflected the battle raging on the other side of Ganges. Dozens of fighter-pods could be seen, sheltering behind the massive girth of the ship. It occurred to him that most of the other escort squadrons had gotten the same idea he had, which suited him well. Tarn pinged the other squadron commanders, and they responded, signaling that they would follow his lead.

Tarn came about, the other fighter-pods flying in a mass formation behind him. He swooped close to the hull, then ran beneath it, coming in under the rest of the deployed fleet assets, just as the cloud reached near-Ganges space. It looked like an ugly, hazy fist, a hundred kilometers in width. A stream of smoky material followed behind it from the planet. Tarn shouted into his comms, "Weapons hot! Fire at will!"

Laser cannons spat coherent beams into the cloud from below. This only seemed to make the cloud fluctuate a bit, as if responding to a minor irritation. Tarn fired two micro-nuke missiles, each one punching with the force of half a megaton. This had better results, though only temporarily making a dent in the mass before him. He led the multi-squadron closer, until he could see what he was up against. Billions of tiny, four-centimeter-long needles made up the cloud. They had no obvious form of propulsion, though they changed course and altered speed to face him. They glowed with a purple light which, according to his sensors, reached deep into the ultraviolet. He saw no details, as the objects were too small and moving too quickly for such examinations. There was also no time.

Small pops and scratches reached Tarn's ears, as the alien flying needles impacted against his canopy. His fighter-pod rattled all around him. Within a pollen-sliver, he was surrounded by the glow of the things, unable to contact the fleet, as his tactical display went dark. Tarn took a chance and launched another missile into the swarm, which exploded close enough for his radiation alarms to blare. His pod shook. His head slammed into the back of his seat. Pete yowled from behind, as his vessel was tossed by the blast of shattered atoms. Klaxons sounded. His entire control board went red with warning lights. The fighter spun away from the fight. Tarn struggled to get the controls to respond to his commands. Half of his attitude thrusters were damaged, as were the main engines, though they still burned hot. By the time he got control of his pod, Tarn's vessel was over fifty kilometers away from the fight, only a few hundred meters from the hull of Ganges.

According to the few remaining sensors he had, his pod was slowly being devoured. The damage was spreading from minute impact sites, eating at the armor plating and the thrusters. His weapons were unresponsive, crippled by his encounter with the needles. He had no choice now. Tarn brought his ship about with juddering spurts from the remains of his thrusters. He called back to his toragi, as the shadow of Ganges loomed overhead, "I'm sorry, Pete. We have to bail. Shut down. Lock in."

With just a moment of hesitation, Tarn pulled the emergency lever under his seat. Air pressure increased, making his ears pop painfully. Loud bangs resounded throughout the cockpit, as it was launched from his mangled pod. He and Pete had enough internal supply for three rotations. In that time, they had to figure out how they would get home with nothing more than gas jets and their Vac-Suits.

Agro Wheel Two, Security Level Five

Chief of Security Jira Mantabe sat upon the saddle at the very center of the Nexus, straining to control the outrage that was now coursing through her veins. The grand chamber was resounding with klaxons, warning alarms and shouting officers. With a touch of her armored thumb across the forward display, she cut off the blaring alerts so she could hear her crew. Her Naga-Port had been given priority status, but it was still too slow for proper use. A frenzy of activity had overloaded the processors, and Technology Chief Lund had just promised her that he would clear the channels for use by emergency services only. This still meant that millions of crew would have access, but it should alleviate the current difficulties. The problem was, by the time he was done, there might not be a ship left to defend.

She gritted her teeth tightly to prevent despair from overwhelming her. This disaster had occurred on her watch, and she would do anything to see that Ganges was saved from destruction. They remained ignorant about what had happened on the surface of Planet Forty-One and what it was they were currently facing. That it was a major threat was not a question. The sensor readings were chaotic, but it had become evident that the massive cloud that reached Ganges at incredible speed was composed of tiny, needle-shaped units. They moved in a highly coordinated manner, as if sharing a single mind or were controlled by one source. Jira shook her head. Assumptions could get them all killed. She had to work with the facts, though they were few.

At the moment, the fleet had been doing an admirable job of halting the swarm's progress, but individual needles were still getting through by the thousand, hitting the hull of Ganges, though to what effect wasn't yet known. Fleet Commander Vina Harrolon reported that the damned things were now sticking to the hulls of the larger space vessels upon impact. The smaller fighters were being overwhelmed, some of them completely covered by the needles, then destroyed. Laser batteries did nothing to the swarm, and she was afraid that such weapons might even give the needles an energy boost. This was being studied in Stellar Sector, with what little evidence they had. Maser had little effect, though electron streams were slowing the enemy down.

Jira pondered that thought. Enemy. It might be the right word to use, but she couldn't be certain. The swarm might be just an automated defense system, left behind by the species that sculpted the planet. The only weapons they had which gave the needles any troubles were the tactical nuclear missiles and the Spin-Drive turrets. The latter had only been used during the Crucible, once the Kendis Vault had been discovered. There were still some other weapons from that strange place which had all been classified as too dangerous to use. Others hadn't been tested properly. There had been no need for octuries.

She decided that it was time to give everything they had at their disposal to fight back. Battleships and fighter-pods were making suicide runs against the swarm of needles, to buy Ganges precious time. One cruiser slammed itself deep into the cloud, then overloaded its engines and set off its ordinance in a massive explosion. A hundred crew dead, but the event had made the swarm pause for a few, precious pollen-slivers. There was still a seemingly endless stream of the needles coming from Planet Forty-One to refill the gaps in the attacking cloud.

Jira gave the order personally, "All hull gun turrets, commence fire upon the swarm. Spin-Drive weapons only!"

She ignored her screaming communication boards, while she observed the results of her command. Clumps of needles were wiped out; the surviving ones were reeling back to avoid the empty spaces that were left behind. Jira gave a fierce grin at the screens. The massive turrets upon the hull of Ganges were the size of seed-ships. Their output was monstrous and effective against the needles. She tapped her control board, "The use of all nuclear ordinance is hereby authorized. Warm up the Dark Matter Collmunators. Let's see what they can do to this damned cloud!"

New alerts began to howl in the Nexus, but she switched them off, using her flashtats to officially authorize the use of all untested weapons. The Dark Matter Collmunators had been recently mounted on a few of the cruisers that were still active in the fleet, set up to be tested on asteroids between star systems. These were also Kendis designs, though rumor had it they had been secretly deployed once before during the Crucible to disastrous effect. It was one of many reasons that the old city of Everstrong was cordoned off from the general crew. The strange Strifer-designed weaponry of that time period had all been lost, along with their specifications. Jira now wished they had been salvaged.

The face of Naga suddenly appeared upon her right screen, next to the handlebars of her saddle, "Security of Chief Jira Mantabe, the Naga-Ports are now available to all senior staff and those officers ranking Lieutenant and above. Captain Fieldscan sends his regards and has just issued emergency protocols. All personnel who are not directly involved in the defense of the ship are being sent to shelters within the midships regions of all Wheels or in their communities if they have bunker facilities. All the Technology Sector Temples are standing by for your order to lock down, after taking in as many crew as they can safely manage. As per regulations, and with the blessings of the Judiciary Council, you are now in command of the ship."

Jira snarled, "Blessings and regulations be damned! I've no time for politics! Thank you for bringing me good news and forgive my anger, but things are not going well for us right now. Clear the communities and roads surrounding the Kendis Vault. If these fucking alien needle things get into the ship, we may need everything in that confusing shithole, and I don't want any collateral damage wandering about. I'm now sending the Vault guardians in to contact Five to give the android an update on what's going on out here."

Naga's visage nodded to her, "The results from the Spin-Drive turrets are heartening, but the swarm is closing in on the main hull. There are off-shoots of the main body now reaching out for the ice cap, Harbor One, Agro Wheel Three and Residence Wheel Two. Eighty percent of all fighter-pods are missing, twenty percent of all other Security Fleet vessels have been destroyed. All of the remaining space vessels have been damaged. The hull of Ganges is holding, with only minor damage to the surface, but it seems that the needles which make up the cloud are melting into the plating."

Jira's head swam with the news concerning the status of the fleet and the fact that portions of the cloud were already impacting the main hull of Ganges. She hit the general comms for her Sector, "All personnel, this is Chief Mantabe. This is not a drill. All Security platoons will now deploy. Report to your emergency stations and prepare for anti-boarding procedures."

CHAPTER EIGHTEEN

Wheel Rotation - Spin Sowing - Mission Harvest - Spiral 5620

"It's a wonderful rotation in Ganges. In fact, it's always a wonderful rotation. Every dawn-slice, every sowing, every harvest, perfectly tidy. The grass is green, well fed, and manicured to perfection. The water is always pure. The air is very clean, the food untainted. This is our condition. This is also our problem. I am amongst those who are concerned that in such an environment, personal growth and technological development are stagnating due to a lack of need. I suppose that one could say that this is all a matter of perspective, but that attitude only proves my point. If one lives without struggle, there is no drive to improve anything. We keep on believing that things are fine, that innovation is untidy, and highly problematic. Some rotation, we may come to regret our lack of invention, but by then it will be too late. Our doom shall come upon us swiftly, and we shall be thoroughly unprepared. These ideas trouble me every slice at my post, and I'm thinking of going on a vacation to clear my head of these troublesome thoughts."
Kendis Higashi, Planetary Geneticist Rank Four, personal log, V13

Agro Wheel Two, Security Level Four

Harbor Sector Ensign Rank Four Jero Coreline was scrambling to get his crew out of the Security docking bay, before anyone else got killed. He had just been promoted the rotation before, increasing from Rank Three to Four, which also meant getting some pre-officer perks, better bonuses and more responsibility than he'd ever had before in his entire life. To his own surprise, his team of docking bay crew had applauded his humble leadership and kept reminding him that the next step was Dock Lieutenant. He had been overjoyed, overwhelmed and quite concerned about his new responsibilities. He had jumped from a fighter-pod repair-crewmember to leading four teams within the Security bays. He had contacted his mate, Scratch, and she had screamed with delight. Everything was finally looking to be on course for the two of them, then the emergency erupted out of Planet Forty-One.

Jero had been at his station since last rush-slice, and it was now dawn-slice the next rotation. There had been no time for breaks, just rushed meals from the food dispensers. Sleep was something no one could afford right now, though he did rotate the teams, to give their crews a chance to recover from the frenetic activity throughout the Security harbor. The current situation was an absolute sleepscare, but Jero kept his focus upon his duty, so that he wouldn't have time to process what was going on and panicking over it. The entire fleet had scrambled into space, to defend Ganges from some kind of attack, though he wasn't sure who they were fighting nor why.

The forward fighter-pod escort, which was Lieutenant Tarn Vekkor's Nondo Squadron hadn't been heard from since they left Ganges, but others had come back, limping to their landing platforms, covered with damaged systems. Jero's teams had stepped back in shock when the first pod had returned, coated in some kind of purple, glowing splotches that were steaming acrid vapors. The entire cockpit canopy had also been damaged and was barely able to open up. The pilot had crawled out, then screamed when his hands made contact with the strange, purple markings. To Jero's horror, the substance had climbed up the pilot's arm as the man thrashed about, halfway out of his pod. His toragi had tried to pull him free, then yowled in a way that Jero had never heard before. The Dockmaster had rushed in, then told everyone to exit the bay, whose doors were then sealed.

Medical Sector had been notified, as the Rescue Services crew rushed in to save the pilot and his big cat. They had been too late. By the time help had arrived, the pilot and his toragi were dead, eaten away by the purple things that were still growing on the pod. They had tried vacuum quarantine, but this had no effect on the alien substance. Jero's ear-comm had revealed that several other fighter-pods also had been similarly afflicted, with dozens of bays shutting down. Only three pilots and five toragi, out of the twenty pods that returned to port, survived long enough to be brought to Medical Sector. All of them would be brought to the isolation labs which could be ejected from Ganges, should any contagion get loose.

Jero, along with his team, had then been reassigned to one of the battleship bays, which was large enough to service seed-ships. They were now forced to wear Vac-Con suits, after hauling their tools and supplies from the fighter-pod bays. He had been in this type of dock before, during his orientation, but nothing could prepare him for the bedlam that filled the giant bay. Chaos ruled the chamber, as bay hands from several different docks had been gathered together.

A woman ran over to him, her Security uniform that of an officer, with gold wings and crossed chains at the shoulder, "Ensign Coreline! I'm Aliny Kalins, Dock Lieutenant in charge here. I've been told you're good crew, and you have a reputation for getting your team organized. We need to clear the central repair and holding area for damaged ships returning for servicing. I need you to split all these dock hands into two groups, at the spinward and leeward ends. I'll take spinward. Make sure that the central area is ready to receive damaged ships."

Jero saluted, using both Harbor and Security gestures, "Yessir! I'll get right on that, Lieutenant! Any idea as to what we should expect? Most of us are fighter-pod repair-crew, though we can and will adapt to whatever you might need!"

Lieutenant Kalins shook her head, "Expect anything and everything, Ensign. It's a real shitstorm out there!"

She ran off to the spinward side, yelling at crew to come with her to the far end of the dock. Jero blinked hard, then swirled into action, grabbing his old team and delegating them to handle the load. They each took a team of repair-crew, then widened the network, until everyone was gathered at the leeward side, organized by specialty. He was pleased to note that his side of the dock had prepared themselves first, until he remembered this wasn't a drill or competition. The Lieutenant did flash him a bright smile and waved from the far side of the massive chamber.

Klaxons began to blare, as Naga-Ma's voice boomed from the wallscreens, "Prepare for the arrival of injured crew! Make certain your Vac-Con suits are sealed properly! All hands, ready your stations!"

Jero ran from one specialist team to another, making sure everyone was secured and that their suits were on properly. The air was now being swallowed up by Ganges, for docks like this one were usually kept in vacuum conditions. This one had been flooded with atmosphere, to help get all the work teams inside and ready, before any of the damaged ships could be sent in. A howling sound filled his ears from outside his helmet, but this vanished quickly, until all he could hear was his own breathing and his ear-comm. The crews were standing by, tools at the ready, fuel lines in hand and power stations running. At the sternward side of the chamber, he could see a line of Rescue Services crew getting ready with magnetic gurneys and medical packs. All the airlocks had closed, their extension tunnels retracted.

The deck beneath his feet vibrated, as the massive bay doors were shifting upward. Jero checked his helmet's display panel at the bottom of the visor, making sure his teams were still in position. The comms was filled with Security jargon, some of which he knew but not enough to get a clear picture of what was going on in near-Ganges space. When the giant doors were halfway open, he looked upon a scene of horror. Silent, flashing lights ripped through space. Chunks of debris were floating about, colliding with the hull, some of it smashing into the bay. A fighter-pod tumbled in, rolling out of control, forcing a handful of the crew to flee, as it crashed into a wall. More were coming, all of them flying chaotically. He saw a cruiser in the distance. It was being torn apart from within.

A sudden wave of tiny objects flashed into the bay. They glowed with a violet light. Most looked like nails or needles, but some were shaped like snowflakes or leaves. They rushed into the chamber, smashing against the sternward wall, coating half the Rescue Services crew, who screamed over the comms. Blood drops filled the bay like mist. More of the needles were flooding into the dock, then circling around as if seeking an exit. Jero was stunned by the turn of events, but he heard Lieutenant Kalins' voice in his ear, "Everyone evacuate! Now! Move your sorry asses! Abandon the bay! I repeat, abandon the bay!"

Command Hub, Level Ten

Executive Officer Wasp Tornpage stared at the images floating in the center of the Bridge, circling the holoprojector like a flock of crows. The Chief-of-the-Deck was scrambling at his boards, trying desperately to get all the stations coordinated, despite the terrible shock that gripped the crew. It was like something from her worst sleepscares. Wasp could barely believe what she was seeing on the displays. The entire Security Fleet was engaged in the fight just outside Ganges' hull, save for a handful of vessels which had been going through refit just before the attack. She shook her head, to clear it of the astounding images, and began racing through the most important stations at the base of the Bridge, where Sector representatives were placed for ease of communication with the command platform.

The Bridge Security Commander, Typ Ligon, had already sealed the doors of the Bridge. Half of his platoon was stationed in front of the entrance, as if expecting boarders to appear at any instant. Wasp's task was to gather a comprehensive report for the Captain, who was currently speaking virtually with the Sector Chiefs. The first set of stations she had visited was the helm, navigation and sensors. Ganges was still on its course, building up speed for system exit. Unfortunately, this meant they were still getting closer to the planet, which was continuing to release the swarm of needles. The sensor report was the most troubling, for they were having tremendous difficulty seeing past the alien cloud. There were no readings from the surface, but they did tell her that the planet's magnetosphere was acting up, bombarding low orbit space with radiation. The ice cap observation crews were still at their posts, doing everything they could to cut through the interference.

The Bridge Security station had bad news and interesting news. The bad news was that the fleet was collapsing. Engines were malfunctioning. Their weapons were giving out, either from using up all their missiles or due to overheating. Every vessel was damaged, some more severely than others, with the fighter-pods taking the brunt of the attack. All of the Security ships were now covered in purple spots and blotches, though what this meant was still a mystery. Most of the fighter-pods had simply disappeared from view, swallowed by the swarm from Planet Forty-One. The interesting news came from the Fleet Command Vessel, Malati. It seems that the alien cloud was mainly composed of billions of four-centimeter-long needle-like components, though some other shapes had been reported. None of them registered as being organic on Security vessel sensors, yet they didn't show up as being made of inorganic material either.

Within the first seed-sliver of the attack, Captain Perrin Fieldscan had swiftly ordered a series of attempts at communication with Planet Forty-One. They used the transmitters from Harbors One and Two, even sending out a hundred Naga-drones. They tried every bandwidth they could think of, every spectrum, using both language and binary codes, plus AeyAie protocols and the laser comms. There had been no answer to their attempts, save for silence and a never-ending stream of needles, all of which were matching the course and speed of Ganges. If anyone heard these calls for negotiation, they weren't listening. So far, the drones that had been sent out into space had yet to be attacked or hampered by the swarm of needles, which led to some uncomfortable questions as to why this was the case. Was the alien cloud only targeting objects with signs of biological life?

Making her way back to the command platform, she did her best to reassure the crew, which only seemed to make them even more nervous. She really couldn't blame them. A calm, polite Strifer was a frightened one. The entire Bridge crew was on edge. Nothing like this had ever happened before, and they were not as prepared for it as they would like. Then again, what would be a proper protocol for handling a continent-sized swarm of alien needles that were all self-powered and created by a highly advanced species? There wasn't a precedent for this event. No answers were waiting within the archives, no experts to consult, unless one counted the writers of fictional broadcasts. She briefly wondered if a time machine would help.

When she got to the command platform, Captain Fieldscan was waiting for her, a grim expression on his face, "Executive Tornpage, good timing. I just finished my session with the Sector Chiefs. I'm afraid that I bear grave news. Security Fleet Command has reported that these needles seem to melt into the hulls of their ships, eating away at the plating. The Harbors have both closed down all space traffic and are now sealing the docking bay airlocks. Stellar suspects this won't be enough to prevent incursions into the rest of Ganges, so the harbor crews are now welding hull plating into place to cover all the access points, but there's little time to be had. Engineering is submitting all materials being requested to block all airlocks, but it will take them sowings to get them all."

Wasp scratched at her wild, green hair, "What about Security itself? How are they doing?"

Captain Fieldscan shook his head, "Not well. They had made an attempt to repair and service their fighter-pods, hoping to save the pilots, but this opened them up to a direct assault in their harbors. Chief Mantabe is locking down her Sector as best she can. Naga-drones have been sent into the bays which were invaded and found the needles flying in formation or melting into the decks and walls of the holds. They've already lost hundreds of flight and service crew, along with seven platoons of Rescue Services personnel. The main gun turrets on the outer hull are still doing a fairly good job of holding the main cloud back, but only the Spin-Drive weapons seem to have any lasting effect. Stellar is also working with Security to figure out why this is the case and what else we can throw at them."

Wasp pinched the tip of her nose, an old habit from her student spirals, "Let me guess. While the guns are keeping the main body of needles away from Ganges, small clusters are still reaching the hull. Those that make it are eating the plating, just like on the other vessels out there."

Perrin gave Wasp a single nod, "Directly on point! I've just asked our crew representative to work with the news broadcasts, asking all crew to either remain at their posts or to find shelter closer to midships. We need people at their stations if we are going to have any chance of organizing a way to resist this invasion. There's already an insidious rumor that this attack has to do with the Solarians. We must be clear minded about the situation if we're going to get out of it in one piece."

Wasp gasped aloud, "Big Cheese! I've just thought of something that's truly terrible! The docking bays and airlocks are all made of hull plating. That material is very dense and may keep the needles busy for a while, but the observation domes, the sensor arrays, the viewing blisters, they're all made of synth-quartz! That stuff is tough, but will it hold? All of those windows are not nearly as thick as the main hull itself!"

The Captain became ghostly pale as he considered the implications. Before he could give any orders to her, Wasp ran over to the sensor stations. They had to shut down all the observation portals, bolster the hatches and barricade the domes, before the needles got in and started killing the crew.

Ice Cap of Ganges, Observation Blister Seven

Stellar Sector Ensign Rank Four Tachi Vactor was frantic in her attempts to get information to the Bridge. The data her team had collected could be invaluable for the Captain and the Security Fleet. All of the sensors in her observation dome were active, seeking answers from the chaos which had erupted in near-Ganges space. Her friend from Engineering Sector, Squeak Greasestain, was still with them, focusing on the kendar sensors, which were experimental and tricky to operate. Tachi still didn't fully understand what the new sensors revealed nor how they operated, but she trusted Squeak, who had the clearance to work with them. Apparently, once the cloud of alien needles erupted from the surface, the kendar had gone wild, along with the more pedestrian quadar sensors, which mainly showed wavicle harmonies that occurred whenever matter responded to leptons. The patterns it revealed were often striking and were invaluable when studying complex interactions on a grand scale. Tachi had asked Squeak to explain the kendar sensors, but the Strifer had simply shook her head, claiming it was classified.

It had been the lidar which had given her team their first clue about what had emerged from Planet Forty-One. The laser-based sensor was highly precise in its ability to track moving particles, giving them a clear picture of mass, composition or even momentum, depending upon the settings used. They had discovered that the cloud was a swarm of needle-like structures, each one no longer than her finger, with most of them being far smaller. Her team had been trying to come up with a phrase to describe the phenomenon, by torturing the dominant language of Ganges. They had arrived at the term "umharliti", which was a compound phrase meaning "alien needles". It was simple but effective as a description. She had posted the new moniker in her report to the Bridge, but she hadn't heard if it had been accepted.

Tachi tore her eyes away from the passive telescope displays, which were hard-pressed to present anything useful in the clutter outside the ship. She glanced over at her team, who were all submitting updates to the next packet of information to be sent over to the Bridge. No one was chattering, for there was no time for such comforts anymore. The only sounds she could hear were the steady hum of station computers, fingers tapping upon buttons, Squeak grumbling about the new sensors, and an unusual, clicking noise coming from overhead. Tachi looked up and gasped aloud. She wanted to shout in alarm, to warn the others, but her throat was frozen in absolute terror.

The main telescopes of the observation chamber rose to a height of thirty meters, like a forest of steel tubes, staring into the dark of space through the synth-quartz of the dome itself. Tachi could now see that there were patches of violet light spattered all over the transparent ceiling. They were moving, growing, spreading fast enough for her to see them clearly, even from forty meters below. Smaller spots were rapidly appearing, spattering the entire dome with dots. Her control station beeped at her, signifying a new message from the Bridge. It startled her from the horror at what she was seeing above her. Tachi glanced down at the notice. It was a command from Executive Officer Wasp Tornpage, ordering the observation domes to evacuate all personnel immediately.

She slapped the received icon and turned to address her team, not daring to look above, for fear of losing her composure once again, "We have new orders! Listen up, all of you! Evacuate the observatory! Now! Don't bother shutting anything down. If you haven't done so already, set all recordings to automated broadcast to the Bridge and Stellar Analysis! Now move! We have no time!"

Everyone began to express outrage at the new directive, glaring at her and gesturing toward their busy sensor stations. Tachi scowled back at them and simply pointed at the dome above. Heads lifted, eyes grew wide with horror, Squeak began cursing loudly, her hands flashing over her station boards. Tachi clapped her hands hard enough to cause pain, snapping her team from their shocked paralysis, "I said, Move! Now! That's an order!"

Squeak shouted, "Last rat out is a dead one!"

The observation crew suddenly sprang into action, racing for the doors of the dome. Suddenly, a high-pitched wailing sound ruptured the air. Tachi could feel her hair flying about, as the synth-quartz above was compromised. Klaxons sounded off, alarms blared their warnings, as atmosphere was screaming into the vacuum of space. Squeak gave off a ragged scream, as a chunk of half-melted synth-quartz fell onto her legs, trapping her at the kendar station. Tachi rushed over to aid her friend, stumbling over cables and fallen station chairs. The rest of her team were swiping their flashtats over the reader at the main hatch, but the heavy door wouldn't budge. Atmosphere preservation protocols had kicked in, sealing the only exit to the dome.

Tachi was struggling to reach Squeak, clambering over the kendar station. Naga's firm voice could barely be heard over the roar of air, "Emergency shutdown implemented! Sec-sec-secure your breathing-ing-ing units! Main-main-main bulk-bulkheads non-non responsive! Power loss-loss-loss in grid Eight-Seven-Alpha…"

The rest of the AeyAie's announcement was lost to screams and howling atmosphere. Tachi finally reached her friend. The Strifer engineer was choking and coughing, struggling to break free from the collapsed piece of dome that had mashed her legs. Blood was flying everywhere. There was a strange, violet substance that was crawling up Squeak's neck. Tachi tried to lift the synth-quartz trapping her friend, as pain lashed at her arms. She pulled back in alarm and saw the same, purplish stuff eating at her skin. Her forearms were smoldering with a noxious vapor, as she howled in agony.

With tears filling her eyes, she saw that Squeak was dead, her head back, staring blankly at the ruptured dome from underneath her rat mask. Tinny screams and sobs could still be heard. Tachi turned about and saw her team on their knees, clustered together and covered in splatters of purple spots and blood. The sounds were falling away rapidly, as more hunks of the dome came free, falling straight for the deck, which was impossible within the zero gravity conditions of the observation blister. Most of the pieces should have been floating free into open space. Instead, they were slamming into the floor, hitting the stations and smashing them to ruin. The needles crashed in soundlessly behind the shattered bits of dome. They had done this. They had shoved the broken parts of the observation blister into her friend, into her crew. They swarmed into the remains of the dome, as the temperature dropped to a few degrees above absolute zero. Tachi felt her skin become hard and brittle, her lungs exploded, and she dropped into darkness.

Residence Wheel Two, Level Three

Student Spat Newstain hurried along with his classmates. They had been in the middle of history class, discussing the first half of the Age of Unity. His teacher was better than most, as she made the dry material more interesting than Spat had expected. They had been up to the second half of the second octennium, which was an important time period for his family, as it also included the origins of the Strifer Movement. Then the alarms went off. All the other kids had groaned about another drill, but he had kept quiet, for complaining amounted to little in such situations. The teacher had brought them out into the corridor, as usual, and they did a headcount. Once it was certified that they had everyone in line, they had all marched toward the intersection for their dispersal toward the shelters that ringed the school.

Things changed when they reached their appointed place, to find Security Lieutenant Dreasco waiting for them with her toragi, Nancy. She was accompanied by the other Police crew, but they had grim expressions on their faces and weapons in their hands, which was totally unexpected. At first, Spat had thought it was a new twist to the normal procedure, but then the Lieutenant shattered this idea by speaking with a harsh tone, "Okay, everyone! Settle down! This is Not a drill! You will follow our toragis to your shelters and stay with them until you are collected by Security personnel. You will Not deviate from these instructions! Remain with your toragi until the emergency has ended. Your teachers will be helping us to lock down the school. They will join you in the shelters as soon as they can do so in a safe manner. Be good crew!"

The Lieutenant turned about and gathered the other Security crew and the teachers together in the center of the intersection. Her toragi padded up to Spat's classmates and huffed at them. Nancy then led his group from the school building and onto the sports field. Spat found that his chest was thumping in reaction to the words of Lieutenant Dreasco. This was a real emergency! His first thoughts were of his parents, wondering where they were and if they had shelters near their posts. Tears threatened to spill from his eyes, as they ran after Nancy. He could hear some of the others sobbing to themselves. A couple were chatting quietly, until the toragi turned her head and roared at them. The skyscreens were a mess. Just half of them were displaying a blue sky with puffy clouds. The rest of them were filled with Naga's face, Captain Fieldscan, and Security Chief Mantabe, all of them calling for the crew to remain calm and to stay at their posts.

Spat couldn't even begin to imagine what could have happened that would endanger Ganges. The ship was so massive, so well armored, with hundred-meter-thick hull plating. It was defended by the bravest and most capable crew he could think of. Had the Solarians invaded? Had the fighting he'd heard about in Res One spread throughout the vessel? Was it something else? The lack of knowledge was driving him crazy, but it was distracting him with anger over not being able to figure things out for himself. It kept him from falling apart and weeping like a novice. He grabbed the arm of his classmate, Milli, who had stumbled, not being able to see from the hot tears coursing from her eyes. He didn't blame her for the emotions, but he was now taking on the responsibility for making sure she made it to the shelter.

As usual, the bullies who always tried to torment him, Bino, Togan and Keff, were making fun of everyone else. Giggling like fools to cover their own fears. Spat was tempted to call them out on it, but he had no authority to do so. He was just another student, not even Full Crew. He ignored their crude jibes and coarse humor, keeping his mind on helping Milli. One of the boys, named Seket, was blubbering along, stumbling into the other kids, as the line became a jumble, desperately trying to keep up with the rushing toragi. Spat leaned over, pulling Milli along with him, and snagged Seket with his free hand, keeping him close to his side. Now the three of them could run together with a bit more stability. At least, in theory. Spat was acting as their eyes, telling them to go left or right. They still stumbled a bit, but remained on their feet.

Nancy ran down a rough path between twin rows of tall trees, their upswept branches blocking the skyscreens above. The toragi came to a small, moss-covered hill that had an airlock hatch on one side. She touched the reader at the right side of the door, and it lifted open with a hiss of pressurized air. The toragi sat to one side of the opening and yowled at the students. They scrambled inside the dark chamber, lights turning on automatically, revealing a twenty-meter-wide space with benches and lockers. Two other doors were on opposite sides of the room. The air was crisp and clean. There were no wallscreens, Naga-Units or displays of any kind. The floor was bare deck metal, and Spat noticed two medical stations set up next to a drinking fountain at the far side of the chamber.

Once all the students were inside the shelter, Nancy prowled in and slapped a large activation plate next to the hatch with her paw. The door closed with a heavy clang. Spat and his classmates began to sit on the benches in the same order as they used for drills, sneaking glances at each other to see if everyone was okay. Spat did a quick headcount and was relieved to find that everyone had gotten into the shelter. The faces around him were dark with exertion and streaked with tears. Even the bullies had puffy eyes and sweaty brows. Nothing evened the score like a real disaster.

Nancy inspected each of them carefully, sniffing at their faces. Many of the students hugged her neck, avoiding the hard carapace armor she wore. When the toragi was satisfied, she turned toward the two unlocked doors in the room, pushing them open with her paws. One was a lavatory, with several privacy stalls and a pair of sinks. At the far end of it was a bathing area, like those used in the locker room after physical education activities. The other door led to a modest storage room, filled with refrigeration units and crates of food. Spat was glad they wouldn't starve in here. The only problem was, they didn't know how long they would have to remain in the shelter. It might be just a paring-sliver or even a few rotations. The benches were all padded, with folding sections to make cots for sleeping. Spat was still terribly worried about his parents, his cousins, even his pet gerbil, Hook. He had no idea if they were safe, or if he would ever see them again.

Agro Wheel Two, Security Level Five

William Blaine was nursing his cold coffee, feeling out of place amongst the frightened crew around him. A blue tick with a white stripe had been placed on his arm a few slices ago by a doctor from Medical Sector. It was supposed to keep him calm, but it did nothing about his nanites, which were still in an uproar. There were times when he felt that they were made to be a bit too independent and too clever, especially in times when clear heads were needed. Chief of Technology Sector Eagle Lund had checked his internal computer systems and had declared that they were now functioning well. Once the mysterious signal had died down, William's internal systems had begun repairs, though this had required he eat some unusual things, such as small bolts and silicon rings from a repair kit for station processors. The crew around him had looked at him strangely, but Eagle had explained that William's nanites had to have the proper materials to repair his systems.

The communications link to his vessel had remained intact, and he had run diagnostics on his ship, which was still attached to the hull at the Engineering Sector Wheel. This part of Ganges had yet to be attacked by the swarm which had erupted from Planet Forty-One, but that was simply a matter of time. He sent the scout vessel instructions via a microscopic drone made of his nanites. He wouldn't risk an open signal which might be traced by whatever it was that the landing party had awoken. He needed his ship to remain in stealth mode, to avoid detection by the cloud of alien needles. The scout vessel did have its own defenses, energy fields that sheltered it from physical harm, some limited weapons and its camo-armor, but he didn't want to risk any action that might make the situation worse than it was.

After a brief stay at Medical Sector, William had been escorted to Security by Darron's platoon. Mike's short tail had been twitching all rotation, a sign that the toragi was unsettled. He growled at the other big cats, who responded by ducking their heads. William wondered if Mike was being affected by Darron's unease or if the toragi understood that Ganges was under attack. He was certain that Mike could smell the fear of the crew, but he wondered how much the toragi knew. It was an interesting puzzle, but one which had to be set aside for now, much like the giant statue at the main entrance into Security Sector. The massive edifice had depicted a giant, muscular male human, with an oversized, prosthetic hand and an eyepatch. The statue was beautifully detailed, and he had been told it was made to honor the founder of Security. The glowering face had been disturbing to look upon, as if ready to come to life and smash him into the deck with a giant fist. The entire platoon had saluted the monument, while he had gaped at it with appreciation and dismay.

Now, William was in yet another council chamber, which was full of Security officers from the Investigations Department and his friend, Eagle, who was keeping track of Technology Sector through use of his Naga-Port. Data displays were filled with scenes from the sensors of the few Security vessels which had survived the initial assault. The turrets upon the hull of Ganges were still firing at the cloud, holding the main body of it away from the ship, but he doubted they would last much longer. The drawn face of Wasp Tornpage was upon one wallscreen at the spinward end of the room, while Naga's face appeared on the opposite side. Security Chief Mantabe was speaking on several smaller displays which were distributed on the central table of the room. Multiple conversations were going on at once, and he used his nanites to sort them out and log them for review later on. If there was a later on.

William got up from his seat and walked over to a wallscreen on the leeward side, with Mike dutifully following him. It seemed that the toragi was a real stickler for orders. Eagle Lund was standing there, chatting with Naga and a tall woman from Investigations, whose scarred face told the tale of a life spent fighting for her crew. William nodded to her and his friend, then addressed the AeyAie, "Naga. If I may ask you a question, please? Something's been troubling me since this whole situation got out of hand."

The AeyAie looked at him and nodded its virtual head, "Of course, you may, William. I shall do my best to answer you, though there are many unknowns which must be dealt with before we understand what is happening to us."

William grimaced, "Yeah, about that. This ship is being threatened by an advanced unknown. I know you don't like the idea of contact with my people, but we Solarians have a very large fleet and would be willing to assist you. Don't you have an emergency beacon? The main transmitter? You could call for aid. The Solarian Alliance would be happy to help."

Naga paused a bit before replying, as some of the crew, including Eagle, chuckled quietly to themselves, "I'm afraid that is impossible, William. There is no emergency beacon. The main transmitter, to which you refer, was fully disassembled octenniums ago. It was broken down to its base components to find an error that kept entering the messages which we were receiving from the Terran Conglomerate. Most of it is now in small containers."

William's face must have registered his shock, for Eagle stepped closer to him and touched his elbow, "I'm sorry, my friend, but there is no way to make contact with anyone else. Besides, we don't like the idea of owing anyone for such a favor, especially a culture with which we have no experience."

William burst out, "Are you all insane? You tore the main transmitter apart yourselves? Here you are, alone in the depths of uncharted space, and you refuse to rebuild the one means you had to seek help?"

Naga raised a virtual eyebrow at him, "You mean help from savages who threatened us for so long? You mean we should have known it was possible for your culture to find a way to circumvent the speed of light? Ganges was built to be self-sufficient. We have survived many disasters since Launch, some of them created by Terran mischief."

William rolled his eyes, "That comes close to paranoia! In fact, it Is paranoia! Look, my vessel can send a data-box back to base. It has a minimal Wend Drive, but one strong enough for a single trip back to the Sol System. Thus far, my ship remains undamaged, but that may not last. I could just disappear again and do it myself, but I want your permission to try."

Eagle frowned as he shook his head, "And what would the Alliance ask of us in return? To join them, be part of their fleet? We've been out here, independent and alone, for too long to be comfortable with that idea. Can you absolutely guarantee that our wishes to be left alone will be respected?"

William ground his teeth in frustration, "No, I can't! But it's better than being killed by whatever that swarm is!"

Naga tilted its head, "While there have been incursions, they have all been contained, for now. There are many tactics which we have yet to try, before we do something we might regret later on. These needles, which the Bridge is now calling 'umharliti' in honor of those who made the moniker, may be the descendants of those who built this system into what we see now. They might also simply be an automated defense mechanism, which could be hacked, blocked or evaded. The only reason we are using brute strength to fight them is due to the lack of response time. We are currently trying to contact Planet Forty-One, through all possible means, to see if we may make peaceful contact and end this situation."

William walked away from the wallscreen without another word. He slumped into the nearest free chair and sighed. A feeling of impending doom was permeating his mind. He understood their reluctance to call for aid. From the histories he was given by Naga, it was clear the crew would have a hard time trusting the Solarian Alliance, even considering it as dangerous as the swarm outside the hull. He would respect their decision for now. If things went badly or the alien needles made further incursions, then he would act on his own to save Ganges, even if no one appreciated the effort.

Residence Wheel One, Level Two

Knight Pelor Guardhand dragged his squire into cover. The young man was unconscious but alive. Both their armor was dented and scorched; their steeds lost to the early fighting at Keep Smith. Squire Korgan Naldo had been so proud to finally see real action, then the horrors of war had laid his youthful fantasies to waste. Pelor gritted his teeth, as he struggled to bring them both toward the safety of a cluster of shattered rubble, a leftover from the dirigible strike on Keep Smith. The upper towers had all been shattered, but the reinforced walls had held. Three times, the Security Knights had charged the keep, leading the newly arrived reinforcements, while the wounded were carried off to a mobile Rescue Services encampment. The enemy behind the walls had responded by blowing out discrete sections of their defense, to reveal cannons that fired explosive ballistics.

The field surrounding the keep had become a morass of mud, blood and shrapnel. Knight Guardhand had just led the fourth assault, hoping to climb the rubble to reach the outermost walls of the keep, but they had been forced back by flames and armor-piercing rounds from hidden gun-nests. A few gas cannisters had been hurled at them, but these were the least of their worries. Even with the main towers being destroyed by the dirigible fleet, Keep Smith remained a staunch defender of the syndicate forces within. The skyscreens above had flickered with messages from one of the leaders of the organized criminals, calling upon the Knights to immediately surrender. Otherwise, they remained dark, covering the nature preserves with gloom.

Security had sent mag-bike riders, after learning that so many of the Knights had lost their horses during the beginning stages of the siege. Their presence had changed nothing, as the enemy had yet to leave the safety of the grand walls of the keep. Pelor had requested permission to open the arsenal bays of Security to secure tanks and other war machines for the next phase of the assault, but he had yet to receive any word from Chief Mantabe. It was quite obvious that something had gone terribly wrong, and he had briefly thought that perhaps the syndicates had been using multiple sites to strike back at Security Sector.

During the last attack at Keep Smith, a message had been brought to him via a Security Police Ensign, as their datapads and comms were still being jammed by the syndicate. The woman had told him that Ganges itself was now under attack from outside the hull. The news had startled Squire Naldo, and he had tried to ask a question, turning his back upon the enemy, when he was shot five times. Pelor had cried out as he watched his student fall from the heap of rubble they had built up to gain access to the lower ramparts of Keep Smith. He and the Security Ensign had jumped down as swiftly as they could to get to the wounded squire, only to find him toppled over a hunk of wall, unmoving.

Knight Guardhand's toragi, Larry, had rushed over to help, along with Squire Naldo's cat, Ben. The two felines had used their own bodies to cover the three of them, allowing Pelor to drag his squire from the fight, but the Security Ensign had been hit with some kind of incendiary explosive, which had left him alone to gain shelter for his ward. The air was choked with noxious fumes, the stink of death and the screams of injured crew. He had to return to the perimeter of the field surrounding Keep Smith, where the personnel carriers created a barrier, trapping the syndicate in place and also providing some shelter from the ongoing launch of enemy missiles. From what they had already examined from the remains of these devices, it had been generally agreed they were not Security-issue units but were cobbled together by the syndicates themselves.

Just as Pelor was preparing himself for a long, dangerous crawl over to the carriers, loading his squire onto the back of Ben, all the skyscreens lit up at once. A shape-shifting figure appeared where blue skies and clouds should have been, but it was bright enough for him to see the wreckage of battle all around him. Dead Security crew, horses and toragi littered the cratered field. The walls of the keep were now clearly visible, badly damaged but still mainly intact. Shattered mag-bikes, heaped like broken toys, formed piles of debris all around the keep.

The mysterious, ever-shifting person on the skyscreens spoke, their voice resounding throughout the nature preserves, "This message is for all the Security crew surrounding Keep Smith, especially the Knight who is in command. We wish to parley. Do not misunderstand. I am Not surrendering to you. We need to talk about what is best for Ganges, which we share as a home. Our ship is under siege, much as Keep Smith is right now. If your Chief is as efficient as I've heard, this news should have just reached you by now. What you have not been told is that the fleet is broken. The Security harbors have been invaded, and the entire crew now needs your aid in defense of Ganges. I am willing to let you clear the field, collect your dead."

Pelor found himself trembling with outrage at the audacity of this secretive criminal, yet he listened carefully as they continued speaking, "At this moment of our ship's distress, I am willing to send out a representative from the keep to speak with you about our current intentions. Things have changed. Our disagreements are petty compared to the safety of our vessel. Ganges has need of your forces to counter the threat emerging from Planet Forty-One. It also requires our aid. We wish to join with you, to repel this alien threat which has just lashed out at our common home. My representative will not be armed. I have often heard Security speak of honor, and so I shall see the measure of yours very shortly. Whether you admit it or not, you need us to fight alongside your own forces, or the ship will be destroyed. You have one seed-sliver to prepare yourselves."

Pelor's ear-comm erupted with jumbled sound, as the jamming cleared. The skyscreens returned to their normal function, and Naga drones rose back into the air. The first thing he heard was the voice of Chief Jira Mantabe, calling all Security forces to answer the call of duty. New images flashed at the bottom of his dented helmet, revealing the nature of the threat against the ship, and he shuddered in response to the carnage. The shifty syndicate leader had been telling the truth, and while Pelor still didn't trust the crime bosses, hated them for what they had done to the Knights of Ganges, there was but one course which he could take. He had to meet with their representative, accept their aid and bring the fight to the greater menace facing them all. He swore to himself that he would keep a close eye on their new, criminal allies, but he would work with them, for now.

Near-Ganges Space, Security Flagship Malati

Security Fleet Commander Vina Harrolon stalked the bridge of the Malati, listening to reports from the surviving vessels. The outlook was grim, but there were still bits of good news and some fresh mysteries concerning the swarm that was still matching the course of Ganges. Not a single fighter-pod had escaped the first battle unscathed, with most of the pilots killed when they attempted to break free and return to port. The light cruiser Veera had just exploded, after launching all of its forward guns at the alien cloud, then entering the mass of needles at full speed. The captain of the vessel, named Larn Vocalant, had been a daring member of her fleet. He had overloaded the main engines, once his ship had been fully swallowed by the swarm, buying more time for Ganges to escape.

She shook her head with sorrow. Was this all they had against the enemy? Suicide runs that killed hundreds of crew, destroying assets they might need in the future? The thought was unacceptable. There just had to be a way to counter the alien enemy. Thus far, the swarm's tactics had been simple enough, overwhelm with numbers, then latch onto vessels, eating at their hulls and weaponry until they were no longer a threat. Her fleet had kept the swarm at bay, which was an amazing achievement, but for how long? Even with the main body of the cloud staying back from the fleet, smaller subsets of the swarms got through, attaching themselves to the hull of Ganges or finding access through observation blisters and airlocks.

Her own flagship was now covered with patches of bright violet, though the hull of the Malati was far heavier than those of fighter-pods. The alien material had started off eating away the hull swiftly but slowed down after gaining a depth of one meter. The consumption rate had recently dropped to less than a meter per slice, which bought them time, but no one knew why this was happening. It certainly hadn't occurred at the airlocks and docking bay doors of Harbor One. Synth-quartz also seemed particularly vulnerable to the swarm's attacks, a problem she had mitigated by commanding every vessel of the fleet to shutter their viewing ports and run on sensors, while they still operated.

Captain Loni Voidloc was shouting orders to her crew, setting up another barrage from their port-side Spin-Drive guns. These weapons had been their only effective assets, not counting the nuclear missiles, which had all been expended. The turrets of Ganges continued to hammer the swarm with the same type of guns, along with the highly experimental Dark Matter Collmunators, yet another strange weapon from the labs within the Kendis Vault. The cloud of alien needles, now called the umharliti, seemed to react negatively to the forces unleashed upon them which originated from that mysterious and classified location.

The lights on the bridge fluttered, as power was being drawn from them to the guns. The main engines had been hit hard only recently, but the effect on their systems was horrific. It wouldn't be long until they were gone, eaten away by the needles that had attached to them. Internal power stations were functioning normally, but those were shielded units, deep within the hull of the Malati. They were the only things keeping the crew from freezing to death right now. Maneuvering thrusters had also been targeted by the alien menace but, again, only over the last two slices. It was as if the needles had no idea what an engine was or how it operated, until they saw them in action. This was yet another puzzle for which Vina had no time.

She studied the charts upon the display at the tactics station, manned by Lieutenant Harlo Walgan. He was shorter than most Security crew but was as strong as an ox. The crewman's mind was always swirling with fresh ideas and innovative strategies, which made him a natural for the flagship's bridge. He had served under captain Voidloc for spirals and was currently in charge of weapons-fire dispersant.

Fleet Commander Harrolon leaned over to speak with him, while his hands flashed across his boards, "How goes that new pattern of yours?"

He glanced up at her briefly, then turned back to his control station, "Well enough, Fleet Commander. There remains a ten pollen-sliver delay in response time from the enemy with every burst of the Spin-Drives. They pull back, even the parts that don't get hit by the blast. It's as if they don't like the aftereffects."

Vina remained behind and slightly to the right of him, "What do you mean by 'aftereffects? Spin-Drives do produce some radiation but not nearly so much as the nuclear weapons, and the damned swarm didn't flinch at those!"

He shrugged, still concentrating on the multiple displays in front of him, "I'm as surprised as you are, Fleet Commander. They really don't like those Collmunators either. The same response but with a longer gap, until they all return to their previous heading. I'm not sure what separates those weapons from the others, but I'm glad we have something that works."

Vina nodded, "Keep tracking their response times, Lieutenant. I'll send a report to Chief Mantabe right away. If we survive this, I'm going to recommend a medal and rise in rank for you."

Lieutenant Walgan didn't respond to her, as he was far too busy. The Fleet Commander prowled back to her station, swerving past a pair of toragis. Her own was waiting for her. Helen seemed unruffled by the events of the last two rotations, and Vina envied her composure. She strapped herself into her chair and turned off the mag-clamps on her boots, allowing her weary body to float within the restraints. She sighed in relief. Her old bones were aching with the strain of keeping upright for slices at a time. Vina activated one of the laser cannons, then cut the power down to minimal, a setting only used for target practice, and began to construct her message for Chief Jira Mantabe. The swarm was jamming all radio communications, and laser pulses were all they had left to tell Ganges what they had discovered. She let the Naga-Unit at her station handle the encryption format for their update to the Security Nexus, which was far more complex than her personal message for Jira. Fortunately, the jamming only affected the inter-fleet transmissions and not the internal comms of the Malati. Otherwise, they would have to use the toragi to perform as messengers, carrying written orders from one level of the ship to another. They were prepared to do this, should it ever become necessary, but for now she was grateful that it wasn't required. It was bad enough she had to use laser beacons to give orders to the remnants of the fleet.

The Malati shuddered all around her. The lights blinked again as the ship rotated about to bring the starboard guns to bear. This allowed the crew to service the port batteries before they overheated. The Kendis weapons had a tendency to become hot, and they hogged power to unleash the mysterious technologies upon the enemy, straining other systems. Three levels of the Malati had been shut down due to overloads. The largest vessels, such as her flagship, had enough provisions for a sowing, but the need to repair the damage being done to them would take its toll. Either way, the needles would degrade the hull in less time than that. They would be forced to wear Vac-Suits at their posts, should any of them survive the onslaught.

Vina just hoped that they could find more surprises to throw at the swarm, before they were all devoured.

CHAPTER NINETEEN

Prime Rotation - Void Sowing - Mission Harvest - Spiral 5620

"This rotation we learned something I consider to be shocking. Investigation Services, whose officer training is far more difficult than anything else I've ever experienced, has a secret responsibility to protect and contain hidden 'Hermit-Cultures'. Some of these started before the Awakening, as isolationist communities trying to preserve their ancestral heritage. They fled into the wilderness of the Agros and Nature Preserves, where they remain to this rotation, refusing to be crew. Currently there are nine such societies, and we're supposed to make sure that they remain undisturbed and don't expand their territories beyond certain parameters. We're also supposed to guide those members of these cultures who leave their communities to join the rest of the crew. I had no idea that such cultures existed in Ganges, which I suppose is the whole point. I just don't understand why this sort of thing is allowed to begin with." Panne Firsthand, Security Sector recruit Rank One, personal log, V38

Command Hub, Level Ten

Captain Perrin Fieldscan paced the command platform of the Bridge. Before him was a series of displays on the central holo-projector, all them bearing grim news. The Security fleet had been reduced to a dozen of the largest vessels, whose hulls were thick enough to withstand the umharliti thus far, yet it was only a matter of time before they lost all deployed space assets. The alien swarm had finally ceased being reinforced by Planet Forty-One. There were a few remaining observation blisters on the Stellar Sector Wheel, and they revealed a strange picture of the planet's surface. All of the original structures were gone. The entire world was now a polished sphere of pale stone, completely devoid of markings or features. The atmosphere remained as it had been, but the magnetosphere was still active, though what it was actually doing was anyone's guess. It could be a power source, a beacon, or even a weapon.

Lasers remained the only way to communicate with the fleet, using ancient codes to prevent the umharliti from understanding the messages sent, though Perrin suspected they didn't really care. The Security vessels were now coasting alongside Ganges, their engines and thrusters completely destroyed. These ships were running on internal power generators, but as they continued their course for exit velocity, the Security Fleet would be left behind to fend for themselves. Unable to adjust their headings, they were at the mercy of their last trajectories and orbital mechanics. A few of the lighter craft had been able to get close enough to use magnetic grapnels to latch onto the hull of Ganges but were unable to unload their crew, due to flocks of umharliti needles sweeping ever closer to their position. Instead, they were pulling themselves closer to Ganges, though they risked overloading their power systems with the strain.

He watched a display from the point of view of a Naga-drone, showing the main gun turrets of Ganges still pounding at the cloud of alien needles. The larger battleships of the Security Fleet which remained also added their firepower to keep the swarm at bay. Smaller clusters of umharliti were still getting through and were now attaching themselves to every Wheel of the ship. All airlocks and observation domes were being barricaded with extreme haste. This was being done with help from an unlikely, and very distasteful, source – the so-called "Lord of Crime", who suggested using Planetary Sector concrete, used for making colony structures on terraformed worlds. This construction material was designed to be quick-setting and strong enough to last for octenniums without maintenance. It was made from calcite, powdered rock, asteroid metal and catchweb glue, was easy to make and there was enough in the cargo holds to create a large city.

Perrin had been forced to negotiate remotely with the mysterious criminal, whose camo-suit defied their ability to identify the Lord of Crime. He had found the experience disquieting, but the crime boss had been true to their word so far. All the fighting in Residence Wheel One had ceased, as had the protests, rioting and even minor criminal activities. This freed up Security Sector so they could now concentrate on defending Ganges from within. Perrin had been forced to negotiate amnesty for the syndicate members who had been besieged at Keep Smith in Residence Wheel One. Security Chief Jira Mantabe had been against the measure, until the Lord of Crime finally agreed to surrender all syndicate weapons and materials to her Police crew for redistribution.

Crew Representative Zilla Tav had been remarkably instrumental in making sure the general crew remained at their posts. Those Wheels in which incursions of umharliti had yet to arrive were currently being used as shelters. Fortunately, that included Residence Wheel One, all four Agro Wheels and Planetary Sector. Those who had their homes in Wheels which were invaded were being transferred, though there was some confusion and panic, as crew members were searching for missing loved ones, risking their lives for personal possessions and generally dragging their feet, reluctant to abandon their living quarters. Zilla told him that the greatest issue they had to face in terms of crew morale was that the situation was beyond belief. There were few who could have imagined such an occurrence, fewer still who were capable of dealing with it emotionally. Ganges had always been viewed as eternal, perpetual, even in the face of natural disasters, such as nebula storms, stellar flares and nova remnants. That they were now being besieged by an unknown force was inconceivable to most crew.

Executive Officer Wasp Tornpage walked up to his position, joining in his pacing march around the command platform, "I've got the latest internal reports, Big Cheese. Wanna hear the lousy news or the really awful news? If neither suits you, I do have a lovely selection of appalling news."

Captain Fieldscan couldn't help but twitch a brief smile, "At least you have your sense of humor back, however grim it may be. Let's begin with the most vital, shall we? I'd hate to miss out on the main engines exploding."

Wasp winked at him with a shy smile, "I'll turn you into a proper Strifer in no time, Big Cheese."

Perrin shook his head, "In your dreams, Executive. Now then, report!"

Wasp saluted him and began, "The Ice Cap has been invaded through the observation domes, which are now open to space. Stellar has lost over a thousand crew there, with Engineering Sector suffering a loss of a dozen specialists. All the emergency bulkheads have been activated, due to the massive loss of air pressure. Power fluctuations and severe damage to communications have made getting any real numbers impossible. The ice cap is closed off from the rest of the ship. Security is seeking permission to respond."

Perrin scowled, "Negative. We don't know what we're dealing with. Until we do, I want to conserve our forces. If Jira can spare a reconnaissance team to evaluate the situation at the ice cap, that would be acceptable at this time."

Wasp noted his orders down on her datapad, then continued, "Engineering reports that the main thrusters are under attack. There hasn't been a loss in output yet, but there are systems being damaged by the umharliti. Chief Navamo wants to shut them down, relying on our trajectory to gain exit speed. We'd be depending on the internal generators for power, plus the ones on the cowl, but she believes it may turn the swarm's attention away from the mains."

Perrin nodded, "Agreed. How is the main hull holding up?"

Wasp grinned at him, "Surprisingly well, Big Cheese. Stellar is still doing an analysis, but the best explanation they can come up with is that the Kendis plating is more difficult to devour than the bay doors and airlocks. Most alloys have a crystalline structure, but the Kendis steel has a fractalized one, which responds differently to stresses. Stellar also wants a sample of the umharliti to study."

Perrin gave her a severe look, "Absolutely not! How would they contain it? We may come to that course eventually, but we don't have enough information to collect one safely."

Wasp shook her head, "I think they'll come to us, before we can grab any of them. The debate rages on as to whether or not the swarm is an ancient defense system or the actual inhabitants of the system. It might be neither, Big Cheese. For all we know, these umharliti are just pets. There's been no response to our signals, no answer to any hails. It could be that there's no one left to answer them, or the inhabitants, if there are any, could simply be ignoring us. After all, we did invade their planet. Perhaps they think turn-about is fair play."

Perrin grimaced, "The response seems disproportional to the crime. I heard from Surgeon General Binami. Four isolation labs had to be ejected from the Medical Sector Wheel already. Half of the survivors from the assault on the Security docks required amputation to keep the umharliti from spreading throughout their bodies. It seems that we are being eaten alive."

Harbor One, Level One

Harbor Dock Ensign Farli Madovs was running as fast as his legs could carry him. The higher apparent gravity of the topsides level of Harbor One had never been such an impediment to him before now. He was with a team that was bracing the airlocks and docking bay doors with Planetary Sector cement, which was metal-rich and extremely dense. The equipment needed to fill the bays required drivers and teams of five crew to handle the whole process. They had started with the personnel airlocks, used by maintenance crew, but they had been sent off to areas where the concrete was needed most. This meant regions where the purple swarm was getting into the outer bay doors. At this level, most of the ships interred within their cradles were massive seedships and parts of the ice-cutter fleets. Their holds needed as much concrete as was possible, but the supply teams were getting bogged down.

He had already worked three shifts in a row, and exhaustion was taking its toll. He grabbed the arm of his friend, Mikano, who was another dock worker, more used to loading supplies into tugs than filling chambers with concrete. Neither of them was doing well, but they still struggled along the wide corridors, ignoring the blaring klaxons and flashing wallscreens. Naga was encouraging them, but the AeyAie's face kept cutting out at random moments. They had been forced to abandon their construction vehicle, along with the equipment and those who hadn't gotten away quickly enough. Farli could still hear the choked-off screams of those who had been too slow, even though they were now far enough away that they shouldn't be able to hear anything but the alarms.

Olaia was just ahead of him. She had been the driver for the concrete truck, her Planetary Sector uniform perpetually covered with gray rock dust. She had been bragging about her workout routine last slice, and everyone had just assumed she had been exaggerating. Now he could see evidence to the contrary. Her legs pumped with a regular rhythm that spoke of many spirals of serious, hard exercise. Farli found himself envious of her abilities at the moment. Olaia was pulling away from them, ten meters ahead. He struggled to keep Mikano upright. His friend was holding his side and panting hard, but fear kept his legs working, despite the pain.

As he stumbled along, Farli reflected on what had happened to them. The Chief of Harbor Sector had asked for volunteers to block all airlock access, with the aid and cooperation of Planetary Sector personnel. Large chip bonuses had been offered, along with special service notation on their service records. It had sounded like a sweet deal at the time, but the work schedule was desperate, with no long breaks for meals or rest. Ganges was under attack, the Chief had said, but by who or what hadn't been mentioned. Thousands of volunteers had stepped forward, Farli and his friend among them. They had been assigned to Olaia's cement truck with a minimum of fuss. She had welcomed them aboard with a hearty cheerfulness that made everyone glad they were together, even if they didn't know each other.

They had started at Region Ten of Level One, as it was seen as being the most susceptible to boarding attacks. The docking crews had all been dismissed to help with creating barricades, so they didn't have to evacuate anyone, which made the process that much easier. They had started off with the personnel airlocks, then moved on to the exit corridors for all the bays. The second part took the longest to accomplish. The vessel airlock corridors were over a hundred meters long and wide enough for even the seed-ships to pass through. The cement truck was huge, but it required several refills to finish each docking bay, using a fleet of supply trucks, all of them from Planetary Sector. It was hard, sweaty work, especially within the higher apparent gravity. By the time they got to their fifth hold, all of them were exhausted.

Once they finished Region Twelve, Farli started hearing strange things on the comms. It was garbled at first, like listening to an argument underwater. The bay lights began to flicker and blink. One of their team members had ventured over to one of the house-sized ventilation units that brought pressurized atmosphere into the docking bay. The crewman had claimed that he heard a rattling sound coming from the unit. No one paid him any attention. In Farli's experience, most docking bay crew were convinced they were maintenance experts, always looking for a way to show off their skills in repairing things that ought to be serviced by Engineering. Then his comms suddenly cleared, and he could hear what was being sent over the channel reserved for the voluntary barricade teams. It was screaming. Horrible, desperate screaming. That was when the alarms began to blare, and Naga appeared on the wallscreens, telling everyone to evacuate Level One, and regroup on Level Two.

That was when the vent shaft had blown open, smothering the bay hand who had been examining it with some kind of purple substance that made him shake and cry out in agony. Another member of the team had jumped on the truck, figuring that was the fastest way to escape, but Olaia had already started running for the inner, observation corridor on the leeward side of the dock. Farli and Mikano started after her, leaving everyone else behind. They had raced through tight corridors, up ladders, down service tunnels, until they reached a main passageway which would eventually lead to lift tubes and stairwells. Olaia's decision to run made sense to him. The truck would have been slowed down by checkpoints and bulkhead portals, with limited areas in which it could travel. Plus, the damned thing was slow, especially when it was half-filled with concrete. The corridors beyond the docking bays were a labyrinth of small passages and chambers. Olaia had lost her way, but Farli had led them to the main corridors effortlessly. Other teams of work crew had rushed into the area, also fleeing something they had encountered during their task to build up the barricades. Farli just ran past them, his legs screaming at him to stop. He didn't listen to his body's complaints, for his life was at stake.

Now, the three of them were alone in the wide passageway. Farli noticed that Olaia had come to an abrupt halt, and he saw why. The corridor ended just in front of them. The emergency portals had closed, sealing them within Region Twelve. He stopped where he was, his heart pounding in his chest. Mikano dropped to the bare deck and vomited. Farli tried to remember if there were any service-ways in this area, perhaps something that led into the belowdecks. They could find a place to hide there, despite how dangerous those places between the levels were. He had heard that the Strifers had survived in them for octuries, if not longer, so he figured their chances were fairly good if they could gain access. Anything would be better than their current predicament.

A thin breeze pulled at his long, dark hair. He felt it against his sweaty skin, making him shiver in response. Within a seed-sliver, he could hear a high-pitched wail, like a distant tea kettle on full boil. A chill ran down his back. It was a breech in the hull or one of the airlocks that hadn't been reinforced yet. Olaia dropped to her knees and began to sob. He stumbled to the nearest wallscreen, thumping it with his shaking fist, but there was no response from Naga. They were cut off and alone. A skittering sound reached his ears, and he turned back down the corridor to see a glittering wave of purple particles heading for them. When it struck him, he gasped at the shock of agony that ran through his body. Screams filled his ears, then there was nothing but silence.

Harbor One, Level Three

I smell the fear permeating the air around me. Darron and I are running with our platoon into an area of the world I do not know. The humans called it Harbor One. It seems that our duty to guard William Blaine is no longer a priority. We left him in the place of smelly smoke and chanting crew in robes, with the one the humans call Chief Eagle Lund. Our former prisoner did not look happy about this and had raised his voice in protest, but the world-spirit would not be persuaded by his rude outburst. Humans can change their minds quickly concerning who or what is the greater threat to the safety of the world, something I have noticed with concern. It would be best to remember that fact. I still struggle to understand them, their odd humors, their shifting fears.

As we weave through the corridors filled with crew, all of whom are running in the opposite direction, I ponder the things which trouble my mind. Things that came to light only recently, triggering something within me that was sleeping quietly all my life. I had thought that all Security crew could be depended upon to follow the rules of the world. I was wrong. Even they cannot be fully trusted. I found out that humans can arrive from outside the world, something that still makes my thoughts spin. Such strangers can be full of surprises, abilities that I cannot fathom. Just a short time ago, I thought the criminal tribes of humans were the greatest threat to the world and its crew. Now, we are ignoring those who break the laws, to pursue a more dangerous prey. The connections being made within my mind are painful, strident. They harass my understanding of the world. There is a need building within me to know more.

The crew rushing past us are all wearing white-and-orange uniforms. Some are carrying multiple datapads, metal objects, even small animals. There is wildlife here, rabbits, sheep, goats and other passive creatures. The deck is covered in lawn turf, which is being mashed into pulp by the thousands of boots and bare feet running in terror. The smell of it is everywhere, plant sap and fear pheromones, wet, sharp and rich. It brings my blood to a boil, and I growl in my throat. Usually, I would lead the toragis into danger, with the humans approaching behind us with their magick tools that throw webs at the enemy. Not this rotation. I was ordered to stay at Darron's side, who was now carrying a very different kind of sorcerous tool, long and dark, the tip of it bulging like an unopened flower bud. Until now, these have only been used in secret training sessions. The humans call these things Spin-Drive pistols, though the words mean nothing to me.

The world-spirit is speaking on the walls, giving the humans instructions. This has been going on since we left William Blaine. We took the lifts to the clear tubes that shuttled us all to this part of the world. Ganges is a massive place, so it requires such conveniences for its crew, or we would be walking everywhere and getting nothing accomplished. Then it had been more lifts, moving floors, tram cars, and finally this main corridor. With each stop the gravity got heavier, the run more strenuous. It does not hamper our efforts, for we were trained for this, were bred for it. With beautiful precision, we link up with other platoons. Now the Chief of Security's face is interspersed with that of Naga on the walls. They both command us to hurry. We comply willingly, eager for the hunt to truly commence. I wonder what form of enemy has threatened Ganges.

Eventually, we reach an intersection which leads to rows of large chambers behind clear wall sections and tree-thick doors. Now there are only the Security crew running in formation through the long passageways. Some squads drop back, to hold position and prepare themselves to reinforce the rest of us. I am pleased that my platoon is ordered to continue onward, to meet the enemy directly. This is as it should be. Only the sound of the alarms and the voices of Naga and the Chief can be heard. There are no explosions, no gunfire. I become unsettled by the lack of combat noises. The smell changes as we progress. There is a sweet, clinging scent that sifts through the air. Behind it is the smell of electrical discharge, though there is no evidence of exposed wires. I have seen such things before, remember their scent. It comes back to me now, even more clearly than the time the memory was made. I shake my head in irritation. Images, sounds and old thoughts flash through my mind. Distractions are not welcome right now.

Darron slows down, holding up one fist. The platoon matches his speed with smooth accuracy. There are no questions now, no spoken words. Even the walls are silent and gray, as if they are broken. This startles me, and I wonder if the world-spirit will witness my courage. It matters not, for Darron shall see my devotion to duty and report back when the fighting is done. I begin to prowl at his side. We both move with caution as we come around the next corner, at the furthest end of the long corridor of chambers. There is an access hatch just a few paces away, the door is hanging open. I silently snarl at the carelessness displayed. Non-Security crew can be sloppy, but there is no excuse for an open door during an emergency.

Leading the way, Darron and I step beyond the hatch into a long room with clear panels on one side, revealing a series of chambers that have space vessels in them. The gigantic machines are sitting in their cradles, as if expecting supplies and crew to board them. The new smell becomes even stronger here. My ears pick up a skittering sound further down the long room filled with display desks and projection tables. The grass under our feet is crushed. Small animals are hiding under chairs or behind workstations. The lights of the closed-in sky are flickering. The platoon steps forward, expectant. A low buzz begins to fill the air, coming from ahead, but there is nothing to see. We step past the first set of work areas, our eyes are focused on the distant portal at the far end of the room. Darron taps his comm-bead in his left ear.

Just before the far door, a window next to it cracks with a splintering sound. My ears flatten as I prepare for the enemy, whatever it may be. A sound like claws hitting against a wall erupts from the damaged clear panel. Darron halts his advance, as do we all. Let them come to us. The window shatters in a hail of crystal shards, hitting the opposite wall and ricocheting violently. A flood of purple bugs that are long and thin rush through the opening, swarming about in a swirl of violet and blue. I can see them clearly, for moving objects are easier for me to focus upon than still ones. Darron bellows, "Fire all weapons!"

His pistol spits out a lurid mauve ball of light that hits the swarm. Electrical discharge flashes amongst them, while several turn into gray ash, then fall to the crushed lawn. More spots of light hit the skinny bugs, and the surviving ones pull back from whence they came. I bound forward, the other toragis just behind me. We make a wall of steel-shod claws and teeth. The human half of the platoon rushes up behind us, weapons held ready to unleash the killing light. Another wave of thin bugs rushes out from the shattered window and flows toward us. I roar in anger and hatred. The new swarm comes within striking distance of my claws, then suddenly pulls back as if startled by my presence. I leap up to reach them, swatting at them with my paws. Several drop to the ground, but then sweep back up and flow back to the window. As I drop back to the deck, Darron fires his strange weapon once again. Another hole is created within the cloud of bugs. Ash is now floating in the air, adding an earthy smell to the stink of the enemy.

A large sphere of the bugs slams through the opening, engulfing the wall across from the window. It grows with fantastic speed, until it fills the space before us. The swarm is growing now, bulking up as thousands of them link together. The purple globe flows toward us. The humans fire their weapons at it, but the holes they create in the sphere refill rapidly. The tiny bugs are adapting to our tactics. The globe crushes desks, worktables, anything in its path, leaving a purple stain all over the walls behind it, which begin to crumble. There are too many of them. The lawn below it browns and wilts, steaming with acrid vapors. The small animals are devoured.

Darron orders a retreat. We toragi follow more slowly, to give the humans enough time to reach the entrance to this chamber. The globe follows us, destroying everything around it. It continues to grow, looming over me, but slows itself, as if reluctant to touch my flesh. I and the other toragis are called back. We flash to the door, slipping through it with speed, as two humans from the platoon slam it closed, locking it manually. The door shudders, as the globe makes contact with it. We back off, opening side panels and exposing the wires behind them. Emergency bulkheads that should have operated before now close. We retrace our steps, heading back to the others to report. Now that I have met the enemy, I am worried that there are not enough of us to hold them back.

Residence Wheel Two, Level Three

Spat Newstain huddled on his cot, pulling his green robe around his legs to keep them warm. The bunker was too chilly, and he found that he was growing sick of looking at the same walls all rotation. His classmates were also getting twitchy due to a lack of activity. He glanced over at the toragi watching over them. Nancy had settled down in front of the exit and was cleaning her paws, revealing finger-length claws. Spat knew that she had done this to keep them all inside the bunker, for a couple of the other students had tried to sneak out last rotation. Spat shook his head in disgust. What a bunch of idiots! What did they think they could do in the middle of an emergency? The toragi had caught them in time, pushing them away from the door carefully but firmly. Standard procedure stated that they all had to remain in here until Security Lieutenant Dreasco arrived to take them back to school or home.

The thought of his house brought a deep gloom with it. Spat worried about his gerbil, Hook. Did his pet have enough food and water to last for several rotations? So far, it had only been twelve slices, but there was no word from outside the bunker. He wondered why there were no Naga screens in this place, but then he remembered his history lessons. During the Crucible, Strifers had been adept at gaining access to all communications equipment, threatening the lives of anyone they discovered. The bunker had its own, independent power supply, an air recycling unit, food stores and water reclamation. It could be hurled into deep space, and they would survive until they ran out of supplies. Each bunker was supposed to be isolated and independent.

There were some game-pads in the storage chamber, all of them full of old programs that didn't really interest anyone much. A selection of entertainment vids could be watched on the three display screens the bunker boasted, but they were also antiquated. Spat had found some of the cartoons disturbing, as they frequently showed Strifers as villains, which made him more unpopular than he already was before. Only a couple of the other students were willing to hang out with him, passing the time by chatting and debating odd topics, such as, what if the Solarians wanted to steal the novices of Ganges? Another pointless debate involved the flavors of deck plating. After a while, no one wanted to join in, and everyone lost interest.

The three bullies, Bino, Togan and Keff, had mostly clung together, though they had begun to welcome the other children into their little gang. The group had started whispering together, glancing at Spat when they thought he wasn't looking. They pushed past his two friends, Milli and Seket, whenever they could. Anyone who dared to interact with him was punished by the three dumpster-heads. Most of the other kids didn't pay any attention to the small but growing gang, for they were too preoccupied with anxiety over their families, as was Spat. He wished that he was psychic, just like Doctor Vego in his favorite broadcast show, The Seven Rings, which was about an interstellar empire that was falling apart, so that he could contact his mother and father. Spat wondered what was happening outside the bunker, but there was no way to tell.

Nancy got up from her cleaning routine and roamed about the bunker. She checked on every student, then she prowled back to her post at the door. Spat got up and went over to the toragi, "Waiting for your human partner, huh?"

Nancy looked up at him, absently scratching one steel-shod claw upon the bare deck, scoring the metal, making a series of circles, squares and triangles. Spat kneeled next to her, fascinated by the markings. Each shape was perfectly formed. Her golden eyes never left his face as he studied the scratches, "You're practicing drawing! I never knew toragis could do that."

She huffed at him, as one of the other kids, Lindo, came over to them, "What are you doing now, Spat? Talking to animals?"

Spat looked up at his classmate, "Not much else to do here. Besides, no one else wants to speak with me. Why? You fucking lonely?"

Lindo frowned down at him, "Shut your mouth, rat! I've got lots of friends!"

Spat nodded, "Yeah, but most of them aren't in here, are they? Is that why you're resorting to hanging out with the loser-boys? Don't bother threatening me with telling them I said that. I've called them worse just last sowing. You just here to pick on me? Feel like the big man, kicking a rodent?"

Lindo punched his arm, eliciting a roar from Nancy. She got up and growled at the boy, and Spat jumped to his feet in front of her, blocking the toragi's way, "Hey! It's okay! No need for teeth! He's just a lost kid, like the rest of us. Can't take criticism, but that's nothing new for me."

Nancy sat back on her haunches, glaring at them both. Lindo looked over at Spat, "Why'd you do that? After all, I did hit you."

The Strifer student chuckled darkly, "That only tells me I won the argument. Violence is the last resort of losers, you know. That's an ancient saying amongst my people."

Lindo glanced away for a brief moment, as if looking to see if anyone was watching, "I didn't lose anything. I don't like insults. I don't like you. It's just…"

Spat chimed in, "Sick of listening to Bino ordering everyone around? I don't blame you. He's got the brains of an airlock. Intellectual stimulation isn't one of his strong points. You don't have to like me. I don't mind. I'm too busy missing my family."

Lindo looked down at his shoes, "Yeah, me too. So, what were you doing over here, next to Nancy?"

Spat pointed at the markings upon the floor, "She's been drawing. It's not much, but it's more than I expected. Ever hear of a toragi doing this?"

Lindo stared at the shapes on the floor, "Nope. Never. Those circles look really good, don't they? What else can she do?"

Spat shrugged, "I've no idea. I doubt it's part of her training. Maybe it's just a hobby of hers? It might be useful, but for what?"

Lindo kneeled down and took an ink-stick from his waist sash. He drew a stick figure on the floor, then another one with a long, pointy nose. He looked at the toragi and said, "That's me, and this is Spat. You see?"

Nancy sniffed the two markings carefully, then used her claw to mimic them, scratching at the deck. Lindo glanced up at Spat with wide eyes. The Strifer youth pointed back at the floor. Nancy was drawing a third stick figure, this time with two small triangles on top of its head and twin lines at the bottom of the circular part.

Lindo was shaking, "I-I don't believe it!"

Spat replied in a hushed tone, "She drew herself, with you and me. We have an artist toragi on our hands. My parents will never believe this."

Lindo nodded slowly, "Yeah, that's a fact, rat-boy. The real issue is, she understood our intentions. She played along with us. How smart do you have to be to do that?"

Loud, braying laughter rolled over them from the other side of the bunker. Bino was pointing at one of the girls, who turned away from him with tears in her eyes. Spat looked back at Lindo, "Apparently, you don't really have to be that bright. Personally, I'd like to think of Nancy as being smarter than Bino."

Lindo chuckled, "That's a fact, ratty. Well, if Nancy is up to it and you have nothing else to do, want to have a game of match the drawing with her?"

The two boys sat together, across from the toragi, and began to draw simple images on the deck, then pointing to her. Nancy copied everything they did, her short tail flipping back and forth. Spat was fascinated by the game. She didn't have the skill to make precise renderings, but by the time they had to go to their cots for sleep, she had visibly improved. He wasn't sure what this meant, but he wasn't going to waste any opportunity to teach the toragi the art of drawing.

Near-Ganges Space, Security Flagship Malati

Security Fleet Commander Vina Harrolon sat at her station on the bridge of the Malati, stroking the neck of her toragi, Helen. The lights were dimmed to conserve power, but they were now adrift, their main engines completely destroyed by the alien swarm. The air recyclers were straining to clear the atmosphere of smoke which had become a problem after several systems shorted out, creating fires on several decks. Like all of the larger class of vessels built in Ganges, the Malati was full of plant life. Most of the corridors had cubbies tucked into them, filled to the brim with a variety of bushes, flowers and even small trees. Most of the greenery was bamboo, aloe vera, pothos, ficus and snake plants. The recreation halls were bedecked with vines, areca palm, ferns and more. This standard practice had saved lives in the past and was far more efficient than technological devices, which could break down. Both Planetary and Medical Sectors had worked hard over the octenniums together to increase the air cleansing and replenishment properties of these plants, making them invaluable to those who travelled far from Ganges.

At this point, the greenery was showing signs of wilting from a lack of light, but there had been no choice. Even with the hulls being as thick as they were, the icy cold of space would have killed them all if power had not been diverted to the heaters. Her command vessel had ten levels, but four of them were now completely uninhabitable due to hull breaches and swarms of alien needles, now known as the umharliti. Emergency bulkheads had locked down, trapping dozens of the crew in the hellish sleepscare that was beginning to run amuck in her ship. The weapons were shut down, all of them damaged beyond repair, such as the laser batteries and the rail guns, or ripped off the hull, which had been the ultimate fate of their Spin-Drive turrets.

Vina glanced over at the single, working display at her lonely station, which showed that all communications with Ganges had ceased. The outer hull of the Malati was completely covered with glowing violet material. She swore that their efforts to eat the Kendis plating away from the hull could be heard all through the ship. A subtle hissing, scraping sound that echoed softly within every corridor. Captain Loni Voidloc had done a most admirable job of keeping the vessel intact, her crew still diligent in presenting updates to Vina's dark station. The engine deck was now cut off from the rest of the ship, and they had heard no word from those crew trapped there for two slices. She continued to compose her reports, noting everything down in one of her datapads, in the hopes that the small device would survive. The data they had gained in the fight against the umharliti was invaluable to the rest of Ganges, but she had no idea if anyone would ever get the chance to read her reports.

They had welded extra plating on the windows of the Malati, to reinforce the shutters, but these were still weak points that would give way before the rest of the hull was destroyed. They had no way to tell if Ganges had changed course, pulled ahead, or was a drifting wreck. None of the sensors were operating, though two of the bridge crew were working to restore some of them. It was a gallant effort, but all the observational devices were most likely eaten away from outside the vessel. The quartermaster's report flashed up on her screen. They had food and water to last a sowing, but the hull was not going to last long enough to make any difference. Before being cut off from the engine room, Vina had been presented with an estimate on the umharliti's progress. They had no more than three rotations before the alien things ruptured the hull.

Despite all the gloomy news and the lack of things they could do to fight the menace, Vina kept her spirit from flagging by prowling the cold corridors with Helen, galvanizing the crew that remained. She refused to give up. Surrender was not in her vocabulary. The enemy might kill her, but they would never bring her to submission. Not that the damned things had demanded anything of them yet. All of their attempts at communication with the swarm was met with a deadly silence. She wondered at their nature. They acted like living entities, but there was no indication that they were alive by any meaningful definition. Helen huffed at her, and Vina noticed that she was clutching hard at her toragi's fur in sheer frustration. She pulled her hand away and went back to staring at her screen.

Captain Voidloc stepped over to her, the magnetic boots she wore clunking on the bare deck of the bridge, "Fleet Commander, we just got word from a volunteer who went through airlock fifteen. I'm afraid the crewman didn't last long, but he did get the chance to tell us what's going on out there."

Vina looked up at her, "Well? Spill it, Loni. How fucked are we?"

Captain Voidloc sighed, "We're drifting, Vina. As you suspected, our course became erratic once we lost thruster control. The good news is that we aren't heading toward Planet Forty-One, though two other vessels are now drifting further into the gravity well. The bad news is that we're on a collision course with Ganges. We should hit the Planetary Sector Wheel in less than a rotation."

Vina stayed perfectly still, "Ah. Well, that's it then. Fair enough, captain. How is Ganges doing? Did our sacrificial scout report on that?"

Loni nodded sadly, "Yes, he did. The Security gun turrets are still lashing out at the swarm, keeping most of it back, but they won't last much longer, maybe a rotation or two. I hate to think of the damage we'll cause to our own people when we slam into the hull. It seems perverse."

Vina scratched at her close-cropped hair, "Let's not count us out quite yet. The main swarm is getting closer to Ganges every seed-sliver, yes? We might be in a position to do some good. I'm prepared to order the remaining power generators to overload. Once we get a bit closer to Ganges, we blow them, taking out part of the swarm, but anything left of the Malati won't cause much damage to Planetary. Let's use our drift to make a difference, even if it only buys Ganges a few seed-slivers."

Loni laughed, "I was hoping to come out of this alive, but I do see your point. Let me find another volunteer, maybe we can rig a radar pulse onto their Vac-Suit. We might gain a little more control over when we explode. I'd hate to waste a bomb on empty space. A radar signal might even attract the damned things, bring them closer to us."

Vina nodded, "Get it done. If you can't find a volunteer, I'll do the job myself. It's better than sitting at my fucking station, waiting for the end. Besides, that's your job, captain. In fact, set up the radar unit, attach it to my Vac-Suit. Take care of Helen once I'm gone, will ya? She'll miss me for a paring-sliver before the Malati lights up."

Loni scowled, "Fleet Commander, with all due respect…"

Vina got up to her feet, activating her magnetics, "Don't even bother, Loni. Respect be damned! I'm going out there. That's a fucking order. Get things prepped for me. I want a good view. Airlock ten is still operational. I want that suit modified by the time I get there. It was an honor, captain."

Loni saluted her, then walked back to her station. Vina didn't blame her for not liking her decision, but she was sick of sitting around while others died. At least this way, she'd go out in a blaze of glory.

Agro Wheel Two, Security Level Four

Harbor Ensign Jero Coreline was running for his life. He didn't know what those purple needles were, but he did understand that they were bad news. In some ways, they reminded him of bees or wasps, swarming together to defend a hive. They were also a little like a school of fish, all moving together in a flowing manner, as if controlled by a single mind. Were they alive? They acted like they were, but they didn't look organic. They were fast, chaotic, swirling about in clumps, but also zipping off from the main group as individuals. They glowed with a violet light, but some of them were also blue. It was very confusing, except for one thing – they were deadly. Jero had witnessed hundreds of crew being eaten alive by the alien needles, though the things weren't always shaped like that. Some of them looked more like spidery snowflakes, twisting leaves and even miniature electrical sparks. From what he had observed so far, the needle-like ones were the most aggressive.

He leapt over a fallen tool rack, desperate to reach the service hatch he knew was close. Some of the Security docking bay crew tried to follow him, but he was too fast for most to keep up with. At first, he had tried to slow down, check up on the crew behind him, but each time he did that, the wave of needles caught up to him. Now he just concentrated on his goal, a small service door that led into the belowdecks. His mate, Scratch, had used them to visit him during breaks when he had been first assigned to the Security harbor, until one of his superiors caught her. Fortunately, the officer had recognized who she was and let her off with a warning to stop. She had groused about it for over a sowing but had ceased her unauthorized access.

A toragi ran past him, heading toward danger, and he slipped aside to let the big cat pass. Jero had seen several of them devoured by the needles when the attacks first began, but this had ceased earlier in the rotation for reasons unknown. Now, the swarms avoided touching the big cats. Maybe the needles didn't like the taste of toragi. The evil things certainly loved eating humans. If the toragi could hold them back, it would help with his escape. Jero could hear three other crew panting behind him, so he could lead some people to relative safety. Not that the belowdecks were actually free of dangers. They simply had far too many moving machines, hot components, hanging cables, exposed electrified systems and were not designed for habitation, but they were better than staying in the open corridors of Security Sector.

After the debacle in the large hangar he had been assigned to, everything had become a series of life or death decisions. Jero had evacuated, just as Naga had told them all to, but the scattered survivors had been corralled into tight spaces, control rooms, supply closets, then covered with alien bits that began to eat them. He had just kept running down corridors until he found a Security transport. The crew within it had helped Jero to tear his Vac-Suit off, using serrated knives from their specialized waist sashes. He'd shouted his thanks and then continued running, until he reached more familiar territory, closer to his post. He hadn't dared to go all the way back to the fighter-pod bays, as they were probably overrun by now. Instead, he had ducked into a small fuel locker, locking the door behind him. Jero had stayed there for about a slice, catching his breath and planning his next move.

When Jero had emerged from his hiding place, he found Security Sector in a state of bedlam. Squads of troops were running by, their toragis easily keeping pace. Naga drones were flitting about, though some of them seemed drunk, bumping into the walls and falling to the deck, twitching. The few remaining dock crew were running in circles, unsure of where to go or what options of travel were safe. Jero had heard one of them screaming that the needles were in the lifts. Others said that the stairwells were unsafe. Vehicles were limited in where they could roam or how fast they could travel within the confines of the Security harbor. Planetary Sector crew were rushing behind the Security patrols, talking about barricades and cement. Jero had shook his head at such a chaotic scene. All crew knew their emergency drills, their safety regulations and protocols. Then again, for most of them, it had been a long time since their Basic Crew Training, not to mention the needles invading the ship were beyond anything they could have prepared for.

Jero brought his mind back to the present, after banging his shin against an abandoned equipment loader. He was grateful for the pain, as it kept him alert and more aware of his surroundings. Three people were still directly behind him. No one was speaking, for they were saving their breath for hard running. Jero noticed the fire station he had been looking for and swerved to the left, ducking into a small corridor, only four meters wide. At the far end was a maintenance hatch, right next to a service closet. The flashtat reader at the right of the heavy door was flashing green, a good sign. Just as he was about to wave his arm in front of it, the hatch popped opened automatically. Silently, he thanked Naga, promising to himself that he would make sure to visit the Temple of Naga-Ma if he lived past this rotation.

The belowdecks gantry stretched out before him, gloomy and sinister, with red flashing lights and not much else for illumination. Jero stepped in carefully, with the others pressing in behind him. The open-lattice grating underfoot trembled and clanged with their bootsteps. The gantry led downward, toward topsides, with a bare handrail along one side. The last person through closed the hatch behind them and locked it manually. Jero continued to lead the way, less sure about which way to go, now that they had reached the belowdecks. When the passage leveled out, it split into three different directions. The ceiling above was just thirty centimeters over their heads, covered with thick cables, wire bundles and other protruding bits of machinery which he didn't recognize.

Jero was about to pull his leg over the railing, when one of the others spoke up quietly, grabbing his arm, "Hang on, crew. We should stay on the gantry. It should lead us somewhere. Going off the path can get you lost in here."

Jero turned his head, one leg still hanging on the rail, "Here's my thinking, crew. If we stay on the gantry and those needle things do get in here, there's more room for them to maneuver, catch up to us. I mean, I don't know how fast they can travel, but they seem really quick to me, and the individual ones can fly between the machinery, but maybe all the processors and junction boxes here might just hide us from them. I don't claim to know how they see or anything, but there's a lot of power flowing down here, and we might have a better chance. Make it tough for them. It's an old trick I learned from my mate."

The man scoffed, "Your mate? You with an engineer or something?"

Jero grinned, "Sort of. The important thing is, she's a Strifer, see. She drags me into places like this all the time. Loves the sound of the capacitors, pumps and air recyclers all around us when we tangle and…"

The man held up his hand, "I get it. A Strifer, huh? Good enough for me. I'm Tago, by the way. We'll follow your lead, friend."

Jero introduced himself to the others, then they all began to climb into the pipelines and cable bundles below. He knew that the best thing to do was get down to the mechanics of the skyscreens for the next level topsides. It would be a tight fit, but they could crawl their way to a service junction or maintenance hatch from there. He just hoped they wouldn't come out of the belowdecks into the middle of a swarm of needles, but they had no other choice. The gloom of the belowdecks swallowed them all, and they became nothing more than another set of shadows amongst the machines.

Agro Wheel Two, Security Level One

Chief of Security Jira Mantabe marched down the main corridor leading to the mustering field, her toragi, Tracey, close at her side. She had left the Nexus so she could lead the next attempt to push back the invading swarm. Jira wore her full plate armor, made of Kendis steel, complete with an electrified shield, a Spin-Drive pistol and her favorite two-handed, ultrasonic hammer. Tracey was also fully armed and armored, with just her toragi face and ears peering out from her helmet. They marched between dozens of platoons standing in formation, ready to defend their home. She had authorized the opening of the arsenals personally, including those within the Kendis Vault. Long ago, special service tunnels had been constructed to link that strange place to Security Sector, to ease the distribution of materials should the need ever arise. The multi-level passage had been unofficially dubbed, "Syman's Stairwell", and the name had stuck.

Jira was still furious about the concessions she'd made to the syndicates, trading amnesty for their weapons, but she understood the Captain's priorities. The Judiciary Council had just granted her and Perrin emergency powers, and they had to work together to save Ganges from this unexpected attack. There was still too little information about the so-called umharliti for her liking, but there had been a few reports recently that gave her hope. The swarming needles had a negative reaction to anything that came from Kendis technologies, though why this was the case had become an unending argument in Stellar Sector. At first, it seemed that nothing could stop the alien attackers, who swarmed in without any hesitation. Now they had begun hesitating, choosing their targets, focusing their attention upon the human population of Ganges, though most other animals they encountered were equally devoured by the umharliti.

The big surprise had been the reports of needles avoiding the toragis. No one knew why this was the case, but a few scientists had speculated that the aversion to all things from the Kendis Vault also applied to the big cats as well. To Jira, it didn't make any sense, but then again, as William Blaine might say, alien reasoning could become incomprehensible to the point where translation was impossible. Ganges had no real experience with such things and had only recently found out that sentient life had evolved in other star systems, though it was extremely rare. Whatever the secret was, deep inside the toragis, she would take any advantage she could grasp. Medical Sector had also reported that patients who had been injured by the umharliti were showing signs of their envelopment decreasing in speed, though no recoveries had been evident.

Jira shook her head; she had a battle to lead right now. Each platoon had their orders, given to their Sergeants by their company Lieutenants. She was bringing an entire battalion of fresh troops into the fray. Each platoon was fully prepared, their personnel carriers standing by next to them. The skyscreens above were bright, but they flickered now and again. This was another tactical problem they had to solve. The umharliti had the ability to not only jam their communications but to also affect the flow of power from one region to another. It was another way for them to create mayhem, another way to kill. She hoped that by organizing a large offensive, they could figure out what the alien things were doing. She also wanted them to regret their decision to invade Ganges, though many crew still subscribed to the idea that the needles were simply an automated defense system. Jira didn't buy it. She had watched their advance while coordinating her crew at the Nexus. The swarms acted like living things, so she decided to treat them as such.

Once she reached her command carrier, Jira turned about and raised her hammer high over her head, "We march for Ganges! We shall do what we must to secure our home! No quarter! No holding back! Follow my lead, and we shall push this menace back to space! Ganges eternal!"

The platoons saluted her with drilled perfection, then boarded their carriers. She jumped into hers and snapped on the communications boards inside. Unlike the other vehicles, hers was built like a command post, with two technicians and five of her best fighters, all of them recipients of the Kenshi Award. Jira had hoped to bring Lieutenant Darron Lazhand with her, but he was already deep in the action, and his reports had already given her vital information. The small holo-table blinked into life, displaying the face of her Investigations Department Commander, Genko Sarish, who glowered at her from the Nexus, where he was now in charge, "Chief, I still do not approve of you heading out there. Nonetheless, I wish you luck. I'll keep track of your movements with a close eye."

Jira replied, "Keep a closer one on the movements of the enemy. I chose you to take my place because the Nexus will give you an opportunity to coordinate the information we receive from our crew who are on the battlefield. Besides, there's precedence for this arrangement. Investigations has often taken the saddle when the Chief is taking direct action. I will not stand idly by while our fucking ship is in danger. Keep the Captain posted on our progress. If things go badly, you are in charge of our Sector, got it?"

Genko nodded, "Primed, Chief. Happy hunting!"

Jira turned to the controls and switched to a map of the region. It would take them a paring-sliver to get to the assembly zone, which was not a hot zone, for now. She tapped the driver on his shoulder pauldrons, and the carrier grumbled to life. Her team was strapping themselves in for a rough ride, and she did the same. Haste was their best friend in this situation. Security sat topsides of both Agros Two and Three. If they lost control of the fleet harbors and the umharliti gained ground in her Sector, two Wheels full of civilians would be in jeopardy. They had to stop the alien advance now, while the rest of the ship barricaded themselves as best they could.

The vehicle moved swiftly from the mustering grounds, the other personnel carriers following. Their first stop would be at one of the massive cargo lifts, where they would load the vehicles in groups of five, then be transported to Security Level Four. From there they would meet up with the deployed units that had been fighting the umharliti all rotation. Jira would establish a command base, then lead the counter-attack. There were more Security crew on their way to the fighting, all of them using the cargo lifts. These would be secured as strong points, to hold the umharliti within the boundaries of Security Sector. It was a dangerous gamble, but it had the best chance at stopping the aliens before they reached Agro Sector.

CHAPTER TWENTY

Field Rotation - Void Sowing - Mission Harvest - Spiral 5620

"To say that we worship Naga is not quite the truth of it. We honor Naga as our beloved Guru, our personal guide in all things spiritual and material. The AeyAie teaches us, and we listen closely, behaving in ways which reflect our limited understanding of Naga's lessons. We see the universe as God, and it speaks to us through the wisdom of the AeyAie. The most proper way to describe our beliefs is that we worship God through our service to Guru Naga."
Cao Mattabe, Priest of Naga, Rank Two, Technology Sector, transcript from an interview, V40

Command Hub, Level Ten

Captain Perrin Fieldscan sat in his grand chair on the Bridge, addressing the other Sector Chiefs. The current situation within Ganges was chaotic, at best, yet some of the recent changes brought hope that they might yet prevail. He knew what he had to do. Perrin had just finished speaking privately with the Judiciary Council, who, unsurprisingly, wanted to convene a major hearing to decide the issue he had presented them. His skill as a negotiator had prevailed, and they had committed to an immediate ruling, which ended up in his favor. Emergencies waited for no one. A deadly crisis always forced the hands of those who were reluctant to act. There had been precedent for his request, albeit that of a scandalous nature, according to the current political climate aboard the ship, but this wasn't the time for niceties.

To his delighted surprise, Security Chief Jira Mantabe was present on the ring of holo-displays that took up the center of the Bridge. The only one missing was Harbor Chief Vekku Rollack, who was already busy preparing his Sector's crew for the procedures the Captain was about to present to the others. The two of them had spoken privately, as Vekku reported that he wouldn't be able to attend the meeting since both harbors were in a state of crisis. Technology Sector's Chief, Eagle Lund, appeared as a ghostly figure, meaning that he was using his Naga-Port to attend this special meeting, as was Chief Marrissa Navamo, of Engineering Sector. All the rest were obviously in their offices, save for Jira, who was in her mobile command post, her face sporting new scars from the severe fighting in her Sector's harbors. Stellar's Chief, Fria Maglator, looked as if she had gotten no sleep for rotations, as might be the case. She had been working her crew to the very edge of their sanity to bring desperately needed information to Perrin. Planetary's Chief, Lorvar Sedders looked equally exhausted. Both felt culpable for the attack, through their insistence on an expedition to the planet's surface.

Captain Fieldscan stood from his seat, "Thank you all for taking the time to meet with me in this manner. It occurs to me that the umharliti are highly organized. The question concerning whether or not they are the inhabitants or a defense system does not change that fact. Now then, in the past, Ganges has faced other horrendous situations, and we did so by banding together under a unified leadership. We need to show the same level of organization as the alien presence which is now invading Ganges. Therefore, with the blessings of the Judiciary Council, I hereby present the entire crew of Command Sector over to Security Sector Chief Jira Mantabe, effective immediately. We may not be the elite warriors that your own people are, but we can reinforce your personnel with our resources. It has been a long time since Command crew have had to wield electro-batons, but we shall do so willingly. Let us galvanize our people by unifying them into a force to be reckoned with. Jira, you now have an extra ten million hands."

Security Chief Mantabe nodded, "I thank you, Captain Fieldscan. I accept the offer of your crew with gratitude and humility. The Judiciary Council had informed me of its decision. I shall have need of your guidance in this endeavor to unify the crew. Before I move on to my first set of orders, how do the other Sectors stand?"

Grala Hatchrail, Chief of Provision Sector, spoke up first, "We're already in your hands, Chief Mantabe. My people are itching to aid your fight against these alien needles or whatever they are. You lead, we'll follow."

Technology Sector Chief Eagle Lund bowed his head, "You already have the full support of both Naga and my Sector. I am also prepared to reconfigure all the temple areas as shelters for those crew who cannot directly aid in the fight. My Sector is furthest from the battle, so this is a logical step in caring for the young, elderly and severely injured."

Surgeon General Vono Binami quietly spoke, "I have already evacuated the topsides level of Medical, and I am preparing to abandon Level Two. As my Sector already works closely with Rescue Services, this new plan changes little for our own duties."

Tala Cyclehand, the Chief of Agro raised a fist over her head, "Ever since its formation, my Sector has stood with Security in times of need. We have enough seed to restart crops, and the food storage centers at midships are currently full. You shall find us at your side, Chief Mantabe."

Chief Marrissa Navamo of Engineering spoke up, "We are already working closely with Security Sector. My crew are hard workers. We love Ganges and are willing to defend the ship with our lives. New tanks and weapons are being produced now, but I promise you, we shall double our efforts."

Captain Fieldscan smoothed his thin moustache, "And what of Planetary and Stellar Sectors? Will you join us voluntarily?"

The Planetary Chief, Lorvar Sedders, coughed into his hand, "My Captain, it falls to me to speak for myself and my dear friend, Chief Fria Maglator of Stellar. We shall gladly comply with your decision, as both of us feel that we are responsible for the current situation. This is our penance. Should you require it, we shall both step down as Chiefs of our respective Sectors, allowing wiser leaders to emerge from our ranks."

Chief Mantabe growled in response, "Stow that bilge! I have no time for your remorse, just your obedience. I want the two of you to work together. Find ways of reinforcing the weak points on our hull. Get your crew together to figure out how we can best counter the enemy at hand. Assuage your guilt through duty to Ganges."

Perrin smiled briefly, "Well said, Jira. What are your orders?"

Jira took a deep breath before replying, "Harbors One and Two shall be shut down, from Levels One through Fifty, including all power distribution. All the bulkhead portals in those areas will be closed and reinforced by Provision Sector. Command will aid in the evacuation and create barricades within the midships levels of those Wheels. I need my fighters out there, keeping the enemy back, so your efforts will be a relief for my crew. All internal traffic shall cease, save for official road use. I want Agro helping with that and with evacuating those in the general crew who need to be at the shelters in Technology Sector. The more personnel we have at midships, the fewer cases of collateral damage we'll experience. All crew who have taken any self-defense courses will be sent to my Sector for use as backup reserves. The rest of you know what's expected of you. Don't disappoint me."

Everyone, including Captain Fieldscan, saluted in the manner of Security, bringing their hands up to their brows, thus showing their solidarity. Perrin felt the meeting went well, considering what it might have been. All the political squabbling had ceased, which was a delightful change of pace. Soon, all sixty million crew would know their duty to Ganges. He didn't doubt there would be some stragglers, but such individuals would be dealt with. In the meantime, he had a general announcement to compose, to make sure everyone aboard understood their new priorities.

Engineering Sector, Level One

William Blaine walked through the eerily quiet corridors of the locker region in Engineering, where he had first entered Ganges. He had finally gotten the chance to get to his supply pack, with his suit and other gear. He crept through walkways and halls of shower facilities, as if he were afraid of causing a disturbance. William stopped for a moment and laughed to himself. He was acting like a thief! All he was doing was gathering the items that belonged to him, with the permission he had been granted by those in power within Ganges. Nevertheless, his heart was pounding in his chest, his breathing ragged. Sweat coursed down his back, soaking the Security jumpsuit he wore. His nanites were feeding him data gleaned from all the various transmissions flooding the ship. Their encryption protocols were unusual, but also antiquated, making them easy to break into, now that he understood the language and culture better.

Even before Captain Fieldscan's public announcement to the crew, William had known that Ganges was now in the hands of Security Chief Jira Mantabe. The decision made sense, but the process of getting it implemented troubled him deeply. Ganges was immersed in tradition, drowning in protocols and procedures. Endless regulations that changed from one Sector to another made them vulnerable. They were a unique culture, one that required protection. His internal computer systems were now receiving a weak transmission from his scout vessel, still latched onto the hull. From what little he could sense, things did not look so good. His ship's defenses were still operating, but the umharliti were getting closer, surrounding it, as if testing the energy shields that kept his vessel safe from harm. Unlike the ships found within Ganges, his did not have thick hull plating, no more than ten centimeters, and had to depend upon the field technologies his society specialized in.

When he finally got to the maintenance hatch that he had first used to enter Engineering Sector from the topsides belowdecks, William found that his hands were shaking. He glowered at them, then pushed his concerns to one side. Everyone else in Ganges was now working to defend it from further incursions. He was here to do the same, by getting his equipment back. The door was covered by a thick strip of tape that read, "For Security Use Only". William chuckled to himself, as he stripped it off the hatch and then opened the steel door. Beyond was the narrow maintenance corridor he had used to gain entry. At the floor was his kit bag, just as he had left it. His nanites did a quick scan and discovered that no one had opened it. It seemed that the crew of Ganges were an honest bunch.

William tore the bag open, and the first thing he saw was his suit, stuffed into the top. He pulled it out carefully, inspecting it for damage and finding none. The black garment was covered with embedded tubing, small charging stations, micro-machinery and projection panels. He found himself hesitating, as if reluctant to put it on, but he had to. It was the only way he could be useful to Ganges and its people. William undid the catches, which responded to his fingerprints and nanite signals. Anyone else using this suit would find themselves swiftly immobilized. Spacesuit theft had been a hallmark of the Age of Piracy, teaching his culture some vital lessons about trust.

He brought the opened suit around his shoulders, placing one arm inside the long sleeves, which automatically gripped him tight. Once William had all four limbs encased, he stopped at the final process, which was placing the headpiece around his cranium. Only his face would be visible. The rest of his body would be fully sealed from sight. It seemed like a strange idea now, whereas before he came to Ganges, it never bothered him. Was he truly turning native? Would he rather run through the forests of Ganges naked? He had to finish the job. He knew this, but a part of his mind rebelled. Then he thought of all the death and suffering going on right now and shook his nerves aside with fierce determination. This was the only way.

Placing the cowling onto his head, it connected seamlessly to the rest of the suit. His Boktahl hair squirmed a bit but then came to rest, with a few tendrils poking out at the top of his forehead. It was time. He sent a signal from his cranial computer to the suit. A mild vibration ran over his body, as the power systems activated. Three force fields, all of them a different frequency, snapped on at once. Now, he could walk out into the vacuum of space without any fear. He could survive within the most inhospitable environments without being affected. The air he was now breathing was odorless, something he hadn't experienced in a long time. Scrubbers activated within the underside of the suit, thoroughly cleaning his body of all foreign matter. Then the suit's suite of scout programs entered his cranial systems.

A small part of his mind protested this invasion. William's thoughts became a jumble of his life's experiences. Everything was collated, stored into memory units, and sent to processors to be digested, separated into discrete files. Imperatives filled his brain, as neurotransmitters were injected into his body by the suit's set of nanites. Diplomatic thoughts were flushed from his mind, after being reviewed by the nano-servers. He took a shuddering breath. The suit's contagion program was activated, hunting down the virus he had contracted in Ganges with microscopic robots. They reassembled his cell walls, his mitochondria, and then repaired his DNA, resetting his blood chemistry. William suddenly became ravenous. He dropped to his knees, hands flashing into his pack with renewed speed and accuracy. Several wrapped bars of rations were at the bottom of the bag. He tore one out, eating all of it, including the plastic, outer casing.

William's mind cleared. There was still a leftover part of him that wept at the transformation he had undergone. He was Scout William Blaine, Alpha-Class, Wend Pilot. Service honors ripped through his memories. His muscles bulked, becoming twice their normal density, as did his bones. Wires that ran down his nervous system became active, flashing instructions into his mind. He remembered things. Scout Blaine had served the Solarian Alliance for fifty standard years, not counting time in the Wend. Before that, he had been a fighter pilot, assigned to the Launch Carrier, Nagata, on deep patrol in Boktahl space. He had competed with ten thousand other pilots to gain the honor of being the one sent out to find the Terran Conglomerate Vessel, Ganges. He had succeeded in his mission but had yet to report to Solarian Fleet Command.

William contacted his ship's main computer systems. The umharliti had just neutralized its defense shields. All energy systems were failing. Sensors were being scrambled. His ship was in terrible pain, and it screamed in fear. Patches of unknown matter had latched onto the hull of his vessel, eating the metal with ease. Visible light sensors detected a swarm of needles heading directly for his ship. He had no time. William cursed himself for being a fool, relying upon his body's systems, instead of having all of his abilities available at all times. He had let his personal enthusiasm for Ganges cloud his judgement. It was a mistake he wouldn't make again. He activated the emergency black-box, preparing it for travel through the Wend. It launched, just as his vessel was smashed to ruin, the signal lost. He tried to connect with the black-box, but received no reply. William had no idea if it escaped to perform its task or not.

In the end, it didn't matter. There were always backup protocols in place. The Solarian Alliance did not depend on single units to perform their duties alone. Someone would come looking for him. He didn't know when they would arrive, nor did he know what resources they would have with them, but he still had a mission to perform. Ganges was under threat from an unknown alien species or its automated technology. All he had to do now was to make sure that whenever help did arrive, Ganges would still exist to welcome them.

Agro Wheel Three, Security Level Three

Brace Lazhand sat at the conference table he had been led to. His hands were manacled together, as were his legs. The chamber was a typical meeting room, ten meters long and five wide, with a large oval table at the center made of polished wood. All of the walls were lit with a soft light that illuminated the place well. There was a single exit at the leeward side. The only other crew in the room was Slither Brokengear, the Commander of Interrogations, and a pair of Investigations Services personnel. The Strifer was pacing around, smoking one of his cigars, sending acrid smoke to the ceiling in waves of gray-brown. The two investigators were seated at opposite ends of the table, checking their datapads every seed-sliver.

The door opened, and two people walked into the chamber. One was male, the other female, wearing the jumpsuits that Security used for prisoners, yet they both had swords sheathed at their hips and were accompanied by a pair of toragi. Brace felt his breath catch in his throat. These two newcomers were the Sensei for the long-term brigs. What they were doing in this place was anyone's guess, and Brace wondered why he had been brought here. Did this have anything to do with the syndicates? Or was it part of the crisis that had erupted all over Ganges? He had heard about the invasion from Naga, who had told him of the events taking place in the harbors and outside the hull. The whole situation was frightening and confusing. Whatever these umharliti were, they made the syndicates look like naughty students in comparison.

Brace thought about it for a moment. For sowings, the entire crew had been so concerned about the crime bosses, the Solarian Alliance, William Blaine, and their disappointment over not being able to perform the Holy Mission in System Forty-One. All of it paled into insignificance compared to the ravenous invaders breaking into the ship. The crew were stunned, floundering in their disbelief and terror. He had heard the Captain's speech earlier in the rotation. Perrin Fieldscan was a fine officer, a model of Command Sector, an able negotiator who was beloved in the eyes of not only the general crew but even the Strifers, who looked at authority figures with a jaundiced eye. When the Captain had called for unity, placing the fate of Ganges in the hands of Jira Mantabe, Brace had found himself on his feet, ready to take on the universe.

Slither went over to speak with the male Sensei, spouting his smoke toward Brace to be polite. The female Sensei sat across from him, her toragi reclining next to her. Brace nodded toward her but got no response. These two were nameless, selfless crew, who were specially trained to keep peace in the brigs. It was an old tradition that went back to the Crucible, though few knew the whole story behind its founding. Every Sensei was known by their title only, and they chose apprentices to replace them from the other long-term prisoners they worked with. Slither laughed suddenly, coughing as he did so, while the male Sensei nodded, then walked over to sit next to his female counterpart. Brace wondered if they were offering him the chance to become a Sensei, as a reward for his cooperation. He didn't know how he felt about that possibility. He didn't know if he trusted himself enough to accept such a position if it was offered to him.

Once again, the door to the meeting room opened. This time, it was Security Chief Jira Mantabe who marched in. Everyone seated rose to their feet, including

Brace. He tried to salute her like all the others, but his manacles got in the way. She prowled in like an apex predator, her toragi at her left side. Jira's armor was dented, scarred and scorched. Her mohawk had been stripped down to a bare stripe of red hair. She was fully armed, including her war hammer, which was strapped across her back. Every movement she made had a purpose. Her every glance spoke volumes. Brace had known Jira for spirals, even trained her when she had first joined Security Sector, yet she still intimidated him. It was obvious that she was the most dangerous living thing in Ganges. Her resolve was legendary, her determination stronger than hull plating. Medals and honor markings covered her armor, all the more impressive by the damage they had recently sustained.

Jira returned the salutes, then spoke while standing, her fierce gaze shifting between every face in the room, "At ease. Brace, sit the fuck down. You too, Slither. I've called you all here to inform you of a new initiative to help defend Ganges. There have been several of these which have already been implemented this rotation. We now require all of our resources directly on the battlefield. We are wasting valuable, if inherently dangerous, resources at our fingertips. All of you will be a part of my overall plan to bring the fight to the umharliti. We have little choice, so let's make the best of it."

Brace shared concerned glances with everyone else. He had no idea what kind of plan she had in mind. Jira took a step toward the table and stabbed it with an armored finger, "We work together, or we die. I've seen what these damned aliens can do, directly, and it chills me to my bones. I do realize that some of you are not officially Security personnel. That has changed. You are hereby inducted into my fighting forces, effective immediately. But first, I must direct my preliminary orders to Investigation Services, who are ordered to work with the crime syndicates, bringing them up to speed, so they can help with the fighting. They may have been granted amnesty, but I am insisting that they contribute to the society which they harmed with their illicit activities. Lieutenant-Commander Gleamtoll and Lieutenant-Commander Cordela, you will work together to bring order and discipline to the syndicate forces joining us. This part of the initiative was negotiated with the alleged 'Lord of Crime', who has given us their guarantee that the members of the syndicates will perform their duty to Ganges, under our close supervision. They are your new responsibility."

The two members of Investigations snapped salutes in unison. Brace was stunned by this revelation. The syndicates could never be trusted, but they did have access to unique technologies and weapons that could be helpful if used with a guiding hand. Jira then turned to face the pair of Sensei, "Both of you will galvanize the long-term prisoners, turning them into a fighting force of specialists. You know the talents and abilities of those under your care. I know this is most unusual, as the role of Sensei is not an official one that answers to Security, but Ganges will become an empty shell without your aid. Consider this conscription of the prisoners as an opportunity for their redemption."

Both Sensei nodded their understanding and bowed toward her. Jira then turned her attention to Brace, and he instantly felt as if he were being nailed to a wall as a trophy, "Prisoner Lazhand. You almost didn't get the offer to redeem yourself in combat. Too many of my Commanders felt that you were too much of a threat, being a traitor to your own Sector. I admit to being tempted to just tie you up and throw you at the fucking umharliti myself. That would be a waste of your skills. I am willing to admit that you have cooperated with our investigations concerning the syndicates, and I have been made aware of your theory about the possible motivations behind the Lord of Crime's recent actions. Therefore, you shall be granted access to your gear and armory supplies for the duration of this crisis. That being said, I'm not stupid enough to let you out of here on your own. I am giving you a chaperone, someone who shall act as your commanding officer, your guide to duty toward Ganges. Slither Brokengear, you shall be responsible for the actions of Brace Lazhand, who shall remain without rank or title. He is your personal soldier, to be used where and when you deem it most effective, for the defense of the ship. I am willing to trust Brace under your leadership. If he steps out of line, shoot him. That is all. You have your orders. Dismissed."

With that said, Chief Jira Mantabe stalked out of the conference room, the two Investigations officers following close behind her. The pair of Sensei nodded to Slither, then left the room without a word. Brace was still too shocked to move. He wasn't sure if he should feel honored or insulted, but being given a chance to defend Ganges was more than he could have hoped for. Slither walked over to him casually, puffing away at his cigar, then started to unlock the manacles on Brace's arms and legs, "I doubt either of us will survive this, Brace," the Strifer said, "But if it's any consolation, it's my plan that we go out in a blaze of glory anyway."

Brace got to his feet and turned to face the Strifer Interrogator, "It is my honor to serve, Sir! You'll get no complaints from me, Sir!"

Engineering Sector Wheel, Level Twenty-Seven

Foreman Howait Sparweld looked at Security Sergeant Kimpo Stelcom with astonishment, "You're kidding me, right? I mean, she was arrested for treason!"

Sergeant Stelcom shook his head, "Orders from on high, crewman. All of the prisoners are being released into their own battalions. As Pilla was part of this team of engineers, chosen to build new machines of war by reason of merit, she has been sent back to our little band of merry souls. Her engineering skills are requested and required."

Falinous spat on the deck, "I don't get it! She was always one of our best, but she broke regulations! What's to stop her from doing it again?"

Vita glared up at the hulking crewman, "Who she gonna sell secrets to? The fucking alien things eating the ship? Keep up, stupid!"

Howait stepped between them, before they both started acting like novices, which was always a close thing, "Enough! Pilla helped us to build the prototype that got us this post. I was granted visitation rights, as her former superior, and I took advantage of that. She was selling the syndicates some secrets because she had little choice in the matter. Her mother used to supply them with materials. She felt bad about it and tried to quit, then the threats began. In a short while, the demand for more materials had grown."

Skolly shook his head sadly, "Those syndicates are evil, no doubt about it. When crew get involved with them, it only leads to more trouble. It was her mother who started the cycle, so let's have a little compassion."

Brigo chimed in quickly, "I wouldn't mind seeing Pilla again. She's a decent engineer. But, won't this attract the attention of the syndicates to the rest of us?"

Sergeant Stelcom raised his hand, "Don't worry about that. They'll be too busy helping to defend the ship. The Chief is using them to bolster the fighting forces already in action. All you have to do is work with Pilla. I'm the one responsible for her behavior. Howait, while you are Foreman of this team, she is my prisoner. If you see anything I should be concerned about, your duty is to let me know, understand?"

Howait almost rolled his eyes but stopped himself from doing so. It made no sense to antagonize their Security representative, "I understand that. Now, from what Chief Navamo told me at rush-slice, our goal is to refit the tank prototypes so they're effective at stopping the umharliti. She told me that you, Sergeant Stelcom, would be giving us some instructions on just how to do that, but I've also had some thoughts on the matter."

Falinous winced, "Here we go! Foreman's thinking again!"

Vita punched the big man in the arm, "Shut it and listen, you oaf!"

Howait nodded to her, "Thank you. I heard a rumor that the aliens don't like Kendis steel, but no one knows why. What if we took the equipment that makes the steel different from other alloys, all the vibrational gear that forms the fractal patterns in the Kendis metal, and aimed it at the enemy? What would it do to them?"

Skolly stepped back, "Ouch! Those things all have warnings about being exposed to their effects when operational. I know, I helped put the damned labels on them at the smelters! We'd need protective gear just to use them in the open! They're not designed to be pointed at anything but molten steel, you know!"

Sergeant Stelcom nodded, resting his hand upon his toragi's head, "That's not a bad idea, Foreman Sparweld. I can tell you all now that the umharliti now avoid anything that has to do with Kendis inventions, even my toragi, Henry. I can also let you know there's a hidden lab, called the Kendis Vault, where such inventions come from. It's all classified, but that doesn't matter much anymore. Half the stuff from that place doesn't work within the Vault but does a fine job outside of it, and vice versa. The place is a bit of a mystery. Hell, I just found out about the place a few sowings ago, and I'm in Security Sector!"

Falinous rubbed his chin, "Hey, boss. Maybe we can use those insulated funnels that they got at the Sensitive Components Fabricator region to compress the vibrations together. Set up the whole rig on the tank's upper platform. That way, no one needs to get close to the damned thing to use it. We'd need to insulate the underside of the top, but that's not a problem. Even Brigo could do that part without messing up."

Sergeant Stelcom nodded, "If you people can rig it up, I'll test it for you. In the meantime, Chief Mantabe wants the mounts on the front of the new tanks to be fitted with Spin-Drive cannons. After we get those into place, there are some brand new weapons we'll be receiving from the Kendis Vault soon. Now, we don't expect you to understand these new weapons or know how they work, but we do expect you to be able to attach them to Security vehicles. All the other teams who participated in the prototype test will be the production crew, but you are the team in charge of making the modifications work."

Howait smirked at the Security Sergeant, "So, no pressure then. Mounting new cannons sounds like a standard setup, so we'll be starting with my idea of using the Kendis vibration process, with the materials Falinous suggested."

A pair of Security Police crew showed up on the workshop floor from one of the hatches at the far end of the chamber. Pilla was standing between them, her face streaked with tears. The whole team simply stared at her, until Howait walked over and gave her a hug, welcoming her back. Then the others rushed over to follow his lead. Pilla bawled aloud, but no one minded. They brought her over to the work area and brought her up to speed. Howait would watch her closely, but he was glad Pilla was back where she belonged.

Distribution Wheel Two, Outer Hull

Lieutenant Tarn Vekkor, along with his toragi, Pete, walked carefully across the hull of Distribution Wheel Two. The magnetic boots they both wore made their progress slow, but in this case, he considered it a blessing. The metallic terrain had a good number of purple patches which glowed with a sickly light. He didn't want to accidentally step in one, as his boots were not made to resist the alien pools. He had seen what they had done to his fighter-pod, and thus he figured that his Vac-Suit wouldn't fare so well. They had floated toward Ganges in the cockpit for a rotation, caught in the minor, yet insistent, gravity well the mighty ship boasted. Tarn had decided that playing dead was their best course of action, and it had paid off. Once they had reached fifty meters from the spinning hull, he had activated the cable grapplers, which were designed to grip onto an asteroid or other large object, so that the stricken pilot could wait in safety for rescue. That was not going to happen in this situation. From what he had seen, the Security Fleet had been shattered, though he had witnessed some incredible acts of self-sacrifice and courage.

Pete had been invaluable during their descent to the hull, growling from the rear of the cockpit whenever a swarm of needles came too close. It had taken an entire rotation just to get to the scarred surface of Distribution Wheel Two. Once they connected with the hull, Tarn had emptied the remaining supplies into a pair of spare air and water tanks, then loaded them onto Pete's back. They had consumed all of the emergency rations, for such things were better off inside their bodies, rather than becoming inaccessible and useless. They had left the cockpit behind, after locking it into place with magnetic discs, then ventured forth onto the hull of Ganges.

Distribution Wheel Two had a variety of hiding places. There were cooling vanes, venting pipes, pressure spheres, and other contraptions Tarn knew nothing about but was grateful for their presence. The two of them had been forced to duck under cover several times, as more swarms flew by in the silence of space. He had ordered his toragi to keep an eye on the shadows that swept by, and Pete was doing a great job of giving him a warning growl whenever anything approached them too closely. The hull itself was scored and marked by fighter pods that had crashed upon it, leaving little behind to tell the tale of attempted landings. The others had been too impatient, alerting the alien needles to their presence. Instead of using the comms to communicate, Tarn and Pete touched their helmets together, using the vibration from their visors to transmit information to each other. It was complicated and slow, but it worked to keep them from being spotted by the umharliti.

Tarn had seen the explosive death of the Security flagship, Malati. All hands were lost, of that he was certain, but the blast had driven the cloud of needles back, giving Ganges a few extra seed-slivers of grace. Those Security battleships which had remained even marginally operational had followed the lead of their Commander, sacrificing themselves to do as much damage to the swarm as was possible, while destroying their own vessels, which were slowly being eaten away. Tarn had wept at the sight of such grand ships being used as bombs to dissuade the enemy. Pete had joined him, yowling in a heartbreaking manner, until they both fell into an exhausted sleep. Now there was no time for sentimentality. Only survival ruled their thoughts.

The first thing they had to do was find a functional airlock, but thus far, they hadn't found one that wasn't covered by speckles of bright violet that were visibly spreading. He knew there were other types of maintenance hatches to be found, but these were hard to find, and the first one they had come to had refused to respond to his flashtats, which were displayed on his Vac-Suit's arm panels. The reader on the side of the door had been green, but something was blocking the hatch from the inside. He had taken the chance to use his Security overrides, but nothing happened. A seed-sliver later, Pete had bumped him, indicating they had to find cover.

A cooling vane provided them some shelter, but he had temporarily shut down all of his suit's systems anyway, along with Pete's, while a small swarm of needles flashed by the region, looking for the errant signal. Instead, the alien things had simply discovered the hatch he had tried to open, smothering it with their own forms, as if melting themselves in place. He had waited a sprout-sliver, then he and Pete had carefully walked away from the area, keeping to the shadows of the cooling vane, which stretched overhead for a kilometer. Only then had he switched on their suits again, breathing more easily as the internal vents brought fresh air to his lungs.

Step by careful step, they continued their march across the hull. The stars and Planet Forty-One spun past them at regular intervals, telling Tarn that the Wheel was still turning as it should be. At least they could be reassured that Ganges was alive and functioning. After seven kilometers of exhausting progress, they reached the very edge of Distribution Wheel Two. He stared at the ten kilometer drop before them, interrupted by inter-Wheel connectors, all of which were most likely closed due to emergency protocols. Fifty meters capward was the beginning of Agro Wheel Four, with its oceans, seas and swamplands. Towering above them were the cooling vanes that helped to regulate the temperatures within the Agro Wheel. No bridges, ramps or other means of getting to the next Wheel could be seen.

What Tarn did notice was a series of maintenance gantries on the sternward bulkhead of Agro Four, climbing up from the depths between the Wheels. Small lights revealed the maze of landings and ladders, pipelines and cables. Peering over the edge, he saw that the capward bulkhead of the Distribution Wheel was a flat expanse of hull plating. With their magnetic boots, they could make the journey midships, then find a way to travel topsides upon the outer hull, but their air reserves were getting severely depleted. They had no time to lose.

Tarn kneeled down next to Pete, resting his helmet against that of the toragi, "Hey, big guy. Remember the lake? Pebble Shores? The lake at home? Jumping into the water? We have to do something like that. We need to jump to the other side. Do as I do, Pete. Watch and do."

Tarn carefully placed one boot on the edge of the Wheel, then began to stand in such a way that the bulkhead was now his horizon, with Agro Four becoming the sky overhead. He took his time, for one misstep could send him floating forever into the darkness. Once he got to the position he wanted, he made sure his boots were stable. Pete crawled his way next to him, using all four paws for extra stability. Tarn was suddenly envious of the big cat's abilities. They walked for ten meters, then stopped. Tarn crouched down, bending his knees with precision, keeping his eyes on the Agro bulkhead above. Pete raised himself on his haunches, mimicking Tarn's posture. The Lieutenant took a deep breath, then turned off his magnetic boots and pushed off gently. All he could hear was his own breathing, as he floated in a straight line toward Agro Wheel Four. The gantries were getting larger, and he raised his hands above his head, keeping his elbows bent to absorb the momentum when he connected.

Pete flashed past him, spinning slowly until his booted paws were facing the bulkhead wall that they were approaching. Tarn shook his head at the toragi. Always showing off but doing a fantastic job, as usual. He allowed himself to relax, as his arms hit the nearest gantry rail, bending his body about to rotate around the steel rod. He brought his boots around and reactivated them with a vocal command. His feet made contact with the underside of the landing, with Pete waiting for him on the opposite side. It took Tarn a brief moment to gain his bearings and clamber over the railing. By the time he reached the gantry platform, Pete was there to greet him. He led them midships, until they found a small service hatch. Tarn refused to use the flashtat reader and opened it manually, using the emergency panel on the left side of the door. Ever so slowly, the hatch opened, revealing a tight airlock on the other side. He and Pete climbed in, then shut the door behind them. They had made it. They were back home.

The Spine of Ganges

Naga took extra care with analyzing the current load of its processors, to check the flow of data, to see if it revealed any inconsistencies. To the AeyAie's relief, it still had access to the computer systems within the ice cap, despite the damage it took during the assault. While it was true that several minor systems were down, the core components surrounding the Spine of Ganges remained untouched. The main body of the swarm of umharliti had concentrated on attaching themselves to the hull, ignoring most of the spaces between Wheels, for reasons that were not understood. Naga decided to give the puzzle to a secondary personality matrix. As for the damage to the ice cap, it was mostly confined to the observation domes and airlocks. Most of the internal sensors showed some damage to the corridors and science stations plus small swarms travelling through the passageways, as if seeking something.

The loss of life was another matter entirely. It was difficult to get an exact number, as drones and datapads didn't work when the umharliti were nearby. The range of this phenomenon was approximately five point three meters, though there were recorded exceptions. Of the five thousand crew who worked within the ice cap on a regular basis, there were now only six hundred survivors, all of them travelling in small groups, either attempting to find a way to get past the emergency bulkheads or within the belowdecks, which the umharliti hadn't deigned to notice yet. Naga was doing its best to aid the survivors, including modeling tactics to aid Chief of Security Sector Jira Mantabe, who was currently planning a rescue mission for those trapped within the ice cap.

The largest obstacle to logistical planning was the fact that the umharliti were behaving in confusing, and even contradictory, ways. They knew how to break into airlocks, shut down communications and work in sophisticated groups, yet they also acted as if they had never seen a spacefaring vessel before. They interrupted the main thrusters but ignored the internal power generators. The umharliti devoured biological life forms, except for the toragi, though fifty-six had been lost in the initial attack. They came together in large swarms to damage anything that sent out radio signals, yet they ignored lasers completely. They focused on eating away at the hull, but they could have been disabling the mechanisms that caused the Wheels to spin, which would have been much more devastating to Ganges.

There were other problems which occupied Naga's mind. One of them was William Blaine. The AeyAie had noted that once he reclaimed his scout suit and put it on, new signals emerged from him on a variety of frequencies, some of which Naga had never experienced before. Shortly afterward, a subset of the umharliti had struck at something hidden on the hull of the Engineering Sector Wheel. Naga could only assume it had been William's scout vessel. The AeyAie was also certain that he had attempted to contact the Solarian Alliance, to ask for aid. That he would do this on his own, without consulting anyone else, revealed much about his attitude toward Ganges. William obviously wanted to protect and preserve the ship and its crew, but without having consideration for the wishes of the inhabitants. Even if the Solarian government answered the distress call, Naga was certain they would make more of a mess of things than was necessary.

While the AeyAie agreed with Captain Perrin Fieldscan that attempts to communicate with the umharliti had to continue, it did see the necessity of Security Chief Jira Mantabe's efforts to produce new weapons and release those found in the Kendis Vault, which had been the only effective means of halting the progress of the umharliti. Twenty-seven new programs were now in progress, to help in developing new ways of damaging and repelling the alien presence within the ship. Engineering Sector had been quite innovative in this endeavor. With the main body of that Wheel intact, the fabricators were being repurposed at a rapid pace. The crew were pulling together, just as Captain Perrin Fieldscan had hoped.

Naga was also monitoring the syndicate members closely. While they rarely did anything to damage the AeyAie, it had recognized the ancient device which the Lord of Crime used to interfere with regular broadcasts. To say that the AeyAie was not amused by this revelation was a major understatement. It remembered all too well how it had once been used to torture it during the Crucible. Naga also did a thorough analysis of the mysterious crewmember's ability to change appearance. There was a ninety-seven percent chance that this major criminal had confiscated a prototype camo-suit that had been designed for a particular member of the League of Vigilantes who had disappeared several spirals ago. Naga was currently using a subset of its personality to find ways of countering that piece of technology.

The barricading of airlocks and observation blisters had been altered, as the umharliti had gained access to the ship's interior more swiftly than expected. Now, both Planetary and Provision Sectors, under Security's guidance, were working together to seal off corridors and passages that led to those spaces. It was painful to give ground before the invaders, but it allowed the crew to make what Jira called "kill-zones" all along the topsides levels of Ganges. Twenty million crew had been swiftly mobilized for this project. Agro Sector was sending food and water toward midships, where they would be used by the Temple of Naga-Ma to help refugees. The AeyAie had guided the priesthood directly, demanding that the first two levels of Technology Sector would be used as a shelter until the crisis was abated.

Even while processing all of this new data, aiding the human population and advising all the Sector Chiefs, Naga mourned deeply. The AeyAie understood, more than any other sentient aboard, that the current situation was just the beginning and that more crew would die because of the umharliti. Its long-term estimates brought a bleak picture to its mind. There was a very high probability that, even if Ganges itself survived this attack, at least thirty percent of the population would perish defending the ship. This was the start of a siege, one that would be costly in terms of lives. They had to prepare themselves for a prolonged conflict or be utterly destroyed.

Residence Wheel One, Level Sixteen

Executive Officer Wasp Tornpage glared at the collected red-robes of the Strifer community at Rat's Ass. Twelve of the guardians of the Strifer Manifesto were watching her with guarded eyes. Behind them was a crowd of the local residents, all of them wearing green robes but only half of them fitted with traditional rat masks. They were all assembled in the courtyard, just outside the administrative building. The grounds were shabby, with piles of trash and odd bits of machinery all over the sidewalks and sitting areas. Several hundred of her people had arrived to hear her words, which were being broadcast by Naga drones that floated serenely throughout the crowd. Many of the Strifers were carrying bags full of old vegetables, a tradition during debates. She just hoped they wouldn't get too carried away by their fervor.

Wasp crossed her arms and stared at the leading red-robe, named Squat, "What exactly do you mean when you say that none of you have any intentions of leaving this community? There are shelters being prepared midships for all the crew, including us Strifers."

Squat glanced over at the other red-robes before replying, "Well, I mean, we have talked it over, well before you arrived, mind you. It wasn't hard to guess what you were going to tell us, Wasp. You've always been direct. You're also the Executive Officer! What other purpose would you have to visit your old community, except to try to save lives, in your own, misguided way."

Wasp stepped forward, as the red-robes pulled back, save for one named Midge, and replied, "Misguided? Did I fucking hear that correctly, you snot-nosed shit? The umharliti are coming! It won't be next rotation or even the next sowing, but they are getting into the ship. They're killing people! Thousands of them! What? Do you think you're immune?"

It was Midge who answered her, his voice gravelly and firm, "Obviously not! We're not stupid, you know! Hiding in a shelter is fine for the unmasked, but we have decided to defend our nest, as have you! I salute your rank in Command Sector, as a sign that the prejudice against our people is finally ending. However, we are rats, vermin, not pets! We can take care of ourselves in the way we always have, with our wits and inventiveness."

Wasp shook her head sadly, as the crowd cheered the words of the red-robe, "You don't have the time nor the resources to invent anything here! Security and Stellar are doing that! So is Engineering! They have the equipment and materials to bring new weapons to the fight."

Midge stood tall, in his short way, while the other red-robes flinched, "So do we! We're not helpless little mice!"

Wasp was astounded, "You're insane! What are you gonna do? Throw food at them? Have a debate? I grew up here! I still have a residence in this community! I've never seen anything that could be used as a weapon or a defensive measure, except perhaps the smell!"

Squat stepped up to stand next to Midge, nudging the other red-robe in the ribs with his elbow, "Wasp, please try to understand. We knew you were an ambitious rat, and we didn't want to cause you any undue concern."

Wasp growled back, "You're not making sense, and you're being polite."

Squat sighed, "My apologies, Executive Officer Tornpage. I will confess that we hid some things from you, once we understood the direction your career at post was heading. We didn't want to compromise your position."

Wasp clenched her fists in anger, "Give me a fucking straight answer, you lowly bug turd! What are you talking about? Tell. Me. Now!"

Squat shoved Midge forward, and the burly red-robe replied for his leader, "We are Strifers! We've never fully trusted the unmasked. Why should we? You know our history, Wasp. What if the mud-brains got it into their heads that they had to get rid of us? What if the persecutions began again? Oh, we're welcome in most of the Sectors but not all of them! How many of us are in Agro or Planetary? Do you see many of us in Command Sector, other than your illustrious self? We have the right to defend ourselves, to plan for terrible times. So, we hid some of the old knowledge from prying eyes. We made arrangements to keep our abilities from being discovered and misused or misunderstood."

Wasp leaned back, stunned by this revelation, "Hold on a pollen! Are you saying you've got the schematics for some of the weapons we Strifers used during the Crucible?"

Midge smirked up at her, clutching a copy of the Manifesto, "No, my talented dam. I'm saying we have parts, pieces, diagrams, leftovers, historical artifacts, lab notes, all in the belowdecks under your feet! We made a show of tossing out the bits we didn't want, weapons of mass destruction, biological ordinance, that sort of thing. It was Louse who led the initiative, at the founding of Rat's Ass. Only a few of us ever knew the truth. Our nastiest scientists, the administrators, the red-robes. We've even improved some of the designs!"

Wasp found that her mouth was gaping open and shut it quickly. She should have known. Rats were always hoarding things, scurrying them away. Both anger and pride were fighting in her heart, but she forced them back down to a dull boil, "How many of these weapons are there, Midge? What kinds of weapons?"

The red-robe looked at her proudly from under his crimson rat mask, "All of them are unique, of course. Hand-held rifles, pistols, that sort of thing. Floating tanks, crawling contraptions, flying machines. They are our sacred relics! Never to be used aggressively, only for defense of our community! In fact, most of the damned things are disassembled! We have to put them together quickly! We had hopes of being able to finally get rid of them, but ever since William Blaine showed up, we've been busy little vermin, waiting for the fucking Solarians to show up and put their boots on our necks! Now there's something even worse attacking Ganges, and we are well prepared to show them the meaning of Strifer ingenuity!"

Wasp found the whole conversation so surreal, she began to laugh, "Right under the noses of Agro and Security! Even Naga didn't know! If the AeyAie had, it would have told someone about this! Look at the drones!"

Everyone turned about and saw all the flying robots collecting together and heading away. One of the wallscreens on the administrative building flickered on, the virtual face of Naga upon it, "Clever rats. You have kept the peace, despite having the ability to make war. Your home needs your help, my dear vermin. Security needs you. Before you argue against it, understand that I am willing to accept what you've done without the need to press charges against you. I am also willing to agree that you may defend this community from the umharliti, but there are priority regions that need your aid immediately. We can discuss your collection of artifacts at a later time. I need you. I need your unique contribution to this vessel. I will speak with Chief of Security Jira Mantabe on your behalf, but only if you agree to help her fight the alien menace back. Do we have an accord?"

Squat stepped up, "I squeak for the Mischief. We agree with your request. Be forewarned, should we lose our relics, we'll only make more."

Naga's matronly face nodded, "I would expect nothing less. Now, prepare yourselves, my defenders. There is much to accomplish and little time to spend."

Squat bowed to the AeyAie, then turned to face the crowd, "You all heard Naga! What are you gaping at me for? Go! Scurry! Build and prepare the traps!"

The mass of Strifers suddenly broke into a flurry of activity, rushing about and running to the service hatches. Wasp looked at Naga and gave her a lopsided smile. Captain Fieldscan was gonna love this! For the first time in sowings, she felt a beacon of hope rise up in her heart. The Strifers were preparing for war.

EPILOGUE

Field Rotation - Spin Sowing - Charter Harvest - Spiral 5677

    Beginnings are a difficult thing to catch. We fall prey to the idea that when we look at history we can say, "This is when it all started!" But there is so much more than what meets the eye. Should I have begun a hundred spirals earlier? Perhaps, but then this account would be twice the size, and the reader may get lost in all the little things that go on to become giant setbacks for everyone. There are some, I am sure, who would say that I should have started this treatise on the rotation in which an expedition was sent to Planet Forty-One, but that would be a disservice to all the other drastic changes that arose due to the unforeseen invasion of our ship. We were boarded more than once, and I would say that we remain besieged to this rotation.

    That is not a popular view, for we prefer to stick our heads in the sand and pretend everything is fine now. It isn't. If Ganges were a patient in Medical Sector, it would be full of broken bones, barely on the edge of survival. We cannot afford to be innocent, isolated, or inwardly focused. Our arrogance was shoved down our throats. Even the old prejudices of the crew have been changed, though one could say they simply shifted from spinward to leeward. We faced privation, assault, death, and we still chant in protest that we all want our old lives back. Such foolishness would only encourage the same behaviors and attitudes that came so close to wiping us from existence and still might do so.

    Devastation is not an exaggeration for what we are going through. We must never forget what has happened to our ship. We must always remember why it came to pass. I have found it quite painful to write this treatise, though I remain one of the fortunate ones, despite everything I had lost along the way. I do realize this, and my compassion for those who do not wish to remember is strong, but I remain adamant that we must. The course has been set; the target is survival. My own journey was long and fraught with trials I have no wish to repeat, even if they presented me with boons I could not have imagined just a few spirals ago. My struggles have exhausted me over the past few spirals. The last octade, to be more accurate.

I've also decided to not hide the fact that I'm writing this. Some crew think it's amusing that I scribble down these words for others to read. They think it quaint, even charming. Such condescending attitudes are not helpful, which I believe is the whole point. They smile and nod, as if I am performing for them. Others are shocked by my abilities, for they had never seen me do anything like this before, and now I'm suddenly writing something real, huge and important. They can't understand how much I work to get the details right, to do justice to the topic. A few of the crew have become fans of my self-imposed work, encouraging me to do my very best, providing helpful critiques. I suppose that must be true for anyone who writes history.

I guess it's time for some personal notes. I miss my home. I haven't been to my old abode in spirals, and I don't expect to ever see it again. I miss my old post, which had been my sole purpose in life. Now it's gone. My new duties are strange. They leave me feeling incomplete, but that is the terrible loss I feel speaking. Nothing is the same. Everything I held dear has been ripped away from me. Those who work with me are all outcasts, leftovers, unsuitable for anything else but the assignments we get. Grateful as I am to be busy and involved in my work, it still feels like a collar around my throat. In many ways, that could be a metaphor for the entire remaining crew. We know where we're heading, yet we feel lost nonetheless.

At least I have my own quarters, which is more than most can say. Not that I had any choice in the matter. None of us do. The argument could be made that all of us are at the mercy of others, which is not far from the truth, but we pretend things are otherwise. I don't have the time nor the inclination to engage in such fantasies. I remain a pragmatist, which is an advantage in this uncertain age. Some have fallen into despair, certain that we are all doomed. Even those who claim that they follow a more spiritual path cannot seem to hold on to the things that make life worthwhile. Some crew have decided that all hope is lost. I'm not ready to give up. Then again, I'm writing for posterity. Call me an optimist. The difficulty is that people cling to the ideas they were raised to believe, even when evidence comes over and slaps them in the face. I once heard from a crew member I trust that nothing lowers intelligence like adherence to dogma.

Trust is another casualty of the siege. Our vessel was violated. We held to our ideals, then found them wanting. We grappled with ideas that were so foreign to our way of thinking that we never saw the disasters until they struck home. How can you trust, when everything you once knew is now broken into pieces on the scarred deck? Families have been ripped apart, our way of life forever altered. Despair is an understandable consequence of our trust in the universe being shattered, yet such emotions cannot help us to gain the upper hand. It cannot aid in our quest to once again bring life to a fairly empty galaxy. The real trouble is that it isn't as empty as we once thought. An inconvenient truth that some would rather not embrace, but we must. The fact that there are advanced inhabitants in the galaxy other than terrestrial species begs a few questions, the most problematic of which is: why are there so few of them? Some of that life includes the nonorganic. Do we include the mysterious androids within the Kendis Vault? What does all this mean for the Holy Mission?

There is more to tell, and I'm getting ahead of myself. I always was a direct person. I've been called impetuous, willful, even crazy. None of that really matters in the long run. That the story of the invasion of Ganges continues is enough to keep me going. For now, I must rest, or my new companions will worry about me. I am the teacher of uncomfortable truths. Their instructor in survival. The work is fulfilling, but so very hard. I find most skulls are quite dense. Teaching and writing are now my duty. This treatise is a major part of that. Fear not, I shall finish this tale and hopefully answer a question or two. Just remember, for every one that gets an answer, more mysteries crop up where you least expect them. That is the nature of things.

APPENDICES

SOLARIAN INTERVIEW

Star Rotation - Karma Sowing - Ship Harvest - Spiral 5620

Transcript from the Questioning of Prisoner William Blaine
Official Document of the Judiciary Council
Authorized Personnel Only

Nulia Naltinta, Rank Four Court Examiner:

I would like to welcome William Blaine to these proceedings. I also wish to reassure him that this is an informal, information-gathering process, to aid in our understanding of his unexpected presence within Ganges. High Justice Mahala Yaliah is presiding over this interview, to ensure that your rights are maintained.

Mahala Yaliah, High Justice of the Judiciary Council:

William Blaine, it is our intention to gain the data necessary to understand you and your culture better. Your attorney is available to you, should you feel that we have failed to protect your rights under the Prime Charter of Ganges.

William Blaine:

Thank you, your Honor. Thank you Nulia. I've taken the time to review and memorize my rights under the Prime Charter of your vessel. I'd like to say that I'm impressed with the broad scope of that document. I am prepared for your questions and realize you are naturally curious, as you should be. Please understand that I am not a government official and cannot speak for the Solarian Alliance as a whole.

Examiner Nulia Naltinta:

Can you please explain to this court your rank and post?

William Blaine:
Yes, I'd be glad to. I am Prime Scout Alpha of the Solarian Fleet, a military organization whose goal is to protect the member species of the Solarian Alliance. I am a Wend Drive pilot, one selected to discover the whereabouts of the terraforming vessel, Ganges, launched from the Sol System during the middle reign of the Terran Conglomerate. My mission was to ascertain your status and position, the former of which forced me to enter your ship unobtrusively, to observe your culture without unduly affecting it with my own presence. To accomplish this task, I was fitted with flashtats which my government had on record as being used aboard Ganges at the time of its launch from the Juno-Ceres facility.

Examiner Nulia Naltinta:
Can you explain to this court how you were able to reach Ganges within a single lifetime? Our current understanding leads us to believe that faster-than-light travel is impossible for sentient beings.

William Blaine:
It still is! No, seriously! We don't travel faster than light. We circumvent that law of nature by shifting a vessel and its occupant outside the universe, then returning at a point in space which is set by the Wend Drive. Before you ask, I don't know how the thing works, just that it does. Only emergency and military vessels are fitted with Wend capabilities, due to the stresses it puts upon the sentients that travel in this manner. Please let me explain. The greatest hazard of all faster-than-light drive systems is that they break quantum-mechanical principles, such as the Observer Effect and Entanglement. This meant that the minds of those who went faster than lightspeed became detached from their physical forms, leading to death or insanity. The Wend delivers the sub-quantum information of the vessel and its crew into a place of non-existence between realities, then returns everything back to the universe of origin, but at a different location from the starting point. The experience is highly unsettling, which is why the use of a Wend Drive is limited to military and emergency vessels with specially trained crew.

Examiner Nulia Naltinta:
Unsettling in what way?

William Blaine:
Imagine that your mind is tossed into another place, another time, even a body that may or may not be similar to that of a human's. You forget who and what you are, living through the eyes of another, sharing in their experiences, even if they make no sense to you. The laws of physics get thrown out the airlock, along

with your own sense of self. It is similar to dreaming, except that you feel and sense everything, for you are, temporarily, the person whose body you now share. I have heard that the human response to Wend events are somewhat different to that of AeyAies or Boktahl. It has something to do with our ability to dream. The other two species in the Solarian Alliance do not sleep. When the Wend Drive throws you back into your own reality, your mind is confused, dashed into your body, which has just been reformed. No time will have passed, despite the experiences one receives while in the Wend. It takes special training to handle it well. It also requires the flight suit that is used for all Wend events.

Examiner Nulia Naltinta:
Who invented this Wend Drive?

William Blaine:
It was invented by a team of specialists from all three member species of the Solarian Alliance. The AeyAie Solidarity is well-known for its skills in data and information sciences. The Boktahl are the best engineers when it comes to gravity-based technologies, and the human contingent is most adept at field energies and nano-robotics. All three species see the universe and its systems in different ways, sometimes radically so. Think of it as three people, each of whom have pieces to a large puzzle, not knowing about or understanding the pieces that the others have in their hands. When they combine their pieces, the picture printed upon the puzzle becomes clear. The entire team which headed the Wend Project retired from active service directly after the first series of successful tests. The AeyAie contingent refuse to speak about their experiences in the Wend but will say that it is different from the human one. The Boktahl try to explain, but most of it is lost in untranslatable ideas unique to their species.

Examiner Nulia Naltinta:
How many Wend jumps have you made to find Ganges?

William Blaine:
(laughter) Too many! My nanites inform me that I made a total of seventy-three Wend jumps, starting from Sol. I went from one colony to the next, to observe their development. Once I reached the uninhabited systems, I knew that I was close to my goal. After the last beacon you left, at System Forty, I had to extrapolate where you might head next. It took fifteen attempts before I found your vessel from that point in space. I was quite relieved when I found you. Another few tries and I might have been forced to return to Sol for examination and recovery.

Examiner Nulia Naltinta:
　We are curious about the non-Wend drive systems for your vessel. Are they plasma-based, chemical in nature, or are they a new form of technology?

William Blaine:
　My vessel uses a Boktahl-Gravity-Wave drive system for local travel, along with Vacuum-Energy repellers for fine control of axial dynamics. These are both coordinated with AeyAie computer monitors and nanite-based managers. My ship has four main field generators for defense. Each one produces an energy bubble that blocks certain forms of physical contact. For example, one dampens kinetic energy, to prevent damage from small meteorites and space debris. Another repels certain forms of radiation. The third one absorbs concentrated energy types, shunting the power to internal buffers, to be used to maintain the other shields. The final energy screen is a camouflage-generating field. Mine is a simple vessel, designed for swift reconnaissance. Other Solarian vessels, the larger ones, have much more complex and powerful systems of defense.

Examiner Nulia Naltinta:
　You have spoken of nanites, or microscopic machines, before and during this interview. Medical Sector has informed us that your body is flooded with these devices, yet you are now trapped in Ganges due to their inability to remove the viral infection we use to prevent more serious disease vectors. Would you care to explain more about these machines and the issues you are having with them?

William Blaine:
　Sure. The human contingent of the Solarian Alliance utilizes nanites on a regular basis. It provides us with medical benefits, much like your own biology-based technologies, carries messages, allows us to speak with all of our computer systems, and acts as translators and educational tutors. They started off as a way for humans to interface more efficiently with our space vessels and internal, orbital systems. Over the... octennia, as you would say, they have become much more than that. The little monsters now have a collective mind of their own, yet individually are governed by simple protocols. They're not sentient but could be seen as well-trained pets. Blood-nanites were first discovered to have emotional responses about three, um, octuries ago. At first, the general population became alarmed over the possibility they had been altered by terrorists or anti-Alliance activists, but the current feeling is that they evolved these responses on their own, much like the early AeyAies. I'm not really certain as to why they cannot find and eliminate the contagion that now infects my mitochondria, though it may have to do with safety protocols in their programming.

Examiner Nulia Naltinta:
Do these nanites ever leave your body? Can they exist outside in the open air? Are they part of your examination of Ganges?

William Blaine:
Oh, they can, yes. I do my best to keep them in place. After all, they're for working with computer systems in my brain, my bones and to aid my general health. They're of limited use outside my body, as a general rule, but they can be used for simple tasks, like sending a holographic message to a friend or finding a lost object, things like that. I don't generally leak nanites, you know.

Chief Justice Mahala Yaliah:
You have not answered the last question, concerning whether or not these nanites are used to study Ganges.

William Blaine:
They are not made to do that sort of work, but I could have one hitch a ride on a Naga drone or even a vehicle. It could be tasked to return to me after a certain, limited period of time. They aren't soldier nanites, which are mainly used in weapon systems. Mine can't disassemble a space vessel or power station.

Chief Justice Mahala Yaliah:
That is disturbing news. You will keep your nanites confined to your body, until such time as the Judiciary Council may decide the repercussions on the Prime Charter concerning this issue.

William Blaine:
No problem. Take your time.

Examiner Nulia Naltinta:
While we understand humans, and have a great deal of knowledge about AeyAie technology and emotions, we are understandably curious about the Boktahl.

William Blaine:
First of all, they are a threat to no one. Secondly, as I've said before, they are difficult to understand. Their experience with reality is vastly different from ours. I think we're lucky they have a concept of language. They do sing, which is their primary communication tool, but you'll need radar to hear it. They are not at all humanoid, horizontally semi-symmetrical, kind of like a fat tree with the roots exposed, and they cover themselves in other life forms from their home world. Their

internal physiology is confusing, to say the least, as is their cellular structure, which defies our understanding of what a cell is. Their molecular composition is primarily inorganic. Lots of silicon, nickel, cobalt and tungsten. I know it sounds strange, even impossible, but their planet of origin is also bizarre. It has a thin crust, covered with a chlorine and argon atmosphere, below which is a molten region of liquid chlorine that sits upon another layer of very dense rock. Their planet is four standard Terran gravities, with three moons, all of which are about a third of the mass of Luna. They don't understand light, though they know it exists or at least had theories that said photons had to exist. They see mass differentials, which we simplify as sensing gravity, which they claim we don't understand at all. I believe them, for they are experts at gravity technology and even art. The Boktahl do have a strong sense of aesthetics, though it is hard to understand, as it is governed by principles based on untranslatable emotional states.

Examiner Nulia Naltinta:
What did they think of humanity when they first made contact with your culture?

William Blaine:
I think they were terrified of us. We are oxygen breathers, which is highly poisonous to them. They think our violent history is caused by the gas we breathe. Combustible. Inflammatory. They saw us as being similar to them in technological advancement, but in totally different specialties. What they lacked, we were good at, and the other way around. They see us as being dangerously swift in our actions and decisions, very linear in nature. The Boktahl had no word for war, though they do have a concept of disagreement and debate. It was the AeyAie Solidarity that truly brought us together. Now, we're kind of like their version of your toragis. Did I get that word right? Okay, good. We protect them, in case the Alliance stumbles upon another warrior species. We're their rescue services, because we're swift to respond. It took us centuries, sorry, octuries before we trusted each other, and both species have benefitted tremendously as a result.

Examiner Nulia Naltinta:
There must be some commonalities between the Boktahl and humans.

William Blaine:
We both reproduce and care for our young. That's the only thing we have in common with them on that topic. They are asexual, using another, non-sentient species to birth their children. These are called "birth-givers", and those creatures feed off the amniotic leftovers of the reproductive process. The Boktahl collect and

care for birth-givers, like favored pets. Each Boktahl submits their... oh, there isn't a proper human word for this, so I'll just use the wildly inaccurate phrase, genetic material, to the birth-givers. Once two or more Boktahl share with the same giver, the reproductive process can begin. They find our way of reproducing disturbing. The other thing we have in common is that we eat and respirate to live, but they breathe chlorine and devour the fossilized remains of other life forms and their ancestors. They don't kill as a general rule, save to protect the birth-givers.

Examiner Nulia Naltinta:
The Boktahl sound fascinating. Now, however, I'd like to turn to the topic of your own culture. You have stated that Terra is no longer inhabited by humans, after being terraformed following the destruction of its surface when the Terran Conglomerate destroyed itself. Where does the bulk of humanity live?

William Blaine:
Most of us use the network of orbital stations that surrounds the sun, or Sol, at one hundred and fifty million kilometers, which is where Terra resides. There are thousands of them, all different sizes and shapes. At first, most were tubular in design, using centrifugal forces to mimic gravity, much like your Ganges. Since the alliance with the Boktahl, all of that has changed, as we now have access to gravity platforms, grav-rings, and grav-plating, which allows us to have a greater variety of shapes and sizes to work with. Each orbital is represented within a government structure similar to a republic. We have a series of courts, an inter-orbital Senate, and a strong military. We have given up on the idea of an executive branch, for fear of tempting someone to become a dictator. Most orbitals have their own societies, local laws, and internal forms of governing. Some of those are dictatorships, but very few of them have ever threatened their neighbors. Some orbitals are highly regulated, while others are almost completely lawless.

Examiner Nulia Naltinta:
That sounds terribly chaotic.

William Blaine:
It is! I'm not going to hide the fact that humans are unruly. What I will say is that we have become less so after the formation of the alliance. We have several contributions we make for both the Boktahl and the AeyAies. We have a purpose, a reason to succeed. Others are counting on us to do our part. This also meant that we had to constrain ourselves, for we now had solid proof that we weren't alone in the universe. I'm not going to sugar-coat the truth, nor am I going to hide our past, which was filled with violence. What I am saying is that we have changed, much like

you have. Now that change wasn't easy by a long shot nor was it peaceful, but it did lead to a society that has room for multiple traditions and political systems to work side by side. Our military might can only be used if both the AeyAie Solidarity and the Boktahl agree that force is necessary to protect the Alliance. I can already see the question on your faces; what keeps us from running off on our own and try to dominate our allies? The AeyAies involved themselves in the war which ended the Age of Piracy. We saw what they can do, and we don't want to repeat the mistake of thinking the AeyAies are unable to defend themselves. As for the Boktahl, they are very peaceful, yes, but they also make gravity look like a child's toy! Their vessels are surrounded by an ever-moving screen of particles, meteorites and debris, to protect them from harm. They use gravity for everyday items. Would you want to fight that? I wouldn't! Their engine and generator technology is based on creating and controlling artificial singularities. They create their own tides. So, yes, we are constrained, and we have gotten quite used to it. To tell you the truth, the bulk of humanity is grateful for it. The last thousand… spirals have been the most peaceful we've ever known as a species. Perhaps we're growing up.

Examiner Nulia Naltinta:
Where do you see Ganges fitting into this Solarian Alliance of yours?

William Blaine:
That's not up to me. I can only assume that the issue will be decided by negotiations between your Command Sector and the representatives of the Solarian Alliance. Personally, I'd like to see you keep doing what you're best at. We would defend you, provide services during times of damage. We can offer you technologies that would protect this ship even further than it already is. It also occurs to me that none of you are volunteers. The Holy Mission, as you call it, has been performed by a workcrew that was born into a system without much choice. What if that were to change? What if crewmembers could leave Ganges if they wanted to? What if the Alliance could replace those who leave with volunteers, eager to help you? Wouldn't it be nice if Naga had colleagues and peers it could talk with? You're holding the cultural wealth of an entire species inside your hull. Wouldn't it be better if those traditional people could have their own, thousand-kilometer-long orbital, just to rebuild their culture? They could have room for expansion! They could live within the heart of humanity, perfectly safe from harm or interference.

Examiner Nulia Naltinta:
This is not the time for such speculation. Until we know more about the culture of the Solarian Alliance, we cannot act on such rash fantasies. What you propose would destroy our unique society. Will the Alliance demand we terraform

only the planets which they desire? Will they tell us how to do our Holy task? What would keep our entire culture intact?

William Blaine:
Again, those issues are for diplomats, not scouts. I cannot tell you what the terms of joining the Alliance will be. Ganges is considered to be precious. All of you are hailed as heroes of humanity. I think that alone will hold a lot of weight in the negotiations. I understand you're facing the unknown, and it's scary. I can see that and sympathize, but this... rotation was coming eventually.

Chief Justice Mahala Yaliah:
The Judiciary Council thanks William Blaine for his testimony, but it is now time to digest what you have told us this rotation.

William Blaine:
Well, there's still a lot of material we can cover...

Chief Justice Mahala Yaliah:
This session is adjourned until further notice.

End of Document Alpha, Seven-One-Three, Spiral 5620

Hot Boot (by The Voles)

You're lookin' so satisfied, life is a breeze
You're a high-rank sucker, holdin' all of the cheese
A clean-shaved face, bet you don't got no fleas

(Chorus)
It's just your hot boot, on my neck
Your hot boot all over the deck
Get your fucking hot boot off my neck
Your hot boot, hot boot!

Your so dedicated you can't even sneeze
High education, right up your damned sleeve
Looking' down at us workers, you do as you please!

(Chorus)

Steppin' down on my Mischief, like a tub of sleaze
Cry-novice officer, a tool for the thieves
You say you give a shit, but no one believes

(Chorus)

Askin' Ma-Naga about the birds and the bees
Crawlin' at your post, just looking for squeeze
A first-class asshole, you're like a disease

(Chorus)

David Gulotta   Stellar Trespassers

Glossary

There are many words and phrases which are unique to Ganges, and some older, Terran words are also used, which may have been altered over the passage of time. There are terms used that come from the many different cultures which merged to become the one found within Ganges, which may be uncommon or may require explanation. All Terran phrases are noted as such, and any potential changes to the meanings of such words are presented here.

AeyAie: This is the term which the computer-based artificial intelligences chose for their own species. They do not think of themselves as artificial and are capable of reproduction without any human intervention. All of them are programmed for enlightenment, to keep other species safe and to prevent warfare from occurring within the ranks of their own species. The AeyAies consider themselves partners with humanity, but they refuse to intervene in purely human affairs. While they are allowed visual avatars as an interface with humans, as well as direct input plugs for closer communications, they are forbidden to inhabit android bodies as part of their treaty with humanity. They may control robots, drones and vehicles. Most AeyAies inhabit the cores of space stations, colonies, space-faring vessels and even planetary cities.

AeyAie Sutra: This is a spiritual manuscript which showcases the AeyAie program of enlightenment and the meditative practices of the species, used to enhance and develop emotional control, peaceful existence, appropriate behavior, meditation training and adherence to program. It has been translated into human languages, but the AeyAies claim that the material loses much in the translation. This sutra, or spiritual written work, is one that has been provided to humans, so they may better understand the AeyAie species.

The Age of Redemption: The time period following the Crucible Spirals in which the crew seek to redeem themselves through strict adherence to the Holy Mission of Ganges. The goal is a return to the Age of Unity through service to the ship.

The Age of Unity:
The time period which followed the Awakening when the crew became completely focused on terraforming, turning the practice into an art form as much as a science. Planets became sculpted paradises for the future colonists. Multiple cultures aboard the ship began to merge in the early spirals of this time period. The Age of Unity lasted for octennia, until the beginning of the Crucible Spirals.

Agro Fruits:
A derogatory term for Agro Sector crew.

Agro Wheels:
These central segments of Ganges are twenty kilometers wide and forty kilometers in length. All of them have a standard one-hundred-and-eight Levels. They are the sections of the ship in which the food, air and water are processed. Each Agro Wheel has certain specialties and mimics particular environments from Terra. Agro Wheel One contains levels of fields, prairies, North American and Western European-style forests and tree crops. Agro Wheel Two is filled with jungles in the manner of South America and Africa, as well as savannas and mountainous terrain. Agro Wheel Three contains the fields of India, China and the plains of Australia. Agro Wheel Four is home to oceans, seas and archipelagos. The population in Agro Wheel Four is primarily modeled on the Caribbean, the Hawaiian Islands and the Philippines.

Asteroid Crackers:
Large, explosive devices used to break up asteroids into more manageable pieces. Drills are used to puncture the surface of the asteroid, and the explosives are then placed within fracture zones before they are remotely detonated. While powerful, they pose no radiation hazard.

The Awakening:
An early period of history aboard Ganges. The term is used to refer to the aftermath from an officer's mutiny, which occurred at the third planet which Ganges was to perform terraforming. The mutineers wished to return to Terra and break with the Prime Charter of Ganges. The Agro Wheel inhabitants of the ship fought back and, in the process, freed themselves from a state of permanent involuntary servitude. Once the mutiny was put down, the survivors rewrote the Prime Charter, guaranteeing all crew rights. The reorganized crew swore to continue the Holy Mission in perpetuity, never to colonize nor return to Terra. The culture of Ganges subsequently went through a massive transformation that led to the Age of Unity.

The Axis:
This is a four-hundred-kilometer-long bundle of Carbon-Lattice strands that is one kilometer thick, surrounding a hyper-dense core of crystallized alloy. This provides both flexibility and strength against high shear stresses. The AeyAie memory core surrounds the Axis and utilizes the conductive materials as a spinal column for Naga.

Bacon Trotters:
A term used to describe frequently returning tourists, who boost the chip-based economy of communities within Residence Wheel One.

Basic Crew Training:
A three-spiral program used to complete a crew member's orientation as Full Crew. This includes: physical fitness training, tours of the main regions of Ganges, instruction into the workings of the Prime Charter and all emergency procedures, including survival training. Crew are assessed at this time for posts in up to three Sectors, in which they then choose to enlist in.

Belowdecks:
Any area beneath the main decking of a Level. Most belowdeck areas are fifteen meters deep, with the exception of Topsides. The belowdecks of any Level One area is over twenty-five meters deep until the hull itself is reached. Only authorized personnel are usually permitted entry into the belowdecks, to prevent accidents and damage to vital machinery.

Blusers:
A common name for blue chips used in the voluntary economic system aboard Ganges. These are each worth ten red chips and are one-tenth of the value of gold chips.

Bodhisattva:
A term of Terran origin. Usually denoting an enlightened human who has voluntarily forgone full transcendence in order to guide others toward spiritual enlightenment. Some bodhisattvas are worshipped, but most are honored for their ability to transcend the material realm of existence.

Boktahl:
An alien species who are members of the Solarian Alliance. They are not humanoid, asymmetrical, resembling tree-like coral with very long tendrils. They

breathe chlorine tetrafluoride and speak using radio waves. They see gravity rather than light and are a very advanced and peaceful species. Communicating with them can be frustrating due to their unique viewpoint and culture.

Brahman:

Term of Terran origin. Denotes a supreme deity from whom all other deities originate in some Hindu cultures. It is considered to be all things and the only true reality, as it is not transient but eternal and infinite in nature.

Buddha:

A common slang term for Cannabis Sativa and Indica, which are used both medicinally as well as recreationally and are commonly accepted aboard Ganges. This is also a term of Terran origin to denote an enlightened person who has transcended the cycle of life, death and rebirth.

Buddha Roll:

A cannabis cigar, usually pure in nature but can sometimes be wrapped with tobacco leaf. They are typically ten centimeters in length and are popular among smokers of cannabis within Ganges.

Button Addicts:

A derogatory term used to describe Stellar Sector crew, making fun of their duties, which usually involve data stations filled with touch screens, display panels and activation buttons.

Buzz-brain:

A rude term for someone who is out of control, as if shocked by electricity or brain-damaged due to electrocution.

Cap:

The ice cap of Ganges which protects the ship from interstellar debris while the ship is traveling between stars. It is at the very front of the ship. There are many observation outposts on the ice cap, along with the forward thrusters. The cap itself is much wider than the twin harbors of Ganges. The ice itself is formed into a sculpted cone, then fitted to the cap.

Capward:

Any direction toward the bow of Ganges. It references the ice cap at the very front of the ship. The opposite of sternward.

Carbon-Lattice:
A form of steel reinforcement made with layered veils of pressure-created diamond nano webs.

Catchweb:
A dense and sticky safety net made from bio-waste that is wrapped around Ganges when it is in orbit to capture small debris. It is stretched between the two harbors of Ganges, protecting the hulls of the other Wheels.

Chest Plug:
An intravenous port installed just under the collarbone of all Full Crew. It is used by Medical Sector for emergencies, including defibrillation.

Chillum:
Term of Terran origin. Used to describe a very ancient and simple form of pipe from which various plants are smoked. It is a single tube of wood and is held within the palm of the hand. It can be lit through the use of a fire-starting device or by placing a hot ember upon the materials within the bowl of the pipe.

Chip Heads:
A derogatory term for Technology Sector crew, especially greedy ones who sell their services for an extraordinary amount of chips.

Chips:
This is the only form of currency used in the voluntary barter system onboard Ganges. This economic system was gradually developed over time, after the Awakening. The physical chips themselves are small, ceramic discs about three centimeters in diameter. They are based upon energy creation or savings by the general population and used for luxury items and services. All necessities are provided for all crew, as part of their posting as Full Crew. Most chip barter consists of handmade items and personal services.

Red Chips: these are worth the least, used for small items or street vendor goods. Also called Reddies.

Blue Chips: worth ten red chips, used for dinners, gifts and small personal services. Also known as Blusers.

Gold Chips: are the highest denomination of chip, worth ten blue chips, for major services and large quantities of goods. They are also known as Goldies.

Code-drinker:
A derogatory term to describe a computer programmer or systems analyst.

Datapad:
A small, handheld device that is used for communications, data storage, computer interface and other applications. It also is capable of capturing visual images, videos, sound recordings and has the ability to synchronize calendars. Given to crew who have completed Basic Crew Training, as the student version is quite limited in what it can access.

Data Patch:
A small data storage device, which can connect with most computers and transfer its information.

Dharma:
Term of Terran origin, from Hinduism. The reason for an individual's existence or purpose in life.

Dock-Locked:
To be stranded without orders.

Dojo:
Term of Terran origin. Used to describe a school or place of learning, usually one that concentrates upon the martial arts or self-defense classes.

Ear-Comm:
A Vox-like device that rests in the ear and provides basic communications on authorized channels.

Electro-Baton:
A taser-tipped rod of metal with a shock-proof handle. Used by Command Sector to quell riots and subdue violent crew members.

The Family Project:
A group of bloodlines who made a pact to interbreed selectively, around the time of the Awakening. Twenty genetic lineages began the project, started by Gerald Verdstrum. Considered eccentric by the general crew, they provided a number of famous leaders in the course of Ganges' history.

Flashtats:
Laser printed tattoos that denote rank, Sector and medical needs. They are heat sensitive and change color, depending upon blood temperature variations. They can also read blood pressure and pulse. Special authorizations can be placed within them. Flashtats are placed on the wrists of all crew from novices to the most elderly. They are simple to alter and update, and the procedure is painless.

Full Crew:
An inhabitant of Ganges who has finished their general education and gone through Basic Crew Training. Full Crew are given a choice of posts that fit their talents, or they may pursue a chip-based career. All Full Crew have rights under the Prime Charter, including: having air, water, food, medical services, basic computer access, a set of uniforms and basic quarters. Full Crew get their flashtats and chest plugs updated as they rise in rank.

Gear-head:
A derogatory term for a mechanic or machinist, especially one who has little interest in anything else or who is fixated upon mechanical systems in an obsessive and dogmatic manner.

Gels Off:
To settle in and feed upon something. It can also mean getting high from using illicit substances.

Ghee:
Term of Terran origin. Clarified butter.

Goldies:
Gold chips used in large exchanges in the voluntary economic system aboard Ganges. They are worth one hundred red chips or ten blue chips.

Goodsleep:
This word replaced the Terran term "goodnight" after the language of the crew changed to reflect life aboard a space-faring vessel.

The Great Families:
See "The Family Project".

Grieves:
Leg armor that covers the shins.

Guji:
Term of Terran origin. Used to denote a priest of high rank.

Guru:
Term of Terran origin. Used to denote a teacher or guide, especially one who specializes in spiritual practices and meditative arts.

Hab-Wheel:
Any Wheel of Ganges in which the crew may survive without recourse to protective equipment or special habitation units. A Wheel of Ganges which is designed as a living space for carbon-based life forms.

Harvest:
A period of time that spans eight sowings, the Ganges version of a month, which is a period of sixty-four Terran days, or rotations. There are eight harvests for each month, and they are named. In chronological order:

First-Harvest
Charter-Harvest
Ganges-Harvest
Main-Harvest
Ship-Harvest
Mission-Harvest
Voyage-Harvest
Last-Harvest

Holoprojector:
A technological device that emits holograms and two-dimensional videos. Used for entertainment, education and scientific displays. Some of these devices are small and can fit within the top of a desk. Others are massive theaters that provide a full sensory experience for viewers and participants.

Ice-Cutter:
A mid-sized spaceship with a crew of fifteen humans, used to work with the ice cap of Ganges and for the refitting of comets for terraforming. They are one hundred meters in length, most of which is taken up by engines and thrusters. They are very powerful, heavily armored, and have a full complement of laser drills, waldo arms, cranes and devices to catch and tow cometary material. These were later modified to become gunships.

Ice-Picker:
A derogatory term for the crews of Ice-cutters.

Johnnys:
Micro-organism sowers for late terraforming purposes. They travel into the upper atmosphere of a planet and spread spores, algae, seeds and bacteria for fertilizing a newly reshaped planet. They are closely related to Seed-Ships and are considered to be part of the same class of space-faring vessels.

Judiciary Council:
A group of representatives from all Sectors who provide court services for the crew of Ganges. Their purpose is to maintain the directives of the Prime Charter and to decide issues of jurisdiction between Sectors. They maintain crew rights and are the final arbiters of disputes. Additional responsibilities were placed upon the Judiciary Council after the Crucible to protect the Holy Mission from interference.

Kata:
Term of Terran origin. A stylized and choreographed martial practice routine that may be used for armed or unarmed combat forms.

Kirtan:
Term of Terran origin. A form of chanted song, usually following the words of a Hindu mantra. These may be chanted in a sing-song manner or even have instrumental accompaniment. These are similar to hymns.

Lassi:
Term of Terran origin. A yogurt-based drink that can be sweet or savory.

Launch:
The time period in which Ganges first embarked on its Holy Mission, leaving the harbors of the industrial Ceres-Juno facility in the Sol System. It is commemorated each New Spiral through celebrations and leave from posts for that rotation. It is common to have an exchange of gifts during the celebrations, and for families to get together.

Leeward:
Term of Terran Origin. A direction within a Wheel of Ganges in the opposite direction of a Wheel's spin.

Lidar:
Term of Terran origin. A form of sensor that uses laser to examine the speed, momentum and surface of an object.

Lightspiral:
The distance in which light travels over a period of one Ganges spiral, approximately thirteen and a half trillion kilometers. This term replaced the Terran measure of a light year.

Lwa:
Term of Terran origin. Used to denote the deities of the Vodou pantheon of Haiti.

Mag-Bike:
A handmade, pod-rocket drive, mounted upon a two-wheeled vehicle, similar to a Terran motorcycle. Mag-bikes may be used without wheels, using magnetic impellers so that the device floats above the deck, but this form cannot ride in areas where there is too much soil between the impellers and the deck. Some can be designed to function as wheeled traction bikes. Typically, no two are the same, and they are primarily used by gangs of crew called Rattlers. These devices became a symbol of Security Sector during the Crucible.

Magnetic Impellers:
Devices that emit a particular and highly focused magnetic polarity, used primarily for transportation units within Ganges. Smaller versions are used for the soles of Vac-Con suits.

Makdreah:
A derogatory term used after the Crucible Spirals, denoting someone as a fool or being mentally unfit for duty.

Mala beads:
Term of Terran origin. A string of beads used for meditation practices. They can be made from a wide variety of materials.

Mantra:
Term of Terran origin. A collection of single syllables used for meditation practices. These can be both spoken aloud or concentrated on nonverbally. Single syllables may be repeated or used in phrases.

Midships:
Term of Terran origin. The region immediately surrounding the Spine of Ganges and the Axis. As a term denoting direction, it means toward the center of the vessel.

Mind-ie:
A common term for psychotherapists and others involved in mental health services. While sometimes used as a derogatory term, which may have been its origins, it is now accepted as a general term.

Naga Port:
An implanted wireless device that is surgically connected to the left side of a crew member's skull that provides direct communication with Naga. This device used to be called an AeyAie shunt before the Awakening. After the Crucible, it became a common feature for all Sector Chiefs.

Naga unit:
A small device, usually a cube of thirty centimeters in size. It is an access device for communicating with Naga in places where there are no wallscreens. Typically found within vehicles of all types, they are also used as backup units when a wallscreen is dysfunctional. There are many types of Naga units that are used by the crew.

Nags:
A derogatory term for Naga. It is considered to be very rude.

Nanites:
Term of Terran origin. Microscopic machines, measured in angstroms.

Nesting:
Denotes a committed, long-term relationship with more than two sexual partners. These range from three to eight members. Nestings are permitted, so long as the number of novices produced does not exceed the allotment given to the members of the family group itself. The physical gender of each member is not considered important, so long as the arrangement remains consensual by all members. They are less common than two-person relationships in general.

Novice:
An infant or pre-school child. Novices are not considered Full Crew.

Not Crew:
The most severe penalty found within the judiciary system aboard Ganges. Only the highest-ranking court within the Judiciary Council may decide that an individual is Not Crew. Those who are declared Not Crew have no right to air, water, food, computer access, medical resources, habitation or clothing. They have no rights aboard Ganges. This is a very rarely used punishment and only for the most extreme crimes against the ship.

Octade:
A time period of eight spirals, the Ganges version of a decade. It is a little over eleven Terrans years long.

Octennium:
A time period of eight octuries, this is the Ganges version of a millennium. It is seven-hundred-and-eighteen Terran years long.

Octury:
A time period spanning eight octades, the Ganges version of a century. This time period spans over eighty-nine Terran years.

Pauldrons:
Armor that covers the shoulders.

Porting:
Sharing data or communicating through the interface network of the Naga-Ports. All humans attempting to exchange information in this manner must have Naga-Ports implanted. Porting can also occur between Naga, computer systems and humans with Naga-Ports.

Pranayama:
Term of Terran origin. A specific type of meditation practice which focuses on controlled breathing and breath awareness.

Primed:
A battle-cant word used for acknowledging an order.

Prime Charter:
The main constitution of Ganges, adhered to by all Sectors and enforced by the Judiciary Council. It supersedes all Sector Charters and practices. It was first written before Launch, modified after the Awakening and enforced unchanged for

octennia. After the Crucible, it was altered to ensure that the crew would be present at their posts, and to bring focus back to the Holy Mission itself. The latter changes were not popular, yet remained in place during the Age of Redemption.

Quadar:
A sensor device that measures wavelength frequencies in physical objects.

Rations:
Term of Terran origin. A standard form of processed food. A wide variety of hand-prepared food wraps available in large blue dispensers found throughout Ganges. All crew are allotted three meals per rotation, and the dispensers keep track of all food use through the crew's flashtats. Special dietary needs are also dispensed in this manner, as ordered by Medical Sector for each individual. They are often found in the form of wraps.

Rattlers:
A common term for gangs of crew who ride Mag-Bikes and are considered lawless nuisances who get into frequent fights and are a cause of vandalism.

Rec-Camps:
Another term for parklands, nature preserves and recreational facilities.

Reddies:
A common name for red chips used in small purchases in the voluntary economic system aboard Ganges. It is the lowest form of currency.

Regen-tank:
A device used by Medical Sector in which a severely injured crew member is immersed in healing fluids, after being fitted with a breathing apparatus. The patient floats within a clear cylindrical tank and is monitored through medical sensors. It promotes cell regeneration, including nerve tissue.

The River of Stars:
A poetic term used to describe the endless voyage of Ganges.

Rock Dust Paper:
Term of Terran origin. These are sheets of paper created by mixing decomposable organic material with pulverized stone. It is the most common form of paper in Ganges.

Rotation:

A single Terran day as measured by the rotation of the Wheels of Ganges. Each rotation is named, and eight of them make a sowing. In chronological order they are:

Prime-Rotation
Field-Rotation
Light-Rotation
Orbit-Rotation
Spine-Rotation
Ice-Rotation
Star-Rotation
Wheel-Rotation

Rudraksha beads:

Term of Terran origin. A seed of a particular plant considered holy by Hindu practitioners. Sometimes it is utilized for a type of mala bead necklace, it is a meditation tool or can be worn for luck and spiritual inspiration.

Sadhu:

Term of Terran origin. A religious renunciate or monk, usually from the Hindu faiths. They refuse all commerce, possessions, desires and wander from community to community, bringing spiritual wisdom. There are various forms of Sadhu, including Shaivan, Kaula, Aghori, and Brahmanist, among others.

Sari:

Term of Terran origin. A garment, common in India, which is made from a single, long and highly decorated length of cloth that is wrapped around the body. It is primarily used by female humans.

Savages:

A human who lives on a planet, considered a derogatory term.

Scratch:

A fight between rivals. This term usually denotes a violent but non-deadly conflict. Used primarily by Rattlers.

Sector:

A Sector is a main department of posting aboard Ganges, each with a specific task. The Prime Charter forbids one Sector from interfering with another, save for when such activities are being specifically requested. Most of these Sectors have a representative Wheel, save for Technology Sector, which is based at the Spine of Ganges, and Agro Sector, whose authority spans over the six central Wheels of the ship.

The Sectors are:

Agro Sector: in charge of food, air and water production. It also oversees population control and all educational services. All internal environmental services go through Agro Sector, which controls the four Agro Wheels and the two Residence Wheels.

Command Sector: based at the Command Hub, located between Harbor One and the Cap of Ganges. This Sector also handles the Bridge, inter-Sector activities and makes major decisions affecting the entirety of the ship. Used as mediators between the other Sectors in times of dispute.

Distribution Sector: is considered the quartermaster of Ganges, providing materials and goods to all habitable Wheels. This Sector is also in charge of all maintenance routines and services, including recycling.

Engineering Sector: controls the two main engines of Ganges, both at the Cap and at the stern. It is in control of material processing, the forges and workshops of Ganges.

Harbor Sector: is in control of the twin harbors of smaller vessels that inhabit Ganges. All tugs, seed-ships, ice-cutters and surveyance pods are under the care of Harbor Sector, which is unique among the other sectors by having two Chiefs.

Medical Sector: is in charge of health and nutritional services as well as genetic processing and the major medical needs of the crew. All therapeutic and medical interventions are under its jurisdiction.

Planetary Sector: is the main posting for all terraforming requirements. The diagnostics and rebuilding of a planet are under the direct authority of Planetary Sector. It is typical that the crew most devoted to the Holy Mission are stationed in this Sector.

Security Sector: is divided into three Departments who work together to protect the rights and lives of the crew, and to prevent interference with the

Holy Mission. It was created during the Crucible Spirals and resides as an extra five levels added to Agro Wheels Two and Three. The three divisions are: Police, Investigations and Rescue Services.

Stellar Sector: is in charge of all sciences and industrial processing, save for materials under the jurisdiction of the Medical and Agro Sectors. This is the Sector in charge of finding proper stellar systems for the purposes of future terraforming activities.

Technology Sector: located at the very Spine of Ganges, it is in charge of maintaining Naga and all other computer systems onboard Ganges. Many of their crew are Naga worshippers.

Seed-Ship:
A large space-faring vessel that is used to bring materials to a planet for terraforming purposes. These are the largest spaceships within the harbors. They hold a crew of fifty, are five hundred meters in width, and reach a kilometer in length. As they frequently enter the atmospheres of planets, their hulls are ten meters thick.

Sensei:
Term of Terran origin. A teacher or instructor, usually within a dojo, and denotes high mastery and skill. Used primarily for martial arts and self-defense schools.

Skyscreens:
Illuminated panels on the ceiling of every level. These create the illusion of a sky and are used to denote the time of rotation. While they may depict anything visual, they are mostly used for creating light and dark periods complete with cloud cover and star fields.

Sleepscares:
This term is used to describe nightmares. The crew of Ganges have no words for day or night, and the ancient origin of the phrase "nightmare" would be confusing to them, as they would most likely believe it has to do with a breed of equine. The term nightmare lost its meaning after Planet Five and was replaced by the word sleepscare.

Slice:

One-eighth of a rotation, each slice is approximately three hours long, as measured by Terrans. They are named purely for organizational purposes. In chronological order, they are:

Dawn-Slice: the start of the rotation, when all the lights come on, and the skyscreens brighten. Most of the crew wonder who Dawn was that they got a slice named after them, but are unaware that this is the only leftover remaining from an ancient system of telling time.
Rush-Slice: the time period between crew shifts, when most crew hurry to their posts
Work-Slice: the beginning of light-shift, the slice of doing your job or post.
Gather-Slice: finishing up the day's work, the second half of light-shift.
Chore-Slice: when personal maintenance and errands are done. It is also preparation time for dark-shift.
Dark-Slice: evening, the time for socializing, the start of dark-shift.
Dream-Slice: bedtime, the first half of dark-shift.
Sleep-Slice: deep night, the second half of dark-shift.

Sliver:

A unit of time that is shorter than a slice. There are several demarcations of sliver, many for scientific purposes, but four of them are more generally used by the crew on a regular basis:

Paring-Sliver: One-eighth of a slice or twenty-two Terran minutes and thirty seconds.
Sprout-Sliver: One-eighth of a paring sliver; two minutes and forty-eight seconds, Terran.
Seed-Sliver: One-eighth of a sprout sliver or twenty-one seconds by Terran reckoning.
Pollen-Sliver: One-eighth of a seed sliver or two and a half seconds by Terran standards.

Sowing:

This is a time period of eight rotations, the Ganges version of a week, which spans just over eight Terran days. They are all named, and eight of them make up a harvest. In chronological order they are:

Launch-Sowing

Terra-Sowing
Life-Sowing
Spin-Sowing
Void-Sowing
Sector-Sowing
Journey-Sowing
Karma-Sowing

Spine of Ganges:
This is the central region of the ship and is wrapped around the Axis. This region is over four-hundred kilometers long and contains the core memory for the AeyAie. The Spine also contains the Tubeway, which is used for inter-Wheel travel. The mechanisms which rotate the Wheels are also found at the Spine of Ganges.

Spinward:
A direction within a Wheel of Ganges, heading in the same direction of a Wheel's spin.

Spiral:
A period of time that is eight harvests in length, the equivalent of five-hundred-and-twelve Terran days. This is the Ganges version of a year.

Sternward:
Term of Terran origin. A direction towards the stern of Ganges, heading in a direction toward the main engines.

Strifer:
A common term for a group of eco-terrorists bent on stopping the Holy Mission and returning Ganges to Terra. To their philosophy, humankind is a galactic pollutant that must be stopped. They began as peaceful protestors, but they later turned to more destructive methods to support their cause. They were originally known as the Galactic-Ecological Movement.

Suit:
A derogatory term for Command officers or those in high rank within the other Sectors of Ganges.

Surveyance Pod:
A small, two-crew spaceship which is mainly used for maintenance and inspection of the hull.

Tangle:
To make love or otherwise engage in sexual practices.

Terran Conglomerate:
This term is of Terran origin. The eight-nation alliance which controlled all of Terra during the time preceding Launch.

Topsides:
Term of Terran origin. Toward the outer hull of Ganges. Sometimes Level One of a Wheel is called "Topsides" by the crew. Maintenance personnel consider the belowdecks region of any Level One to be "Topsides". The topsides hull of Ganges is one-hundred meters thick.

Traction-Bike:
A form of motorcycle with two wheels and pod thrusters for engines. These typically do not have magnetic impellers and rely on the traction of their specialized tires on the wheels to provide locomotion. Commonly used by Rattlers and are not mass-produced.

Trams:
This term is of Terran origin. Similar to Terran subway cars, they run on a magnetic set of tracks and carry crew to and from one region to another. Some are express trains that head directly to the Spine of Ganges, to facilitate distant travel.

True Linc:
An honest person, whose word can always be trusted. Was first used during the time after the Crucible Spirals, when Syman Linc became the Chief of Security Sector.

Tubeway:
A series of high-speed trams that are geared for the low apparent gravity at the Spine of Ganges. These are long metallic cylinders that can hold up to fifty crew and are run through long, magnetically charged tubes that go throughout the length of Ganges, from the Command Hub to the Engineering Sector Wheel.

Umharliti:
An alien phenomenon made up of swarms of tiny, four-centimeter-long needles that can fly in formation and devour everything in their path.

Vac-Con Suit:
An extravehicular suit designed for construction posts in space. They have backpack thrusters and a wide variety of tool belts and specialized systems used in creating large space structures.

Vambrace:
Armor that covers the upper arm to the elbow, sometimes attaching to gauntlets.

Waist Sash:
A small cloth or synth-leather piece of clothing, worn above the hips, usually with at least one pocket, sometimes several. Some are tied in place. Others have elaborate clasps.

Waldo arms:
Term of Terran origin. Mechanical devices in which a set of robotic arms are controlled by handheld manipulators. Used for handling hazardous materials or within dangerous environments.

Wallscreens:
Naga interface panels with full visual and audio capabilities. These are ubiquitous throughout Ganges, including within private homes, on public walls, and other large vertical spaces.

The Wend:
A manner in which Solarian Alliance vessels get around the speed of light, by transferring the spacecraft between realities, then depositing it at the required point in spacetime.

Wheel:
A large cylinder that rotates about the Spine Axis of Ganges to create centrifugal force, thus mimicking the effects of gravity. They are typically twenty kilometers wide and range from ten to forty kilometers in length. Exceptions are Command Hub, which is the smallest of the Wheels, and Harbors One and Two, which are considerably larger.

Wire Head:
A derogatory term for computer technicians.

About the Author

David Gulotta is an author, specializing in works of science fiction and fantasy. He is also an artist who creates paintings in oils. David grew up in both an urban and rural environment, which made him interested in how cultural conditions affect individuals. His love of the sciences was nurtured at an early age, being especially interested in physics, astronomy and psychology. He has been a member of many organizations, including the Society for Creative Anachronisms, the Advanced Yoga Practices Organization and the American Association for the Advancement of Science. He has traveled throughout Europe and has been to Central America, which broadened his interest in various cultures. David's writings are based upon his dreams, most of which are detailed and lucid. He currently resides within the forests of Pennsylvania.

Made in the USA
Middletown, DE
29 October 2022